THE TONGA LEGENDS SERIES

A
PROVIDENCE OF
WAR

JOSHUA TAUMOEFOLAU

A Providence Of War

Copyright © Joshua Taumoefolau 2009
2nd Edition 2012

www.tongalegendsseries.com

Photography: Yvane Fifita
Cover Design & Artwork: James Campbell
Map Illustrations: Joshua Taumoefolau
Character photographs: Yvane Fifita, Ebonie Fifita, Ruha Fifita, Mercy Kafalava, Lani Wolfgramm and Joshua Taumoefolau

A catalogue record of this book is available from the Australian National Library

Sydney, Australia

ISBN: 978-0-9807916-1-7

Dedicated to my son, Musashi.

Forever may my paths in life reach into unknown vistas -
forever will they lead back to you.

Special thanks to

my family for believing in the promise of this book, to Carla, who has never
doubted me,
and to Elizabeth, who afforded great support on the 2nd Edition

Written in honour of

the ancient history of Tonga and all the historical characters in this book,
whose voices and deeds, have been lost in the passage of time.

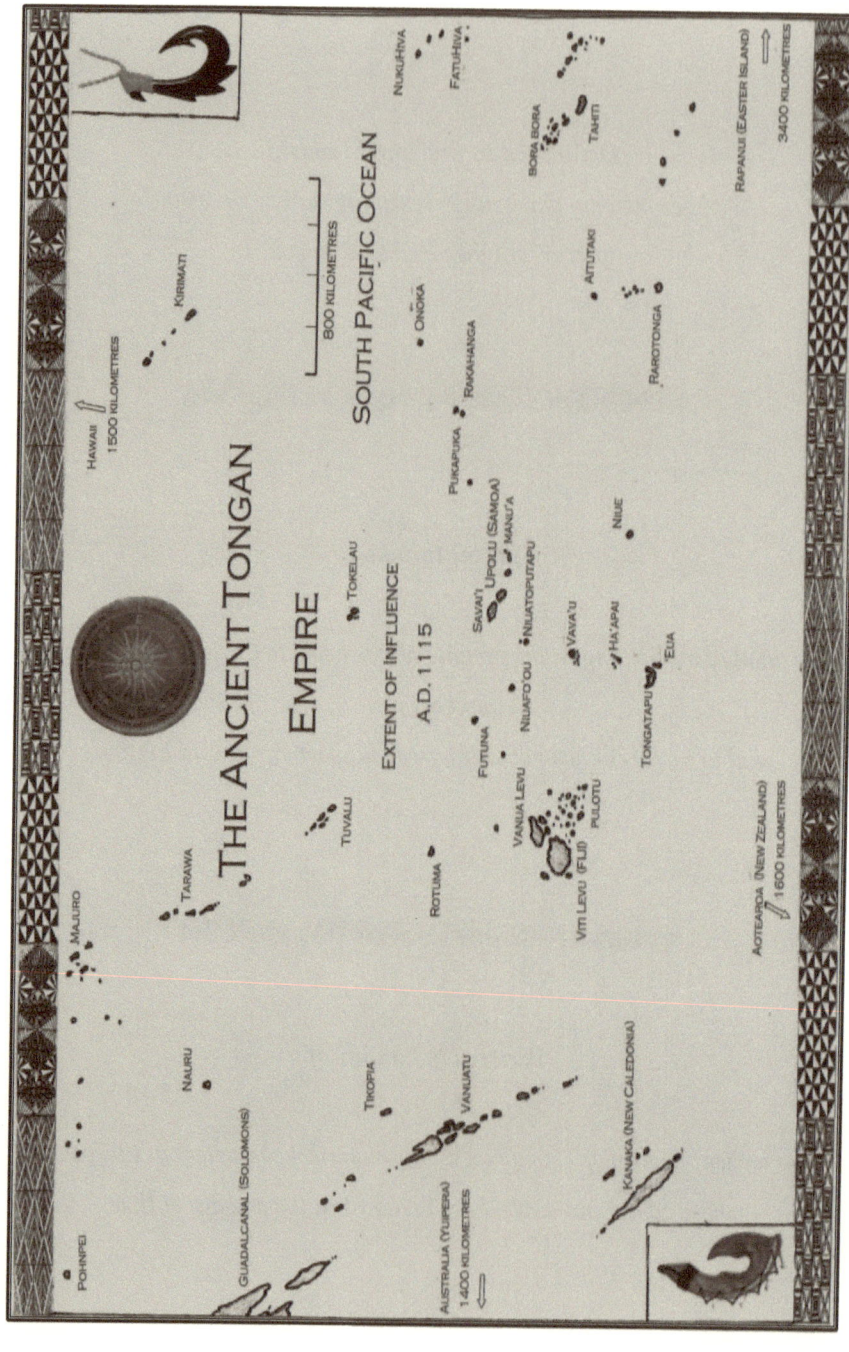

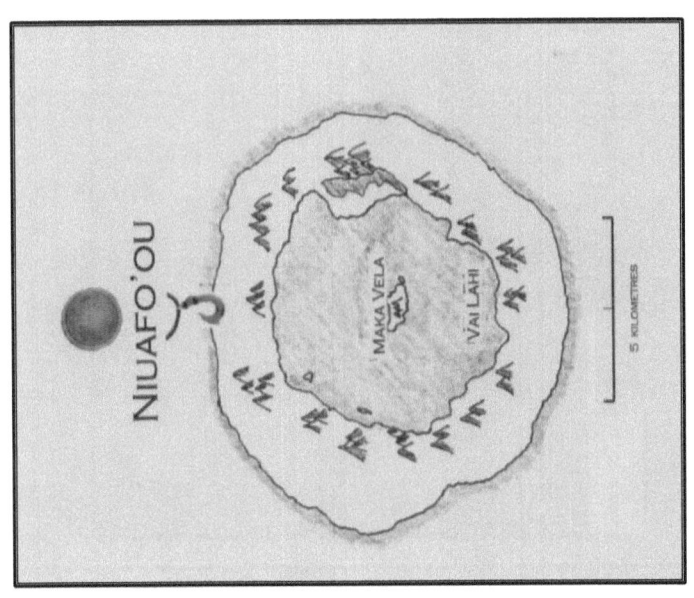

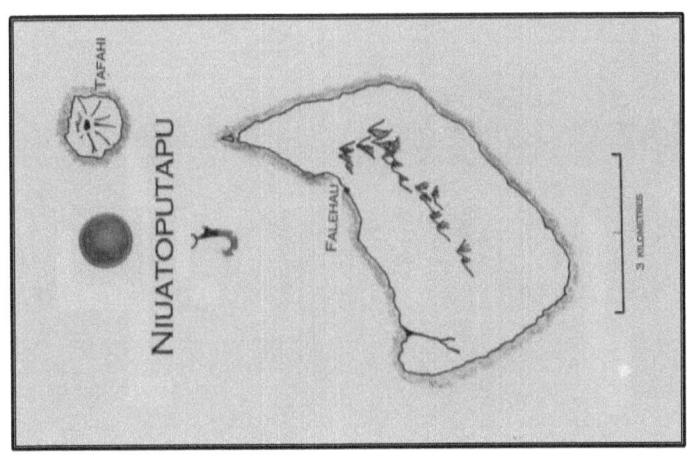

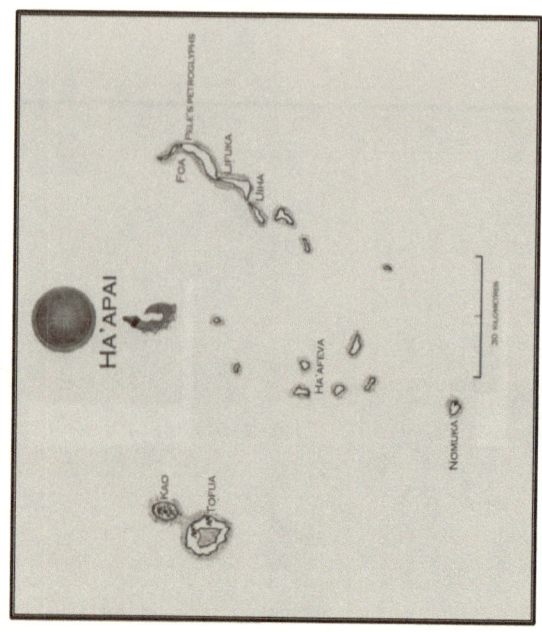

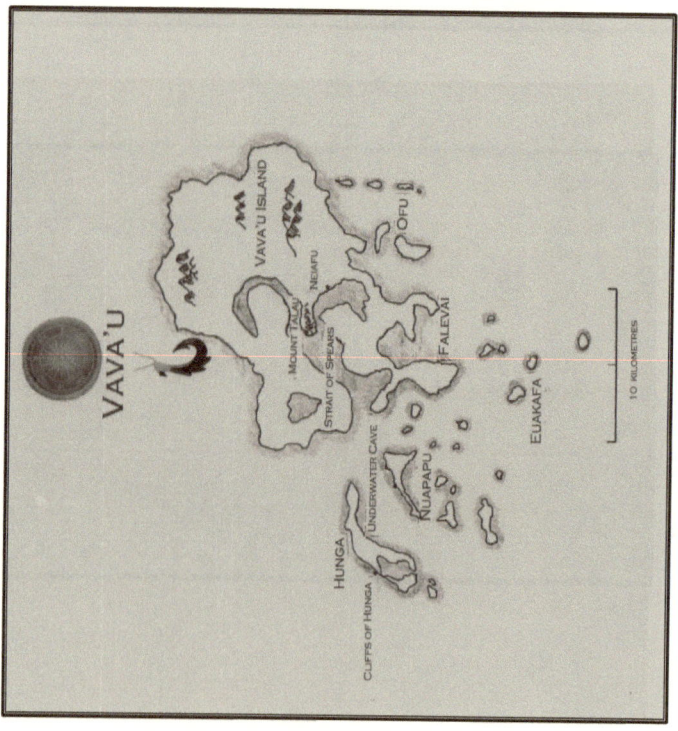

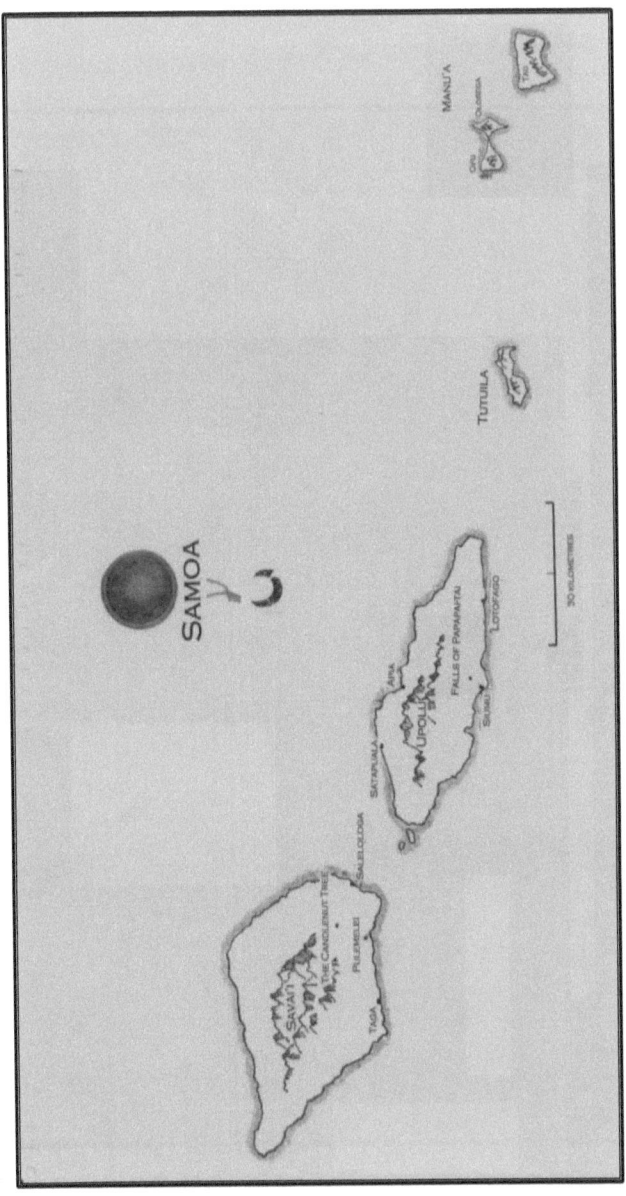

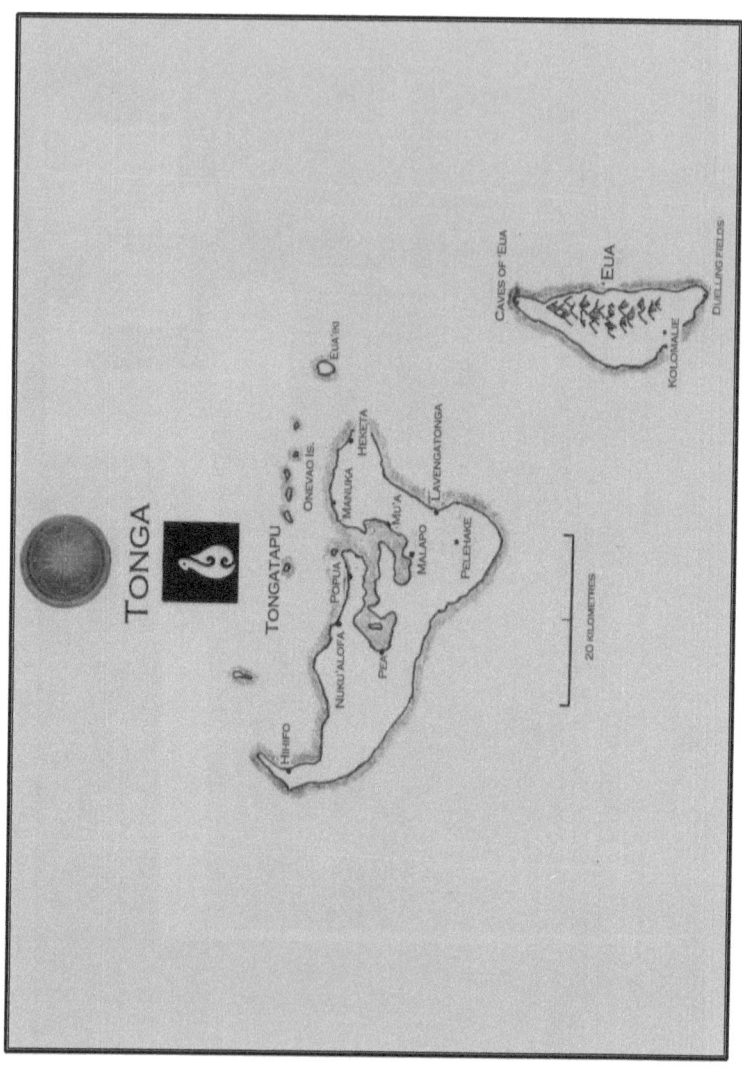

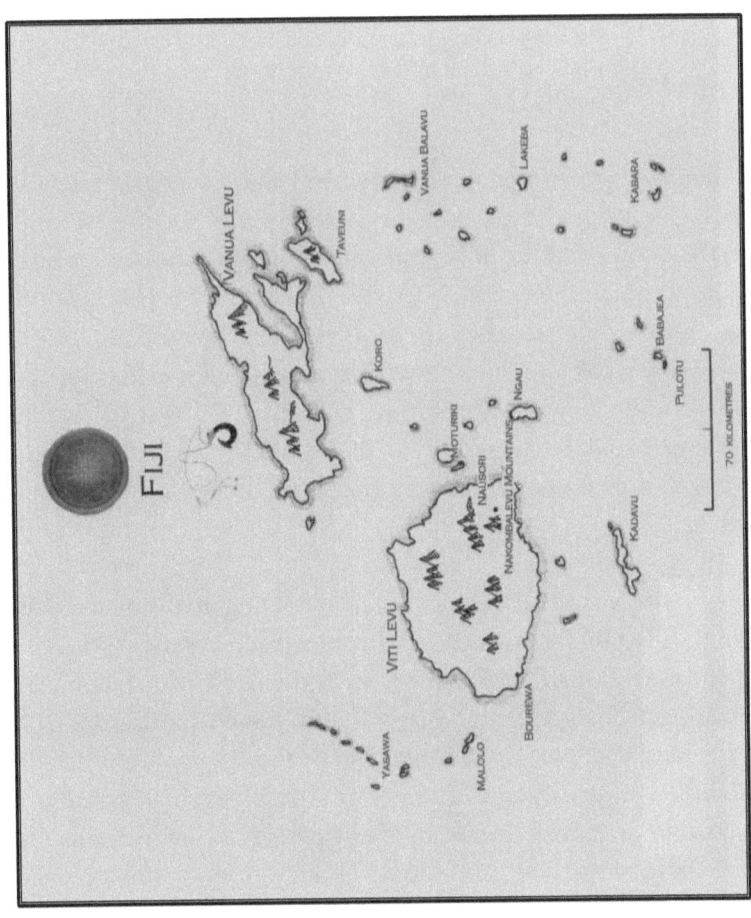

PREFACE

A thousand years ago, was the period known as the High Middle Ages. The Order of the Knights Templar rose in succession of the First Crusade to the holy land and a unified Scandinavia ceased Viking raids in the British Isles. The Byzantine Empire was ruled by the Greek Komnenos Royals, and the Song Dynasty fought the Jin Dynasty for rule of China. The Moors had conquered most of North Africa, and the Toltec Empire rivalled the ancient Mayans in Mesoamerica. The largest ocean in the world, the Pacific Ocean, was dominated by a warrior society that was unparalleled in power and ambition.

In the year A.D.1100, the ancient Tongan Empire reached its zenith, ruled by its powerful Tui Tonga (Sacred Kings) lineage. In no other time did the Pacific nation reach such epic proportions through the impact of its mighty warriors and skilled navigators. It was a fierce feudal civilisation: Devoid of iron and steel. A rich culture without gold or silver. A successful farming society, without beasts of burden or horses. In the harshest part of the world, the Tongans were born from the ambitions of an ancient warrior race that conquered the seas since the dawn of time. At this point in history, the Tongan Empire's influence stretched almost three and a half million square kilometres: equivalent to an area stretching from Turkey to Spain, and from Sicily to Sweden.

When we look back into the ancient history of a culture, it is easy to accept a collective view on the social interaction and stratification based on ancient written accounts and decrepit physical evidence. These two parallels are typical examples of classic human historical interpretation. They are accounts written from a biased view or founded on individual objects, created only in a personalized style that may have contradicted the reality of the social norm at the time.

This theory of "interpreted history" is more emphasized when cultures, such as that of the ancient Tongan, had no conclusive written language to record events or trail of timelines, nor concept of time itself, in the classical sense, to verify certain periods.

Another historical explanation of transformation, within a race or culture of people, can be shown with the rise and fall of their civilizations. The intricacies and advancements of social contexts of those civilizations can vary between certain periods of history. A great civilization might one day crumble, and only years later never reflect its previous grandeur. In some cases, ancient civilizations rose, fell and then vanished altogether.

Factual cornerstones, on which this book is based, are only corroborated through verifying accounts of other Pacific nations, and substantiated by extensive literature that has been dedicated to the preservation of ancient Tongan culture itself. However factual certain milestones that are outlined in the book may be, the lifestyle and the complex fabric that made up the ancient Tongan Empire, are vivid and largely unknown during this period in history. This grounded my belief that although various stages in the book are supported by certain historical events, actual places and some historical characters; the plot would always be fictional and based on my historical interpretation and imagination.

PART 1

PROLOGUE

The night began with a slight chill. Over the brine sat a sullen moon, tarnishing its surface with a road of yellow ribbon. Tafahi, rose from the sea with compelling strength. Her skin, dense with vegetation, concealed her charcoal surface beneath: a distant memory of her last eruption perhaps two hundred years past. Dark wings spiralled from her peaks. The shrill chorus of bats echoed across the sea that separated her from Niuatoputapu. The larger island was a morbid, black mass on the horizon. Within its centre was a dim light, which pulsated like an irregular heartbeat. Faint bellows and song were like whispers from afar.

The Falehau Winter Feast was a grand banquet of food, kava and sexual indulgence by all who were invited by Noble Anga'uli. These invitations were met without decline by all merchants, warriors and townsfolk, annually called to celebrate the end of winter. Roasted pigs, fish and other cooked delicacies lay presented within the village feasting area.

The day had been filled with mantras of voice and dance, showmanship of club matches, wrestling and spear throwing. As the sun had begun to set, the kava began to flow with opulence and the mood of the guests became sullen and inebriated.

Paea crept from the shadows. His face was a lather of sweat and grime, his body skin and bone. He would startle and flinch at the occasional moans from nearby lovers somewhere in the shrouded darkness. He nervously remained within the outer limits of the feasting area, hugging close to a refuse heap behind an umu pit. The fresh smell of sun-spoiled fruit and vegetables lingered among the unused remains of slaughtered animals. The boy had much choice. The small, tattered pouch around his waist was filling quickly. His hands scurried across the garbage as he kept his eyes posted on a nearby group of intoxicated warriors. He felt a vicelike grip around his wrist.

"Boy."

A bolt of fright shot up his spine. He yelped and slipped backwards to the ground. The warriors momentarily looked in his direction. Paea felt his heart burst through his tiny chest as his first instinct was to flee. Instead, wide eyed and wheezing he slowly propped to his knees and faced the man before him. Collapsed on his side, the stranger could barely lift his head from the earth. Paea could see a gaping wound in his chest. In the darkness, it glistened with oily black blood.

The stranger beckoned to him. "Boy, come closer so that I may not shout ..."

Paea looked about slowly, then crept forward. The stranger spoke with a noble tongue and was dressed in well made tapa. *Men garbed in such a manner could only hail from the Imperial Army,* Paea thought.

The warrior gazed at him with desperation, reaching out in a dying plea. "There's no time, you need to - " he stopped, coughing thick blood. "A matter of utmost urgency - a matter of the Empire..."

"Yes, Master?" Paea swallowed nervously.

The warrior struggled to summon the strength to reach into his vala to reveal a parchment of thin tapa.

"This is - guard it with your life, you must take it to Tongatapu. It must get to the - King Tu'itatui - promise ..." his gaze slowly drifted into oblivion.

Paea stared at the body for a moment then whispered a short prayer to Tangaloa. He looked blankly at the parchment. He traced a finger over the strange pattern of shapes and symbols, their meaning a mystery. He shoved it into his pouch and turned to the corpse in resolve.

"I will do what you ask, but forgive me if I ask for your possessions as payment." He halted for a moment, wondering if he had asked too much of the dead warrior.

Shaking his conscience aside, he replaced his tattered rags with the man's vala. His belongings included a length of twine, two well carved throwing clubs and a beautiful dagger made of obsidian. Before he could inspect them, however, there boomed a fierce shout from across the umu pit.

"You! Maggot! What are you doing there?" a warrior repeated and began to head in Paea's direction.

Paea juggled his newly acquired possessions and tripped through the refuse into the darkness. The warrior brandished a spear and began to run, leaping over the umu pit in pursuit.

"What are you doing?" his companions laughed. "It was just a tu'a! Let him be."

The warrior halted and slowly wiped his mouth, still greasy from feasting. He squinted through the dark foliage before conceding the chase. With a belly stuffed with swine and much kava his senses were not sharp. He grunted and gradually returned to the firelight, unaware of the slain warrior at his feet and that within Paea's tattered pouch lay the darkest secret of the Tu'i Tonga Empire – one so powerful that it threatened to tear the great nation apart.

CHAPTER 1

Heketa, Tongatapu
Winter, A.D.1120

"Catch it, Your Highness!"

The young women ran through the royal courtyard. Their faces gleamed with joy as they shuffled against one another playfully. Ahead of them was a large, blue butterfly that teased as it bounced through the air just beyond their reach. One of the women leapt towards it only to have it slip through her arms. When she fell and the others toppled over her, they all burst into fits of laughter. They lay sprawled on the grass as their laughter subsided.

"I almost had it!" Princess Fatafehi wiped tears of joy from her cheeks.

"Yes, Your Highness, but do not worry, I am sure it will be back!" Lupe grinned.

"I hope so." Fatafehi's thoughts suddenly went to her brother. "I hope he will come back."

The maidens quickly saw the change in the princess's mood and gracefully stood to help her stand.

"This way, Your Highness. Let's prepare for the feast tonight."

"No." She smiled to them. "Go and prepare yourselves. I will call for you soon."

Left alone with her thoughts, Princess Fatafehi strolled through the royal gardens of Heketa. Anxiety filled her mind, and the memory of her father's words echoed deeply. The prospect of being married was a frightening concept. In ancient Tongan society, it was

16

generally accepted that a woman was ready to wed at her first menstruation. At fifteen, Fatafehi was well bloomed and her father was eager to match her with a young chief. There had been much discussion on the matter and it annoyed her. She would much rather continue playing her games with the other girls.

The beautiful Heilala flowers were blooming. They brought vibrant colours to the trimmed hedges and surrounding greenery. She picked one gently from a branch and inhaled its sweet scent. She smiled as she adjusted her long, black hair and placed it behind her ear. Somehow they always brought her happiness.

"Soon you must give away your girlish games," crackled the voice of Queen Sialeataongo.

She was Fatafehi's aunt; a war widow and a dark shadow across the royal family. Never seen without her harem of old women, all who had lost their husbands to war, she emerged from the entrance of the courtyard, draped in tapa dyed black from crushed ash. Bulbous eye bags shadowed down a hard and worn face, filled with a history of gloom and pessimism, and crowned with silver hair that reached her large waist. From the time she was a child, Princess Fatafehi had always been frightened of her, believing she was ghost among the living.

"Y-yes Auntie, I know."

"It's time you were wed and do your duty as a woman. Your father, the king, agrees and I have spoken to him at length of a possible mate for you."

Princess Fatafehi nodded as she cautiously edged her way around the brooding group of old women.

"Despite your father's lack of support in the past for the picking," she clicked her tongue, "he's recently returned from Ha'apai with surprising news of a possible future husband for you -"

"Yes, Auntie," she had made it to the exit of the courtyard and skipped away, "I'll be sure to speak of it to father!"

The Royal Reception Hall was enormous. Fatafehi paused before stepping inside silently, hearing the strong voice of her father.

"I have heard enough of that nonsense. If Manusiu wishes to remain out of the Empire's affairs, then that is his decision. The old man has served the Empire for more years than I can count. I do not want to hear anymore about it."

"Yes, Your Majesty." High Priest Toutai bowed and moved aside.

Fatafehi appeared unannounced before the court filled with noblemen, warriors and priests. At the head and principal position, she saw the King of the Empire, King Tu'itatui. Sitting against an ancient giant clam shell the size of a man, carved and fused into a spectacular throne made of ironbark and polished whale ivory, he personified authority and supremacy. His face bore the years of battle, hardship and sacrifice. He was a warrior king of old: who, like those before him, would carve his destiny upon the sands of time and set them in the heavens above. At sixty years old, seven foot tall and one hundred and twenty kilograms of muscle, King Tu'itatui was still a formidable man. He wore his hair out and it was soaked and dried with coral. The result made it resemble a great mane, which accentuated the size of his head.

"Fatafehi! Come here, my daughter!" He stood from his throne and stepped down into her arms.

"Sorry to interrupt, Father. I ... I just wanted to see you."

"It is no interruption." Tu'itatui embraced her and gazed into her eyes. "Ahh, you are a welcome sight for these weary eyes."

"F-Father..." she began, "You haven't been talking with Auntie about a future husband for me...?"

"Ah, yes! I met a fine young man in Ha'apai, Sisimataila'a, despite being a commoner, perhaps the most handsome man I have seen in a while. Fatafehi, you'll like him!"

"But Father-"

"Your Majesty." Lord Fasi'apule stepped forward and bowed. "I beg your pardon, another issue must be discussed; suspicion of overlords in the outer kingdom."

"Enough talk of politics today, my brother," the king waved his hand.

"No, Father, I will go," Fatafehi quickly kissed him. "You have important things to discuss. I will talk with you later of this."

He sighed as he watched his favourite daughter skip out of the court. *She has grown up so quickly*, he thought. She'll make a good wife to a lucky man.

"I assume you speak of Niuatoputapu?" He turned to his half brother and frowned.

"Well, yes, that's *one* island."

"What proof do you have of these accusations?"

"None but rumour." Lord Fasi'apule's tone was cautious. "But I see it as potential trouble should it be left unchecked."

In the not so distant past, districts, outer islands and foreign occupied islands in Tonga were ruled by rich and powerful 'overlords'. Similar to dictatorships, though in scores of segregated regions, the power struggle between these men had slowly eroded Tonga's economical state. The overlords enforced their own laws, taxed their own people harshly and fought with one another regularly. This age-old rulership came into being when the 'Togafiti', powerful overlords who spread across the South Pacific from Pulotu, conquered Tonga and split its islands among themselves.

The greatest overlord was a powerful man named 'Aho'eitu. Following a campaign against other overlords, he became the first Tu'i Tonga in A.D.916 and came to reside in Popua, Tongatapu. Over the next two hundred years, the other overlords begrudgingly accepted 'Aho'eitu's royal line and often conspired to defy his rule. Occasional wars and skirmishes followed as a result. However, they knew Aho'eitu's power was too great to overcome. They continued to pursue their own interests in order to grow self sufficiency in their communities. They established the ability to govern and provide for themselves through trade. Indeed they competed for social and agricultural advancement.

Unfortunately, in later years, the descendants of the original Togafiti overlords became so tyrannical that the population began to suffer; more tributes were demanded, famine followed which in turn gave way to disease. The people could do little for their plight and their cries of abuse and cruelty fell on the deaf ears of rival overlords. Cannibalism thrived. The overlords became even more ruthless. Change was needed desperately.

It eventually came with a major transformation, designed to restructure the country's social and political system with the rise of the great Empire. 'Aho'eitu's tenth descendant, King Momo, dreamed of a better country: one that was united. The transformation was simple. Only one king should rule the country and govern its people. Only when this was achieved could they begin to re-develop the internal social structure.

When his foes had thought him dead, Momo returned from a distant sanctuary, and with the support of his powerful son, Tu'itatui, he was empowered with an unwavering vision for the absolute unification of the Tongan Empire. It was fuelled by his thirst to uproot all of the traitorous kings who had persecuted their own people. He ruled as a military genius, gaining overwhelming respect and support from friends and foes alike.

His resolute focus for change tore through the political structure, surprising even close friends and advisers by his impulsive, yet wise, decisions. In response to this, the overlords refused to acknowledge either the Tu'i Tonga line, or the rise of the visionary King Momo and his son, Tu'itatui. Such acts were taken as treason which marked the beginnings of the Kaimana War.

Powerful overlords and kings to the east and south erupted in resistance to Momo's plight for unification, amassing armies by forging alliances with other foreign warlords in the region. Limited royal forces from the north pushed southward for months, but were unsuccessful amid guerrilla warfare in the jungles of Tongatapu. In the summer of A.D.1085, the Great Battle of Pea saw the breaching of the village by more than ten thousand imperial warriors.

Though this was a dramatic turning point in the war, the overlords evaded every attempt of capture and thwarted social acceptance in the 'royal cause' for the following three years. Pro-royal propaganda washed through the Tongatapu islands like a religious exorcism. The root of the strategy was to sway the minds of those who had wealth and status, and those who had been threatened and blackmailed to withhold the whereabouts of the overlords. Despite this, King Momo was unwilling to pressure the masses because of a rotten few and opted for patience over a forceful transition.

This decision was to later earn him the respect of thousands. After five years of royal occupation, the scattered support for the fugitive overlords vanished. Most of them were never found, or captured, rumoured to have moved to the islands of Kiribati, Tahiti and Rarotonga. The people, however, had a huge change of heart towards the royal occupation, and their hopes for a brighter future were realised under a unified country.

In the year A.D.1095, the 'Ten Years of Rebirth' marked both the passing of Momo, the crowning to his powerful son, Tu'itatui, and the implementation of Tonga's greatest social change, which would last for the next thousand years.

Among the innovations inspired by his grandfather, Lo'au, King Tu'itatui introduced the traditional kava ceremony. This particular ceremony was a pivotal strategy to emphasize and enforce the new ranks within Tongan society: the royal bloodline, the nobles, the chiefs and the commoners. The practice itself achieved this through strict procedures that enforced rank acknowledged privileged invitations, seating arrangements and even the actual presenting of the kava. As sub-categories of class existed within the four main classes, it meant that even in a commoner kava circle, seniors of rank had to be recognised.

Surprisingly, its implementation was not resisted, but rather accepted by all ranks of society. It was an ingenious method of slowly educating society of the importance of respect, reverence and loyalty and thus ensuring the stability of the Tu'i Tonga. This new, governmental structure was revolutionary in the king's plan to create the most powerful Oceanic Empire the world had ever seen. This semi-feudal system provided the people with the protection and wealth of the Empire, in return for all services rendered to the king himself.

In this time also, King Tu'itatui initiated the 'Great Expansion'. In an effort to expand his kingdom, Tu'itatui launched imperial armadas in all four directions of the winds. It was a legendary era of conquest filled with countless tales of discovery, wonder and occupation. Even the king captained one of the armadas that led east to a fabled kingdom called Mapuche.

Following the expansion, the Tu'itatui government masterminded serviceable grants, incentives and provisions for the higher classes of citizens and ritual tributes. Favour was given to those of prodigious service, for as the Empire grew, so did the people of Tonga reap the rewards. For the first time in history, men from the lowest to the highest class no longer wished to strive for personal gain, but to serve faithfully under the eleventh Tu'i Tonga. It was all in the name of the Empire.

"Leave us." King Tu'itatui stood from his throne. "All of you."

He placed his arm over Lord Fasi'apule's shoulder before pacing slowly to the centre of the court. His big hands rested on his hips when he turned and faced his brother.

"What news of Anga'uli and Niuatoputapu?"

"Growing concern," Fasi'apule cleared his throat. "It has been three months, Your Majesty."

"Are you sure? How time flies these days." The king shook his head.

"I fear for the worst. Moa'uli'uli will not return."

"Perhaps I should have sent more spies with him."

"He was the best because he worked better alone, Your Majesty."

"And the rumours?"

"That Anga'uli supports the Pulotulahi."

"Careful brother," Tu'itatui said sharply. "Such accusations are treason if they are heard by anyone in the court."

"Under your laws, Your Majesty."

22

"What good are my laws if they do not apply to everyone? Do not try my patience, Fasi'apule. Our agreement was thus until we received word from Moa'uli'uli. No, we cannot allow these rumours to tarnish our vision without proof."

"But they must not be allowed to build doubt in the people's minds."

"Doubt? What would they have to distrust?"

"Your Majesty, the Pulotulahi have grown in numbers the past year, recruiting countless renegade warriors and foreigners alike. Recently they have attacked imperial tongiakis and publicly challenged the Empire. They have been clawing their way through the social ranks, Your Majesty. You and I both know it is only a matter of time before they bribe a noble. Once this happens, the people's faith in the social structure will crumble."

"All this based on common rumour," Tu'itatui frowned.

"Seven summers ago, rumour whispered of the old Pulotulahi allegiance rising again from the past. Soon after it was confirmed they had returned. Two winters ago, rumour had it warlord Kamohoali'i was involved with the Pulotulahi. A month later it was verified. He and his band of rebels had taken leadership of the evil movement! Your Majesty, in my experience there is always dark truth in rumour."

"Mmm."

"We cannot take this chance. There is too much at risk."

The king finally nodded in agreement and the two stood silently for a brief moment, knowing what must follow.

"Who will you send to Niuatoputapu, Your Majesty?"

"The only warrior I can trust in this matter."

CHAPTER 2

Falehau, Niuatoputapu

A small fleet of tongiaki banked slowly at the port of Falehau, Niuatoputapu. The sails that bore the imperial insignia were secured to the masts, and preparations were made to disembark. The winter sun was setting, yet the chill on the breeze had already begun to form. Only the volcanic summit of Tafahi appeared beyond the reach of cold, still basking in the rays of the failing light.

Twenty soldiers leapt into the water, the lapping waves splashing against their powerful bodies as they heaved their crafts further up the wet sand. Three senior warriors moved ahead of the group: two captains and a commander. From where they gathered on the beach, they could take in thousands of kilometres of view; the great Pacific Ocean pillowing out into a darkened velvet horizon, the palmed beach surging westwards along the coastline, ahead the forests of the island that marked the edge of the 'Inner Empire'.

The Inner Empire included the islands: Tongatapu, Ha'apai, 'Eua, Vava'u, Niuatoputapu, Niuafo'ou, and Niue. The Middle Empire covered Samoa and Fiji, Futuna, Rotuma and Tokelau, Rarotonga, Kanaka and Vanuatu. The outermost regions of the Empire reached Tikopia, Guadalcanal, Nauru, Tarawa, Tahiti, and Kiribati. Stationed within each of the islands that lay within the inner and middle regions of the Empire were imperial governors. They were posted as representatives of the king though had little to do with the local affairs of each island. Although there were no official diplomats posted on islands within the Empire's outer regions, Tongan residents lived and thrived locally. They were loyal to the Empire assisted with tributes sent to the capital.

The commander stood confidently in the sand ahead of his men. He adjusted the tapa that covered most of his body with a thick, broad girdle made of sandalwood bark. Pausing for a moment, he turned and faced his soldiers and took a heavy breath of accomplishment. He reached for his weapon, raised it abreast towards the early evening sky. It was a beautifully carved club of rare make – four feet of intricate incisions and cuts, banded shapes and symbols that told an ancient story of courage and valour.

It was lacquered in a potent mixture of both coconut and sandalwood oil. This darkened to a thick molasses that hid the depths of its carvings. But its design was unlike anything common at the time. Although three feet of the club was tubular, its end was fashioned like a European broadsword; a double edged blade with rings every three inches and a flat head. The hardwood was called to'a, the hardest timber throughout the islands. Polished and treasured, its flawless appearance disguised its antiquity. It was a family heirloom: legend had it that the old King Momo returned to Pulotu in a time of suffering and returned to Tonga with it to restore peace. Like all weapons used by warriors in ancient Tonga, they were given names. King Momo named it 'Fakamelino', which meant *the peace maker*. The man who now wielded it, was the crown prince of the great Tongan Empire, Talatama.

The captain lightly stepped towards his prince and commander. "Milord…"

"Out of the water," Talatama stated, as he turned and strode forward, quickly surveying the area.

Talatama was the first of King Tu'itatui's four children by his mother, the principal wife. At the age of twenty one, he was the epitome of warrior elite. Standing six foot-eight and one hundred and twenty kilograms, he possessed a taut and muscular body which complemented his warrior spirit.

His position as commander of the Imperial Army's Fourteenth Legion for the last two years was a substitute for stewardship. A stewardship had been offered in recognition for his efforts in the Imperial Army, one that promised governorship in the south-western districts of Tongatapu. Though this was an incredible honour, he declined, on the grounds that he best served his father as a warrior in the field. The next oldest brother, Prince Talaiha'apepe, who was also serving in the Imperial Army, accepted the stewardship instead. Agreeing that the disposition of his eldest son would not cater for an administrative role, King Tu'itatui promoted him to commander of the Fourteenth Legion under General Ngongo and administered Talaiha'apepe as the assistant governor of the Fua'amotu district.

Over his two years as commander, Talatama had brought glorious honour to his father and reaped the rewards of prestige and respect. He was hailed a hero in western Viti Levu after quelling bands of raiders between the waters of Fiji and Kanaka, only six months past. He had single-handedly rallied the pirates with an iron fist, crushing their hopes to overthrow the stationed outposts and invade the island. His bravery had saved hundreds of lives, mostly women and children.

Unmarried and never having been with a woman in courtship, Talatama, was the most eligible bachelor in the Empire. He was handsome: bearing a noble face and strong chin. His chestnut eyes against his smooth, caramel complexion enhanced a captivating glare. His long hair was as black as midnight and was tied neatly in a bun at the pinnacle of his skull. Modest to the degree of finding a compliment annoying, Talatama refused all hands in marriage from noblewomen bluntly, making no excuse for his manner. Deep down, he believed he had no time for a wife or family. His army superiors often expressed that although the way of the warrior demanded that a soldier should expect death at any given moment, it should not act as an impediment to marriage or having a family.

Despite his strong demeanour, he was in some ways soft-hearted, and it was for this reason that he felt it unhealthy to

26

undertake marriage in his position. He felt that love could very well make him sloppy in battle, cloud his judgment and soften his spirit. The very thought made him queasy and defenceless to an enemy which he had no way of defeating. He avoided any advancement, especially when he felt the throb of unfamiliar sentiment in his chest, around such prime females.

It had taken them almost six days to reach Niuatoputapu from the capital. He was discreetly elated to finally reach the northernmost province of Tongan soil. He chose not to remove his headdress of shell, mother-of-pearl and sharks' teeth. He shouldered a cloak of fine, flowing black tapa, which enveloped his large frame and shielded him from the slight chill.

Before long the colours of dusk had gone and the moon had risen. The tide had come in, leaving little beach for the imperial warriors to stand on. Passing villagers had scuttled by nervously, whispering as they stared at the warriors. It was a well known Polynesian social custom that commoners were not to approach the warrior class unless summoned. It was also a custom to meet an imperial visitation without delay.

"Perhaps the good Noble is engaged," Captain Mateitau joked, as he searched the water at his feet for shellfish.

"What could be more engaging than our arrival?" Kunamoana, the other captain began. "Surely he could have sent an emissary or the like."

"We were presented with a better reception in the enemy camp on Kanaka!" Mateitau laughed.

"Only because you had just killed their last general," Talatama said.

"Then perhaps I should seek out the general of Niuatoputapu, milord!" Mateitau remained chuckling to himself.

Talatama and Mateitau were close friends, beyond bounds of military decorum. Having shared years of service, they had endured the dangers of political ventures and bloody wars through changing times. Together with Kunamoana, Mateitau's younger brother, the three had been the inspiration of leadership throughout their successful campaign in Fiji.

"Milord, I should seek out ..." Kunamoana began, walking forward.

"No. We wait," Talatama said firmly. "We will let this rudeness be seen by all."

Finally, a messenger appeared in the night from the road that lead from the village. The young man scuffled up the sand holding a flaming torch. Talatama did little to correct himself as the man fell to his knees.

"Is it Niuatoputapu hospitality to keep an imperial commission waiting on such an eve?"

"M-my apologies, Milord. Lord Anga'uli has been engaged," the young warrior stammered.

Mateitau glanced at Talatama as the rest of the men chuckled to themselves. After smirking with his warriors, Talatama glared at the young man, "I'm not impressed."

"Please, by your will I shall lead you to Lord Anga'uli's house immediately," he bowed his head low.

"Lead!" Talatama shouted as they marched forward.

A pale trail of dust followed the group as they made their way down a worn track from the beach towards the township.

As night drew older, the temperature dropped quickly and the wind almost seemed to send shivers through the trees. It howled and violently fanned the fires, as if in defiance to their heat. The moon was high in the hazy night sky, encompassed by a celestial ring.

The ancient ramparts around the House of Anga'uli glowed under the large torches lined along its base. It had been an old fortress during the Kaimana Period. Its ramparts of solid ironwood ascended at least ten metres high, and rose magnificently from the deep moat, mud and water refuge. Surrounding the house, beyond the small moat, were the domiciles of the village headman and high priest, senior chief and their regiments of soldiers. These quarters were also home to the servants who served in the house, the township assemblies and the living abodes. The house was illuminated like a seaward beacon that could be seen for kilometres.

The outer reception room was comfortably tepid, warmed by small hearths that smouldered neatly in every room. Talatama and Mateitau sat refreshed after a wash down and a thorough oiling from female servants. They were led into a large adjoining kava house where their hosts sat in ceremonial positions around the kava bowl. Seated at the head was Noble Anga'uli, and to his sides were the senior chief, Talo, village headman, Ilamaki, and high priest, Ulikaite. When Talatama and Mateitau seated themselves within the circle, the kava was passed among the men.

"Welcome to Niuatoputapu, Commander Talatama," Anga'uli smiled broadly.

"I hope that you have had a safe journey to my shores and that your stay will be pleasant." His smile was unmoving, as if permanently pained across his face.

"Pleasant enough to have been kept waiting on the bea-"

"Thank you for your welcome, Noble Anga'uli," Talatama cut off his captain. "My stay, however, will be swift, as I hope to accomplish my orders and return to Tongatapu as soon as possible. Be assured, I do not have time to pass with simple pleasures so I hope that all cooperation is granted."

"Well, I am glad you see it well to dispose of the pleasantries. I agree there is no need to pretend." Anga'uli frowned immediately.

"Understand that I have a township to serve, so I'll be direct. Your coming here is like spitting into the wind, Commander Talatama. I suggest rather than being a nuisance prancing around, you and Ilamaki can settle this officially right now."

"How dare you!" Mateitau produced a jagged dagger of whale bone and took position to pounce across the large kava bowl at Anga'uli.

"No, Captain." Talatama quickly took hold of his friend's shoulder.

"This is your Crown Prince you speak to, worm!"
Talatama pulled Mateitau back to the floor.

Dozens of shadows appeared around the fale, and the sound of many men shuffled nervously.

Anga'uli sat back and jeered, "How is it I should receive you, Talatama, by virtue of Crown Prince or Commander? Would an enemy care on the battlefield that you are a Prince? I think not. I have heard that you made the decision to refuse the life of decadence as a 'royal son'. So as you chose to serve as a Commander in the Imperial Army, I therefore outrank you."

Talatama tapped Mateitau on the shoulder reassuringly, who was still seething with fury.

"True," he returned a stern gaze, his chestnut eyes glowed in the firelight. "And I never use heritage as a pedestal. Be that as it may, your rule of this province is the reason I am here, my lord. My presence should pass without hindrance if I am to favourably discern a report of Niuatoputapu."

"I think you forget yourself, Commander. I am -"

"My orders are from King Tu'itatui himself, Noble. I think it would be wise to adhere to the fact that we come here on an imperial commission."

Anga'uli leaned forward, blood seeming to flow into his eyeballs.

"Commission?" Ilamaki shot. "What is there that demands for a comm —"

"I don't give a damn about your petty imperial commission nor your father's wishes," Anga'uli sneered.

"That is sedition!" Mateitau snapped and leapt to his feet.

In an instant all the men were standing around Anga'uli and hordes of his men flooded into the hall and surrounded the imperial officers. Weapons were drawn. Talatama remained seated and regarded the warriors with a mild amusement. A fight would end in their swift deaths, but he was ready to go to Pulotu courageously. The Polynesian afterlife paradise of Pulotu was a place of eternal beauty, feasting and indulgence. It was the promised heaven where all chiefs and warriors travelled to after death, carrying the heroic deeds of their lives.

Anga'uli knew the prince was ready for death and he knew it would bring undue attention to Niuatoputapu.

"I thought you were smarter than this Anga'uli," Talatama said with a grin. "If you kill us, you'll have the entire Imperial Army wash over this island like a sea of blood."

A long silence befell the hall.

CHAPTER 3

After a brief but loud discussion outside the kava house, Anga'uli's head was finally cooled and focused. Ilamaki and Talo returned within and persuaded Prince Talatama to re-commence their awkward meeting.

"I wish to take back those hasty words, Commander Talatama." Lord Anga'uli bowed his head in false submission.

"For the sake of greater purposes, I will pretend that did not just happen," Talatama started. "But I cannot ignore that you all seem preoccupied. Is there something that I need to know about here?"

"Prince Talatama, w-we have a few local laws that we have worked on for the last year, that will be put forward soon," Ilamaki said.

"Local laws? You are aware you must have the king's consent to introduce laws, even local ones?" Talatama gave a suspicious glance to Anga'uli.

"Yes, of course. That's why we were hoping that you could take word back with you to King Tu'itatui, and have his reply returned by messenger," Ilamaki lied easily.

"I hardly see myself as a courier of local laws, village headman," Talatama returned his gaze to the noble.

"I have more pressing matters that I will begin tomorrow, by your leave."

"So what is it that you have come to plague us with then, Commander?" Anga'uli huffed disrespectfully.

"Briefly, my duties are to assess the local trade including your offerings, distribution of political power and state of general commerce," Talatama projected.

Momentarily stunned by this response, Anga'uli returned Talatama's unflinching gaze.

Ilamaki was shaking with fear behind his comical face. He had not gone over an approach to the meeting with Anga'uli before the warriors had arrived. It had been over a year since Niuatoputapu had been sent an emissary from the capital, as their assessment usually came from a bribed political advisor from Vava'u. News of their visit was only days in advance, giving Anga'uli and his cronies little time to compose a cover plan. This late delay hinted that Niuatoputapu was under suspicion and was in need of imperial assessment. With their plans about to bloom amid the political side of the village, the visit was nothing short of a blatant threat to their positions and lives. Anga'uli and his military officials were blind to this threat in their arrogance: an arrogance that could bring down years of planning. What made matters worse, was that Talatama was steadfast in his purpose.

A hint of a bribe could have the entire Imperial Army upon Niuatoputapu, and Ilamaki knew it. He was clearly chosen as the best man to conduct the assessment. He was a man that held no loyalties but to his king, his father. He represented the latest standard of elite warrior, not just muscle with a club, but a sharp and intelligent diplomat, able to conduct political inquiries. Ilamaki's only hope was to assist and cooperate so that their stay was indeed swift.

"I will hand over power to Ilamaki," Anga'uli finally motioned. "Who will personally assist you in anything you may need."

"That is all I ask," Talatama bowed with Mateitau, then stood and excused them for the night.

Anga'uli fumed as soon as they were out of sight.

33

"The swine, offal, dog-shit!" His clenched fists vibrated the wooden floor.

"Lord Anga'uli —" Ilamaki began.

"Shut up, Ila, not another word from you!" Anga'uli turned to Talo. "I want them leashed tighter than a diseased pig, you hear! I want to know what they are sticking their noses into and their whereabouts at all times!"

"Yes, Milord."

"Of all the times to send a damned emissary!"

Anga'uli rose to his feet and paced the length of the room. He then stopped and turned to his advisors with conviction.

"If they step out of line, kill them."

"W-w-what?" Talo stammered.

"You heard me."

"Lord Anga'uli —" Ilamaki stepped in.

"Ila, if you say anything more, I'll take your life."

"Master, you cannot be serious about this. He is the son of the king," Talo stated.

Anga'uli began walking towards the exit.

"I'm not about to let some buffoon stand in the way of our plans. Besides, it will not matter soon. He'll be just another dead warrior."

Before Anga'uli could depart, Talo shuffled to catch him up at the exit. His voice was a curt whisper so their conversation was theirs alone.

"Master, I have growing concerns. What pressures you so?" Talo pressed lightly. "I know you to be a level headed man."

The priest half expected Anga'uli to sweep a club across his head. Instead, the noble turned to him with an anguished look.

"Lady Rongaueroa – her husband is Lord Toi," he stuttered. "He and I once – we were once ..."

"Master?"

"I have broken an old brotherhood." Anga'uli disappeared through the exit. "I will burn in hell for what I have done."

Talatama sat quietly with his three seniors among a few low burning torches. Their chatter ceased when a young female servant entered their fale with fresh coconut milk. They said nothing while the woman served the drink slowly, all staring at her movements as if they were watching it for the first time. Once she had finished, she respectfully stepped outside of the house and knelt with her head bowed.

"Milords, I have sent for our most beautiful women to tend to your desires. They are currently lathering in sandalwood and will be here—"

"No more interruptions." Talatama did not hesitate. "That will be all."

"Yes, Master." She bowed, stood and disappeared into the night.

All eyes went to Talatama impatiently.

"It's a clear cut case of what happens when these nobles get too much power! We're going back to the days of the rogue kings and the Kaimana War!" Mateitau, red in the face, tried to keep his voice down.

"Such disrespect cannot be swept aside!" Kunamoana exclaimed.

"Mateitau is right. I can already smell the reek of treachery against the king from the looks of those seniors," Oliame, a lieutenant said, looking from face to face.

Talatama rubbed his chin and took a sip from his coconut.

"As warriors representing the Imperial Army, we supersede any local warriors of higher rank. Trust no one under the noble's rule. Remember we are on an imperial mission under the direct order of the king. Underhanded conspiracies and plans will be put to rest once we have the evidence to expose them all. There is no room for failures." Talatama took another sip.

"We all have our work cut out for us the next few days. Keep your heads up and your eyes open. There is much we need to do here." Talatama glanced at Mateitau. "So I need to know that you all will carry out all orders as requested. Is that understood?"

All warriors quickly answered and nodded.

Hours later, Talatama stood next to a young palm in the inner courtyard. Standing between the dark shadows of palms that lay scattered about, his was bathed in moonlight. He peered at the pale moon and took time to remember an old acquaintance.

Moa'uli'uli was not a close friend, but had known Talatama for long years in Tongatapu, as a peer under the same military leader. Moa'uli'uli was not a warrior, but a senior spy who dealt, not in assassinations, but covert reconnaissance missions and inductions into imperial conspiracies. Talatama knew his loyalty was unquestioned.

Mateitau joined his commander in the courtyard. His steps were laboured and could be heard a mile away. He placed his hands on his hips and sighed with exhaustion.

"You're not tired, Milord?"

"No, I've much on my mind. Go and sleep. It's been a long day."

The captain turned to leave, but hesitated.

"Permission to speak freely, Milord?"

"Granted."

"We're not here to check the damned politics of trade are we."

"No."

"Then wha—"

"Do you know of Kamohoali'i?"

"The criminal? Wanted for mass murder, rape and pillaging, extortion, arson and who knows what else?" Mateitau frowned. "He's one of the most wanted men in the Empire, Milord."

"Indeed."

"Is he here?" Mateitau's face beamed with new vigour. "If I—"

"I've told you enough. I'll reveal all in a few days time. Go and sleep."

The captain bit his tongue and bowed in respect. He knew the prince always gave him important information because of their friendship and not as his captain. He would never wish to abuse that.

"Good night, Milord."

Talatama's thoughts remained on his objective. He would go ahead as planned and conduct the assessment of the village. He would leave the secret investigation of Moa'uli'uli's disappearance, and Kamohoali'i, to Oliame. Only he and the king knew that Oliame was, in fact, a spy. His disguise as a soldier was flawless. This was common in the way of a spy, as most spies held various positions in all walks of society in common view, to hide their real occupation. Within the next couple of days, Talatama and his captains would preoccupy Anga'uli and his men to provide better cover for Oliame's work.

To Oliame, his mission was personal. Moa'uli'uli was his mentor and the man who introduced him to the occupation of spying. They had shared the secrets of the art and bound a relationship, like father and son. Before the group had left Tongatapu, Oliame had made a vow; to either expose the corrupt government accountable, or kill Kamohoali'i if he was responsible for the murder. Talatama knew this, but also knew that although it was personal to Oliame, he was professional enough to conduct his investigation without giving in to reckless vengeance.

As Talatama leaned his weight against the palm, he moved out of the moonlight and melted into the shadows. Folding his arms, he began to recap the order of his duties for the following days. Dreamily staring down at his folded arms, he was startled when a beam of moonlight flickered on his forearm. His gaze shot upwards, quick enough to see a lone figure glide across the rooftop of the fale.

His mind went straight to Oliame, but he was quickly discounted. He had not yet given him the order to begin the investigation. From where Talatama stood, he could clearly see the figure make its way across the thatched rooves towards him. As the spy approached, he was definite it was not Oliame; this spy was far more elegant. As he was discerning this, the spy disappeared from view momentarily, just before almost landing on top of him in the courtyard.

The figure must have dropped down at least ten feet, with no more sound than a soft pad. With its back towards Talatama, the spy stood only an arm's length away. It was garbed in a fine, silky tapa that covered the body and the head. It peered through the archway that led into the outer reception room. At such a close distance, Talatama immediately detected an unmistakable scent; that of a woman.

His mind raced with speculation. No local spy would be prancing about on the noble grounds, unless returning from a mission. This had to be a spy from another island, from her obvious disorientation and caution, but from where? Had King Tu'itatui added to his mission and sent another spy to investigate as well? Unlikely - whoever she was, the importance of her mission was serious enough to breech the House of Anga'uli. Had he wanted, Talatama would have had little difficulty reaching out and snapping her lithe neck. Arms still crossed, he decided to reveal himself.

"Good evening," he grinned.

With a gasp, the spy leapt forwards in a blur, spun and threw an object at Talatama's face.

"Wait!"

Adorned with sharpened edges, the shell sunk into the soft bark of the palm where his head had been. He straightened and nonchalantly watched the spy race across the courtyard. She scaled the south barricade in a feat that would put any man to shame.

The prince scratched his chin. For a fleeting moment, they locked gazes under the moonlight. Her eyes were icy pale, gleaming with determination and fearlessness. But there were sudden feelings that were exchanged: strength, defiance, curiosity, interest, and attraction.

Frustrated that he had not acted following their confrontation, he clicked his tongue. What was he thinking? Her gaze was so – incredibly captivating. He was instantly reminded of the dangers of women. He yanked the shell from the tree and inspected its sharp edges. He shook his head, and paced out of the courtyard in the opposite direction to that in which the spy had fled.

CHAPTER 4

The spy made her way through the dark outskirts of the village with ease. It took little time to reach her camp on the northern side of Niuatoputapu. Cupping her hands around her mouth, she whistled the call of a Tavake bird. Seconds later, it was returned. She entered the camp and carefully placed her weapons and tools beneath the shelter that her comrades had erected for a single night's purpose. As she sat down on the thin tapa, she removed the tapa covering her face and looked at her two comrades who were opposite her.

One of the men reached out and handed her a young coconut which was recently opened. She lifted it to her lips and sculled the sweet milk.

The other man sat silently and watched her as she took her fill. He could wait no longer.

"What news, Mahina?"

The woman lowered the coconut from her mouth and placed it to her side. She took a deep breath and exhaled slowly.

"I found her."

"Bastards!" The man's effort to remain discreet dissolved as he swore.

"H-how did she look? Is she alive?" the other man asked quickly.

Mahina did not answer immediately. She had to summon the strength of heart to continue with the news of their Lady's condition. It was long breaths before she spoke again.

"She – she does not look well, my friends. I saw her within the main compound, in an old and ruined fale. She was bound hand and feet ..." she paused.

The men edged forwards as the hiatus sounded the heart beats of all three.

" ... And she appeared to be tortured and raped. I barely saw her body rise and fall with breath."

This time there was no answer from the two men. The senior companion was visibly shaking. The other man sniffed as he wiped tears from his eyes, glistening in the moonlight.

Finally, the senior comrade stood in a fit of anger and picked up a club. Mahina jumped to snatch the weapon from his grasp.

"No, Tarapu! You can't go there!" she exclaimed, her voice filled with emotion. "I would have saved her, but it's too well guarded!"

The other man rushed forward to help restrain Tarapu. He struggled for a moment before succumbing to grief, and then fell to his knees and began to weep. The other man comforted him. Mahina wiped her face of tears and stepped away from the men in the direction of the village.

"Tarapu, Piri. You must both return to Ngatangi'ia and give word to Lords Toi and Whatonga," she said. "You must leave now – tonight. I will stay here and watch over our Lady and prepare for a battle when you return with warriors."

She turned and approached the two men. She held both their heads and gently pressed hers against theirs, sharing the anguish of their noblewoman's capture and suffering. Within a few minutes, Tarapu and Piri had prepared their tongiakis for sail. Under the dim moonlight, they cast off shore and bade a silent farewell to Mahina. She stood on the dark beach and watched as the tongiakis vanished into the black horizon.

Mahina, was a stepdaughter of Lord Toi, the ruler of Rarotonga and the large village of Ngatangi'ia. An orphan as a child, her mother had been a fourteen year old village girl, too young to properly provide and care for her. Lord Toi, who had lived only a short walk from her mother's fale, took her to join with many of his young children under proper care and tutelage.

As she grew, she was treated as an outcast within Lord Toi's noble family, not greatly mistreated but left to perform menial duties around the compound, and last to be fed. Regarded with a mild neglect from the other daughters of Lord Toi, she learned at an early stage to become calculating and clever in ways to achieve what she wanted.

Lord Toi bore her no false mood. He kept busy with his important responsibilities as chief. So much so, that he barely spent any time with his children. It was his wife however, Lady Rongaueroa, who displayed the only affection towards her as a child.

As the other daughters spent time playing in the forests, down by the beach and flirting with boys, Mahina kept the company of Lady Rongaueroa, who would entertain her with fascinating stories of adventure, humour, and romance. She was mesmerised by the stories and used to fall asleep during the evenings under the warm, summer breeze. However, when the daughters and sons returned home, she was reminded again of her subservient position among them; a worker, a plaything and a servant to the will of them all. As much as the daughters used to tease her, so did the sons play fight and treat her roughly.

As the years passed through the cycles of the seasons, she grew into a strong and firm teenager and developed an immunity to the insults and taunts from her sisters, who at this time had been long married with their own families. Her brothers, over the years of tough handling with them and often accompanying them on boyish adventures of their own, regarded her as a real sister and one of the boys.

More years passed and Mahina became a woman. Some of her brothers perished in battle, some finally settled down with families. Only she and her older brother, Whatonga, remained living in the compound with Lord Toi and Lady Rongaueroa. Whatonga had become one of Rarotonga's greatest warrior navigators: a proud and resourceful right hand to his father. She too had become a skilled navigator, but behind compound walls had developed into an apt spy. She was graceful, powerful, dextrous and deadly.

As weapons, she favoured two throwing clubs made of ironwood, which were tied to her waist, and a vicious whalebone dagger. The two clubs were each one and a half foot in length, etched with the intricate designs from the Rarotongan culture, with thin handles that grew bulbous at the ends. On the spherical end of each club protruded crude spikes, carved and sharpened from the original piece of wood. Each spike was approximately five centimetres long and shaped to avoid snapping off easily.

The clubs, despite their cruel appearance, were used primarily for throwing. Notwithstanding her physical strength, she was no match for an average male warrior, and thus strategy omitted her from conducting close quarter combat. She was an outstanding thrower of the clubs and rarely missed her mark. If, however, after throwing two clubs she was still unable to avoid a close attack, she employed her whale bone dagger.

Practising, day by day, in the art of using the dagger in close quarter combat, she had pinpointed the precise areas of the body to attack for greatest damage. The movements focused on short and rapid slashes, stabbing strikes and cutting motions. Her dagger was made from the bone of the great Pacific whales, a white tooth-like weapon with a sharpened point and a double serrated blade. During her time of limited youth, she had taken many lives in battle.

Her beauty was defined by her shapely figure and her honey complexion: a perfect face of jade eyes, warm, full lips and a smile that had in the past, torn the hearts of young men. And despite a full decoration of spiralling Rarotongan tattoos around her body, she remained a model of sheer charm.

Standing in the moonlight, where the sand met the grass, Mahina was garbed in tapa that covered her midsection to her upper thighs. She removed her upper garment and tossed it next to the camp, revealing her full, round breasts, which were outlined perfectly in the faint luminosity.

She knelt down on the tapa first and then rested her body down on her side. She supported her head with her warm garment and looked out to sea. Her thoughts returned to the sight of her mother, only hours before. It was a heart-wrenching sight, like a glimpse of a terrible nightmare that one prayed not to come true. Yet she was helpless. The immediate compulsion to embrace Lady Rongaueroa and run with her from this dark and evil place was irresistible. Ironically, it was her very upbringing that brought about her decision to do nothing. It was the natural impulse to withhold the heartfelt emotions and think logically about how to achieve the best outcome: That was to take the information of her Lady Rongaueroa's location to her father and brother, not risk losing her own life and the life of her mother.

As she comforted herself for her actions in hindsight, she remembered the man she had encountered in the outer courtyard as she was making her way out. She frowned as she recalled his unusual actions as she appeared before him. Surely he was not a retainer or guard. He made no effort to subdue her, or call for reinforcements. Instead he smiled. She involuntarily placed her index finger to her lips. He was handsome and imbued goodness about his being. Looking into his eyes she felt an immediate attraction to him, a sentiment one acquires when feeling a loved one display affection. She felt herself blush.

She sighed and was suddenly reminded of her fatigue. Despite this, her mind continued to race in a lurid turmoil. She raised her weary eyes to the open sea. Somehow it always calmed her. She did not know how long she gazed out to the black sea stretching out into nothingness: a seaward infinity that gifted her troubled soul peace.

CHAPTER 5

Vaohoi keeled over, clutching his stomach. His high pitched whooping reached a climax. His boyish face beamed a crimson colour as tears sparkled in his eyes. He could not remember when he had laughed so much. The comedy, much to his companion's amazement, won the humour of passers-by. Many chuckled to themselves.

The fisherman slowly picked himself up out of the sea of squashed breadfruit and yam on the road. He was covered from head to toe with muck. He had also sustained a bump to the leg during the cataclysm of ripe produce. As well as totally demolishing the fruit farmer's corner store, the fisherman had also managed to lose the thief whom he had been chasing. Fuming at the mouth, the fisherman glared at Vaohoi, standing across the narrow road.

"You! What are you laughing at?" he growled, then looked around in the hope of locking gaze with another amused bystander. Not finding one, he glared back at the young man.

Vaohoi spluttered and waved a hand in defence.

"Oh, my – I'm sorry – heeheehee," he wiped the tears from his eyes.

Finally coming to the end of his painful spasm, he momentarily corrected himself, failing to see the fisherman stride angrily in his direction.

He took a deep breath and stood upright. Vaohoi slowly looked up to see the fisherman looming before him. The fisherman's strong hand clasped around his neck and he suddenly felt himself being lifted off the ground.

"Well, you clown, I have an idea that you won't find amusing. Since you decided to laugh rather than help catch the thief, you can make up for what he stole!" The fisherman's rancid breath was mixed with the smell of wasted staples, which dripped from his head.

"W-well, I don't see how that's fair, besides, I have nothing to offer," Vaohoi choked.

After peeling the young man with his eyes, the fisherman's grip became stronger.

"That's not the right answer, you whelp. It looks like there's only one other way to even this out then." He readied his fist for a blow.

Finally, Vaohoi's companion came to stand beside both of them.

"My good Sir, please forgive the outburst of my friend. I will make amends for your loss of face and the rudeness of Vaohoi here."

The fisherman, expecting an accomplice troublemaker, turned in surprise, the old mu'a standing with an outstretched hand full of beautiful shells.

Looking quizzically from the shells to the mu'a, the fisherman slowly placed Vaohoi back on the ground and released him. He wiped the muck from his face and was instantly pacified by the old man's presence.

Shooting Vaohoi a final glare, he placed his hands together in respect and faced the mu'a.

"Forgive my outburst. I cannot accept your offering." He turned and quickly disappeared within the crowds of townspeople.

Vaohoi giggled and looked up to Lo'au.

"Ha-ha, it's quite handy, you being a mu'a. No one has the nerve to upset you."

"I am saddened that you see it that way, Vaohoi. Knowing that he wouldn't take the shells, I saved him face nonetheless because of my position, and managed to save you from a lot of bruising."

"Tsk-tsk, are you upset because I was laughing?"

"No," the mu'a smiled. "But I'm concerned about his reaction. I've noticed many people here are tightly wound. I wonder..."

Once Vaohoi realised he was not in trouble, he ignored the rest of the old man's words. He waved his nose about to the south end of the road, before kicking his heels together.

"Mm, there's an umu with pork, I can smell it! Great Tangaloa smiles upon me this day!"

Lo'au breathed in deeply and smiled, as he watched the young man dodge village folk and disappear beyond sight. He began to hum an old tune, smile at passing villagers and walk in the general direction Vaohoi had gone.

Lo'au was from Manu'a, an island group amongst the beautiful isles of Samoa, located in the northern region of the Tongan Empire. He was a mu'a, a chief, skilled in the art of the adze and artistry. A highly skilled carver and maker of statues, shrines, houses and other items such as sacred weapons, pendants, fishing hooks and ceremonial kava bowls.

More than a master artisan, Lo'au had been a high priest to Tangaloa, the great god of the sky, for the past twenty years. Some say he held the highest order across the entire kingdom, though long ago refused to remain faithful to one single temple, people or king. Many say he had wandered across the oceans for decades as a humble pilgrim, providing aid to all who needed his help. Though bearing no actual position in the religious circles of worship, Lo'au was at all times, greatly respected and revered by other priests and orders. Prior to that time, his life was a mystery.

A physically able man of ancient years, Lo'au bore fine features compared to the common man. He had wavy shoulder length hair that shimmered with silver and lacquer, as if permanently damp with coconut oil. He had kind eyes: deep and filled with the memory of joy, laughter and humility. Beneath a grey and regal beard were fine, strong teeth, which beamed when he smiled. His voice was low and assuring, calming and influential.

He was adorned in a basic garment of heavy tapa and wore woven bracelets and anklets. The most significant item was something only a grandmaster of artisans would possess: a large medallion that he wore around his neck. It appeared to be pieces of whale ivory, mother-of-pearl, and obsidian moulded together to form a magnificent collage of intense colours and emblematic carvings. In a backdrop of shimmering pearl, was a prominent carving of cream ivory in the image of the sun, and beneath it, the representation of the a crescent moon, cast in black obsidian. On both sides of the sun and moon were carvings of symmetrical birds in flight: one made of bone, the other of stone. By his side was a long staff made from ironwood, inlaid with shining ivory, set with the constellations from the night sky. Like his medallion, his staff bore considerable and most sacred worth, believed to contain the power and blessing of the gods.

It had been four weeks since Lo'au met Vaohoi in Futuna on the cusp of autumn and winter. He was there for days, awaiting the tongiakis that carried the young boy from the neighbouring island of Rotuma. Vaohoi was the grandson of Nasili, a mu'a who had been Lo'au's friend from times past.

Before Nasili had become a devout mu'a and artisan, he had taken a wife and bore a child in Samoa, both of whom left him because of domestic and financial hardships. A decade later, Nasili was reunited with them just before his passing. Nasili's last wish to Lo'au was for him to provide guidance to his only grandson. Although both men knew that Vaohoi was undisciplined and would probably never become a mu'a, this course of guardianship was needed now more than ever.

At thirteen, Vaohoi was a trickster and a flirt who knew nothing of the world. He wore his hair cropped and erect, painted half his face yellow and wore a crazy assortment of pouches and clothing that would raise eyebrows. His face was comical, loose and could contort in ways that would have warriors keeling with laughter and children gawking in amazement.

Sneaky and calculating, Vaohoi often found himself in the nests of trouble and disorder, none of which, he argued, was any fault of his. Although his greatest vice was girls, his games of seduction and romance were uncouth, yet highly successful. In times past, it was the contest of winning the heart of a young woman that excited him beyond measure. His luck with this, according to him, was ever opulent. On every occasion he managed to find trouble, he also found much luck; the fundamental reason why the young man had not been yet killed.

The noonday sun beamed down on the island of Niuatoputapu. Sea birds called and circled the glittering coast amid a cloudless sky, searching aimlessly for fish. The northern wind was still brisk, despite the sunshine that did little to cool the temperature of the sea.

Lo'au savoured the thick smell of his hot broth that was wrapped in banana leaves. It consisted of pork, breadfruit, salted kelp and taro. His serving was infinitesimal compared to the countless portions laid out in front of Vaohoi. The youngster had taken enough cooked portions to sustain the crew of one hundred tongiaki on the sea for weeks. For the one thing that Vaohoi had inherited from his father was his spendthrift disposition. His father, a wealthy and respected mu'a of Futuna, had passed away leaving Vaohoi with more than enough riches to barter with throughout his travels with Lo'au.

"You sure you don't want any diced squid with that broth, Master?" Vaohoi pointed his greasy finger.

"No, no, Vaohoi. This is enough for me. I am forbidden to overindulge with food, remember?"

"Oh, yes, that's right," the youngster said candidly, reaching to one of the furthest portions greedily.

Lo'au grinned under his thick beard.

The pair sat out of the sun under a small palm tree on the edge of the market. They sat on a small rise, able to look over the people going about their business.

"So where are we going from here?"

"I'd like to stay for a while. I feel that my presence is needed here." Lo'au peered over the milling village folk of Falehau.

"Here? Why?"

"Something – a feeling ..."

"What feeling?"

"There's something amiss here, Vaohoi, despite the obvious."

"The obvious? You mean people going about their own lives? Everything looks normal to me," Vaohoi chomped into a whole fish.

"What is obvious, are the souls of all the people here. The obvious is the anguish, the scared, the hopelessness. I've just discovered that Anga'uli has squeezed them to the point of leaving the island – perhaps even worse."

"So what? They're common folk!"

Lo'au concealed his disappointment as he sipped the milk from a young coconut.

"Vaohoi – they have a right to be here," he started. "No one deserves to be treated that way, no matter what class. This world should be a shared one. A crawling ant has just as much right to be here as we do. Life is as precious as it is short. It should not be filled with depravity or forced destitution."

Vaohoi looked at Lo'au briefly between mouthfuls. "What? That doesn't make any sense at all, Master," he shook his head in disbelief.

Lo'au ignored him and bunched the remaining food together to eat later. The youngster continued feeding his face without comment.

A young girl who had served the food approached and knelt beside the two.

"More coconut, Master?" she asked politely.

"No thank you, my child," Lo'au smiled.

"Young Master?" She turned to Vaohoi.

The youngster motioned towards his broken and empty coconut, as he chewed with his mouth open. Once she had replaced the coconut, she stood and bowed to leave. Vaohoi stared at nothing but the girl's body and grinned wickedly.

"Excuse me, my dear, could I have a word with you?" Lo'au shifted on the grass and faced her.

"Yes, Master, of course."

"Do you know where I could find a young boy by the name of Paea? He is about so high, and is about ten or so."

The young woman paused, and then looked around as if being watched.

"In the south-western district there is a small fale kava, facing an old trail that leads to the eastern side. If you ask the men at the fale kava, they should be able to help you," she said.

When the girl had left, Lo'au slowly turned and took a final apprehensive bite at his food.

"Who's Paea?" asked Vaohoi.

"Someone I met when I arrived here in Niuatoputapu last week. He is a very endearing young boy. I'd like to see him again."

"What for, Master?" For the first time Vaohoi stopped eating. "I want to get out of this dump of a town and head south towards the capital. I hear that the Mid Winter Festival is a blast in Ha'apai. Lots of pretty, young girls!" He raised his hands in exclamation then resumed his feast. "Plus, I've never been there before."

"We will stay here until I have satisfied my curiosity, Vaohoi. Niuatoputapu is on the brink of administrational collapse. There's going to be plenty of potential violence here. It's imminent, I can feel it." Lo'au folded the banana leaves around the bones and uneaten food.

"Fighting? Ah, well. That's a good enough reason to hang around," Vaohoi took a loud sip of coconut milk, however, Lo'au was not listening.

An unnerving sensation rushed through him like a slow, electric pulse. There was something very wrong about the village. Something greater was at work than the political pressures of a cruel noble. It raised the hair on his back. He turned sharply to his rear as if to face an attacking opponent. The wind brushed the palm leaves, and the sensation passed momentarily.

CHAPTER 6

The dark politics of Niuatoputapu ran deep. For the past five years, Lord Anga'uli had turned the island into a ripe source of personal income; wealth to fund his plan to conspire against the king. Though as each year passed, no sum could levy his courage or the courage of others to make a move against such odds. Most who knew his secret plans condemned them. Regardless of his ambition, he was still a coward. His advisors questioned why he would risk all that he had: after all he virtually lived like a king in Niuatoputapu. He was once a great captain of the Empire's Northern Armies, but had sunken to become nothing but a greed-driven politician.

The last year had been ill fated however. The whale and pearl trades had, after years of continual exploitation, ceased to provide the opulence they once had. Furthermore, the sea merchants and traders had slowly begun to steer clear of Niuatoputapu's shores because of his oppressive manipulation. These socio-economic shortfalls came slow and virtually unforseen to Anga'uli and his political advisers, and were irreversible once they had begun.

He had become steadfast in his resilience, proclaiming the start of outrageous new offerings to which all citizens of Niuatoputapu were beholden. The great village of Falehau, consisting solely of soldiers, traders and artisans, was overwhelmed by the sudden demands. No one dared oppose the noble or his wishes, openly or otherwise. All feared the sudden spark of Anga'uli's wrath and short temper. His savage ways of "solving a problem" were well known.

Although most of the population of Niuatoputapu consisted of soldiers and merchants who were middle-classes in the social structure of the Empire, there were the lower-class citizens, known as tu'a. These classes of people made up the general population across the Empire: servants, farmers and labour-oriented occupations. Tu'a had no birthright and received no respect from other classes. In the eyes of cruel warriors and nobles, their lives could be taken on a whim.

The tu'a of Niuatoputapu had been badly affected by Anga'uli's growing greed. The priests from local temples, who in the past had provided them with food and shelter, could not continue their benevolence, because of the growing need. Other social groups and kind merchants were also unable to afford their weekly offerings for charity. As a result, classes left the island in droves. But for the tu'a, who were too poor to leave, it was a cruel and sad time. Now they were very few in numbers.

The night laid its clear and paved roads of the heavens across the sky. The thin clouds that weaved above the land were kind in their opposition to the constellations, much less than their forbears, who had recently ravished the northern islands with torrents of rain. However, the winter had not been as harsh as previous years. The glow from the village lights warmed the shadowy jungle that concealed it from the north winds. Spirals of smoke rose slowly from the dozens of fales, smoke that searched casually towards the far stars. The moon had risen and was only partly visible through the night clouds.

From where the two boys sat, they overlooked the entire village. To their eyes, it was a foul dwelling of evil and villainy, for it had always been this way, or so they thought.

"It's a nice night," the chubby boy remarked.

"Yeah," the other replied.

The two had been sitting in the giant palm tree for at least two hours. The chubby boy glanced at his friend fearfully.

"Do you want to go out tonight? Because if you don't -"

"Maka, we're going out tonight," the slightly older boy said with a sigh.

Maka hung his head in resolve before gazing up slowly, as if hoping to see something different about the village. But he saw what he had seen for every night of the past years: the shimmering lights of a corrupted township and the pitiful faint sounds of stupor and laughter, shouts and wails. Paea turned and looked at his friend with a resolute, yet tired, smile.

"You know we have to do this, Maka. I know that sometimes it's hard," he paused. "Alright, it's hard all the time."

Seeing his sarcastic gaze, he continued. "But we have to do this, for us, for the others ..."

Maka had heard it all before, but thought he would try his chances again anyway.

"Did you -"

"Shhhh!" Paea crouched and peered cautiously to the ground below.

From the shadows of the night appeared a small figure. Paea and Maka had their small clubs in hand, watching as the shadow paused and looked up to them.

"P-Paea?" came the voice of a young girl.

Maka's eyes rolled and Paea clicked his tongue.

"Paea ... Maka?"

"What are you doing here, Heilala?" Paea tucked his club into his vala and began climbing down the tree. He dropped from about six feet next to the girl and put his hand on her shivering shoulder.

"I -"

"You know you're not supposed to follow us. It's dangerous!"

"I know. But ..." The girl could say no more as she buried her face in Paea's chest and began to sob quietly.

"Maka, it seems you will get your wish. I need you to take Heilala home."

"Okay."

"I'll go alone," Paea said as he rocked his sister tightly to keep her warm.

Moments later, he stood quietly as he watched them disappear into the night. It was not a safe part of the village for them to be in at this time of eve, he thought, and it had not been the first time his sister had followed him outside during the nights. He was beginning to worry about her.

Paea, a tu'a of ten summers, had supported Heilala alone since their mother had died five winters ago. He and Heilala had a younger brother too, not long passed. Paea glanced up to the silver brilliance of the moon and remembered their loss.

He was young, unskilled, and had supported two siblings during that time. As he had no way of growing crops, or earning food, he turned to thievery. Desperate and starving, it was not long before he was caught and thrown into slavery on a nearby island where, remaining a boy slave for two long moons, he managed to escape as a stowaway on a trade tongiaki that sailed to Niuatoputapu. But he had returned too late. Heilala, and the baby brother, had gone without food without his support. She was unable to walk for three weeks, suffering from malnutrition and the baby had died from starvation. Heilala never recovered from the loss of her dead brother, and Paea never forgave himself. He swore that he would never again leave his sister and would do anything to scratch out a living for their survival.

As he made his way through the dark night, he was suddenly reminded of the dying warrior in the garbage pit a few weeks earlier. Little did he know that the encounter would change his life forever. On that night, he had carefully examined the items he had taken from the dead warrior and observed most things were common items: items that would not fetch him a great exchange for food. But it was the tapa cloth with strange symbols that puzzled him. Why had it been so vital to the dying warrior? What was its significance? Its importance was hidden within the symbols, and it frustrated him not knowing. He decided he would do his best to decipher it.

The next day Heilala, having knowledge of tapa design and artwork, stared at it blankly. He then took it to a trusted friend, who had previous experience with tapa symbols. The friend concluded the particular symbols and design appeared to be imperial, and if they were, that only royalty and men of high rank could construe the mysterious meanings. He also gave a word of caution: it was dangerous to be seen with such writings, as the late king had outlawed all but royalty to practise the ancient writing.

For weeks, Paea deliberated whether to ask an imperial soldier if he could take the parchment to Tongatapu, but as time passed, he considered the trouble if he were found in possession of it. He could well be blamed for the death of the warrior, if not the theft of his possessions. He could not risk walking into guaranteed capture, assured slavery, or death.

Despite this, he had made a promise to the dead man that he intended to keep. For the last week, he had been collecting as many valuable items as he could, to trade for passage to the capital, Heketa. Soon he would have enough for Heilala and Maka to accompany him. He planned to deliver the tapa to the king himself, if he could.

CHAPTER 7

Savai'i, Samoa

The midnight sea was choppy, and amid its velvet cloak it occasionally revealed a reflection of the heavens above. The sand was black under the moonless night, and waves lapped onto the soft shores at the base of the sand dune. Behind it, the light of a camp fire flickered through the whispering surrounds of the beach and the slight tussles of the palms. Sudden bursts of reddened shards drifted up through the flames and slight wisps of smoke blew from the crackling wood.

To the side of the dancing fire and within the hot coals sat a small bundle of banana leaves. Acting as an outer shell, the broad leaves were bound around a small piece of breadfruit, a couple of sweet potatoes and fresh fish. The leaves protected the food from the brazen flames and, through tight insulation, baked the meat without losing the natural juices. Every so often, the cook carefully shifted the bundle with his bare hands so as to ensure it was evenly heated. The alluring smell of roasting fish and sweet potato drifted down the dark beach. It could have summoned all the devils from hell to fight over the scraps. Instead, it drew a dozen Samoan warriors armed with the deadliest intent.

The cook sat comfortably on an old shredded piece of tapa cloth, and against a woven basket bulging with ripe coconuts. Standing behind him was a large, pronged spear used for spear-fishing, with its end stabbed into the sand like a flagstaff. Within arm's reach lay a dark and powerful weapon: a great war club four feet in length. Curves and sharp incisions on its surface formed synchronised bulbous studs. It was both a formidable weapon and a master's artwork that surpassed any woodcarver of the current day.

The weapon's symbolic patterns and designs were pre-Empire and it was undoubtedly a weapon more than a few hundred years old. It was made from a rarest form of ironwood: one of the hardest timbers found in the Pacific. It was lacquered with a mixture of sandalwood and coconut oil, and left to steam in a volcanic cavern of toxic sulphur. Within the grooves of its design were the darkest shades of black - the blood of a thousand men dyed its core over the centuries. The weapon was called 'Mohemamahi', which meant, *the painful sleep.*

The warriors crept slowly in the seaward direction so that their approach was shielded by the dune. Armed with spears and single-handed clubs, they were members of a rogue group of nationalists. They often operated covertly and defied the imperial reign of the Tongan Empire in Samoa. Earlier in the evening, they were told a Tongan warrior had been sighted sailing from the North and had set up an encampment at dusk on the western beach of Upolu. The simple task of the ambush was to murder and take possession of the warrior's property, including his watercraft.

The breeze ruffled the dry palm leaves and the waves lapped consistently onto a wet shore. Their silent and unseen approach was easily achieved and they had no difficulty taking position on the lip of the dune, covering all routes of escape. Their fierce hatred coursed through their blood, making the air thick with the silent building of testosterone and warlike rage.

As the warriors began to approach, the cook reached into the fire and pulled the bundle of banana leaves from its embrace. When he peeled back the leaves, a sudden punch of delicious aroma exploded through the camp. The baked fish laced with kelp and the heavy smell of sweet staples was intoxicating. Strangely, there was also a distinct smell of burnt food skins. The cook placed the small feast in front of himself and inspected the results. He picked out one of the sweet potatoes which was charred and blackened. He smiled as he brought the overcooked potato to eye level.

"I shall waste naught of your whole, my little friend. But your skin shall pay the price of death tonight. I have not the mood for it."

The leader of the warriors crouched into a pouncing position and quickly glanced around to the others. Another slowly adjusted a long spear in his palm, judging the distance of a fatal throw. He began to bare his teeth and share the electrifying fury among the eyes of his comrades. His gaze fell over a warrior furthest from him, and he felt his heart skip a beat. The warrior's enraged expression had been replaced by disbelief. The battle fury dissipated in a matter of seconds, as a wave of dread washed over the entire group of warriors. Their raised weapons gradually touched the sand slowly as they crouched, both poised and stunned by the sight that lay before them.

With one swift jerk, the cook had ripped his left thumb nail from his hand and began to quietly sing an old love song. The milky, red blood flowed from his torn thumb and soiled the blackened potato he held. With his right, he commenced using the severed fingernail to scrape off the charred skin. When half of the potato was cleaned, the cook tossed the used nail into the fire and ripped off his other thumb nail in the same fashion. Again, without a single sign of pain, the cook never faltered his song and continued to scrape the charcoaled potato.

When the potato was freed of its burnt crust the cook's forearms dripped with blood, his stumped thumbs caked with the maroon colours of the clottish mess. He smiled as he finished the song, turned and scanned the bare sand dune where the warriors had been. He stuffed the remaining potato in his mouth and climbed atop the dune. The entire beach was deserted and the vastness of the ocean lay out before him.

"Only on nights like these can you really appreciate time alone," he laughed, and walked back to the campfire.

He sat down and tore off small parchments of tapa cloth from his own clothing. Using his teeth, he tightly wrapped each length of tapa around his wounded thumbs and knotted the ends. Within seconds, the blood from his thumbs stained through the light brownish material. He leant against the net of coconuts and reached for his club.

With both hands he inspected the club with an eye of scrutiny, running his fingers through the grooves of its carvings. He then held it out in the open palms of his hands.

"Mighty Mohemamahi, I know you yearn for more lives of men. Forget tonight. There will be more important lives to take soon enough," he smiled and placed the club next to him, folded his arms and closed his eyes.

An hour before dawn, new light hinted amid the darkness of the horizon. The wind had subsided in potency, gently kissing the pre-dawn like a loving mother. The air temperature had dropped suddenly just before dawn. Its brisk touch felt refreshing to the cook as he packed his belongings together.

He made several short trips through the sand to his tongiaki, throwing an assortment of fishing nets, utensils and tapa cloth into the aft of the sail craft.

Although unusually styled, his tongiaki still retained the equal double hulls that totalled eighty feet in length. They were strengthened by supporting ribs from aft to bow. The cross sections of supporting beams secured a sizable deck, one which secured two main masts that curled out in a mailu claw. To the rear of the deck was a decent sized housing in the shape of a tiny fale, capable of sheltering up to a dozen men. Towards the bow was a large fireplace: a crucible of stone, fashioned into the deck and secured with wooden railings. The vessel was clearly made beyond that of average standards.

He heaved the nets of dozens of coconuts over his shoulder and tossed the bulk of what would have weighed twice that of a man, into the tongiaki. He paused directly at the aft before striking the sail craft with his large hands and his body weight. In seconds, he pushed the entire craft ten metres across the dry sand and back into the calm morning sea. With the embrace of the cool water, the craft took float and he leapt out of the water like a projectile onto master deck. He made the preparations to untie the huge sails.

Dawn had arrived. The stars across the sky began to fade amid a beautiful mixture of pinks, oranges and turquoise. The apex of the sun peeped over the horizon. The tongiaki was hundreds of metres from the shore. It had turned in the direction of the open sea, its lone master facing the marble of the Pacific Ocean and the rays fell upon his face with warmth and welcome. He smiled, as though greeting the morning for the first time.

Had the rebels, during the night, known the identity of the cook, they would have either bowed to their knees, or fled as they did for one reason alone. The man was renowned across the entire Pacific. He was regarded as a living legend, folk hero and the last of a mighty warrior lineage from the dawn of Polynesian ancestry. A warrior without equal and allegiance, his name was Maui Atalaga, a mortal descendant of the great Maui himself.

He was of average height, about six foot ten inches, built with a strong frame of well sized and defined muscle and in perfect proportion. He neither appeared of Tongan stock nor other Polynesian race. He was perhaps a mixture of all. His age could be put between thirty and forty, though there seemed to be an ageless quality about him. His hair was a dark brown colour, straight and wavy, and hung to his shoulders. Painted across his body were the tattoo styles of every Polynesian race across the Pacific. Typical designs included intrinsic sharp, angled motifs from the Tongan and Samoan peoples, the undulating spirals and curls from the Rarotonga and Tahiti peoples and the symbolic totems from the underworld, Pulotu. The designs also represented a mythology of Polynesian gods and told the story of their origins.

There was a pantheon of gods in the Polynesian mythology: gods of the winds, the ocean, the sun and harvest and of creatures such as sharks, lizards and birds. The most powerful triumvirate of

Polynesian gods, being Tangaloa, Hikule'o and Maui, had drawn up all the Pacific Islands with powerful hooks and were the creators of all things.

Tangaloa was the eldest and most revered, ruling the realm of the everlasting sky, sun and moon. He was well worshiped across the Pacific Islands and was renowned for his kindness, humility and compassion for man. The religious following of Tangaloa was the most common and popular among the people. Offerings included the burning of aromatic flowers, leaves, fresh fruit and bird meat.

Hikule'o was the powerful and feared ruler of the underworld, Pulotu. Hikule'o was revered and respected through fear from the living, an ever-present dominance on mortal minds. The god was the taker of life, a malevolent deity who yearned for all souls to be taken to the underworld, where most would exist in pain and suffering for all eternity. Only those mortals who showed dominance and power over others were given concessions in the afterlife. Offerings and tributes were often human sacrifices, appeasing the god for his thirst. These would give the people times of peace from his rueful taking.

According to the myth, when Tangaloa was not watching, Hikule'o threw all the volcanic islands across the Pacific Ocean from the sky and he laughed at man's horror in his tiny sail craft as he did so. In turn, his brother, Maui, tossed his magical fishing hook into the ocean and pulled up all the great islands of the Pacific to save man and provide exploration and habitation. Hikule'o scorned Maui for spoiling his cruelty, at which Maui simply laughed.

Maui was the least worshiped, not because he was less revered, but because the god represented freedom, diversity, autonomy and free will. The very meaning of Maui and what he represented cross-grained the idea of formal worship and veneration. Those who adulated him did so in an individual, private manner and during times alone, without fanfare or ceremony. Maui gave favour to all warriors and travellers who lived life with courage, optimism and daring, those who rebelled against a hardened life of law and order.

Legend had it that following the ascent of the elder gods from the material world, each god left behind a progeny of descendants.

Maui Atalaga was said to be the only remaining progeny of these ancient times. His stories had spread far and wide, and like his fathers before him, Maui Atalaga was of neutral alignment, which neither favoured good nor evil.

Tales of his wanderings across the seas as a folk hero, slayer of monsters, and protector of man were widely known. Though as a man he was introverted and indifferent, neither professing to his great deeds, nor acknowledging his fame as a hero of lore and mythology. He lived his life seemingly with no purpose in the world but to travel the open seas, seeking duels as a warrior and discovering that which lies beyond the yearning horizon.

He gazed up at the majestic morning sky and looked at the fading stars, then lowered his head and looked in a particular direction on the vista. He reefed the beam of the lower mast sharply and swung it to capture the rear wind drafts. The tongiaki turned slightly and bore a new course.

"Niuatoputapu," he said.

The tongiaki cut through the calm brine like peeling skin on a cooked potato.

CHAPTER 8

Strong voices came from the House of Anga'uli. Within the large reception room they were chillingly sober.

"Master, please!" the servant girl wept, cradling a baby.

Anga'uli stared at her bluntly, his male retainers lined against the walls of the room. Suddenly, over the soft wails of the girl, rose his cruel and heartless laughter. He sat cross legged in the middle of the room with a kava bowl in front of him. He sneered when he could laugh no longer. His words slurred with inebriation.

"My, my. I haven't heard such news for a while. Well, since the previous girl left the house last month!" He couldn't contain himself as he and his retainers roared with laughter.

The girl, no more than fifteen years old, tried to see through the blur of her tears and mockery of men.

"B-b-but what am I to do, Master?" she cried in vain.

Anga'uli stopped laughing and glared at her sourly.

"Think, woman! Perhaps feeding it would be a good idea!" he cackled. "You could comfort it with this thought – it isn't the first bastard born from drunken lust!"

"But, Master, it is *your* child!" the girl exclaimed in tears.

There was a cutting silence.

"GET OUT!" The noble leapt to his feet as the kava bowl tore across the floor. "If I see you again, I will flay you lifeless!"

His voice was so powerful that the girl almost fainted. Her wailing had become uncontrollable and she was paralysed. Anga'uli fumed at the mouth when she did not respond. He eyed two retainers and ripped his throwing club from his waist.

"Get her out now, damn you!"

He stormed from the fale towards his private quarters and swore angrily. The punch of night air sobered him somewhat as he inhaled deeply. By the time he returned to his abode, his fleeting moment of anger and guilt had evaporated. The goodness that was once the mortar of a dignified commander had all but been forgotten. The surge of carnal desire lit in his loins suddenly. He felt the evil cloak of yearning, which he could no longer control, envelop him with intoxicating power.

As he stumbled into the fale, he glanced at three servants waiting patiently against the walls. His eyes caught his prey. He snatched the young girl's wrist so hard he almost snapped it. She squealed in agony.

"Get out!" he roared to the others.

Before they scuttled away, Anga'uli threw the girl, no more than thirteen years old, to his sleeping area. She crashed on the wooden floor hard, knocking her head with a thump. The noble was on top of her. He ripped the tapa from her quivering body and gorged her breasts with his mouth. The girl bit her lip as she tried to control the pain and fear, daring not to displease her master. His rough hands crushed her suppleness and his nails drew blood as they tore her flesh. With a grunt, he flipped her to her knees and struck her forwards. He moved in behind her like an animal. Reaching out, he seized a handful of long hair and yanked her head backwards. As he did, he thrust himself into her with a slap. She could no longer contain her screams.

Had the soldiers been partially sober from kava as they swayed at their posts, they would have noticed the small dark figure move across the entryway behind them. Paea was silent as he skimmed along the ground with incredible dexterity. He had learned much since his escape from slavery and living a life of thievery.

The old timber made no sound as he clambered up the steep framework to the roof of the high priest's house. The fale was the easiest house to penetrate within the Noble Compound because it lay closest to the entryway and was barely ever guarded. It was also a house Paea was familiar with...

The rustling of the thatched roof gave an inconspicuous sound. His form melted with the dark shadows within massive cavities of the roof inside the house, as he carefully reshuffled the thatched roofing – one of the first rules of his trade – to always cover your tracks. There was no light in the large room, no sound. The constant tickle of the cold wind outside made the insides of the room seem deathly silent, and made his eyes water.

As he sat in silence, he reminded himself of the reason he was there. One more visit and he would have enough bounty to leave Niuatoputapu. They would leave as soon as the next day. The faint, musty smell of the thatched roof and the polished ironwood reminded him of the adrenalin of his previous visits. The smell coursed his blood, and he began to hear the sound of his heartbeat. He dug his weight onto the beam as he slowly slid down the pillar.

Suddenly, a soft voice of clarity rose over his thoughts, the voice of a wandering mu'a he had met a few days ago.

"What you are doing is a miracle to those you love. Despite the thievery you are beholden to, to think of others before yourself, is a quality few men in this world possess."

The mu'a, an ancient man with plain cloth, had confronted Paea for directions in the south end of the village and yet after short moments, Paea had recounted to him his whole life. He was not the kind of boy who would normally open up to anyone, in fact most people regarded him as withdrawn and guarded. He felt a peace around him, the kind of peace a son would have in the presence of his father. The benevolent mu'a offered him a handful of mother-of-pearl before they departed company, which he had subtly refused and blushed with embarrassment; no one had ever offered valuables to him for nothing. The boy remembered Lo'au's words as they parted.

"Just remember, Paea, there is strength in all of us. As long as you have hope, your strength and spirit shall prevail. May the good of Tangaloa guide and protect you."

The glowing embers did little to illuminate the reception room, and Anga'uli who lay limp in the corner, was weary and glazed. Following hours of ravaging the young girl, he had come to the high priest's house to discuss the dubious position of his favour in the eyes of the gods. The assistant of the village headman, an honest and truthful man, had opposed Anga'uli's economic strategy for more offerings. The idea was ridiculous to the assistant, a man who also frequently spoke his mind, despite his dictator's view.

Anga'uli came to the high priest to discuss whether the gods favoured the assistant headman and whether they would frown upon a plot to murder him. Should the gods smile on his death, it had to be done carefully, for the man was popular with the townspeople. Only two days ago, the high priest had told Anga'uli he would be absent from the island in order to attend a family funeral in Niuafo'ou, and as Anga'uli often ignored personal matters of his advisers, he had forgotten that it was mentioned to him.

Arriving in the fale and remembering this, he decided that under the circumstances, he would spend the night drinking kava at the empty house anyway. He had begun to sing to himself in a self-induced delirium amid a floor covered with empty cups and pools of the spilt kava.

Suddenly he heard movement from the shadows across the room. It shook him from his inebriated state.

"You tremble, *son of worm*," a grinding, hypnotic voice echoed from the darkest corner of the room.

He recognised the voice and whispered a prayer to Hikule'o that he was not alone.

"K–Kamohoali'i?" Anga'uli stammered as he stood and took a blind step forward.

"Anga'uli," another voice, deep and low resonated from the other corner of the room.

There was the sound of clicking fingers, and suddenly, red sparks hissed and showered to the floor. The flames on the torches began to grow and reveal two men facing the nobleman. Anga'uli fell to a knee in respect.

"H-Hail the Pulotulahi!" he quivered, failing to hide the fear in his voice.

General Kamohoali'i, the right arm to Lord Tu'ipulotu, the overlord of the Pulotulahi, paced to the centre of the room and crossed his arms. He was a short, stocky man for a Tongan, standing about six foot two inches, with a large stomach that slightly overhung the tapa around his waist. He appeared to be a man around his mid forties, covered in a patchwork of terrible scars that told a story of battle, sun and sea.

Despite his girth, he possessed strong arms and even more powerful legs that seemed to root him to the ground like a giant palm. Less impressive to the eye than younger, fitter warriors, he commanded the dominant presence of a warrior who had lived and survived through a long life of violence and cruelty. His experience on the battlefield was a skill greater than any warrior of greater youth.

"I overheard your less than cordial conversation in the kava house," Kamohoali'i's voice was like a light tremor of an earthquake.

"Yes – well – I-I'm," Anga'uli stared at the floor.

"You're close to feeling the bite of my club is what you are." The second man's hypnotic voice carried like a manifestation from a nightmare.

Anga'uli could not summon the courage to even look in his direction. Though he followed Kamohoali'i as a dog does his master, he feared Havea, Kamohoali'i's warrior chief, far more than any man.

As Havea advanced, the shadows seemed to follow him like a creeping darkness. The warrior chief wore no clothes. However, he was never naked, as his entire body was swathed in a myriad of intricate tattoos and symbolic Polynesian designs. He appeared to wear ancient rings of bone and obsidian, bracelets, anklets and a necklace that sported the skulls of human foetuses.

Havea's physique was a perfect balance between skin and bone. Long limbs and tattooed skin pulled tightly over elongated sinew that resulted in a gaunt appearance. His neck and face bore the most striking tattoos of jagged lines twisted in a fierce and vivid style. They bulged significantly from his skin as if the ink were arteries that pumped the black blood through his body. Even stranger, he did not seem to possess pupils in his eyes nor iris; his eyeballs seemed black in their entirety.

His midnight hair was unkempt, hanging wildly about his shoulders and upper chest. His age could be put between thirty and forty, however his presence gave him greater years.

"What sort of trust do you think I should hold for you, Anga'uli, when I find you in such states?" Kamohoali'i was immovable.

"I-I have no excuses, Milord. Please forgive me."

Havea smirked from the corner and with his hands made the sound of strangulation around the grip of his club. Just as he stood and motioned for the two warriors to sit with him, there was a flicker of shadow that faded into the darkness behind them, and unknown to the three lords, there were now four in the room.

Paea could barely breathe as he squeezed into a space between the corner wall and tapa cloth that hung from one of the high beams. He quivered slightly, trying to suppress the fear of certain capture as he was forced into the reception room. Having headed straight for the high priest's personal room where the fief of the household lay, he nearly collided with a horde of retainers who appeared from the rear entrance.

Evading the plodding servants with ease, he had slipped into the reception room, unaware that it was occupied. Once the retainers had left, however, he realised he was trapped. The entrance was in plain view of the three lords who had seated themselves. Only dark shadows lay in the corners of the long room, one of which, Paea had made his hiding place. Squashed in the darkness, the boy had no option but to keep still, keep quiet and listen.

Kamohoali'i slowly placed his large hands on his thighs and glared at Anga'uli with big, gruelling and merciless eyes.

"Now," he growled. "Tell me. How have the plans gone?"

CHAPTER 9

Nausori Highlands, Fiji
Autumn, A.D.1120

The wind picked up around the warrior priest, teasing his tapa robes of soot and auburn tones. The cloth rippled in waves as he tirelessly made his way along the high and treacherous mountain path. Alongside it were deep chasms covered in wet moss and clumps of ferns, and between the chasms swirled the heavy morning mist that coveted the streams below. The trail of black river stones wound and twisted as it rose higher and higher to its peak. The warrior priest followed it around a precarious and narrow edge then paused to take in his view.

The summit was sparse and flat, falling short of the surrounding mountains, which loomed and darkened behind heavy mist. Two or three vesi trees that looked to have stood during the time of creation, guarded the entrance to the tiny glade, which was spotted with giant timber totems bearing religious symbols and intricate carvings. They too seemed to have stood the test of time: all soaked with age-old wounds of years of weather beating and moss growth.

In the centre of the clearing was a small fale that overlooked the entire southern island of Viti Levu. It was of simple design: floored with polished sandalwood, cornered by four short beams of ironwood that supported a contemporary thatched roof of ancient Fijian style. In the four corners of the fale, lay red-clay pottery of ancient Lapita design; inside of each burned the sweet scent of oil. Tiny strands of tinged vapour rose from the oil, smelling of warm coconut and crushed Heilala flowers. There was a single, perfectly cut, stone step, which led onto the shrine where the warrior priest stood and waited.

The initiate sat motionless in the shrine, absorbed within the tranquil surroundings. Covered in auburn drapes of tapa and hood, the body of the initiate seemed to flow onto the shrine like layers of melted lava. The initiate ended the meditation without rush and recited a few lines of the religious faith, before stepping out of the small fale. The initiate stood unfazed before Emori, a member of the Degei warrior priests.

Emori lifted both hands to draw back the hood of the initiate, revealing a stoic, yet attractive, female face.

"Adi, your time has come," he smiled.

Far below and hidden within the forests of the Nausori Highlands, was the infamous bure kalou of Degei. The huge structure was said to have been built by the first brethren of Fijian voyages from Kanaka, a few hundred years ago. It sat in a perfect axis at the foot of the crag and was constructed of solid ironwood and black palm, decorated with sennit and cowry shells. The site covered an area of ten acres and rose as high as thirty feet, its massive halls that carried the echoes of eons, and lofty heights that rivalled the tallest trees, made it an ancient wonder amongst the people of the Empire.

The greatest of all Fijian gods was Degei, the Snake God, who created man and taught him how to cultivate the earth and live life. According to legend, Degei also created Viti Levu and all the small islands. The Degei priests had long been the guardians of the bure kalou and Keepers of the Stars. The Way of the Stars, as the Degei called it, was a path of spiritual embodiment that emphasized the simultaneous development of mind and body, which led to understanding and enlightenment. Thus their main goal was ultimate control of their own spirit and achieving harmony between mind and body.

The warm autumn sun shed beams through the tops of the tall palms, painting the forest floor in patches of jades and ochres. Adi and Emori strolled along the green forest trail, the initiate always a step behind her protector. The fifteen years of study and attainment within the bure kalou had been hard and somewhat of a trial for Adi. Being among the few women within the order, she had always been treated as an outsider, despite her vivid past. Her family had been too poor to support her and, as a result, her father had begged the Degei to adopt her as an acolyte at the age of four.

Three hundred Degei disciples sat cross-legged in the centre of the bure kalou. Sitting in rows of perfect lines, the sheer numbers did little to occupy the hall; like a convergent of ants on the floor of a large room. Clad in the disciple level of yellow and white tapa, the disciples had been chanting the melodies of Degei, songs that outlined the meaning of disciplinary accomplishment. The chanting was loud and hypnotic, personified by the great number of priests. It echoed through the bure kalou in a low vibration that seemed to resonate from the cowry shells themselves.

In front of the disciple body, were the four priests holding the title of Master. From the left sat Masters Koroi, Vunibaka, Adi, and the last, Lemeki, Master of Snakes. Congregated in the form of a crescent moon, were the heads of the Degei. Seven priests in all, facing directly adjacent to the four Masters and the disciples. To the left sat the Masters of the East, West, North, and South Winds and to the right were the Masters of Summer and Winter. In the centre of the half circle sat the Grandmaster. Every initiate in the bure kalou, with the exception of the seven, had chanted the song that usually took about three hours to complete. It was a chant sung only during times of promotions and recognitions of courage and service. On that day, it was to honour Adi's attainment of the title, Master of Snakes.

The chanting finally ended and the disciples opened their eyes. A single word was roared by the hundreds of disciples as they clapped their hands together. The Grandmaster spoke only when the powerful echo had died.

74

"Adi, Superior Master. Rise," he said in almost a godly voice.

The young woman made her way into the space between the Seven and the Disciples.

"Adi, over the past few years you have proven yourself as a wise and powerful teacher of the Degei and the Way. You have given yourself completely to the discipline and religion. You are now presented with the amulet of the Superior Master," he stood and approached her.

The Grandmaster produced an old parchment of tapa cloth, which he unwrapped slowly to reveal a true treasure. A shining, green stone necklace, the size of a human eye, sparkled in the half light like a northern star on a velvet horizon. He extended the necklace and placed it around her neck.

"You have now earned the title – Master of Snakes. This path is beset with its own quests and challenges, and will be a difficult responsibility," he finished, extending his hand, palm upwards.

"Yes, Grandmaster. I am ready to take that responsibility," she fell to both knees and bowed her head until she was asked to rise.

The river flowed peacefully, parting for stones that protruded from the glistening surface. The evening sun gazed through the azure palms, casting warm spots of sunlight on the moving water. There was a slight breeze: one that carried the scent of sandalwood incense that wafted from the bure kalou. Adi sat by the water and stared, lulled by the moving water.

She had become a woman of the Degei with the power to accept life's trials and deal with them with an overwhelming spirit of both strength and clarity. Despite this, she knew that she was but half way to attaining true enlightenment. The mountain peak was still as far as the distant ground below - she was now considered a true Degei, at the beginning of life's quest. Fifteen years of training was now over. Those years were merely instructions and preparations for that day, the day when she would transcend the initiation, and begin her true destiny. Having completed the first stage of the Degei, she would now begin the last stage, which would take the rest of her life.

Emori gently sat down beside her by the river. When she did not acknowledge his presence, he shared the silence and looked at the water as she did. Emori, a man of his late twenties, was a tall and handsome Fijian from the island of Vanua Levu. His dark features made him alluring and there was a peace in his eyes that could ground any troubled soul in solace.

Brought to the bure kalou at six months old, he was the abandoned infant nephew of the Grandmaster, Nakaunicina. The Grandmaster's youngest sister had been raped by brigands in their home village during the civil wars. She had wanted to kill the baby when it was born, however, in a twist of fate she died giving birth to Emori. He was then dumped at the steps of the bure kalou with the family tapa design, identifying the baby as Nakaunicina's kin.

Throughout his whole life, he had to accept the fact that he was a product of a fiendish act; a rape, which had killed his mother and dishonoured his father. This shame and dishonour had him searching for answers in the stars for years, unravelling the anger and humiliation of his history. But instead, he found peace and acceptance, a medium that showed no blame or malice. This, he knew, was the core of his existence; a series of unfolding events that wrote his life without consciousness. This unconsciousness became his understanding and this understanding to him was enlightenment.

"How are all the pressures of responsibility setting in?" he grinned.

"Emori, do you ever wonder whether destiny is – predetermined?" she asked, ignoring his question.

"Well, the Way tells us that all things are predetermined, Adi, even our destinies. You know that." He took on a more serious tone.

"I know the teaching. My faith is untarnished. But I have just been thinking about it the last few days."

"That is no surprise. You just completed your grading, something that is not an easy accomplishment. During these times you ask yourself a lot of things. You sometimes doubt the obvious. It's natural," he smiled warmly.

"So each man does not control his destiny?" Adi could not take her eyes off the river.

"Not directly. His choices create the illusion that he is sewing his own path. But in reality, his choices are a result of the predetermined destiny of the stars. If a man throws himself off a cliff to his doom, it was meant to be, despite any impulsive actions that may have caused the event."

The pair sat again in silence.

Eventually she turned to him and took his hand in hers. She looked into his eyes. A rush of feelings was shared between them, an unspoken bond of loving friendship. There was no one else Adi confided in or cherished as she did Emori. As childhood friends, they were inseparable. As adults, they had become as close as kin.

However both knew that once Adi attained the Master of Snakes, their years together would end. As the Grandmaster's grandchild, Emori held a respected and unyielding position as commander of the Warrior Priests in the Nausori Highlands. The Grandmaster cared nothing for the bond he and Adi had for each other, and had repeatedly stated that he was to stay at the bure kalou in Nausori permanently.

"You will do excellently, Adi. This is your destiny that has been bestowed on you. Never lose your focus; remember, the best teacher in this world is yourself," he said as they both slowly stood.

"I wish you were coming with me," she whispered, sounding like the young girl she once was. "How do I learn to live without you?"

"No one, not even the Grandmaster knows the true paths of destiny. I can only hope that destiny may bring us together again, my soul mate."

The two embraced, and then parted.

Emori disappeared along the forest trail, only moments before another man came from the other direction. Adi had resumed her daydreaming when the senior warrior priest stood respectfully behind her.

"Adi, Master of Snakes. I believe we have met, a number of years ago. But firstly, I would like to congratulate you on your promotion and express my delight that I have been given the honour to escort you to begin a new bure kalou in Niuatoputapu." The man wavered, uneasy that she had not acknowledged him.

"I'm sorry, what was your name?" she apologized as she stood to face him.

"I am Duvuduvukulu, Captain of the Red Earth."

"Yes, I know your face from the units. Pleased to meet you, Captain." She motioned him to sit, as she and Emori had.

"Tell me, Captain Duvuduvukulu, have you waited long for this commission?"

"Ten years."

"Your destiny, Captain," she said.

"Well, yes – a warrior priest may wait his whole life and never be commissioned. I consider myself very honoured," he ended hesitantly, not know where the conversation was going.

"How many warrior priests are accompanying us?"

"Just twenty-five for this initial journey. We will be stationing one hundred once we build the new bure kalou."

Adi paused as she mentally composed herself. She had not given a thought to their meeting, knowing well the predicament they were in. Duvuduvukulu was, by reputation, a bully of sorts among the warrior priest ranks. Though upstanding and ambitious, he was known to subtly defy the Way.

The predicament was that Duvuduvukulu had been the best friend of Vunibaka, an arrogant man at the same rank as Adi. Over the years, Vunibaka had taken a dislike to Adi and considered her a rival within the Degei.

"Well, Captain Duvuduvukulu, I look forward to leaving next week. In my opinion, both of our positions will be put to the test during this quest. I'd prefer if this mutual understanding could be used for the benefit of our goal," she said sternly.

"I could not agree more, Master Adi." He rose before her, bowed and left.

"We shall see," she said when he was gone.

Her first task as Master was to travel to the island of Niuatoputapu in the northern part of central Tonga. She was to travel to the island to find a place to build a Degei bure kalou, and if successful, establish her subsidiary there on the grounds.

The task was a great one: though the Fijians were under the rule of the Empire, Fijian religion was seen as inferior to the pantheon of Polynesian gods. Despite this, the Tongans withheld the cares of how Fijians or other Pacific Islanders in the Empire practised their religion. Regardless, only a master could be suited to such a task on a Tongan island.

When she had notified the Grandmaster of her willingness to become the next Master of Snakes, he knew that building a subsidiary was forthcoming. Under his judgment, no one deserved nor suited the honour more than she, and despite the fact that the cost of this bure kalou would be more than they could afford, he would find a way to make it possible. He had many reasons why he decided to send her to Niuatoputapu.

He knew that if anyone had the potential to develop a bure kalou anew, it would be she. She was also a woman: an unprecedented promotion as the head of a bure kalou. Yet in view of drawing such criticism, he believed she had proved to be an outstanding example to other women, and thus deserved the responsibility of such a task.

Perhaps it was destiny, he had surmised.

CHAPTER 10

Early morning, perhaps a few hours before dawn, Maka shuffled between the thick shrubs and the looming wall of the domicile. Only two torches lit the main entryway to the high priest's house, however, the inner courtyard seemed very dark. He decided not to take any chances anyway; plunging headlong into the residence would be suicide. He slowly peered up at the walls to search for a suitable niche for his makeshift grappling hook.

Minutes later, he was shrouded in the shadows of the great fale. At the end of the high walls were wooden statues of Hikule'o: impressive monuments that were lined all along the inner walls. Between the statues and the building, was his usual covert position on most nights. It was an excellent hiding place as it was out of ground view and provided access to countless entryways. On most occasions, he stood as the sentry, as Paea slipped through the house like the evening breeze.

Memories flooded back as he sat still catching his breath, times of close encounters, of miraculous escapes and wealthy thefts. This fale, he thought, was the easiest abode they ever had the pleasure of returning to, time after time. There were, by far, more heavily guarded houses in the village than the high priest's abode. Never before had they had much trouble with this house, he assured himself; they knew it like their own. He had memorized the number of steps from the entrance to the hallway, from the hallway to the "treasure room".

He unconsciously began biting his thumbnail. Had he been older and wiser, he would have realised that he was making excuses for what he feared. They were excuses, which doubted certain capture; reassurances that explained Paea's disappearance. Paea had not returned home by his usual time and had been out for over four hours. It had been too long a period to be a normal visit to the high priest's residence.

His instincts urged that he was still inside. The thought that he may be dead never crossed his mind. He had learned that imaginings were a dangerous thing, especially if you did not have the willpower to ignore them. Such thoughts had taken his hopes away his entire life, and he had thus adopted the habit of ignoring such presumptions and accepted reality as it came to him. This, unfortunately, taxed his efforts to act on his own accord as he followed Paea's orders blindly, and did little to question his actions. It was the very reason that he sat on the wall and did nothing.

Almost half an hour passed before he heard the whole house awaken. Shaken from his blank and incomprehensible musings, he peered fearfully down to a blaze of torches that lit the area suddenly and pierced his eyes. A dozen shouting retainers sprinted out like hungry dogs, followed by Anga'uli and Kamohoali'i. Maka could hear them from where he lay.

"Damn you fools! Which way did the kid go?" Anga'uli's face was red with fury.

"This way!" one of the retainers barked, as he led the mob out of the courtyard and into the outer perimeter.

The noble was left with the general.

"Do you think he heard–" Anga'uli started.

"He heard everything, you imbecile. Do you have warriors guarding this fale or flower girls? He was hiding in there the entire time!" Kamohoali'i seethed and turned to leave. "I will take care of this myself."

When he disappeared and the noble began to follow the searching retainers, Maka slowly stood and leaned against the wall. He swallowed hard as his stomach churned, and his face went pale.

Nothing like this had ever happened. Never before had the household of retainers been alerted to their presence, let alone the ruler of the island and a powerful lord. Taking a few seconds to check that he would not be sick, he took a deep breath and vanished into the shadows of the roof.

On the other side of the domicile was a small courtyard that opened onto a large garden. The fale itself came out as far as the adjoining courtyard, looming over the stone fixtures in an unorthodox design. Maka peered over the edge carefully, looking for a safe, possible way to climb to the ground. Latching his strong hands around a groove in one of the statues, he turned and placed his foot slowly over the edge.

Suddenly there came a piercing roar from beneath him, and he could do nothing more than catch himself falling from fright. He stared down into the courtyard, to see his friend stagger against the wall. Paea paused to find somewhere to hide, but was too late. An arrow thumped into his left shoulder in an impact that spun him to the ground.

Three retainers raced out of the domicile howling as if they had caught a prized animal. They raised their clubs to finish the young boy off before a shrilling scream came from above, followed by the giant statue plummeting amid them. The weighty thud was a mixture of splintering bones and heavy earth. The last retainer took the chubby boy's weight with a hefty crash.

"Paea! Paea!" he cried, lifting the dying boy over his shoulders.

As he did, another arrow zipped past. Maka turned feverishly and saw General Kamohoali'i standing at the entryway, casually stringing another arrow to his longbow.

Crying in vain, he staggered through the courtyard with Paea over his shoulder. He felt another arrow claim the body as he slipped and sprawled into a shallow pond, sending Paea's body flopping forwards. But he did not stop moving. Wiping mud and water from his face, he heaved the body again and lurched through the pond to the other side. The added weight of his friend and momentum sent them smashing through the rear bushes from the garden and out onto a dusty trail.

He made an effort to rise but his body did not respond: he lay utterly fatigued, shuddering with each breath. The thumping of blood through his head was deafening and his vision blurred with muck and tears. The echo of angry voices seemed distant and for seconds he dared to believe he had escaped them. He flinched as a yell shot down the dim trail, followed by a young man carrying a bag of woven banana leaves. As he leaned over to inspect Paea's pierced shoulder, another voice came from behind. Before he lost consciousness, he recalled the bearded face of an old mu'a peering down at him.

Around noon the following day, Maka awoke suddenly, saturated in perspiration. The air he breathed was stale: the confines of the small fale were stifling but for two exits on either side. Rising slowly and peering from its main entrance, he recognised the old fale kava down along the busy waterfront. Clothing himself properly, he limped around his headrest and approached the other exit. Pulling aside a tapa curtain that led into an adjoining fale, he saw Lo'au sitting next to the pale body of Paea. The old mu'a had rested his right hand on Paea's forehead and was whispering something indiscernible. The arrows had been removed and his body had been washed and clothed. When he entered the room, Lo'au opened his eyes and smiled.

Maka hesitantly returned the smile, and seated himself close to his friend. Lo'au lifted his palm from Paea and placed both hands in his lap.

"Good afternoon, young one."

"S-s-sir."

"My name is Lo'au. Do you remember meeting me from a few weeks ago with Paea?"

He was silent.

"I took you in this morning after your daring escape from the high priest's residence."

Verbally reminded of the horror, he lowered his head and then cast a glance at his friend.

"Is – is he dead?"

"No. He is unconscious. His recovery is doubtful though."

"So – h-he's going to – d-die then?"

Lo'au sighed and answered truthfully.

"I am uncertain. I believe that the arrows were poisoned."

Maka put his hands together and bowed his head. As he did, Vaohoi casually appeared through the curtain.

"Ah, he's awake at last," he blurted, and threw himself at the foot of the body.

Maka gave him an apprehensive look before turning to his unconscious friend.

"Hey, what the hell were you two doing last night?" Vaohoi started.

"Vaohoi—" Lo'au raised his hand in annoyance. "Just let me handle this."

"Maka, who did this to Paea?" The mu'a spoke with a confiding voice.

The boy answered by hanging his head. Sweat ran down his face and, with mucus, dripped off his nose.

"You must tell me."

"T-t-he Dark Lord ..."

"Dark Lord? What is his name, child?"

"I-I don't know. I have heard other men talking about him. He's old, but really big and looks like the god of death. He used a bow..." The boy shivered.

"Kamohoali'i, a General of the Pulotulahi. I heard that he was seen in these parts. Well, that explains the poison," Lo'au's gaze became unfocused. "I wonder what he is doing here – and at the high priest's house."

"Maybe they're old buddies?" Vaohoi shrugged and giggled.

Lo'au ignored the sarcasm, "Maka, was Paea there to steal?'

"Y-y-yes, sir ..."

"Well, that's strange, because I found no fief on his body. Still, that could just mean that he was spotted before he could lay his hands on anything."

"Humph, that's a poorly trained thief for you." Vaohoi clicked his tongue.

"Paea is the best!" Maka shouted defensively. "I don't understand, we've never been caught before. He's always got the goods!"

"That's because you've never had a big, bad, ugly Dark General in there!" Vaohoi taunted.

"Vaohoi, please," Lo'au warned for the last time.

"Maka, do you remember anything different about last night? Or something the retainers may have said during your escape?"

"I – I remember something the Dark Lord said. He said that Paea 'had heard everything' and they were angry about it."

Lo'au nodded and looked down to the dying boy. He then rose and searched his worn travelling pack.

"I think I know a proper antidote, now that I know the type of poison."

"How do you know that?" Vaohoi was genuinely impressed.

"When the Kamohoali'i broke away from the Imperial Army twenty years ago, he adopted the use of poison in his arrows, well-known to his enemies."

"Poisoned arrows? Never heard of such a thing," Vaohoi said seriously.

"So can you cure him?" Maka leaned towards Lo'au pleadingly.

"It's not as easy as that. The poison is in his blood now. I am not going to make any promises."

Maka hung his head again.

"There is some warm fish and taro wrapped in banana leaves in the next fale. When you've finished I'd like you to go and find Paea's sister."

"Heilala?"

"Yes, and bring her back here. Also, bring anything of personal value back here if you're able to carry it."

As Maka stood quickly, Lo'au raised a hand.

"Be careful when you go out." He paused, glancing at Vaohoi. "On second thoughts, Vaohoi, I'd like you to go with him."

The young man shot a displeased look and kicked his feet. But he then smiled and agreed, "Sure, I'll go," his secret agenda known only to him.

Lo'au glared at the adolescent.

"Vaohoi, stay out of trouble."

CHAPTER 11

A servant boy dashed through the courtyard with blinding speed. He glided up the steps into the reception fale in a single leap and came to a stop at the entrance to the secret underground domicile. Breathing heavily as he composed himself, he dared not peer down the dark staircase that led below.

"M-M-Master ... your allies have just arrived," he stammered.

"Good. Show them in," Kamohoali'i shouted from below.

The old crypt was primarily used to store food, weapons and tools during hurricanes and famine. It was large enough to house about fifty men and appeared more like a torture chamber. A single torch lit the area, its flames dancing irritably from a cold draft. The sound of water dripping from the ceiling onto the cold floor echoed through its walls. The stink of wet earth and decay suffocated the room. Kamohoali'i sat in the centre of the dark and dank crypt, with his hands on his thighs. Behind him, stood the terrible Havea; deep shadows illustrating his fearsome appearance.

The first person to step down into the surreptitious den was Kupe, 'The Weeping Assassin', a man originally from the island of Raiatea nearby Tahiti. It was said that when Kupe was a young warrior, he had sailed to a great island and battled with a giant bird creature that stood upright on two legs. With its immense talons, it clawed Kupe's face, leaving horrific scars and rendering him blind in one eye. The damage had turned his retina a pale blue and it forever wept tears as a living wound.

Although in his late fifties, Kupe was well-proportioned and well defined. Standing at six foot-three inches, he emitted an air of hidden confidence and cruelty behind a hunched frame with rolling shoulders. Tucked within his short vala were complicated weapons of ruthless design: tools that had helped him build the feared reputation as the Empire's most ruthless assassin.

Omani leapt into the den with a quick thud. Standing straight from his crouched position, he arched his back, rolled his neck with the sound of grinding bones before glaring at Kamohoali'i. The great warrior from Nuapapu, Vava'u was a renowned fighter of unique skill and ability. Slightly taller than Kupe, he was built like an impenetrable chunk of volcanic rock; chiselled and powerful. Most noticeable was his hair: cut short, pasted erect with tree sap and dyed dark mustard.

Streamlined tattoos twisted down his limbs in a distinctive fashion as though his arms and legs were tapa cloth themselves. The warrior's wrists and fists, ankles and feet were bound in what appeared to be the raw bark of the mulberry tree. His shins and forearms sported multiple lengths of whalebone plates bound together to form shield-like gauntlets for protection against club strikes. All who had fought the great warrior understood the reasoning: he was famed as the only man in the Empire who did not employ a weapon in battle. Rather, he combined devastating strikes from his hands and feet in what was described as a system of unarmed techniques that often maimed or killed his opponents.

The 'Unarmed Warrior' stepped to the side and from behind him appeared an extremely tall woman, at least six foot ten. Mo'unga's origins were unknown. Speaking a multitude of Polynesian dialects, she had served her time in far and distant lands in the name of the Pulotulahi. She was recognised as existing both in the spiritual and material world, with legends of her being the daughter of Seketo'a, the demi god of the sea. A woman of noble, yet dark, guise with a vacant expression, she stood naked with flowing blue-black hair that hung to the nape of her back. Her body was adorned with a combination of kelp, lei, and mother of pearl shells. Her beautiful breasts were small but full, crowned by erect nipples; a sexuality that betrayed her dark persona.

In her right hand, she gently held a cudgel that swayed at her side like the motion of the surging sea. The cudgel was jagged with sharp shells that could cut through skin and bone. But it was not her fighting ability that made her a feared adversary: she was the mother of all sharks and some claimed she, through a mysterious spiritual connection, had the ability to summon and control great sharks at will. It was said that her champion was a monstrous great white shark and all who had crossed her, had been devoured by it.

The fourth warrior to step into the room, with over two hundred kilograms of weight, rattled the headdresses and kava cups on the floor. Ganilau dwarfed the other villains, looming at over seven feet. He plodded out of the shadows into the dim firelight, revealing his grotesque appearance. His massive body was wrapped in thin pieces of tapa, stained of claret from bloody blisters caused by the affliction of leprosy. His face was partially covered to conceal a horrible sight: the remains of a flesh eaten nose, bleeding gums that revealed jagged yellow teeth, his bloodshot eyes and peeling skin.

His entire being ached with pain from enlarged nerves and swollen lymphs, which emitted a constant stench of decay. Revolted by his very presence, but daring not to insult, his comrades kept a wide berth. Ganilau was a formidable foe despite his suffering. He possessed incredible strength and the source of this was his unparalleled anger: a terrible fury that could not be stopped once begun.

General Kamohoali'i looked at his loyal warriors, nodded in approval and motioned for them to sit. Nodding, they came together as one and faced their general. The boy who had been ordered to prepare the kava could not summon the courage to approach. He trembled and turned on his heels in utter terror. Kupe reached for a weapon to throw. Mo'unga raised her hand and turned to the general.

"I will honour our circle with kava."

"Granted." Kamohoali'i nodded then turned to his commanders. "Time is at hand, my brothers. The Pulotulahi will rise again and rule over all."

"Aye! Hear, hear!" the group of evil warriors chorused.

"How go the plans, Milord?" Kupe queried.

"Siateki and his group are in position. The bait has been set and soon the trap will be sprung. Pele will arrive shortly, completing the circle of our strength."

Kava was passed among them. All drank from their cups and began to sing a dark and wicked melody known only to the Pulotulahi. The lyrics told a story of the spirits of the dead becoming trapped forever in the underworld, and that paradise would only be achieved when all of humanity was there. Their deep and haunting voices echoed through the cavernous abode and trailed out into the open air like the whisper of a ghost.

A few kilometres from where the villains sat in communion, Vaohoi pressed through a polluted area of the island. His feet slipped across fresh mud and filth making it difficult for him to balance.

"You live here?" he pinched his nose to block the reek of sewage.

He and Maka made their way down through the dark and rotting shrubs into the poverty stricken area.

Three hundred years past, Falehau was but a coastal village of near primitive villagers who made their living from fishing and hunting. A community of less than two hundred, all the original abodes lay around the beach at sea level. But as the years passed, structural additions were made instead of dismantling old fales and trails. Over a greater time, they began building on top of the areas of the original structures. Matters were made worse by the steep hills that surrounded Falehau, preventing it from expanding. In the passing of large population and economical growth over three hundred years, Falehau was literally built upon every stage of advancement.

Another small village sprung up further along the coast of Niuatoputapu, but it was Falehau, which remained as the epicentre of its economy. Still, the vile areas of wastage and disparity were not without their advantages. They provided a home for the tu'as, safe from the reaches of the political changes around them.

"How much further?" Vaohoi had given up holding his nose and subdued himself to the revolting smell.

"It's just up ahead."

As they made their way through the maze of dilapidated shrubbery, the pair passed scores of tu'a. All were the absolute depiction of filth: matted hair, rotted teeth and bodies racked by malnutrition. Most had spent their entire lives outside the village and knew nothing of social order or decorum. They owned naught but the rags that sparsely covered their bony backs.

Their accent was short, rough and in most parts indiscernible. Beholding the poor excuses for human beings, Vaohoi's negative and boisterous opinion of tu'a wavered somewhat. He glanced across to his chubby friend with a renewed outlook, never before in his sheltered life had he been witness to such poverty.

He followed Maka a little further into a hidden alcove of tightly intertwined shrubs. Within the recess, was a home of paltry regression; old tapa so worn that it had become part of the soil, and the smell of damp air and campfire trapped by the foliage. Huddled to the side of the alcove, Vaohoi noticed a small girl of poor appearance trying to sew a basket of dry reeds. When she looked up and saw Maka, her eyes filled with hope. Vaohoi stood and watched uneasily as Maka told Heilala of the events that had transpired over night.

A long silence ebbed when he finished. Heilala sat cross-legged on the tattered tapa with her hands cupping her face. Her sobbing shook her thin shoulders as Maka reached out and embraced her. The news of Paea had been given to her gently – her response expected. Maka started to cry softly as he hugged her.

Vaohoi looked around and shifted uncomfortably. He tried to avoid looking at the two poor children so cursed by poverty, living in such miserable and heart-breaking conditions. Now, to have the tragedy of this news brought to their home to add to their plight. Vaohoi swallowed hard and fought to suppress tears in his eyes.

The young man had never seen such scarcity in Tonga. Being the son of a wealthy and respected man, his experiences of the world had been ignorant of destitution and helplessness. The very thought of such was as unfamiliar to him as hardship or sacrifice, and he found himself confronted with emotions so foreign to him, perhaps forever obscure to him, that he could not help but be struck by the barefaced reality of these deprived children. It felt like a stake through his heart.

He turned away quickly and raised his fist to his lips as if to cough. He closed his eyes, and his jaw shook slightly, before clearing his throat. After composing himself, he turned and faced the young children, his eyes damp with tears.

"Hey! You guys, stop that crying! I tell you what I'm going to do – I'll help find the antidote for Paea and then we'll go and slap the face of this damn general! What do you say?"

Maka and Heilala paused in their grief and peered up at the young man in confusion.

"Don't worry about a thing! Uncle Vaohoi will take care of you guys from now on! Understand?" The young man continued the momentum.

"Have I told you that I'm the most feared warrior in the entire kingdom? The bravest, the most daring!" He pulled a ridiculous face that failed to be fierce.

"And – did I mention the most handsome?" He strutted foolishly around in a circle and earned warm smiles from the children, their tears of sorrow drying up.

"So! Leave it to the professional warriors like myself, and I'll make the dark general pay so dearly, that he'll be swimming back to the mainland with sharks biting at his backside!" He mimicked the jaws with his hands. "RRraaagh, RRraaagh, RRraaagh!"

The children burst into laughter as they watched him scuttle around the tiny alcove, his hands clutching his behind.

"Yeeoooowww!" he screamed and laughed with the children.

When he stopped, he fell and embraced the children in fits of hoots and giggles. When he eventually got back to his feet, he noticed dozens of young tu'a had surrounded the camp. Their faces beamed with contagious smiles, eager to join the fun. They gazed upon Vaohoi with anticipation. The young man poised himself and straightened his posture now that he had a crowd to please. He paused long enough for a throbbing silence to fall over the area.

"YYYYIIIHHIIIEEEE!" he exploded in an ear-splitting cheer, leaping from the ground and throwing a fist in the air.

In an instant, a chorus of thrill and elation from the children exploded from the area, so sudden and unexpected, birds shot from the nearby trees.

CHAPTER 12

The market place was bustling with life. The trade tongiakis had arrived in the early morning. Since they came to port only once a week, it was usually a busy day for venders and traders alike. Sandalwood, tapa, fruits, kava, and precious stones were the main commodities of Niuatoputapu, as well as an array of woven mats from across the Pacific. All of these imports had always been in high demand for Niuatoputapu, since the geography of the village and its bay area could not support proper cultivation.

Talatama stood next to a small gift vendor at the edge of the crowded market. The group of imperial warriors who were escorting him through town loitered a few yards away. Talatama was speaking sternly with an old man and they were at the end of their conversation.

"So what is generally asked of you?"

"Almost my day's trade!" the elderly man exclaimed. "Please help me."

"Mmm. That's outrageous. Thank you for your time." Talatama nodded and turned into the milling crowds. "I'll see what I can do."

He pushed his way to where his men were, but had disappeared.

"Where have those fools gone?" He put his hands on his hips and squinted in the sunlight as flies buzzed around his head.

The weather had been unusually hot. The humidity was heavy and although he had donned a light vala, he was still dripping with perspiration.

"Commander," Oliame approached.

"What is it?"

Oliame leaned close and spoke in a whisper. "From what I've gathered from numerous accounts, I'm sure Kamohoali'i is here in Niuatoputapu. And while I have no evidence, my guess is that Anga'uli is keeping him in hiding."

Talatama rubbed his chin as he gazed at the ground.

"Only Lord Anga'uli could hide him, especially if he's here with his vagabond of fools. If they're somewhere in the compound then we can take Anga'uli down with them." The prince grinned. "This could well be a prosperous visit, my friend."

"Yes, Milord."

"Be sharp, there's —" he stopped short.

Oliame was glaring at something behind him. The commander inconspicuously turned and frowned. He saw nothing of interest about a lavish looking teenager, a chubby tu'a and a young girl making their way through the marketplace.

"Oliame, what is it?"

The lieutenant seized his arm. "Commander – follow me."

Lo'au produced a tired smile as Vaohoi, Maka and Heilala appeared through the entrance of the fale kava. Heilala scattered her belongings across the floor, and rushed to her unconscious brother. She cradled his hand in hers, bowed her head and began to cry. Maka knelt on the other side of Paea as Vaohoi placed his hands on his hips and looked at the patient sideways.

"Master, he's looking better," he said surprisingly. "Much better."

Lo'au smiled, as he squinted at the mu'a quizzically.

"You found the antidote, didn't you?" he chortled.

"Yes, and administered it just in time. He will improve," he said. "He needs his rest now. In a day or two he'll be amongst the living again."

Both Maka and Heilala leapt to their feet and rushed to Lo'au and embraced him lovingly, "Thank you, Master!"

Vaohoi, with his hands still on his hips, smiled and shared the gratitude. Though Lo'au did not see it immediately, he was to later learn of Vaohoi's newly acquired sympathy, a story of humility at the tu'a camp. Vaohoi now felt just as responsible for the children as he.

As Vaohoi began to get teary-eyed again, there was a sharp crack at the entrance. His hand went straight for his short club. Lo'au and the children looked up in surprise.

"Hold!" came the voice from the first man who entered the fale. He was immediately followed by five armed imperial soldiers.

The warriors rushed in, cornered them and thrust their spears in their faces. Talatama entered the fale, with an open hand extended forwards.

"Stay your weapon boy, or I'll have you killed on the spot," he growled at Vaohoi, "All of you stay where you are."

The mu'a and children froze as they watched Oliame ruffle through Heilala's possessions on the floor of the fale.

"I found it, Commander," the lieutenant exclaimed.

"Found what?" Vaohoi peeped.

Talatama gave the boy a scornful look, "You have a lot of explaining to do." He gave the signal for his soldiers to secure the fale.

By the time Talatama concluded his interrogation of Lo'au and Vaohoi, it was past midday. The revelation of the tapa parchment was obviously news to the pair. Once Talatama had ascertained the innocence of their story, he sent his warriors to complete their daily duties, in order that they might openly confer about private matters. Maka and Heilala played in the next room away from the talk of men.

"I couldn't believe it when I saw the girl carrying it," Oliame shook his head. "The imperial symbols were unmistakable."

They all gazed at the tapa cloth, laid out in the centre of the circle in which they sat. It was the thin parchment of brown tapa cloth containing black, imperial symbols which the spy, Moa'uli'uli, had given Paea, months ago, prior to his death. It was the very clue Talatama and his men were looking for. Written on it were the hieroglyphs of what transpired in Moa'uli'uli's last hours.

"Would the girl be lying?" Oliame looked at Talatama.

Deep in thought the prince gave no answer. He finally squinted at the old man.

"No, she did not lie," Lo'au said. "She would have no reason to."

"Well I could think of one, old man," Oliame retorted.

"You imperial buffoons are all the same: deaf and dumb," Vaohoi interjected.

"Watch your tongue, you little upstart!" Oliame glared viciously.

"I believe what the girl says," the prince said before the contest erupted.

Vaohoi huffed towards Oliame as though it were his victory.

"Master, she – those kids – they're all tu'a. Steal from the living let alone the dead!" Oliame hissed loudly.

"It matters not, my friend. Moa'uli'uli is dead – there's no doubt about that now. How the children came into possession of his belongings is beside the point. The important thing is that we have the tapa," Talatama said as he looked at the symbols and began to rise to his feet.

"Do you know what it says?" Lo'au asked with a strange expression.

"No. These hieroglyphs are a secret language known only by the king and his chosen spies," Talatama returned slowly. "It must be given to the king as soon as possible."

"You're the Prince aren't you?" Vaohoi began. "Why can't you read the symbols?"

"One more word ..." Oliame clenched his teeth and turned to Talatama. "Master, shall I teach this boy –"

"Just try it, moon-face."

"Vaohoi!" Lo'au shouted in a volume that startled everyone in the room.

The adolescent's tongue fell cold, and the imperial warriors regarded the old man with surprise.

"The language of the ancients is almost forgotten." Lo'au began slowly. "Long ago when the kings came from Pulotu to Tonga, they discovered the old ones had the gift of written language. Conquering the old Tongans, the new dynasty learned the language and announced a taboo for anyone to practise the writing. In time, only the royal bloodline of the Tu'i Tonga possessed the knowledge of this vanishing writing."

"Why didn't they let others learn?" Vaohoi asked innocently.

"Power. Once, long ago, the power of writing proved the undoing of a king and from that time on, it was reserved only for the king's line."

"I assume you know this information through your travels, old man?" Talatama said as he eyed the old man suspiciously.

"Long, long years of travel, young commander."

Talatama motioned to Oliame, "Wait for me outside. I wish to talk with the mu'a alone."

As the warrior bowed his head and departed the room, Lo'au looked at Vaohoi and indicated that he should follow.

"W-h-hat? I should stay, Master. You might need my expert advice," he jeered.

He received no response from Lo'au, and after puffing and clicking his tongue, Vaohoi disappeared also.

Talatama did not speak until he and the old man were alone. "What is your connection to these children?" he asked.

"It is as I told you, Prince Talatama. I am a wandering mu'a, and I am here to help the children – and to unveil the evil that besets this place."

"You know who I am?" Talatama looked surprised.

"Yes, and I also know why you're here," Lo'au said gravely.

"Oh? And how do you know that?"

"Talatama, you will learn in time that my ways are difficult to understand. Be content that your secret is safe with me."

Talatama paused. He had heard many stories about Lo'au the great priest of Tangaloa, knew he was a man of kind and trusting repute. Though he had never met him, the mu'a was all the prince had imagined; benevolent and wise. He also knew he could be trusted. But he chose to withhold signs of respect and acknowledgement in the matter. Doing so would diminish his position, and he could not afford to lose his composure so close to achieving his goal.

"I will be back tomorrow to talk with the sick boy. I'm trusting that you and the children will not vanish overnight, o' wise Lo'au." Talatama picked up the tapa cloth and began to walk out. "And I doubt what you said – I will not be in your company long enough to learn your ways." He grinned and departed the room.

"We shall see, good Prince," Lo'au smiled.

CHAPTER 13

Towards the southern tip of Niuatoputapu, in a large clearing of rolling mounds, Adi sat and rested her weary legs. She stretched out on the warm grass, leaned back on her hands and raised her face to the sun. Her dark skin glistened in the sunlight and smelled of oils and flowers.

"What a beautiful morning!" she exclaimed.

Captain Duvuduvukulu stopped as he caught up to Adi's position and looked down to her, then turned to monitor the two dozen Fijian compatriots slowly following up the gentle incline.

"Master Adi, we should continue until we reach the rise over there."

"Look at the sky, Captain. The trees, the grass, this whole island," she slowly stood. "I couldn't have come to a more beautiful place."

Nofu was an elderly local priest of Tangaloa, who had met the Degei mission in the earlier hours of the morning. He caught up with the pair, breathing heavily from the persistent trek through the woodlands.

"Nofu, you are blessed to claim Niuatoputapu as your own." Adi smiled to him.

"Yes, Milady, we have lived in peace and contentment in the past -"

"In the past? What about now?"

"The Noble of Niuatoputapu, Lord Anga'uli, has - "

"Excuse my interruption, dear priest, but perhaps such things could be discussed when we reach the site," Duvuduvukulu interjected.

"Let us talk of politics later, my friend," she smiled at Nofu and walked ahead with him, ignoring the captain. When she pushed past him, he grinned before facing the long line of Fijian men following in single file.

"Move it men!" he barked. "No one is to rest until I say he may!"

The missionaries arrived at the site around midday. It was an opened and levelled area, trimmed in a circular section from the forest and laying way to a perfect site to build a fale bure. The site was perhaps close to the centre of the island, greatly elevated from sea level and surrounded by a picturesque landscape of colour and sunlight. A dozen of the Fijian labourers had already begun to construct the first shelter of the mission.

The warrior priests ventured into the nearby forest while others managed the labourers. Other subordinate priests unloaded their possessions and quietly chatted about the beautiful island.

"Come with me, Nofu." Adi took the old man's arm into hers. "Let us talk of many things."

Duvuduvukulu noticed her intention immediately. "Master Adi, if you would stay -"

"Captain, that will be all!" She spun on her heel and pointed at him. "Do not talk to me again this day."

All turned on hearing the master raise her voice. Most of the warrior priests began to make their way back towards them.

Duvuduvukulu gritted his teeth and bowed slowly. "Master ..."

"Be careful, she has the venom of a snake." Another warrior priest shot him a wry look and chuckled.

"What she needs is a good beating and a hard fuck. Then she will know her place."

"Are you the man to do it?" the warrior priest laughed.

"Perhaps. We shall see." The captain's eyes narrowed as he glared at her.

Adi walked on with Nofu, ignoring the sly whispers. As they neared the edge of the glade, the old man pointed to a path heading north.

"Master Adi, this leads to the township of Falehau," he said.

"Yes, of course," she returned. "Come, Nofu, let us sit a while." She led him to the side of the forest trail and leaned against a tree.

Nofu groaned as he sat, smiling as he did so. "Ohhhh, I'm reminded of my age every day. I fell from a coconut tree when I was young and I've never really recovered."

"Veneration is something well earned, Nofu," she returned.

"Ahh, you are as kind as you are beautiful, Master Adi. I am so pleased that you have come to the inner realm of the kingdom," he sighed, "I have always respected the Degei, and have visited the Fijian Isles on many occasions. Your peoples are a proud and traditional race, like our own."

"Indeed, Nofu," she frowned, "But I can't help but feel there's something wrong here."

The old man picked up a fallen twig and began to inspect its thin bark, its twists and natural shape. He contemplated his words that could have grim consequences.

"I must be truthful with you. You have come to our beautiful island at a dire time."

"Please tell me." She leaned forward and touched his hand.

"The politics of the island have never before ruled the level of living, Master Adi. Lord Anga'uli has become the most ruthless noble this island has ever known. His ways are cruel and heartless, and his greed will destroy the people."

"But surely the king will not stand for such tyranny? The nobility were put into position to replace the warlords, a position used for the betterment of the Tongan people," Adi recounted modern history.

"Yes, I know. Such stories rarely go far from this island these days. But from what I've heard, an imperial fleet directly from the capital has only just arrived. Our hopes and prayers lie with the commander of this fleet. He is said to be here to conduct an inspection of the island and to search for such corruption."

"That's good news, Nofu. Perhaps I shall go into the township soon and speak with this commander."

"No! Please Master Adi, you must not tell him what I have told you! I will be killed outright if the noble discovers my treachery!"

"But he must know! That is the only way we can rid this island of his rule!" She ignored his plea. "Do not worry Nofu, I will not give away who gave me the information."

The old man seemed somewhat accepting. He nodded as if he had resigned to his fate in any case.

"Master Adi, please excuse me, I must be getting back to the township," he said, as he struggled to his feet.

She helped him and held his hands in hers. "Must you go now?"

"I will be back in the morning to see you again. My followers shall return here this evening with food and water." He paused.

"Yes, of course. I thank you again for such warm hospitality."

"You are welcome, my Master Adi. Peace be with you." He kissed her on the head.

The Fijian priestess watched the old man disappear down the forest trail and felt the mission was now tainted by Nofu's account of the island's political situation. She had not heard of the internal problems and it was difficult to imagine the omnipotent Empire allowing such tyranny to exist. Though it was commonplace that religion and politics were kept separate in most ways, she could not help but worry about how the situation would affect the mission. Perhaps she and the Degei should keep to themselves in this secluded area for the immediate future, until such toil subsided. She decided, however, that it would still be a wise move to make contact with the Commander of the Imperial Army.

He may have more answers for her.

CHAPTER 14

Morning was high. The sun was shining from a winter apex, the sea wind was subtle and a half moon hid shyly on the horizon. The greenery of the overhanging palm trees projected from the golden sand and the brown of the earth. On the northern shores of Niuatoputapu, close to where hundreds of tongiaki and kalia lay moored, a dozen craft bearing the unique designs and symbols of the islands of Ha'apai approached.

As swiftly as the sea crafts banked on the sands, so the two dozen warriors leapt onto the wet sand and made their way onto the busy beachside area. The fervour of the strangers caused locals to stop and stare: their faces were painted dark green on one side, wore grassy loincloth and were adorned with traditional ornaments of ancient Tongan heritage. It was known that the Ha'apai and Vava'u islands produced some of the fiercest fighters in all the Empire.

At the head of the group came forth the leader. She was a woman of proud stature, a powerful feminine build, an attractive yet rough exterior, with a count of scars equal to any warrior at her side. Her name was Pele, a she-warrior of renowned ability, strength and skill. Daughter of the famous warrior chief, Alama, and trained by the greatest warriors in the kingdom, she had the fury of a man with the will of a woman scorned.

Standing at six foot-four inches, Pele's body was devoid of fat or unused flesh, gleaned with auburn skin, etched in male tattoos over muscular thighs and stalwart arms. Her black hair was a waterfall of braided plaits that hung to the middle of her strong back and crowned her stoic face.

Across the Polynesian Islands, the ancient Tongans were the only warriors to employ the bow and arrow in warfare. They adopted the weapon through constant war with the Melanesian races of Vanuatu and Kanaka, who had introduced it to the Pacific. From a young age, Pele was instructed in archery and its effectiveness in combat. Over the years of battle, she had become a true master. Her longbow, a superb carving of ironwood, was tightly secured across her back with a quiver loaded with feathered arrows.

Tucked in her loin cloth was an equally distinctive weapon. The war club of black granite was a two foot masterpiece of creation. It was fashioned and polished to a narrow and sleek finish, designed so that, despite its weight, it could be wielded in rapid movement. Said to have been created in the underworld of Pulotu, its rarity and unique existence equally matched its owner.

Pele walked through the Niuatoputapuans with her head raised high and with the airs and graces of a true warrior-chief. Her devoted warriors followed closely behind, returning glares with distaste. They strode through the village of Falehau and before long, entered the ramparts of the House of Anga'uli. The noble's warriors bowed and hastily shuffled out of her path. Most did not risk a glace in her direction. Once inside the compound, Ilamaki appeared from one of the large fales to greet the warrior.

"My lady, what an unexpected surprise," he stammered.

Wiping the sweat from her forehead, she was irritable and in a foul mood. She twitched her head to make her braids swing from her face before glowering at the village headman. Her look sent a chill through him.

"Food and board, fresh water. Send girls to tend to the needs of my men."

"Yes, my lady." He bowed swiftly and signalled the dozens of retainers to come forth and escort the warriors away.

The she-warrior strode towards the guest fale, used only by senior officials and important visitors.

"My lady? Where are you going?" Ilamaki stumbled.

When she ignored him he chased her quickly.

"My lady – m-my apologies but you cannot stay in that fale. It is being used by another."

"By whom?" she turned to the headman impatiently.

"I am." Talatama appeared in the entryway of the domicile and stared at Pele as though he were expecting her.

Unstartled, she gave an exasperated sigh. "So who are you?"

"Commander of the Imperial Fourteenth Legion," he ignored her rudeness. "And you?"

Without responding, she turned on her heel and strode away. Ilamaki stepped in quickly and made apologies.

"Commander, her name is Pele - "

"- perhaps the greatest woman warrior in all the Empire," Talatama interjected. "Yes, Ilamaki, I've heard of her. Interesting ..." He smiled and retired within the shelter of his fale.

Following a swift bow, Ilamaki hurried after her and finally caught up with her in the garden, laying in the shade of a mango tree.

"My lady - that was Talatama, Crown Prince of the Tongan Empire."

"Oh? I didn't know that." She showed little concern. "How should I know what any of the princes look like? They hardly leave the royal compound in Tongatapu, playing their pompous games and gorging their faces with food."

"My lady, Prince Talatama is not like that." Ilamaki hesitated. "Not like that at all."

"I care not for imperial concerns, Ilamaki. Now leave me."

The village headman knew no amount of convincing could sway the warrior.

"Is there anything else you require, my lady?"

"Tell my brother I wish to have an audience with him tonight."

"Your brother?"

"Don't play the fool, headman. I know Kamohoali'i is here, and I didn't just travel a hundred kilometres to be fobbed off by you."

"O-of course not, my lady! I shall seek him out immediately."

She closed her eyes and relaxed in the shade, feeling the warm breeze that carried the scent of nearby frangipanis. She breathed in deeply, her breasts rising and falling and her mind went to difficult matters.

Behind her bold front, she harboured a weight of guilt and culpability that tainted her very soul. Memories of the past haunted her waking mind and chased her in nightmares: deeds she had done, both terrible and unthinkable. She was a stalwart warrior of unequal parallel but she could not escape the shame of events that she had sewn. They were evil campaigns in which she had played a key role, campaigns calculated and construed by her elder brother.

For many long years, Kamohoali'i had directed and controlled her in every major plan he had fulfilled in the name of The Pulotulahi. She had manipulated, murdered and supported the downfall of his enemies without question and in return, he had constructed her roles so she could remain relatively free of any repercussions. He accepted he was an infamous criminal and did not want that fate cast on his sister: her uses as a free woman proved more valuable to him than an equally hunted criminal. Nevertheless, he did not hesitate to employ her and her warriors whenever the need arose.

Over her twenty-five summers, she had seen much and experienced much of what life offered. Born into a renowned family steeped with honour, she could have chosen any path in life. But the moment she had become a student of war and the philosophy surrounding life and death, her destiny was set. Little did she know that with this destiny came the burden of her brother's influence. In the past year, she had struggled with the reality of her predicament, bound to her brother's will, seemingly without escape. Thoughts of betraying his trust weighed heavily on her mind and pre-empted hypothetical repercussions should she do so.

Struggling for many months, she cursed to herself that her internal struggle was like that of a child who laboured to escape the control of her parents: parents who had become too accustomed to dominating the life of their child. Her mother had died giving birth to her and Lord Alama had not provided her with much direction as a parent. He had become distant in his old age and cared nothing for her wellbeing, nor the affairs of Kamohoali'i.

Her goal to confront Kamohoali'i in Niuatoputapu was simple. She was no longer his weapon or tool to use as he willed, no longer beholden to his decisions, free from his manipulative and malevolent plans. She was to sever the bond with her brother forever.

CHAPTER 15

It was early afternoon when Talatama returned to the fale kava to seek Lo'au. Vaohoi was sleeping in the corner of the room, snoring loudly, and Lo'au, Heilala and Maka sat together with Paea in the centre of the room. Next to them were small bundles of hot food that produced wisps of steam into the air. Paea regarded the prince with obvious apprehension and although conscious, he remained weak but showed signs of recovery.

"I see you've regained some strength, boy," Talatama said as he approached the group.

"Y-yes, Milord."

"Lo'au, you seem to be both a priest and a healer," he smiled at the old man.

"The indulgence of an old man is always through compliments."

"So, now that you're awake, I'd like to ask you some questions." Talatama turned to Paea and held out the tapa parchment, "Firstly how you came to be in possession of this."

As the boy squinted at it, Mateitau and Oliame rushed through the entrance to Talatama.

"Milord ..."

"Wait. I'm just getting started with the boy."

"Milord, there is a situation out in the market. You need to see this," Mateitau said quickly.

"A situation? That sounds interesting!" Vaohoi woke up immediately and rushed for the exit.

Talatama sighed with annoyance. "I'll be back shortly."

A clearing had been made in the village market. Hundreds of people had congregated around a few men.

"Make way!" Mateitau shouted, forcing a passage for his prince.

Talatama and his officers came to the edge of the crowd and saw four of Anga'uli's soldiers, armed with spears and clubs, facing a single man.

"Drop your weapon now! This is your last chance!" The leader of the soldiers shouted at the stranger.

Talatama beheld the stranger and his eyes widened: he was one of the largest men he had ever seen. Leatiogie, a chief from the island of Upolu in Samoa, stood at eight and a half feet tall and would have weighed close to two hundred kilograms. His figure was an explosion of gigantic muscles, tattooed skin and war scars. He was, perhaps, one of the most physically powerful men in his lifetime, dwarfing Talatama and the majority of other men around him.

His chiselled jaw and squared face was crowned with short hair pasted in an off-yellow dye. His ears were pierced with bones from an assortment of sea creatures, and around his powerful shoulders draped a tapa cloak patterned with Samoan designs. He was probably in his early twenties and still possessed young features, which seemed to ease the initial shock of his size.

He wore an impressive whale bone breastplate that protected his entire chest and abdomen: armour that appeared incredibly well made, furnished especially for his unique frame, which secured any threat of pointed or edged weapon. The bone itself appeared old, and though covered in dents, cuts and punctures, it was nonetheless robust. His torso was draped in a fine tapa and he wore wooden rings, bracelets and anklets.

In his right hand he held another item fashioned solely for him. His war club was a five foot trunk of ironbark wood, carved only to incorporate a satisfactory grip, so as to leave the natural curves and bulbous knots from its original state. The weight of it looked tremendous and its results in battle left nothing for the imagining.

"Come and taste the bark from my club, puny guards," he growled.

"Hold! Soldier, what is this man's crime?" Talatama stepped forward.

The soldier's anger turned on Talatama. The imminent fight had clouded the soldier's vision and he had failed to recognise Talatama's rank.

"Stay back!" Saliva sprayed towards Talatama, before he turned to Leatiogie. "I said, drop your club!"

"I said hold!" The prince's hand moved to his own weapon. Mateitau and Oliame poised at his side.

"I say let them fight," came a strong voice from the crowd.

Maui Atalaga smiled from the far edge of the circle. Surrounding onlookers gasped as they recognised the famous hero standing among them.

"I agree. I'm in need of some good entertainment," returned a firm female's voice from another section of the crowd. Pele stood proud, with three of her warriors, leering down her nose at the men. A greater crowd began to gather.

Vaohoi pushed through the milling people and laughed at the soldiers who were huddled together in front of the giant. Talatama ignored the comments.

"I am Commander Talatama of the Fourteenth Imperial Army. I order you to lower your weapons. Lower your weapons!" he boomed, finally getting through to the soldier.

"I-I –Yes – Err."

"Leave now! I will take care of this."

"Ignore that order!" Afi Kakaha, General of the Niuatoputapu Army appeared, with twenty warriors and began dispersing the nosy onlookers.

"What is going on here?" the general shouted angrily. "You! Samoan! What is your business here?"

"As I told those idiots, I come to warn Niuatoputapu of danger," he stared at the general.

An instant realisation appeared across Afi Kakaha's face and he leaned forward to seize the Samoan, "Right, come with me."

"No, he's not. He's coming with me," Talatama said, stepping between them.

Vaohoi egged on the crowd excitedly. "Let's have a fight!" he shrieked.

"Commander Talatama, you have no local power here," Afi Kakaha stated, his twenty warriors amassing around him.

Mateitau and Oliame poised their weapons for a battle.

"I have absolute, imperial power here. Under the Imperial Empire, I have higher discretion - only the Noble of Niuatoputapu can supersede my order." Talatama edged forward, "Don't doubt that in two days, I can have the entire Imperial Army of five thousand warriors arrive here and sweep the island clean of anyone who displeases me!"

Onlookers waited anxiously for a move. The general remained silent then began to fall back.

"Wise decision," the prince said, seeing his words ring true.

Afi Kakaha's face winced then took the shape of rage, "Keep your fine words, Talatama. I'll be back for that Samoan," he growled and swiftly departed with his warriors.

Murmurs and whispers echoed from the crowds of onlookers.

"There's no more to see people! Back to your business!" The prince waved his hand.

Pele and her warriors shook their heads and left the area. Maui Atalaga had disappeared. Vaohoi approached Talatama with a broad grin.

"That was impressive!" he jeered.

"Be gone you upstart," he sneered with distaste before turning to the giant. "You, what is your name?"

"Leatiogie, Matai of Tuamasaga. Call me Atiogie."

"Come with me then, Atiogie."

CHAPTER 16

Talatama, Atiogie, Mateitau and Oliame were huddled in a small forest glade not far from the village and spoke in whispers. In the centre of the glade were the two giant menhirs of ancient origins, named Fakafafa and Tauloto. Across their surfaces were strange and undecipherable symbols of a language long lost. Mythically, the first Maui was said to have placed it there in tribute to the beautiful island. The glade was considered sacred to the ancients and was rumoured to be haunted by the spirits of old. As such, most people avoided it.

"I don't know what that fuss was about." The Samoan frowned as he scratched his large head. "If you two have a bone to pick with each other, that's not my business. I came here to warn you people of danger and I get threatened for my efforts."

"Forget that, there's more politics here than you'd care to know. All you need to know is that you're safe with me."

The prince motioned for them to sit on the short grass. "What news do you bring? What is this imminent danger you speak of?"

"I am Atiogie, the son of Matai Feepo, Chief of 'Aele. We are a proud and peaceful people and we have never defied the Empire. However, we have many enemies," he paused. "To the east of our clan lie the peoples of Saleimoa. Among the chiefs there is a general called Va'iga, an evil mercenary who sells his murder to anyone who will pay him."

"I've heard of him," Talatama nodded.

Before Atiogie continued, Mateitau and Oliame, who stood guard, raised their weapons to the forest, "Who goes there!"

"It is only us." Lo'au and Vaohoi suddenly appeared through the trees into the private area.

"This is an imperial matter and therefore private." Talatama stood to stop the two men.

"Sit down, my son," Lo'au said calmly. "Your clandestine ways need not apply to us."

Despite his natural apprehension, Talatama had come to trust Lo'au quickly. The mu'a's reputation as a man of integrity and piety was widespread and his aura of decency was felt in his presence. Still, having the mu'a tangled in the affairs of the Empire was not a favourable option. Talatama sighed. Being far from a mood to carry on with more disagreements, he resigned to allowing them to stay.

"Two weeks back, I learned that Va'iga and his army, maybe a thousand warriors, were setting sail to Niuatoputapu. My people think that they may be working for the Pulotulahi."

"Who?" Vaohoi cocked his head.

"What more do you know?" Talatama edged forward, now twice as interested.

"I followed them for days along the northern coast of Upolu, then one night they sailed south between the Savai'i straits. Tailing a tongiaki through the night is near impossible without being seen. The next morning I'd lost them, but I know they were headed in this direction. Maybe they bypassed the island altogether. Unless – have you seen them?"

"I've not seen Samoans here, let alone a thousand warriors," Lo'au said.

"Why do you bring us this news? What do you gain from this?" Talatama asked suspiciously.

"I am a good man, respected and loved among chiefs. Va'iga is my enemy. If he has come here, then I will fight him."

"There's more isn't there, Atiogie," Lo'au said.

All men glanced at the old mu'a and the giant stared in astonishment. He then relaxed, as if his charade had come crumbling down.

"Yes I admit. As his enemy, I represent my people and our interests. My father believes the army may be here to make alliances in the inner kingdom and return to Samoa with a greater force to crush us. I was sent here to spy," he swallowed. "But once I arrived, I couldn't bear the thought of slaughtered villagers at the hands of General Va'iga. I had to warn of their coming."

"The king will know of this," Talatama said.

"With respect, the Pulotulahi have grown in numbers. We don't expect the Empire to rescue us if Va'iga becomes allies with the Pulotulahi and makes a move on Samoa."

"Can't expect the Empire to do anything, I say," Vaohoi spat.

"Who else knows about this? Who else have you told?" Talatama ignored the boy's comment.

"No one. When you found me, I was stopped in the market while making my way to Noble Anga'uli's house."

"Thank Tangaloa I found you first," Talatama breathed. "Listen very carefully. You must not tell anyone else about this, least of all Noble Anga'uli or men in his employ. Do you understand?"

"Why?" the giant asked.

"That goes for all of you now you've heard this." Talatama glared at all present. "Because I have a strong suspicion that Anga'uli may be harbouring men of the Pulotulahi. That is all you need to know at this stage."

The prince got to his feet and the others followed suit.

"Come with me, all of you. Atiogie, I need you to stay with me. I can't risk the Pulotulahi discovering your identity and with any luck, I'm hoping Afi Kakaha didn't guess the reason you're here."

"It doesn't matter if he did," Atiogie said and clenched his massive fist, "I would have crushed them underfoot!"

"But had you gone with him to Anga'uli's house, they would have murdered you by now," Talatama warned before raising his hands towards the men in the glade.

"Listen up everyone. Before we leave, I have an admission to make. This imperial investigation of the island and Noble Anga'uli is a crucial mission in the interests of the Empire and King Tu'itatui. So far I am pleased with the progress I've made to unravel this evil. However, it's been at the cost of involving innocents such as you..."

"Much has been discovered, and it has implicated you all in one way or another. Knowing this, I cannot have your deaths on my conscience. Whether you like it or not, we have to stick closely together for the next day or two until I've exposed Anga'uli."

"You don't trust us to be letting us out of your sight either, now we know what's going on," Vaohoi lashed.

"This is true," Talatama shot the young man a disapproving look.

"I trust your judgment," Lo'au replied immediately.

"I do also," Atiogie added. "Don't forget that I have my own interests at heart for my clan."

"Agreed," Talatama nodded.

"Welcome to the group." Vaohoi smiled and gazed up to the giant.

Just as the crowd began to depart the glade, the Samoan Chief glanced to a nearby tree.

"Spy!"

Immediately all warriors brandished their weapons and Talatama rushed to a large mango tree surrounded by dense shrubbery.

"Show yourself!" he shouted.

"I-I-I'm sorry! I-I didn't mean to intrude, Milord!" came a petite female voice.

A young woman appeared from behind the tree, a woven basket filled with fruit was tied to her back.

"Come here immediately!" Talatama ordered, as she hesitantly approached the group and hung her head in respect, her long black hair covering her face. Clothed in typical garb, she appeared to be a local village girl in the forest collecting food.

"M-my apologies, great warrior. I did not hear that there were others in the area. "

Talatama extended his club towards her, the tip of the Peace Maker touched the top of her head.

"What did you hear? Speak!" he snapped.

"N-n-nothing, Milord! Just voices. I came closer out of foolish curiosity - I heard nothing," she stammered.

"She lies," Vaohoi stated.

The young woman glanced at Vaohoi angrily.

"N-no, I beg of you, Milord, I am no threat!" She threw herself towards Talatama and touched her forehead to his feet.

"Who are you?" Talatama took a step back.

"I am Ofa, I live in town with my mother." She began to cry. "Please don't punish me Milord! You all startled me as I was picking fruit. Please forgive me. I heard nothing. Please!" she grovelled.

"Get to your feet," Talatama didn't lose his tone, "Be gone! Don't let me catch you around here again!"

"Thank you, Milord. Thank you, thank you!" she repeated in joy, as stumbled through the long grass, fruit bouncing out of her basket.

When she had disappeared through the jungle foliage, Talatama motioned to Oliame.

"Follow her," he said, "The rest of you, follow me."

CHAPTER 17

The sun had begun to set on the western horizon. Stunning shades of pinks, oranges and purples coloured the evening vista and the seaside palms swayed in the gentle breeze. Towards the north-east point of the island, Mahina arrived at her hidden camp not far from the beach on the eastern side. She de-robed from the garments of tapa and threw down the basket of fruit next to her belongings. She sat and peeled herself a mango, smiling as she thought of how she'd successfully disguised herself in front of Talatama and his companions.

She remained grinning as her mind went to the night they had first met. How she had wondered who he was and what he was doing at the House of Anga'uli. *So, he was a Commander of the Imperial Army from Tongatapu here investigating the corrupt noble himself?* If he was not involved with Anga'uli and Kamohoali'i, then he was no threat, she thought. Could he help her? Or would his meddling stand in the way of her rescuing Lady Rongaueroa? His interests were only in the Empire and its imperial business. He would not care for the issue of Lady Rongaueroa, and how her kidnapping had insulted the Rarotongans. No, he would not help, she thought. If he got in the way of their affairs, he would be swept aside.

As she sunk her teeth into the sweet mango, she gazed out to sea and mulled over what the Samoan Chief had revealed. Who was this Va'iga leading a thousand warriors from Samoa? What was their purpose? Did they have a connection with Kamohoali'i as he had suspected? As she pondered the news from the conversation, she noticed a lone warrior banking on the shore a few hundred metres south on the beach in the twilight. She recognised the man immediately and a shiver went through her body as she conjectured why he had returned.

Tarapu approached the hidden camp, breathing heavily from heaving the tongiaki ashore.

"You're back so soon! What has happened?" She confronted the man quickly.

"Mahina, news from Lord Toi -"

"What is it old friend?" she pressed.

"Only a night's sail from here, Piri and I intercepted Lord Toi and Lord Whatonga with over a thousand men," Tarapu breathed.

"How is that possible?" she gasped with joy.

"A week after you and I departed Ngatangi'ia, the lords could not wait for news to come to Rarotonga. Their love for Lady Rongaueroa brought them on hasty winds," he stated.

"Tangaloa be praised! That cuts weeks off waiting! Where are they now?"

"Directly east. The lords and the men lay just over the horizon. I have told them we've discovered Lady Rongaueroa's location and state," he paused. "Mahina this is important: Lord Toi and Whatonga send word that we attack the island tomorrow at daybreak."

"Excellent news. I am ready."

"Lord Toi wants you to stay on shore prior to the attack. Before dawn, you are to breach the House of Anga'uli and free Lady Rongaueroa. Wait for the battle to start and then make your escape through the main entrance," he drew lines in the sand.

"Good."

He placed his hand on her shoulder, smiling with a certain relief.

"At last, my good friend, tomorrow we shall free our queen, revel in a grand victory and return to Rarotonga," he beamed.

Short moments later, the pair sat, preparing some light dinner. Tarapu drew forth some fish and octopus from his basket.

"How have things gone the last few days, Mahina? Have you kept eyes on Lady Rongaueroa?" Tarapu asked.

"Yes, I've been seeing her every night. She's slowly gaining strength. I've told her that Lord Toi is coming," she said, collecting the fruit from the camp.

"That warms my heart, Mahina! She is well!" he gasped. "Then tomorrow will not be too late. Tangaloa be praised!"

"I've also made accidental contact with Lord Talatama, a Commander of the Imperial Army," she started slowly.

"Who? What happened?"

"He's the man I saw many nights ago in the courtyard of the Noble Compound," she smiled.

"Yes, I remember. You mentioned, and I've known you long enough to have noticed a liking ..." he teased.

"Well, yes, he is very handsome. I overheard a conversation and he questioned me. I managed to escape."

"I'm sure you did," Tarapu chuckled.

"Enough!" She laughed and gave him a shove. "The important thing is that he and his companions spoke of a Samoan army in the area."

"So? We have no quarrel with the Samoans. Relations between Samoa and Rarotonga have always been friendly," he shrugged. "It was probably talk of other things."

"All that matters is Lord Toi and your brother are here, and tomorrow we will gorge ourselves in a glorious victory!" He cried before eating his fish raw.

"Mmm," she nodded and looked towards the sea, deep in thought.

Just beyond their position were prying eyes. Two men, unaware of each other, lay hidden in shadows gathering all the information they required. Kupe, the Weeping Assassin had hidden behind ancient volcanic boulders. He slowly departed the area, under the cloak of darkness with rich tidings. The other, Oliame, sat perched in a nearby tree, grinned at the irony that he returned the eavesdropping on Mahina. She had done well concealing her identity from Talatama, he thought. Satisfied with the information, he silently disappeared from the area also.

Kupe sat in the reception room in the Noble Quarters, guarded from the outside and the rest of the compound. With him sat Noble Anga'uli, General Kamohoali'i, Havea, Afi Kakaha, Siateki and the she-warrior, Pele.

"General, the Rarotongans have arrived. They lie just beyond the eastern horizon and will attack at day break," Kupe grinned.

"Already? They are persistent bastards. They were probably not far behind their scouts." Kamohoali'i nodded his head. "Good work, everything is falling into place."

Kupe accepted the praise and wiped tears from his ruined eye. Kamohoali'i turned to his corrupted Imperial Commander, warrior - chief Siateki.

"What of Va'iga and the Samoans? Are they still moored close by? What news do you bring Siateki?"

"The Samoans harbour on the far side of Tafahi, Milord. They await your command," he responded.

Noble Anga'uli sniggered at the news. "This is brilliant, Kamohoali'i. When you ordered Havea and Kupe to kidnap Lady Rongaueroa from the Rarotongans, I thought you were mad. Now that they have taken the bait, we are ready for them with the Samoan warriors!"

"Extra muscle that we don't need," Afi Kakaha spat.

"Don't underestimate the Rarotongans. A vengeful heart is a greater weapon than that of pride," Kupe warned.

"What is your plan, brother? What is this twisted fate that you've construed this time?" Pele frowned, having just arrived at the meeting and was ignorant of the Pulotulahi's plans.

"I am to rectify my standing in the eyes of King and Empire," he grinned.

"What?" she laughed. "What does that mean?"

"My dear sister, Pele, I will reveal my plans to you in good time." He took a mouthful of kava.

"Keep your secrets – it doesn't concern me. I need to speak to you of why I have come ..."

"We will talk of that later Pele, I have a special role for you," he said as they all stood.

"Siateki, go immediately to Va'iga and his men and prepare for battle at first light. Kupe, be ready for Mahina to rescue Lady Rongaueroa. Kill both of them when you have the chance. Afi Kakaha, prepare your men for the conflict tomorrow and remember they must paint their faces with green paste. The Samoan warriors will need to know their allies in the fight. Havea and I will wait for the right moment to appear."

"Milord, what about Prince Talatama and his men?" Siateki asked before he departed.

"His visit was no doubt an inquiry into your rule, Anga'uli," he growled. "Nevertheless, he will undoubtedly be caught in the melee tomorrow. Anyone who can bring me his head shall be rewarded with ten slaves."

A cheer erupted from the room.

Only two hundred metres from the reception room, Talatama sat with Oliame, Mateitau, Kunamoana, Atiogie, Lo'au and Vaohoi. The night was dark. Crude torches barely lit the room that completed the stage of their underhanded meeting.

"I can't believe we remain here, Milord," Kunamoana said.

"We don't want Anga'uli to suspect that we know his plans. If we left abruptly he'd guess something is amiss. We will stay here for one more night," Talatama returned.

"What do you make of the Rarotongans attacking tomorrow, Milord?" Oliame asked.

"I'm unsure." Talatama rubbed his chin. "I can't work out why Anga'uli would provoke the Rarotongans by stealing their headwoman."

"I feel that it's a trap," Oliame stated.

"A trap? But for whom? It's a blatant call for war. It doesn't make sense," the prince frowned.

"The mechanics are in motion, Lord Talatama, a manipulative and cunning plan. I have no doubt Kamohoali'i and Havea are behind this, but for what reason, I do not know," Lo'au said.

"And what plan Va'iga and his men have with Niuatoputapu remains a mystery," Atiogie pondered in confusion.

"I feel the answer staring at me in the face! I know it!" Talatama punched the floor in frustration.

"What shall we do then, Milord? What shall we do about the battle tomorrow morning?" Mateitau persisted. "Shall we make battle preparations?"

"We'll be crushed if we're not cautious." Talatama placed his hand to his forehead. "I need to guess Anga'uli's plan. I can't confront him and prematurely throw accusations. We must wait for the right time to confront him and it might not be until the last minute."

"I say we sit back and watch the Rarotongans kill Anga'uli and his bastard cronies," Vaohoi laughed.

"Has anyone heard of Kamohoali'i or Havea being seen on the island? All this is speculation," Talatama threw the question.

"Lord Talatama – Paea, the wounded boy tu'a," Lo'au said clearly.

"What about him?"

"His wounds were caused by, what he says and I firmly believe, Kamohoali'i and his men. He said that he overheard them talking about their plans the night he was almost killed," the old man ended.

"What? I thought his wound was from a local scrap! My interest in the boy was in light of the tapa parchment. You didn't mention anything about him overhearing Kamohoali'i's plans or his appearance on this island!" Talatama jumped to his feet.

"You didn't ask. Nor did you reveal to us that Kamohoali'i was your primary focus," Lo'au said calmly.

"Damn! Where is the boy?"

"Still at the kava house, I think," Vaohoi pitched.

Talatama and the group of men sprinted out of the fale.

CHAPTER 18

Maui Atalaga stood before the great gates of the House of Anga'uli. Four guards blocked his path, spears drawn. The moon was not out, making the night seem blacker than usual. Scores of burning torches spotted along the ramparts barely illuminated the gates and the hero garbed with naught but a tattered vala around his midsection. Resting over his right shoulder was Mohemamahi, his soul and spirit reincarnate in the exalted war club.

"I am telling you, you are not allowed inside," the senior of the guards said again.

"Why?" Maui Atalaga asked like a curious child.

"You are neither a guest nor a recognised official of the Empire," the soldier stammered.

"But I go where I please. This is my land, after all," he returned matter-of-factly.

The soldiers looked at each other in disbelief.

"I'm telling you to leave!" the soldier summed up the courage to shout.

"Havea! Havea! I have come for you!" Maui Atalaga suddenly shouted at the top of his voice.

"You're mad! Who are you shouting at?" the soldier cried as he and the others stood back.

"I'm looking for my cousin, Havea. I know he's here somewhere ..." the hero proclaimed. "Havea! Havea!"

"We've never heard of him! Now get lost you crazy fool!" The soldiers pointed their spears at Maui Atalaga and one of the tips jabbed at his chest.

The hero rested his eyes over the soldiers and his childish demeanour evaporated. His face contorted and projected an aura of peril. A cloak of fear washed over the soldiers like a frozen chill. The sudden shift from a nonchalant stranger to a living horror was mortifying and their faces reflected their trepidation.

"So ... you want to meet death so soon ..." he said slowly, his voice sounding like a dreaded whisper on the wind.

The men were petrified. A sudden shout came from the inner courtyard as Noble Anga'uli appeared and strode down to the main entrance with almost forty guards.

"What is going on here?" he shouted.

Maui Atalaga stood back and returned to his inquiring purpose, the shadow of death slipping away.

"I'm looking for Havea. Bring him to me," he leered to Anga'uli.

"Yes, I could hear your rants from the castle. There's no one here by that name - you must be mistaken. I am Noble Anga'uli of Niuatoputapu, this is my house and these are my personal retainers. I don't know anyone by the name of Havea," he lied.

Maui Atalaga regarded the noble with a blank stare.

"I'm sorry, great warrior, is there anything else I may assist you with?" Anga'uli pressed.

Without answering or a sign of understanding, the folk hero turned and walked away into the darkness of the night. Some of the soldiers laughed as he disappeared. Anga'uli turned to them and smirked, "He is of no consequence."

When the noble left with his house warriors, the original four soldiers finally broke from their paralysed state. The youngest soldier, only eighteen years old, fell to his knees and sobbed like a child. The other men, eyes wide and pale, shivered with a chill and did not utter a word, as they slowly made their way back to the ramparts.

Inside the inner chamber of the House of Anga'uli, Kamohoali'i paced the length of the room, his big frame thumping the floorboards that echoed each footfall. At the other end of the room stood his sister Pele, leaning against one of the huge pillars that supported the high roof.

"So what is it you want to discuss, Pele? You'll have to make it quick, I wish to tell you about your role tomorrow," he said as he flicked the remains of kava from his kava bowl out into the courtyard, then tossed the bowl into the corner of the room. He paced towards her, adjusting his tapa, which wrapped around his powerful torso.

"Brother, I've come to tell you that I am leaving your service," she swallowed.

Putting his hands on his hips he turned around. He then turned and faced her again with a confused look.

"What did you say?" He cocked his head and took another step towards her.

She pushed herself off the pillar towards her brother.

"I said I'm leaving your service," she raised her chin, "I've allowed myself to be your pawn all my life – no longer! All her emotions began to run free. "I will live my life without your evil schemes and find my own destiny."

Kamohoali'i's hand shot at her head, and although she defended in time, the strength of her brother's strike flailed her across the room. She adjusted, rolled to her feet and glared back at him.

"How dare you, you upstart little bitch? I am your brother, your father, your life!" he growled.

She swiftly drew her obsidian axe and instinctively swung it as she would on the battlefield. She breathed heavily and her heart swelled with the pain of sisterly agony.

Kamohoali'i took a step towards her and finally raised his hands in surrender. His raging expression suddenly turned to that of apology. In her mind, childhood years flooded back when he used to come to her aid, helped her with difficulties and took pity on her. His face was almost compassionate.

"Now, now, Pele, let's not quarrel about this." His voice was calm and gentle.

She slowly lowered her axe but kept her distance.

"Come now, let's talk," he said with almost a smile. "I'm sure we can come to an agreement."

Perhaps Kamohoali'i's greatest asset, even over his power as a warrior, was his proficiency for fork-tongued deceit. He was charismatic and a natural leader: his ability to conjure and attract willing followers was to be admired. For the last few years he had raised many warriors to his cause. Pele slowly tucked her weapon to her side, composed herself and raised her eyes towards him.

"There is no agreement or discussion." She cleared her throat before exiting the fale, "I leave in the morning."

Kamohoali'i stood silently for long moments as he digested the gravity of his sister's words. After all the long years she had supported his endeavours, he had provided for her when they were younger and their parents cared little for their upbringing. He arranged for her to be trained by the best fighters in the land, provided the base for her spirit to grow, to be forged in the fires of success, reward and bounty. He clenched his teeth and spat.

He shook his head and admitted that he had noticed a change of heart, when she recently refused to partake in killings in the Vava'u Islands. He had conceded that she was perhaps going through a testing time as a female leader in the Pulotulahi. Now he knew of her desire to sever her bond with him, he accepted that it was not an impulsive move. She must have decided to leave him for some time. Although her harsh words were swift, he knew there was no turning back.

As he pondered his reprisal, Havea seemed to melt out of the darkness to approach him.

"All is ready for dawn," he reported.

"Good."

It was long moments before he faced the dark warrior.

"Summon Kupe, Afi Kakaha and Anga'uli. I must speak with them at once. There will be a small change in plans for the morning."

Pele stormed into the courtyard quickly and ended up under the large mango tree in the northern corner. She struck her forearm against the tough bark and rested her head against her arm, staring at the ground. She took in a deep breath, then another.

"Milady," came the voice of her captain.

She straightened, but did not turn to him. She wiped her eyes, awash with tears.

"Prepare the men. We leave for Ha'apai in the morning."

"Yes, Milady," he bowed and left the courtyard.

The she-warrior turned in the direction her captain had gone and folded her arms. She had done it. It was over. Now she could start her life anew. The prospect was unfamiliar and seemed empty without the shadow of her evil brother. But it excited her.

CHAPTER 19

Close to dawn Talatama stood with his head bowed in the fale kava. He kicked the kalis across the floor and cursed. Hours prior, he and his companions had learned that the children; Paea, Maka and Heilala had disappeared without word. He and the giant Samoan, Atiogie, remained in the fale kava while he sent Lo'au, Vaohoi and his soldiers out to scour the village for them.

"Time is growing short," he sighed.

"Perhaps I should be out searching also." Atiogie scratched his head.

"You don't know what the children look like, and let I remind you – you are safer with me."

"No, I mean search for Va'iga and his men," the giant returned.

"I wouldn't worry about that. I'm sure they'll show up," the prince's eyes widened immediately, "Wait – it can't be a coincidence that the Rarotongans are here at the same time as the Samoans. It is logical that Anga'uli and Kamohoali'i are using Va'iga and his warriors to fight the Rarotongans - but then - why stage the battle? What do they gain?" he stared at the ground again.

"I've never been that clever, but I feel that we're missing a clue in their plans," Atiogie conceded.

"Damn! I almost had it," the prince swore.

Lo'au and Vaohoi appeared through the entrance, looking exhausted and unsuccessful. Vaohoi flopped himself on the floor and curled up in the corner.

"Sleep time!" he hollered and in less time he was snoring loudly.

"I had higher hopes for you two in your search," Talatama said as he approached the mu'a.

"Something has happened, Lord Talatama. They said to me they would stay here until Paea was healed," Lo'au returned.

"We can't wait any longer." Talatama saw further failure as Mateitau and Kunamoana entered the room.

"Where is Oliame?" he asked.

"Still out searching, Milord."

"Mateitau - round up the men," Talatama fastened his ironbark girdle, took hold of his headdress of shell, mother-of-pearl and sharks' teeth and placed his cloak of black tapa over his shoulders.

"Be ready for battle. We meet back at the quarters within the Noble Compound."

Atiogie assembled his large breast plate and prepared himself with Talatama.

"What do you want of us, Lord Talatama?" Lo'au asked.

"Stay here in the fale kava. Guard the entrances. It's likely that the battle might spill into the village," the prince warned. "Tangaloa be with you."

Shades of light began to rise from the eastern horizon as dawn showed signs of arrival. The island was illuminated in the half-light and the cool morning air welcomed the coming of the sun. The forest path appeared easily in the dawn, making the walk from the Degei camp easier as Adi, Duvuduvukulu and a few other warrior priests trundled towards the village. Mildew on the trees and grass sparked softly in the pale light. Morning birds chirped and sounded the coming of a clear and fine day.

"Master Adi, are you sure it is wise to make ourselves known to Noble Anga'uli, especially after hearing the stories from Nofu?" Captain Duvuduvukulu asked as he followed the Fijian priestess.

"Yes, Captain, I understand your concern. Our visit this morning is simply to make a peaceful contact in a respectful gesture before we continue our mission here," she said firmly, "If the stories are as bad as they say, then we will not hinder the internal affairs of the island following this visit."

"I value your insight, Master Adi," the captain returned, "Though I want to make it known, that I do not agree with this, for your safety and mine."

Adi stopped and turned to the Captain of the Red Earth.

"I tire of our disagreements, Duvuduvukulu. Need I remind you that we shall be working together for a long time, so perhaps swallowing your pride might save us both torturous and laboured quarrels in the future?"

"Yes, Master Adi." Duvuduvukulu glared at her from behind.

Before long, the Fijians entered the village and beheld a typical early morning; villagers starting their chores for the day, merchants preparing the village market, fishermen preparing their kalias, women in social groups assembling woven ware, children playing here and there, and scattered warriors and soldiers milling about searching for breakfast.

The Degei priests wandered among the Niuatoputapuans as visitors, pacing slowly and taking in the various activities and sights.

"Which way do we go?" Duvuduvukulu asked.

"Excuse me, Sir, which way to the House of Anga'uli?" she stopped and asked an old man with an approachable look.

Lo'au turned to face her, holding wrapped banana leaves of cooked meat and vegetables in both hands. Just taken out of the umu oven, the succulent smell and heat produced steam from the packages.

"Good morning. Would you care for something to eat?" Lo'au smiled and spoke in Fijian.

"You're most generous, Noble Chief," she said, taken aback from the sudden invitation in her own language. "But I need to meet with the noble of the island as soon as possible."

"What brings you here, Priestess of Degei?" the old mu'a asked, still smiling.

"How do you know that we're Degei?"

"I might also like to know how you know that," " the captain pitched in.

"This morning is not, let's say, an appropriate time for you to meet with Noble Anga'uli. Please, I invite you to join me in breakfast," he said seriously. "There's enough here for all of us."

There were many customs shared by all island nations across the Pacific. One of them was that it was considered rude to refuse an invitation to eat.

"Well, yes, of course. Thank you, honoured mu'a," the Master of Snakes accepted and followed Lo'au. Duvuduvukulu clicked his tongue in disapproval and huffed as he followed in turn.

Vaohoi yawned as he rose from the short hours of sleep. He arched his back, stretching, stood up and rubbed his sleepy eyes. While scratching his backside, he peered around and saw no one in the fale kava.

"Where did everyone go?" he said to himself.

Lo'au walked into the fale holding the food and brushed off the mud from his feet. The smell from the meat carried in and struck Vaohoi in the face.

"Chiiiihii! Whale meat!" he shouted as he stretched. "Master, you're a godsend!"

"Morning, Vaohoi. Prepare for guests please."

"W-wha-" the young man froze as he watched the Fijians follow Lo'au into the room hesitantly. He had never met a Fijian nor seen the dark and proud Melanesian races beyond the Fijian Islands, and their sudden appearance excited him immensely. Once he had ceased staring at the priests, he fumbled around organising mats and bowls.

The Fijians relaxed and accepted portions of braised whale meat with kelp and sweet potato served on fresh green banana leaves. Vaohoi rushed around and handed young coconuts to drink and gave Adi special interest. He stared at the priestess with genuine interest and curiosity.

"Master, do they speak 'common'?" Vaohoi asked Lo'au.

"Yes, we speak common," Duvuduvukulu answered quickly.

During this point in history, most of the Polynesian nations spoke virtually the same language; there were very little differences in words and only slight accented pronunciations. The term 'common' language referred to the one broad Polynesian tongue, different to the dialect used by Fijians and the Melanesian cultures.

"Thank you." Adi smiled at Vaohoi for his extra attention. "Noble Chief, I must—"

"Please call me Lo'au," the mu'a interrupted, as he served out more delicious food.

Adi glanced at her Degei priests in shock.

"Y-you are not ... the Great Lo'au, of the Priests of Tangaloa?" she hesitantly asked, leaning forward.

Lo'au looked at Adi, smiled and continued to eat slowly.

"Master, they know who you are!" Vaohoi guffawed.

Adi glanced quickly to the other priests, swiftly placed their food down and stood. They bowed reverently. "You honour us, High Priest of Tangaloa."

Among the distinct orders of religion and piety across the Pacific cultures, some men were lauded and known to all sects by their deeds of kindness, insight and devotion to the religion. Lo'au was perhaps the most renowned high priest of Tangaloa to have ever lived. His peers were among the highest echelons of the religious circles. His close friends included Adi's Grandmaster of the Degei, Nakaunicina.

"Please sit down", Lo'au motioned.
"Eat up. You're going to need your strength."

Adi could not hide the mix of joy and respect as she returned to her seat.

"Master Lo'au, I am honoured to finally meet you," she started. "My name is Adi, Master of Snakes. I hail from the Nausori Highlands in Fiji and have been charged to establish a bure fale in Niuatoputapu." She motioned to her comrades, "These are some of my brethren and Captain Duvuduvukulu of the warrior priests."

"I see, I see," Lo'au smiled. "I am pleased to meet you all. Welcome to Niuatoputapu. As you may have heard, I am a wandering priest these days and by happenchance, sailed into Niuatoputapu a few weeks ago. This is my travelling companion, Vaohoi."

The boy raised a hand and pulled one of his ridiculous faces.

"Well met," offered Adi cordially, a characteristic of hers. "Master Lo'au, I now see that my coming here this morning was the will of the gods. We have been in Niuatoputapu for only a couple of days, and I've come to let the Noble of Niuatoputapu know we are here," she paused. "However, I have heard disturbing news of politics on the island."

"You don't know the half of it!" Vaohoi laughed.

"We have been involved with much of the plight that the people are facing here, Adi. And your help is needed also to make right the wrongs of this strife." Lo'au looked sternly at the Fijian priestess.

"Now wait a minute. With respect, perhaps its wiser we just stay out of this internal discord," Captain Duvuduvukulu put forth. "We're not here to become tied up in politics of the Empire."

Lo'au continued finishing off the morsel of whale meat. He then regarded the Fijian captain in a way that made him uncomfortable.

"You are already a part of a destiny that will change your lives forever."

CHAPTER 20

The sound of bellowing men woke Emori with a start. Lying on the sand next to his kalia, the Fijian warrior priest shifted up onto his elbows and squinted out to the early morning brine. He shook his head so the sand could filter off his frizzy hair. He took a deep breath and dared to imagine the repercussions of the decision he took to desert the Degei Order.

Many days ago, Emori, warrior priest of Degei and kin of Grandmaster Nakaunicina, had abandoned his order and set off to find his true love. The decision to leave his chiefly post toiled his consciousness for sleepless nights, but in the end the truth of love, a love that ruled his heart, could not be ignored or swept aside. His passion, adoration and unconditional love for his soul mate, Adi, was irrepressible.

When they parted company in the Nausori Highlands, the warrior held his emotions tightly concealed, knowing the charge Adi had been given was a far greater purpose than his own desires. He saw in Adi's eyes that she too dreaded the times ahead, accepting a life without her beloved. But the Degei had been their whole lives, the mortar of their bond as children, the foundations that had given them hope, purpose and direction. And yet despite the strict and reverent faith, love sent his sense of direction and purpose wayward. Would he have purpose without Adi in his life?

A respected and charismatic warrior among his peers and across the Fijian islands, Emori's plight was known to many brothers of arms and friends. And though his decision was supported by them all, he refused all offers of companionship on his journey to Niuatoputapu. His quest was that of love, a destiny that no man may make, other than on his own. His legion of over one hundred Fijian warrior priests fought with the prospect of allowing their leader to voyage across dangerous seas alone. But it was his fate.

He pushed himself to his knees and brushed off the sand from his dark skin. He stood and placed his hand on his sea craft and squinted out northwards, to see the great volcanic island of Tafahi many kilometres away; the famous landmark of Niuatoputapu.

"All revere! All make way! All bow down!" echoed the same voices that woke him from his slumber.

He felt the two nights without rest begin to catch up, despite his brief reprieve before dawn. He rubbed his eyes from the glare that reflected on the brine from the morning sun, as a dozen tongiaki moved slowly into, what appeared to be, the main port of Niuatoputapu along the next beach. Standing abreast of the sea craft were extravagantly dressed men, brandishing brightly coloured banners and sails. The men at the bow were obviously announcing the arrival of someone of importance. From what the Fijian warrior could see, their approach was causing a great commotion to the people ashore.

He quickly heaved his small kalia up to the shrubs and palm trees and gowned his native Fijian tapa, girdles and his infamous spear. The spear was over seven feet long, carved from strong palm wood and dyed in the rich honey of sandalwood oil. The spear tip was renowned among enemies and allies alike: three giant stingray barbs protruded almost twenty inches in length, bound by way of tie and smoulder. Each sported smaller stings jutting forth to create additional damage on a successful thrust. Its ability to pierce through most armour made it a powerful weapon. Within the first few weeks of fixing new barbs to the spear, they withheld the natural venom that inflicted terrible pain and partial paralysis. The

Fijian warrior took a deep breath and began to stride towards the village, spear in hand and love in his heart.

Talatama, Atiogie and Mateitau stood in the noble guest fale within the compound, waiting impatiently. The prince had given up searching for the children and had returned to the Noble House to confront Anga'uli in the hope of discovering his plan. Shortly after sunrise, they arrived at the compound and were advised that Anga'uli's whereabouts were unknown. Talatama began to pace, the feeling of impending danger rising under his skin.

Kunamoana stepped into the fale quickly and approached the prince.

"No word, Milord. I cannot find Anga'uli, or any of his chiefs. The House of Anga'uli is empty save the she-warrior, Pele. She and her men are preparing to leave the island."

"And the village?" Talatama asked.

"The people are going about their daily business."

"Perhaps Anga'uli has fled the island in fear of the Rarotongan attack," the giant Samoan put forward.

"Not likely. Come, let's leave this place," he said angrily as he stepped out of the fale into the courtyard and towards the main entrance.

Just as the four men exited, Oliame appeared, sprinting up the hill toward them.

"Where have you been? What news do you bring?" Talatama demanded answers.

"Milord! I found the children!" He stopped to catch his breath.

"Maui be praised! Where? Did you speak with them?" Talatama grasped his lieutenant's arm.

"Milord, you must hear this immediately – I spoke with the boy, Paea, about what he recalled," Oliame breathed. "He confirms the identity and presence of the Dark General, Kamohoali'i, his commander, Havea, and others on the island."

der"Yes Oliame – and ...?"

"Milord, Paea overheard some of Anga'uli and Kamohoali'i's plans, most of which involved luring your brother, Prince Talaiha'apepe, to the island."

Just as the words escaped Oliame's mouth, they heard the faint chorus of a royal heralding from the distant waterfront. The chorus was followed by a faint cheer from the people. A sudden realisation hit Talatama in a wave of dread.

"They plan to assassinate my brother!"

The prince sprinted down the hill, Atiogie and his lieutenants struggling to keep up.

The royal tongiakis banked slowly on the sand as hundreds of townsfolk milled around on the beach and bowed down. The royal herald, a matapule, continued to proclaim the arrival of the royal fleet of a hundred warriors and His Royal Highness, Prince Talaiha'apepe. An entourage of retainers jumped from the central tongiaki and heaved a portable dais from the sea craft: a wooden masterpiece of lavishly carved designs that formed a royal chair, circled with wreaths of flowers and jewellery. Upon it sat the second son of King Tu'itatui.

Talaiha'apepe was a large man for his young age and possessed a slightly larger frame than his older brother, Talatama. He showed visible signs of a life of decadence; overweight and unaccustomed to travel, he appeared bloated, pale and weary. Wearing the finest tapa and adorned in the most valuable jewellery in the kingdom, he epitomized the wealth, power and profligacy of the royal family.

Behind the royal herald, the entourage of strong men carried the dais and the prince ashore to where the sand became soil. All villagers present remained on their knees and bowed their heads to the ground. There was no sound but that of the matapule singing in baritone, the lapping of waves and the sea breeze through the palm leaves. Noble Anga'uli, Senior Chief Talo, Village Headman Ilamaki, and Ulikaite, the high priest, had appeared. They knelt down in welcome to meet the prince in support of dozens of bowing retainers.

"Your Royal Highness, Prince Talaiha'apepe. As Noble of Niuatoputapu and steward of its people, I extend a humble greeting. Welcome to Niuatoputapu," Anga'uli said as he bowed low, followed by all his men. "We are honoured beyond deserving to receive you to your faithful island. I am your willing and most loyal servant, Lord of all Things."

"Greetings, Noble Anga'uli, you are a favoured man among many nobles in the kingdom." Talaiha'apepe's voice was deep and carried a clear and defining tune. "Oh to live on such a fecund island. I look forward to seeing more of Niuatoputapu. But for now, I wish to rest my weary soul and the souls of my men from many days at sea," the prince ended, closing his eyes somnolently.

"Yes, my lord, of course and without further delay," Anga'uli returned, slightly distracted by something out at sea.

"Noble Anga'uli, kalias approach – are we expecting another fleet of royal visits?" Headman Ilamaki said as he pointed out the fast looming sail craft that seemed to double in accumulation as they appeared in sight.

All men on the banks of Falehau, including the royal entourage, gazed out to the armada heading towards the beach at a speed that warned this was not a casual approach to shore. As if suddenly, the fleet was close enough for them to discern war-cries that revealed the intent. A thousand Rarotongan warriors thundered towards the shores of Falehau, like a billowing hurricane of devastation. Anga'uli paused with his men and said nothing for long moments, acting though they were shocked into paralysis. Village women began to scream in high pitched wails of fear, a sound that broke everyone from their state of fear.

"Attack – we're under attack! Back to the village! Protect the prince!" the noble finally shouted.

Discordant cries of panic erupted from the townspeople, suddenly scattering in all directions. The air was filled in a chaotic frenzy as battle came on sails of death. The royal entourage panicked as they tried to shuffle their prince along the uneven ground.

Looming down upon Niuatoputapu, Lord Toi and Lord Whatonga stood strongly at the bow of the largest tongiaki, which carried over two hundred warriors. The aged King of Rarotonga laid his hand on his son's shoulder as their craft screamed towards the shore.

"We take no slaves. Kill anyone with a club." His steely eyes met his son's.

"Find Noble Anga'uli and crush him along with all his men. Search for Mahina. She will rescue your mother and will be seeking you forthwith. Not until the Lady is aboard this craft do we cease our campaign," he finished calmly in the face of imminent battle.

"Yes, Father." The handsome Rarotongan Prince nodded solemnly.

Whatonga turned and faced his steadfast warriors packed into the massive tongiaki, raised his club skyward and emitted an ear splitting cry. The matching thunder from the hundreds of loyal warriors ready to die for their prince rippled their skin. Seconds later, a hundred vessels hurtled into the sands of Niuatoputapu. Boiling over the edges, leapt a thousand painted Rarotongan warriors filled with the rage that fuels revenge.

Had any of the Rarotongans noticed at the time of banking ashore, they would have been curious to see an equal amount of vessels only a few hundred metres away, approaching from the North. The Samoan tongiakis numbered about one hundred. Floating motionless between Niuatoputapu and Tafahi, they were filled with some of Upolu's finest warriors. General Va'iga stood at the helm of the main tongiaki among his fleet with his Captain, Sooalo, his lieutenant, Nam'ulu, and Kamohoali'i's commander, Siateki.

"They've hit the beach," Sooalo jeered.

"Haste, we must make haste! I starve for battle!" Nam'ulu edged forward, eager for the forthcoming fight.

"Prepare for full sail!" Va'iga turned to his mast-man.

"Hold! Not yet. Not just yet. Let the Rarotongans lay waste on the village for just a few moments longer," Siateki, the Fallen Commander smiled.

CHAPTER 21

The morning sun beamed from a cloudless sky, though did little to heat the wind of the winter day. The light kissed the islands of paradise as though blessing its beauty. But the beauty of the day was ravaged by human storm clouds that loomed over the island of Niuatoputapu. Shrill screams of women and children echoed across the island and the air was thick with fear and death.

The Rarotongan warriors swept up the beach in a matter of seconds. They slew a dozen defending soldiers and flooded into the township like a river of murder. Hundreds of townsfolk ran in all directions: women scampering and screaming, carrying young children, men shouting and searching frantically for their families. Terror gripped the souls of the helpless villagers. The midst of battle was terrifying. Niuatoputapu soldiers were slain without question.

Talatama, Atiogie, and the imperial warriors made a path through the scattering villagers with difficulty. Talatama rounded up a handful of fleeing children into his arms and ran to the nearest fale.

"Get them inside!" he yelled to an elderly woman.

"Battle calls Talatama! We must fight!" Atiogie gripped his massive club with fierce eyes.

"No! Not until -"

Through the chaos he spotted his brother still seated upon the dais – his men trying to escape the carnage and protect the prince as best they could.

"There he is! Follow me!" he shouted as his soldiers dodged and ran towards the royal entourage.

But the surge of fleeing villagers and the mulch of warring men made it impossible. An attack exploded from their right and one of Talatama's men fell; Kunamoana was killed with a single blow, his body destroyed in a bloody heap of skin and red. Talatama shuddered, the target of rescuing his brother momentarily forgotten at the sight of his lieutenant's death. A sudden dread swept through the warriors as the man-terror appeared and the prince felt an irrepressible chill surround him. He was unlike anyone he had faced before.

Havea lifted his giant club from Kunamoana's corpse and faced the terror stricken warriors. The weapon was a thing of both horror and amazement, five feet of wood, jagged from hilt to tip with rows of large sharks' teeth. It was already spattered with the blood of men. The eight foot warrior lifted his head and surveyed Talatama, saliva dripping from his gaping mouth.

"You meddling fool," he exhaled, seeing the effect he had on the horror struck warriors, "I'll enjoy picking your bones tonight."

Mateitau broke from the seizing fear, the sight of his fallen brother too much for the terror to restrain him. His sudden action liberated the group from the invisible grasp. He leaped towards the giant in a blind fury.

"Attack!" Talatama roared, his eyes blinking with battle rage.

A dozen imperial soldiers assaulted the warrior simultaneously, their clubs flailing in a combination of heaves and thrusts. The sound of wood cracking together and war cries lifted above the screams of the villagers.

The prince whirled to Atiogie, "Flank him!"

The Samoan weaved incredibly quickly for his size and already repositioned himself with the same plan. Guarding beyond the monster's reach, he bore witness to the rising and falling of Havea's club and there was no sign of falter. As every second passed, one of his men fell in sickening sounds and mists of pink. And though vastly outnumbered, the demon-warrior did not relent. Left and right the dreaded club swept, collecting the bodies of imperial soldiers, ripping through their flesh with jagged, bitter-white teeth... Any strike that landed on Havea bounced away like hollow wood.

"He's too strong," Talatama swore in disbelief.

Atiogie rose behind Havea and released a gut wrenching roar as his giant club throttled down to the menacing head. Talatama leapt towards the giant, winding up for a killing stroke. But in one deft movement, Havea swept aside Atiogie's attack, grabbed him by the neck and brought their faces together, locked in a fierce glare. Havea clenched his fangs and stared into Atiogie's soul with pitiless eyes. Stricken with fear, Atiogie gave a last attempt to strike him with his fist, but missed and felt himself being lifted off the ground. With an almighty heave, Havea hurled him through the air and sent him smashing through the side of a nearby fale in an explosion of splinters.

The Peace Maker swept across the back of the evil warrior, cleaving ribs and opening up his leathered skin. He roared with fury, arching his back in pain. It was Talatama's only chance to fell the unstoppable terror, his strike true and strong. He reefed back the Peace Maker to make the final attempt but in the moments between seconds, Havea recovered. With a deft backhand, he aimed his club straight for the prince. Talatama's carnal reflexes shot up the Peace Maker in defence. The sound of the two clubs colliding together cracked through the blood-pungent air, and with it created such impact that Talatama's headdress was thrown from his head and he was sent hurtling into scattering villagers with a crash.

Far from the melee, within the compound of the Noble House, Mahina raced through the deserted fales towards where Lady Rongaueroa was kept bound. The ceaseless chorus of screams and cries echoed in the distance, faint and irrelevant to her ears. The beautiful Rarotongan grasped her throwing club in one hand and her whale-bone knife in the other, as she crept across the floor of the reception fale. Halfway across, two of Anga'uli's soldiers appeared at the exit before her. One of the men grinned and turned to the other as the thought of raping her was more tempting than taking her life.

The other stepped forward into the throwing club that had somehow closed the distance between them. The hard and bulbous end throttled into his forehead with a hollowing smack, snapping his head back and dropping him lifeless to the floor. His companion glared in disbelief, and in the moments it took him to consider his next action, Mahina had dashed towards him and sank her dagger into his flesh. She retracted her weapon and moved aside, leaving a gapping puncture in the side of the neck that spewed bursts of blood.

Mahina leapt from the reception fale's exit and reached the prison where, upon peering inside, she shuddered, seeing Lady Rongaueroa laying beaten and gagged. The queen's eyes watered with tears at the sight of her daughter. Their eyes met and between them rushed a mutually devoted love.

"Mother..."

Sadness streamed down the woman's face as she shook her head. She knew she had seen Mahina for the last time. Her eyes reflected her surrender.

"Mother? Wh-wha—"

There was an almighty snap and a whipping sound outside the fale. Like the gods snatching a life, Lady Rongaueroa was reefed skyward by a rope around her neck. The power of the rope pulled the woman straight through the roof of the fale, sending wood and leaves in all directions.

"Noooo!" Mahina fell back in horror before racing outside to see her lifeless mother, high amongst the trees. The twine had been tied to a massive tree trunk that had been dropped as a counterweight to cause the fiendish trap to work.

"N-no ..." Mahina fell to her knees.

A warrior casually stepped out from behind the tree that caught the dead woman high in its branches. Kupe approached her with a curious look, a single tear trickling from his blind eye. He cocked his head at her.

"Oh, you didn't like my little trap?" he said, regarding the body of Lady Rongaueroa with amusement.

A flash of white bore the fruits of death. Mahina's whalebone dagger swiped, but Kupe was too quick. He stepped aside and struck Mahina in the side of the head with his fist, sending her sprawling across the ground, her dagger rolling from her grasp. She gritted her teeth and supported herself with her arms first then slowly regained her footing. She faced the Weeping Assassin groggily: her vision awash with tears and stars.

A sudden memory of her training came back to her, times of hardship, sacrifice, determination, of the relentless pursuit to become a warrior. *Lose your concentration and you will die*, she remembered. She took a deep breath and faced Kupe with her two throwing clubs.

"Behold Princess, my instrument of death," he grinned as he unravelled one of his deadly weapons; a long length of rope with a combination of coral and spiny sea urchins bound to the end. The coral was as hard as rock, with modelled swollen bulbs, while the dozens of urchin spines were at least four inches long.

He began to swing the rope in circles above his head as they faced each other and moved around adjusting positions. Mahina glared at him, her attractive face contorted by pure hatred. He returned an unemotional gaze of total absorption, as they poked feints at one another in hope to commit a forced assault. Dust from the earth smoked about their feet as they altered their footwork.

Coral and urchin screamed at Mahina's face with astonishing speed. She ducked quickly and moved in to capitalize on an over extension. Kupe twisted and yanked the rope sharply, causing the dangerous end to come screeching back towards her. She deftly abandoned her counter attack and opened the distance again as he cackled and continued to weave the weapon through the air.

She needed to edge closer to her dagger where it lay on the ground, but Kupe saw her intention immediately. Pushing her ground caused him to step back, and as he did, she rolled and nimbly snatched up her dagger. But it had sacrificed her footing. The coral and urchin combination whirled down and glanced the side of her legs before exploding beside her.

She leapt up in a blur: her throwing club cracked off Kupe's shoulder as he attempted to protect his face. He spun to strike her with his off hand. Tripping to avoid being hit, her second club barely found its mark under his jaw. The impact smashed his jowls together and shattered teeth. As he stumbled from the blow, she felt the sharp blow on the back of her shoulder. The coral and urchins sank into her skin and spun her to the ground.

After what seemed like hours, she gradually got to her feet again, her vision trembling with dark corners of unconsciousness creeping in. The blurry shape of Kupe on one knee was a few feet from her, head bowed and blood dripping from his mouth. She stretched down to collect her weapon and almost fell as she did. The thought of trying to finish him off was too much; she could not survive another clash. She swayed as she stood, tucking her weapons to her side and hearing Kupe cursing in her direction. He had collapsed again after an attempt to get to his feet. Dizzy and close to unconsciousness from fatigue and lament, Mahina stumbled towards the village.

CHAPTER 22

Pele and her warriors from Ha'apai negotiated their way through the carnage. She had ordered them not to engage in battle with the Rarotongans unless forced, and made it clear that their only interest was to return to their isles over the southern sea, leaving her evil brother behind to deal with his making. Their tongiakis lay only a few hundred metres away as she entered the centre of town and spotted her brother amid a cluster of large fales, accompanied by Afi Kakaha and dozens of Niuatoputapu warriors.

Almost immediately, a large group of local warriors moved to surround her and her men. Kamohoali'i strode towards her, garbed in battle ware, holding forth his club and revelling in the omnipresent chaos and terror. He glared at her with wicked eyes; a look that reflected tenacity.

"Come to see me off, eh, brother?" she spat defiantly.

"Yes, I have. Your decision is your own, and with it comes repercussions. You'll die knowing this," he motioned towards his men.

Pele was a warrior before a woman, and despite their bond, his order for her death did not hinder her action. It was as though their sibling bond had never been.

"You bastard! Fight me!" she screamed into his face.

Without falter, the Niuatoputapu warriors armed with long spears closed in. At least half of her men were skewered instantly.

Her captain escaped the spears and broke through the circle of death, followed by half a dozen at his rear.

"Pele, follow me!" he shouted.

But instead of fleeing, the she-warrior bounded towards her brother. As she leapt in Kamohoali'i's direction, Afi Kakaha and his warriors stepped into her path and momentarily overwhelmed her in a blur of fighting bodies. Her plaited hair flailed in the melee as she swung her axe in natural movements that cut through flesh and bone. In the work of moments, she had slain six warriors while on the back foot and outnumbered.

Afi Kakaha took a step backwards, as a circle of tentative warriors formed around her, her dazzling skill taking the old warrior by surprise.

"Don't underestimate her," Kamohoali'i laughed as he watched his sister fighting for her life.

Afi Kakaha wove a hand in the air towards his warriors and stepped into the circle to face her. The sounds of violence and war cries surrounding Pele did not cease, though the old warrior's challenge seemed desperately isolated. She raised her chin in defiance and regarded the warriors with abhorrence.

"Look at you all, you cowering dogs. Do you think you can kill me here and now? How dare you insult me? Run back to the bush and tend to the taro, you bunch of farmers!"

A nearby group of fales burst into ash and flame as if to support her defiance.

"You insolent, little bat-shit! I'll kill you!" Afi Kakaha leapt towards her.

She grinned as the old warrior took the bait so easily. She stepped to the side as he attacked her. Her obsidian axe arched downwards and sliced through the tough ligaments and tendons in his knee. Though the old warrior showed no sign of pain, he roared out in fury as he swiped with his club. She shifted effortlessly to let him over extend and miss before her axe came down vertically to split his head open like a ripe watermelon.

Without a moment's hesitation, she drew her bow and an arrow fired silently towards Kamohoali'i like a bolt of lightning amid the stunned warriors. The general, however, knew his sister's extraordinary skill and pre-empted the shot. He yanked a young warrior in front of him as a shield, and at the moment he was struck, the general discarded him to the side.

"Kill her!" he bellowed.

The Niuatoputapu warriors jerked into sudden action and as they did, Pele nimbly dodged the attacks and raced back towards the ramparts through a frenzied landscape of fire and devastation.

Emori waded his way through the fleeing townspeople of Niuatoputapu and the burning town. By the favour of the gods, the warrior priest had caught a glimpse of his love, Adi, through the crowds in the distance. He immediately discarded his belongings, gripped his spear in hand and sprinted towards where he had last seen her.

"Adi! Adi!" he cried, a lover's anguish in his voice.

Lo'au gripped Adi's hand as he careened through the chaos, Vaohoi, Duvuduvukulu and the Fijian contingent of priests close behind. The old mu'a led them from the fale kava into the heart of the town, where he searched desperately for Talatama.

The fire had spread through the village like a swarming wave of obliteration. The smoke rose from the island like a beacon that could be seen for hundreds of kilometres. Burning houses meant the villagers had no place to hide and the amount of people in the open streets tripled. Duvuduvukulu suddenly snatched Adi's hand and pulled her towards him. His face was a mask of fear and anger, incapable of negotiation.

"Stupid woman – you listen to me! We must leave this place now, leave these people to die in their own doing!"

"Let go of me!" she ordered, as she yanked back her arm.

Suddenly, a handful of Rarotongan warriors rushed them. Adi shuddered at the intent of the warriors, the closest warrior thrashing down a Fijian warrior priest in a single blow. Duvuduvukulu and his warrior priests paused in fear. He snarled at Adi in a fulfilling emotion of betrayal.

"Stay here and die then, stubborn bitch! I am done following your orders!" he snarled and fled with the remaining warrior priests.

She was silent as the weight of mutiny fell over her. Turning to stare straight into the eyes of her killers, Lo'au stood in front of her, protectively, with his staff. Vaohoi brandished his club and stood by her. As the warriors approached the three, the leader laughed at the sight of them putting up a show of bravery.

"Look at this! Who wants first spoils of the woman?"

"You horrid sons of whores! Why did mighty Tangaloa create such ugliness!" Vaohoi spat back at their laughter.

"Such daring, you little grot," the leader seethed before a spear thumped into his chest with an impact that threw him backwards. Emori leapt over burning wood and smoke into the fray. In an instant he retrieved his spear and commenced combat with the remaining Rarotongan warriors. The first gurgled and fell to his knees as the poisonous barbs shot through his mouth. Emori adjusted his stance and thrust the deadly weapon forward again, taking down a second warrior. He resumed a solid stance with a look of concentration and focus towards the remaining Rarotongans who hesitated, and then retreated.

"Emori!" the priestess exclaimed as she abandoned herself into his ready arms.

"Adi, my love ..." he breathed heavily.

"How? How is it possible? Where - how ...?" She could not comprehend the sudden appearance of her betrothed.

"Adi, I must get you to a safe place," the warrior priest glanced to Lo'au desperately.

"I know a way. Come, follow me," the old mu'a said with assurance.

The roar of a thousand Samoan warriors ripped through the air like the clapping of forceful thunder. Siateki and Va'iga stood at the forefront of the beach landing, raising their weapons skyward.

"Spare no Rarotongan! Slay them all!" Siateki roared.

The waves of Samoan warriors continued to amass across the beach towards the burning town, battle-lust and fury burning with every step. The wild hoots and violent charge of the hundreds was a terrifying sight as they shook the ground with their stampede. Siateki and Va'iga followed the last hundred men in the direction of the village.

Whatonga stood blood-clad with his generals, breathing heavily from the violent clashes. Another wave of Niuatoputapu warriors surged towards them, blaring like wild men as they did. He and his generals formed a crescent moon to invite the rushing warriors to their line and as the warriors filled the circle, they realised too late they were ensnared. Whatonga shouted the order as he and his generals moved in for a quick kill. It took moments before they stood victorious, if only for a brief reprieve.

"Rarotongan!" hollered a call from the fray.

Lord Whatonga beheld Noble Anga'uli standing close by, defiant and surrounded by an entourage of his soldiers. Though he had not met Anga'uli before, he guessed his identity immediately. He amassed his men to face the noble in a stand-off.

"So – you must be Prince Whatonga," Anga'uli scoffed. "You look like your father. How it bleeds my heart."

"And you, Noble Anga'uli."

The two leaders glared at each other, warriors of both sides edging to meet one another in battle.

"You've come a long way for nothing. All this," Anga'uli motioned around the burning town, "And your feeble effort to rescue your mother is in vain. But she's been a welcome guest here with us.... she's provided much pleasure – whether she enjoyed me or not."

"Anga'uli – if you were on your knees begging for forgiveness, I would still tear the life out of you," Whatonga seethed. "And as such, I now swear for all to hear that you Anga'uli have offended my family and people beyond reconciliation."

The warrior prince heaved deep breaths of violence and looked to his generals.

"Die!"

Before Anga'uli could respond, Whatonga snatched a spear from his general and javelined it towards him. Anga'uli, taken aback by Whatonga's lightning reflexes, tripped slightly and received the spear through his right shoulder. He reeled from the impact and his soldiers stepped back to watch him fall.

"Help me! Help me, you fools!" he screamed as he writhed on the ground.

"Leave him!" Kamohoali'i shouted from afar.

Anga'uli's soldiers hesitated as they made way for the approaching general. They stepped back from the noble and left him to his fate.

"No! No! What are you doing? Help me!"

Whatonga leapt at the opening. He pounced above him as his club swooped down left to right, then back again. Sprays of blood, teeth and bone from Anga'uli's face sprayed with every clout. Three strikes from Whatonga and the noble was never to rise again. Anga'uli's men retreated to Kamohoali'i and paid no heed to their fallen leader.

As Whatonga stepped away from the slain noble, he spotted the Samoan army loom through the narrow opening towards the village. A dread filled his heart as the realisation struck.

"Ambush ..." he whispered to himself.

His astonishment turned to anger. Still surrounded by his generals, he raised his conch and pressed his lips to the shell. With every last ounce of breath he blew, causing it to blast forth a resounding trumpet of alarm to his Rarotongan warriors.

"To the rear!" he boomed, before lowering the conch from his mouth.

Almost immediately, hundreds of blood-drunk Rarotongans turned position with astonishing synchronization and faced the oncoming Samoan warriors. Whatonga and his generals stood at the front of the Rarotongan contingent, weapons drawn, blood curdling as they watched the hundreds of Samoans race towards them. Blazing fire set the background of the battle, and the land that lay between was blood soaked and matted, as if to prepare for the ultimate confrontation.

Kamohoali'i raised his hands in the air in exultation. His plans were coming full circle.

Whatonga raised the conch to his lips for the last time and punched his weapon in the air, as the shell-horn reverberated like a call to the heavens. His generals roared with war cries that shook the earth with ear splitting volume, rippling every man's skin with goose pimples. Their voices were upheld by a thousand valiant and loyal brethren looming behind their position. A single Rarotongan broke rank and raced solely towards certain death. It was the enactment that spurned the charge of the Rarotongans, leaping forwards like an inescapable force of raged men.

It was an engagement that echoed from the corners of the island. The two armies charged towards one another, neither diminishing in speed, nor voracity. The earth shook as the two thousand men trampled the ground towards one another. The distance between the armies shortened as the leaders at the front quickened their pace. Suddenly, there appeared a man from the side of the burning fales; a warrior who casually paced out into the middle of the two sides. Once in the centre of the land that separated the two forces, Maui Atalaga regarded them with amusement. Any onlooker would have believed the man out of his mind.

He held out Mohemamahi to his side and took a deep stance. He then dug his feet into the earth and produced a roar that shook his body and gleaned his teeth. In the next instant, the thousands of rushing Samoan and Rarotongan warriors collided together in a bone crushing clap of violence. Maui Atalaga disappeared in the mulch of warring men. Ferocious battle consumed the village like it had never seen, cries of fury and death erupting so loud that it could be heard across to Tafahi. The thousands of warriors, locked in brutality, swayed and moved like a single body of vigorous life struggling to exist. Neither side seemed to prevail as the body counts stacked and created a high mound of dead from both sides, essentially stopping the warriors at the rear who pushed forwards.

The monstrous pile of dead in the centre of the melee caused single strains of warriors to filter to the sides to reach their adversaries. War parties formed and thrashed through burning fales to the side of the open area. Siateki and Va'iga led their own group of eighty men, bringing up the rear and confronted the opposition who had breached the Samoan horde. Siateki fought with recognizable skills, taught through the years of training in the Imperial Army, while to his side, Va'iga fought, relentless and untamed, an attribute forged through years of barbaric murder.

Whatonga continued to fight alongside his valiant generals. Their skill and ability to fight in unison proved too great for the battle-blinded Samoans at the head of the army, as wave after wave of Samoan warriors collided into their position. Those not slain, washed to the sides to push forward onto easier skirmishes. The Rarotongan prince realised that although they held their position, the relentless push of the hundreds would eventually uproot their stand. He turned to his generals and yelled above the deafening noise of battle.

"Arrow head formation!"

In unison, the Rarotongan's generals called out to all warriors within the order. Every Rarotongan who heeded the call obeyed spontaneously and formed to the left and right of Whatonga's position, marking Whatonga and his generals as the tip of the arrow. It seemed that in an instant, a contingent of over seven hundred Rarotongans had assembled into the arrow head position. Once Whatonga established the formation, he blew his conch again with all the air his big lungs could muster. The Rarotongans emitted a singular shout with trained timing, and as they did, the whole body of warriors now formed as an arrow head, lurched forward.

In an awesome sight that demonstrated the distinctive Polynesian war tactic, the Rarotongan forces pierced through the body of the Samoan army in the form of a giant arrow, escaping their trapped position and making for their kalias.

CHAPTER 23

Blood and sweat smeared Talatama's eyes, stinging and blinding him. He felt himself supported by Atiogie, the giant Samoan pulling him from under the arm and defending with the other. Following the death of all Talatama's soldiers, it took the limit of Atiogie's great strength to pull the prince from the fire, escape the wrath of Havea and retreat. Both warriors were blood-clad, wounded and battle weary. Their lungs burned from fatigue, smoke-filled air and the lactic acid that muddied their muscles and crippled them.

Talatama wiped the grime from his face and summoned all the strength he could to hold his own weight. He gripped the Peace Maker with both hands and continued to aid his giant comrade in their plight to stay alive. As he thrashed to and fro, he claimed victims at every strike and felt himself gathering a second wind. His senses began to return to him.

"By the strength of mighty Tangaloa, I will not die this day!" he grimaced.

The giant Samoan hooted, enlivened by his renewed spirit.

The two warriors continued to fight side by side, discovering a combined rhythm of deadly sequence as they dealt with all oncomers. Amid the melee, Atiogie realised the warriors who they had been battling were now mixed with Va'iga's Samoan army. All Samoans that came before him hesitated when they recognised one of their own. Atiogie did not waver however; his remorse for Va'iga and his men was greater than any enemy.

Seconds seemed like hours, minutes like days. Somehow over the battle cries and screams of terror, Talatama heard his name being called. He looked about between parries and thrusts and spied Lo'au, calling and waving his hands from an elevated position behind a large burning fale.

"Atiogie!" he shouted and pointed towards the mu'a with his club.

The two warriors, strength rekindled with new purpose, launched themselves through the carnage towards his desperate friends. As the prince came closer, he realised a Fijian warrior and Vaohoi were the only defence for Lo'au and what appeared to be a Fijian priestess. As he and Atiogie defeated the enemy swiftly, they united and enjoyed a brief reprieve. He glanced at Emori and Adi without question, assuming there was no time for introductions.

"Where are your men?" Lo'au was having trouble breathing.

"They're gone." He turned towards the mu'a and tried to think. "Have you seen my brother, Prince Talaiha'apepe?"

The group shook their heads and he silently cursed, the likelihood of finding his brother alive was slipping through his fingers. He surveyed the burning village. The anarchy was ceaseless; murder continued in the streets and anyone was free game. The giant Samoan shook his shoulder.

"There's no time to waste – enemies are everywhere! If we want to live beyond today, we must leave this island now!"

"My idea exactly!" Vaohoi snapped.

"We won't make it back to our vessels," Talatama hollered as he continued to defend the mound from new attackers.

"Don't you have a sea craft?" Lo'au turned to Atiogie.

The giant Samoan winced as his mind worked slowly. "I have a tongiaki banked on the other side of the island."

"Make to the forest trail!" Talatama ordered, "Atiogie, lead the way!"

Emori cast a glance to Adi and nodded his head in approval. The group shuffled their way through the back streets of burning ruins, however, they were slowed as they confronted more enemies. As the prince continued to fight, another nearby skirmish caught his eye. A wounded woman was struggling to fend off two warriors' intent on play before killing. She stumbled as she swung her club wildly and missed her tormentors. They laughed as they savoured the cruelty. Her need was dire.

"Wh–Where are you going?" Atiogie looked over his shoulder in mid battle to see Talatama dash in her direction.

"This way!" Lo'au called and led the group behind the warrior prince.

"B-but we must - I thought -" the giant shouted but followed.

Empowered by the spirit of virtue, Talatama struck down the two warriors swiftly. The men were still twitching on the ground when he stood before the woman, breathing heavily.

"Lady, you must seek shelter, head for the—" He stopped as recognition washed over him.

The woman, a warrior herself as it appeared, regarded Talatama with feverish eyes and raised her club weakly towards him. He could not mistake those green eyes, which had confronted him many nights ago in the Noble Courtyard, as those of the woman who had enchanted his nights ever since.

"Milady, I mean you no harm! Come with me - I will get you to safety." He opened his palm to Mahina in submission.

She hesitated before his gesture, his face slowly becoming familiar through the haze of anguish. Her eyes rolled and she slumped to the ground before Talatama could catch her. He gathered her in his arms and turned to the group who had been watching.

"Let's go!" he shouted.

"Who is that? We haven't got time to pick up stragglers!" Vaohoi squawked.

"Keep moving, Vaohoi!" Lo'au managed to shout.

They breached the outskirts of the village as enemies hoarded from the seaward side. When they halted to repel the attackers, they realised the enemy's focus was on warrior just beyond them. Pele was a matted mess of crimson. Glistening with sweat and fresh blood, she slew mercilessly all who appeared before her. Talatama recognised her immediately as the fight began to flurry into his group. In the split second of identifying him also, Pele used them as defence and with renewed strength Talatama, Atiogie and Emori grimaced as they clashed with new foes.

To the detriment of the companions and their plans to escape, many Rarotongan warriors, unable to hear the call for retreat, had remained at the far end of the village. A hundred or so who remained locked in battle continued to slay all who came in their way. A short distance to the south of their position, the Rarotongan warriors turned to face the companions. Vaohoi and Lo'au at the rear were the first to see the approaching danger.

"Dog-shit!" Vaohoi shouted, "Talatama! Back here!"

Talatama gritted his teeth as he continued to fight with Mahina over his shoulder. The mere sight of the Rarotongans approaching quashed his hopes instantly. It was obvious they could not escape, not this time. He carefully set Mahina on the ground and raised his chin towards the Rarotongan warriors, his lungs making a horrid sound at every breath. Atiogie, Emori and Pele struggled against the enemy. Emori toiled as he slew each and every foe before him: a deep wound to his leg was taking its toll. Pele and Atiogie had also suffered taxing wounds. The companions were in their last moments of struggle. With the Niuatoputapuans in front and Rarotongans behind it would be soon over for them. They pulled together more tightly as they fought for their lives, like a last patch of dry land against rising water.

As if straying from a dream, a lone warrior appeared from the fire and smoke behind the enemy. Covered in the paints of battle and sinew, he walked casually towards them. His tattooed body glistened over a perfect sculpture of might and muscle. Maui Atalaga invited the local warriors to turn and face him. As they did, they parted a way for him in panic. His unseen cloak of fear was intoxicating, like a cold, snapping wind that strikes the heart. His effect disrupted the encroaching enemy. The companions could not help but stand in amazement at his power. Suddenly Lo'au stepped forward and motioned to him.

"Brother! We are in need of your aid! Help us!"

The warrior regarded them with vague interest but, as he did, he spotted someone beyond the group. The Rarotongans had stopped their advance and cowered in the presence of another lone figure. Havea was covered from head to toe in crimson blood and sported severed heads of victims that were tied by their scalps around his neck. He imbued the same aura as Maui Atalaga: a cloak of fear that immobilised the common man and chilled him to the bone. All who witnessed the spectacle stood in awe, as the two warriors eyed each other from afar.

Talatama glanced to Atiogie with a dire expression. "Damn, he still lives."

"Surely", the prince cursed, "The gods have abandoned them".

"Havea! I have found you! Let us end this!" Maui Atalaga shouted.

"After all this time, Atalaga, do you not understand, you cannot end my line!" Havea returned.

The dark warrior then took a deep breath and arched his back, releasing a demonising roar of unearthly terror. Such was the blast that everyone close-by clasped their hands over their ears. As his voice carried away, all enemy warriors flew into a frenzy of violence and the threat to the companions was once again real.

Maui Atalaga grinned at Havea and began to head for him.

"Atalaga! Help us!" Lo'au shouted in vain.

The hero paused at the sound of his name as he faced Havea then glanced back to the group, struggling in a losing battle. Lo'au's plea had struck a chord with him, and for an unknown reason the conflict within him was apparent. He confronted his nemesis again, fervent with the desire to face him, and when the frustration of indecision caused him to hesitate, he gritted his teeth and sprinted to the companions.

With a few mighty blows of Mohemamahi, he reached the group, demolishing the Niuatoputapuans, and with them, the immediate threat. He glared at the fatigued warriors and enlivened their resolve with a single gaze.

"Follow me," he said calmly.

The companions responded immediately and spurred at his heels. Talatama heaved Mahina over his shoulder and Adi assisted her beloved Emori. Pele, however, continued to fight, her braided hair flaying about with every strike, refusing to accept help. Maui Atalaga paused and glanced back to her.

"You fight well, warrior-woman," he motioned towards Havea, "But you're no match for him!"

Pele shot the hero a fierce stare, and with a last strike from her obsidian axe, she fled with the companions. They glanced back and saw that the dark warrior had turned on the Rarotongans in a vicious progression of murder. The battle, fire and death echoed behind them as they plunged deep into the forest, trampling through the wild scrub, in what seemed to be a directionless escape. Be that as it may, no one in the group could summon the effort or courage to question their saviour's plans. Vaohoi tripped and juggled himself over roots and vines that marred the way. Beams of sunlight pillared through the canopy of overhanging trees as they dodged and weaved through the green foliage. But the sound of the enemy began to loom at their heels.

Pele brought up the rear and paused to shoot at pursuing Niuatoputapuans. With every loosened arrow, a warrior would fall. Again and again, she picked her targets skilfully.

"Come on!" Vaohoi shouted, noticing Pele was falling behind at the expense of her shots.

She about-faced and hastened her retreat, her athletic body propelled through the forest strongly, a glorious sight of perseverance and purpose.

The group burst from the forest onto a deserted beach. A cool wind kissed their burning bodies and the sun reflected off the sand and sea, blinding them momentarily. A single war-tongiaki was moored just off the sand bank; the representation of their salvation. Pele crashed through a tall shrub, sending leaves everywhere. She rolled in the sand and swiftly fitted an arrow to her string. A Niuatoputapuan warrior burst from the shrubbery, but as her arrow thumped through his throat with the sound of pierced flesh, a second enemy appeared with a spear aimed towards her chest. She scrambled to refit an arrow but had no time. In a blur of movement Maui Atalaga swiped at the airborne warrior and struck him squarely in the side. The impact shattered ribs, punctured internal organs and caused blood to explode from his mouth before landing. The hero quickly ended the dying Niuatoputapuan clutching the arrow at his throat.

Pele crawled quickly to defend herself, kicking sand as she retreated. She gazed up at the great warrior, her breath quick and laboured. He motioned towards the tongiaki that lay moored in the shallow water.

"To the tongiaki," he pointed.

The companions staggered into the shallow sea, splashing and spluttering water in all directions. Blood that covered their bodies filtered through the pristine water, marring it with pink and cherry. On the verge of collapse, Talatama fell to his knees in the water with Mahina over his shoulder. Atiogie groaned in pain as he grabbed his girdle to reef him back to his feet. The companions threw themselves on the tongiaki as Maui Atalaga pushed the craft out to deeper waters.

As he jumped onto the sea craft, they turned and watched dozens of men pouring out onto the beach, screaming curses and insults. A few attempted to throw spears but were well out of range.

The wind cracked the sails into full breadth and the companions felt the great war-craft lurch forwards at a strong and steady speed. Adi nursed Emori's head in her lap and stroked his face. Atiogie thumped himself against the main mast, slid down to his backside and winced as he slowly removed his dented breast plate. Pele, resting at the far end of the tongiaki, laid her head against the hard stern and closed her eyes in fatigue. Vaohoi somehow found the energy to jump up and down, shout, pull faces and return insults to the Niuatoputapuans on the beach.

Talatama lay sprawled on deck beside an unconscious Mahina. With one hand he sheltered his eyes from the high sun, the other remained holding her hand. He took a toiled breath and finally accepted that they had all escaped certain death. Seconds after, he lapsed into an exhausted sleep.

PART 2

CHAPTER 24

The shadows were but fleeting wisps across the ground. It was the same blackness as the rest of the night's shadows – sharp and blotchy silhouettes that patterned the grass across the imperial compound. They faded from greys to blues under the dim moonlight and gave life to the stillness. The shrubbery and trees were immaculately trimmed, and the grass was finely cropped. Only in the Royal Household in Heketa would one find such a perfectly kept estate.

The sounds of buzzing insects and light footsteps permeated the minds of the three nameless men. They weaved through the foliage with impressive dexterity, always mindful of where the others were, their nearby enemies, and of their ultimate purpose. They dodged the moonlight that streamed down from the canopy in columns of white as if they were solid stone. The leader stopped. The others converged and crouched to a knee.

Their heartbeats thumped in their heads. They faced in all directions, their eyes shooting from side to side, perspiration trickling down their faces. They tried desperately to control their laboured breathing, and the surge of adrenaline pumping through their veins. Then the high-pitched buzz of mosquitoes reached their ears. They could not see them, but they could feel the blood scavenging insects flitter around their heads. The leader turned to his companions and gave a signal. The three darted forward into the night.

The sullen sentry walked across the compound as he had done a thousand times. He arrived at his usual position, with his back to the trees and thumped the butt of his spear in the ground to lean on.

"Hey."

He snapped alert and faced one of the men behind him. The distraction was successful. The other man landed his club at the base of the sentry's skull with a crunch, as the third man caught the body and dragged it into the shadows. The three glided across the cropped grass like sea hawks.

Murmurs echoed in the outdoor court area as King Tu'itatui sat on his stone throne, 'Esi Makafakinanga, and deliberated with High Priest Toutai and half brother Lord Fasi'apule. It was long into midnight and they had spoken of the island of Niue for some time. The king lifted his hand to his forehead and rubbed his weary face.

"I've had enough of politics," he said. "I'm tired of having to make these decisions."

"It is the will of the gods, Your Majesty," Toutai answered.

"Then perhaps they should pay tribute then," Fasi'apule stated.

"They are still Tongan people, brother," Tu'itatui said. "The grand tributaries are expected from foreign lands, not our own regions."

"With respect, Your Majesty, the past one hundred years has allowed the people in Niue to grow their own state of affairs," Fasi'apule stated. "Yes, they are Tongan by origin, but have strong influences from Samoa and Rarotonga now. These influences mould the shape of their culture, which I said, is slowly becoming independent."

"That's only natural," the king replied, "Niue's trade with Samoa is thriving. More and more Samoan merchants and families are migrating there. As for Rarotonga and Tahiti, it's the bridge-way between the inner kingdom and the far eastern edge. Travellers will always navigate through Niue as a port of call."

Tu'itatui rose from his throne with a groan and stood next to his advisors. He caressed an old wooden ring he wore, memories of his kin flooding back.

"My grandfather, King Afulunga fell in love with Niue. That's perhaps why he pushed for our people to remain there," he turned to Toutai. "What then is the future for our people in Niue?"

"Lord Fasi'apule speaks words of wisdom Your Majesty. The gods concur with his logic."

"I don't care what either of you say. As long as I'm king, our people in Niue will have the same rights and privileges as our people here in Tonga. If, and when, they become separate from our society, then my future descendant can make that decision."

"Yes, Your Majesty." Both men bowed.

"Now what I want is for –"

"Assassin!"

The king turned in time to see the three nameless men sprinting towards him from the other end of the court. His bodyguards leapt out from the darkness and intercepted them. A fierce fight erupted, and as the leader of the group tore away from the melee, Lord Fasi'apule stood protectively in front of the king. Toutai shrieked and ran.

"Death to the king!" he bellowed, enraged with murder.

"Your Majesty – get back!"

A warrior swiftly appeared from the shadows closest to the king. Toa was Tu'itatui's chief bodyguard and greatest fighter. He had not been in the service of the king for twenty years by way of idle manner. His club blocked the assassin's attack with a crack and continued in an arc to smash at the knee, crumbling the patella instantly. Toa blocked again and again. As the assassin fought on, it was only moments before Toa feinted and landed a decisive blow to the temple. The assassin went rigid and somewhat paralysed. Toa reefed his club down and shattered his skull like the shell of an empty coconut.

"Kill them!" Toa spun and shouted to his men who had overcome the two other assassins.

By this time, King Tu'itatui had gathered his war club and ran towards the fighting. Fasi'apule held him back in time for the warriors to make the final kill.

"Let go of me!" the king shouted.

"You must not engage in battle, Your Majesty!" his brother shouted over the violence.

The king broke free, but it was too late. The three nameless men lay dead: their bodies sprawled across the ground, bent and twisted. Toa and his men immediately formed a circle around Tu'itatui. When the warriors saw there was no more threat, they slowly fanned out and called for reinforcements. The king lowered his club and sighed, before glaring at his brother and storming away. The torches burned into the night.

Morning came promptly and there was slight dew on the ground. The king sat in the garden with his daughter, Fatafehi, on a dry blanket of tapa, singing songs with the morning birds. He had dismissed the servants and maidens, to spend private time with whom he loved most.

"My King," Lord Fasi'apule said as he slowly approached.

Tu'itatui concealed his annoyance but said nothing. He ignored him and continued to sing.

"Your Majesty," Fasi'apule said.

Fatafehi's voice trailed off and she smiled warmly to her uncle, but Tu'itatui continued to sing. The governor did not hesitate.

"Ko'au!" he shouted the king's name as a youth.

"Were you not my brother," the king growled as he turned, "I would have your head on a pike."

"It is your head I'm here about. We must discuss last night's attack."

"Wh-what happened?" Fatafehi rose to her knees.

"Nothing."

"Another attempt was made on your father's life."

"What? Father?"

"Please leave us my dear..." the king said delicately. "We will talk later."

"But, Father — "

"Fatafehi." He became firm. "Leave us."

170

The princess stood and left abruptly, her face awash with shock and worry.

"You didn't tell her."

"I didn't. Why should I worry her?"

Lord Fasi'apule put his hands on his hips and looked down at his brother like an admonishing father.

"That's the third assassination attempt this year," he began. "How many more are you willing to allow before you do anything?"

"I'm thinking of dismissing my bodyguards permanently."

"Are you mad?" Fasi'apule balked. "They are the only defence against your certain death! If you dismiss Toa and his men, I will only re-appoint them under my command."

The king stood and faced his brother. He then peered off in a distant gaze.

"I was once the greatest warrior king that ever lived. My father and I forged this nation, out of warring tribes and backwater villages. With these hands, I've taken the lives of men beyond count."

"It's not a question of your fighting ability, Your Majesty. It is your reckless death I am concerned about."

"What of it? Should I be killed, Talatama will become king. He will make a strong king ..."

"Why do you speak of your life so cheaply? Your son is not ready, Your Majesty," Fasi'apule sighed. "You have not even taught him the secret hieroglyphs of the ancients. It is your life we need to protect, and we must gather intelligence to discover the root of these assassination attempts."

"They're nothing. They're scraps of men who've held grudges since the time of our father's reign. They'll keep coming no matter what we do. Killing is a way of life."

"It is a way of life for common folk, Your Majesty. Not for royalty."

"Nonsense. The blood of warrior kings runs through my veins – runs through yours!" He stood and faced his brother. "All men face death at the hands of violence."

"We do not live in times of war any more, Your Majesty." Fasi'apule turned to walk away. "I find your lack of concern for your own welfare distasteful."

"I care not."

"Obviously. I'll look into these assassination attempts and I'll personally oversee all actions taken..."

Fasi'apule paused before departing the garden.

"... Because, Your Majesty, were you not my brother, I would turn a blind eye while the assassins put *your* head on a pike."

CHAPTER 25

Late afternoon was setting in. The blue in the sky had begun to fade into dyes of violets and wisps of cedar. Short-winged tavakes flew overhead, their calls echoing the empty beaches that surrounded the island. The ocean was tepid and the short waves lapped onto the soft sand of Niuatoputapu as it had done since the dawn of time. Nature, it seemed, had restored all that had turned the day into a nightmare and the blaze of violence to a peaceful calm.

Further towards Falehau, the smell of smoke and burning corpses lingered and seemed to taint the very forest that surrounded it. The remaining Samoan and Niuatoputapuan warriors had dragged the dead into large masses and had commenced burning them. There were multiple burning mounds. Others helped clear the wreckage of ashen fales, desecrated shrines and destroyed forest.

The villagers had begun to rebuild fales, even in the fading light. Men struggled to erect new pillars and structures of palm wood, while the women scoured the forests for leaves to thatch the roofs. The children, who normally would be out playing, stayed close to their mothers. The mood remained sombre. Late in the afternoon, Ilamaki had gifted the leaders of the common folk, twenty hogs to be cooked during the night; food for all the villagers as compensation and in victory to those who had survived.

Although this gesture had lifted the spirits of the villagers, the memory of those killed was still fresh. No songs were sung as the men cooked enough food for the weary and the homeless. The village leaders did what they could to provide support.

Prince Talaiha'apepe sat surrounded by his remaining escorts and royal entourage within the House of Anga'uli, in perhaps one of the only sections of fales untouched by the battle. Before him sat the Senior Chief, Talo; Village Headman, Ilamaki; High Priest, Ulikaite; and at least a dozen retainers. They all sat in ceremonial positions.

Astoundingly, Prince Talaiha'apepe had escaped serious injury during the great battle. The sudden attack of the Rarotongans had placed him in dire peril because he had not travelled with many warriors, and despite the overwhelming odds he could not ignore the fact that he was saved by an equally surprising intervention.

The arrival of the Samoan army and their abrupt counter attack on the Rarotongans fortuitously provided Talaiha'apepe the chance to escape certain death. Had the Samoan numbers not equalled the Rarotongans or provided a stout and aggressive opposition, the island of Niuatoputapu would have certainly fallen to ashes. It was obvious Prince Talaiha'apepe owed his life to the leader of the Samoan war party.

"I summon, General Kamohoali'i," the prince said loudly.

The dark general lingered at the rear of the hall with his arms crossed, shouldered by his entourage of vile warriors; Havea, Siateki, Kupe, Ganilau, Omani, and Mo'unga. All within the great hall stared at the menacing group, yet all knew through the eyes of the Empire they had been the saviours of the son of the king.

"General Kamohoali'i of Ha'apai, come forward and be recognised." The Imperial Matapule, standing to the left of the prince, called forth the general.

Kamohoali'i paused before striding through the staring onlookers towards the prince. He stopped short of Talaiha'apepe then fell to a knee and bowed his head low.

"Your Highness. You honour me with your recognition," he said, head still bowed.

"Rise, Kamohoali'i."

"Your Highness," the general stood and looked proudly at the prince.

"Answer me this: are you responsible for the Samoan war party that came to the shores of Niuatoputapu today?"

"I am."

"Are you responsible for their actions, their deeds, and the decision for them to repel the Rarotongans?"

"Yes."

"Then you are responsible for saving the lives of thousands of Niuatoputapuans and the life of a prince."

"You honour me with your words, Your Highness."

Prince Talaiha'apepe sighed deeply, his face dark and full of thought before he finally motioned for Kamohoali'i to be seated at his side. The general shuffled as he remained in a kneeling position and the prince glanced to one of Ilamaki's errand men. He had entered the fale and bowed with urgent tidings.

"What news do you bring?" the matapule asked for the prince.

"Your Highness, I have terrible news. Scouring through the dead, I found the body of Lord Anga'uli."

An explosion of gasps echoed in the great hall.

"I also found his war chief, Afi Kakaha, and many others slain."

The Imperial Matapule turned towards the prince for direction.

"Terrible news indeed," Talaiha'apepe looked at the errand man and shook his head. "It is truly a dark day for the Niuatoputapuans, and the Empire."

"Your Highness," the errand man touched his head to the floor.

"I need time to contemplate this," the prince continued slowly and rubbed his eyebrows.

A long silence elapsed over the great hall.

"Your Highness -" the matapule motioned towards the general.

"Oh, yes, General Kamohoali'i - stand."

"Muni, what are his past crimes?" he asked his matapule.

"Your Highness, General Kamohoali'i is wanted for murder and treason, but to name a few."

"Then let all know across the entire Empire, that I pardon all of his crimes," the prince announced.

An uproar of disapproval forked through the ranks of the imperial entourage. Disrespect following the judgement could not be hidden.

"B-but Your Highness – Kamohoali'i is ..."

"Do any of you stand against my will!? The prince of the greatest Empire ever forged?" Talaiha'apepe stood enraged.

"You shall all share my gratitude towards this man, for whatever past misdeeds he has done, today he has saved the life of your prince!"

"Y-yes, Your Highness."

"And therefore, without further interruptions, I again state that Kamohoali'i is a free man and pardoned for all his crimes," he ended with a boom in his voice.

The Imperial Matapule and the entire hall of hosts bowed down and acknowledged their ruler's wishes.

"My deepest gratitude, Your Highness." Kamohoali'i looked up towards Talaiha'apepe. "My deepest gratitude," and under the cover of his bowed head, a grin spanned from ear to ear.

The general and his warriors burst from the Noble House into the streets of Niuatoputapu as free men. The stride in Kamohoali'i's gait was long and proud as he breathed the free air, as if it were for the first time. His evil warriors followed him with equal liberty as they too, basked in the exalted grant of an imperial pardon. All the years of villainy sewn through his twisted plans were finally bearing fruit.

They walked briskly to the beach where Kupe had prepared a light tongiaki for sail. The sun had fallen and twilight was upon the island. Stars had begun to dimly glitter across the heavens and the cool air had begun to swiftly drop the temperature. Kamohoali'i glanced to Kupe then looked over the craft.

"Is her body on board?"

"Yes, Milord," the Weeping Assassin answered quickly.

"Siateki, Omani and Mo'unga, go with Kupe." He had reconsidered the potential risk of the plan.

"I don't need them, Milord," Kupe stated.

"You need Omani and Mo'unga for additional strength and Siateki for his diplomacy."

The three warriors bowed their heads and complied before boarding the tongiaki. Ganilau grunted as he pushed the craft from the sand bank into the darkening velvet brine. The three remaining watched as the sail craft drifted into the horizon towards the island of Tafahi. Kamohoali'i then turned and headed back towards the village, the two warriors Havea and Ganilau striding in his shadow.

On the north side of Tafahi, seven hundred Rarotongan warriors made camp on the beach and prepared umus for the evening feast. The men were in good spirits, having been advised by Lord Toi and Whatonga that Anga'uli had been killed during the battle. Anga'uli, the rancid noble who had kidnapped their revered Lady Rongaueroa was dead, slain by none other than her son, Whatonga.

Further inland from the beach, Lord Toi, Prince Whatonga and their generals sat in a circle of discussion. A warming fire crackled in the centre. The faces of over a hundred men guarded their backs. They nursed their own wounds of battle, drank the milk of young coconuts, gnawed at cooked hog meat off the bone and spoke with optimism of a second attack in the morning.

"We were taken by surprise, Milord – that's all!" one of the generals continued.

"The Samoans were lucky to arrive when they did! The gods were favouring their side today," said another.

"Nonsense! The Samoan army was there by Anga'uli's bidding! He knew we were coming and he hired their help. And look what good it did him? He's now wandering the underworld without a face!"

The group of fifteen Rarotongan leaders burst into laughter.

"Hold, hold," Prince Whatonga held his hand to diffuse the amusement. "Firstly I commend all of you for your courage, your strength and most of all your discipline today. Our tactical advantage over the enemy was our winning edge, if indeed it was a win," he spoke as a true leader.

"Don't ever underestimate an enemy. Make no mistake – had it not been for our superior training and focus, we all would be wandering the realm of the dead. That was a trap we blindly walked into, a trap meant for our total obliteration." The firelight emphasised the intent on his face as his words rang true.

"Tomorrow we will attack with greater strength and greater precaution. Our aim is to search for Lady Rongaueroa and Mahina, if they still live ..." his voice trailed off.

CHAPTER 26

Further along the beach on Tafahi, a group of Rarotongan warriors spotted a lone sail craft in the darkness heading towards the coast. A call was made, and in seconds, hundreds of warriors rushed to the shore with flaming torches and spears with the intent to kill. One of the captains blew his conch to alert the entire Rarotongan army.

The tongiaki dug into the sand and four occupants jumped into the shallow water. Torchlight illuminated Siateki walking forward, his hands open in a non-threatening manner. At least fifty angry Rarotongans lunged towards him with long spears.

"Hold! We come alone and in peace," he began. "We bear no threat to you. I wish to speak to your leader immediately," he stated calmly with verve.

The Rarotongans eased their advance but remained standing, with their spears in hand.

"Your leader, I wish to speak to your leader!" he repeated.

"And so you shall, Tongan," Whatonga said as he appeared from the crowds of fiery warriors, accompanied by ten of his generals.

"Milord." Siateki bowed reverently. Kupe, Omani and Mo'unga followed suit.

"So foolhardy. You come alone, with a handful of companions." Whatonga peered over the small sail craft. "Are you giving yourselves up to be sacrificed in our fires tonight, or do you bring news of surrender?"

"Milord, firstly may I introduce myself. I am Siateki, Commander to General Kamohoali'i. My companions here are also under his command," he paused. "We are not Niuatoputapuans, we are not kin to the Empire nor do we hold allegiance to Noble Anga'uli and his minions. We represent the Pulotulahi, an organised group of warriors that rival the Empire."

"Go on." Whatonga frowned.

"Secondly, we come to you in deep reverence and respect, both with a gift and valuable information." Siateki signalled to Omani.

The Rarotongans eyed the Unarmed Warrior warily, poised to spear him at the slightest false move. He carefully gathered something together on board the tongiaki, lifted it and carried the tapa wrapped object towards the Rarotongans. He stopped before Whatonga and carefully placed the large object on the sand. He then gently unveiled the pale face of Lady Rongaueroa.

"Mother!" Whatonga fell to his knees.

The Rarotongans growled in a chorus of deep and vibrating crescendo at the sight of their dead queen. Siateki and his companions stepped back with their hands raised in defence as the generals rushed around the slain queen. Whatonga gently took up her head in his lap. He kissed her forehead and hugged her tightly to his chest, his face contorted in silent grief. He then released her slowly and motioned for his warriors to take her body. He rose slowly and faced towards the Tongan warriors, eyes wet with tears.

"So tell me, soldiers of the Pulotulahi, why shouldn't I kill you right now?" he said with incredible self-control.

"Milord, a thousand condolences ... we are truly beset by grief in your loss." Siateki stepped forward again, diplomatically. "But we have news surrounding your mother's death and important information regarding your retribution."

The prince stared at Siateki with a gaze that would have pierced stone.

"For now you have earned my patience with your words," he stated. "And you may yet leave this island with your lives. Follow me."

The four Pulotulahi warriors sat with Whatonga and his generals at their camp. The Rarotongan warriors continued to eat and drink without an offer to the Tongans. The air between the two parties was filled with distrust and suspicion. One of Whatonga's retainers approached and knelt beside him.

"Milord, Lord Toi is preparing the pyre for Lady Rongaueroa."

"Good." Whatonga returned.

The prince regarded the four warriors with distaste, eyeing each and every one of them cautiously. The flickering firelight over their faces was an illustration of unknown intent.

"So, after a battle that saw the demise of that noble dog, you bring back the body of my mother. On the face of it, it shows you're no ally of the Niuatoputapuans. They would have sported my mother's body for their leader's death."

"That's correct, Milord," Siateki answered politely.

"Interesting," Whatonga took a gulp from a young coconut shell, "And how is it that you came to be in possession of my mother's body? And what business did you have in Niuatoputapu in the first instance?" he shot back.

Siateki shifted as he digested the question and judged the Rarotongan prince. He was certainly a magnetic leader. It was obvious that his charisma did not merely come from his good looks and fighting ability; his acumen was evident, and it was not until that very moment that Siateki understood how the Rarotongans escaped defeat. He knew that he had to use quick wit to answer Whatonga. A false word could result in their swift deaths.

"Milord, we were in Niuatoputapu in preparation for the arrival of Prince Talaiha'apepe, son of King Tu'itatui. We planned on assassinating him," he said proudly.

"Oh?" Whatonga raised an eyebrow.

"But when he arrived this morning, you and your soldiers attacked the beach and we did not get the chance to kill him," he paused. "Though throughout the enduring battle, we witnessed your strength and skill and admired it greatly. We realised that you and your brethren would make powerful allies to the Pulotulahi."

Whatonga maintained an unflinching glare.

"We quickly learned that your queen was held captive in the House of Anga'uli, and following your retreat, Kupe here –" Siateki pointed to the Weeping Assassin sitting beside him, "found your mother shortly after her death and stole her away from the Niuatoputapuans."

Siateki paused to allow his story to be digested.

"We knew that, despite your terrible loss, returning your queen would place us in good stead – a gesture of our good will and intent to make you an ally."

Whatonga allowed his thoughts to linger on the Fallen Commander's words. It seemed an incredible story, he surmised, perhaps they really were seeking a loose allegiance. But for what reason, he frowned.

"We shall see, we shall see." He leaned forward. "But first, what more tidings do you bring? What more do I have to learn from this dark day?"

Siateki took to a knee, his eyes a reflection of the dancing flames.

"Milord, I have the name of the man who killed your mother, and the circumstances that surrounded her death."

"And who may that be?" Whatonga sneered.

"His name is Talatama, and he is none other than the first born Prince of the Empire."

Whispers and shock erupted from the circle of men. Whatonga leant back, glanced at his closest general and broke into a grin.

"That's nonsense. I've met Talatama, not three years ago when a royal fleet visited Ngatangi'ia. I remember him to be a noble man. There was not the germ of evil in him. Besides, what reason would he have to kill our queen?"

"Milord, your question leads me to the disturbing information I have tell you," Siateki paused. "Days ago in Niuatoputapu, Talatama met and fell in love with a Rarotongan spy by the name of Mahina."

Whatonga's preposterous expression vanished immediately.

"What did you say?"

"Talatama and Mahina fell in love with each other, conspired and killed your mother. They fled the island during the battle."

Whatonga and his warriors leapt to their feet and seized their weapons as the Pulotulahi warriors stumbled backwards, readying themselves for a fight.

"No! No! Milord – what I say is true!" Siateki pleaded.

"How dare you! How dare you accuse my sister of murdering her own mother!"

"Milord! What advantage would I gain creating such an outlandish lie?" he tried to reason.

The Rarotongans edged closer to the terribly outnumbered Tongan warriors. Siateki began to realise that he may not be able to talk them out of the situation. He slowly began to reach down for his weapon.

"Hold! There is proof of our claim!" Kupe suddenly pitched in. "One of your other spies knows of this! His name was – was – Tarapu!" he recalled quickly.

Whatonga was astonished in the midst of heightened emotions. He looked around wildly, as if he had seen Tarapu only moments before.

"Tarapu! Where is Tarapu? Bring him here immediately!" he shouted.

"I hope you know what you're talking about," Siateki whispered in Kupe's ear and eyed the Rarotongans bent on killing the lot of them.

Half a dozen warriors shoved a reluctant man forward into the circle of the quarrelling chiefs. Tarapu peered at his angry prince and immediately fell to a knee.

Whatonga was beyond patience. He stepped to Tarapu, grabbed him by the neck and lifted him so that he could look into his eyes.

"What do you know of Mahina and this Prince Talatama!" Whatonga growled.

"N-n-nothing, Milord," Tarapu trembled.

"He lies!" Kupe shot.

"Tarapu – I will only ask you once more. Speak!" Whatonga's grip tightened.

"Milord! M-milo-" He began to choke.

The prince finally released him and watched as he clutched his throat and heaved in deep breaths. He quivered at his feet as a beaten dog might before a violent master.

"She – she – fancied him, Milord," the spy uttered. It is... it is not her fault. I beg, Master. She was innocent of her feelings. I know nothing more!" Tarapu tried to defend her, unaware of Kupe's accusation.

Whatonga stood staring at the ground. His blood was boiling beneath his skin, "Be gone with you! Out of my sight!"

Tarapu tripped as he pushed his way through the circle of men. The rage of Rarotongan warriors had risen to shouting level as Whatonga glared at the ground in disbelief until the deafening noise finally broke him from his confusion.

"Enough! All of you leave my sight! Now!" he roared, glowering around at all of his warriors, including his generals.

He kicked the edge of the fire, sending glowing embers showering across the area. His countrymen scattered immediately, many casting enraged looks over their shoulders towards the Tongan warriors. The bulk of them melted into the darkness and many made their way back to the beach. Whatonga's generals remained in the shadows just out of sight, eyeing the Pulotulahi warriors who were alone with their prince.

The firelight gleaned over Whatonga and the Tongan warriors who stood solemnly and without words. Siateki and his companions reflected the disturbing news and empathised with the prince.

"Milord, what are your thoughts?" Siateki asked after what seemed ages.

The prince did not answer. He stared into the glowing embers of the fire.

"Milord, we offer you our services. It would honour us, as your allies, to assist you in your retaliation against Prince Talatama."

Whatonga regarded Siateki for the first time with an expression of understanding.

"We have tongiakis ready on the shores of Niuatoputapu to leave immediately. Omani and Mo'unga, two of our chiefs will lead a group of our warriors in the direction in which Talatama and Mahina were headed. They are at your disposal," Siateki offered.

"Agreed," the Rarotongan prince nodded, "Amosa! Amosa!" he shouted into the darkness.

"Yes, Milord," the general appeared from the tree lines and approached the group.

"Assemble three assault groups and ready them for a voyage to locate Talatama and Mahina."

"Siateki, we'll go with him," Omani put forward.

"Your will," Mo'unga added.

"Granted – Prince Whatonga?" Siateki looked for the Rarotongan's approval.

"Yes. This is one of my generals, Amosa. They will go with you now and fetch reinforcements from Niuatoputapu. Once that is done, join together and hunt down these defilers," he grabbed Amosa's shoulder to emphasise his point.

"Yes, Milord."

"I will be making this island, Tafahi, our base for the next few days until you return," Whatonga said. "And make haste."

He then turned back to Siateki and Kupe and motioned for them to leave.

"Leave this island now and return to Niuatoputapu. There's already been enough grave news this evening lest I continue to be reminded of it by looking at your ugly heads." He began to walk away into the shadows. His voice echoed in the darkness.

"I'll send out a messenger at first light."

CHAPTER 27

The face of the moon was parted. A scoop of milk filled the lower side of its quartered surface, the murky body that appeared full and ripe. It was glazed with the background of a million stars that formed the great Milky Way, sparkling and dazzling the heavens that looked down from above. Thin wisps of night cloud occasionally drifted across the silver lining of the moon, illuminating them and showing their transparency. The sea breeze was gentle, the waves slight and the air warm. In all directions, the great Pacific Ocean unfolded out to the horizon, shadowed in the darkness of the night and the black galaxy that existed beyond it.

The tongiaki melted silently through the brine, cutting the surface all so gently. Her speed was constant and true, neither waning nor heading promptly. The massive tapa sails were curved with a moderate breath of night wind, the sounds of the masts creaking against the stern and the lapping of the water at the bow. In the centre of the sail craft was a large, elevated platform, which housed a fireplace. It was furnished from a huge limestone crucible that protected the wood of the tongiaki and was heaped with logs that burned with steady flame and warmth.

Long hours had passed without conversation, hours that provided little recovery for those weary of battle, scarred from betrayals and wounded from combat. The mood had somewhat lifted with nightfall, the smell of grilled fish on the open fire was enough to lighten the ambience from any darkness.

Vaohoi sat closest to the fire, holding a total of five skewers of coconut oiled fish grilling on the open blaze. The crackling and the aroma of the succulent meat and coconut was intoxicating. The young man could barely wait as he tried not to burn the skin.

"Ohhh, blessed Maui ..." he murmured to himself, stripping the food with his bulging eyes.

Lo'au sat cross-legged next to him and smiled. In the face of such horrifying events, food to Vaohoi was always the catalyst of happiness, with the power to wash away all evils.

The giant, Atiogie, was pushed up against the youngster; a child spoilt by the fruits of war. He gobbled away at half cooked fish, stopping only wash it down with coconut milk. He had proved to Vaohoi he was a staunch adversary in the ways of food consumption. The two relished every morsel of the victuals they could cram in their mouths. They laughed at themselves as they tried to out-do one another, yet despite Vaohoi's valiant efforts, he could not physically consume as much as the giant man.

Lo'au pondered the events that transpired and occasionally gazed over the companions. The calamity that had brought them all together may have been fate, the bidding of the gods, or perhaps even a bit of mortal intervention. He chuckled to himself and peered over his shoulder to Maui Atalaga, standing at the bow of the craft. He took a deep breath and picked up three pieces of cooked fish, which lay on a large taro leaf, and passed it to Emori.

The Fijian warrior priest accepted the food graciously and placed it down by his side for a moment's time to cool. He and Adi were huddled together, covered in a Fijian tapa blanket as they watched the flames in silence. The two had not spoken much since they all departed Niuatoputapu. The finality of finding one another amid such deadly strife was beyond their understanding: they sat in quiet veneration to the gods that they did. Emori frequently looked down at his beloved who had her head snuggled against his chest. His fingers stroked her hair tenderly.

Beyond the fire, lay the beautiful Mahina. Her body was covered with a blanket of warm tapa, her head rested softly on a folded parchment of vala. In the early evening she had regained consciousness and, though appearing to make a recovery, remained distant and dark for her own reasons. Unknown to the companions, her mind was completely haunted with the vision of her mother's death and the brutal battle with Kupe. She could not remember much of what transpired following the encounter. She returned to the image of Talatama's face to keep her strong. Periodically, she would open her weary eyes and gaze into the dancing flames of the fire.

The warrior prince sat against the portside of the tongiaki, barely illuminated in the flickering firelight. He sat pondering the day's grim events, daring to accept his brother may be dead and that he had failed to defend him. Though he was a leader, trained in imperial tactics and strategies, blessed with a military focused intellect, leadership, courage and the ability to face adversity, he was often too hard on himself. It was a self-induced psychology that had grown with him since childhood.

He shook his head, cleared his thoughts temporarily and looked over to Atiogie. The giant man, in such a short time had proved to be a trusted friend and formidable fighter. Despite being a heavy handed brute, he could prove to be a powerful ally in bringing down the Pulotulahi.

Pele, the she-warrior, approached the open fireplace from the aft. After long moments alone staring out into the open sea, she was perhaps, one of the first of the companions to understand the chaotic events and accept their fate; whether that was to perish out on the open sea or die in some distant land. Her sentiments had completed their transformation to stone. Only days ago she was one of the greatest enemies of the Empire, evil and bent on killing innocents for the prosperity of the Pulotulahi. Now, her heart was an impenetrable chunk of rock that had bled its last tear of anguish. Severing ties with her brother, followed by his ultimate betrayal – that of ordering her death – meant nothing would ever to touch her opaque heart again.

She stood over Vaohoi and snatched a skewer of coconut oiled fish from him. The young man stared up at her with an annoyed expression.

"Hey – don't be rude. You could have – "

"Shut up, boy," she returned and continued to walk to the other side of the war craft.

He looked to Lo'au, who was smiling and Atiogie who had stopped eating. The giant then broke out into a fit of laughter as the young man stared back at his grilled fish and pouted his bottom lip.

"I don't see anything funny about that," he muttered.

Pele slowed near the bow as she saw Maui Atalaga leaning out over the craft towards an unfolding horizon. His body was outlined both by the firelight and moonlight, edges of his skin glowed and his wavy hair swayed in the sea breeze. As he jutted out over the craft towards the darkened night horizon, it seemed he yearned to reach the infinite expanse before the sea craft could carry him. It was almost as though the dark unknown was a craving for him, like that of a child with an expectation of a new gift.

When he did not acknowledge her presence, the she-warrior stepped closer to him.

"So – I wager you'll want a reward for saving my skin. Or demand me to be in your debt," she started sharply, "You'll be getting neither from me."

She bit into the cooked fish on the skewer, waiting for her statement to provoke banter. Maui Atalaga heaved his body with a swift swing back to the deck and landed directly before her.

"Yes. I'll be expecting compensation of some sort," he said. "Though not for saving your worthless lives, but for interrupting the course of my destiny."

Pele stopped chewing and returned the glare. She then broke into laughter.

"Devise your own excuses," she scoffed. "I know men of your ilk – bent on profiteering and nothing more. As I said before, I'll give you nothing for this escape from Niuatoputapu."

The folk hero winced in a sort of misunderstanding and annoyance. He then shook his head and began to walk away.

"Your heart is black, *daughter of man*. Do not infect my senses with its polluted consequences. You understand nothing."

She grimaced as though cracks shot across her stone heart.

"HO! Come forth and gather around the fire!" Lo'au stood and yelled to everyone. "I have things to say and things we must discuss as companions."

Pele brushed off the insult and began to walk towards the old mu'a. Mahina slowly rose from her sleepy haze and made her way over to sit next to the fire, with the tapa still draped around her. Talatama groaned as he got to his feet and joined the meeting. Maui Atalaga did not sit with the group but remained leaning against the main mast, his arms crossed.

The new companions all reluctantly gathered around the fire and sat in a perfect circle; all newly locked in a fate with little choice and devoid of hope. Thrown together in such accidental probability and scarred by the individual pains that affected them all. It was all but the gift of life that had dulled the bitter taste of defeat and reminded them of the fragility of mortality.

The companions stared into the flames and occasionally at each other. Lo'au nodded his head and gave Talatama a signal to commence. The prince straightened his posture and raised his chin to speak. His words were gentle.

"Before we start, I bid you all join in lament for those lost today."

He began to sing in a deep and strong voice, a well-known tribute to fallen warriors.

> *"Behold the gods of old, behold the great sea, behold the warrior,*
> *Here stands the warrior before you, long wandered long struggled,*
> *Through life, a child of Tonga, a heartbeat of the earth, a joy of the sun,*

Forever yearning to find that one place, that eternal land of restful sleep."

As Talatama came to the chorus, Atiogie, Lo'au and Vaohoi joined in harmony.

"Welcome this warrior, welcome his brothers, welcome his family,
Bid him fortune, bid him bountiful reward, bid him a place in the eternal land,
Forever keep him satisfied that all was won through the mortal sacrifice he made.
As one day we will all be there to share the rest of dreams in the land of sleep.

Welcome this warrior, welcome his brothers, welcome his family,
Bid him fortune, bid him bountiful reward, bid him a place in the eternal land,
So brave and stout, facing the enemy side by side in fire and rain,
Remained standing till the last hour when only giants will fall,

Welcome this warrior, welcome his brothers, welcome his family,
Bid him fortune, bid him bountiful reward, bid him a place in the eternal land,
Forever keep him satisfied won through mortal sacrifice he made.
As one day we will all be there to share the rest of dreams in the land of sleep.

'Behold the gods of old, behold the great sea, behold the warrior,

Here stands the warrior before you, long wandered long struggled,
So the hour has come, and brothers lay to waste, their heads filled with sleep,
Ready they were to make the journey, beyond the realm of pain and suffering,

Welcome this warrior, welcome his brothers, welcome his family,
Bid him fortune, bid him bountiful reward, bid him a place in the eternal land,
Forever keep him satisfied won through the mortal sacrifice he made,
As one day we will all be there to share the rest of dreams in the land of sleep."

The men's strong voices faded off and there was silence among the group. Talatama paid silent tribute to his brave lieutenants; Kunamoana, Mateitau and Oliame. Streams of tears laced Mahina's face as memories of her mother tore her heart. Emori gently rubbed Adi's back, as both Fijians empathised with their comrades in grief. All those who had lost a loved one hung their head in sorrow and, after long moments, Lo'au broke the mournful silence.

"Thank you, Prince Talatama," Lo'au stood and bowed his head. "May the dead find their way to eternal peace." He raised a hand to the heavens.

The night wind picked up and teased the flicking flames for a moment. It then died away slowly. The old mu'a then made eye contact with Emori, Mahina and Pele and smiled warmly to them. "I am Lo'au, High Priest of Tangaloa. My friends and I are allies of the Empire and men of good will. Welcome! Welcome to our company."

"Friends become enemies, enemies become friends. What madness is this?" Pele said, as if to herself.

"I agree. You've been an enemy of the Empire for years with your sick, malevolent brother Kamohoali'i. Why is she here?" Talatama glared back at Lo'au.

"Do I get to throw her overboard?" Atiogie stood up, slowly holding his club.

"Just try it, you dumb oaf," she returned.

"No Atiogie, stay your weapon," Lo'au interjected. "For she must understand, whether she likes it or not she is an enemy of the Pulotulahi and their evil allies now."

"What business do you know of this, old man? Don't presume to speak on my behalf!" she leapt to her feet angrily.

"From what I saw, you were fighting the Niuatoputapuans when I saved your worthless hide," Maui Atalaga stepped in. "Niuatoputapuans who are allied to the Pulotulahi. That makes you an enemy of our enemy. So you're either a friend or a fool."

"You! I've had about enough of your forked tongue, heathen!" Pele grabbed her axe.

"Enough!" Lo'au's voice was like a great clap of thunder that almost stopped the wind.

"Pele, you owe him your life." The old mu'a stepped forward and glared at all present. "We *all* owe Maui Atalaga our lives. His intervention is the only reason we're all still among the living. Don't believe for a moment that the Niuatoputapuans, Rarotongans nor the Samoans would have speared our lives."

A long silence ebbed.

"Lo'au is right. Lord Maui Atalaga, I thank you for your aid. You will be rewarded by the Empire for your service." Talatama winced as he stood and faced Maui Atalaga proudly.

"Well, I guess that means me too," Atiogie followed suit.

"I seek no reward," the hero replied.

Vaohoi remained seated, eating with his mouth open. The rest of the companions got to their feet and all bowed in thanks to the Polynesian hero. Pele lowered her club and shifted weight from side to side as she glared at him. She licked her lips and breathed heavily, the inner turmoil evident on her face. She said nothing before facing the fire. Maui Atalaga pushed off the mast and faced the companions, feeling an explanation should be given.

"I have nothing to say to you," he said candidly. "What happened today was a twist of fate, nothing more. And with that, all of our lives were spared."

"All *our* lives – what do you mean? Surely you were not destined to die then?" Talatama said.

"Yeah! You seemed to be doing fine against those warriors!" Atiogie laughed.

The hero put his hands on his hips and gazed out to the eternal ocean, splashed with silver.

"Havea, the great monster you saw," Maui Atalaga paused. "He is my arch nemesis. I have been warring with him my whole life and today was to be our final battle."

Pele turned her head slowly and watched the great warrior, the anger gone from her face.

"It is the tumultuous balance of the universe that the sons of gods remain in the land of men. Monsters like Havea and his ilk have been lingering in this world far too long and our time is at hand. Soon it must be done." Maui Atalaga suddenly walked away from the group to the bow of the war craft once more.

Vaohoi nudged Lo'au with an elbow and looked at him with a raised eyebrow. The old man patted his shoulder before catching up the mysterious warrior, as the rest of the companions sat back down and gathered warmth from the fire. Lo'au rested his arms on the bow of the tongiaki with Maui Atalaga, and they both stared out to the open sea.

"What fanakenga do we navigate?" he peered out to the darkened horizon.

"There." Maui Atalaga pointed to a low-lying star. "'Tis the zenith star of Niuafo'ou."

"Do you want me to count the corresponding stars with you?"

"No. I'm used to sailing alone."

"I remember well the last time we voyaged together," he laughed. "Are my companions not so different now?"

"What game are you playing at, old man?" Maui Atalaga suddenly turned.

"I have faith in these men and women," he returned. "The stakes are too high now."

"You waste your time. They are all doomed. It is the way of men."

He paused as he gazed back to the companions around the fire. They had begun to talk openly: Mahina was engaged in conversations with the rest of the group and Pele had joined with Talatama and Atiogie in hesitant chatter. The companions had become a fellowship, ready to face whatever fate had to deal.

"And would I be otherwise if I didn't believe you?" he turned back to the hero and smiled.

"No." Maui Atalaga finally turned and broke a broad smile. The two men laughed and embraced each other strongly.

"It's good to see you after all these years," he said.

"Aye, though you've grown older and uglier," Maui Atalaga teased and patted him on the back.

"So Tu'i Manu'a Lefolau, I see you still go by your new name," the hero said.

"Mmm. It's been a long time since I've heard my old title."

"*Lo'au* sounds simple and without acclaim."

"The way I want it."

The hero smiled and nudged Lo'au in jest.

"So the time is almost at hand," he breathed with a grin. "No mighty anticipation, no grand salute?"

"We'll – I'm sure I can wait a little longer." Maui Atalaga smiled and folded his arms. "Just a little longer."

"Do you have someone to carry your line?" he turned serious.

"No. I am the end of it."

CHAPTER 28

Midnight. The night was pitch-black. So black, that murky darkness of the universe was a lighter shade than the shadows that hung over Niuatoputapu. From above, the faint screeches of giant bats echoed the silent roads of the scorched village as they flew over. A dull cold crept through the island, a chill that seemed to infect every corner of it and into the hearts of those who lingered after the battle.

Omani, the Unarmed Warrior, walked silently between the fales within the burned village. Occasionally, he would leer into the destroyed ruins. He saw scattered human remains that lay beneath the ash and blackened timber. He came to a narrow path at the edge of the village that disappeared between the trees. At its end, was a large fale amid the dark forest. It too had been partly burned and destroyed.

The Unarmed Warrior glanced back in the direction of the distant village before entering. He stepped carefully through the collapsed beams and avoided the hanging thatches. From within, he spotted a dim light pulsing like a heartbeat. In the centre of the fale were the remains of what appeared to be a kava drinking room. The smell of ash and smoke still lingered, but it was the stench of death that made the air thick.

To the edges of the room slumped three dead men. They had been posted against the wall, placed so they stared vacantly to the centre of the room with lifeless eyes. To the other side was a dead woman, an old man and an adolescent. They too had been positioned in the same manner. All had been slain through vicious bludgeoning. Many were mutilated and covered in blood.

"My lover..."

Mo'unga stepped out from behind the flickering candle in the centre of the room. He smirked as he watched her come slowly towards him. She was naked: even her assortments of crude jewellery were absent. She lifted her head and shook her long hair so it fell behind her, revealing her supple breasts and dark nipples. Her fingers found her mouth, and with a sliver of her tongue, they slowly parted from her lips with dripping saliva. They snaked down and stopped between her legs. She beckoned him.

"Tonight we have an audience."

It took one of his nimble hands for his loincloth to drop at his feet, before heaving her into the air and impaling her before they fell to the floor. Her long legs wrapped around his waist, which throbbed on top of her. His powerful arms lifted his torso and arched his back, their union never deeper. With one hand he snatched at her neck and began to strangle her. As he throttled her body he glared feverishly aside to the dead who watched on. Their bodies were slick with sweat, the smell of their sex twisting with reek of death. It was not until Mo'unga almost lost consciousness that they shuddered together in a sick climax. Sprawled across the floor, her wicked laugh echoed the ruin.

A figure stirred outside the large domicile Kamohoali'i' had made for his temporary residence. Siateki stood at the entrance and peered inside.

"General Kamohoali'i," he said quietly.

Silence. Suddenly a resonating voice echoed in return.

"What is it you want, 'betrayer of man'?" Havea appeared from the darkness, chewing on food. When he came into the dim light, Siateki saw his mouth was lathered with blood. Clutched in his hand was a human arm, severed at the shoulder and half cooked.

"Nothing that concerns you. I wish to speak with Kamohoali'i alone." Siateki raised his chin to the monster.

"You waste your time, defiler. He has gone to meet with the Dark Lord," the monster grinned. "And had I wanted your information, I would have torn it from your mouth."

"You don't frighten me like the other men, Havea."

A dark shadow loomed from behind the fale and it drew near the dark warriors without halter. Ganilau regarded the two with disdain.

"Have you not satisfied your thirst for death, Havea?" the giant leper said.

The monster ignored him and snapped into the human meat, tearing the flesh with his powerful jaws.

"Is it true?" Siateki asked, "Is the Dark Lord here on this island?"

"Yes. He came while you were at Tafahi," Ganilau continued walking.

"That is good, he'll be able to see our victory." Siateki paused, glancing at Havea, who remained looming over him.

"Know this, Havea, we may be allies now but I'll never condone your contemptible ways."

"Kamohoali'i wishes to have you within our corral. When the day comes for his mind to change, I will eat your heart while it still beats," the terror snickered with a hollow growl.

"You vile creature." The Fallen Commander walked away.

Not far from the Noble House and within an unkempt part of the forest, lay the dark entrance to the ancient langi, tomb of the Niuatoputapu noblemen. It lay within a graveyard more than a thousand years old, was no longer used and had fallen into disrepair. The dark stone slab had been pushed aside to expose a steep staircase that led down into the blackness. Voices were heard from within the tomb, which wafted into the night air. Below in the darkness, the most evil designs were discussed and conspired.

The tomb was significant in size, enough to accommodate a large score of men. The bodies of the fallen lay carefully stacked to the sides of the room on stone slabs, all wrapped in cocoons of tapa. The stench of the dead had long dissolved over the years, and all that remained was the dust, reek of decaying tapa and stifled moisture. To the rear of the tomb, a single torch was lit, providing scant visibility within the overpowering darkness.

Kamohoali'i knelt on one knee before his master, his head bowed for some time. There was movement in front of the torch, causing the flames to flicker. Heavy breathing echoed. A creeping evil emanated from the man who sat before Kamohoali'i. The repulsive negativity could be felt from anyone who came close - a presence of hate and malcontent.

Tu'ipulotu, Lord of the Pulotulahi, studied Kamohoali'i with a dark and unseen expression. He was a large man and his overweight physique was evident under a black tapa cloak. From beneath his hood flowed black hair, resting down about his shoulders. He wore simple girdles and adornments and wielded a long staff made of solid whale ivory. Though it was hard to distinguish any particular characteristics in the half-light, Tu'ipulotu's well-spoken and gruff voice was unmistakable. It denoted intelligence and purpose. Typical of a leader bent on subversive designs.

Towering beside him were his guardians; two disfigured and mutilated men of untold origins. They appeared more creature than man. Hideously powerful, deformed and forever bound to the will of the Lord of the Pulotulahi.

"Sit, General Kamohoali'i."

"Yes, Master," Kamohoali'i complied swiftly. "Master, I trust you had a safe journey."

"The journey was necessary. The manner of its quality matters not."

"Yes, Master."

"Tell me, how have the plans gone? That buffoon - Prince Talaiha'apepe – was he fooled by your timely intervention?"

"Yes, and as a reward, I have been pardoned of all past crimes."

A deep chuckle coughed forth, "Excellent. That was easier than I'd planned, he's more foolish than I'd expected. And what of Noble Anga'uli?"

"I've exploited his existing power to gain a foothold here. Little did the idiot know I'd dispose of him once his usefulness expired. He fell under the fury of the Rarotongan prince, Whatonga, while his men deserted him," he laughed, "I saw the despair on his face when he realised my betrayal."

He reached for a sack of tapa and once untying the knots, he revealed the grotesque decapitated head of Anga'uli. The jaw drooped and glazed eyes stared upwards. Blood and fluid still oozed from the trunk of the neck.

"Good. He was weak, vulnerable under the people's lack of support. They will not miss his leadership."

"Yes, Master."

One of the guardians walked forward and gathered the head by a tuft of hair. He inspected the skull and turned to the Dark Lord expectantly.

"You may cook it tonight for yourselves," Tu'ipulotu said offhandedly to the guardian. "But bring me part of his brain with taro and some skin, once it's cooked."

The guardian snickered in a gurgled sign of pleasure, before retaking his position at the Dark Lord's side, still clinging to the head.

"More importantly, what of Prince Talatama? Was he disposed of in the battle?" Tu'ipulotu asked curiously.

"No, Master. He escaped with the help of strangers."

"What?" The air suddenly turned vile. "He was outnumbered and without aid. What more did you need, you fool?"

The Dark Lord rose slowly to his feet and was visibly shaking. His breathing was laboured and a growl seemed to vibrate from his core.

"My apologies, Master." Kamohoali'i paused, carefully choosing his words. "I have taken care of things. My warriors are hunting him down as we speak. We have manipulated Prince Whatonga and his kin from Ngatangi'ia - they will not fail us."

"Understand, Kamohoali'i, eliminating Talatama is paramount. He is the only thorn in the side of our success to come."

"I understand, Master."

"Do not fail me again - he is only one man."

The Dark Lord stood for a moment before slowly seating himself upon an old stone slab again. A long silence ebbed and the sound of his guardians shifting at his side echoed the tomb.

"Master, what is your will?"

"The next phase of our planning. Stay close to Prince Talaiha'apepe while he is here on the island. Gain his total trust. Offer your service to him for greater responsibility. With Niuatoputapu leaderless, push the prince to appoint you as guardian of the island. Only then can we hope to look southwards with political strength."

"And what of the Samoans?"

"Promise them riches and plunder in battles to come, nothing more. They are mere mercenaries. Their ears will tune finely to the sound of wealth," he waved a hand, "However, if you feel they can be turned, become more persistent in recruiting them to our cause."

"I understand, Master."

"So, we have the combined strength of the Samoans, Rarotongans and the Niuatoputapuans at our beck and call. We are fortunate to have accomplished this position."

"Prince Whatonga is not easily fooled from what my commanders tell me, Master," Kamohoali'i added. "It may not be long till he discards our loose allegiance."

"Use him while you can then. Be prepared to betray and kill him and his men once that allegiance is done."

"Yes, Master."

"And your commanders, Kamohoali'i, are they in order?"

"Yes. As you said years ago, the greed of men can be used to drown them in the pursuit of that greed. They all stay lured to the assurance of their own desires." The general lowered his head. "However, I lost one."

"Killed?"

"No. Left our ranks..." Kamohoali'i paused. "It shames me to tell you that it was my sister, Pele."

Kamohoali'i braced for an uproar from his evil lord that never came.

"I see," the Tu'ipulotu started slowly. "You of all men should know by now that life is full of betrayals."

"To add to my shame, my spies tell me she is in the company of Talatama and his companions."

"She is truly like fire itself," Tu'ipulotu laughed, "Fearless, deadly and unpredictable. Beneath her amiable façade and loyal demeanour over the years, I always felt that one day this would happen." He leaned forward. "Your paths will cross again. It will be to her regret to have left the Pulotulahi when that day comes."

"Yes, Master."

"That will be all. In the morning before sunrise, I will make for Vava'u, and prepare for your coming."

"Your will."

"Remember, Kamohoali'i, do not fail in slaying Talatama. Once he is gone and we are within reach of the king, we will remove him from power by force and take control of the Empire." The Dark Lord began to raise his fist. "Once we have control of the Empire we shall crush all who come across our war path of pillage and destruction!"

The general lowered his head to the ground in reverence.

"I will have the throne, Hikule'o be my witness."

CHAPTER 29

The morning sun beamed down from a cloudless sky. The wind was strong, making for choppy sea. The war tongiaki smashed through the waves with ease and at an impressive ten knots. The massive tapa sails were plump and the hull scattered white sprays of sea.

The companions were scattered around the deck of the large craft, engaging in idle conversation or attending to their own affairs. Vaohoi, Atiogie and Maui Atalaga stood at the aft of the sea craft, wild hoots and whistles coming from the group.

"Tiiiiihhiiiiii!" Vaohoi screamed as he gripped a rope that extended out into the trailing sea.

Atiogie helped grip the long line and laughed loudly as the two scuttled from side to side, as the rope disappeared into the white-wash. Maui Atalaga stood by with his arms crossed, watching the pair stumble around. He laughed at their excitement, "Don't let it go!"

Suddenly their catch, a colossal two hundred kilogram marlin, exploded from the sea into the air, only thirty metres from the tongiaki. The massive fish squirmed in mid-flight then plummeted into the sea again, causing the rope to swerve to the opposite side of the hull. It sent Vaohoi and Atiogie slipping onto the deck to trip over each other.

The commotion drew the attention of the rest of the companions who had gathered to witness the furore. Adi raised her hand to her mouth as she broke into contagious giggles, and Emori and Pele laughed out loud at their misfortune. Mahina and Lo'au looked on with an amused smile. Talatama observed, but reflected no emotion.

"Atiogie! If you let go, I'll never forgive you!" Vaohoi screamed as he lost his grip of the rope and hit the side of the deck.

The line then yanked the Samoan forward and hurtled him to the aft with a crash. The impact caused him to release the line, but just as he did, Vaohoi recklessly threw himself onto it. In the melee, the youngster's foot flicked up into the Samoan's head with a smack. Another chorus of laughter exploded from the watching companions.

"Watch out, you imbecile!" Atiogie shouted, as he gripped the line again and rubbed his head.

Again the rope whizzed to the other side of the craft at incredible speed. But this time it ripped out of the Samoan's hands and flipped Vaohoi onto his back again, while the remaining rope zipped away and the catch seemed inevitably lost. Maui Atalaga leapt to their aid and stomped his foot onto the last few feet of rope, snapping it tight with a twang. The hero bent down and took a hold of the rope with both hands and seemed to contain the wrath of the giant fish effortlessly. The two men sprawled across the deck, bruised and sore, peered up to him in astonishment.

"Atiogie – your club – get ready!" he shouted.

The Samoan scrambled to his feet and armed himself with his huge weapon.

"Do I get to hit something?" he chuckled.

"Be ready, I'll bring him in fast," the hero replied with a grin.

The Samoan glanced at Maui Atalaga in misunderstanding: surely he would need help with the rope. Suddenly the great hero exhaled a sharp roar and commenced reefing in the rope at a staggering speed. The amount of force expended to anchor his feet to the tongiaki and pull in the marlin weighed the craft down into the water.

With one last yank, the giant marlin blasted out of the sea straight towards them. The Samoan took a quick step backwards and swung his club with all his might, hitting the airborne marlin square through the bill, causing an explosion of fish head everywhere. The great body crashed to the deck beside Vaohoi, and though killed instantly, it thrashed around and smacked Vaohoi across the legs.

"Ooowwwwww!!!" he howled.

The companions, who had shielded their eyes from the impact, gazed in disbelief at the destroyed marlin. Vaohoi wriggled away from the thrashing fish, clutching at his legs which brought forth another eruption of laughter. Maui Atalaga shrugged his shoulders and squinted back to the group.

"Good work, boys!" he said.

Vaohoi cackled in uncontrollable laughter as he rubbed his legs.

The companions began to cheer. Talatama frowned and turned away, his mind elsewhere. Atiogie looked down at the marlin then back to his club, which was covered in a gooey film of blood and muck.

"Nice hit." Maui Atalaga shoved the giant in good sport.

Hours later, the midday sun shone from a hazy position. Light clouds stretched across the sky and muted its exposure. The strong morning gale had lessened to a fervent breeze, diminishing their speed and the roughness of their voyage. The craft glided across the brine clean and smoothly. All fronts revealed nothing but the broadened Pacific Ocean, pillowing out to a soft horizon.

The companions had gathered around the fireplace once again, the centre of the hearth glowing red embers and smouldering heat. Lo'au busied himself around the companions and the fireplace, playing the host in what was a wondrous meal. The old mu'a braised the succulent steaks of marlin with sea salt, kelp and coconut milk, and served it with baked sweet potato and taro that Maui Atalaga had stored in a compartment of the tongiaki. Everyone ate heartily and with restored appetites.

"Master, this is delicious!" Vaohoi smiled with a mouth full of food.

"Humph," Atiogie murmured, incapable of eating and speaking at the same time.

"Indeed, Lo'au, you've made an impressive feast from scant provisions," Emori agreed.

"Thank you. More coconut milk?"

Lo'au crouched down beside Mahina, who was tentatively eating the food, and offered her a young coconut.

"Young lady - here." He gave her the coconut. "This will help you regain your strength."

"Thank you, honoured priest," she said submissively.

"Please, call me Lo'au." He stood and faced the rest of the companions with a smile. "That applies to all of you. My name is Lo'au, and among friends, I wish only to be called as such."

"Prince Talatama, where are we headed?" Mahina asked, her voice silencing idle talk and drawing interest.

"We are sailing to the island of Niuafo'ou. We shall take refuge there," he said softly. He searched her alluring eyes for something more than navigational curiosity.

"Refuge? We don't need to hide or seek help from anyone," Pele stated proudly.

"I agree! Those dogs we left behind won't find us. They probably didn't even notice our escape except for those fools on the beach," Vaohoi pitched in.

"I don't think we have anything to worry about," Atiogie said offhandedly.

"From what I saw, I doubt that an insignificant group of warriors would be of much interest in the great scheme of evil that happened yesterday," Emori added.

"Yes, I think so too," Adi agreed.

"Speculation." Talatama regarded the companions with frustration. "I'm not acting on anyone's speculation. And I'm not taking any chances. While you frolic around laughing and playing, you forget the predicament we are in! I have no doubt they are searching for us, and they could be just over the rearward horizon!"

The companions fell silent by the prince's sobering words. He brought back the reality of pain that was so recent.

"Talatama is right. We cannot know for sure if the enemy seeks our whereabouts," Lo'au added. "But in my experience, it's always wise to ere on the side of caution."

"You're all doomed," Maui Atalaga said.

"Now there's optimism," Emori returned.

"Listen up everyone. I'm stating this now," Talatama stood and took centre stage, "Those who wish to stay by my side when we reach Niuafo'ou are welcome. I am in need of strong warriors and good companions. However, those who wish to go their own way on our arrival, so be it. You're not expected to join me in this fight."

"I'm with you," Atiogie smiled and nudged the prince.

"We're with you too, Talatama." Lo'au spoke for himself and Vaohoi.

"So am I," Mahina said suddenly, looking into the depths of Talatama's brown eyes.

He returned her gaze with a surprised look, and then felt himself lose focus on the peripheral. His vision encapsulated nothing but Mahina's jade eyes, which swelled with wanting. Attraction shook his very soul. He was instantly reminded of the first night they almost collided the Noble's courtyard. The moment was chiselled into his memory. He felt a stirring in his stomach and could not help but be aware of its primal effects. Suddenly he felt he was being watched. He shook his head slightly and looked away from her.

"Well – as I said, you're all welcome." He coughed and changed the subject, "Lo'au, thank you for the meal."

"Certainly," the old man smiled; an amused knowing in his eye.

Midday turned to afternoon, and afternoon to early evening. The sun had trailed its magnificence across the clear day and finally hung into the horizon, as if bathing in the sea. The spectacular light reflected off the distant waves and painted colours of pink, orange and violet. The teasing winds tossed the sails to and fro, stretching up to a fading sky that was spotted with the evening's first stars. The short moments of dusk that lay on the open sea were breathtaking. Adi and Emori stood at the bow of the tongiaki and held each other's hands, watching the picturesque sky. Talatama and Lo'au joined them.

"For all the years I have walked this earth, I shall never cease to marvel at the beauty of our world." Lo'au smiled to the others as they all enjoyed the last peaceful rays of sunlight. Adi and Emori returned warm smiles to the old mu'a.

"Yes, it's delightful," the Fijian priestess admired.

"Peaceful," Emori added.

"It makes me forget about war and the troubles of the Empire," Talatama added in an unlikely, passive tone.

The four companions, for a brief moment in time, shared a silent sentiment of tranquillity before the setting sun. Recently all strangers to each other, they were beginning to regard one another with familiar friendship and trust. In its dying minutes, the sun had fallen beneath the horizon and the moment of serenity was gone. The four companions smiled to one another and left the bow.

CHAPTER 30

"Come to the fire, everyone. Let us share in the telling of tales." Lo'au smiled under his grey beard, a joyful pitch in his voice.

"Oh, goodie! Master, can you tell us the one about the sea dragons?" Vaohoi stood quickly from the floor with excitement.

"Maybe later, my boy," he grinned as he sat himself slowly on the deck.

The rest of the companions gradually gathered from all parts of the sea craft, and sat in a casual circle around the fire. Maui Atalaga, for the first time, wandered towards the fire and joined them, resting next to Pele. Adi smiled and began to pass fruit around, and Mahina offered young coconuts to thirsty comrades. Atiogie began to gnaw the leftover meat from their midday feast. His appetite was insatiable.

The embers in the fire crackled softly, occasionally spitting forth tiny pieces of glowing cinders that drifted high into a velvet night sky. The firelight reflected off the companions' faces. They had begun to enjoy each other's company despite the horrific events that had brought them together. Most of them had begun to accept the others as lasting friendships, regardless of where the journey would take them.

Lo'au picked up a piece of wood and began to stoke the fire. Everyone made themselves comfortable and gave him their total attention. The old mu'a continued to stir the glowing ash, as though to establish consideration towards the words he was about to share. He then turned to his friends and emanated a manifestation of wisdom, illustration and captivation.

"A long time ago, when I was a young child, my father told me a story," he began. "Let me say, there are not many memories I have of my father. He was killed before I became a man, but I recall a tale he told me when we were in distant lands and during different times. He stroked my hair and smiled down to me as he spoke, on a calm and peaceful evening like this one. He said, 'My son, I will be gone soon and I would like to tell you one last story.'"

"Beyond what we know of old, it began with two brothers, up there, in the black," he pointed into the night sky. "Two brothers were born from the murky womb of nothingness – both unable to live without the other in dynamic opposites. The first brother is what we know as 'Existence', pure and simple. The other brother is what we know as 'Time', the very power itself."

The old mu'a shifted and cleared his throat as he continued.

"One day when the brothers were young, Existence told his brother, Time, that he decided he would create matter, being all physical things." Lo'au motioned to the sea and sky and tapped the wooden boards of the tongiaki. "Following that, he then created life."

"But Time was quickly jealous of the beautiful things that had been created, and so out of spite, he exhumed all his strength and laid the most powerful effect over all things – time. For Time knew that his power over all reality would cause all physical things to age, decay and die."

"Realising his brother's jealous intentions, Existence blessed all living things with natural procreation; the ability to leave behind generations of offspring that would live on. He imbued man with the greatest spiritual strength of all, a spirit that entwines through every man's continuation of family – maintaining that his line would live forever."

"Our ancient lore is rich with families naturally blessed with enduring power through the ages. The most powerful of these families, imbued with spirit and strength, emerged from the dawn of time from a far distant land. The first and eldest was the formidable Hikule'o family, ruled by the ruthless, Havea Hikule'o. The second was the mighty Maui family headed by Maui Motu'a, the strongest warrior who ever lived. The third, and last, was the Tangaloa family, spawned from Tangaloa Eiki, the most wise and kind. The three fathers were brothers – kings and powerful warlords of their distant lands."

"What distant land?" Vaohoi asked. "I thought they were gods?"

"Ahhh, but even gods have their origins," he smiled. "Tales tell of a beautiful and great land of sweeping valleys, lush forests and an opulence of fruit and game. It bared forth a great civilization of music, peace, prosperity, advanced sophistication and unification. It was one of the first great civilizations of man. The great kingdom was called Pulotu."

"You mean the underworld?" Vaohoi said. "You mean to say it once existed?"

"Hey, pipsqueak. Stop interrupting!" Atiogie grumbled.

"You speak of it as though you've been there," Pele interjected.

Lo'au smiled but didn't answer. "It - doesn't exist anymore. One day in Pulotu and Babajea, there began a terrible civil war. It tore the lands apart and thousands perished. During the war there was a great cataclysm and the island of Pulotu sank into the sea. The three great families became estranged following the catastrophe and were split over the great loss. Hikule'o Havea had deceived Tangaloa Eiki and Maui Motu'a, his actions almost destroying their two family lines," he turned to the folk hero.

Maui Atalaga nodded slowly.

"Havea Hikule'o's offspring were blessed with unparalleled strength but had been tainted with evil. The children of Tangaloa Eiki and Maui Motu'a were also blessed with unique abilities of their own. However, they could not easily rival Havea Hikule'o's monstrous offspring."

"For hundreds of years, the three great families continued in their rivalry, spreading their influence within the world of Polynesia," he took a deep breath and exhaled slowly.

"So what happened to them, Master?" Vaohoi asked.

"Over the expanse of time, the families of Hikule'o and Maui dwindled in numbers. Once great and proud men of honour were disappearing, many of them slain in the ancient feud."

The companions looked at the deck solemnly.

"That's sad," Adi said. "I hadn't heard that story before, Master Lo'au."

The mu'a shook himself from thought and returned her gaze. "Oh, it's not so sad." He began to poke the fire again with the wood. "After all, we have one sitting among us from the great line of Tangaloa," he chuckled at Talatama.

"Me? I think you have me confused, mu'a. My line comes from Aho'eitu – the first Tu'i Tonga."

"Tangaloa Eiki was Aho'eitu's grandfather," Lo'au smiled. "You are from the great family of Tangaloa."

"It all makes sense now," Talatama whispered in disbelief.

"And what of Hikule'o's evil lineage?" Emori frowned. "Is there a generation alive today?"

"Indeed. You all saw him yesterday," Lo'au said quickly.

"That monster we fought in the village," Atiogie pitched. "That has to be him!"

"Yes," Lo'au sighed. "Havea, the monster you saw, is the descendant of Havea Hikule'o."

"He carries all the dark powers of a true demon," Pele added. "He'd be impossible to kill."

"I don't doubt for a moment," Atiogie laughed slapping his leg. "He picked me up and threw me around like a child!"

"There is but one man who can defeat him," Lo'au glanced at Maui Atalaga. "The last of the Maui line."

"The last?"

"Then you must be the only one to stop him." Talatama turned to the folk hero.

Maui Atalaga looked away from the companions and for the first time appeared to bear an inner burden. The companions fell silent as interest turned solely to him. A long silence followed and it seemed that the great warrior accepted his story would ease the understanding of his new comrades. He looked up to the companions, his face illuminated by the flickering firelight, his eyes reflecting a misty past of unspoken history full of strangers and ancient lands. But no words came. He remained silent.

Pele glared at him intently. The great warrior suddenly stood, strode to the far end of the craft and disappeared into the shadows of the mast.

"Wha – ?" Vaohoi said in surprise.

Following a silence from the companions, Lo'au began to speak in Maui Atalaga's stead.

"Maui Atalaga and Havea are destined to fight until the end," he paused. "It will end the ancient feud between their families, once and for all."

"After yesterday, its obvious Havea is deep within the Pulotulahi leadership. I will do what I can to support Maui Atalaga fulfilling that destiny," Talatama said.

"Count me in!" Atiogie boomed.

"I will also." Pele smiled as she raised a clenched fist, the compelling story obviously touching her.

"I'll be able to do something too!" Vaohoi threw in.

Lo'au laughed and patted the young man on the shoulder. "Not so hasty, young one. We all have a part to play in this story before it ends."

Maui Atalaga slowly appeared again before the group. He regarded them with an awkward smile.

"I'm – grateful for your words – all of you," he said. "Consider yourselves all welcome on my tongiaki."

The group cheered and began to sing a well known song farewelling warriors off to war. When the song finished the companions continued their hearty conversation and before long, the prince concluded a discussion with Atiogie and patted him on the back.

"Comrades, I am retiring for the night," he said as he stood. "So you all know - we should be arriving in Niuafo'ou tomorrow. We shall make the preparations to moor and seek the support and council of the Noble of Niuafo'ou who is a trusted uncle of mine. Good night."

The prince left the firelight and walked to the portside of the tongiaki, placed his hands on his hips and looked out to sea. His heart was filled with anxiety, his mind with confusion.

"Ah, Prince Talatama." Lo'au approached slowly. "A wonderful night, is it not?"

"Yes, I suppose it is." His voice was edged with the desire to be left alone.

"This is just the beginning. Don't burden yourself too quickly."

"How — ?" Talatama turned in surprise. "Well - I have much on my mind, mu'a."

"Do you think they pursue us?" Lo'au looked over his shoulder.

"Yes I do," he said without hesitation. "They will not risk me making it back to the capital alive to tell the tale."

"We'd be well ahead of them by now," Lo'au said.

"That won't stop them - you know that," the prince became more edgy. "With the great numbers they had - they'll hunt us down. I know Kamohoali'i's mind. I've no doubt he's killed my brother too."

"You don't know that ..."

"I am unsure of many things at present, old man." Talatama clenched his teeth, his inner turmoil bubbling at his patience. "Not to mention even those in our own company ..."

"You don't trust her, do you?"

The prince couldn't believe his words.

"Is it that obvious?"

"Pele is alone, Prince Talatama. She does not act for the enemy."

"And how do I know that, Lo'au?" he said frustratingly. "How do I not know she is a spy among us?"

"Becau—"

"Because you say so? Why should I listen to you? Why should I accept your council?" his raised voice reached the companions and they casually glanced in his direction. He breathed deeply, cooling his mind.

"I'm sorry," he whispered. "She – she is from the echelons of the enemy commanders, she is Kamohoali'i's sister, by Tangaloa."

"Then 'trust' shall be your first lesson." Lo'au smiled with wisdom. "Goodnight, my Prince."

An hour later, the fire had smouldered and the dark of the night cloaked the war tongiaki as it streamlined through the black brine. The companions lay asleep, scattered around the craft. Vaohoi slept against the aft, curled up in the foetal position. He rustled from his slumber and turned, opened his eyes and saw the outline of Maui Atalaga standing at the mast. He was gazing in the direction they were headed. As he shifted again, he glanced back and suddenly saw a glimmering light behind them on the horizon. He jolted awake with fright and his skin turned to goose pimples but as he scrambled to a knee and rubbed his sleepy eyes he couldn't spot the light he'd seen.

"What is it, boy?" Maui Atalaga said.

"N-nothing. I thought I saw something ..." Vaohoi breathed.

He continued to search the blackness of the night with his weary eyes and finally shook his head and lowered himself again to the deck. He began to close his eyes and as Maui Atalaga watched him fall back to sleep, he regarded the dark horizon with a smile.

CHAPTER 31

Maka Vela, Niuafo'ou
Spring, A.D.1120

Over two hundred years before the rise of the Empire, and during the peaceful years between the Pacific nations, there was a legendary last stand that took place on the island of Niuafo'ou. In that time, there ruled a stout Tu'i Tonga by the name of Lihau, loved dearly and respected greatly by all in the Kingdom of Tonga.

Unlike the powerful King Tu'itatui, King Lihau, was an adventurous man, a pioneer, preferring to spend his years searching for discovery than to rule a kingdom. As it was for most of his rule, he lived away from the throne of his Tonga, allowing his trusted governors to preside over the people.

Legend had it that in the last years of his life, Lihau and his army of loyal warriors sailed to the ends of the earth. What transpired there was largely unknown. Years following his long disappearance, locals of Niuafo'ou one day saw King Lihau reappear on the horizon with but a handful of his original army. The people received him with open arms, overjoyed to see their king alive and returning to the kingdom. However, they soon realised something was terribly amiss when the king landed ashore the black beaches of the western coast.

Lihau leaped from his war tongiaki with his warriors, bearing a panicked expression. He shouted for the villagers to make for Vai Lahi, the name of the great lake in the centre of the island. Following

216

the king's swift landing, it was said that the locals then saw the western horizon lined with thousands of giant and strange ships unlike anything they had ever seen.

"Prepare for battle! Make for Maka Vela!" the king shouted.

The entire population of Niuafo'ou immediately traversed the great crater lake to reach Maka Vela, a single large island in the middle of the lake. Fortifications were prepared and the men were ready to fight not a moment too soon. The villagers gasped in terror as thousands of foreign warriors came, wave after wave and from all sides of the lake to reach Lihau. However, as the king had proven in times past, his military genius prevailed. All the foreigners were stopped and defeated from his position of strength in the middle of the lake. Hundreds by the hundreds were shot by Tongan bowmen before they could reach the shores of Maka Vela.

After a day of desperate battle and slaughter, the foreigners began to retreat. King Lihau and his handful of brave soldiers were victorious in holding off thousands. The foreign leader, as legend had it, was adorned in strange armour and was a man with flowing black hair, pale complexion and almond eyes. He came to the edge of the lake and called to Lihau in a sharp and foreign language. The king exchanged words in the strange language, before the foreigners returned to their ships and disappeared into the horizon with the setting sun, never to be seen again.

In the following years, when asked about the events that led up to the Battle of Vai Lahi, King Lihau often declined to share his story. However, from that day forward, the people of Niuafo'ou were treated as kinsmen by Lihau and the royal family. In the century that passed, the Niuafo'ouans gained the reputation among Tongans as people of high loyalty and virtue. The noble warriors, who that ruled to the day of King Tu'itatui, were direct descendants of the warriors who aided King Lihau on that mysterious and fateful day.

The morning sun shone down across the volcanic island of Niuafo'ou, its steep-sided rim rising jagged and undefined. Spread across the centre of the island was Vai Lahi, its waters wide and vast.

In the centre of the great lake lay the infamous stronghold island of Maka Vela, a multitude of fales, abodes and temples and supporting about two thousand people. In the very centre was the Noble House, perched on a tall hill. It was a fortified stronghold built to withstand an attack from any adversary.

The domicile stood with a grander brawn and design than the Noble House of Niuatoputapu, having being built exclusively from Fijian timber and constructed by Tonga's greatest craftsmen. Its polished and superior architecture was exceptional in comparison to other regal structures. Voices echoed in the large halls of the reception area.

"Milord! Milord!" came the voice of Sia, the high priest of Niuafo'ou.

In the great hall sat the Noble of Niuafo'ou himself, Papani'ai tau, who was tending to the lacquering of his ancient and revered weapon.

"What is it?" he returned disinterested, continuing to polish his club with cloth.

"Milord -" Sia breathed heavily when he reached the side of his master, "News from the outposts."

"Hmmm."

"We have a royal visit."

"What?" Papani'ai tau dropped the mastic lacquer. "Why wasn't I notified earlier?"

"My apologies, Milord, it seems like an unannounced visit. Prince Talatama arrived moments ago with a small entourage."

Papani'ai tau rose and faced the village headman, his weapon clutched in his hand. Standing at seven feet tall and one hundred and forty kilograms, he was noble born warrior-elite and second cousin to King Tu'itatui. His heart and integrity was as strong as the obsidian forged in the bowels of the volcano itself, and his sense of duty was untarnished and focused.

"I have missed his arrival. It's but shame on us that we were not there to greet him when he arrived," he cursed, "Bring Prince Talatama and his group to the house immediately. Provide them with food, water, ointments and the aids they need after a long journey. Call the chiefs to prepare a feast immediately. Send word to Lafa and Mata Ita so that they may join me in reception."

"Yes, Milord," Sia complied.

"Sia, no delays. Bring them here immediately."

Maui Atalaga's tongiaki was banked upon the only beach on the island. The black pebbled beach, a representation of the island's volcanic heritage, made it easier to drag a sail craft to shore, especially one as large as Maui Atalaga's war craft. The rest of the island, however, was beachless, rocky and without favourable ports in which to dock vessels. The companions were greeted by scout warriors from a nearby outpost, and on identifying Prince Talatama, one of the soldiers was sent running to hail his coming.

Following brief directions, the scouts led the companions through kilometres of jungle, heading inland. They followed a path that wound up a mountain ridge through thick vegetation. A number of times during their ascent, flocks of malau scuttled across the path ahead of the companions. Their feathers blended from greys to brows. From their bright yellow beaks chirped a loud unison. Their song carried through the jungle.

"Look!" Vaohoi pointed. "Hairy running-birds!"

"Yes, they're all over this island." Lo'au smiled as he watched the *megapodius pritchardii*. "Flightless birds that lay their eggs in the earth. But not like *Moa Tonga*."

"Are they good to eat?" Atiogie asked.

"They're too small. They'd have little flesh," Pele laughed.

"Once, long ago, there were many species of those birds." Lo'au looked down as he continued to walk. "Many of them were much larger."

Finally reaching the summit, the companions paused in an area that revealed a picturesque view of the entire island: abundance of bright green fauna, sharp mountain ridges that ringed the island, Vai Lahi in the centre that spanned over ten kilometres in diameter, and the impenetrable Maka Vela island fortress.

"That is beautiful," Adi remarked as she looked back to Emori.

"It is an island within an island, Master?" Vaohoi asked Lo'au.

"Indeed. You know there's a story behind that, my boy." Lo'au smiled.

"I have never seen anything like it," Mahina said.

"This is perfect, Talatama." Atiogie nudged the prince and motioned to the fortress. "What more protection do we need against our enemies?"

"Perhaps," he replied, his mind full of troubles.

"Keep moving you great lump. You're breaking my stride." Pele pushed past the giant Samoan.

As the companions began to move on, Vaohoi looked around and back towards the direction from which they came.

"Master? Where is Maui Atalaga?"

"He remained down by the beach. You'll find he cares little for political or social affairs."

The journey from the summit took less than half the time to descend, on the worn mountain path. The earth was a deep brown colour, moist and fertile, and on both sides of the path crept lush ferns and tropical shrubbery filled with blooming crimson and golden flowers. The companions made a final march through a shaded canopy, before exiting into a sunlit area on the shores of Vai Lahi.

From ground level, the companions agreed, Maka Vela appeared further from the shore than it appeared from an elevated position; it was perhaps over two kilometres from the banks of Niuafo'ou.

"I could not swim that!" Vaohoi laughed looking out over the water.

"It is probably full of sharks anyway," Atiogie scoffed.

"Actually the lake is fresh water and has very little fish," Lo'au said.

Atiogie scooped a handful of the water into his mouth.

"How can that be, old mu'a?" Mahina asked curiously.

"Because, we are standing in the mouth of a volcano. This very lake is the crater. No life can sustain itself in there."

"So these crazy people built a whole village, out there in the middle of the volcano!" Vaohoi partially asked, partially laughed.

"Vaohoi, my boy," Lo'au chuckled and patted the young man on the back, "The volcano has not erupted for a thousand years."

The scout waded out into the shallow water and prepared a large canoe that was moored under a hanging palm.

"This way, Milords," he bowed.

The companions marvelled at Maka Vela's appearance of an unspoiled island, lush with greenery that had been cropped and trimmed to perfection. The grass, ferns and trees were groomed and sculptured to complement the dominion of its people, emanating a sense of tranquillity. The neat paths wound through the uneven, olive earth. Fales presented character and charm to its visitors. The domiciles were erected spaciously to provide for open spaces, decorated with garden beds of bright flowers and ancient stones. Here and there, various buildings and temples peeked out from the pockets and tree hidden areas.

The path gradually led the companions into the Noble Compound and the reception area. Before they could remark on their surrounds, they saw a large man exit from the main hall, accompanied by many servants and warriors. The man fell to a knee before Talatama and then stood to face him.

"Prince Talatama, you honour us with your visit," Papani'ai tau said quickly.

Talatama reached for the noble, pressed their faces together and inhaled, initiating a more casual greeting.

"It is good to see you, old friend," the prince grinned warmly.

The noble smiled with genuine cheer, honoured by the display of trust and familiarity from the prince.

"My Prince, please. Follow me."

Vaohoi, Mahina, Pele, Emori and Adi were offered the luxuries of bathing, lathering of coconut oil and refreshments by a multitude of servants. While Vaohoi revelled in the attention and the company of young women tending to his needs, the others were content to rest weary bones and receive remedial care for their wounds.

In the great hall sat companions, Talatama, Lo'au and Atiogie as guests of Papani'ai tau. In the centre of the circle sat a chosen woman of ceremonial custom, directed to serve the kava. She showed grace and skill as she ground the kava root, soaked and prepared the drink for the men. Once the kava had been served to all the men, Papani'ai tau turned his attention to the prince.

"My Prince, news from the capital has grown sparse through the winter months. How is His Majesty's health?"

"My father is well. His troubles bear their weight on my shoulders these days, however." He grinned. "But the duty takes me far and wide, so I cannot complain about it."

"Yes, well it's been far too long since your last visit. Tonight we shall feast and celebrate your arrival!" the noble turned serious, "But truth be told, I was shocked to hear that you arrived earlier without herald. And finally seeing you and your companions with the recent wounds of battle, I fear your need is desperate. What's happened?"

The prince did not answer for long moments. He glanced at Atiogie and Lo'au briefly then took a deep breath. He finally confided in the men with a tone that sent shivers through the Niuafo'ouans.

"Noblemen, there is an evil dominion who call themselves, the Pulotulahi. They are the remnants of an old rebellion against the Tu'i Tonga and have now sacked the island of Niuatoputapu with the support of a mercenary army. I seek aid from those who would stand against this evil – for we are hunted."

CHAPTER 32

A lone kalia sat some fifty kilometres from the shores of Niuafo'ou. The two fishermen stood patiently on the edge of it and watched the massive school of ocean perch swim beneath them. The multitudes of fish clouded the waters with darkness below the bow. Although the afternoon sun glittered on the choppy sea, the fishermen had no difficulty seeking out their aim.

"Now!" one of them shouted.

Both men swiftly threw barbed spears into the school of fish simultaneously, puncturing the surface of the water and finding easy targets. The dark cloud of fish separated and fanned out immediately and in an instant, the school of perch had vanished but their fishermen's prize had been won. Their two spears floated to the surface and twisted about in the water. One or two fish thrashed about as they remained pierced on the barbed ends. The pair dove into the sea to retrieve the spears and catch.

"What's your count?" the younger man grasped his spear and raised it above the water with two impaled fish.

"Three!" the other shouted with glee as he raised his own.

But just as he began to swim back to the kalia, the third fish succeeded in uncoiling itself from the barbs and plopped back into the sea, quickly shooting away.

"It's a draw!" the younger man exclaimed.

The older fisherman pulled a sour face as they both made it back to the kalia. Wading beside it, the men threw their spears and catch into the hull of the craft, then swiftly heaved themselves aboard. Their bodies were slick with water, wetting the dry deck as they kept their footing. The younger man made for his short club and proceeded to bludgeon the writhing fish, as the older fisherman began to ready the sails to return to Niuafo'ou.

"Get those fish into the baskets quickly. I want to make it back well before sundown. I do not ..." the man's voice trailed off suddenly.

"Hey, do not take it so hard," the younger said, throwing the fish into the large woven basket. "Next time," he looked up to see his friend staring out to sea. A large fleet of tongiaki had silently loomed from the horizon.

"Who is it?"

"I do not know. They do not look local, nor like imperial tongiakis."

They stood staring, their kalia swaying gently in the sea.

"I do not like the look of them. We should head back," the younger fisherman stuttered.

"I think you are right. We will notify Lord Papani'ai tau immediately."

The two fishermen began to prepare the sails and masts for the swift retreat, sporadically glancing back in fear to the approaching vessels. Suddenly their kalia began to vibrate from impacts beneath the water. The dull thuds began as random cuffs, but in seconds became a repetitious beat of frightening thumps.

"Wh-what is that?" the younger man exclaimed.

"Merciful Tangaloa – help us!"

Hundreds of tiger sharks circled them in a school that formed a mass so dark, that it blackened the water to night and outlined the kalia from above like a tiny pupil on the eye of the sea. The sharks splashed about on the surface and violently struck the bottoms and sides of the kalia. In an effort to quicken their escape, the young fisherman leapt from the hull to the narrow platform to reach the rear mast. Failing to notice that the platform was wet from their initial resurfacing, he slipped before he could reach the mast.

"No!" the older fisherman screamed as he saw his friend slip and fall.

The young man threw himself swiftly against the platform and struck his head hard against the hull. His friend made a desperate lunge as his body began to slip limply overboard, but was too late. The older man clawed at the deck to prevent himself falling in as he watched in horror, the grey and white viciousness rip his friend's body from the surface.

He made it back to the masts and managed to snap the sails into shape but the ferocity of the shark attack on the small kalia began to take its toll. He began to hear creaking and snapping of old wood and suddenly felt the hull lurch under a massive impact. The front end of the right hull splashed into the water that had sent it reeling, and a long splinter shot through the centre platform.

"Damn you!" he cursed, his face pale and breathing haggard.

Just as he grasped the main mast, another huge impact struck the hull with a force that lifted the aft from the water. As the hull plunged back into the blue, the centre platform could not withstand the heavy contact, and splintered instantaneously. He quickly swung from the mast as the collapsing platform caused the hulls to turn inwards and forced them to take in gushing ocean. A mass of teeth and hunger thrashed about in the centre of the sinking kalia. With it sank his hope. He reached for his spear, made his ground on the high shell of the aft and began valiantly spearing the moving sea of sharks.

Before the kalia was beneath the surface, the fisherman finally gave up. Careworn with every breath, tears of helplessness running down his face, he made a final throw. The spear disappeared into the thrashing brine without effect. The sound of breath being thumped from him echoed off the waters before the terrors ripped his body beneath a reddened sea. A kilometre away the advancing tongiakis slowed their pace; the onlookers seeing the kalia sink into the stirring ocean.

Mo'unga stood tall at the bow of the tongiaki, her right hand stretched out towards the sunken kalia. Her eyes were rolled to the back of her skull, exposing the whites that matched her snarling white teeth. She slowly lowered her arm and returned to the reality of the moment.

"They are no more," she said in a resonating voice.

"Good. They would have alerted the enemy of our presence," the Weeping Assassin whispered with a sniggering smile.

"Well done, Mo'unga," Omani, the Unarmed Warrior smiled.

General Amosa and his lieutenants stood in disbelief and many of the Rarotongan warriors whispered fearfully as they turned back to their duties.

"That is a godly gift," Amosa said, staring at the woman.

"That is not all she can do either," Kupe slapped the Rarotongan general on the shoulder.

"I'm happy to hear that. Come," the general replied as he beckoned his lieutenants and the Pulotulahi warriors to sit in a circle on the main platform of the tongiaki. Once everyone was seated, he regarded Kupe and his evil companions with intent.

"They have taken refuge on the island there in the distance: the island of Niuafo'ou," Kupe pointed at the scant line on the horizon.

"What can you tell me about this place?" Amosa started, "Apart from it being the anus of the world?"

"We cannot approach the cursed island from any direction without being seen, due to its geographical shape; it is almost a perfect circle, with elevated mountains ringing the inner land. They have lookout posts on the peaks."

"Not to mention Prince Talatama would have alerted the locals of the battle and they will be on their guard," Omani added.

"You have not told me who travels with the prince besides his deceiving whore, Mahina," Amosa spat.

"Our warriors on Niuatoputapu said that he is in the company of an old mu'a, a young upstart and two Fijian priests —"

"That does not sound impressive," one of the lieutenants scoffed.

226

"Not so fast. He is also rumoured to have at his side, a giant Samoan warrior of incredible strength. Also Pele, the she-warrior, fights with him—" Omani broke off with distaste.

"Who is that?"

"Pele was our peer within the Pulotulahi, General Kamohoali'i's own sister. She's unparalleled in the echelons of archers."

"So the group is full of mongrels and deceivers," Amosa sneered.

"Beware my friends," Mo'unga whispered, "for they also hold the company of Maui Atalaga."

A silence fell upon the group. The Rarotongans looked at each other with astonishment. The Pulotulahi warriors frowned.

"You mean Maui Atalaga, the hero?" one of the Rarotongan lieutenants gawked.

"No! She means a man who claims he is. He is nothing but another deceiver and trickster. He holds no weight," Kupe said quickly. "Make no mistake – they are of no great threat. They are small in numbers. They will put up a feeble fight and revenge will be ours."

"What is your plan then?" Amosa nodded.

"We shall drift here on the edges of the horizon until nightfall. Then we shall make our move. Pray the moon does not show its face for we need the black of night to hide our advance."

"Once we are ashore, we will make a hidden camp and ascertain their strength. We will then notify General Kamohoali'i of our location and need, should we require it."

"There won't be time to send a messenger all the way back to Niuatoputapu," the general chuckled.

"Do not worry about that. We have other means." The Weeping Assassin wiped a tear from his cheek. "For now, let us rest up and prepare for tonight."

As dusk fell the three Pulotulahi warriors sat in the hull of one of the great tongiakis, consuming a cold meal. They sat in silence for some time, tearing at the raw flesh.

"Perhaps I should notify Kamohoali'i now of our progress," Mo'unga whispered.

"No. Not until we reach the shore safely," Kupe said annoyingly.

"It may have been a better decision if all of us had come," Omani added.

"We will not need them, not when we have these fools to fight for us," the Weeping Assassin motioned towards the Rarotongans. "Our plan has worked well so far."

"Perhaps." Omani ate his food with much appetite.

"And you," Kupe pointed angrily at Mo'unga, "Next time you want to tell us of your visions, ask me first. Your talk of Maui Atalaga almost had the Rarotongans turning back to Ngatangi'ia."

"It is the truth, Weeping Assassin," she returned without heeding his words.

"Just do what I say, the both of you. If we're to succeed in killing these *heroes*, we must work together."

CHAPTER 33

The afternoon came quickly for the companions. Talatama, Lo'au and Atiogie sat for hours with Papani'ai' tau and his warriors in the main hall. The severity of the incident in Niuatoputapu was discussed and a counter attack from the island was explored. The noble and his entourage walked through a rear exit quickly to make arrangements for the evening, while Talatama, Lo'au and Atiogie gradually emerged from the main entrance into the courtyard.

"By Tangaloa I am tired," Atiogie yawned as he swaggered from the fale.

"Atiogie." Talatama nudged the giant. "Try to stay awake next time we sit in a war council."

"I cannot take much talk of battle tactics – at least not for that long!" he returned, "Just tell me who to hit."

"Do not worry, there will be plenty of times for that," the old mu'a patted him on the back.

The three strolled from the courtyard into a larger courtyard, edged with fine cut stone and designed gardens. In the centre of the courtyard were the rest of the companions; Mahina sat talking and laughing with Vaohoi under a handful of mape trees that were ripe with berries, while Adi and Emori stood close by a garden rich with frangipanis. Vaohoi's face beamed with joy when he saw Lo'au appear.

"Master!" He jumped to his feet. "Master, you are not going to believe what we did this afternoon!"

"Oh? What is that?"

"We were bathed in hot water and coconut milk by maidens, then lathed with tea tree oil and had our hair groomed." The young man paused for air. "Then we sat down for a banquet of fruit and fish—"

"Hey *pala*, I do not want to hear anymore," Atiogie snapped.

"- and we ate and ate until we couldn't eat any more!" Vaohoi shrieked as he ran away from Atiogie's swipe.

"What? Did you not get that treatment?" the youngster taunted the giant. "Okay, okay, I am sorry."

Vaohoi pulled a puppyish face and stood next to the giant. Suddenly loud flatulence erupted from Vaohoi's backside and the smell immediately struck Atiogie in the face.

"Why you little – come here so I can knock your teeth out!"

Lo'au ignored them and stepped towards the Fijians, failing to notice that they were engaged in a serious conversation. "Excuse me."

"Oh, Master. My apologies, I did not see you come." Adi turned with a warm smile.

"Can I assist with anything?"

"N-no thank you, Master."

"I just wanted to let you know about the feast tonight: it will be held just past dusk. I will come to get you both so we can go together."

"That would be wonderful. Thank you," Emori and Adi said in unison.

"Hey," Talatama began as he breeched the group. "Where is Pele?"

"Have not seen her." Emori looked about.

"I saw her leave the compound not long after our arrival," Mahina said, joining the conversation.

The prince frowned immediately at Lo'au. He then glanced to Mahina, "So only a few hours ago you think? Alone?"

"Yes, but—"

"Damn it! Atiogie, I want you to go with Mahina to find her immediately."

"What? Why me?" Atiogie objected.

"I do not trust her. In all probability she has gone back to the outer rim to meet with a Pulotulahi war party!" He turned to Lo'au. "I knew we should not have trusted her."

"I would not worry about her, Prince Talatama," Lo'au said calmly.

"I do not hold the same faith in people, old man," he focused on Atiogie and Mahina again. "Two of you go – now."

The giant sighed deeply with a hurtful look while Mahina stared at him with a concerned expression.

"I will go with Mahina," Vaohoi piped up suddenly. "We will make it to the rim and back in time for the feast!"

"Granted. Now go!" Talatama shouted.

Vaohoi and the Rarotongan assassin rummaged together their possessions and disappeared in the direction of the compound exit. Talatama stood quietly, fuming over the possibilities of Pele's disappearance. If she'd betrayed the group, she could destroy all of the plans he had devised that afternoon and threaten the very lives of everyone. Could she be trusted yet? Over the past few days the companions had created a unique bond with one another, yet her tainted past could not be ignored. He clicked his tongue and shook his head. No – he did not trust her and never would. He turned to face the remaining companions, only to realise he was suddenly alone.

The setting sun hung above the western sea like a fiery teardrop that would inevitably fall into the melting horizon. The sky glittered with peeping stars and cirrus clouds stretched among them like the wings of heavenly hosts. The soft shimmering of the ocean's surface was comforting and the light breeze that carried the scent of palms and brine was soothing.

Pele sat on a grassy ledge that leaned out over the jagged rocks and gazed out to the beautiful sunset. Cross-legged, the she-warrior cradled her jaw in her palm as she rested, deep in thought. Her long braided hair hung about her powerful brown shoulders and partly hid her strong face. Within arm's reach lay her axe and her longbow. Her tools of war were never far from reach.

Her mind was still numbed with the thought of her brother, Kamohoali'i and his betrayal. Despite knowing that her decision to leave would invite great difficulties, she had never dreamed his violent actions would guide her into the welcoming arms of the enemy – allies of the Imperial Empire. She had not prepared herself for that outcome. Her plans were to simply return to Ha'apai and gather warriors to a new cause of adventure. Until now however, the unforeseen destiny that had influenced her friendship with the companions had not become so apparent.

"Farewell, oh mighty Sun, till we meet again tomorrow," came a strong voice below her.

Broken from her thoughts, she snatched up her bow. Standing with his heavily tattooed back to her was Maui Atalaga, gazing out to the fading dusk. He took a deep breath through his nose and exhaled slowly, his hair blowing lightly in the breeze. He was without weapon and naked but for a loincloth of tapa around his waist. She remained watching him silently until he turned to her, and in light that turned his skin the colour of melting honey, struck her with his handsome qualities. He smiled, eyes filled with zeal and purpose. He slowly approached her position from below.

"You speak as though you've only witnessed the sunset a handful of times," she forced herself to say under her sudden rush of attraction.

He broke from his intense glare and maintained a warm contact. "Perhaps it's because I may not live to see another."

She returned an amused smile and shifted nervously as the folk hero moved slowly to her position. His eyes did not waver from her.

"And though you may not live to see another day, you continue to be rude to people," she baited, as he walked up the steep grassy hill to reach her.

"I'm not rude, I just speak my heart's mind," he smiled as he finally made it to her ledge.

"So you say your heart's mind can't be rude?"

The warrior did not respond as he sighed, sat at her side and gazed out to the setting sun. The two leant their bodies together and shared the moment, absorbing the final moments of the sun's dying rays. The moment was long and comforting between them, so different in their personalities, so alike in their fiery thirst for battle, so attuned to their feelings towards one another.

"I feel that you've much burden on your mind. I've seen that from the beginning," he finally said as he turned to her.

She glanced at him and became suddenly aware their faces were only inches from each other. She did not recoil as she might have done in the past, rather kept her position and accepted the closeness. She could feel herself becoming familiar with a physical attraction.

"Yes. You probably heard Prince Talatama speak of my treachery in the past. He speaks of my brother Kamohoali'i and my allegiance with him and the Pulotulahi."

"Mmm."

"It is not that which troubles me."

"Then what troubles you Pele?" he called her by name for the first time.

"I have consorted and befriended the enemy of the Pulotulahi – Prince Talatama and his companions."

"And so?"

"They are the nemesis of the Pulotulahi."

"And you just said that you have abandoned them. So they are enemies no longer."

"It's – it's – I find myself – enjoying the company of the enemy," she paused. "And I feel torn because it feels very wrong to me, despite what happened between me and my brother."

The warrior engulfed her with his eyes and placed his hand onto hers. He smiled again with an irrepressible wave of wisdom and amiability.

"Throughout all my years, I have always watched the ebb and flow of the hearts and minds of men. I have seen such betrayals and tragedies like you cannot possibly believe, witnessed the most miraculous sacrifices and acts of love like you cannot possibly imagine. Yet the one thing that fills me with the greatest sadness, are those who do not follow their hearts."

Pele sat silently, concentrating on his words.

"Because it's the following of the heart that leads to truth, be it for good or for evil." He smiled and searched her eyes. "So I see that by following your heart, you've found the goodness that lay beneath the weight of evil that has lingered all your life."

The she-warrior looked down to the ground slowly as she pondered his words. He then placed his hand on her shoulder and stroked her arm.

"And when following your heart leads you to places that feel unfamiliar, have the strength of mind and spirit to accept the unfamiliarity."

She looked up and met his gaze, filled with a kind and content expression. He knew his words had rung true.

"And what if my heart leads me to places beyond my control?" She edged closer to him.

"Then you must trust your heart has made the right decision."

Pele moved towards the warrior slowly. The last rays of sunlight vanished between their lips softly touching together. An instant cloak of loving desire swept over them as they kissed and embraced passionately. The bed of grass was yielding as they rolled onto each other, and as he pinned her down with his powerful arms he stared into her eyes, fierce with passion. His head shot forward and their mouths joined quickly. Their tongues danced together as their heads fell to the side. With a yank, she buckled his arms and mounted him. She grinded her hips against his groin and he felt the very depths of her being. As she arched her back, he sat up and embraced her, their lips coming together again. He squeezed their naked bodies together so hard they were as one.

CHAPTER 34

From the edge of the forest watched a pair of jade eyes, peering onto the ledge where Pele and Maui Atalaga lay. Over many years in the occupation as an assassin, Mahina had naturally developed the skill to locate people quite easily; it was an instinctive gift, an inner compass that guided her to the person she held in mind. Her targets, laying together on the seaward ledge and oblivious to her presence, were an easy find. She sat crouched in a thicket of mulberry bushes and leaned her weight against the trunk of the largest shrub.

For a brief moment, as she watched the two lovers caress one another, her mind drifted to Talatama and her stirring feelings towards him. The thought of his strong hands grasping her body, the firm vice of his embrace and the determination in his eyes as he stared into hers, came suddenly to her. Despite where her mind was, her gaze could not be broken from Pele and Maui Atalaga making love amid the fading sunset. Her mind went further and her own hand wandered. She bit her lip as it did. Abruptly, as one receives a physical blow on the head, Vaohoi's voice knocked her from her fantasy.

"Mahina!" the youngster shouted from afar.

She almost slipped from her position as she spun and saw Vaohoi making his way through the forest towards her. She glanced back to Pele and Maui Atalaga who had also heard the shouts and stared in her direction. She felt flushed and hot beneath her skin and caught herself breathing heavily as if she had been holding her breath for the past few minutes. Composing herself, she negotiated her way out of the thicket.

"Mahina! Where are y—" Vaohoi saw the assassin finally appear. "Oh, there you are."

"I'm here, boy," she said angrily. "Why are you making that racket?"

"What's wrong with you?" He looked perplexed. "We're looking for someone, not hiding!"

His logical words suddenly doused the fire from her.

"Where is the sea?" He ignored her reaction and looked about in despair, "It's got to be around here somewhere!"

"Just beyond the tree line there," she pointed.

"Did you see anything?" he sighed and wiped the perspiration from his brow. He threw himself onto the ground and hung his head.

She did not answer.

"The sun has set. We're never going to find her now," he said in dismay. "I'm going to let Lo'au down."

"Don't worry, I'm sure she'll turn up," she smiled and patted him on the shoulder.

"Hey, what's going on over there?" came a strong voice from the seaward direction.

Pele thrashed through the bushes to glare at the both of them. She too, looked hot and flushed, though no thanks to a foul mood.

"Well? Speak up!" She glowered at the both of them.

"We came looking for you, you hot-tempered grouch," Vaohoi returned.

"Wait till I meet your father you little upstart. I'll crack his skull for raising such a cheeky little bastard," Pele lashed.

"Okay that's enough," Mahina interjected. "Yes we came looking for you. Prince Talatama is directing that we all be present during the feast tonight on Maka Vela. They hold a gathering in our honour."

Pele stood silent for a moment, then slung her bow across her back and tucked her obsidian axe into her girdle.

"Fine. Let's get going then," she stormed through the bush towards Vai Lahi.

Mahina did not hide the surprise from her face when she looked at Vaohoi, but the youngster retained his own frustration. He jumped to his feet and followed the great warrior in a huff, as the assassin paused and smiled to herself. Her witness to Pele and Maui Atalaga would remain a secret. She turned and followed her two companions through the forest of twilight.

The torches that were posted on the sides of the paths on Maka Vela illuminated them like a fiery serpent, coiled around the whole island. The township was even more enchanting at night: a fastidious eye for detail in the garden arrangements and land design was even more prominent in the warm firelight. As a sign of respect to the visiting prince, the entire island had posted decorative torches of quaint motifs atop selected positions. The illumination bequeathed a great sense of peace and harmony.

Mahina slowed her pace once she began to make her way through the township. Even Pele slowed and occasionally looked about at the wonderful designs. Vaohoi's boyish face beamed.

"It's beautiful!" he exclaimed.

"Yes it is." Mahina's eye caught the fancy of a particular arrangement, then another. "It's like walking through a pathway in the stars."

The Noble House on the summit of Maka Vela was illuminated by bonfires along each side. Its surrounding fales were equally lit with complementing purpose and illustrated the greater design of the structures. In the grand courtyard, a great many tapa cloths were carefully laid out on the grass in an oval shaped arrangement. In the centre of the oval, was a single line of the most decadent of foods available; a dozen succulent roasted pigs, countless boiled and braised lobster and crab, mountains of steaming sweet potato and taro, an abundance of stone-grilled fish, a forest of fruits that bore the colours of the rainbow and much more. It truly was a kingly feast.

At the head of the oval, upon the most decorative of the tapa designs, sat Prince Talatama and Niuafo'ou Noble Papani'ai tau and the rest of the companions. With Papani'ai tau sat High Chief Sia, High Priest Lafa and General of Niuafo'ou's army, Mata 'Ita. Completing the circle of dignitaries was a combination of high ranking soldiers, priests from various creeds, honoured artisans and luminaries from visiting islands. In the centre and around the display of the banquet were two dozen beautiful to'a's who politely served portions from every selection of food.

"Ho! O Great Prince, O Great Noble, I wish to speak," Mata 'Ita straightened his back and raised a cup of kava.

Chatter and conversation ceased at the general's introduction. Everyone collected their cups and raised them with both hands.

"I, General Maka 'Ita, on behalf of our great Noble Papani'ai tau and the good folk of Niuafo'ou, wish to extend a deeply respectful and honoured welcome to our Prince of Warriors and the Great Empire: Prince Talatama."

"Hear, hear!" Papani'ai tau added.

"I also wish to extend a warm welcome to his companions. You all honour us with your presence. May the good light of mighty Tangaloa shine upon you always – thank you greatly!"

"Thank you greatly!" everyone cheered.

Upon lowering of the cups, a band of musicians who were set in front of Talatama and Papani'ai tau began to play a score of rhythmic melody. Seated at the foot of the musicians were a dozen men who chorused a mighty song and clapped their hands. During the music Talatama caught the gaze of Mahina and motioned to her. His chestnut eyes burned deep into her soul and she suddenly felt herself blush. She carefully knelt down behind the prince, her face close to his.

"Mahina, what did you see down by the sea? Did you see any ships? What was Pele doing?" his questions were quick and abrupt.

"N-nothing, Prince Talatama," her heart sank. "I saw no tongiaki save Maui Atalaga's. They were both in conversation by the sea. Nothing more."

"Mmm, thank you."

For a fleeting moment she entertained the thought that perhaps, just perhaps, he had wished to unburden his caged love, his longing and desire for her. She lowered her head in disappointment and returned to her seat. The clamour of conversation rose as the banquet commenced in a buzz of grand company, delectable food and jovial song.

Hours later the feast had dwindled and many continued to chew on morsels, pick at fruit or commence heavy drinking of kava. Song had been replaced with enthusiastic dance routines of dazzling entertainment. Dignitaries began to relax and converse in deeper conversations and the companions debated subjects together, laughed and enjoyed the luxuries of being honoured guests. Atiogie still ate with an infinite appetite, while Vaohoi lay on his back having almost gorged himself to illness. Lo'au smiled and chatted in conversation with Talatama and Papani'ai tau and, despite her earlier mood, Pele sat together with Mahina and laughed about some of the greatest loves they had had.

Emori and Adi sat side by side solemnly and irregularly looked about to others. Adi had hardly eaten throughout the night and had begun to nibble at a slice of watermelon. Emori had eaten little also and declined to partake in any conversation. He stared at the ground in front of him and occasionally sighed deeply. Suddenly, Adi threw her watermelon down, bowed towards Talatama and Papani'ai tau and left the banquet area. So deep in laughter and conversation, none of the companions noticed her departure. Emori watched her leave, and following a long pause, pursued her.

He found her standing alone in a small, adjoining courtyard and walked to her gradually, allowing her to notice his approach. Though she did, she ignored it.

"My love," he said delicately in their language.

The Fijian priestess did not answer.

"Adi, my love. Please —"

She turned towards him and then lowered her eyes to the ground.

"I love you, Emori," she started, "and the quirk of fate that has brought us together after all these years has been long awaited."

"Yes, my love."

"But I can't ignore the faith that rules my soul," she whispered.

"Adi, you know what I say is true," he began. "This conflict is an imperial crisis. Even you cannot deny that."

"I know."

"Then let us leave this struggle for power to the Tongans and the Empire. It is too dangerous to go on with Talatama and the others," the warrior priest pursued, "I almost lost you in Niuatoputapu."

She remained silent. He sighed and paced about, frustrated with the ironic situation.

"After all these years of being separated, we are finally together and in a position to steal our love away and start a new life as one. And yet now we have it, you hesitate for the sake of strangers!"

"They are strangers no longer, Emori." She finally turned and engaged him with a glare. "And I do not flee across the sea, back to Fiji for the sake of fearing our future. I stay with Talatama and his companions because they fight for that which is right."

"But your post, your commission to Niuatoputapu – that is lost now. The island has been sacked. You cannot complete your destiny there, and that is why we should return home."

"You are wrong," she continued. "There is a greater purpose for my destiny. Perhaps it is not a physical location, but the journey itself that leads to my enlightenment and fulfilment. And what I feel now is to continue my journey with Talatama and Lo'au. I feel that my destiny is intertwined with what happened in Niuatoputapu and what brought us all together."

"But—"

"No, Emori. I have made my decision. I love you but I cannot ignore my faith and where my faith leads me. I'd hoped you of all people would understand that."

"I – I have never had much in life. My duty and commitment to the code was what forged my spirit in the absence of family, honour or prestige," the Fijian warrior raised his head and looked at the stars above, then lowered it to the ground, "But then you came into my life and gave me purpose. I have never known a love like ours. I can truly say that what we have is ours and no one can take that away. But I understand; now that I have the chance to take you away and keep you for my own, I have lost sight of what *you* want."

The Fijian priestess placed her hand into his and peered into his eyes.

"And what I want is to be with you, my love. To live my life with you and to one day... one day be married in a union of eternity," she paused. "But please, I need you to follow me that much further before we do."

The Fijian warrior inhaled deeply and regarded Adi with a resolute reflection.

"Then, I take my new charge. The greatest of all charges a warrior priest can have: the duty of protecting the one priestess he loves unconditionally," he took to a knee and kissed her hand.

"My love, I will follow you into the far depths of hell to protect you if I must. Until that day we can be together as one, I will not fail you in this duty."

A single tear trickled down the priestess's face as she looked down at her man and embraced him.

CHAPTER 35

There was nothing at first. Nothingness that stretched out and encompassed all that was. It was murk that held no colour, no shape and no form. Silence prevailed, a silence that was stifling and enclosed like that of suffocation. Yet there was peace. As morbid as the reality was, there was an emptiness of emotion and worldly fears. On occasion, there were slight movements in the murk, and the confinement of sound began to open.

The murk began to take colour, albeit a dark and troubled grey. It started to show signs of slow movements in its womb, twists and swirls. Uncertain shapes began to form amid the movements like silhouettes in shadows, bulbous and phantom like. The asphyxiating absence of sound was gone and, in its place, had come the unyielding sense of exposure. Scant murmurs of wind crept through the murk.

In what was perceived as moments across lifetimes did the murk reveal an approaching mist. The creeping fog was a dull and dark blue, yet struck a significant contrast against the grey murk. With the mist came the increasing sound of the wind and the echoing of mind-numbing hollow. The blue fog then encapsulated all that was, and the murk was but a foreground to its presence.

The deliberate mist began to swirl chaotically within itself. It flowed here and there, as though bearing a will of its own. Despite the sounds of eerie hollow, the foggy movements were not affected by the resonance of churning wind. Suddenly the blue tentacles of mist slowed their movements. A form swirled in the centre of all that was. The form melted from the murk as a darker shade, like the heart of a storm cloud. It took shape. The subjected mist swirled around it and sustained its presence. The shape became more clearly defined. The shape formed into that of a woman.

Her naked body was slender, with smooth dark skin. Her hair was long and her face was beautiful, but haunted. She appeared to be suspended in the air and supported by the swirling mist. No sounds were made with her entrance. She rolled her head back and extended her arms as if to caress the power she possessed. Arms spread to the sides, her legs together and feet overlapping, she resembled the position of surrender and sacrifice.

Slowly, she began to float forwards. The mist began to double in density and its energy seemed to personify. The darkness amid the blues and greys quickened. The subtle sounds of the wind began to rise. The woman who remained in the transposed position came closer. Her definition became larger. Scurried whispers in the wind could be heard in the rising sounds. Haunting echoes reverberated across the scene. Closer still she came. Closer until her very body was all that could be seen, then her unseen face looking skyward.

Chillingly, her head snapped forward with a jolt. Her eyes had been torn from the sockets and from her mouth spewed forth black mud. A word came from her charred lips.

"Kamohoali'i ..."

General Kamohoali'i shot up with a start and reached for his club. His chest heaved up and down, perspiration weeping from his forehead. He looked about the dark and empty room where he slept. The whisper of the gentle breeze could he heard outside, the sway of the palms in the midnight air. The striking dream seemed to fade away as reality set in, though it was not the first time he had experienced the same unnatural nightmare. He slowly caught his breath and sat up straight. He wiped his brow with his forearm, and after a short moment of deliberation, wrapped a single sheet of tapa around his naked waist and approached the exit.

An hour later, dawn arrived. The morning sun tried desperately to permeate the shapes of great cumulous clouds that sat lazily on the horizon. The clouds were thick and dark, carrying within their bowels the hint of thunder and rain. The beach was slightly wet from the morning dew as Kamohoali'i waded from waist-deep water to the shallow shore, lathering his head and face with seawater. On the shore gathered his remaining commanders: Havea, Ganilau and Siateki. Havea and Siateki de-robed and walked into the sea towards their general, however Ganilau, cursed by leprosy, used a canoe to paddle where Kamohoali'i had swum.

All four of the Pulotulahi ventured far from the beach in waters below eight feet. All that could be seen were their heads above the water, facing each other and Ganilau standing on the canoe. Occasionally, the sun poked through the clouds and illuminated the sea around them like silver on a starlit surface.

"Council of the Sea," Siateki said.

"Indeed, Fallen One," General Kamohoali'i returned. "There's growing suspicion among the people about our new found freedom. No place is safe to discuss matters but by Council of the Sea."

It was known among people of the Empire, that in times of war and strife, councils were vulnerable to prying ears of spies and assassins. A practical method of eliminating that threat was to wade out into the open sea and conduct the council, whereby no approach could go unnoticed and privacy was guaranteed.

"Men, I have news," Kamohoali'i started. "My meeting with the Dark Lord last night bore us great favour."

Ganilau and Siateki smiled in acknowledgement.

"He is happy with our progress and impressed by our victory."

"Hear, hear!" the commanders sounded.

"But it is time to move forward. There is still much to do."

"Is the Dark Lord still here, General? Will he stay and oversee our next move?" Siateki enquired.

"He departed just before dawn to prepare for our successes in the next few weeks. So with this in mind we cannot fail." He paused. "Before I go further, I had a vision from Mo'unga in the early hours of this morning. Her message changes the plans I had for the next few weeks."

"They are in need of aid," Ganilau guessed.

"They are. They've tracked Talatama and his companions to Niuafo'ou."

"A natural fortress," Havea growled.

"Correct. And though they haven't been spotted yet, they have little hope of breaching the outer rim. Even if they do, they don't have then men to assault a fortification like Maka Vela."

"What do we do then?" Siateki asked. "Take the Samoan army there and besiege them?"

"I'll go to Niuafo'ou and attack the island," Havea snarled. "They won't be able to stop me."

"No. Following today, all our commanders will be well spread across the Inner Empire. I need you by my side more than ever," Kamohoali'i turned to Ganilau. "You too."

"Then I shall go," Siateki knew it was his calling.

"Yes, but not alone. I want you to meet with Prince Whatonga and convince him to go with you. Convince him to take his entire army there," he said. "Perhaps it is good timing. The Rarotongan Army is camped too close to Niuafo'ou, too close to the Va'iga and his men. We can't have them talking."

"Yes, Milord."

"Sail to Niuafo'ou and unite with the others. Once there, take charge of the forces. With the strength of Whatonga's army and the other commanders, you cannot fail."

"I will not, Milord."

"Remember this, Siateki, the Dark Lord specifically stated that Talatama's death was of utmost importance. When you have slain the prince, return with the men to this island. I have further tasks for you. Do you understand?"

"Yes, Milord."

"We will remain here to manipulate and gain further favour of Prince Talaiha'apepe," he turned to Havea and Ganilau, "We must do this with haste, while he remains here on the island."

"Ganilau, I want you to rally the common folk on the island and convince them to make me steward in the absence of a leader."

"Yes, General."

"Take the men loyal to our cause with you. Go to the people and show them great deeds of strength to inspire. Influence them so that their cheers of support find their way to the prince's ear."

"Havea, I want you to seek out those still devoted to the Empire and in mourning for Anga'uli. Find those who will not support us, those who will stand in our way of taking this island," the general grinned. "Then during the night, kill them."

"With pleasure."

"Siateki, leave this morning," Kamohoali'i began to stroke back to shore.

Siateki stood on a prominent rise on the volcanic island of Tafahi. The rocky ledge was blackened by lava that had spewed forth hundreds of years ago, now hidden under a green blanket of grass. Beyond him was Prince Whatonga, gazing upwards towards the mouth of the volcano. He stood solemnly, his long hair blowing in the wind, his mind deep in thought. He wore a grass skirt that covered his groin and exposed his fine and strong body.

Siateki noticed there was a large dais erected where the ledge met the side of the mountain. It was newly built and adorned with decorations of flowers, pearls, and a great amount of valuable tapa. However, it stood now charred and burnt. The flowers were grey and covered in ash and the tapa nothing more than layers of powder.

"The funeral pyre for my mother withstood the flames last night," Whatonga said dreamily.

"The pyre represents my mother as in life: strong, well built and decorated with the most beautiful of embellishments. Even in death, her spirit remains steadfast and unbroken.

"My father, Lord Toi, will return her ashes to Ngatangi'ia and plant them under a Heilala tree. There, my mother's spirit can bloom with the beauty of the Heilala flowers each spring, and be reborn again and again forevermore."

"I am sorry I missed your mourning," Siateki bowed his head.

"It was a private funeral. I would not have allowed you to be present." The prince shook from his vagueness.

He turned and approached Siateki, with eyes like burning flames and placed his hands on his hips.

"So, you say they need aid," he said.

"Yes. The island is well fortified."

"How do you know this?" He turned from Siateki and gazed out to the open ocean.

"One of our commanders has the ability to send word via dreams," Siateki stammered.

"The witch? Yes, I remember. She appeared possessed by spirits."

"Mo'unga has many gifts."

The prince stood for a short moment as if to ponder the words of the stranger.

"I agree to your plan. The desire for revenge burns my soul like a hot rock that I can't remove from my throat," he seethed in unrelenting rage.

"But know this, man of the Pulotulahi, if ambush awaits our arrival I will seek you out and give you a slow death."

"No ambush or betrayal, Prince Whatonga. We want Prince Talatama killed as much as you desire it in vengeance. Together we can achieve this."

"I'll tell my father to return to Ngatangi'ia without me and my men," he nodded.

"Come then, let us make preparations to leave."

He and Siateki bounded down from the rocky outcrop towards the beach far below.

CHAPTER 36

Dawn. The twenty war tongiakis sat floating together far out at sea, bound by rope and husk, side by side, front and back. Seen from above, the ships formed the shape of a large square. The Rarotongan men passed from one tongiaki to the other freely, amusing themselves with an assortment of games and interests to pass the time. On the centre tongiaki sat the war council, deep in conversation; Omani appeared oblivious to the task at hand and Mo'unga reflected nothing but the absence of reality. Amosa, the Rarotongan captain frowned and shook his head in disapproval, while Kupe appeared frustrated and his voice carried the edge of impatience.

"Are you sure?" Amosa pressed.

"Yes. It took an hour to find a landing. The entire island is guarded by impassable rocks and cliffs. It's virtually impossible to land tongiakis there," Kupe hissed.

"No beach at all? That's hard to believe," one of the Rarotongan lieutenants said.

The Weeping Assassin shot him a deadly look and turned to Amosa.

"Tell this idiot to leave this council before my impatience gets the best of me."

Amosa nodded and motioned for the man to leave.

"I'm not going to repeat myself any longer, is that understood?" He glared at all present.

"What's our plan then?" Omani asked.

"Hit them during the night. We'll have to hit them swiftly."
Amosa leant forward.

"The night could be an advantage..." Kupe murmured.

"We should wait for the others to arrive," Mo'unga's voice
echoed.

"What?" all said simultaneously.

"They'll be here tomorrow," she finished.

Two tears trickled from Kupe's blind eye, which was now
bloodshot. He had spoken to Mo'unga about holding off contacting
General Kamohoali'i. He had made it very clear: he was in charge
and all decisions were to be made by him alone. Her disregard was a
blatant show of insubordination and her request for assistance
would have showed Kamohoali'i that they had failed, failed with
him as the leader of the campaign.

Over all the long years as an assassin, he had mastered the art
of self control; it did not mean that dousing his flames of anger was
an easy matter, however, his wrath bubbled inside him like the
festering of a dormant volcano waiting to erupt. His control proved
greater, and his fury at Mo'unga subsided, suppressed, but never
forgotten. One day, he swore, he would return the mark of
underhanded infidelity.

"So - it would seem we have a few choices," Kupe started.
"Choices that will bid different outcomes."

His eyes shone with the energy of calculating evil and latent
aggression. He leaned forward and engaged the other commanders.

"Our numbers will account for nothing against such defences
and odds. But there is another way to win this battle," he sniggered.

"Come closer. I have a *new* plan ..."

Noon was swift and the sun was directly above. The day had
remained relatively cool with a consistent breeze, as the village on
Maka Vela was active, abundant with the daily chores of commoners
and chiefs alike. Within the Noble Compound, Talatama sat with the
companions in an audience with Papani'ai tau. They were discussing

leaving the next morning with a thousand Niuafo'ou warriors to return to Niuatoputapu and reclaim the island.

Suddenly, distant conch horns interrupted their discussions and within short moments, horns from within the compound blasted through the air. There were shouts and screams echoing from everywhere and everyone jumped to their feet and grasped their weapons.

"Horns of war," Papani'ai tau turned to Talatama.

The prince and the noble ran to the entrance and were met quickly by Mata Ita, who was out of breath.

"Milord – we are under attack."

"Bring me my weapons!" Papani'ai tau roared.

Prince Talatama raced to the companions and regarded them with a fierce passion.

"My friends – they have found us," he breathed. "Atiogie, Pele and Emori, come with me."

Mahina and Vaohoi anxiously stepped forward.

"No. The rest of you stay here. We can handle this - Lo'au, look after them."

"I will. The gods be with you." The old man nodded.

The four warriors sprinted across the courtyard and joined with Mata Ita, who led them up a wooden staircase that guided them to an observation platform that extended out into the open air. Papani'ai tau was already standing on the platform. His attendants adjusted his armour and adornments, before he excused himself quickly and disappeared in the direction of the staircase.

"Talatama, see here!" Papani'ai tau called to the Prince.

From the platform, built into the roof of the highest building in the Noble Compound, the warriors could see the entire island around them. Their observation extended down the main road of Maka Vela to the great lake Vai Lahi, and beyond to the high rimmed mountains that ringed the larger island of Niuafo'ou.

Papani'ai tau pointed towards the main harbour of Maka Vela and beyond it, Vai Lahi. A dozen tongiakis were already half way across the lake, brimming with Rarotongan warriors bellowing at the top of their voices. The ridgeline billowed smoke, which rose from the forest canopy.

"The outposts wouldn't have stood a chance," the noble cursed.

"There are only a dozen tongiakis there," Talatama pointed out.

"The rest of the army must be within the forests on the other side of Vai Lahi," he turned to the prince. "Attacking in broad daylight, they must have great numbers to assault Maka Vela!"

Talatama frowned and turned to his companions. Pele and Emori reflected no emotion whatsoever while Atiogie rolled his shoulders and cracked his neck from side to side. He patted his great club and grinned at Talatama.

"Well? What are we waiting for?" he laughed.

"Right, let's go." Talatama clenched his teeth.

"To the lake!" Papani'ai tau shouted.

The warriors could already see the main contingent of soldiers led by Mata Ita, swarming down the main road, past the formidable walls and towards the harbour. Papani'ai tau, and Talatama with his warriors, leaped down the stairs and towards the exit.

Amosa stood at the bow of the tongiaki ahead of the other sea crafts. He glared at the fast approaching shores of Maka Vela, the winds of war blowing his long hair and renewing his breath. He turned back to his loyal warriors and released a terrifying war cry, one that was returned by a deafening roar of two hundred voices. Next to him was Omani, the Unarmed Warrior who stood strangely calm, arms folded and squinting under the noon sun towards the scrambling warriors on shore.

"Men! Take heart and prove your bravery! We shall be the first to conquer the defences of Maka Vela!" he boomed.

Papani'ai tau and the companions, accompanied by fifty warriors sprinted through the township towards the gates of the village defences. The gates were locked tight with hundreds of men manning the walls of the great barricade. Once the noble warriors were close, Papani'ai tau screamed at the guards.

"Open the gates!"

With a loud groan, the heavy gates opened and the warriors rushed through to the other side. Talatama saw the harbour one hundred metres away, lined with Mata Ita's forces of about five hundred men. Beyond them approached a force of twelve tongiakis headed directly towards the shore. They were not supported by any further contingents.

The Niuafo'ou warriors parted their ranks as Talatama and his companions ran through the battle formation to reach Mata Ita at the forefront. Papani'ai tau faced the entire warrior contingent, a shortness of breath evident in his voice.

"My fellow warriors of our proud island Niuafo'ou. Forever have our ancestors guarded this island down through the ages! Forever have they defended it! Forever has it withstood the onslaught of countless attacks!" he roared with the infectious charisma of a warrior chief. "Now prove yourselves worthy of our ancestors! Prove that you have the strength of heart to continue our legacy! Show your Prince, who stands here with pride, your strength, courage and us! Fight for the Empire!"

Five hundred warriors, electrified with adrenalin and pride screamed out a thunderous war cry that echoed the rim of Vai Lahi and Niuafo'ou.

The Rarotongan tongiakis banked onto the muddy shores of Maka Vela and hundreds of blood-mad warriors poured over the edges to rush the Niuafo'ou legion. But the local warriors were masters in the art of defence. About seventy men at the forefront of the legion simultaneously pitched their spears at the oncoming warriors. At that range, almost every spear found its mark, impaling an equal number of Rarotongans. The spear throwers then stepped to the side, allowing the ferocious close quarter combat to begin.

With it came the shrilling cries of fury, the dying and of the victorious. The Rarotongans surged forward into the centre of the Niuafo'ou legion. However the legion seemed as immovable as a mountain, causing mounds of dead to form quickly and forcing the Rarotongans to fan out to the edges of the battle. A conch horn blasted from somewhere amid the war cries and the rear lines of the legion took two steps rearward. Every man in the rear lines then fit his short bows with arrows and angled his aim to the bulk of the Rarotongans. Swift twanging sounds snapped the air and a shower of arrows rained down upon the moving mass of warring men.

Talatama reefed the Peace Maker through the air rapidly, crushing the chest of an attacking warrior before turning towards his comrades.

"Move to the left!" he roared.

Atiogie and Pele nodded and followed him through the carnage before facing fresh warriors across the left wing. Talatama took down a warrior with every stroke, his weapon finding its mark with deadly accuracy. Here and there, his strikes shattered limbs and occasionally exploded skulls, while the mighty Samoan fought with renewed strength; such a marvel of strength it was to witness. With single swipes of his gigantic club, he would claim at least two victims, often lifting them from the very ground. Pele weaved through the chaos like an unstoppable phantom of death. Her obsidian axe glistened wet with blood as she seemed to pre-empt attack and to counter-attack simultaneously.

Amid the fray, Talatama realised Emori had not followed their lead from the centre of battle. He searched desperately for the Fijian warrior, to no avail.

CHAPTER 37

A young Niuafo'ouan boy, perhaps ten or eleven years old, crept through the light shrubbery towards the edge of the water. He pushed back the foliage and stared at the single tongiaki that had banked to the western edge of Maka Vela. As he approached, echoes of battle from the other side of the island resounded across the great lake. It caused him to shudder as though the battle were at his heels. Perhaps it a parent's admonishment that scared him more: he had ignored his mother's strict instruction to stay at home when the alarms called. But the tongiaki, which sat banked before him, was of puzzling interest.

From a distant path he had spotted the seemingly unmanned tongiaki float to the shore. He had made his way closer, in an effort to make out persons within it, but as he approached it was clearly abandoned. With a troubled look, he stepped into the shallow water and placed his hands on its sides. He lifted himself on his toes and peered into the empty hull.

As the boy shrugged and turned to walk away, the water beside the tongiaki swirled. From the unseen depths rose a water apparition, revealing itself with deathly conviction. The boy looked over his shoulder before being struck with an impact that crumbled the side of his head. A length of coral and urchin ricocheted off his skull and dropped into the water. Kupe waded forward, snatched the lifeless body with one hand and pitched it into the hull.

"The dead cannot warn the living..." he snarled.

Three Rarotongan warriors rose from the water and grinned with devilish approval. The Weeping Assassin coiled his weapon together and tucked an assortment of other tools into his girdle. Peering up at the elevated island, he and the three warriors sprinted from the shallow water and disappeared into the bush that concealed their incursion.

There was a monstrous spread of warriors lying lifeless between the grass of Maka Vela and the shallow water of Vai Lahi. As a result of the human mound, two separate infiltrations sparked to the left and right wings of the landing. Separated from the others, Emori had joined Papani'ai tau and Mata Ita, who fought valiantly against the leaders of the Rarotongan war party. But the strength of the enemy was in General Amosa. His bulbous club was a lethal extension of his fiery spirit, against which, no Niuafo'ou warrior could prevail; such was his indomitable determination.

Papani'ai tau stepped forward boldly. In his left hand, he gripped his lance and in his right, his paddle club. He was a dynamic sight, possessing a lethal combination of weapons; enemies at a pace could be speared and those who came close, fell victim to the blunt edge of his club.

"Come forward, brave warrior! You and I shall dance the way of death!" Papani'ai tau pointed his spear at Amosa.

"Accepted!" the general shouted, straightened his back and wiped the sweat from his brow.

Papani'ai tau poised, as the Rarotongan general lurched forward. He gleamed with the excitement that only warriors possess: the thrill of meeting a fate of either life or death in the next moment. His spear tip shot forwards and narrowly missed Amosa's chest. The general stepped to the side with incredible timing and speed, parried the attack, rotated and swung his club viciously. He ducked, allowing the weapon to glide over his head within a hair's breadth. He then launched himself up, and with all his might, rammed Amosa in the solar plexus with his shoulder.

The force sent the general landing on his back with a thud. With the wind knocked from him, Amosa still had the presence of mind to keep focus on his enemy. Papani'ai tau leapt in the air and came down with his spear arm cocked. Unable to breathe, Amosa summoned all his strength to shift his body from the path of his doom and the noble's lance impaled itself in the ground with a thump. The Rarotongan rolled to one knee, slowly found his feet and recovered the regularity of breath. Papani'ai tau, breathing heavily, corrected his footing from his awkward landing. They locked eyes momentarily, and shared a knowing that their skill and determination could well be matched.

Atop the observation platform, the rest of the companions looked on with anticipation. Lo'au appeared strong and confident, as he watched the battle from above. He gripped his staff and held it as if it bore the silent victory within it. Adi was clinging to the old mu'a's arm with anxious concern. From their distance, it was impossible to make out individual warriors amid the battle. The Fijian priestess gazed out aimlessly. She whispered a prayer to the Great Degei for mercy. Her decision the previous night to remain with the companions, weighed heavily on her mind, knowing it risked Emori's life.

However, Vaohoi and Mahina stood apart from the mu'a and priestess, feeling quite the contrary; the young man huffed and puffed in frustration. The Rarotongan assassin, reflecting similar frustration, preferred to look elsewhere than the conflict. The two companions, though not seasoned warriors, were irritated with the decision for them to be omitted from the fight. Little did they care the prince had done so for their protection: Vaohoi for his inexperience and Mahina for his secret affection for her. Vaohoi began to throw twigs off the platform in tedium. Finally, he looked at Mahina and the pair struck the same idea. They both beamed at each other in acknowledgement.

"Master, Master."

"Yes, Vaohoi," Lo'au answered without averting his gaze.

"Mahina and I – we're going to search for some food," the young man lied, "We'll be back soon."

"Don't go far. And don't be long," he frowned.

"Yes, Master."

He turned to Mahina with an enormous smile as both tiptoed across the platform then glided down the staircase. The pair swiftly returned to their abode and collected their weapons and items. They jumped from the entrance into the courtyard and began to sprint across the grassy area. Suddenly Vaohoi halted and grabbed Mahina's arm, pulling her to a stop.

"Wait! Wait! I forgot my dagger – wait here!" he panted and raced back to the fale.

"Hurry!" she replied nervously.

The beautiful assassin waited in the centre of the courtyard and adjusted her tools on her girdle. Tying a length of twine around her waist, she caught movement from the corner of her eye. Like a knife tracing up the spine, she knew something was wrong. A Rarotongan warrior leaped out into the courtyard, his fierce face leering with the want of murder. He raised his arm quickly to protect his face as the sharpened sea shell sunk into it. Mahina reached for another as she faced him with conviction.

But when she realised the man was a Rarotongan, the spark dimmed from her attack and she slowed in confusion. The warrior cursed as he ripped the shell from his bloodied arm and glared at her. She recognised him as a warrior in her brother's army.

"Mahina!" Vaohoi yelled.

Broken from her confusion, she saw Vaohoi run out of the fale towards her. Another Rarotongan warrior appeared, and with a hard punch to the youngster's face, swiftly knocked him unconscious.

"Guards!" Mahina screamed.

Again, her senses alerted her of imminent danger, but this time her enemy was too quick. Kupe glided across the courtyard behind her and by the time she turned to face him, his club bounced off her head with a pop. When she collapsed, Kupe motioned to the third Rarotongan warrior to collect her over his shoulder. Guards armed with bows appeared in the courtyard, as one of the Rarotongans shrieked and fell into the gardens with an arrow lodged in his chest. The other wounded enemy evaded the zipping of arrows, stumbling as he followed his comrade for an exit. The Weeping Assassin covered the escape and faced the amassing guards.

First, he reached behind his back and produced a thin, long reed. He crouched down and placed it to his mouth. With sharp breaths he fired poison-tipped darts at the grouped guards. In his crouched position he made for a small target. Arrows failed to mark as he rapidly discharged darts into open flesh. Here and there, guards fell before he swiftly tucked the reed away and rolled towards more appearing adversaries.

As Kupe leapt to his feet, his right hand reached into a pouch and swept it towards his enemies. From it sprayed a cloud of volcanic ash which blew straight into the guards' faces. Many clutched at their eyes and wailed, while others held their positions and tried to shield themselves from the haze. Given the distraction, Kupe unravelled his deadly weapon of coral and urchin with a smirk. It whirled and claimed defenceless victims. More followed. The rope pulled tight and the coral and urchin ripped through the throat of the last guard. He took a step back from the killing, and when he saw Lo'au and Adi appear with dozens of guards, he let out a cruel cackle and disappeared through the foliage.

Talatama and Atiogie found themselves fighting with the backs against each other again. Assaulted from all sides, the two warriors comfortably defeated the onslaught of Rarotongan warriors, while Pele, who preferred to fight alone, battled close by. Emori had finally caught up with the companions, lancing his foes with every lunge. Following a flow of failures, the remaining Rarotongans halted their attack and made way for a lone warrior, walking ankle deep in the water. Talatama and Atiogie stared at the warrior in disbelief, for he possessed no weapon.

"So, we meet at last, Prince Talatama?" Omani, the Unarmed Warrior goaded.

"You - you're no Rarotongan. You must be one of Kamohoali'i's cronies, bent on the promise of the Pulotulahi," Talatama spat.

Pele concluded her duel and joined the companions, "Omani, you arrogant bastard," she cursed.

"Pele, the betrayer and deceiver. I'll kill you and return your head to Kamohoali'i," he boldly approached the group.

"He's not even armed!" Atiogie laughed.

"I'll lance him." Emori gritted his teeth.

Pele eyed him carefully. "Be wary, he doesn't use weapons becau – "

Omani suddenly rushed at the companions and with astonishing speed leapt in the air towards Atiogie. He thundered down on the Samoan's chest with a kick that sent the heavy warrior crashing to his back. Landing with incredible finesse, he ducked a swipe from the Peace Maker and drove a fist into Talatama's kidney. The prince winced in pain and swept the weapon again. Omani evaded once more. His lightning fists struck the prince in the sternum, another arcing to the temple. A kick shot from nowhere, striking Talatama in the abdomen and sent him to the ground.

The Unarmed Warrior turned and continued executing startling kicks and strikes to oncoming Niuafo'ou warriors. Many of them were killed, others ended lame or unconscious. Pele lunged at the warrior rapidly, expecting her first attack to miss her target. Once it did, she then ripped through her second so he could not evade. Instead, his vice-like grip ensnared her arm and with a slight movement of his feet, he shifted and twisted her wrist. She flipped off her feet and crashed to the muddy earth, her braided hair exploding everywhere. Without hesitation, he leant down and attempted to punch her face. She turned her head, as his fist glanced off and ripped at her ear. With her innate fury, she collected both her feet on his chest and fired him into the air.

Papani'ai tau and Amosa faced each other desperately. Their breathing was haggard and their fierce intent sapped their energy.

The surrounding Niuafo'ou warriors grew impatient and broke into a cheer. Papani'ai tau was the first to attack. He shuffled forward jabbing his lance, which Amosa parried and countered with a deft back-hand blow, barely missing his jaw. Papani'ai tau's club weaved through the air and clipped Amosa's shoulder harmlessly, but it gave him time to line up a spear thrust. Amosa launched into another attack but could not move in time to avoid the spear. As the lance impaled him through the side, Papani'ai tau received a blow across the head. A sudden ringing and loss of sight consumed his head.

He stepped back and tried to shake off the effects. The feeling of warm blood ran down the side of his face as the image of Amosa blurred before him. The Rarotongan keeled over, nursing his stomach wound, unable to summon the strength to attack. The noble realised he was slipping into unconsciousness and had no choice but to launch again. Amosa too broke from the wounded reprieve and parried the predictable spear jabs, but missed a club strike that came down in an arc. The paddle club split the skin on Amosa's head with a crack before the spear penetrated his body again. Both combatants dropped their clubs and grabbed the spear with both hands. They glared hypnotically at each other in the last moments until finally Papani'ai tau, collapsed on his hands and knees, and Amosa, in death. Immediately, a roar of victory erupted from the Niuafo'ou warriors. The Rarotongans, devastated by the death of their general, looked about at one another, leaderless.

CHAPTER 38

Omani landed on his haunches in a cloud of dust. Using the momentum, he rolled backwards and flipped himself to his feet. He regarded Pele with annoyance then faced a new threat, as Emori rushed at him and lunged with his spear. He effortlessly evaded and spun around the length of the spear. His leg then stretched up and struck Emori across the head, sending the Fijian's world hurtling. Another kick and the spear shot from his hands. Emori did not see the last one that landed on his chest, flailing his arms as he flew backwards like a rag doll.

Pele, Atiogie and Talatama slowly found their feet. Suddenly a cheer erupted from the centre of battle a hundred metres away. Omani spotted Amosa dead at the feet of Papani'ai tau and his animation vanished. Strangely, he looked skyward towards the sun, back to the village of Maka Vela then back again.

"Back to the boats!" he shouted, "Retreat!"

A single conch blasted out from the tongiakis in repetitious resound. Its call signalled the immediate withdrawal of the enemy forces. The Rarotongans scrambled back into the shallow water and leapt onto their crafts as they fought. Many tried valiantly to drag their fallen comrades back to safety in the tongiakis. Omani faced the three companions with a defiant reflection before melting in with the fleeing enemies. Talatama frowned and looked over his shoulder up to the village. He had noticed Omani's strange reaction prior to his retreat.

"Come back and fight, you cowards!" Atiogie chased the warriors into the shallow water.

The prince squinted beyond the fleeing warriors to the far side of the lake. There were no supporting contingents, no further attacks or raids from their army. This battle was a palpable loss on their part from the beginning.

"Why the sacrifice to no end?" Talatama posed to himself. The prince deliberated, as the Niuafo'ou legion roared in victorious cheers and song. Papani'ai tau, blood-clad and staggering to the companions with Emori, reflected well earned jubilation. Pele stood at Talatama's side and remained silent, wiping the blood from her axe with a dirty rag.

"Something's amiss," Talatama murmured.

Suddenly it came to him. The colour in his face drained as Papani'ai tau reached out to embrace him, before sensing a wrongdoing.

"My Prince?"

"A diversion!" The prince spun towards the village.

As he did, the call of alarm conches could be heard from the village.

"What?" Atiogie shouted from afar.

"Oh no – Adi..." Emori shuddered.

"The battle here was a diversion! They've attacked the village!" The prince sprinted back towards the gates, Papani'ai tau, Emori and the comrades at his heels.

As the hundreds of warriors milled hastily back into the ramparts of the greater Maka Vela, Pele remained on the shores of its harbour. The scuttling Rarotongans had reached the other side of the great lake and were vanishing into the forest beyond. The warrior continued to polish her beautiful axe, surrounded by countless dead. For a moment, her forlorn figure that loomed over the fallen seemed surreal, like an immortal standing over the fragility of mortality.

Night came quickly. The village of Maka Vela illuminated itself typically with glorious torches of wondrous design. But there were no songs of victory, nor chants, or feasts of conquest or of the brave. The village shores and walls were tripled with soldiers and posted guards. The impact of the enemy's deception caused them to over compensate security, making the island an even greater fortress. The companions and noble deputation congregated in the great hall. There was no kava in the centre of the circle. No food and no drink was offered.

A call from a senior soldier resounded through the halls of the house and was followed by the shuffling of feet across the wooden floors. The leaders in the circle turned and watched three soldiers enter the large hall.

"Milords, an emissary under a banner of truce," the senior stated, "wishes an audience to bear word from his masters."

"Let him in," Talatama said quickly.

A scrawny Rarotongan warrior carrying the recent wounds of battle knelt before them. He bore a respectful disposition, notwithstanding his demands.

"Milords, my leader brings word from our mooring at sea," he paused, "and an ultimatum."

"Out with it, cur!" Papani'ai tau snapped.

"You are to sail out at first light. Sail east until you come to our moorings. You are to come out in one tongiaki; one tongiaki alone." The man swallowed. "We will exchange the life of Mahina for the life of Talatama."

"There is no bargain to be had there, Rarotongan! The life of a prince is not worth the life of a foreign woman!" Papani'ai tau barked, finding support in other members in the circle.

"Continue," Talatama ushered.

"Prince Talatama, you are to be accompanied by one other and no one else is to be on board. If you do not come after first light, she dies. If we see signs of an ambush, we'll make her suffer before her death," the Rarotongan warrior paused. "We know her value, good Prince -"

"What nonsense," Papani'ai tau and the others spoke in unison. "Guards! Take this lying scum out the back and take his life."

"No!" Talatama got to his feet quickly. "Lead him to the shores of the island. See to it he returns safely."

No one argued with the prince. The soldiers bowed and swiftly escorted the emissary from the hall, and once gone, words of bitterness erupted from everyone in the hall.

"Enough!" Talatama voice raised the roof. "I've heard enough – everyone get out except for my companions, Papani'ai tau and Mata Ita."

He stared at the solid beams that supported the great hall, followed them up to the high ceiling where the framework arched and met the thatched roofing. Though he looked at it, his mind was elsewhere. He sighed and placed his hands on his hips, as if he was waiting for the answers to come from the fale itself. He then returned to reality and sought counsel from his companions, regarding them slowly, one after the other. The loyalty in their eyes was clear and they awaited his leadership. His words came to them as equal comrades.

"You all know my mind – I'll not leave her to die," he paused. "I will save her and risk my life trying."

The warriors lowered their heads. Adi knew Talatama's words belied his conviction. She nodded and with a single look she shared her understanding with the others.

"I say again as I did many nights ago, my actions are my own. Do not feel compelled to follow me into what may be my last fight," he said.

"I laugh in the face of death," Atiogie scoffed.

"Death is but the beginning," Lo'au's voice echoed.

The prince broke a warm smile, the fragility of his spiralling emotions showed.

"You've all become... good friends."

Pele raised her head and looked away, finding it difficult to hear his sentiments, perhaps in fear of what she yearned. The others knew what it meant for Talatama: divulging and sharing his feelings revealed his trust and closeness to the group. This was unprecedented from a crown prince to friends of but a few days. Strangers they were no longer.

"I must admit parting company now would be -" he paused, "welcome if it gave me peace from Atiogie's snoring at night."

They all burst into a friendly laughter, the comment breaking the tension and seriousness of the crossroads they had reached. Atiogie shook his head and giggled like a boy.

"Or the constant chatter from Vaohoi or the dry prophecy from Lo'au ..."

"Hear, hear!" the Samoan laughed.

The prince allowed the jovial moment to pass before he returned to their reality once more. "My friends - make no mistake," his steely gaze penetrated them all. "I *will* save Mahina."

"I'm with you, my Prince. She's one of us, she's a companion of ours," the Fijian priestess leaned forward pleadingly. "There's no hesitation in my mind."

"I go with Adi," Emori said quickly.

"As long as there's more fighting," the giant Samoan added.

"Let's get those bastards. Kill as many as we can as we steal her back," Vaohoi growled, his black and bruised eye lending his words weight.

"She still holds a valued destiny with us, Prince Talatama." Lo'au nodded. "But I warn you - you risk altering your own."

"My destiny is here and now," he returned.

"No it is not." Lo'au became stern. "Your destiny lies in the hearts and minds of others in your future. There is more at stake than you know. Don't throw that away for reckless notions..."

"If my destiny lies with what I know is righteous then I cannot fail."

The others were taken aback by the old man's change of heart. For unknown reasons he had become indifferent, being the first time he had openly disputed Talatama's decisions.

"I disagree with your actions, Prince Talatama, but I will not stop you," he sighed.

"It will be a hard fight," Pele interjected.

"My plan is to ambush them of course, steal her away unharmed and escape capture," Talatama said.

"Easier said than done. One tongiaki, no aid from Papani'ai tau or the Niuafo'ou army," Pele continued.

"I know. The fight will be difficult. Outnumbered and fighting on sea craft will be testing."

"We will need the help of Maui Atalaga," Pele added. "We can't do this without him."

The prince glanced at her and despite his inner suspicions; he knew her words were true. He turned to Lo'au, who nodded in agreement.

"I have a plan. Come, let us make preparations – we leave at first light."

The companions concurred and departed the hall as Talatama signalled for Papani'ai tau and Mata Ita to come forward.

"We're going ahead," he said.

"But my Prince, you can't seriously entertain the thought of giving yourself up or risking your own life," the noble exclaimed. "You'll be killed. That's a certainty."

"Today our enemies taught us a lesson about diversions. We will see if they live up to their own methods."

Mahina began to open her eyes groggily. Her vision was smoky and weary. The rocking, she realised, was not from the blow to her head but the sea. Familiar tongues harped around her, native to her homeland Rarotonga; sharp voices filled with aggression, uncertainty and frustration. She could smell the abundance of many men, the scent of tea tree oil on festering wounds and, above all, the stench of death. Then came a voice that haunted her nightmares, an unforgettable hiss that shattered her very consciousness.

"Be quiet! She is waking."

The Rarotongans hushed and leered down at her in the hull of the tongiaki. She shook the unconsciousness from her vision and wobbled to her feet, to face the dozens of men. She recognised the Rarotongan craft she was aboard and that she was surrounded by her countrymen. Suddenly there was an immense wave of relief. But in the centre of them was the man she had hunted for years. The Weeping Assassin glared at her in the torchlight, his old white eye weeping a single tear that shimmered down his face.

"Princess Mahina. You wake," he hissed.

"What's this? What's this madness?" she glared at her Rarotongan warriors. "Why are you in the company of this man?"

"They are here to avenge the death of Lady Rongaueroa" Kupe said.

"What?" Tears began to well. "Then why –"

"You are responsible for her death, Mahina. You shame yourself beyond words," Kupe continued.

"No! He is the –"

The assassin's backhand swiped across her face with a smack, knocking her to the floor of the hull.

"How dare you! These men here, your countrymen, know the truth, Mahina! You stole your love away with Prince Talatama! You betrayed your mother to escape capture with him in Niuatoputapu!"

"No," she whimpered in the darkness.

"You whore!" shouted the Rarotongan warriors as they spat at her. "You dirty whore!"

"Your mother was then killed because of your selfishness, your wickedness, your betrayal!" Kupe was now shouting.

"You lying bastard!" she leapt towards him in a fit of desperation.

This time, one of the Rarotongan warriors struck her from the side, then another, until she collapsed into the hull again in trembling silence.

"Enough! She can wait until the morning," Kupe lowered the aggression. "Bind her hands and feet – and gag her."

The Weeping Assassin sat on the centre platform with Omani and Mo'unga, as torchlight illuminated their faces with a fitting, sinister reflection. With them sat Ruakere, the Rarotongan lieutenant, placed in charge by the loss of General Amosa. He was a more scheming and calculating warrior than his predecessor, quickly agreeing with the ways of the Weeping Assassin.

"They will come for her," Kupe said as he sat down.

"Will they?" the Unarmed Warrior doubted.

"Yes – the prince's love for her is too great. He is a chivalrous man with much pride," he remarked.

"So we can prepare for another battle tomorrow," Ruakere pointed out.

"Maybe. Maybe not. He could prepare a trap for us," Omani pondered.

"Either way, he makes fallible plans should he attempt to rescue her. Remember, our goal for tomorrow is to kill them both. Our guise of exchange is simply to lure the fool to us – close enough to kill. If he boards our tongiaki, the easier it will be," Kupe grinned.

"You have set this up well, Kupe. You've turned the calamity of this situation into a possible victory. Lord Kamohoali'i will be pleased," Omani praised the old assassin.

"Talatama is your business. I want to kill Mahina myself," Ruakere growled.

"Beware the cunning of the prince. His passion will over rule our plans," Mo'unga whispered.

The warriors gave the woman an uncomfortable glare. The Weeping Assassin regarded her with an unwelcoming scowl.

CHAPTER 39

An hour before dawn, there was a chill in the air. A grey sky lay on the eastern horizon, hiding the faint stars in the dawning heavens. But as the warmth of the sun's rays foretold their coming, the morning was far from calm. An unforseen southern wind had picked up. It swayed the great palms of Niuafo'ou and chopped the sea's surface into messy whitewash. It matured into a gale and it obscured the island's appearance. Here and there, dark forms of grey twisted and grew within the irrepressible clouds that stretched across the sky.

The positions of the Rarotongan tongiakis became precarious. The lines of rope that bound them together groaned under the stress of natural heaving, as the sea swelled rapidly. A tense yawning apart would then follow with a crash as they came together again. Ruakere's voice shrieked over the howling wind.

"Bind those ropes! Tighten the knots! I want all tongiakis to float as one!"

Just as the men scurried about the tongiakis to prevent disaster, a swift, cold shower struck the sea. The rain whipped around in the direction of the wind, pelting men in the faces as they tried to fasten the twine and bindings. Another loud crashing of vessels came together and cracking wood suddenly caused a mast to topple and smash the centre platform of a tongiaki.

"Get those ropes bound now or I shall throw you all overboard!" Ruakere roared in the whistling wind and rain.

"Damned weather," Kupe swore as he stood quietly on the centre platform with the Unarmed Warrior.

"Omani, keep your eye out for an approaching vessel," he ordered, as he left the platform to seek Mahina.

It was not long before the weather conditions became worse. From their position, the haze had totally cloaked the distant island of Niuafo'ou. Despite the grey curtains of rain obscuring the direction of their threat, Omani stood focused and resolute. Judging by the dim light, he estimated it was an hour beyond dawn and wondered if they should give the prince more time on account of the unexpected weather. Mo'unga appeared next to him and gazed out to the howling brine.

Kupe reappeared on the platform with Mahina from below deck. The princess was emotionally broken – defiled. She walked unsteady on the wet and slippery platform, with her hands still bound. Omani peered back to the Weeping Assassin and knew what he had done. He snorted and resumed his watch, as Ruakere jumped onto the platform and shielded his eyes from the rain. He looked doubtfully at Kupe.

"He won't come," he said. "We should kill her now."

"There!" Omani yelled and pointed out into the haze.

From within the heart of rain and sea appeared the shadow of a war tongiaki. It lurched up and down with the surges but held its course towards the Rarotongan fleet. The craft was alone in the gale and seemed to carry only two figures. The two men could be seen clambering about, trying valiantly to control the thrashing masts under the windstorm. As they approached, the Rarotongan warriors could not guess the design of the tongiaki. It was not an imperial vessel.

"See? I knew he'd come," Kupe shouted over the wailing wind. "Prepare the starboard side. Prepare to moor with the craft!"

Mahina squinted under the wailing rain towards the approaching tongiaki and bit her lower lip, praying for her saviour. She closed her eyes and imagined Talatama before her, and stealing her away from this nightmare. She fell to her knees with a thump, her head striking the deck hard. But the hurt was insignificant against her want for his embrace. As the rain dripped down her face, she whispered his name.

Rarotongan warriors cursed and scrambled about the decks, preparing to secure the approaching craft, and as they did the enemy tongiaki turned its position and ceased its advancement. The two men had suddenly halted the tongiaki's course and their sails were fixed to the craft.

Kupe, Omani, Mo'unga and Ruakere leaned forwards and peered out to the two men. They all recognised Prince Talatama standing next to the mast. The rain glistened off his muscular brown skin as he glared back. To his right was another man, at the helm, but whom the warriors did not recognise.

"I see you've kept to the bargain, Prince Talatama!" Kupe yelled.

"I have, you spineless cowards!" the prince returned. "Stealing a woman to extort, instead of fighting like warriors. You have no shame!"

"Your words hold no weight, 'Prince of Thieves'! You're not one to lecture on stealing!" Kupe turned to Ruakere with a grin.

"My words and purpose shall be judged soon, cur! But before I do that, do me the honour of your name!"

"I am Kupe! Remember it well, Prince, for when you go to the underworld you can join the countless dead I've sent there!"

"So, you are the old deserter. I know your past. It is stained with dishonour and shame beyond forgiveness! It's no wonder you've duped to kidnapping innocent women and murdering for the Pulotulahi!"

"Shut your mouth, insolent whelp! You know nothing of my history that transpired with your father!"

"Some say you returned to Aotearoa under a second campaign!" Talatama continued, "What lies! You stole away the great Matahourua, killed Harapua and stole his wife!"

Kupe began to slowly reach for his blow darts, his face contorting in a reflection of uncontrollable fury. Omani touched him on the arm.

"Not yet. We have to get him closer."

He struggled to curb his fury and swallowed before he spoke again, choosing his words carefully.

"The past is the past, *Prince*! We are here and now!" He cleared his throat. "Moor your craft against ours and your woman can go free!"

"It will be done!" Talatama agreed, before turning to Maui Atalaga. Despite the hero's face being pelted with the wind and rain, he gave it no heed. He scowled as though immune to the weather and regarded the prince with indifference.

"If you fail, I will not come back for you," he said.

Talatama nodded and peered over his shoulder to the hull of the far side. He saw Vaohoi covertly slipping back on board from the sea, breathing heavily. They exchanged a silent confirmation and the muscles in Talatama's jaw eased. *Good boy*, he thought. Vaohoi drew a dry tapa blanket around himself under the shelter of the hull roof, where all of the companions lay hidden.

"Take us to the tongiakis," Talatama shouted to Maui Atalaga.

The hero unveiled the great masts on the tongiaki and the craft lurched forward. The hundreds of enemies edged closer to the hull, eyeing Talatama as if he were an imminent feast bearing down upon starving men. The Weeping Assassin hauled Mahina to her feet and looked about to his men.

"Be ready!" he said excitedly. "Watch for enemies from the hull!"

There was no sound but the irrepressible howling wind and whipping of the rain, the creaking of the tongiaki's wet wooden frames, the slapping of waves against the hulls of the crafts and the distant clap of thunder. All men squinted against the whipping rain as Maui Atalaga's vessel came within metres of the enemy craft, close enough for Kupe to see the glare in Talatama's eyes.

"Get her ready!" the prince directed. "When I step aboard, you must release her onto my vessel!"

"Agreed!" Kupe roared devilishly.

Talatama nodded, then motioned for Maui Atalaga to moor the tongiaki against the enemy vessels. It then grew closer still, within jumping range.

"Bring her to the edge!" Talatama yelled as he stepped precariously to the side.

Kupe did as commanded and led Mahina next to the warriors on the hull.

"Come to me, Prince Talatama. Let me shut your eyes forever," Kupe whispered.

Suddenly the tongiakis crashed together with a deafening boom, then as the great surge passed they yawned apart. The warriors lost their balance and some fell back into the hulls. Using his powerful legs, Talatama leapt across the gap and snatched Mahina with all his might. Kupe went to strike him. Within the same movement, he kicked off the hull and together with Mahina plunged into the raging sea. The violent water was immediately pierced with spears and arrows by Rarotongan warriors. Kupe screamed with rage and pushed some of the warriors into the water after them.

"Kill them!"

As it happened, Omani and the others beheld the masts of Maui Atalaga's tongiaki open and catch the full breath of the wind. The vessel was hurtling away from the fleet of Rarotongan crafts with the power of the bitter wind.

"Let it go!" Omani yelled. "Concentrate on the water! They are still in the sea!"

The Rarotongan warriors who had been thrown into the brine appeared on the choppy surface, flummoxed as they looked about frantically, unable to spot Talatama and Mahina.

"Where are they, you fools!?" Kupe screamed as they scanned the chaotic waters.

Just beyond the floating warriors, the prince and assassin surfaced in the white wash, clinging together in an embrace.

"There!"

As the warriors began to swim to them, Talatama and Mahina were suddenly hauled away by an unseen force, violently skimming in the direction of Maui Atalaga's tongiaki. The enemy watched on in astonishment, finally realising they had taken hold of a well placed rope underwater; a cunning escape plan that dragged them quickly through the water. Vaohoi had done well.

"Damn it! After them!" the Weeping Assassin screamed. "Strike the masts!"

"We can't!" Ruakere roared. "We are knotted to the other vessels!"

The Rarotongan leader scrambled around with his men in an effort to unbind the ropes that had protected them, but now killed their movement. Every moment they fumbled with the ropes, Maui Atalaga's vessel widened the distance between them. The two bodies clinched together in the water, streaming through the choppy sea, disappeared from sight.

The realisation struck Kupe across the face. He felt his fury consume his entire being. They had escaped. He stared at the moving sea in dismay, his hand still in a position that had held Mahina moments before. Omani and Ruakere's loud orders echoed in the distant corners of his mind, as the words came as whispers to the right of where he stood.

"You have failed, Kupe," Mo'unga said, staring at him.

As the rainwater streamed down his face, his eye wept in spite of his cold, stale rancour. The moment of despair passed and he returned Mo'unga's glare.

"I'm not finished yet, witch," he spat.

He then confronted the warriors and hurled insults towards them in an effort to get their vessels released, but by the time the ropes and bindings had been released, Maui Atalaga's vessel had vanished behind the curtain of wind and rain.

The powerful storm had chosen no sides in the battle. Its unified force swept down upon Maui Atalaga's tongiaki with voracity as the folk hero leapt around the vessel clutching ropes and heaving the huge sails. Atiogie groaned as he pulled forth the rope that bore Talatama and Mahina, still clinging to their lives. Lo'au and Emori stood next to him, wincing under the rain that swept across their faces, peering out into the blurry whitewash for their companions. Pele assisted Maui Atalaga in an effort to tame the straining masts against the wild gale.

"Slowly! Bring them in slowly, Atiogie!" Lo'au yelled over the howling wind.

The mighty Samoan gritted his teeth against the weight of the rope, as massive muscles bulged from his arms. Finally, they saw the white wash.

"There they are!" the Fijian pointed.

Both he and Lo'au fell to their knees, ready to grasp their companions. With one last heave, the Samoan lifted the two bodies aboard with the help of the others. Talatama and Mahina hit the centre platform hard and sprawled across it in a spectacular finality. Vaohoi briefly appeared with Adi from the shelter of the hull and cheered in victory.

Their reflections of joy vanished when they saw Talatama had fallen unconscious – and gravely wounded. The prince was pierced with arrows; one lodged in his thigh, one in his shoulder and an arrow had penetrated through his back and protruded from his abdomen. He had thrown himself in harm's way to protect Mahina and being dragged through the sea had drained him of much blood. The Samoan shot Lo'au a pleading look when he saw the severity of Talatama's condition. Mahina was barely conscious and repeatedly reached out for the prince in delusion.

"Get him below deck! Adi will tend to him – take them both quickly!" Lo'au ordered.

CHAPTER 40

"Lo'au!" Maui Atalaga bellowed.

The old mu'a turned and saw the hero pointing out ahead of them in the misty rain. Dark forms materialised across the curtain of the downpour: tongiaki beyond count heading directly towards them. Even in the poor visibility, the companions could still identify the approaching crafts as Rarotongan. A feeling of trepidation swept over Lo'au. Ahead, hundreds of enemy tongiaki blocked their path to Niuafo'ou; behind, Kupe and his fleet just beyond the haze of rain.

"Maui Atalaga! Steer us north!" the old man shouted. "We can't make it back to Niuafo'ou!"

The great warrior swung from the ropes that took him across the large platform. When he landed, he took a wide stance and heaved with all his might. Pele grimaced with fury, as she leapt over to aid the hero shift the sails, while Lo'au scrambled towards the sheltered hull where the other companions rested. He poked his head down into the hull, rain pouring from his face and down his beard.

"Hold on!" he yelled.

Suddenly there was an explosion that sent the tongiaki reeling. The abrupt turn of direction lined the vessel up against a giant wave that struck the sides with a crash. Lo'au was flung across the vessel. He barely caught the edge of the hull with one hand, his frail body dangling over the side of the tongiaki, while its shape angled over the monstrous surge of the wave's follow-on. But there was more to come. The mu'a's eyes widened as he spotted another wave equal to the first, loom before them. In an instant, Pele took hold of the mu'a with both hands and heaved him aboard strongly, only to slip and fall into the open hull. He groaned from the awkward fall and put his hand on Pele's shoulder in a gesture of gratitude. The she-warrior nodded and quickly got to her feet, ready to hurtle herself back on deck, before Maui Atalaga shot her a grave look.

"Stay in the hull! You can aid me no more!" he roared.

"Let me help you!" she returned.

"Stay with the others!"

Lo'au grabbed her by the wrist and motioned for her to return to safety. She squinted back at the hero, her heart wanting to join him in the dangerous melee.

"Pele, we need you here," Lo'au said.

The armada of tongiakis that headed towards Maui Atalaga's craft loomed like a growing darkness of evil. A strongly built vessel sailed ahead; its superior construction rivalled Maui Atalaga's great craft. On its centre platform stood the Pulotulahi Commander Siateki, Prince Whatonga and three Rarotongan lieutenants. They were all fixed on Maui Atalaga's tongiaki that began to change direction.

"Is that one of yours?" Siateki shouted.

"No – that's not a Rarotongan vessel! Yours?" Whatonga replied.

"No. It's not an imperial vessel either," the commander frowned.

By this time, the ship had made a phenomenal ninety degree turn against the violent storm and had begun to streamline north. By what appeared to be either pure luck, or skill, it had tamed a strong gale that filled its sails.

"Whoever is at its helm is a master shipman!" the same lieutenant gawked.

"Wait," Siateki pondered. "The warriors in Niuatoputapu, who saw Prince Talatama escape, said the craft he took was of unknown design."

The fallen commander's eyes widened.

"It's them!!" his eyes bulged from his head.

"Turn the vessel! Turn north!" Whatonga screamed as he turned swiftly to his lieutenants.

A ripping roar of hundreds of men split the air as evasive action commenced on the Rarotongan armada. Suddenly, groans from the hundred vessels echoed across the rain swept waters as they sharpened their course. Waves of enormous size erupted across the sides of the tongiakis with a crescendo of explosions. Men were plummeted by oceans of falling water like that of a waterfall from the heavens. One or two vessels were capsized in the abrupt turning.

"After them, men!" Siateki voice was almost lost in the wind.

But as effective and courageous as their manoeuvring was, it slowed their momentum and buckled their chase. Within seconds, the Rarotongan armada had effectively turned direction, but the hero's vessel had slipped through the moving sea and disappeared into the shroud of rain.

Just as the armada had completed the spectacular turn, sudden shapes breeched the eastern drapery of rain and a call sounded under the howling of the wind. But as the commanders were fixed on the vanishing position of Maui Atalaga's vessel, they did not notice the other tongiakis until it was too late. Siateki and Whatonga heard a flare of screams to their right and saw the twenty Rarotongan vessels heading straight for them. The wind was carrying them too fast.

"What is -?" Siateki reeled.

"Brace for impact!!" Whatonga seized the main mast.

Across on the other vessels, Kupe and his warriors could not reverse their propulsion.

"Pull back!" Omani shrieked.

"Hikule'o, take us swiftly," Kupe whispered, accepting his fate.

A colossal surge of sea pushed the fleet of twenty tongiaki directly into the side of the Rarotongan armada. Tossed upon the rage of sea, the vessels thundered into their comrades. A deafening explosion that erupted men, timber, tapa and cascades of sea water was scattered into the stormy wind. Screams of men permeated through the wind and rain as almost half of the armada was annihilated.

As quickly as it had come, the surge passed and laid waste to the devastation of tongiakis. Wrecks of the vessels and drowned men littered the foamy surface of the violent sea that did not cease. Siateki and Whatonga's command vessel was untouched as it streamlined ahead of the group.

"Cease the chase! Turn the vessel around!" Whatonga screamed to his helmsman. "Prepare to rescue those in the water!"

"No! We must capture Prince Talatama! Keep our course!" Siateki countered.

The Rarotongan prince snatched his club and poised it ready to strike Siateki.

"We turn around now! Or by Tangaloa I'll strike you dead!" He looked fiercely at his helmsmen, then at Siateki. "Do not ever go against my command of this vessel."

Siateki seethed at the decision, knowing they could still capture the fleeing enemy. He gave Whatonga a frustrated glare and cursed as the command vessel began to turn back.

The hull was overcrowded with all the warriors doing what they could for their dying prince. With his massive frame, Atiogie kept knocking others against the wall as he tried to help. Adi endured the poor conditions, focusing on the arrows in his body; she had removed them all but the most dangerous shaft, which was lodged in his torso. She clicked her tongue in frustration and glared at the others cramming around her.

"All of you – go to the other end of the hull – you're causing a nuisance," she said out of character. "I can't help him with you all here!"

The warriors looked at one another in frustration but eventually complied. Emori sat at the far end of the hull and wrapped himself in a thick blanket of tapa. Atiogie, however, moved out into the open and sat in the rain, unable to take his attention off Talatama.

"The brute is really worried about him," Vaohoi said to Adi.

"So we all should be," she replied. "I will do all I can, but then it will be in the hands of the gods."

The Fijian priestess handed the young man more tapa cloths.

"Here. Keep Mahina dry and warm," she said as she maintained her focus on the prince, "Wrap these around her."

Vaohoi gently covered the Rarotongan assassin and corrected the tapa that had been wrapped around her previously. Regardless of the warmth, she shivered uncontrollably in a broken unconsciousness. He tried to rub her body but she winced away from him every moment he touched her.

"Don't worry. A day or two and she will be back to full health," Adi assured. "Now come over here. I need your help."

"Turn him on his side. And I need you to hold him down," she continued. "Get some tapa and lay it under his wound."

The pair prepared the prince's body for the removal of the arrow from his torso. The chaotic rocking of the vessel was a gruelling impediment to such a procedure. They exchanged places and Adi took hold of the rear of the arrow. She gave Vaohoi an anguished look and quickly snapped the end off. The jolt was enough to break Talatama from his unconsciousness. He gasped from the pain and threw Vaohoi off.

"Hold him down!" Adi glared at the young boy, then over to the giant warrior.

"Atiogie! Come here and help!"

Without hesitation, he scuffled over and knew what he had to do. He regarded Adi sternly.

"I'll remove the arrow myself," he stated as he held down the prince with one giant hand.

"Wait—"

Before the Fijian priestess could stop him, he clutched the arrow head and with a swift jerk, yanked the shaft clean from the prince's body. Talatama shrieked as if his soul had been torn from his body. He then fell senseless against the hard hull. The removal of the arrow was followed by considerable blood that discharged from the open wound. The Samoan slowly retreated out into the rain and inspected the arrow.

"Vaohoi, quickly prepare the leaves," Adi said as she covered the wound.

The young man handed the Fijian priestess two portions of banana leaf, smoothly folded several times and anointed with coconut oil. She carefully placed the leaves on the open wounds and fastened them by wrapping a light piece of cloth around his torso. As she completed this task, Talatama regained consciousness and drearily opened his eyes. He regarded his companions weakly.

"Where...am I?" he said groggily. "Where is Mahina?"

"Hush. You mustn't speak," the Fijian priestess stroked his hair tenderly. "You've suffered a terrible wound. Mahina is safe. She is here by your side. You saved her my prince, but you must rest."

Talatama tried to see Mahina but she pressed him gently. "Rest, rest, close your eyes," she repeated, and before long, he fell into a painful sleep. She covered him with a warm tapa and began to shuffle to the other side of the hull.

"Vaohoi, do not talk to him. He needs to regain his strength," she warned.

Outside, the sea storm still raged without signs of diminishing. Atiogie jumped to the centre platform then leapt over to the other hull where Lo'au and Pele sat. The Samoan told them despite the removal of the arrow, Talatama still faced death if they did not get to land soon and provide proper care.

"Atiogie, we are sailing north, towards Samoa," Lo'au said sternly. "When we come into sight of land, can you guide us to safety?"

"Yes, of course!" he said proudly. "I will take us to my village where we will be received with royal welcome!"

"More feasts and songs?" Pele clicked her tongue.

"Excellent, we are in dire need of that!" Lo'au smiled back at the Samoan.

The three companions gazed up at the centre platform to Maui Atalaga who roared at the top of his voice. The hero, still grasping the ropes of the sails, heaved them with astounding strength. He battled the elements tirelessly, his muscular body lathered with the torrential downpour.

"Come for me, Almighty Laufakana'a!" he bellowed and shook his fist to the sky, "I challenge you to a test of strength!!" he continued in a frenzy of courage or madness.

As he did, the dark sky was lit by a sudden and spectacular display of forked lightning that crackled overhead as if to accept his challenge. The blue lightning illuminated and ignited the severity of the tempest. The companions lowered their heads in fear as the thunderstorm roared and crackled overhead.

"Do your worst!" The hero continued to battle with the very forces of the gods themselves.

Like a tiny fish swimming into the unknown black of the deep, the tongiaki disappeared into the torrential veils of rain, the chasm-like waves and the obscurity of the terrifying squall.

CHAPTER 41

Heketa, Tongatapu
Summer, A.D.1121

"Word has not come yet, Your Majesty." Lord Fasi'apule and High Priest Toutai followed the king down to the rocky beach at Heketa.

The limestone rocks jutted and cragged over the sea. Across their surfaces were natural holes and craters, creating sharp and uneven edges. Over the centuries, these craters had gathered earth that sprouted tiny shrubs and flowers. There were storm clouds brewing in the northern skies as Tu'itatui held his weight on the rock shelf and lowered himself into the shallow sea. The cool touch of the water cleared his mind and gave him peace. It came up to his navel and swathed gently around his body.

"Give him time, he will discover what it is and return," he said.

"I feel a sick bitterness in my throat when I think of this." Fasi'apule sat down on the rocks.

"The signs are random and incomprehensible." Toutai looked out to the dark sky. "The gods do not give me answers today."

"We shall see." The king scooped his head into the sea and flung his hair back, water streaming down his body. He collected water in his hands and splashed his face, took a breath and exhaled slowly before placing his hands on his hips. He gazed out to the calm horizon.

"Do you remember when we were young, brother?" he said strangely, "Not long after we met."

"No. I've forgotten my youth," Fasi'apule smiled. "Did I ever have one?"

"We used to sit down here, at this very spot. Father used to bring us here and tells us stories of war and legend."

"Yes, I remember."

Knowing his place, Toutai knew his presence was no longer needed. He swiftly bowed and left the brothers to their conversation.

"Remember your favourite? It was, was -?" Tu'itatui cocked his head and glanced over his shoulder to Fasi'apule.

"The story of Tuutaki," Fasi'apule finished. "The brave warrior of 'Eua."

"That's right! I remember how fascinated you were in that story."

"Yes, I was, as pointless as it seems now."

"Can you tell it to me?" the king asked, as he turned to face his brother. "I've forgotten the details."

With a sigh, Fasi'apule shifted his seat so he was more comfortable. He knew his brother would not relent to such a nostalgic request, so he picked up a shard of limestone and tossed it into the sea.

"Well, it all started with a warrior named Tuutaki, who lived in 'Eua. For some time, he'd made a name for himself as a great warrior of duels.

"Over time, his duelling had earned him wealth and respect, and before long, he married the most beautiful woman on 'Eua," Fasi'apule grinned. "But success is a beautiful thing itself: people become jealous of it and want it for themselves."

"Ah, that's right," Tu'itatui leaned back.

"At this time, stories of Tuutaki's prowess reached the islands of Fiji. As a result, a party of Fijian warriors, bent on challenging him, set sail for 'Eua. Meanwhile, Tuutaki's success had begun to eat at his wife's heart. She became envious of his attention and could no longer live with it."

"Eventually she conspired with her relatives to kill her husband and take his riches. She told them that he would often sleep under a mango tree of an afternoon, and was therefore vulnerable to attack. One day the relatives followed Tuutaki to the tree and waited for him to fall asleep. When they were sure he was, they attacked, but were unaware that there was a dog eating mangoes on the ground nearby. The dog yelped at their advance and woke Tuutaki: given a chance to correct himself, he fought his way to victory."

"At this time, the party of Fijians arrived on 'Eua, unaware of the events between Tuutaki and his wife. Filled with anger of her slain relatives, the wife set upon killing him herself at their home. They lived in a cave, high on the face of a cliff overlooking the sea. When Tuutaki returned to their home, he was exhausted after the fight with the relatives. He asked his wife to bring him a coconut shell containing water."

"You remember very well Fasi'apule," Tu'itatui murmured in recollection.

"As she gathered the water from a nearby stream, she made sure she only filled it half way. When she returned, Tuutaki was sitting on the precipice of the cliff. He gestured for the water and raised the coconut shell to his mouth, but as it was only half filled, he had to tilt his head right back to finish the contents, and as he did, she shoved him over the precipice."

"But as he lost his balance, he reached out and seized her by the hand - pulling her over the edge with him. She was dashed on the rocky bottom of the cliffs, while Tuutaki himself plummeted into a tree, whereby he was impaled through his anus on an upright branch. Although killed instantly, to people below he appeared to be standing in the tree in a somewhat defiant posture."

"The Fijian party approached the tree and saw Tuutaki standing rigid in the tree, so high and without effort. Struck with terror of such a feat, the Fijian party immediately retreated to their boats and departed 'Eua."

"Ha-ha!" Tu'itatui laughed at the humour. "A good story."

"I can't see how that was funny," Fasi'apule answered.

"Really?" Tu'itatui remained chuckling, "There's a few good morals there; never trust your wife and always look defiant, even when you're dead!"

"Humph." Fasi'apule had obviously outgrown the tale.

"You think too much into things, brother."

"Very true," he finally chuckled. "Then yours brother, your favourite story was about the Legend of Sangone."

"At last we come to my point."

A long silence elapsed between the brothers as a sturdy wind picked up, blowing from the direction of the distant storm. Tu'itatui faced his brother and regarded him with interest, his hair blowing about his face. Fasi'apule frowned and braced for the impact of what he was to be told.

"It was, and still is, an ancient Tongan heirloom," he glared at Fasi'apule. "Its importance to the generations of kings to come is essential."

"Y-Your Majesty, I—"

"You know the story, Fasi'apule. You know the legend. We've dreamed of this quest since we were young men. Now we have the power to go on it."

"Yes, but—"

"Lord Fasi'apule, my governor, my brother, my wisest advisor, I bestow this honour to you. Return to me that which belongs here with us, that which holds the key to all future generations. Do not fail me."

For a short while Fasi'apule said nothing. He finally bowed his head long and low before standing.

"Brother, I understand your wisdom. If it still exists I will find it."

"Your Majesty!" A soldier came running down to the rocky ledge. "Your Majesty, Prince Talaiha'apepe has returned from Niuatoputapu!"

"Not Prince Talatama?" Tu'itatui looked up from the water.

"No, Your Majesty. It is Prince Talaiha'apepe who requests your audience immediately. He says he brings dire news from the north."

The two brothers felt an instant ache in their hearts as they both raced back to the royal compound. The news of Talatama's death would be inconceivable.

CHAPTER 42

Upolu, Samoa
Autumn, A.D.1121

Of all the Polynesian peoples across the Pacific, excluding the vanished peoples of Pulotu, the Tongans were the eldest alongside the Samoans. In B.C.1500, a single culture arrived at the two islands; an enlightened and robust civilization whose name has been lost in the mists of time. They were masters of voyaging great distances and sophisticated in the art of constructing unprecedented tongiakis. They brought with them the knowledge of pottery, fishing, music and tapa making. The islands of Tonga and Samoa became their home of one ethnicity, of one nation, Samoa being the northern kingdom, Tonga being the southern.

Over a thousand years of settlement, peoples on both islands gradually discontinued voyaging. Tonga and Samoa had become the eastern-most inhabited islands in the Pacific and the peoples did not venture further. As such, there began a lengthy period of peace and prosperity. Travelling between both island groups then reduced, and thus began the development of two distinct cultures.

Hundreds of years passed again and there commenced another period of advanced technology and adventurism. With the expansion of the new tongiaki and its design, communications and trade increased between the two nations. But by this time, the one people had become two: Tongans and Samoans. Through the increased trade, flowed the opulence of merchandise such as tapa, oils, fragrances and items of value such as whale bone and teeth, pearls, black coral and bird feathers. The benefits of trade also developed the sharing of language, hunting and fishing skills, tapa weaving techniques and religious customs. This all, of course, spurred an increase of inter-marriages in the chiefly ranks of both cultures.

Sixty years ago, Talatama's grandfather, King Momo, avenged his murdered father, King Afulunga, and forged the greatest oceanic empire ever to exist on the face of the earth. During this rise, King Momo embraced the Samoans as his closest and trusted brethren and continued to extend the relationship of peace and prosperity between the two cultures. In time, even the great King Momo married the Samoan princess named Nua, a true symbol of the commitment between Tonga and Samoa. Over time, and as the Empire grew, Samoa was seen as one of the important vestiges in the centre of the kingdom. The loyalty of the Samoans to the Tu'i Tonga kingship was unquestionable and so the close ties saw the Samoan people share the rewards of the Empire's conquests further afield.

Atiogie's loud voice could be heard for kilometres. The giant was cursing fellow countrymen outside the great fales of his village of Siumu on the island of Upolu, Samoa.

"How many times do I have to tell you?" he snarled and swiftly kicked one of the men in the backside.

"Sorry, Milord!" the three men wailed as they ran away to avoid more of the giant's anger.

"Blasted and brainless, good for nothing."

Talatama appeared precariously from the fale, dressed in a tapa robe. He leaned against one of the great pillars and grinned at the giant.

"You need to curb that anger, Lord Atiogie."

"It's the only language they understand," he shook his head.

The spring day sun was high, moderately warm with slight humidity in the air. A gentle breeze swayed the palms throughout the large village, and the scent of frangipani flowers floated across the coast. Children flocked and played in the open grass, while milling artisans and carpenters went about their business peacefully. The village of Siumu was a tranquil township, with a sense of equanimity and serenity about it.

It had been almost two months since the companions' escape from Niuafo'ou. Reaching Samoa after three days on the wild ocean, Atiogie had guided them to an ally's village called Siumu, on the southern coast of Upolu. The companions decided against sailing back to Atiogie's village of 'Aele as it was an obvious place for the Pulotulahi to search for them. Shortly after their arrival in Siumu, Atiogie's father, Lord Feepo, had discreetly made his way across Upolu to greet the wounded and exhausted companions. It was a considerable effort; the companions were surprised to discover Lord Feepo was totally blind and needed constant aid for movement.

For the first week Lord Feepo had taken charge of the village with the consent of the village chief and he and the villagers spared no expense to provide aid to the dying prince. Over the next four weeks, healers and priests were summoned in secret from the island, in an effort to bring Talatama back to the world of the living.

During that first week, he showed no signs of recovery. His strength failed and a severe fever seemed to draw the very life from him. Both Adi and Lo'au sat by him day and night, to pray to the gods for mercy, but it was the relentless and unyielding nurturing of Mahina, that revealed the strength of true healing. She never left his side. She lovingly remained obstinate by preparing his food and feeding him with a vegetable diet only, gently massaging his body, dressing his wounds, cooling his fever and joining Adi and Lo'au in prayer.

Following her persistent efforts of treatment, the prince slowly began to show signs of recovery. It was not long after, that his strength returned with the increase of meat into his strict diet. He could eventually turn over himself and occasionally sit up for short moments. After weeks of more massage and careful assistance, he advanced to gradual walking within the fale. Within the past few days, he had progressed to caring for himself and walking through the village unassisted.

"Atiogie, can you make the arrangements for us to hold a meeting with your father tonight?" he said, still holding onto the pillar.

"Yes, my Prince," the giant said immediately. "Is it time to discuss our next move?"

"It's time to start planning, my friend," he nodded sternly. "Can you also round up all the companions? Make sure they all attend."

For the past two months, Atiogie had proved himself a true friend and gentleman, albeit in his own rough way. Talatama was astounded by the way he managed the contentious arrival of the companions to Siumu. The giant had done as promised: led them to aid and safety in their moment of need. His command over his people provided the provisions and support the companions desperately needed. This aspect of the giant's conduct was refreshing and welcome to Talatama especially, and on Death's bed, the prince vowed he would never forget the generosity and care he and his family provided him. The rest of the companions all remained to aid their leader in any way they could.

Pele and Emori had taken charge of many of the local warrior groups of Siumu for their security. Emori had devised defence positions and regular patrols along the shores of the south coast. Pele had shared her fighting expertise to provide extra training for the warriors. In the short time the Samoan warriors had been with them, they had quickly come to respect and contribute to their plans and developments.

Vaohoi had intermittently, and perhaps without intention, spread the word of the companions' whereabouts across the entire island. Every day Vaohoi would prey on those willing to listen to the legendary battles the companions had fought and the adventures they had lived through together. Crowds of people would gather around him, curious and fascinated to hear of the just deeds and actions of these heroes. Admittedly, his stories were centred on the truth of the subject, though strayed from reality from time to time. These 'story times' ceased abruptly when Pele discovered him one day and promptly pulled him away by his ear.

No word from Maui Atalaga had been heard since their arrival to Samoa. Following their rush to the village with the aid of the townsfolk, the hero disappeared again on his great tongiaki, and although the companions loved the moody and unpredictable hero as one of their own, they had all come to understand that he would always tread his own path.

Talatama leaned against the wooden pillar and smiled as Atiogie lumbered away. His grin soon turned to solemn reflection as his mind went to weighty matters. He was almost fully recovered and the days grew longer for him. Although grateful for the aid and security the Samoans had provided, he had become restless and agitated. He turned and disappeared into the fale.

The fire illuminated the entire grassy knoll and banished the dark shadows that lingered in the jungle. The stars were littered across the night sky like scattered sand across a slab of black obsidian. The air was filled with jovial song. A large group of male and female dancers performed for Talatama and the companions, Lord Feepo and his entourage of retainers. The audience clapped their hands and sang to the chorus, beaming with smiles and the spirit of song.

The kava was served for a time when the dancers completed their show. As they bowed and left the firelight, the leaders were left to discuss matters of importance. Atiogie sat next to his father, Lord Feepo, and although larger in size, he somehow seemed smaller. Despite his disability, the blind chief imbued a natural leadership and charisma expected from such a leader.

Close to them were a group of Samoans from the village of Toamua, far in the north of Upolu. In the centre of the group sat the leader, a strong middle-aged chief by the name of Ale, who appeared to enjoy the festivities with much humour. To his left was a young woman of alluring beauty, so much so that she had caught the attention of every man present; long flowing hair, perfect caramel skin and eyes that were delicate and bashful. Around her sat maidens who sought her every need and yet even when she was not requiring it, they still cosseted over her. Occasionally she would shake her head in frustration and sigh deeply.

"Who is that?" Talatama leaned over to Atiogie.

"Oh, she –"the big man almost blushed, "she is a prospective ...um, wife for me."

Talatama leaned back and smiled. Vaohoi scorned the sky and slapped his knee, "Are you joking?" he gawked. "She's beautiful!"

"What is her name?" Adi asked.

"Tauaiupolu."

"A beautiful name also," Mahina said.

"Certainly too beautiful for you," Vaohoi giggled at Atiogie.

There was a smacking sound as a leg of meat ricocheted off youngster's head.

"Lord Feepo!" Talatama stood. "I wish to thank you for all of your aid. I wish to thank you for the reception and the care you have bestowed on my companions and me during our time here," he bowed his head cordially.

The aging lord raised his hand quickly and gestured in his direction.

"My Prince, it has been an honour and a privilege to have you here as my guest. To think otherwise would be a sin in itself," his pallid eyes blinking against the firelight. "Though I dare not guess that this means you will be leaving us so soon?"

"I've recovered well, thanks to you and your healers," Talatama said warmly. "But the time has come where I must make plans to leave the island."

"I understand, and regretfully agree. I will make all the arrangements to aid you in your voyage home."

The companions looked at one another and whispers flowed among them.

"Can't we stay a little longer?" Vaohoi whined.

"We cannot leave until you are rested fully," Adi said with concern.

"That's right," Lo'au agreed.

"Well, we can stay here all we like!" Atiogie laughed.

The prince did not engage his companions by their comments. He regarded the old lord with gravity.

"What news of the messengers sent to Tongatapu over a month ago?"

"They have not returned. I fear for the worst," Lord Feepo replied, lowering his kava cup from his lips.

"Then I have to assume that the king isn't aware of what transpired in Niuatoputapu." Talatama hung his head.

"Is it possible they've been held up? Perhaps they're waiting for a decision," Emori spoke up.

"Not likely. Not over such time."

"Perhaps Lord Maui Atalaga might have delivered the message?" Mahina said.

"I don't see Maui Atalaga becoming involved in the current political situation," Pele laughed at the Rarotongan assassin.

"No. I must assume that the messengers were unsuccessful and, therefore, my father could be in imminent danger by now."

"It's only been two months. What could they possibly do in that time?" Adi questioned.

"Don't underestimate my brother, or his vision and desire to overthrow the Empire, priestess," Pele countered.

Talatama almost winced. He was sharply reminded of Pele's relationship with his greatest adversary. He coughed and looked up at his companions, as the old mu'a stepped forward and regarded the prince with affirmation. "Prince Talatama, you must do what you know is right."

He deliberated the decision and accounted for his own recovery as the biggest factor. He anticipated that to act rashly and ignore his recuperation could risk a future failure. He could not face a failure in the company of his companions if it were to reflect a bull-headed judgment. In the past few months, he had learned valuable lessons in the realm of chivalry and wisdom, and they did not often go hand in hand.

"We leave in a week, bound for Vava'u. There, we can gather greater numbers to hunt down General Kamohoali'i and simultaneously send emissaries to King Tu'itatui," Talatama said.

"Agreed." The warriors nodded together.

"A wise decision," Lo'au grinned widely as he put his hand on the prince's shoulder. Suddenly, Atiogie began in song, with a baritone voice and clap his big hands. Across the circle of people, the beautiful Tauaiupolu gazed upon him and smiled with new attraction. With the next verse, all the Samoan men joined in, harmonizing with a force of inflection that permeated the souls of all present. The volume of the voices was such that the song echoed from the very mountains in the distant north. The jovial song was amplified by the enthusiasm of their giant leader, who raised his hands to the night sky and smiled with insurmountable joy.

CHAPTER 43

Tafahi, Niuatoputapu

Morning was unusually humid. Siateki sat in a circle of Rarotongan lieutenants and a handful of his own men, as the towering peak of Tafahi loomed above them. The group of fifty men sat in silence, having completed a few rounds of kava. Some of the lieutenants occasionally leant over to each other and whispered comments beyond Siateki's earshot, while he held his head high and ignored the obvious disrespect.

Finally, Prince Whatonga appeared through the forest beyond the circle with three of his closest generals, exhausted and perspiring greatly. They took their seats in the circle and nodded their heads towards Siateki. Prince Whatonga then gorged himself with fresh coconut milk before catching his breath and facing Siateki.

"So what news do you bring?"

"My lord has departed Niuatoputapu," Siateki replied.

"I see. Then it's time to leave," he continued to gorge himself.

"What do you mean?"

Whatonga wiped his mouth and with him every Rarotongan stood to depart.

"Our allegiance is done."

"But – we have found neither your sister, Mahina, nor Prince Talatama!" Siateki found his feet with his men, "We still have to - "

Whatonga threw the coconut to the ground and regarded the Fallen Commander intently.

"And the lives lost to stoke the embers of revenge have doused my anger," he said as he began to walk away. "As I said, the agreement is over."

The Fallen Commander moved forward to speak as Whatonga and his multitude of warriors walked down the beach. "And if we meet again, don't approach me as an ally."

Siateki stopped to watch the beach as hundreds of Rarotongan warriors set sail into the eastern seas.

The Fallen Commander and his small group of men banked their tongiaki on the beach of Niuatoputapu. Before long, the group made their way up the road and through the Falehau towards the Noble House. The locals made way as they noticed Siateki striding with obvious anger, daring not to invoke his temper. He stormed through the gates and into the large reception hall where his sudden entrance drew the attention of all.

"The Rarotongans have broken our allegiance," he said, breathing heavily.

"Yes, I know," the Weeping Assassin grinned.

Two months earlier, the warriors of the Pulotulahi suffered a brutal defeat at the hands of Prince Talatama. His courage and chivalry resulted in unbelievable victories despite being outnumbered and outmuscled. Their last confrontation on the eastern seas of Niuafo'ou staged the destruction of a fleet of hundreds of tongiakis and the loss of over a hundred lives. Kupe, Omani and Mo'unga were favoured by Hikule'o who spared their lives in the destruction.

Following the cursed day of the mighty storm, the remaining beaten forces of the Pulotulahi sailed slowly back to Niuatoputapu neither knowing the direction of Talatama's escape, nor the destination of his voyage to report to General Kamohoali'i. Scathed and punished, both Siateki and Kupe were blamed for the loss and suffered unbearable shame. In a bid to spare their lives, Omani convinced General Kamohoali'i that neither of their decisions were at fault, and that it was the will of the gods alone that allowed the prince to slip though their nets.

Kamohoali'i, calmed by the Unarmed Warrior's religious view of the defeat, withdrew his decision to kill Siateki and Kupe. Instead he gave them one last chance at the only task that was deemed worthy for them to redeem their honour: to find Talatama and kill him. If they were to fail again, they would be sacrificed to Hikule'o under the cruellest of ways. Omani and Mo'unga were assigned to remain with the two commanders to aid them in this continuing task. As it was now apparent, with his calculated risks, timing and aid of the gods, the prince had shown he was a worthy adversary indeed.

However frustrating and disappointing their failure was to Kamohoali'i, it was only a side task for his immediate plans. Following the departure of Siateki with the Samoan mercenaries two months earlier, Kamohoali'i had laboured his influence on the prince's brother, Talaiha'apepe, in Niuatoputapu.

Every day without fail, Kamohoali'i stood by Talaiha'apepe's side and delicately gained the prince's favour. He would create a dichotomy of problems secretly performed by his commanders in Falehau and advise ways to overcome the task. Among the tales of how his duty and past deeds were misinterpreted, he cunningly illustrated himself as a saint follower of Hikule'o and a reverent servant of the Empire.

In Falehau, his commanders, Havea and Ganilau, tipped the balance of his popularity. Ganilau would gather the people in the middle of town and demonstrate his great feats of strength by lifting small tongiakis and breaking palm trees with his bare hands. He would then march around the village and help those in need by re-building fales, fishing for food and replanting crops in the fields. On odd occasions, he saved the lives of children who were victims of accidents. Soon he became a hero among the people, and he never failed to advise the villagers he owed his allegiance and credit to Lord Kamohoali'i.

Understandably, there were groups of men who either held loyalty to the late Noble Anga'uli or those who thought it inconceivable that Kamohoali'i was pardoned for his crimes. These men would publicly proclaim their distrust of Kamohoali'i and his commanders in hope of gathering more people to their cause. One by one, however, these men disappeared overnight, never to be seen again. There were rumours that they departed the island because of their views, others claimed that Prince Talaiha'apepe banished them because they opposed his pardon.

In reality, they were being abducted and killed in the night by Havea. Their bodies were never seen again. He would peel their skin from their carcasses, drink their blood and eat their flesh. His evil peers often said he could consume a whole man overnight and leave the bones sucked of marrow.

Kamohoali'i would walk the streets with his commanders on occasion and present the people with banquets of fruit and cooked meat as a kind gesture. Within only six weeks, all the villagers of Niuatoputapu were supportive of his presence on the island. Within two months, he had turned his position of uncertainty into that of popularity.

Prior to Prince Talaiha'apepe departing Niuatoputapu, he had to make a decision that concerned the island's welfare and the reinstatement of leadership. After considering Kamohoali'i's initial heroic act of defeating the Rarotongans and saving his life, observing his reputation and fame among the island's people by his benevolent offerings, the prince's decision was clear.

As the island's noble was killed during the Rarotongan attacks and no predecessor was alive to take his place, the prince held a ceremony to appoint General Kamohoali'i as the island's interim Lord and Protector. He stated that on arrival to Heketa, Tongatapu he would present the issue to King Tu'itatui to formally reinstate a Noble for Niuatoputapu. But until that time, General Kamohoali'i was to possess the powers of governing and ruling the island.

Following the departure of Prince Talaiha'apepe, Kamohoali'i sent word for all of Niuatoputapu warriors to join under his banner as loyal subjects. In the short weeks of leadership, Kamohoali'i had re-established the island's army of soldiers and officers. Over a thousand warriors held true to his new rulership and vowed to fight and protect him with their very lives.

Once this was done, General Kamohoali'i, his Samoan ally, General Va'iga, and his armies of fifteen hundred mercenaries, swiftly made provisions for a few nights' sail to Neiafu, the capital of Vava'u. Kamohoali'i then departed Niuatoputapu with his commanders, Havea and Ganilau, and his newly formed force of over two thousand warriors.

He had not attributed forces to Siateki, Kupe, Omani and Mo'unga, as he believed the Rarotongans would stay true to their alliance. Whatonga's breaking of the allegiance did not impact on the general's grand plans; it directly affected the remaining commanders. Their manpower was crippled to nothing but a handful of original Pulotulahi warriors. Their hunt for Prince Talatama would now prove impossible if faced with a large scale battle.

Night fell across the Pacific with the rising of a blood moon that hung on the horizon. Flying foxes screeched as they took flight over the giant palms, their crude shapes outlined in front of the luminous disc. Within the Noble House of Niuatoputapu, torchlight flickered and dimly lit the kava hall where the commanders of the Pulotulahi sat with their trusted warriors.

The to'a in the centre of the kava circle was a beautiful young woman with the grace of a princess. She had been passing the kava to the circle of Pulotulahi commanders for hours, as their kava gathering had become significant and their consumption immense. The reason for their heavy consumption was not just the loss of their Rarotongan allies, but more importantly, the prospect that their task was now insurmountable and the penalty for failure was death.

Large amounts of kava causes the drinker to fall into a lulling and relaxed state, numbing the physical body to all reality, and sometimes providing a condition of euphoria. The commanders had all dropped their corruptible masks of gravity and were speaking to each other freely.

"I've never seen a fighting style like yours. Anyone would think you mad, entering battle without a club. Who taught you?" Siateki leaned towards Omani.

"I learned from an old man from my island who trained me for years. As to who taught him, well that's a strange story," Omani chuckled.

"Why is that?" Kupe said as he sipped from his cup.

"Because he said he was lost at sea when he was younger and came across another culture over the western horizon," Omani scoffed. "He said that the people there taught him how to fight like I do, and when he mastered the art he was sent back to the kingdom."

"Sounds like a fairy-tale," Siateki laughed.

"Be that as it may, the man could kill with those hands and feet!" Kupe countered and wiped his weeping eye.

"And you old man - what is your story?" Siateki turned to the Weeping Assassin.

Kupe sighed and finished the rest of his cup. He then rolled it to the beautiful woman who quickly refilled it.

"When I was younger, younger than you lot, I was filled with a passion for adventure. I learned the arts of navigation and voyaging and with the aid of the gods themselves, I became one of the best oceanic navigators in the Empire."

"The ruler at the time, King Momo, employed me as the chief navigator, assigned to span the South Pacific with the Imperial Army to discover and conquer."

"You? You were an Imperial Navigator?" Siateki gaped in disbelief.

"It seems we are all full of unbelievable stories," the Weeping Assassin continued, "For over a decade my work was instrumental

301

to the Empire's expansion to where the borders of the Empire now reach."

He took a mouthful of a full cup of kava.

"However, once the long years of discovery had passed, I became fanatical about the navigation of our great ocean. I tried to convince King Momo that there was a greater need to send further armadas south to Aotearoa."

"Where?" Omani raised an eyebrow.

"Aotearoa I called it, 'Land of the Long White Cloud'. It is a majestic and godly land beyond imagining. It is a land that stretches out beyond the line of sight, filled with mighty mountains and giant forests, coursing rivers and an abundance of game." Kupe paused as if reliving the moment. "But its shores are too distant."

"What happened then?" Omani said.

"The king laughed at me and said it would be impossible to maintain regular shipping there, even if we were to establish a colony. The fact was, Aotearoa was uninhabited when we found it, so there was no support from other peoples who could pay tribute.

"He stated that he would never approve of such suicidal voyages and, following a disrespectful outburst on my part, I was expelled from duty. Even my best friend and co-imperial navigator, Hoturapa, mocked my passions. Following weeks of ridicule, I could not bear to be ridiculed further. In a fit of rage I killed my friend, Hoturapa, and stole his tongiaki which was one of the greatest sea crafts in the Empire's naval fleet. I also took with me his willing wife."

"I can now see the path of spiralling darkness," Mo'unga whispered.

"I set sail with enough stored food to last us the great journey. After about eight weeks, we arrived in Aotearoa."

"Eight weeks?" Siateki frowned. "That's not a long voyage."

"But I stayed in Aotearoa only a year. During our stay, Hoturapa's wife fell ill while she was carrying our child and died, leaving me on my own. Rather than bearing the loneliness of utter solitude, I made sail and returned to the Empire."

"That's a staggering story," Siateki said. "Were it to be true -"

"I care not for your lack of faith, Fallen Commander," Kupe smirked. "For with me I carry the sailing instructions and navigational charts to return to Aotearoa. I never gave King Momo a copy of these charts. One day I will return there."

The Weeping Assassin reached into his girdle and produced an old parchment of tapa with crude glyphs of charcoal inscribed on it. The Pulotulahi commanders leaned forward and peered at the parchment in wonder.

"It's strangely refreshing to hear you speak the truth – for once." Omani grinned.

After a moment of silence, the Pulotulahi commanders broke into a fit of laughter.

CHAPTER 44

Talatama shifted his aching body and lay on his back. He pushed away the kali headrest and sprawled on the floor, his mind racing with a dozen plans, outcomes, doubts and fears. Although his sleep for the past two months had been terrible, perhaps obtaining a few hours every night, he could not stop his mind from working.

The frustration of his predicament plagued his confidence, robbed him of his action and cast doubt into the future. Despite this, his body screamed for rest and yearned for more sleep. The fact that he recognised this and could not, made him even more frustrated. It made the nights lonely, as his only company was the haunting of his own misgivings. Tired but unable to find further sleep, he grunted as he slowly rose from the floor in his quarters.

He wrapped a loose vala around his waist and stood at the entrance of the fale. The open entrance had become very familiar to him; for long weeks it represented the limit of his mobility. He looked out into the open area of the village and inhaled the clear night air. The moon was high and full, casting down light that illuminated the entire village. He could hear Atiogie snoring loudly in a nearby fale and the murmurs of slumber from the others.

He stepped out slowly onto the village path and straightened his back as he walked, feeling the blood run to his legs and the stretch of his spine. A dull pain throbbed from the left side of his abdomen and lingered like a stubborn rock in the sand. It felt like it reached into his very core. His hand went subconsciously to the spot where the arrow had pierced his body and felt the tough and thick scarring that remained as a mortal reminder of the wound.

He walked while deliberating over a course of action for once he and the companions arrived in Vava'u. He knew the Lord of Vava'u well and he was confident that he would aid their cause and serve his will. But what if the Pulotulahi had already reached Vava'u? Was the lord there in danger or could he be corrupted? His mind then went to his father. A memory came rushing back to him of days in his youth.

He was only a boy of eight years when King Tu'itatui watched over him train to be a warrior. The training of unarmed combat was especially gruelling: blows were served at full strength as it was considered rare to kill an opponent without a weapon. On a particular day, he was faced with three opponents the same age as he. They were the grandsons of a great warlord named Manusiu, who had the privilege of instructing the future king.

The boys attacked him together, fists flying everywhere, most of them finding their mark. He stepped back quickly from the flailing of strikes and winced with pain. He was instantly reminded that his father was watching and that he did not want to let him down. Gritting his teeth, he stepped towards the three boys and threw a few good punches that dropped one of his adversaries. But as he leaned down to continue at his fallen opponent, the other two boys struck him from the side. He swung his arm around wildly and hit his target, dropping the second boy. Again he was struck by the remaining boy, and the first boy easily tackled his legs, causing him to crumble to the ground.

"Enough!" Manusiu snapped.

The boys and the young prince regained their feet and assembled in front of the old warlord. They all bowed to him slowly, and separately staggered away from the training area nursing their wounds. He remained and hesitantly looked over to his father.

"Come here, Talatama," King Tu'itatui said in his deep and powerful voice.

The beaten and battered prince gradually made his way before the king and peered up at him with a swollen eye and a cut lip.

"You fight with too much conviction," he leaned forward from a makeshift stool in the training yard.

"Your mind is preoccupied with too many things. When you fight again, think nothing but the simplicity of movement and effect. Let go of your anger and accept the flow of the battle. Things will fall into place sometimes without you willing them to," he smiled and patted his son on the head.

They were profound words for a boy, but he never forgot them. Even into adulthood, the meaning behind those wise words became like whispers on the wind as if too swift to grasp. Despite this he knew the message was not only relevant to fighting, but to life as a leader. In times of stress and hardship he would always remember his father's advice and try to apply it. It was easier pondered than acted on, on most occasions.

Shaken from his recollection, Talatama glanced around and noticed that he had followed the path out of the village. The faint murmurs of the slumbering village folk and a barking dog sounded far behind him. He had never taken the northern path from the village and he suddenly felt uneasy in his current state. But he remembered overhearing locals speak of a beautiful waterfall within an enchanting grove close to the northern path. Locals had called it the Falls of Papapai-tai. Perhaps a refreshing swim would help clear his head, he thought.

As he walked further north into the jungle, he began to hear the faint sounds of running water. The land was high ahead of him and formed a dark, hilly ridgeline that stretched beyond view. Eventually he came to a point where the sound of water lay off the path, and he reached out and parted the shrubbery, lowered his head and stepped into the thick jungle.

As he came closer to the sound, he had become familiar with the resonance of a constant flow. There was another sound however; an irregular splashing and sweeping that echoed the surrounding rock face. He crept closer still and listened carefully. There was no doubt there was someone in the water below the waterfall as he carefully pushed aside thick ferns and peered down. Below was the pool where the cascading water fell gently from an amazing ninety metres.

From the surface of the deep pool, emerged a woman. She swam to the edge of the pool where there was loose clothing thrown on the rocks. He watched as she untied small ornaments from her hair and threw them onto her clothing. As she turned to swim out into the pool again, he recognised her immediately. Mahina.

For the past long months, the beautiful assassin had not left his bedside. He would never forget the days of lying prostrate, looking up into her emerald eyes as she tended to his comforts. She would carefully prepare the herbs and pledgets for his wounds, wash his body cautiously with wet tapa cloths soaked in brine, cook the vegetables for his strict diet and massage his unused muscles. Then at night, she would sit with him and tell stories of her homeland and her youth.

The assassin and the prince would spend hours sharing emotional memories of the past, and laugh at times shared together with the companions. He would find himself confiding in her about his inner struggle of expectations in the eyes of the Empire. He had revealed the depth of accountability and responsibility he was burdened with as the crown prince to the people and his father. He divulged his greatest fear in the Pulotulahi and his ardent passion to crush the evil faction that threatened his family's legacy.

Over time, the more he revealed to Mahina, the more she consoled him with understanding and wisdom. Her empathy and apperception to his labours promoted trust and conviction between them and the trust grew into something more than affection for the prince. He beheld her as a woman who would be a loyal and devoted wife if she were to be wed. His mind had often tempted the fantasy about such things and it stirred emotions in him that he had never dared venture.

He carefully made his way down through the dark and moist ferns to the pool. He was mindful not to make a noise as he advanced but he soon realised it did not matter. The muffled rumble of the waterfall entering the pool was enough to dull any other surrounding sounds. The mist emerging from the falls tempered the air like a soft haze, and as the columns of moonlight filtered through the moisture in the air, it caused the whole area to glow in a dreamlike reality. It laced the moment with an amorous temptation beyond his imagining.

He stepped out of the shrubbery and knelt near the edge of the pool. He lowered a tree branch that obscured his view and as he did, Mahina rose out of the water like a goddess of seduction. She threw her head back, causing her long hair to sweep over in a spray of water. She arched her lithe back and gradually raised her hands to handle her wet hair. The water glistened as it ran over her supple, naked body as if to caress her very being. Her breasts were full and shaped beautifully in the moonlight, her firm stomach curved with the small of her back, and her smooth, athletic legs were strong and perfectly developed.

Her intense beauty struck his heart like a thunderbolt through his chest. He gasped and barely contained himself as he shuddered. He felt the overwhelming waves of desire rippling under his skin and the stirring of carnal yearning in his abdomen. He could not help but to consciously control his breathing lest he scare her in sudden movement. Watching her for a few more moments, he stepped to the edge of the pool and gazed upon her with a composed expression.

"Mahina."

The assassin spun around instinctively and leapt to the edge of the water where her clothes lay. She snatched up a short length of tapa and made an attempt to cover herself. With the other hand she seized her dagger and pointed it in Talatama's direction. He suddenly felt ashamed looking at her so exposed. He then realised that he was standing in the shade of moonlight and she could not see him.

"Mahina – it's I," he spoke with greater caution and stepped out into the pool, "Talatama."

The moonlight streamed down his strong face and physique, illuminating him like a finely polished statue. Her recognition was instant. She slowly lowered her weapon and stared at the prince, saying nothing as she steadily moved through the water towards him. Her body trembled slightly as she came close. He was uncertain whether it was from the chill from the falls or from startling her, or perhaps something else.

"I'm concerned to see you so far out of the village," he continued the momentum of his words. "You must remember that we're all hunted. It isn't safe to venture out alone."

The beautiful assassin peered up into his glowing eyes. They both paused just beyond the edge of the pool, the rippling water at thigh height. The moonlit mist enveloped them together in a cloak of magical wisps.

"I've been coming here from time to time during your recovery. For privacy, and to be with my own thoughts," she finally said.

"It – it's beautiful." He took his eyes off her and appreciated the enchanting falls.

"Yes, it is. It reminds me of a place in my dreams." She sneaked a smile towards him. "I cannot help but to come here when I can."

The two stood silently and allowed the moment to be cherished. Talatama turned and peered up the great waterfall to seek its peak.

"I know what it is like being with one's own thoughts," he said and turned to her, "To be alone and to ponder all things on the mind. When I was a boy, my father told me much of what the world would expect of me as a king one day. I took it upon myself to forever seek a path that was righteous, valiant and loyal to the Empire -"

"And you have," she stepped closer to him and placed her hand on his chest.

"I have, but at what cost? What cost have I demanded from myself? I've always confused issues in the pursuit of doing what is right. I feel as though I've lost something of myself, and I've begun to question the morality of my virtues."

"Yet your heart remains true, my Prince."

"Is that the price of leadership?"

"To be a leader you must always be burdened with the charge of responsibility. My father taught me that," she searched his eyes for understanding.

"Yes – yet I feel as though I fall short at times. It was my decision that put you all in danger. We are here in Samoa because of those shortfalls."

"My Prince, you're too hard on yourself, you judge your actions too fiercely," she reached out and touched his chin to bring his eyes to hers.

"You must be patient with your actions, your decisions and your role as leader. You have great strength, a commanding conviction and vision. But you must learn patience, forgiveness," she peered from one eye to another.

Her hand slowly caressed his muscular chest as he banished his troubled thoughts, gazing upon her with a longing beyond his words. His eyes lost their steely shine as her beauty destroyed the warrior within him and he felt his heart melt.

"Mahina, you stir a long awaited yearning in me." His languish forced him to gaze skyward. "From which star did you fall, pray tell me?"

When she did not answer, he released the reigns over his heart. "Mahina -" his eyes reflected the rippling water, "I love you... I've loved you since the night our paths first crossed in Anga'uli's courtyard. I ha—"

"Hush," the assassin stroked her finger over his lips. His words struck the depths of her soul and her eyes brimmed with tears. She tore down the wall that surrounded her heart as the tears of joy rolled down her face and her true feelings were exposed.

"My Prince, you saved my life not once - but twice," she trembled. "I had secretly hoped that you had felt more towards me - acted on deeper feelings than an act of princely chivalry."

"Mahina—"

"Talatama, my mind can't resist wandering to thoughts of you! I see your face in every reflection, hear your voice in the wind and feel your warmth in the sun. You've taken my mind as well as my heart," she said in loving anguish.

The prince placed his hands on her shoulders, gripping them to reflect his truth. "Mahina, I want to make you mine."

She did not answer him as the tapa cloth covering her body dropped into the water. Her hand delicately pulled at the front of his vala, causing it to also fall into the water. She peered up into the prince's eyes.

"Take me ..." she whispered as she pressed her naked body up against his. "I am already yours ..."

Their lips came together slowly. His chest pressed against her breasts, his loins throbbed with hers. As they embraced and kissed their hands explored over naked flesh without limits. She moaned as the fire of passion consumed her heart: the strength of his hands over her body fanning the heat in her desire to have him inside her. Memories flooded back that built their moment of obsession; hearing the laughter they had shared, feeling the electricity when they had touched and times they had lost themselves in each other's eyes.

He lifted her and she straddled his waist, and in the instant he penetrated her, they moaned as one. They trembled as wave after wave of sexual desire was sated. The carnal longing behind the modesty of their company was finally unbridled. He could smell the sandalwood oil over her honey skin, the sweet scent of flowers in her long wet hair, the dulcet melody of her yearning sighs, and the hint of coconut on her lips.

She pulled the back of his head so as to press their mouths deeper together. She gave herself freely to the burning chemistry and her desire could not be contained. She was completely drunk with his manly tang and her own craving for his ardour. Her hips curled against him in rhythmic passion as the waterfall's mist swirled around their bodies and wrapped them together in a glowing cocoon of love.

Without ceasing, he gently walked to the edge of the pool and lay her down on the warm grass. Their slick bodies were embraced by the moist sward and they slid against each other easily. Over and over they held each other, sharing feelings that could only be expressed through touch. They descended into the depths of their fervour until they reached a shuddering climax in one final moment.

They lay in each other's arms for hours, finally falling into a wistful sleep where they dreamt of a world that existed only for their love.

CHAPTER **45**

Early evening was setting in across the island of Upolu. The winter sun tempted the ocean's vista as it hung amid a veil of misty, ginger clouds. The southern seas looked dark and starry and a crescent moon rose slightly in the east. The township was scattered with villagers. Traders in the streets pawning necklaces of pearls, wood carvings and large tapa blankets woven with intricate designs were packing up their wares for the day. Fishermen were returning to the shores with their catch of fish they had tied into long lengths of rope to ease its transport. Small groups of children congregated in the grassy areas to the sides of the main road, playing stick games called 'Aigofie'.

Lo'au and Atiogie made their way through the village of Siumu and stopped occasionally to speak to acquaintances along the way. The old mu'a smiled under his regal beard, providing short blessings to those who casually sought favour from the gods. Atiogie stood proudly at his side, choosing whether the approaching people were worthy of Lo'au's attention or not. Lo'au would then ignore the Samoan's harsh dismissals with a polite gesture and listen to those who sought his wisdom. After an hour or so, however, Atiogie was beginning to lose patience.

"Okay, okay. Let's get going old man. I'm getting hungry."

Lo'au finished his prayer with a newly married couple and turned to his giant companion.

"You're right. We need to prepare for tomorrow's departure. Come."

The two made their way back through the congregation of people who had amassed to see them. It did not take them long to reach the chiefs' compound and find some of the companions standing in the private courtyard. Talatama was talking to Adi, Emori and Pele in what appeared to be a matter of some importance. The old mu'a approached the group in his usual and cordial fashion while Atiogie swaggered forward with his hands on his hips.

"Are we changing our plan, Prince Talatama?" Lo'au asked.

The group looked pleased that he had arrived.

"Perhaps, Lord Feepo has just advised me that a small fleet of tongiakis are mooring on the beach as we speak," Talatama was conservatively excited.

"What's special about that?" Atiogie blanched.

"The tongiakis bear the Royal Banner," Adi answered.

"King Tu'itatui?" Lo'au guessed.

"No, I doubt it. My father never travels short of a few thousand men," Talatama began to walk towards his fale. "Those of you who wish to accompany me are welcome. I'll be attending the beach shortly."

The small fleet of four tongiakis parted the wet sand as they came ashore. By this time, the sun had dropped behind the horizon and the faint blue of the sky began to melt away. Royal heralds and servants from the tongiakis leapt from the vessels into the shallow water and proclaimed their arrival. Talatama stood together with Lord Feepo, providing his arm for guidance. A small entourage of retainers and warriors stood behind the chiefs and they watched as men assisted the regalia from the main tongiaki.

Talatama grinned as he watched the leader of the royal party, Lord Fasi'apule, approach steadily with a broad smile as he came close.

"Lord Feepo, greetings from the capital," the lord said with a cultured accent.

314

"Welcome, Your Highness, from my family and the people of Siumu," Feepo kneeled and bowed his head along with the entire Samoan congregation.

The lord then stepped forward and delicately took the blind chief's hands and pressed their faces together in greeting. He then turned to the prince.

"Prince Talatama, you have been gone a long time."

"Much has happened, Uncle - "

Fasi'apule leant forward and whispered in Talatama's ear. "I know. There's much for us to discuss, you're in considerable danger."

"Yes, we are hunted by agents of the Pulotulahi and — "

"It is not that of which I speak. You're in danger from your very own house," Fasi'apule continued to whisper.

"What?"

"I'll say nothing more at this time."

"But, Uncle - "

"I am weary from travel, young Prince. Let us talk of these matters later," he spoke with a sigh.

"I understand." Talatama tried valiantly to suppress his frustration.

"Atiogie, please escort His Highness," Lord Feepo motioned. "We shall prepare the kava for this evening."

The prince frowned as he turned to Lo'au, who had overheard the conversation. There was a strange and uncomfortable silence between the prince and his uncle as they walked back to the village.

Being the older half brother of King Tu'itatui, Lord Fasi'apule was the ruler of the Malapo municipality in Tongatapu. He was a middle aged man of great stature and was well respected for his firm and astute ruling despite the darkness that overshadowed his father's reign. Despite this, he possessed a clever intellect, fast wit and cunning. In times past he had been the mastermind behind countless successful battles fought by the Empire, and during the days of the Empire's expansion of the Pacific, he was a feared warlord who calculated the risk and depth of every voyage, every encounter and every negotiation. He was King Tu'itatui's closest advisor, most trusted friend and governor. The combination of a warrior king with his brother, a master military tactician, made their Royal exploits unparalleled.

As Talatama had grown as a young prince, Lord Fasi'apule had been his mentor and teacher. Fasi'apule had spent years educating the prince in subjects such as geography, astronomy, artistry, history and etiquette. He also enabled him with the skills of agriculture, helmsman, ship navigation and military tactics. During the early years, Talatama remembered him as a patient and understanding man emitting a great sense of wisdom and incredible intellect, much to the aspiration of the ambitious prince. As time passed, and he grew into a man, their time, as teacher and student, faded into the past. Talatama held fond memories and missed his advice during difficult times.

A crescent moon was low in the night sky. The large fale kava was filled with the Samoan Chieftains: Lord Feepo, Atiogie, the high priests and village headmen. With them sat Lord Fasi'apule and his impressive handful of old renowned warriors from Tonga. To Fasi'apule's right sat Talatama and his companions: Lo'au, Pele, Adi, Emori, Mahina and Vaohoi. Little conversation preceded the preparation of the kava in the great hall as they watched the beautiful Samoan to'a complete the gracious kava ceremony and bow to all of the chiefs present. She then commenced serving.

"Hold!" Lord Fasi'apule said in a sudden tone that startled the girl.

She froze and spilled kava on the floor. Idle chatter ceased as a silence echoed through the great hall and the Samoans exchanged curious looks. Talatama knew his uncle's tone well, he was up to something. The prince bowed his head and waited for his old teacher's tricks.

"Tonight, as all of you witness, no one will do the apportioning of the kava but I."

"But, Your Highness —"

Lord Fasi'apule stood and shooed the startled to'a from her position. He collected the coconut shells and started to fill each cup from the massive kava bowl. Lord Feepo expressed a confused look. Talatama quickly returned a comforting smile to appease the Samoans. It was not long before all the cups of kava were passed around to the chiefs in the circle and Lord Fasi'apule raised his own with both hands and toasted to the chiefs. All present raised their cups in honour of the lord.

"Fainting alone in the bush, leaf screeching and whistling," he said proudly then brought the cup to his lips.

The entire hall fell silent a second time. Most of the chiefs lowered their cups without drinking. Talatama and his companions accepted the toast and Lord Feepo and Atiogie ushered between themselves. Feepo turned around and consulted with his chiefs, "What does he speak of?" he whispered.

"It's a riddle, Milord," a high priest said among the blank faces.

"And it's meaning?" Feepo became tense.

"Indeed, good chief!" Lord Fasi'apule said. "That is the question, isn't it?"

Feepo turned to Fasi'apule with an expression that showed his struggle. He chose his words carefully.

"Your Highness – forgive my ignorance. I don't understand your meaning."

Lord Fasi'apule lowered his cup and his enthusiasm seemed to evaporate. He glared at Lord Feepo and spoke candidly.

"Lord Feepo, I seek your wisest man to a challenge of wit," he said. "That is unless someone in this hall can give me an answer to my toast."

Whispers echoed the fale kava as men debated the riddle among themselves. Lord Feepo sat waiting patiently for his high priests and chiefs for an answer. Atiogie stared at the ceiling, not bothering to even attempt such puzzlement. Lo'au rubbed his bearded chin and grinned at Fasi'apule while the prince regarded his uncle with distaste.

"Uncle, you forget yourself. Lord Feepo and his people aided my companions and me when we were in dire need." He leaned forward to Lord Fasi'apule and whispered sternly. "I will not remain seated here if you continue to embarrass them."

"Be silent, Talatama." Fasi'apule shot back. "Do not interfere."

The prince turned away in frustration.

"Your Highness, I fear there is no one here in the hall who can answer your riddle," Lord Feepo finally said. "I must commend you on your astounding intellect. Forgive me if I suggest that I may know of a man who may match your wit."

"If that is so, I will await his answer."

"Your Highness, one of my messengers has just left to seek his counsel," Feepo bowed.

Lord Fasi'apule nodded, "Lord Feepo, my old friend, understand that I mean you no insult through my challenge."

"None taken, Your Highness," the Samoan Chief replied with a warm grin, "but it may take time for us to receive the answer."

"In that case, the kava ceremony will be suspended until we do."

By Lord Feepo's command, all the Samoan chiefs and retainers including Atiogie rose and bowed their heads to Lord Fasi'apule and respectfully exited the fale kava. Lo'au motioned to Talatama that he would join Lord Feepo in retiring. Once most of the fale kava had been emptied, Lord Fasi'apule turned to his nephew and his companions. The prince found it hard to look at him.

"Now we can speak freely," Lord Fasi'apule said.

"What is the meaning of this, Uncle?" Talatama blurted. "I hope there is a reason for this rude charade."

The lord straightened his posture and regarded the companions with interest.

"Do you trust them?"

"With my life," Talatama replied.

"Good. Are you familiar with the Legend of Sangone?"

"Yes. Sangone was the Goddess of Mercy, and the mother of Hinahengi, Goddess of Beauty," Talatama turned to his foreign

318

companions who were not familiar with the story. "And as a symbol of her power and empathy to all that is mortal, Sangone took the shape of a sea turtle to show her compassion for living things. One day, a Samoan chief by the name of Lekapai, used her for a voyage from Tonga to Samoa, and once arrived, had her killed and eaten."

"And the remains of Sangone became a mystery," Lord Fasi'apule grinned. "You remember your history lessons well."

The lord cleared his throat.

"Recently we have received rumour that there is a guardian of Sangone's final resting place, a guardian with a wit of unparalleled cunning."

Prince Talatama looked at his uncle in final understanding. "You plan to outwit him and discover the secret to the burial ground."

"Correct." Lord Fasi'apule took an unceremonious slurp from his cup.

"What's so great about the bones of a turtle?" Vaohoi questioned rudely.

"Vaohoi! Show respect," Talatama shot.

"He's right," Lord Fasi'apule laughed. "Well, apart from being an Imperial Tongan heirloom and a symbol of divinity, the Shell of Sangone is said to hold the magical properties of mercy."

Vaohoi raised his eyebrows once, then lowered his head in silence.

"Your father has sent me to retrieve it for him," he turned to Talatama. "It is a royal quest that I must complete for the king – and I will not fail."

CHAPTER 46

Another hour or so passed with the group discussing the Legend of Sangone and its significance to the Empire. But it was not long before Talatama tired of allowing his uncle the luxury of the subject. He changed the conversation abruptly.

"Interesting, Uncle, and I wish you well on your quest. But to other matters, we had planned to leave in the morning to sail for Vava'u."

"Yes, I thought so."

"I have urgent news for the king. Uncle, the Pulotulahi have gathered in greater numbers and – "

"Before you go further, there is dire word from your father," Fasi'apule raised a hand, "The king has issued an order for your arrest and the arrest of your companions."

The comrades turned to each other dumbfounded. Mahina and Pele exchanged angry expressions and Vaohoi laughed. Adi and Emori just stared at the lord.

"You - you'll have to explain that statement," the prince stammered.

"About three weeks ago, Prince Talaiha'apepe returned to the capital and with him he brought alarming news. He reported that you aided a Rarotongan assault on the island of Niuatoputapu."

The companions exploded in outrage.

"Nonsense!" the prince leapt to his feet.

"Lies!" Mahina exclaimed.

"We've been framed!" Emori exasperated.

320

"They're welcome to try to arrest me," Pele growled.

"Yeah, let them try!" Vaohoi giggled.

"We should give ourselves up. We cannot go against the will of the king," Adi said.

"Speak for yourself!" Pele spat. "Not all of us have glowing reputations, Priestess."

"Adi is right. We cannot outrun both the Empire and the Pulotulahi," Emori stood behind his betrothed.

"I'll not be accused of murder when it was my mother, Lady Rongaueroa, who was killed by members of the Pulotulahi!" Mahina snarled.

"Enough." The prince held out a hand. "Fasi'apule - we were there - but it was a bloodbath constructed by the Pulotulahi! At the time, I feared that they'd targeted Talaiha'apepe for assassination. My men of the Fourteenth Imperial Legion were slain during the battle and we barely escaped the island with our own lives!" he stood enraged.

"According to your brother, a thousand innocent lives were lost that day," Lord Fasi'apule continued. "He claims that you helped the Rarotongan Army attack the island to rescue your Rarotongan lover," he turned to Mahina.

Her jaw dropped.

"And I thought I was good at twisting the truth. How many times can the Pulotulahi use the same lie?" Vaohoi scoffed.

"I've heard enough of this." Mahina rose from her seat and swiftly left the fale kava.

"Mahina wait," Talatama sighed.

"Who could have masterminded such a deception involving the attacks?" Adi shook her head. "Then place the blame on us?"

"And who was then able to convince the Prince of the Empire?" Emori added.

"Only Kamohoali'i could do such a thing," Pele said plainly.

"Interesting you say that. Prince Talaiha'apepe has pardoned General Kamohoali'i of all his past crimes and made him high protector and lord over Niuatoputapu."

"Has the world gone mad?" Talatama exclaimed. "It is because of that man I'm in this position!"

"Your younger brother has always been a little too easy to influence, Talatama. My guess is that Kamohoali'i has seen this weakness in him and capitalised on it. Be that as it may, we have witnesses that corroborate that General Kamohoali'i saved Talaiha'apepe's life in that battle," Lord Fasi'apule paused. "He has gained the ear of the king. You must be sure that your claim against him is true."

"Uncle, not only do I believe he is intending to assassinate the king, but he is planning a complete takeover of the Empire. As I said before, he has increased the number of Pulotulahi warriors and gained the allegiance of Samoan and Rarotongan armies."

"Talatama, those are tall stories to say the least," Lord Fasi'apule frowned. "Surely you can't expect a criminal like Kamohoali'i, despite his renowned manipulation, to gain political control of the Empire?"

"I know how it sounds, but trust me when I tell you it will happen if I don't stop him," Talatama was red with frustration.

For a long time no one spoke. The wind could be heard rustling the palm tree leaves outside and the faint conversations of villagers drifted in on the evening breeze. Talatama remained standing as he peered out of the entrance to stare up to the large crescent moon. He finally turned and regarded the group gravely.

"My plan was to leave tomorrow and gain the aid of Lord Punake in Vava'u. But by now, he would have heard of the king's order of my arrest. He won't help us now."

"Don't be too definitive of your enemies, Prince Talatama," Lord Fasi'apule said wisely. "You possess an honourable reputation and bear respect from both friends and enemies. Though I never believed the accusation against you, you've now supported my belief through your convincing story."

"Then you're not going to arrest us?" Vaohoi pulled a silly grin.

"If I wanted to arrest you all, you'd have been bound, hands and feet, hours ago," Lord Fasi'apule joked.

"Will you help us then, Uncle?" Talatama finally asked as he sat down in front of his lifelong mentor and teacher.

Lord Fasi'apule seemed to glare into his very soul. He then turned to the companions and his own men, "Would you all please excuse us? I wish to have words with Prince Talatama alone."

All present were content to leave following the heated news. Some of the companions appeared disillusioned, others angry and frustrated. The prince watched them file out the fale kava and heard hushed talk from them as they walked away into the cool night. Again, he was filled with a dull sense of responsibility for them and again he began to feel that this rocky road he had brought them on was beginning to take its toll.

He ran his fingers through his hair and untied the length of twine at the pinnacle of his skull. His long hair fell about his shoulders and it seemed to relax him somewhat.

"You were wounded?" Lord Fasi'apule asked.

"Arrow through the stomach," he nodded. "By the aid of Mighty Tangaloa and the people here, I survived."

"Why didn't you go to the Royal Palace to the east? They could have healed you there."

"There was no time. I also feared it would be one of the first places the Pulotulahi would seek us. My companion Atiogie brought me here unconscious. His father, Lord Feepo, then moved heaven and earth to help us."

He paused and stroked his loose hair once again.

"Teacher, I'm feeling overwhelmed. Yet I know this destiny is of my own making, and only I can defeat this evil."

"Feeling overwhelmed is letting your fears take control of your action. Fear can steal the motivation from a man. It can cripple his vision, his judgment and his decisions," Fasi'apule returned.

"Strike the fear from your mind. Take ownership of your decisions, and follow your heart. This has always been the core advice that I have given."

"I understand, Uncle. I've always been clear of mind and stout of heart in the presence of the enemy. But I never prepared myself for a stab in the back from that which I've sworn to protect," Talatama flinched as he spoke.

"All men betray. All men experience the pains of betrayal, many times from those closest to him, those whom he confesses to love, to cherish and protect."

Lord Fasi'apule looked upon Talatama as he did when the prince was just a child. Talatama welcomed the nostalgia.

"But it's the spite, the malice and ensuing darkness in your own heart that completes the betrayal against you. Fight it as you would any other inner turmoil. Take the appropriate steps to right the wrong without involving them."

The prince took a deep breath that shuddered as he exhaled, pondering the words of his old teacher.

"You gain even more wisdom with age, Uncle," he smiled. "Does the extent of your help in this matter end with your advice?"

"I've instructed you all your life. This conundrum of events is your path, your making, and so it must be you who travels it and finishes it. I must, therefore, decline joining you in arms. However as one last act of guidance, I will aid you with the journey you are about to take by contributing to your preparation."

"What do you mean?"

"Stay with me until my quest is complete, then you will see."

Talatama thought about the plans he had made for the next couple of weeks and in an hour's conversation they had been shattered. His plea for aid among those whom he trusted was now pointless. Assisting his mentor, in what might result in better fortune than his current predicament, seemed the only option. He called for a retainer to enter the fale kava. Prior to the young retainer leaving swiftly, he whispered brief orders.

"What was that about?"

"To advise my companions, I've made up my mind," Talatama grinned. "We're treasure hunters now."

CHAPTER 47

Time lapsed into a serene flow of endless story-telling between uncle and nephew. They had caught up on the years they had been apart, and vigorously shared tales of countless exploits and conquests. Once they had exhausted their new adventures, they had begun to enjoy the nostalgia of a time long ago. Fasi'apule never tired of sharing his tales of the Empire's Great Expansion, "It was the happiest time of my life," he said. Before long, hours had passed and the two had consumed much kava.

It was a couple of hours past midnight when a herald's voice called from outside the fale kava. Talatama and Lord Fasi'apule corrected themselves from their casual demeanour and watched as Lord Feepo and his Samoan chiefs entered and bowed reverently. As the chiefs filled the fale, Talatama realised how much kava he had drunk and made a mental note to say little as a consequence.

"Your Highness, I apologise for keeping you waiting," Lord Feepo said graciously. "However, I was determined to fulfil your request."

"Indeed, you've always been resourceful, Lord Feepo," Lord Fasi'apule said with remarkable clarity, "And never fail to honour your word."

Talatama wondered whether the kava they had consumed all night had affected his uncle at all. He watched on as Lord Feepo and his chiefs remained standing for the last of the party to enter the fale kava. He observed two Samoan warriors aiding, what appeared to be, a child through the entrance. But it was not until they came closer that he realised the child was in fact an elderly man. The first thing he noticed was his size: he was a dwarf, standing at only three and a half feet tall.

The dwarf appeared yet more ancient as he came closer. His old leathery skin was wrinkled across his sunken face like a dried mango, and he emitted malevolence like a deep rooted hatred for anything that would displease him. His eyes were like slits between layers of wrinkles, hooded and mysterious. His hunched back cowled his frame, which was supported by a twisted walking stick. The ancient dwarf groaned as he sat on the tapa before Talatama and Lord Fasi'apule.

"Your Highness, may I introduce Lafaipana. His mortal body cursed by the gods, but blessed with both great wisdom and cunning."

"Greetings, Your Highness," Lafaipana said in a wheezing and hissing voice.

"Greetings, wise Lafaipana, I am pleased to have you join us," Lord Fasi'apule nodded. "I have heard much about you."

"You have, Your Highness?" Lord Feepo looked surprised.

"His Highness has heard the Legend of Sangone, and he who guards its resting place," Lafaipana hissed.

"Indeed. And I knew that the only way to get you here was to give Lord Feepo a riddle that I knew only you could answer."

"So it is Sangone you seek, Your Highness? Its resting place has been a secret for over a hundred years, for none have been able to defeat Lafaipana in a challenge of riddles. And those who are defeated are sacrificed, their flesh consumed by Lafaipana himself," Lord Feepo warned.

The ancient dwarf smirked when the sacrifice was mentioned and he began to rub his stubby, old hands together.

"Then I formally challenge you, Lafaipana, in a bout of trickery and cunning," Lord Fasi'apule said proudly.

"I accept your challenge," Lafaipana hissed, a mask of villainy permanently across his dishevelled face. "But know this, Your Highness: I am bound by the will of the gods. Regardless of your royalty and high military position, I cannot reveal the resting place even if you lose. And should you lose, with due respect, Your Highness, I think it fair that you suffer the same fate as those who have failed."

"Wait – I don't think—" Talatama interjected.

"Should I lose, I shall sacrifice myself to the gods of your choice," Lord Fasi'apule agreed.

A wicked smirk creased Lafaipana's leathery face.

"Should I win, however, you will show me the final resting place of Sangone, and grant me one wish, once I have retrieved the remains."

"Accepted," the ancient dwarf wheezed without a second thought.

"I charge Lord Feepo and Prince Talatama to stand as witnesses to this challenge," Lord Fasi'apule added. "So without further ado, I ask again, '*Fainting alone in the bush, leaf screeching and whistling*'".

Lafaipana stared at Lord Fasi'apule before signalling a warrior with a silent task, who disappeared outside. Moments later the warrior returned to the fale kava and with the assistance of other men, placed in front of Lord Fasi'apule bananas wrapped in taro leaves that had been cooked in an umu. The ambrosial scent of food was mouth watering. Steam rose from it and filled the fale kava.

"I present the answer, Your Highness. A wild banana tree standing alone in the bush leans over fainting when the bananas are ripe," Lafaipana said. "The taro leaves give a screeching sound when picked at the stalk."

"Correct." Lord Fasi'apule smiled towards Lafaipana and slowly nodded his head.

He then stood and began to apportion the kava once again. As he did so, Lord Feepo directed a servant to serve the banana and taro leaves for them all to eat. Once Lord Fasi'apule completed apportioning the kava, and the food was distributed, all present sat in the circle and raised their cups in toast. This time it was Lafaipana's turn to speak.

"Your Highness I ask – '*Like a soft earthquake, immovable as a mountain, growling and lying down*'," he stated.

All men present then drank from their cups and commenced eating the food. Before starting his own meal, Lord Fasi'apule turned and whispered to one of his warriors, who then gathered the rest of the Tongan contingent and exited the fale kava. Talatama turned to his mentor with a disapproving look.

"Uncle, this is a dangerous game you're playing," he said low enough for the others not to hear. "And I'll have to honour the outcome, whichever way it ends."

"Let's hope I win then," Lord Fasi'apule chuckled as he began to eat.

Another hour passed, and then another and the royal kava ceremony continued to flow. The small portions of the bananas and taro leaves had been quickly consumed and more and more kava had been drunk. Choruses of song were sung throughout the night, merry and loud, rejoicing songs of old. Their voices carried out of the fale kava and drifted into the night air up towards the stars. Once they had finished a melody, they would engage in more conversation, until a warrior would commence another tune.

Suddenly, Lord Fasi'apule's warriors re-entered the fale kava and with them carried a large, succulent pig that had been spit-roasted over a fire, dressed with coconut milk and laced with kelp. They laid it down in the centre of the circle before Lord Fasi'apule. The lord thanked his men, produced an obsidian knife and began to carve up the roasted pig. He severed the head, the feet and meat from its back and laid them in front of Talatama and his men before portioning the rest of the pig to Lafaipana and the Samoan chiefs.

"Lafaipana, I now present you with the answer: *a hog*. 'Like a soft earthquake, immovable as a mountain, growling and lying down'. My father once had a hog he kept under a mango tree in Malapo. In addition to the mangoes, the greedy pig ate the food the retainers fed him. Eventually it became so fat, it couldn't walk properly, and over time, it could not move at all - so large, unable to budge, lying down. When that happened, it would growl whenever it required feeding."

Lafaipana's eyes reflected a fury of disappointment.

"Correct, Your Highness," he feigned loosely.

The congregation then began to feast upon the succulent pork with much appetite and as they ate, they engaged in more conversation and more song. Talatama and Lord Fasi'apule rejoiced in an ancient Tongan song known by the Samoans that praised the trinity of Tangaloa, Maui and Hikule'o. Another hour passed and the food had been consumed by all the chiefs.

Early morning sunlight streamed into the fale kava, with it bringing the new day. Atiogie appeared in the entrance with Lo'au, Pele, Vaohoi and Mahina; all surprised to see the congregation as they seated themselves beside Talatama and greeted him with excited expressions. Mahina sat close to him, appearing to have discounted the hurtful allegation the previous night.

"Are we going on a quest?" Vaohoi nudged the prince. "The retainer gave us the message last night!"

"Yes, what nonsense is that?" Pele frowned.

"Shhh, all of you," Talatama returned gruffly.

"You haven't been here all night, have you?" Atiogie yawned.

"I have," Talatama said. "Been an interesting eve, let me assure you."

"I overheard Lord Fasi'apule's challenge to Lafaipana. What is your role in this, my Prince?" Lo'au asked.

"A mere witness, but I've given my word that I must see it to the end."

"I understand. It will certainly make our saga more colourful!" Lo'au chuckled under his beard.

"Aye, it's never a dull moment with you!" Atiogie laughed as well.

Another hour dwindled as the men consumed the pig and took part in more kava drinking. Additional Samoan chiefs from afar, loyal to Lord Feepo, had milled into the fale kava as word of the great challenge between the Tongan warlord and the mystic

Lafaipana had spread around the island of Upolu like wildfire. Soon the fale kava was packed to the brim with chiefs, and the house itself was surrounded by all the townsfolk. Finally, Lord Fasi'apule raised his cup to Lafaipana and all the chatter in the fale kava ceased.

"Wise Lafaipana, should we continue to base our riddles on food, I fear we will not only be here all week, but we'll end up sweetly fattened and spoiled!"

The fale kava erupted in a chorus of laughter and even the sour-faced Lafaipana grinned to himself.

"I agree. Let's move on," the ancient dwarf hissed. "Give me your worst."

Lord Fasi'apule cleared his throat and raised his cup again in toast.

"'I move with silent purpose, a thousand lovers have I witnessed, I hide not nor lie not, and though I change my form, my blanket never provides warmth'."

A wave of astonished murmur swept through the fale kava as the chiefs took a drink from their cups of kava and continued to talk. Lord Fasi'apule engaged in limited conversation and was mindful to keep his eye on Lafaipana should he turn to anyone for advice. As the lord was surrounded by Samoan chiefs, he was well monitored should he seek to cheat, so as a counter measure, he positioned two of his Tongan warriors to sit behind Lafaipana. Another hour passed. For the entire time, Lafaipana had not spoken to anyone and had sat with his eyes closed in meditation until finally, he raised his head and spoke.

"Your Highness," his words hushed the fale kava immediately. "A watcher in the night, always visible both crescent and full circle whose light provides no heat. Surely you speak of mother Mahina – the moon."

"You are wise, old dwarf. Correct," Lord Fasi'apule smiled.

Lafaipana exploded in an iniquitous cackle that revealed a mouthful of missing teeth. A cheer rose from the Samoan chiefs and the crowd outside the fale kava. Beaming and excited faces shone from all as the challenge continued to amaze and entertain. The companions glanced at one another, sharing the same feelings of excitement.

"I would never have guessed that one," Atiogie exclaimed.

"Of course not, you oaf," Vaohoi laughed.

"Why you little—"

"This is truly an exciting match of wit and wisdom," Adi said excitedly.

"With deadly outcomes," her partner Emori added.

"Talatama, are you aware of the repercussions to us if Lafaipana loses?" Pele whispered with a dark frown. "We are surrounded by Samoans loyal to the old dwarf."

"They wouldn't risk killing royalty, Pele," Talatama whispered back.

"So why have you been running for the past two months?" she said sarcastically.

"Don't do anything rash. Lord Feepo and Atiogie are loyal to us, that I know. Trust Lord Fasi'apule."

"I don't trust anyone," she sat down angrily as Lo'au patted her on the back reassuringly.

Lafaipana raised his new cup of kava to toast and all conversation ceased. The chiefs present in the circle raised their cups in the same fashion, awaiting his words.

"Your Highness, '*Poor people struggle for it, warriors do not care for it, nobility cling to it, but all end losing it*'," the ancient dwarf toasted.

All then drank from their cups and repeated the same ceremony as an even louder murmur of excitement rippled through the people and into the crowds outside. Following the toast, Lord Fasi'apule served the chiefs more kava. He then took his place in the circle and regarded Talatama and the companions sternly.

"He's not sure what it is," Vaohoi whispered within earshot of Lord Fasi'apule.

"Shhhhh! Keep your voice down, you rude thing," Mahina shot back at the young man.

"I wouldn't have a clue what that is either," Atiogie said rubbing his chin. All of the companions stared at the giant and then looked away.

The morning grew old. Vaohoi became restless and pushed his way through the men to peer outside the fale kava. He returned moments later and leaned over to Talatama.

"There has to be at least a few hundred people standing outside. I can't see a blade of grass."

"Great. That's what we need, more attention." Pele shook her head.

Suddenly Lord Fasi'apule caught the attention of the chiefs and Lafaipana. He raised his chin and stared at the ancient dwarf.

"A clever riddle, wise Lafaipana. The answer, however, must be: 'Life'".

This time Lafaipana did not attempt to smile. He stared back at Lord Fasi'apule and seemed to have frozen.

"Correct," he finally said.

Another cheer rose from the people, loudest from the Tongan warriors and the companions. Lord Fasi'apule laughed as he nudged his friends in congratulations. Lafaipana was not amused, however, and the long standing challenge started to take its toll. Progressing for over twelve hours of kava drinking, eating and under the stress of the challenge, the old dwarf's endurance began to wane. Noonday had passed and the heat of the day came wafting in like an open umu.

"Ask your question, Your Highness," he hissed before the cheering had stopped.

The crowds ceased their chatter and realised the old dwarf had lost his patience. They regarded the Tongan lord with expectation.

"Wise Lafaipana, 'I am a chaotic beast, I feed constantly on the weak, but I can be tamed and controlled, yet I know not one master,'" Lord Fasi'apule stated.

This time he toasted no cup and nor did Lafaipana. They both sat staring at one another in a psychological battle of will and wit. As the two competitors did not touch the kava, neither did those participating in the ceremony. Only the whispers from the crowds of fascinated people outside the fale kava were heard, and occasionally, a warrior would hush anyone who would began to speak too loudly.

For the first time, the villagers of Siumu were completely silent. Faint echoes of barking dogs could be heard, the screeching of lizards in the roof of the fale kava and even the distant sound of the surf. As Talatama and his companions bore witness to the intensity of the combatants, everyone seemed to lose track of time. No one knew how long it took Lafaipana to respond.

"*Fear*," Lafaipana said in a low hissing voice that echoed the fale kava.

Lord Fasi'apule broke his stare, and his eyes dropped to the ground. He looked over to Lafaipana and nodded. The Samoans erupted in a cheer that swept across the room but it was Lafaipana who raised his stubby hand for silence. He wanted to finish his adversary off.

"*What is the sound of singing winds?*" Lafaipana said quickly.

A short gasp of surprise came from the crowd at the short but complex riddle. Lord Fasi'apule for the first time frowned and closed his eyes. Silence reigned. The master tactician and warlord, teacher and mentor to dozens of generals, loved by the Empire, felt a chill of reality run up his spine. The riddle was simple, but its obvious simplicity returned many plausible answers. Within the first minute, he had thought of at least ten possible answers. Before he could let himself become twisted in the riddle, he turned to his old friend, Lord Feepo.

"Old friend, have you heard the answer of this riddle?" he whispered.

"Yes I have, Your Highness," Lord Feepo answered, his blind eyes blinking hesitantly.

Lord Fasi'apule nodded and then resumed mulling. Lord Feepo's answer comforted him greatly, for if Lafaipana rejected the correct answer, Lord Feepo could testify otherwise. More time passed. He pondered the Samoan way of life, the daily activities and past times, ceremonies and how they may differ to the Tongan ways. Some of the answers were Tongan specific, which he quickly discounted. Finally, he narrowed his answer down to a possible five different answers; the sound of the wind blowing through bamboo tubes, the sound of a storm wind filled with rain, the sound of wind through the trees, the sound of a wild fowl flying low over the bush when startled, or the sound of conches blown simultaneously that carries on the wind. When logic failed, Lord Fasi'apule listened to his heart. He sought the truth through his intuition, judgment and instinct. Within ten minutes he gave the quickest answer to the hardest question.

"Singing winds? *It is the sound of a wild fowl flying low over the bush when startled*, wise Lafaipana."

The ancient dwarf looked as though he was impaled through the chest. He glared at Lord Feepo then back to Fasi'apule before opening his toothless mouth, exposing his rotten gums. In burning frustration, he exhaled a high pitched scream of exasperation and struck his walking stick, which skidded across the floor into one of the Samoan chiefs. It was enough for the Tongan warriors and the companions to erupt in a cheer of success, as busy and excited talk amongst all the chiefs of the incredible battle burned through the people. Suddenly Lord Fasi'apule raised his hand for silence. He quickly struck back with a similar and seemingly simple riddle.

"Wise Lafaipana, *'What gives dust when you clap your cupped hands?'*" he stared at the ancient dwarf who was still red with anger.

The silence was deafening. No one spoke, no one whispered, no one moved. Lafaipana sat across the kava circle still fuming with, not just anger and frustration, but with deep rooted embarrassment and loss of face. For his entire life, he had been entrusted by the gods to protect the resting place of Sangone until his wit was to be beaten. Countless men had challenged him, countless men had failed.

For a time, the legend of Sangone was forgotten and Lafaipana lived in peace for many decades in solitude on the Samoan island of Savai'i. It was not until the past twenty years that the legend was rekindled and Lafaipana was called to challenge once again. But he had lost his kind ways. He had grown to relish the taste of human flesh and the enjoyment by which it was cruelly obtained. His evil ways were bent only on the promise of human sacrifice.

But something had changed during this challenge with Lord Fasi'apule. He finally accepted that he may have met his match. The fury and embarrassment had impaired his clarity and crippled his logic. The ancient dwarf regarded the Tongan lord sheepishly and sighed with a wheezing sound. The silence was palpable. Lafaipana groaned as he stood to his feet, then fell to a knee and bowed his head long.

"Your Highness, mighty and wise. I cannot answer your riddle. I concede defeat."

An explosion of deafening cheer erupted from the Tongan warriors and companions. Even the Samoan chiefs cheered and saluted the Tongan lord in glorious congratulations. A roar of joy from the crowds outside the fale kava expressed a deep finality of respect and awe; the challenge would not be matched in their lifetime. Lord Fasi'apule stood before Talatama as they shared the victory through their eyes before embracing hard.

"Brilliantly done, you crazy old fool," Talatama laughed as he held his mentor.

"You know me," he said, returning the elation and relief.

He turned to Lafaipana and resumed his serious demeanour. The dwarf too had composed himself from his short moment of defeat; his face had again become sour and bitter, twisted and evil. The full weight of consequence had begun to set in and he glared at Lord Fasi'apule with hatred.

"Wise Lafaipana, I subsequently hold you to our bargain."

"Yes, Your Highness. When do you wish to leave," the ancient dwarf hissed.

"Now."

CHAPTER 48

By the time Lord Fasi'apule and the companions exited the fale kava it was late afternoon. The heat from the day had dissipated and the feeling of warmth lingered with the falling sun. The crowds of people within the village were mixed with feelings of awe and reverence to the Tongan visitors. Most had begun to disperse and return to their homes, while Talatama held a quick meeting with his companions in the courtyard. He stood before his trusted friends with his hands on his hips, dressed in his full warrior garments ready for travel.

"Friends, time to move on," he smiled.

"Where do we go, Prince Talatama?" Lo'au stood placidly.

"Lafaipana mentioned Sangone's remains are on the island of Savai'i. We will accompany Lord Fasi'apule there for the completion of his quest."

"What then?" Mahina asked.

The prince cleared his throat and changed his tone. He knew his companions had become accustomed to his solemn speeches.

"You all heard what Lord Fasi'apule said. The king has issued orders for our arrest. All he wants is to bring us in for an interrogation of the events that took place in Niuatoputapu, nothing worse than that."

"I still can't fathom how General Kamohoali'i was able to sell this lie," Emori shook his head.

"Point is we can't afford to be captured, halted or waylaid by interruptions to our goal. We've no choice now but to hunt

Kamohoali'i down ourselves and thwart his plans before they come to fruition."

"We can't do that, not on our own," Pele scoffed. "I'm telling you now."

"That's why we will stick with our original plan and sail to Vava'u after assisting my uncle. I trust Lord Punake. He will aid our cause despite the king's order."

"That's risky, Prince Talatama," Adi cautioned.

"At this stage, we have no other choice."

"Why can't you just tell Lord Fasi'apule to return to the capital and tell the king we're innocent?" Vaohoi had to ask.

"Don't you see? Our message of warning, our plea of innocence to the king – that doesn't matter now Vaohoi. The only way we can both vindicate ourselves and stop Kamohoali'i is one and the same: capture him alive. Only now we have to avoid both imperial and Pulotulahi attention. It's going to be more risky and dangerous."

The companions fell silent and the prince knew again that he had to bring up their bonds together.

"I will remind you all again, you're not bound to continue this journey with me. This mission has just become graver and I'll not hold anything against you if you wish to leave."

"I'm with you to the end." Atiogie raised his large chin.

"Me too," Vaohoi giggled.

"Prince Talatama – I – I cannot continue," Adi said slowly, "I must leave."

The companions gasped in astonishment though Talatama and Lo'au did not seem surprised.

"My Lady?" Emori was as stunned as the rest of them.

"My Prince, I continued to travel with you out of our purpose of justice. However, now that we are all wanted by the Empire for the murders of those innocents – I can't go on."

"You coward." Pele glared at the Fijian priestess.

"It was my opinion at the outset to hand ourselves in," Adi defended herself. "I will fight against the persecution of the weak, but I cannot go against the will of the Empire – nor my own faith."

"Followers of the Order cannot be seen to be taking sides in political struggles," Lo'au added.

"I understand Adi," Talatama said coolly. "I commend your respect for authority and the duty to your own faith."

"I will, of course, remain with my Lady," the warrior priest said slowly.

"Are you sure about this?" Mahina touched Adi on the arm softly.

The Fijian priestess did not answer but nodded and averted her gaze from her friends. It was obvious that she was battling an internal struggle between her faith and her camaraderie with them.

"Then I thank you both for your assistance to the Empire, your Prince – and your friend," Talatama said in a personal tone, placing his hands on their shoulders. "With a heavy heart I bid you farewell," he smiled warmly. "You will always be welcome in my fellowship."

The two Fijians lowered their heads to Talatama, feeling the hurt of their parting before each of the companions took turns bidding farewell. Pele stood with her back to the Fijians and with her arms crossed. Vaohoi wiped the tears from his eyes. Lo'au embraced Adi lovingly as one of his own.

"Atiogie, can you organise your people to provide transport for them back to Fiji," Talatama turned to the giant.

"No problem."

"Good. As for the rest of you, prepare yourselves. We leave immediately."

The companions departed the courtyard to gather their things. Once they were gone, the prince turned to Adi one last time.

"Once this is over I will come to Fiji to find you both. Adi, you saved my life. I'll never forget that," he smiled before he made his way down to the village.

The group of six tongiakis sailed out into the melting brine tinged with pinks and oranges. The sun was a burning fireball on the shimmering vista, showing the way to the island of Savai'i. Four of the kalias were Lord Fasi'apule's fleet; one was the companions' vessel and the other, Lafaipana's crude and old sea craft. Lafaipana's tattered old craft was slow and the rest of the fleet had to bind most of their sails to remain behind. Talatama stood proudly at the helm, Atiogie and Pele, his first mates, wrestling with the sails and the fixtures on the craft. Mahina and Vaohoi sat together at the bow of the vessel staring out towards the sunset.

The vessels arrived on the shores of Savai'i under the gleaming twilight of a full moon. Once they moored their tongiakis and walked ashore, one of the Samoan warriors approached the Tongan contingent on the beach and bowed respectfully.

"Your Highness, I request on behalf of Lafaipana, that we stop at the town of Pulemelei and rest for the night. His strength is failing fast and the location of Sangone is many hours travel through the mountains."

"I agree, to the town of Pulemelei until dawn. Then we resume our journey," Lord Fasi'apule said quickly then turned to his men and Talatama. "Prepare for a hike, men!"

Dozens of torches were lit on the beach to part the darkness. The Samoan party, led by Lafaipana, took the lead through the jungle until they found a narrow footpath. The companions, together with Lord Fasi'apule's men, followed the Samoans on the treacherous path by torchlight. Almost two hours passed before they saw faint light through the jungle ahead of them. The light grew brighter and brighter and before long they stopped and heard strong words from their Samoan party and guards ahead. They were then given permission to enter the township of Pulemelei.

It was midnight when they walked through the village, silent and deserted, apart from the wandering soldier or priest. Torchlight ebbed through the township, the low incandescence, exposing many fales and large structures. However, Pulemelei was renowned for one particular monument of importance. As the companions and Lord Fasi'apule's men continued to walk, they stared at the famous stone pyramid that lay amid a sacred area, kempt and trimmed. Firelight illuminated the base of the pyramid next to the visible hearths that lined its length. It was approximately sixty metres wide; its peak was at fourteen metres high and was built from an immense collection of basalt rocks taken from the ancient volcano Matavanu, located in the centre of the island.

"By Hikule'o and his demons, what is that?" Vaohoi exclaimed loudly.

"Keep your voice down, young one," Lo'au said. "It's the great Pyramid of Pulemelei, the greatest monument dedicated to Tangaloa."

"I've never seen anything like it," Mahina whispered.

"It was built about two hundred years ago," Lo'au said as they walked. "The Priests of Tangaloa pray atop of it, burn offerings in the hearths to Tangaloa and conduct ceremonial services. Many followers of Tangaloa come from kilometres around to this place."

"How do you know so much about it, old man?" Atiogie looked down to Lo'au.

"Do you want to know the real story?" Lo'au whispered, and Atiogie leaned closer. "This was once the castle of the great Tangaloa Eiki himself. It was built when they first settled here from Pulotu."

Everyone glanced at Lo'au as Atiogie face was blank. Lo'au grinned with amusement.

"I didn't know you've been here before, Lo'au," Talatama said curiously.

"I've been to many places, young Prince, many different places."

The companions and the group soon passed the Pyramid of Pulemelei and came to the vacant fales provided by the chief of the township. Talatama strode forward to Lord Fasi'apule's quarters and had a brief conversation with him.

"We're taking a risk, Your Highness," one of the Tongan warriors said.

"They wouldn't attempt to murder us," Talatama nodded.

"And their word to lead us to Sangone?" the same warrior asked.

"Prepare for a full fifteen man picket. Watch their every move during the night. Wake me immediately if things go afoul," Lord Fasi'apule placed his hand on the prince's shoulder. "Have a good night's rest. I know I will!"

Morning came quickly for Talatama; he felt he had only slept an hour. He felt a little groggy and somewhat dehydrated, so at dawn he quickly collected a few young coconuts and drank the milk of one freshly husked. He woke the rest of the companions, most of who looked to feel the same. He offered the rest of the refreshing coconuts to his friends, urging them to prepare for a march. Not long after, a messenger from Lord Fasi'apule's group approached Talatama and notified them of their hasty departure.

The trail into the mountains was wilder than the track from the beach; it was abundant with dangerous divots and uneven surfaces and weaved through overgrown jungle that tripped the feet and swung at the head. It led up steep hills and down into gapping chasms. After a while, the Tongans doubted it was a human trail at all. It was more akin to an animal's path, or an ancient path used by recluse men condemned to living their lives in the solitude of the mountain forests. Frequently, Vaohoi would complain about the dense jungle and joke that it was no wonder no one had found the remains of Sangone.

After hours of trudging through the jungle in a direction that the Tongans had given up guessing, a shout from the Samoan group ahead called out. Following a brief reprieve, a Samoan runner appeared before Lord Fasi'apule and Talatama's group and advised them that they had come within a few hundred metres of the remains. Only Lord Fasi'apule, three of his own men, Talatama and Atiogie were permitted to continue. The three chiefs complied immediately, and marched ahead to unite with Lafaipana and three of his warriors.

"This way, Your Highness," Lafaipana hissed, saliva and perspiration flaying from his chin.

The small group turned off the rough trail into the jungle. Lafaipana's warriors struck through the overhanging shrubbery and vines ahead of the chiefs. It was only a couple of minutes walk until the group stepped out into a jungle glade filled with healthy, tall grass. It was bare but for an old, twisted candlenut tree that stood directly in the centre. Perhaps once a grand and fruitful tree, it was now ancient and withered, white in colour and dead in appearance. Lafaipana tapped his warriors aside with feeble strikes and led the way towards it. The Tongans noticed that the ancient dwarf began to walk in a dreamy daze, occasionally murmuring to himself and staring at the tree.

As the group came closer, the Tongans observed that around the base of the candlenut tree were dozens of human skulls. They were bound together by twine, threaded through the eye sockets, and wound around the girth of the ancient tree. Some of the skulls were so old and deteriorated they had snapped from the ropes and lay in fragments. Lafaipana lowered his head and muttered something indiscernible before touching the tree with his squat fingers. He turned to the Tongans.

"Dig here," he pointed at the base of the tree.

Lord Fasi'apule ordered his three warriors to commence digging immediately, as Talatama watched the old dwarf intently. Atiogie seemed preoccupied with his own thoughts and Lord Fasi'apule kept staring around the mysterious glade. As the Tongans dug, the group became aware of an eerie wind that blew around the glade and whistled through the branches of the ghostly tree. The wind had a bite of an unnatural chill, like an icy rancour to an unwelcome guest. The temperature dropped. Talatama, a man with little patience for spirituality, could not deny the glade, even in broad daylight, was filled with a suffocating, vaporous evil that made the skin crawl.

As the screeching wind came to a crescendo, the Tongan warriors exhaled a laborious shout of victory and everyone quickly circled the deep hole they had dug. One of the warriors was on his knees and was uncovering a large amount of tapa with his hands. He found the edges through the rusty earth and finally lifted the buried treasure to Lord Fasi'apule, before they clambered out of the hole.

The lord unravelled the tapa nervously, and privately peeked into its contents. What he saw brought an expression of wonderment to his face as he then passed the treasure to a reluctant Talatama. He turned to face the ancient dwarf with a grim and unmerciful glare.

"Now that I have retrieved the remains of Sangone, you are to grant me one wish, oh Lafaipana."

The ancient dwarf returned a bitter recollection.

"Search your heart, see the evil you have done, feel the pain and suffering you have taken part in, accept your fate in that which you have condemned others to, and die in peace."

There was silence. Suddenly the twisted evil and malevolence seemed to vanish from Lafaipana's wrinkled face. The two sages stared at one another, not in a battle of wit but in a vestige of eternal understanding. Lafaipana nodded and bowed to Lord Fasi'apule before stepping down in the hole from which the remains of Sangone had been buried.

"Let me not lay alone," he asked in a feeble tone. "Grant me a branch for my dove to perch on."

Lord Fasi'apule ordered one of his warriors to lop down a large branch from the candlenut tree. He then heaved the heavy six foot branch down into the pit where Lafaipana stood. The group watched Lafaipana lie down next to the branch and wrap his arms around it.

"Embrace she who has enjoyed the spoils of sacrifice over the centuries, your wife and concubine." Fasi'apule then motioned to the remaining Samoan warriors.

There was no sound but the eerie whistling of the wind as the Tongans stood and watched the Samoan warriors bury the dwarf alive. Once the hole was refilled, the group left the glade with the remains of Sangone. The candlenut tree and Lafaipana's resting place was then forever lost.

CHAPTER 49

The small group returned to the main party on the trail and prepared to turn back. With a melodious song, the Samoan contingent led the Tongans back down the path through the jungle. Hearing their approach, the companions could not wait to ask Talatama what happened.

"Is that the remains of Sangone??" Vaohoi pointed excitedly at the old tapa package being carried by two of Lord Fasi'apule's men.

"Yes, that's it," Talatama said as they walked.

"What happened? Where is the old dwarf?" the youngster persisted.

"We dug up the remains and when we did, the dwarf withered and died at the base of the tree."

"Fascinating!" Vaohoi was absolutely taken.

Lo'au stared at the prince and returned a discernable grin. He understood the reality was a little more detailed.

The journey back to the village of Pulemelei was uneventful. Once they had made it to the township, they were provided with a bounteous feast of fruit and roasted pork in honour of Lord Fasi'apule and Talatama. After enjoying a good meal, they rested in the shade of a large mango tree and briefly discussed Adi and Emori's decision to leave the group. It had only been half a day and the group was already feeling the void of their absence.

When it became obvious the subject would not bring closure, they slowly found their feet and gathered their things. Talatama remained with his back against the tree, comfortable enough to remain for a moment longer. Mahina waited for the others to leave before she captured his gaze and returned to sit with him. Shaken from thought, the prince reflected her hungry glare as they were now alone; such a scarce and precious gift could not be wasted. He reached out to touch her, his intent purposeful. Instead she laughed and slapped his hand away. She playfully opposed his further attempts, until after much exertion, both conceded and laughed together.

"Not so hasty, mighty Prince!" she remained giggling.

Talatama chuckled to himself and savoured the moment. He remained smiling as their eyes locked and their joy slowly melted to sober affection. The prince's heart shook with captivation as he moved towards her lips. Suddenly he felt her hand shove something into his. Mahina leapt to her feet and beamed like a little girl.

"I want you to have this."

Lying in his palm was a beautifully carved ring of whale ivory. It was thin and delicate, etched with fine grooves that depicted a strange motif; birds in flight, evading a giant octopus' tentacles rising up from the sea. It was well worn: its keep clearly sentimental.

"This – Mahina this is too valuable! I can't accept this gift," the prince exclaimed, nonetheless touched to have been offered such a treasure.

"Keep it. It is yours."

"No, I -"

"Often I've pondered over its carvings, what their real meaning was. When my mother gave it to me she couldn't give me the answers."

She turned and walked in the direction of the companions who could be seen in the distance.

"Perhaps you can discover its significance one day and tell me," she smiled over her shoulder.

The afternoon had begun to set in when Talatama and Lord Fasi'apule agreed to move on and return to their vessels. The sun was scorching and the humidity was noticeably greater than that in Upolu. Wiping the sweat from their brows, the group took to their feet and began to march through the township of Pulemelei. As they passed the great Pyramid of Pulemelei, they observed a man at the base of the structure in conversation with a priest. The man ended his exchange and began to walk casually towards them. His stride was so familiar, his appearance, unmistakable.

"Maui Atalaga!" Vaohoi cheered in unison with Pele and others in the group.

The folk hero nonchalantly walked to meet them on the main road outside the sanctified boundaries of the site. The companions patted him on the back in warm welcome, and he grinned without words, so typical of his distant and aloof demeanour. He stood strongly with his long hair tied to the pinnacle of his skull, Mohemamahi strapped to his back and a woven vala that covered his groin and backside.

"Maui Atalaga, well met again." Talatama nodded his head.

"What are you doing here?" Pele asked, his appearance having an obvious effect on her.

"Just wandering," he said hollowly.

"Brother." Lo'au smiled and placed his hand on his shoulder.

Maui Atalaga nodded, "And you?"

"We were here to gather the Shell of Sangone," Atiogie said.

"Finally someone was able to outwit that mangy old fool. About time Sangone's remains were resurfaced, she has spent too long in the earth. She was a god of the sea after all."

"Indeed, her remains will return to their previous grandeur once again," Lo'au agreed.

"Maui Atalaga, we're returning to our vessels to leave Samoa," the prince mentioned, observing that Lord Fasi'apule's group had moved ahead of them. "Will you be joining us again?"

"Which way are you headed?" He squinted and looked into the distance.

"That way."

"Lead on," he nodded.

The companions did not hide their glee to once again join with their mystical comrade. Maui Atalaga paired up with Lo'au and chatted with him as the companions continued their journey out of Pulemelei. They made their way through the jungle once again, and as they travelled in daylight, it took them barely an hour to reach the sea.

Once they had stepped out onto the sandy beach, Maui Atalaga suddenly headed in the opposite direction along the shore, and soon after disappeared around an isthmus. Talatama turned quizzically to Lo'au.

"His vessel is moored a kilometre away on another beach. He will make sail and meet us out past the reef," the old mu'a smiled.

Lord Fasi'apule called out to Talatama as he made his way over to their position. His warriors were already throwing their possessions on board their tongiakis and preparing to set sail. His feet kicked the deep, yellow sand as he trudged towards the prince carrying the tapa package of Sangone's remains. He stopped in the shade of a hanging palm as he spoke to the prince, and his laboured breath did not express the meaning behind words as he spoke.

"Talatama, I told you that I could not join you in arms against the evil that you fight, and the evil from within."

"Yes, Teacher."

"But I wanted you to remain with me until my quest was completed, and it is now complete," Lord Fasi'apule caught his breath. "But I also told you that even though I couldn't stand by your side in battle, I would aid you in your journey yet to come."

He knelt down and carefully placed the tattered tapa package on the sand at Talatama's feet before smiling.

"My gift to you."

Talatama stared at him in astonishment. "But, Uncle, your quest is not complete until you return the remains to my father."

"As I said, my quest is now complete. It will aid you on what dark and dangerous paths you now face. I will presume the return of the remains to coincide with your evidence of innocence and victory – in such timely fashion."

Then without waiting for an answer, the old warlord embraced Talatama fiercely and pressed their noses against each other.

"I pray that I see you again soon." Lord Fasi'apule tipped his head upwards as a farewell gesture.

Talatama knew he could not argue with his old teacher as he sighed and inspected the remains of Sangone. He looked up to Lord Fasi'apule who was already trudging through the sand back to his fleet.

"Thank you, Uncle. Safe journey," he finally said.

"A royal gift," Lo'au said sternly over the shoulder of the prince.

"Yes, well, mine to hold onto until we return it to the capital."

"But until then, we shall make good use of it," the old man smiled. "When we're out at sea I will show you."

The prince seemed to have too much on his mind to fathom Lo'au's words. He watched Lord Fasi'apule and his fleet take to the sea with impressive speed. Within short moments, they had sailed out beyond the eastern headland and disappeared beyond view.

Mahina approached the prince and stood next to him as he stared out to sea. When the others were not watching, she slipped her hand into his and gripped it lovingly. Her touch broke him from his gaze and returned him to the present, her eyes burning with desire and the hope of things to come. She swiftly broke away when the others turned to them. Talatama grinned and turned to Atiogie, Vaohoi and Pele who were awaiting his order.

"Right, let's make sail, comrades," he shouted in a voice filled with new vigour.

After the supplies were loaded on their vessel, the companions pushed the tongiaki into the calm waves and leapt aboard. Atiogie struck the sails and a favourable wind propelled their vessel out from the inlet from whence they came. The late afternoon had begun to end, and the beautiful colours of sunset lit the sky. The ambiance seemed to illuminate what appeared to be a sizable reef beyond the inlet. Its iridescent waters glistened like jewels in the ocean and as the companions' tongiaki came closer, it was apparent the reef was extremely shallow and deceptive to the eye.

Mahina screamed at the same time Talatama saw it: a tongiaki moored off the seaward end of the reef, one they recognised with shuddering recall. It was unmistakably the Pulotulahi vessel used to hold Mahina captive in Niuafo'ou. Lined along the portside were dozens of men, glaring directly at the companions with fierce anticipation. Suddenly, Vaohoi shrieked as he pointed at the hull. Small holes chiselled out in the flooring had gone unnoticed, but had now caused the vessel to take in water that could not be stopped. It was obvious to Talatama - the Pulotulahi had sabotaged their tongiaki and waited for them to flounder helplessly.

"Lo'au and Vaohoi! Try to plug up the holes! The rest of you prepare for battle!" Talatama grasped for weapons.

As their craft drifted closer to the Pulotulahi's vessel, the companions noticed a figure perched on the reef, a fair distance from the enemy. Mo'unga, the dark witch, stood on a coral ridge that barely reached her knees. The shallow shelf created an illusion that she defied gravity and stood on water. Her hands were outstretched towards them as she chanted in an undiscernible language. Talatama squinted in confusion before turning to Lo'au and Vaohoi as they desperately called out to him.

"Talatama! We can't fill the holes!" Vaohoi spluttered as he and Lo'au wrestled with gushing water drowning the hulls.

"We're going down," Pele cursed.

"We're going for a swim!" Atiogie laughed in the face of catastrophe.

"And we won't be alone," Mahina said chillingly as she pointed to the water.

The companions stared in horror. Dozens of grey fins protruded from the water's surface and began to circle their sinking tongiaki. The tiger sharks were great in size, sleek and powerful as they weaved through the dark water. But there was a king man-eater that rivalled the length of the tongiaki; it dwarfed the other sharks and loitered just beyond the end of the reef. The prince regarded their peril with grim determination. He had already noted the speed of their tongiaki slowing, and judging by the water they were taking on, the prospect of reaching the end of the reef was slim. He turned to his companions, his face a reflection of courage.

"Brandish your weapons, comrades. We face a hard fight to escape this."

On the other vessel hoarded dozens of Pulotulahi and Kupe, the Weeping Assassin, with a feverish glower, filled with an appetite for death. Weeks ago, he was paired with Mo'unga to hunt down the companions wherever they may be, while the Unarmed Warrior and the Fallen Commander had followed a second lead in another area of Samoa. Kupe grinned with excitement that he had found them first. He stared out to Mo'unga on the reef.

"Men! Watch on with great detail," he shouted as a wicked cheer exploded from the tongiaki, "It's not every day you watch a prince served to the monsters of the deep!"

Pele had already drawn her bow to fire arrows into sharks that loomed close. Lo'au, Mahina and Vaohoi had armed themselves with half decent spears that they had salvaged from the hull. Talatama readied himself with the Peace Maker and Atiogie, with his weighty club of destruction. In minutes, the hulls were fully submerged and the platform in the centre of the tongiaki was barely above water. They grouped together, back to back, facing outwards as the platform began to dip into the sea, making the footing hazardous and increasing their risk of slipping into the water.

"The shark attack seems unnatural!" Talatama shouted above the scramble of defences. "I've never seen them school against a vessel with such ferocity!"

"It is the shark witch, Mo'unga, who stands there on the reef." Pele called back over her shoulder. "She possesses their minds!"

"Slay her!!" Talatama roared.

Pele shot a glance over to Mo'unga, positioned about forty metres from their sinking vessel and remained poised with her hands stretched out in hypnotic concentration. Pele's blood boiled as she broke the resistance and aimed her bow towards her. However as she fired each shot, the surging platform and the sudden counter attacks from her companions ruined her aim. She fired her third shot and screamed in frustration. Before any of the companions realised, Pele had taken a giant leap from the sinking platform and scarcely landed on the edge of a shallow portion of the reef. Talatama called out to her then saw the emotion on her face; the last time he saw her so riled was during the battle of Niuatoputapu.

She slung her bow over her shoulder, unveiled her obsidian axe and started running across the coral ridgeline, splashes of water resounding with each step. Her face was a reflection of utter fury and bloodlust, but each time she came close to Mo'unga, the shallow ridgeline would end, pushing her to find an alternate route. But her desire for killing was irrepressible: she would not stop. Small clouds of pink and red expanded into the water where she stepped. Her feet had become badly sliced from the sharp coral, but she was numb to the pain. Though Mo'unga did nothing to elude the approaching she-warrior, a score of sharks about the sinking tongiaki swiftly followed her. They waited in the deeper channels between the shallow ridgelines, awaiting one wrong step.

Groups of Pulotulahi warriors shouted aboard the vessel as they pointed at Pele with urgency, but none of them possessed any bows and her position was too far for javelining spears. They watched on as the shipmen tried to steer their vessel towards Mo'unga.

"Do not break our position!" Kupe snapped at the helmsman. "Mo'unga fights alone!"

The warriors glanced at Kupe briefly and resumed their observing. The Weeping Assassin knew Pele would not stop, but did nothing.

"You'd better hope she slips, witch," he muttered under his breath.

The companions' struggle was becoming worse. All were striking the thrashing bodies of hungry sharks continuously seemingly with no effect. Salty perspiration flowed down Talatama's face as his blows and thrusts pierced and crushed before him. He realised the platform was now below sea level and they were all almost knee high in water. It was only a matter of moments before they succumbed to fatigue and terrifying deaths.

Pele finally located the ridgeline that led towards Mo'unga. It did not directly connect with hers however. A deep chasm of water lay between their ridgelines and sharks loitered within awaiting their prey. She felt her quiver for arrows, there was only one left. Without hesitation she positioned her bow, fitted the last arrow and fired. At a mere ten metres, the shot was not difficult for an archer of Pele's skill. The arrow struck Mo'unga hard in the shoulder and spun her into water. But within seconds, the shark witch slowly clambered back onto her coral shelf and struggled to continue her black magic.

Mo'unga struggled to correct herself however, as the arrow protruding from her shoulder was enough to break her hold on many sharks. Most of the man eaters between her and Pele began to swim away, and when Pele saw this, it was enough for her to take the risk. She dived into the water and swam with all her might. In what seemed an eternity, she reached the other ridgeline unharmed. Leaping onto the corral shelf she broke into a sprint towards Mo'unga with the ferocity of the fire goddess herself. Her black axe glinted in the failing sun before it divided Mo'unga's head in two like the splitting of a breadfruit. The witch's long hair suddenly dropped from her body with the rest of the cranium. Spears whistled through the air, narrowly missing the victorious she-warrior and with a thrust of her foot, she kicked the lifeless body of Mo'unga into the deep water. Wild in the opulence of blood, the sharks claimed her in violent thrashes.

At that moment, Talatama looked up from his weary battle and caught sight of Maui Atalaga and his war tongiaki speeding towards them.

"Thank the gods!" he swore.

The companions barely found the strength to cheer at the sight of their salvation; Atiogie was supporting Lo'au in his arms and Vaohoi slumped with fatigue. Across the reef and knowing the witchcraft had failed, Kupe finally gave the order to steer their vessel towards Pele. She seethed and stood her ground, hurling back some of the spears. She even retrieved her last arrow floating in the water and managed to claim another victim.

"Pele!" Talatama shouted, pointing at Maui Atalaga's war tongiaki.

She spotted them approaching and seemed to lose her taste for fighting. She dived back into the reef channel and began to swim. By this time, most of the man-eaters had dispersed from the sinking vessel and disappeared. However, the colossal shark beyond the reef was not so dissuaded, and lingered after. Maui Atalaga's vessel passed it to reach the end of the reef. He wasted no time throwing down ropes for the companions to clamber aboard.

After Lo'au was on deck, Vaohoi fell limp as he tried to climb the ropes. Atiogie caught him and saw the gaping punctures in his left thigh, so deep that he could see his femur. Maui Atalaga grabbed the teenager and hauled him to safety. Pele pulled herself up the ropes after Mahina. Talatama was the last to climb aboard, only after he had rescued the remains of Sangone that were floating in the sea. Once he stepped onto the sturdy platform, the prince glared towards the smaller Pulotulahi vessel. He turned to Maui Atalaga with the fury of a warrior insulted.

"Ram it."

CHAPTER 50

Maui Atalaga laughed heartily. His mighty sails caught the full strength of the wind that blew them towards their prey. Their hulls were built with the hardest ironwood in the Pacific, carved and bound with dovetail notches and the toughest ropes of twine ever woven. The tongiaki was nothing short of indestructible. By the time the war craft struck the Pulotulahi vessel, its wind propulsion was at its height and though only one of the hulls struck the vessel, it was enough. The initial impact smashed the craft into splinters then drove through the centre platform, cleaving it in two. Men jumped for their lives as the tongiaki was totally destroyed and left to sink into the depths beyond the reef. Kupe cursed loudly, even as he dived into the water.

The companions felt the urge to throw their arms in the air and cheer but could not. Most of them were still catching their breath or sprawled exhausted on the deck. The war tongiaki continued its course at high speed as the folk hero swung from one side of the platform to the other, altering the angle of the sails to steer them out towards the open sea. Talatama squinted behind them as the sea wind blew in his face and tossed his hair. The cruel irony of the sight of the giant shark circling the imminent Pulotulahi victims was not lost on him despite his relief. Before they were out of sight, he saw that a few men had made it to the shallow reef and to safety.

Kupe pulled himself onto the coral shelf and watched helplessly as most of his men, too far removed from his reach, were ripped apart. He then glared out to the vanishing tongiaki, his face a reflection of chilling acquiescence not understood by his men scuttling for their lives. At length, he helped those he could up on to the shelf as his weeping eye never wavered from the companions. Once again, they had slipped from his grasp.

A few days passed and the commanders of the Pulotulahi regrouped as the feeling of retribution rivalled the direct orders of General Kamohoali'i. Although Kamohoali'i's instructions were to dispose of the prince quickly and to return to Vava'u, Kupe's news of their defeat instigated understandable commotion from Omani. Though Siateki accepted Mo'unga's death as a frustrating loss, Omani took the news hard. He swore in a bitter rage to capture Talatama, and give him a slow, torturous death.

Had it not been for Kupe's leadership, the Unarmed Warrior would have broken ranks and become a renegade of revenge. Yet the others were surprised to see Kupe regard Mo'unga's death lightly and that in his view, retribution was out of the question. So obvious was this that it began to fester in Omani's black heart.

It was early night as they sat on a deserted beach on the island of Upolu. Dozens of Pulotulahi warriors camped nearby around small fires. Kupe, Omani and Siateki sat together around their own dwindling fire. The Unarmed Warrior had been fuming in silence when Kupe, weary of her passing, did not wish Mo'unga's name to be mentioned again. Kupe could not restrain himself.

"You loved her, didn't you?" he finally mocked.

"You old bastard," Omani spat. "What would you know about love?"

"Enough not to fall for fools," he replied venomously.

Omani was held back by Siateki as he leapt up to his feet. Sand was kicked into the fire during the brief struggle and the flames crackled and flared. Many of the Pulotulahi minions glanced over to them silently.

"Stop it both of you!" Siateki growled with clenched teeth. "Do you know nothing of leadership?"

"Release me!" Omani yelled as he quit struggling and sat back down.

"Only days ago, we lost a third of our men and yet another opportunity went begging. These paltry few remaining don't need to see the friction in our leadership!" Siateki whispered angrily. "Mo'unga is gone. She had her chance. Now is the time for us to rethink our strategy and become stronger in our purpose and minds."

"My point exactly," the Weeping Assassin said, staring at Omani.

"Well it's simple. First, we need to follow them," Siateki continued following a long pause. "They sail to Vava'u – and to certain capture. Then all we need do is prevent them from escaping."

"Agreed," Kupe said. "With the numbers on our side, we'll not fail this time."

"Good." Omani breathed, exhaling the remnants of his grief.

The Weeping Assassin suddenly stood and barked orders to the Pulotulahi warriors. He threw his belongings over his shoulder and indicated his intention to the two commanders.

"Prepare to sail, men! We leave once you douse the fires!"

Beyond the southern horizon on that very evening, the companions continued their journey towards the islands of Vava'u on calm seas. The fire burned brightly in the centre of the platform and it provided warmth on what was an unusually chilly night. Vaohoi sat solemnly, still nursing his wounds and self pity. The rest of the companions sat around the fire and shared stories of their victories and close calls over the past couple of months together. Talatama sat with Mahina, and although the companions may have guessed their union, the prince's conservative standards displayed no affection towards her in public.

Atiogie munched on some leftover food he found in the hulls of the war craft. Maui Atalaga stood over by the masts with his back to the fire, staring out into the blackness and occasionally staring up to the stars. Pele slowly approached the hero, walking with a slight limp from her cut and torn feet. She leant her body and head against his, and he did nothing to avert her affection.

Lo'au smiled to Talatama as he sat down opposite him, cradling the tapa wrapped treasure of Sangone. The old man's smile, bathed in firelight, stirred the prince's curiosity.

"It's time to make use of your kingly gift," Lo'au nodded.

"What do you mean?"

"It was no mere coincidence that this ancient relic came into your possession," the old man said as he began to un-wrap the treasure.

Talatama did not question him further and waited patiently for him to complete the removal of the old tapa. As he watched Lo'au carefully open each of the folds, he noticed that the ancient fabric had become brittle as a result of contact with sea water. A sudden anxiety dawned on him that the priceless treasure could have suffered similar damage during their hasty escape. He sat up and waited with reserve, concerned to accept what may come.

"Ahh, blessed be the holy remains of Sangone," Lo'au whispered in admiration.

"By Tangaloa!" Talatama balked in awe.

The mu'a slowly exposed the remains, brushing away torn pieces of fabric that clung to the treasure. When the firelight touched the pure surface of the carapace, it reflected a glow like soft moonlight off the calm sea. The exterior scales were magnificently polished, sparkling in an untainted smoothness like water poured from a goblet. Its murky brown, hazel and green hues swirled as mist beneath the surface of the shell. Its majesty was unrivalled. Its, was beauty unmatched, and its rarity unparalleled.

"It's the most beautiful thing I've ever seen ..." Mahina whispered in utter amazement.

"I've never seen anything like it," the prince did not realise he had sat up and moved to his knees.

"By the bones of my father's father!" Atiogie exasperated. "No wonder the mangy old dwarf gave his life to defend it!"

Vaohoi raised his head wearily to catch a sight of the shell. Pele turned and squinted in disbelief. Maui Atalaga gave the shell a glance and smiled as though he had seen it many times before. Lo'au ran his hand over its surface soothingly, as if the legendary turtle were alive. He turned and unfolded a new blanket of tapa on the deck to his side, carefully lifted the shell from its tattered bonds and placed it onto the fresh tapa. Beneath the shell was the plastron of Sangone, the flatter, hard underbelly that had been separated from the carapace. Its colour was a creamy white, opaque and supple in texture, and the scales could be seen with finer relief.

The old mu'a repeated the movement and placed the plastron next to the carapace before he threw the old tapa wraps into the sea and focused his attention on the treasure. He sat for long moments staring over the remains.

"Lo'au - what use could this be, albeit a grand and priceless treasure?" Talatama finally said.

"My Prince, you know the legends. The shell, the remains of the Goddess of Mercy in her physical form, possesses a mythical aura; bestowing mercy to he who holds it. Your uncle is a clever fellow." Lo'au smiled. "He knew well that you would need this gift in the destiny that lies before you."

"I understand, but I won't be carrying it under my arm wherever I go. I'd certainly prove the legends wrong by invoking my death soon enough."

"You forget, Prince Talatama, I was once a craftsman," he returned modestly. "Give me one more night and I'll show you."

The night did not linger and neither did the coming of the morn. The sea wind was strong and true and it blew favourably for the companions in their southerly direction. The day passed by quickly and without issue. Before long, the sun had fallen and Atiogie had lit a fire in the centre platform for the evening. The evening had lessened the day's fervent winds and slowed their speed to a slow cruise. The flames flickered under a dark and moonless sky.

Vaohoi had, within the last twenty-four hours, improved greatly in his recovery. His badly bitten leg was wrapped securely in bandages that were replaced every few hours. The youngster had also found his sturdy sea legs and began to hobble around the deck as best he could. His mobility lifted his spirits and it was not long before the companions were subjected to his customary nature. He had begun to sing songs of adventure and women, annoying everyone, Atiogie most of all.

Pele lay by the fire on her back, her arm over her eyes as Atiogie shared the last morsels of food with Vaohoi around the fire. Maui Atalaga stood strongly at the helm, a solitary duty that he welcomed and, indeed, preferred. Talatama was seated across from Lo'au, both sitting cross-legged in a ceremonial fashion.

"Prince Talatama, I have completed my task."

"I'm eager to see it."

"I present to you, the legendary Shell of Sangone, now furnished to aid and provide protection for you."

Lo'au unwrapped the tapa cloth to expose the same shell as the prince had seen the previous night. He saw nothing dissimilar, until Lo'au lifted the shell onto its end and he saw the straps that joined the carapace to the underside. He immediately leant forward and marvelled the artistry that Lo'au had created.

"It is now your body armour, my Prince."

Talatama stood in fascination and lifted it to eye level while inspecting its make. The old mu'a rose and took hold of the other side of the legendary artefact.

"Here, let me help you wear it." He raised the bottom ends of the two piece shell over Talatama's head and carefully lowered it, until the straps held securely over the shoulders. The length of the underside was a perfect fit between the prince's collarbone and his abdomen. The carapace protruded from the nape of his neck and slimmed down to the small of the back, while the width between the shells was enough to accommodate his muscular torso and afford flexible arm movement. Lo'au tied the last straps around his navel and stood back to see his handiwork.

"Outstanding."

The companions immediately congregated around Talatama and were awestruck by the grandeur of artistry. The plastron hugged his muscular chest and stomach like a second skin, its finer scales replacing rippling sinew. The hefty shell around his back made him appear larger and more intimidating, and in many ways, reflected a mythical appearance in the firelight.

Talatama picked up the Peace Maker, lunged forwards and stepped back, shifted and struck the naked air with multiple strikes before slowing to a halt.

"I'm truly amazed," Talatama breathed. "The weight of it is nothing like it looks. And I have complete mobility."

The companions exclaimed their wonder at such a beautiful yet powerful sight and the prince could not disagree, unable to take his eyes off the new armour.

"Lo'au, you honour me too much," he smiled broadly. "Thank you."

The old mu'a bowed his head, "You're welcome. You're destiny is now maturing."

CHAPTER 51

Neiafu, Vava'u Islands
Winter, A.D.1121

The Castle of Ha'afuluhao was one of the principal commissions of the Empire, second largest only to the Royal Castles in Heketa, Tongatapu. The grand ramparts, tiered stone slabs, and impregnable walls were the creation of King Momo almost seventy years prior, during the great Kaimana Wars. The castle was perched atop of Mount Talau, Vava'u's highest peak, built purely to withstand a direct assault from up to ten thousand men. All, assaulting armies in the past had met terrible struggles ascending the difficult incline while defending against arrows and boulders from above.

The foundations in the grounds and construction of the castle itself took almost ten years. King Momo, who had foreseen the need for a mighty stronghold towards the end of the 'Ten Years of Rebirth', had chosen the position and the design strategically. Mount Talau was the bulbous end of an isthmus that stretched to the west from Neiafu. Its position and height presented a perfect view over the only channel of sea needed to reach the capital. This proved a crucial position of defence against approaching vessels and a position of strength against any attacks. King Momo saw its potential immediately.

For years, the summit of Mount Talau was cleared of jungle and the earth flattened to create the grounds. An area of three hundred square metres was cleared for the castle and the garrison that was to surround it. Its natural cliffs provided an advantage against advancement from the sea, tapering off to the rear and towards the capital. Stone slabs were cut from far away coral shores and brought to the site. Each slab weighed from between five hundred and fifteen hundred kilograms. They were placed atop the natural summit in rows of steep steps that acted as yet more impediments against an attack.

Finally, the castle itself was constructed from solid ironbark wood, imported from the isles of Fiji. The walls rose seven metres around the extremities and were solid enough to withstand the strongest earthquakes or feeble fire attacks. The central timberwork of the hawks nest rose to a height of almost fifteen metres. The soldiers who stood guard atop it commanded a view that encapsulated the entire islands of Vava'u, and hundreds of kilometres in all directions.

Only one road connected the castle grounds to the town of Neiafu, a thoroughfare that exited the grounds towards the north east and followed the isthmus into the prosperous township. The majority of Vava'u's soldiers were stationed within the castle grounds at the dozens of garrisoned fales. The other main stations in the group were Neiafu, Feletoa, Pangai, Nuapapu, Euakafa and Hunga.

Noble Punake, third cousin to King Tu'itatui, was the overlord of Vava'u and a mighty warrior chief. Although a man in his mid sixties, he was powerfully built and imbued with a demeanour that demanded the respect. During the final expansion of the Empire, Punake accompanied the king to the great forest Kingdom of Mapuche at the end of the world. He was renowned for his strength and bravery, loyalty and devotion.

The mid-morning brought the heat of the day. The tavakes swooped silently overhead Castle Ha'afuluhao, their white dovetails streamlining through the sky with majesty. Soldiers milled around the ramparts of the castle and its grounds, like proud bull ants over a mighty nest. Within the large council hall of the castle, Noble Punake sat with his commanders, advisors and village headmen from around Vava'u, discussing matters of local concern.

"Milord!" A soldier came into the hall quickly, bowing reverently as he did.

"What is it?" Punake snapped.

The soldier crawled closer to the noble and whispered a brief message before Punake gave him quick orders.

"That will be all for today. Leave me," Punake said to his advisors and village headmen.

Remaining with Punake were his dozen body guards Mako, the General of the Vava'u Army, and Havili, the High Priest of Vava'u. Once the entourage departed the hall, another group of men entered from a separate entrance and seated themselves before the noble.

"My scouts bring word that a vessel matching the description you gave, is sailing down the Strait of Spears as we speak," Punake said to the leader of the men.

"Thank you, Milord," Kamohoali'i smiled with the Fallen Commander and the Unarmed Warrior. "By your leave, I will make the arrangements to meet with Prince Talatama and his companions."

"Granted, but not without my men," Punake ordered and glanced at Mako.

"But, Milord, as discussed, you agreed with my plans to bring Prince Talatama back to the capital and the king."

"Yes, I did, but my men will be present in the arrest, Lord of Niuatoputapu. Mako will assist you, that is final."

"Yes, Milord," Kamohoali'i conceded and with his generals departed the hall. Once they had gone, Mako turned to the noble with grave expression.

"I don't trust him, Milord," he coughed. "Despite the title the king has given him."

"You're still sick, Mako." Punake did not ignore the general's condition. "Perhaps you should let your lieutenants carry out the orders."

"I'm fine, Milord," the old general tried to suppress a fit of coughs.

"This morning the gods provided us with a sign," Havili announced, "A favourable sign of victory and succession."

"Then we proceed as planned."

"But, Milord, we must proceed with much caution," Mako wheezed. "Prince Talatama is the Crown Prince, Kamohoali'i a renowned criminal. I've known the nature of Kamohoali'i for decades and have crossed clubs with him long ago, I distrust—"

"Careful what you say, Mako," Punake shot. "His new title is by the order of the king. He is, therefore, in his right to defend his honour if such insults are heard. I'm not in a position to make judgements on the circumstances of the king's order, nor am I about to take chances against them."

The hall fell silent.

"Mako, assist him in arresting Prince Talatama. Kamohoali'i has succeeded in finding him, so it is his capture to claim. See to it that the prince is brought to the castle once he is apprehended. I wish to speak to him."

"Yes, Milord."

Kamohoali'i and the Pulotulahi commanders returned to their quarters to prepare for Talatama's arrival. They donned their garments and collected their weapons. "Not a moment too soon," he grinned, "More time to prepare would have been preferable."

"We sailed here as fast as we could, Kamohoali'i. Hikule'o be praised that we arrived before them," Siateki said.

"We haven't caught them yet," Omani sneered.

"No you haven't." Kamohoali'i frowned. "Keep an eye on Mako and his men. Where's Kupe?"

"He departed for Neiafu already."

Maui Atalaga's vessel cruised along the Strait of Spears towards the castle and capital. The companions went about the tongiaki preparing for their arrival. Talatama stood at the bow and looked out under the hot sun towards the distant castle. Pele approached the prince and tried to sway his decision again.

"This is madness heading straight for Neiafu, Talatama. You know they'll be waiting to arrest us."

"My Uncle, Noble Punake will aid us. He'll not listen to such rubbish as to Kamohoali'i's newly appointed position. Besides, we'll dock west of Neiafu and avoid the main port on the eastern side. This strait is the only way in or out."

"I still think we should take refuge with allies I have on Nuapapu. I have trusted warriors there who can aid us. We can then assess your uncle's intentions from a place of strength."

"No. We don't have time, Pele. I must speak to Punake before anymore of Kamohoali'i's influence comes."

The she-warrior swore under her breath and stormed away. Soon after, Atiogie stepped next to the prince and gazed into the distance also.

"If I didn't know any better, I'd say that we took the long way to Vava'u," he said seriously.

"Don't start that again. This vessel is one of the fastest on the seas and Maui Atalaga the finest seaman."

"I've made it here faster before."

"What possible reason would Maui Atalaga have to slow our trip?" Talatama turned to the Samoan chief.

"N-none I suppose," Atiogie stammered then attended to other duties.

The prince watched angrily as he walked away. His companions had grown edgy during the voyage back to Vava'u; their nervousness apparent in the knowledge they were wanted by the Empire. Talatama's decision to head straight into the hornet's nest and risk capture was not accepted well once Vava'u had come into view. They had pledged their lives to him, yet as friends would, they showed their apprehension towards those actions. Talatama realised that his sudden anger was in defence that perhaps they were right.

Within half an hour, the war tongiaki sailed into the Bay of Ha'afuluhao and docked on the sandy shores. He had chosen not to dock at Neiafu's main wharf on the other side of the isthmus for obvious reasons. The companions leapt into the shallow water with their belongings and slowly made their way up to the township. Talatama wore his headdress and the magnificent armour of Sangone which drew stares from passers-by. Mahina and Vaohoi walked together, Atiogie and Lo'au followed behind the prince and Pele and Maui Atalaga brought up the rear. From out of the dozens of milling people, Mako and five of his lieutenants appeared to meet the companions. The old general seemed out of breath and was sweating profusely.

"Are you Prince Talatama?"

"Yes I am. I have come — "

"My Prince, please follow me immediately. There is no time to waste."

Talatama frowned and signalled the companions to commit to the general's hasty orders. As they milled through the people, the companions were forced to hurry their pace to keep up with the general and his men. Pushing through the crowds, Vaohoi cringed as he tried valiantly to avoid being struck on his mending leg and as he did, he failed to see Mahina had disappeared from his side.

They were rushed into what appeared to be a common fale on the side of the main road. It was small and confined but provided the privacy the general needed as he and his men, Talatama and his companions squeezed in and faced each other.

"Prince Talatama, I am Mako, General to Noble Punake and the armies of Vava'u. You and your companions must leave at once. You must trust me," Mako wheezed.

"Kamohoali'i." Talatama wiped the sweat from his brow.

"Yes, the proclaimed Lord of Niuatoputapu is here in the township and knows of your arrival. He's bent on arresting you and your companions."

"But my uncle — "

"Is bound by the orders of the king, Prince Talatama."

366

"Surely he can see through this!" the prince growled.

The companions sighed in a heavy sound of frustration. Lo'au did not seem to be affected by the news and as Pele swore out loud, Mako shook his head, recognising her among them.

"Prince Talatama! She is the sister of Kamohoali'i!" he barked as he and his men lowered their spears towards her, "You have an enemy in your ranks!"

"Stay your weapons!" Talatama shouted and raised his hands protectively. "She is no longer a member of his evil group. She is now among my trusted friends!"

Mako and his warriors held their spears hesitantly.

"What madness is this? Kamohoali'i proclaimed a lord, his sister a valued companion of the Prince of the Empire." Mako shook his head.

"Destinies change, General," Lo'au spoke.

"Your wish, Prince Talatama," Mako bowed in acceptance. "Regardless, it doesn't change the situation."

"Our capture is inevitable," the old mu'a stated plainly.

"Nonsense!" Pele shouted.

"Look, I will do what I can. Your uncle's distrust of Kamohoali'i and his men mirrors mine, but he cannot defy Kamohoali'i as the temporary lord, nor the wishes of your father for you to be returned to the capital in Tongatapu. I have been ordered by Punake to assist Kamohoali'i in your apprehension."

"You risk your own honour to aid us?" Talatama questioned.

"I couldn't forgive myself if I willingly aided a murderer and madman such as he."

"I understand."

"Go now. Kamohoali'i and his men will be here any moment."

The companions burst out of the small fale quickly and ran through the crowds towards the beach. Maui Atalaga beamed as he walked casually behind them. Pele yelled to him to hurry as they ran. When she turned again she noticed Mahina pushing through the crowds, finally catching up and breathing heavily.

"Where have you just come from?" Pele yelled, still running.

"N-nowhere," the Rarotongan breathed. "I just got lost."

The companions reached the vessel and threw their belongings on deck before leaping aboard. Atiogie and Maui Atalaga pushed the tongiaki back into the light waves before climbing up to the helm. The mast was struck and the sails caught the breeze of the bay, and in moments the companions were fleeing out towards the Strait of Spears.

"Damn it! I knew we were in for an ambush!" Pele cursed into the wind.

"That bastard Kamohoali'i, I can't believe he's already cooed the ear of my uncle!" Talatama growled.

"How could he have known it was our vessel coming in? There were plenty of other tongiakis around!" Vaohoi was perplexed.

"The Weeping Assassin and his commanders beat us back to Neiafu," Mahina said.

"I told you we took too long sailing back here!" Atiogie yelled.

Everyone glanced to Maui Atalaga who stood by the mast, oblivious to the companions' suspicion.

"We have no time to throw accusations or argue amongst ourselves!" Talatama pointed off the aft of the vessel.

No more than a few hundred metres away, half a dozen vessels set sail from the shore of Neiafu in hasty pursuit.

CHAPTER 52

"Strike the sails, Maui Atalaga!" Talatama was purple in the face. "Let us make these curs cowards and their hearts hollow!"

"Aye! Hail the mighty Tangaloa! Bless us with the winds of fury!" Atiogie thrashed about with the sails.

The energy of the companions lifted at the sound of their leader and his stout confidence. Vaohoi roared in excited glee, Lo'au beamed with a broad smile, even Pele broke into a smile. The camaraderie was unyielding once more in the face of certain capture. The companions rushed about the tongiaki like a highly trained group of sailors. They had learned over the past months every fine skill required to outrun any sea craft.

The tongiaki streamed through the iridescent waters of the Strait of Spears like a bird skimming the surface. All breath of the winds was caught in the tongiaki's sails, expanding them into massive bulbous shapes. Vaohoi laughed with delight and called to the Rarotongan.

"Mahina look!"

Metres ahead of the two hulls were a school of grey dolphins. They glided just beneath the water's surface and took turns leaping into the air, their majestic bodies glistening in the sun before disappearing into the brine. The companions could see their tails moving vigorously to keep pace with the vessel.

"They bring us luck!" Vaohoi hollered over the sound of the moving vessel.

But as the youngster looked behind his heart sank. The six or so tongiakis did not show signs of falling behind; rather, they appeared to be gaining. His glee vanished and he ran to Maui Atalaga at the helm.

"We must go faster! They'll catch us!"

The hero did not listen, nor did he study the distance between them. Talatama and Atiogie were wrestling with the end of a mighty sail and their effort to tame the wind was tireless.

Far behind atop Ha'afuluhao Castle, Noble Punake squinted as he watched the chase with Mako, Havili and chosen lieutenants. They continued watching, as the companions in their war vessel, disappeared from sight. Punake slowly rubbed his eyes.

"Tell me again, Mako. Did you see them before they escaped?"

"No, Milord. I believe they caught sight of Kamohoali'i and his men when they arrived."

"Our men?"

"My best lieutenants are sailing with Kamohoali'i. They will assist him should they be successful."

"Well they're lucky to escape, but it will take more than that to outrun my ships."

"How so, Milord? They hold their course well ahead of our men."

"When I heard of their coming an hour ago, I gave the order to deploy the Neiafu garrisons. Our forces are actually ahead of them," the noble turned to Mako with a stern reflection. "They sail into a trap."

The war tongiaki coasted across the point of Falevai and towards the islands of Nuapapu and Hunga. The open sea winds came in from the north and provided extra strength, propelling it forward as the companions cheered. But their laughter soon evaporated as vessels appeared from the south soon realised their purpose.

"They're imperial vessels advancing to cut us off!" Talatama roared. "I never thought I'd say this – lose them!"

Maui Atalaga shouted and punched his fist in the air.

The bow soared above the waves and crashed with their astounding speed. Yet every moment they progressed southeast their captors loomed closer. Minutes later, the companions could see the men aboard the vessels leering over the sides towards them. Pele swiftly reached for her bow and prepared to fire.

"No, Pele! Do not engage them," the prince said.

Like the shadow of falling water, the imperial tongiakis were set on a crash course with the companions.

"They're going to hit us!" Vaohoi screamed.

"Brace for impact!" Talatama roared.

Suddenly the imperial vessels turned in an evasive manoeuvre to avoid the collision. The instinctive decision forfeited their catch and the surge of water from their direction rocked the war tongiaki from the side and propelled the companions forward. Gritting their teeth and clinging to the tongiaki, they suddenly comprehended their escape and the exhilaration washed over them instantly.

"Chhhiiihhiiiiii!" they all screamed.

The sails of the war tongiaki creaked and pulled the ropes that bound it to the craft. The sea spray swept up from the repetitious diving of the aft and into the companions' faces, the wind tossed their hair and bathed their bodies with refreshing relief. The craft hurtled towards a small island off the mainland of Nuapapu.

"Steer to port! Steer us south! It will take us to my ally's township!" Pele called out.

"No! We can't make the turn!" Talatama pointed to the small island. "Maui Atalaga! Steer us right – between Hunga and Nuapapu!"

The hero leapt from the platform and swung across one of the smaller sails. He exchanged hands and grasped another rope that held the force of the mainsail. In a feat that would take five men, he heaved the taut rope with all his strength. Re-enacting the legend of the wind god taming the breath of the winds, Maui Atalaga single-handedly retched the mainsail rigid, against a wind current equal to that of hauling a fifteen tonne vessel. The sudden shock to the tongiaki caused it to rip through the sea in a sharp turn that lifted one of the hulls into the air.

The airborne hull lingered five feet above the water before crashing back into the sea with an impact that sent some of the companions sprawling across the deck. Pele rushed to the prince as they entered the channel between Hunga and Nuapapu.

"Why don't you want to seek aid in Nuapapu?" she yelled angrily.

"It's not what you think Pele – I do not want innocent people involved in this crisis." Talatama reflected her intense glare. "I have already implicated you all."

For the first time, Pele appeared to be touched by the prince's words. In her single mindedness, she would never have thought of the implications or wrath that would afflict her allies in Nuapapu should they align themselves with them. The proud warrior smiled at Talatama in acknowledgement.

"Maui Atalaga! Is there a bay nearby where we can lose them?" the prince yelled.

"No, there isn't. We cannot outrun them either, Prince Talatama," the folk hero said coolly.

"Nonsense! That sort of talk will get us caught! Pele – do you know of a place we can hide?"

"Yes, I do," the she-warrior answered after a pause. "I think I know of a secret retreat. Maui Atalaga, take us close to the cliffs of Nuapapu and slow us down!"

The folk hero steered the mighty craft close to the edges of the island. The rocky cliffs rose straight out of the sea and shot towards the sky. Atiogie and Maui Atalaga released the sails, immediately slowing the vessel's speed, as Pele leaned over the edge of the tongiaki and peered down into the crystal blue water.

"What are you looking for?" Vaohoi laughed. "There's no bay down there!"

The she-warrior ignored the youngster's sarcasm and continued to survey the depths of the water just below the cliffs.

"Pele -" The prince stepped forward.

"There!" She suddenly pointed.

The companions all edged to the sides and glared into the water. Between the sunlight reflections on the sea, they all noticed a great, dark cavity in the cliff face, perhaps two metres below the surface.

"Quickly, we don't have time!" she said harshly as she gathered her belongings.

"Jump into the sea? That's crazier than my idea of turning to fight!" the Samoan chief blurted.

"It's an entrance to an underwater cave," Lo'au explained. "The perfect place to hide."

"Vaohoi! Grab some food, some supplies!" the prince ordered.

The companions realised, however, that their cunning escape had only one flaw; one of them could not follow. They turned to Maui Atalaga.

"Go now, all of you. I'll lead them away out to sea and cover your escape," he said as if he knew it had to end that way.

Pele launched herself at him and embraced him fiercely before diving into the water. One by one, the companions followed Pele into the sea and Talatama, the last to jump ship, turned to Maui Atalaga and looked at him severely.

"I'd have been a blind man not to suspect your motive over the past few days, Maui Atalaga," he said sternly.

"Do not doubt my actions, Prince."

"When they result in us arriving here in Vava'u late, how can I help but wonder whether you meant for us to be captured."

"Some things are certain, Prince Talatama, not all things."

The prince plunged into the deep water and glided down towards the dark void that emerged before him. The sudden absence of sound as he submerged further somehow eased the predicament they were in. He could feel his heart beat through his ears as he held his breath. He swam behind his companions out of the columns of sunlight and into the dark passage that led beneath the island. Thousands of bubbles from his friends ahead seemed to guide the way through what he suddenly felt become claustrophobic and dangerous.

After swimming perhaps five metres through the tunnel, the prince began to rise towards shimmering light. Suddenly, he surfaced and inhaled deeply in what appeared to be a giant grotto. As he waded in the water, he looked about for his surrounds and saw his companions pulling themselves onto a rock shelf. He swam over to them and took the time to inspect the cave.

Despite the dark cavity they had swum through, the rays stemming from the open sea filtered through to the cavern pool. They illuminated the entire cavern with a gentle luminescence to reveal its uniqueness. Some parts of the ceiling were so high that its end could not be seen easily. Down from the graduating darkness crept thin and long stalactites of all shapes and sizes. From the floor of the cavern and directly beneath the stalactites rose stalagmites, creating an illusion that they stood within the jaws of a colossal shark.

The colour of the cavern stones were grey and dark brown, and occasionally sparkled with an unknown quality. The air within the grotto was stifling and thick, with the strong scent of sea salt and wet earth. From the pool rose a strange ocean mist that lingered above it and winded through parts of the cavern. The combinations of these mystical qualities begged the attention of the companions for long moments.

"Is this the entrance to the underworld?" Vaohoi marvelled.

"I've never been to a place like this," Atiogie said.

"It's surreal," Mahina whispered, "Like the home of the sea god."

"It's a fine place to hide. Well done, Pele," Talatama nodded as he removed his Sangone armour.

"For a short time only – we cannot expect to stay in here too long, Prince Talatama," the old mu'a groaned as he dried himself.

"Well, for as long as it takes," Talatama returned. "Vaohoi, prepare the area for food and sleeping. We'll make no fires in here. Let our eyes become adjusted to the dark."

The rest of the day seemed sluggish and deliberate and when night came to the outside world, absolute darkness reigned within the cavern.

CHAPTER 53

Hours had passed long into the night. The companions had consumed cold taro and bananas during a quiet meal. Following dinner and a quick expedition to the rear of the grotto, which had revealed nothing more than shallow cavities that led nowhere, the companions soon retired. Once the idle chatter ceased, the cavern emanated eerie sounds, deep echoes, strange whispers and occasional rock slippage.

All but one of the companions lay sleeping. Talatama sat at the edge of the pool, with his forearms resting on his knees and his fingers clasped together. He brought his knuckles to his lips and his thoughts spiralled deeper than any underground cavern. He watched the faint glow that pulsated from the underwater passage. Accustomed to the blackness, he observed the smouldering light was enough to provide silhouettes within the cavern; *there was probably a full moon out tonight*, he thought.

"Your thoughts are noisy, Prince Talatama."

"Join me then, old man, so that my words can bring you silence."

The two chuckled quietly as the prince shifted to make room for Lo'au. After a long silence, Talatama dropped a pebble into the pool that sent ripples to the other side.

"How do you deal with betrayal, Lo'au?" the prince turned to the mu'a's silhouette.

"How we deal with, respond to or accept betrayal are all but endless answers," Lo'au said, "because it's your position and your frame of mind at the moment of betrayal that establishes your actions."

"So no matter what you live by, a betrayal could manifest chaotic and unbridled actions, whether that is good or bad?"

The old mu'a sighed and tossed a pebble into the pool also.

"If I told you 'forgiveness' is the way to deal with it, would that offend you?"

"Yes, it does. How can a warrior show forgiveness?"

"Are you a warrior or a man?"

"What is that supposed to mean?"

"Which are you?"

"I'm both!"

"Then if you're both, separate the two, then ask yourself, 'How would I deal with betrayal as just a man'?"

The prince fell silent.

"My Prince, there will be times in your life when being a warrior will have little to do with how you deal with matters, especially matters of the heart."

"Of course it will. As a warrior I'd never show *forgiveness* to an enemy, a deceiver, a betrayer."

"But the essence of betrayal and its very meaning, Prince Talatama, comes not from enemies, but from trusted and loved ones."

When he did not answer again, the mu'a continued to explain.

"And the deeper the trust, so too the severity of the betrayal. The question is, brave Prince, could you be unmerciful to a loved one, as you would a hated enemy on the battle field?

"I - well—"

"I cannot give you the answer you want. And at this moment neither can you. I only hope that if you are confronted by this, Tangaloa forbid, you remember our conversation."

Talatama placed his hand on the old man's shoulder before squeezing it in affection and appreciation.

"Who brings about these thoughts?" the mu'a said after moments of silence.

"Maui Atalaga."

"Why?"

"I've had my suspicions about him for some time. I know he's your old friend. But there are obvious clues that have revealed this. I suspect he knew the Pulotulahi were in pursuit of us before we arrived in Niuafo'ou, and said nothing. Then our voyage to Vava'u, he slowed our trip purposely, allowing our enemies to arrive before us and plan our capture. We're in this blasted cave because of that!"

The mu'a did not say anything and his silence told Talatama he was not convinced.

"How else do you explain that?"

"I agree Maui Atalaga delayed our voyage here, and has therefore led us into this predicament."

"There. You see?"

"He is bound by a greater oath that precedes your time, he cannot overstep this," he paused. "That conversation is best saved for another time. Be comforted his motives are not what you think."

"Motives?"

"If his motive was to have you killed, Prince Talatama, he would strike you down with Mohemamahi without consideration or regret."

"Conjecture, old man. I have to deal with the reality of the situation, sitting in a grotto beneath the sea, without aid, and hunted by my own people. I can't trust the man."

"What about Pele? Is she not the sister of your arch enemy?"

"Pele has proven herself."

Lo'au did not reply. He let time pass between them without words, expressions go without view. He knew the pressures the prince was under and understood his misgivings against those who supplanted his position and those who betrayed his friendship in times of toil. Talatama's heart was great, honourable and just but it had become too easily wounded. More was to come though, he thought but did not say.

"My Prince, you need rest." He patted his friend on the back. "Please, get some rest before sunrise."

Talatama's face was but a black smudge in the darkness but he could feel the warmth and emotion coming from Lo'au.

"I'll keep watch," he said.

"You're right. I'll try to get a couple of hours sleep."

The mu'a watched as the silhouette stood and slowly dissolved into the darkness of the cave.

Morning was but a scant difference of dim light. Talatama woke with a start having drifted into a heavy sleep that had only lasted three hours. He staggered to his feet and looked about with bloodshot eyes. He focused on Vaohoi and Pele who were arguing.

"She's been gone too long," Pele snapped.

"What do you expect?" Vaohoi snapped back.

"What's this all about?" Talatama stepped between them and noticed Lo'au and Atiogie kneeling down by the pool, gazing towards the submerged tunnel. Pele stood with Vaohoi and it came to him suddenly: Mahina was missing.

"Where is she?" he demanded.

"She – went out alone to find some food," Vaohoi said.

"Alone?" The prince hurried down to where Atiogie was kneeling. "How long has she been gone for?"

"An hour or so," Lo'au said.

"Whose decision was it for her to go alone?" Talatama turned to his companions.

"It was hers, she insisted on going alone," Pele looked at Talatama angrily.

"Wait! There!" Vaohoi jumped down to the rock ledge and pointed.

The companions distinguished the blurry shadow of someone swimming through the passage before Mahina burst from the surface and inhaled deeply, the water running off her beautiful face. She swam over to the ledge where the companions stood and stepped out of the pool. She pulled her hair back with her hands and squeezed the water out of it as the prince stepped in front of her.

"You foolish girl, going out by yourself! Do you know who lies out there waiting for us?"

"I know, I -" she could not look at him.

"Do not take a risk like that again - it's too dangerous," Talatama attempted to suppress his frustration. "Here dry yourself. What did you see out there?"

"Thank you. Maui Atalaga is out there waiting for us, my Prince."

"He's come back!" Vaohoi pitched.

"What?" the prince frowned, "Where is he?"

"He's moored just beyond the passage. He told me he lost the enemy around the outer islands."

"Excellent!" Atiogie jeered.

Talatama glanced at Lo'au with a distrustful expression. The old mu'a nodded silently.

"Right, everyone gather your things. We're leaving."

Without falter the companions collected their belongings and dived into the water, and one by one, swam through the passage towards the blinding light of the open sea. Talatama was the last to come through the tunnel and rise into a glary sky that blinded him suddenly. Finally, when his sight returned, a powerful voice shouted down in his direction.

"At long last, we meet the mighty, Talatama."

Surrounding the companions was a fleet of twelve tongiakis, filled with Pulotulahi warriors poised with bows and arrows ready at the aim. A rippling of dread shot through the prince's body and he could feel his face flushing with trepidation for himself and his companions. The realisation of their quandary pounded his chest: there were no imperial tongiakis among the fleet.

His warrior spirit brought forth a sudden urgency to fight, but consideration of his death and the deaths of his companions would bear no honour. His fear melted once he made that decision and accepted their fate. His feelings turned to fury as he glanced at

Mahina who had lied to them. But his love for her well outweighed her deed; they had probably captured her as she searched for food, gave her no choice, he thought.

The leader of the Pulotulahi stood on the bow of the closest vessel and leered down at them.

"And I see you have brought my sister to me also," Kamohoali'i sneered.

Pele returned an incensed stare. Atiogie lifted his club out of the water and prepared to fight.

"Hold! Do not struggle," Talatama said. "We cannot win."

The companions knelt in front of Kamohoali'i. At the general's sides stood the full extent of his commanders – Havea, Ganilau, Kupe, Omani and Siateki. They regarded the companions, lined together on their knees, with abhorrence and distain. They had been disarmed, stripped of their clothes and their hands bound behind their backs. They groaned as blood wept from a multitude of wounds that had been inflicted during their severe bashing. A group of Pulotulahi warriors had pummelled their bodies with bamboo clubs to avoid killing them. Blood from Talatama's forehead trickled down and stained the white of his eye as he glared up at Kamohoali'i.

"You've cost me much, Prince of Princes," Kamohoali'i voice was like the rumblings of a distant rockslide, "And caused me much irritation."

Talatama struggled to stay upright on his knees, breathing heavily; he had received a vicious bashing.

"What do you have to say for yourself?"

"Take us to Noble Punake now!" Blood and saliva hung from the prince's chin.

"Do you think that after months of tracking you and your lackeys down," Kamohoali'i laughed, "I'd just hand you over?"

The Pulotulahi general leered down, only inches from Talatama's face.

"Oh no, your insurmountable nuisances have earned you an honour fit for a prince; the ultimate sacrificial offering to the great Hikule'o."

Talatama turned and saw a man he recognised. Siateki stood grimly next to Kamohoali'i.

"Siateki," Talatama voice was hoarse. "I once called you friend, brother, yet here you stand with these criminals? Did what we have, so long ago, mean nothing to you?"

"You never understood, Talatama. All those years, I hated you, despised you, I've wanted nothing more than to see you fall. Now after all this time, I may yet see that reality." The coldness from Siateki's voice seemed strangely forced.

But Talatama shook with a combination of pain and a struggle to stay conscious before he turned to Kamohoali'i, "My uncle Punake, will be demanding our ..." he coughed sickly, "our return to him. Even you, with your new found claim to power, can't ignore the wishes of the Empire, lest you lose all that you've so murderously taken!"

"Unless, of course, they're unaware. So grateful I am to your actions yesterday. Your flighty escape from Neiafu was successful enough to evade both his and my men. And as such, he believes you're now halfway across the Pacific," the general laughed. "You're all mine."

Talatama hung his head as Kamohoali'i and the commanders burst into a fit of depraved laughter. Their cackle chorused with a gentle sea wind that blew over their naked bodies and reminded them of their delicate mortality. His senses were heaped with claret: the smell of his own blood down his face, the taste of it in his mouth and his vision blurred with it. He felt the sharp pain of his old wound return in his abdomen as if it were struck anew.

He vaguely saw Atiogie had collapsed unconscious against the mast. He had received perhaps the worst beating because of his size. Lo'au hung his head in silent reprieve and Vaohoi sobbed quietly, his lines of tears indistinguishable from sweat and seawater. Pele had, as expected, suffered both physical and mental torment. Yet she managed to keep her head high. Mahina had not been touched. Her face could not be seen through her long hair, overcome with defeat and shame.

"You swine of a man," Talatama growled weakly.

"Don't take it so personally, Prince Talatama. If you wish to blame someone, blame she who betrayed you."

"N-no ..." Mahina whispered.

"Your Rarotongan whore here. She was so easily persuaded," Kamohoali'i motioned to the Weeping Assassin.

Kupe stepped forward with his arms crossed and with a sense of certitude. His blind eye wept a lonely tear as he smirked at Mahina, then glanced at the beaten prince.

"I captured her yesterday in Neiafu, and bought her betrayal with a lie," he chuckled as he regarded her with amusement.

"You did not truly believe we had your brother, Whatonga, captive, did you?" His voice was venom. "He returned to Rarotonga weeks ago and has since erased you from his memory. You have now lost everything."

Mahina knelt before Talatama pleadingly. Her shoulders racked uncontrollably as she wept with cries brought from the depth of her soul.

"She was so willing to hand you over to us," he sneered at Talatama, "over half baked notions and hollow promises. I wondered how deep her treachery would run, Prince Talatama. Obviously quite profoundly, since you're here now, on your knees." He turned and stepped back to Kamohoali'i's side. "What a fool."

Talatama heard words being ordered around him, orders from Kamohoali'i and his commanders. But the words had no meaning or consequence: they were peripheral, insignificant. He closed his eyes and the murmurs of the outside world drifted into the background of his mind. He felt strong hands clutch at him, yank him backwards and drag him away. But the pain was not felt. If his body were full of physical life, like nectar from fruit, it had now been scooped out and discarded, leaving nothing but the shell of a human being. The ache was a void of perpetual hurt, grinding and twisting in places not reached by physical pain and he could barely find the will to breathe.

The innocence of love, blindness of trust and the naivety of betrayal had shattered his soul to the core. All this that encapsulated the prince's heart, forever, remained in the dark underwater cave.

CHAPTER 54

Noble Punake strode the length of the great hall and was followed by scuffling retainers. He entered the council hall and the council of men stood and bowed to him. He took his place at the head of the circle and turned to Mako with a sign of rage.

"So tell me again, how is it you lost Prince Talatama and his companions?"

"Their seafaring skills were—"

"There was a whole armada of you!" he growled, "To catch one tongiaki!"

"Yes, Milord, a tongiaki helmed by Maui Atalaga."

"So I should have sent two armadas?" he stood and threw his hands in the air.

"No, Milord."

The noble rested his hands on his hips and drifted from anger into a daze. He sighed deeply and remained with his thoughts.

"What are you running from, Talatama?" he whispered to himself.

"Milord?"

"Kamohoali'i and his men leave this morning?" he turned to face the men.

"Yes. He has set sail for the Ha'apai islands on his way to the capital."

"Did your men follow him?"

"They did, Milord."

Mako and the lieutenants watched uneasily as the noble swiftly departed.

The fale was sizable but devoid of much light. It was loosely constructed. Nothing more than a thatched roof supported by a flimsy palm frame with woven walls. The thatching was old and rotten and it was without any flooring. The smell of damp earth filled the air, rivalled by the stench of blood, unwashed bodies and the dead. The low light perforating through cracks in the structure suggested it was enclosed by thick bush somewhere in the jungle. The absence of idle village chatter or the sound of domestic animals also suggested it was isolated.

Talatama woke up with a start. He was lying on his side in a dirt patch, hands still tied at his back, body aching all over. He grunted as he slowly sat up and tried to regain his senses. His face was painted maroon with claret. One of his eyes was caked with dry blood that had sealed it shut. He winced as he struggled to gain vision out of the other, but it took long moments before he could finally gain blurry vision and take in his surroundings. He saw some of his companions nearby, Atiogie and Vaohoi lay unconscious, and Lo'au was on the other side of the fale, quietly whispering to others he did not immediately recognise.

"Lo'au," he murmured.

He heard a gasp from the group and a woman stood and rushed over to him.

"Prince Talatama!"

The Fijian priestess knelt down and embraced him the best she could with her arms also tied. She pressed herself against him warmly and did not pull back. He returned the relief and comforted her also. Lo'au and Emori slowly approached and greeted him gently.

"What happened, Adi?" Talatama said shaking his head in disbelief. "Why are you here?"

"Shortly after we departed Samoa, we were intercepted by Kamohoali'i himself," she hung her head.

386

"The bastard knew who we were. He caught us without much fight, killed our Samoan crew and kept us captive for weeks now," Emori said.

"Are you both hurt?"

"No, we're fine. Look to be in much better shape than you – respectfully," Emori smiled.

"I'll live. I probably look worse than I am." Talatama returned a fleeting grin. "Where are we?"

"On the island of Hunga, probably half a kilometre north of the main bay. The village of Hunga lies to the east and Kamohoali'i is camped there with the chief of the island. This fale is a temporary prison guarded by about two dozen warriors."

"Where is Pele and ..." Talatama swallowed, struggling with the thought of Mahina.

"We don't know."

"Who are they?" The prince motioned to the dead men close by.

"I recognise them from Neiafu, Mako's men. They were brought in shortly after our arrival," Lo'au said.

"They probably witnessed our capture and Kamohoali'i had them killed before they could report it," Talatama shook his head and took a haggard breath. "Well, whatever fate awaits us, we shall meet it together."

They all nodded in understanding before a silence lapsed between them as they considered their position.

"Prince Talatama – Lo'au told us what happened with – with Mahina. I'm sorry," Adi said earnestly.

"I don't care, she's no longer a concern of mine," his face contorted instantly.

"My Prince – we knew, we know of the love you both share," Adi pressed gently.

The two men lowered their heads and remained silent as they began to feel Talatama's embarrassment and shame.

"I do not love her! I've never loved her! She's a deceiver and a betrayer, and she's given us up for her own gain!" he angrily stumbled to his feet.

"My Prince —"

There was a bang at the entrance of the fale followed by sharp commanding voices and the sounds of struggle. A small portion of the wall was removed that flooded daylight inside. Mahina and Pele were thrown into the fale, landing heavily on the cold ground. Pele leapt to her feet almost immediately and cursed back in the warriors' direction, as the wall was replaced and the room returned to its dim light.

On first glance it appeared Mahina was unconscious but for her trembling. Her spirit was broken. Pele walked past her and glared at the companions with equal rage. She looked at Talatama with impatience and irritation.

"Have you planned to get us out of here yet? Call yourself a leader?" she kicked dirt before seating herself in the corner.

By this time, Vaohoi and Atiogie had stirred and sat up groggily and groaned over their dull pains. Talatama stood only a few metres from Mahina, incensed and hurt. She slowly got to her knees and feebly shifted her hair aside without the use of her hands. The colour from her face had drained from her skin, her eyes were swollen and her lips were sapped of voluptuousness. Once she noticed Talatama standing before her, her whole body began to shake badly. When she thought she had exhausted all her tears, there were more to come. She hung her head and wept before peeking up to her lover.

"I'm so sorry, my Prince —"

Talatama stood as rigid as an ironbark and refused to look at her.

"Please, Talatama, I'm so sorry for what I have done!" She stumbled and rushed to him desperately, kicking dirt about her feet.

"You - you'll find no comfort here," he snapped coldly and turned away from her.

She fell to her knees and embraced his legs, "Talatama please - please forgive me," she wept.

"Forgive you?" Talatama glared down at her. "You don't deserve forgiveness! You're no different to an enemy on the battle field, no different than – than...–"

He fell silent as he looked into Mahina's defeated eyes. Within them was not the reflection of a liar, neither of a betrayer nor an enemy. They were not the manifestations of evil or malevolent intentions, or the conniving masks that would justify her actions. They reflected the desperation of her love and the admission of her guilt, mirrored in the forlorn and misplaced emotions that had led to their capture and echoed the helplessness of her reality.

It pierced the prince's soul like an ashen spear. Her unwanted betrayal was spurred for the love of her own family and their safeguard. He could feel the stabbing within himself and the pain that it caused. He could feel his heart thumping in his chest and the terrible void that he had felt at her betrayal. As he stared deeper into her eyes, he felt the bridge of exoneration materialise in his mind. His longing for her and his love was a reminder of the past, ever so recent, that prior to their capture he had longed to make her his wife, that after all the years of being alone he would settle down and have her bear his children.

Talatama caught Lo'au's gaze from across the room and remembered his words. He shuddered with understanding and nodded. He knelt down to her as consolation replaced the anger and defiance that was vanishing from his bloodied face. She quickly placed her head onto his chest in a fit of tears. He rested his chin on her head and closed his one good eye.

Adi sniffed back tears and sought comfort from her betrothed which Emori gave. Lo'au smiled with relief, bent to a knee and bowed his head. Pele looked over her shoulder, snorted and faced the wall again. Vaohoi had lay down again and Atiogie stared at the companions with a groggy and blank expression.

"I feel like a smashed oyster. I guess I mustn't be dead," he said.

Afternoon set in. There was a beautiful moon that was clothed in a wisp of twilight cloud. It was surrounded by cobalt sky, sparsely embellished with stars and the tints of darker shades. It was a noticeably humid evening, a welcome gift following the past, colder weeks. The scent of the sea drifted in and enveloped the village of Hunga. It blended with the jungle's tang of local fruit, such as the mango trees and the breadfruits.

In the middle of the village was a cleared area constructed in service of the afternoon reception. Groups of men and women chanted and sang in a thick outer ring of townspeople. Inside the ring, were three fires positioned as points on a triangle. Around these fires sat the villages' warriors, headmen and priests, feasting on the succulent food that had been prepared. In the centre of the whole reception, and protected by the circle of fires, was a kava circle. Around the kava circle sat General Kamohoali'i and his commanders, Hunga's warlord, Kaianuanu, and his lieutenants.

As the Vava'u islands were ruled by only one noble, all outer islands in the archipelago were controlled by individual warlords who were assigned by Noble Punake. These warlords, chosen as natives of their particular islands, were handpicked for their prowess as mighty fighters and united together to form the Vava'u contingent of the Empire's armies. Aside from war, they held the responsibility of administering local laws and customs, providing their people with justice and prosperity.

A young man of twenty-five years, Kaianuanu possessed a wealth of experience on the battlefield. He was a tall man, at slightly over seven foot, wiry and lean and covered in tribal tattoos. His long, black hair that hung plaited to the middle of his back, crowned a composed face unlike a typical warrior of the time, devoid of harsh reflections. It was a face that mirrored the virtues of his soul, insight and acumen.

"Your stay here has been brief, Kamohoali'i," Kaianuanu said.

"I have to make it down to the capital soon with the slaves. I have an audience with the king," Kamohoali'i sat comfortably and drank at his kava.

"An audience with the king is not common these days. I wish you well."

"Thank you, Kaianuanu. And for the generosity you've shown over the last two days. I offer you two the choice of two of my slaves."

"You're too kind. I always have need for slaves."

"On one condition: you have their tongues pulled out on exchange," Kamohoali'i said. "I have a choice of fine men and women."

"Indeed, you're too kind. But I -"

"I'll not leave here with a debt," he smiled, "I insist you take two."

Of all the warlords in the Empire, and unbeknownst to Kamohoali'i, Kaianuanu was among the strongest in the opposition to slavery. He would feign acceptance of the slaves to avoid confrontation to the general.

"You're persistent, General. I accept your gift."

CHAPTER 55

The singing ceased and the area fell silent. Kamohoali'i waved his hand and the circle of singers parted for a dozen Pulotulahi warriors who led the line of slaves into the kava circle. They were beaten to their knees and set before the Hungan warlord as the crackling of the fires curdled and spat embers into the afternoon air. All eyes were on the slaves who had been gagged. Kaianuanu inspected them, scrutinising every detail, while Talatama and the companions glared at Kamohoali'i and his commanders in the firelight, wincing with pain and hatred.

"An interesting group of slaves you have here," Kaianuanu said.

"You have no idea."

"They're beaten and bloodied."

"They tried to escape. You have to remind slaves that they're owned."

"I'll start with that one." Kaianuanu pointed directly at Pele.

"A good choice, warlord. However, she's not for release."

"Then that one," he paused before pointing at Talatama.

"You have fine choice, Kaianuanu, but he is not for release either."

"Perhaps you should tell me which *are* for choosing then, General." Kaianuanu turned irritably to Kamohoali'i.

With gruff hand signals, Atiogie, Vaohoi, Adi, Emori and Lo'au were shuffled forward. Talatama, Pele and Mahina were reefed off their knees and pushed out of the circle.

"These."

"That makes it easy then – those two." The warlord pointed directly at Lo'au and Emori.

"Done. Remove the rest of them."

"No!" Adi screamed as they dragged her away with the companions.

She kicked and struggled against the warriors that held her down as Lo'au tried to calm her. Emori did not fight his captors as they took him away. He expressed his love to her through his dark eyes.

"And remember my condition – their tongues," Kamohoali'i frowned.

"Yes I'll have them cut out immediately. A mute slave is an obedient one." The Hungan Chief squinted against Adi's screams. "Bind her with a fresh gag! I'll not endure a wailing woman tonight. Take them to my quarters. Strike up the music! Let us continue the feast!"

The banquet lingered into the early evening. A majority of the townsfolk disappeared by sunset, leaving the Hungan and Pulotulahi warriors to their feasting and indulging. The laughter and occasional song drifted into the jungle, penetrating the dark fale where the companions were held in isolation. Patterns of light chequered the earth in the fale from the fading sunlight. The companions sat together on the opposite side of the fale where the dead bodies lay. They whispered in low murmurs.

"The Hungan chief didn't know who you were, Talatama," Vaohoi said.

"No, I've never met him. He doesn't seem to have a close relationship with Kamohoali'i."

"No, but he knew who I was," Pele said. "We're acquaintances as neighbouring warriors. He's a good man."

"Yet he said nothing?"

"He didn't because he's an advocate against slavery and didn't want to refuse Kamohoali'i. He chose me first to free me."

"Then we can assume Lo'au and Emori will be freed once we're moved. They're the lucky ones," the prince consoled Adi with a rub.

"Maybe we should request to become Hungan slaves!" Vaohoi squealed.

"Under the circumstances ..." Talatama broke a rare grin.

"Prince Talatama, there's something I forgot to tell you before," Adi sniffed. "When Emori and I were captured we overheard conversations between Kamohoali'i and his commanders."

"What was said?"

"Kamohoali'i spoke of an overlord, a man he was accountable to. He spoke of a man called Tu'ipulotu."

Talatama was speechless, his shock obvious.

"I could have told you that," Pele said.

"Why didn't you?" Talatama cussed.

"It's of no importance – the man is like a ghost. I've never seen him."

"It was obvious that Tu'ipulotu was the ultimate overlord of the Pulotulahi and that he resides somewhere in Tongatapu," Adi continued.

"That's impossible," Talatama reeled. "There could be no such person with that amount of power in the capital. It couldn't go unnoticed. I know of no rebellion or single man with such intention."

"It's Kamohoali'i, that's the true enemy," Atiogie said.

"No. This changes everything," the prince said. "For years we have been hunting Kamohoali'i and his minions as the source of this threat against the Empire. If he is not the true leader, then we have been aiming our spears at the wrong man."

"But he's the real enemy," Mahina said.

"Evil must be cut at the root. He may be the muscle, but the mind and soul comes from someone higher." Talatama slapped his leg in frustration. "It all makes sense. There've been so many times he's slipped though our nets over the years. He's been tipped off by our movements, our plans and our tactics.

"It has to be someone in the Imperial Army." Talatama came to a sudden realisation. "Someone with high military rank ..."

"There's no way of knowing. If he's remained anonymous for this long, it shows he's as careful as he is calculating," Mahina said.

"Like a slimy eel. I relish crushing those sorts of men with my club!" Atiogie growled.

"Does someone come to mind, Prince Talatama?" Adi said.

"I have my suspicions on a couple of likely imposters."

A silence fell among the companions as his mind whirled with a dozen possibilities.

"Get some rest, all of you," he finally said, "We'll need it if we're going to be transported soon."

"My Prince, may I have your audience – in private?" Mahina whispered.

The two quietly shuffled over to the vacant end of the fale where they both knelt in the soft earth and looked at each other tenderly. It was the first time they had been able to share a private moment together since their conciliation in the morning. Mahina gazed into the eyes of her beloved with unparalleled passion.

"My love – I owe you everything."

"Hush, Mahina. You don't need to say anything."

"Yes, I do!" she tried to whisper. "You've given me so much... happiness, laughter, love, my life. You've given me a reason to live after all these years of feeling alone. Now it is my turn to give you something in return."

"You don't have to give me anything. Look, once we get to the capital everything will be fine. We'll start over, make a new life for ourselves."

The beautiful Rarotongan pushed her lips to his. She pulled away, before smiling at him, tears welling in her eyes.

"I will give you a symbol of our love," she whispered. "You'll just have to wait until the end of summer."

"End of summer?" It dawned on him. "You're pregnant?"

"Yes," she cried tears of joy, "With our child!"

"How can you tell? It was only ..."

"I can just feel it," she beamed.

Talatama was struck through his heart with an emotion beyond words. The companions glanced over hesitantly, unaware of what was said and unwilling to pry on their private time.

"That's, that's ..."

"Tell me you're happy. Tell me you want this, my love."

The entrance suddenly crashed open with a rush of noise and five warriors marched into the fale. They strode straight to Talatama and Mahina and tore them from each other, pulled them to their feet and dragged them out of the fale. Vaohoi and Pele hurled curses at the warriors and Talatama reassured Mahina over and over again.

"Where are you taking us?" Talatama growled.

"Shut up and walk." One of the warriors gave him a hard shove.

A dozen warriors surrounded them and struck them in the back at every opportunity, as they were dragged through the jungle on an old path that led west. When Mahina fell once or twice she was kicked to continue moving, while the prince struggled and lashed back when they hurt her. However, each time he was struck over the head with bamboo clubs that resulted in more lacerations and bruises.

Finally they came to a clearing. The first thing they noticed was the view of the outstretched sea, pillowing out into a western ocean. They stood on cliffs that jagged southwards towards Hunga Bay and loomed fifty metres above crashing rocks below. The setting sun bathed the cliffs with dying light over the tranquil vista. The sight was breathtaking.

Standing alone on the precipice was Kupe. He stood facing the setting sun with his arms folded. The light kissed his leathery skin and exaggerated the deep creases on his face. It illustrated the length and breadth of his years on the earth, filled with betrayals, murders, the sacrifice of innocent life and unadulterated sin. He held none of his wicked weapons; he was not adorned with much at all. He turned to them and motioned for them to be brought forwards, but only Mahina was pushed ahead.

With a burst of strength, Talatama broke his bonds and reached out and caught her hand and held it tightly. But as the warriors pulled, his grip began to slip away. Tension along their outstretched arms built up as warriors struggled to pull them back before their hands slipped apart with a pop. Talatama stumbled and fell to his knees from a vicious blow.

"So again you stand before me – bound and helpless," the Weeping Assassin stated.

Mahina said nothing.

"Except this time, your hero won't save you. He kneels there, bound and as helpless as you are," he pointed to the bloodied prince.

"You've taken everything from me," she whispered between clenched teeth.

"Well yes, your mother, your honour among your people, your father and brother's love ..." he smirked.

"But there's one thing you can never take from me, cur. Our love for one another transcends all bounds of reality," she motioned to Talatama.

"Love?" He leered down to her. "Love? Ha! Don't make me sick. You used to be skilled assassin, worthy of a respected enemy. Now I see nothing but a snivelling woman who testifies to love as though it's a reason for being. You're pathetic." His white eye began to weep.

"I won't expect a heartless bastard like you to understand that. All the lies you've woven, all the people you've betrayed, all the innocents you've murdered. You're inept of such purity as love."

"Lies are truth. Innocence is illusion. Betrayal is allegiance, murder is life, and love, – love is hate," the Weeping Assassin stepped towards her with deathly conviction.

"Do what you must." She spat in his face and turned to Talatama for the last time.

The prince saw no struggle as Kupe struck her. Some grass was kicked up from her feet as she disappeared over the edge. The dread cut him like an icy chill straight through his bones, and he remembered bellowing out, a carnal roar that deafened him as he lurched forwards. But there was a cracking sound and suddenly his legs failed. The side of his head bounced on the ground and through the last moments of consciousness he saw a patch of grass, some blades of grass that were taller than others; a distinction that was outlined by the setting sun behind them. It seemed so perennial. He looked at Mahina's ivory ring that remained on his small finger. He clenched his fist over it protectively, and even when he lost consciousness, he didn't let it go.

He was dragged back to the fale and dumped to the ground like the carcass of a dead animal. Fresh blood covered his entire face and his hair was matted into wet clumps. Veins of claret ran in streams down his strong chest and arms and the companions immediately rushed to aid him. Adi had managed to slip her hands free of the knots that bound her and positioned the prince properly on the ground. She cleaned his face and body with tattered rags. The others surrounded their leader with dire expressions.

"Where is Mahina?" Vaohoi dared to whisper. "Wh-why wasn't she returned with him?"

There was a cruel chuckle outside the fale. One of the warriors mentioned something about 'scattered the bottom of the cliffs', followed by another chorus of sadistic laughter. The companions exchanged a sudden shocking comprehension. Vaohoi choked and fell to his side, his mouth open in a silent scream of grief. Adi began to weep. Pele shook her head and cursed quietly.

Atiogie let out a war cry, dashed at the wall of the fale and kicked it where the warriors were laughing. When he smashed out a gaping hole, the warriors ceased their jeer and ran to the entrance and faced the giant Samoan. Seeing the dangerous rage he was in, they looked at each other apprehensively and after short moments, cautiously retraced their steps and left the companions in peace.

Adi wiped the tears from her ashen face and positioned herself ceremoniously in prayer. She lowered her head and sung a lament to Princess Mahina, daughter of Lord Toi of Rarotonga. Her voice drifted out of the fale into the cool evening air, lingered about the numinous jungle and down to where the cliff rocks lay. It then caught the gentle sea breeze and glided out towards a beautiful vista of cherry, lilac and diamonds.

> *Oh Mighty Degei, take into your care the lonely spirit which flies to you,*
> *See to it that she is welcomed with open arms and warm reception,*
> *Make it so that she does not become lost in the realm of the dead,*
> *For we here lament her passing over to you in tears of grief and sorrow,*
> *She was a sister, a daughter, a comrade, a friend and companion,*
> *A woman who's value cannot be replaced nor forgotten to us.*
>
> *Lord Degei, may her soul rest with her people in your land of eternal bliss,*
> *May she find the peace she could not find in this world of evil and tyranny,*
> *May she be at rest from the hardships of this world that burdened her,*
> *May she forever sleep in your loving bosom in the land of the dead.*

PART 3

CHAPTER 56

Early morning had come and gone. The unrelenting sun scorched the Vava'u islands as noon day approached. Ekiaki skimmed above the waves, searching the perilous waters for fish. There was much talk on the island of Hunga: constant whispers, rumours and fear. Inquisitive people from neighbouring islands had come to the village and spread word of Prince Talatama who had escaped Noble Punake in Neiafu only days ago. Kamohoali'i's large fleet of Tongan and Samoan vessels propagated their prying.

Kaianuanu sat in the chief's fale in the centre of Hunga. He was accompanied by two of his captains. While discussing the rest of the day's activities, one of his lieutenants entered the fale and bowed to him.

"Milord, the last tongiaki of General Kamohoali'i's fleet has long disappeared from the southern horizon."

"Good. Free the two slaves. Provide them with their belongings and return here once you're done."

A short time later, the lieutenant returned to the fale and bowed to his chief once again.

"Milord, the two slaves have been freed and —"

"Fine, now come and sit down. I have —"

"Milord ..."

Kaianuanu looked up from his scrawling on the floor and saw the two slaves standing behind his lieutenant.

"What is this?" He frowned at Lo'au and Emori. "You're free to leave. Now go."

"Lord Kaianuanu," Lo'au stepped forward and drew the attention of all with his air of wisdom, "A moment of your time."

But before he began, a soldier strode straight to Kaianuanu accompanied by another chief. Kaianuanu and his men stood quickly with respect.

"Lord Mako, you surprise me!" The Hungan chief bowed respectfully.

"Kaianuanu, I have urgent matters. General Kamohoali'i is in the Vava'u area with a large contingent of warriors. He is here in search of Crown Prince Talatama. I feared the worst when I discovered a few of my men were killed and dumped in a fale to the east."

"Kamohoali'i spent the last two nights here on the island. He didn't have the Prince with him to my knowledge," the Hungan warrior turned then looked back to Mako suddenly. "But he had a group of slaves with him."

All men turned to Lo'au and Emori as the old mu'a smiled and waved his hand politely.

"As I was saying, if I might have a moment of your time, gentlemen."

Days blurred past like transitions of dreams, as Kamohoali'i and his legion journeyed southwards towards the Ha'apai islands. Their captives, the companions, were bound mercilessly, tormented and starved in the dark hulls of the tongiakis like stored livestock. In stark reality, the seas had been calm, weather kind and the sailing peaceful. The breath of the winds, however, had been blowing in a north-easterly direction, slowing their advancement.

In the absence of Talatama's leadership, Pele had taken the role without opposition; her limitless hate and insurrection against Kamohoali'i was the inspiration the companions craved. She protected them from harm with her influence, hurled threats to the warriors and gave the companions hope in her fiery way.

The prince had become a shadow of himself following the death of Mahina. He did not converse with his comrades, acknowledge the hopelessness of their predicament, heed the whims of his captors or show care for their pending fate. While Pele and Atiogie oversaw their protection, Adi and Vaohoi stayed close to him; ushered him to eat and drink and spoke to him in attempts to keep him occupied away from his dark thoughts.

Midday set in across the desolate waters. For the entire night and morning, the winds were frugal, causing the hundreds of warriors, commanded by their frustrated leaders, to strike the paddles and keep the entire armada moving. Marching choruses of song were sung in time with their strokes as they drove across the still sea. Bellows of men echoed across the vastness and grew a unity of evil purpose. Over hours and hours, however, the strength of the men had dwindled and by the time the sun had begun to set, so had their hopes for favourable winds.

"We should keep the men cracking!" Siateki turned irritably to Kamohoali'i.

"We'll have no more strong arms to bear us through another day as this one," the general returned coldly.

"Always about the pride and perseverance, isn't it, Fallen One?" Kupe teased.

"Shut your mouth, Kupe, lest you lose your last eye."

"Siateki, go and prepare the men for meals." Kamohoali'i pointed towards the warriors.

General Va'iga called out from another tongiaki and raised his hand around his mouth to amplify his voice.

"How long til we get to Ha'apai?"

"If this blasted wind doesn't show, perhaps another day."

The Samoan general turned to his commanders and ordered the preparation of fires for cooking. Once the remaining army observed their brief reprieve to eat, they wasted no time. The Pulotulahi armada floated with the backdrop of a still sunset, relishing hot meals to revitalise and nourish weary bodies.

Not long after, a young Pulotulahi warrior stepped down into the deep hull of the main vessel. In his arms he held small portions of meat, mostly breadfruit and one or two taros which he placed carefully on the floor. From the darkness of the roofed hull emerged the Fijian priestess. She knelt down in front of him and smiled.

"Thank you, Nifolahi."

The young warrior appeared hesitant and did little more than return the smile and jump back to the deck. He was a Tongan boy from Niuatoputapu, youthful and naïve; Adi guessed he had been quickly recruited during the Pulotulahi's rapid succession of power over the island. Yet despite the evil he had since been forced to accept, she had witnessed kindness that lingered in him, unlike other hot blooded boys of his age. She quickly collected the food and returned to the darkness of the companions' prison.

As night fell the sky became moonless and black with dark clouds that gathered. Talk between the Pulotulahi warriors was lively. The fires that glowed on the vessels were surrounded by cackling men, boasting tall stories and wishful plights. They laughed, and between them, shared the spoils of their recent conquests: whales' teeth, pearls, embroidery and an assortment of weapons.

Half a dozen warriors reefed Pele onto the deck with brutal force. She leapt to her feet and glared at the warriors with a silent intent to slaughter as firelight illuminated her fury.

"You'll never lose your fiery spirit," grumbled her brother's voice.

She turned and faced Kamohoali'i who was on the other side of the fire, perched on a lavish stool draped with the finest tapa in the kingdom. To both his sides, were his commanders and warriors chosen to accompany him. Pele was surrounded by armed men, spears lowered and brandished to end her life at a moment's notice.

His broad nose became broader when he smirked. Lines creased his leathery face and his hair at the roots had become grey again in the absence of acquiring yellow dye. Despite this, his vivacious eyes and powerful body warned his age was no impediment to physical ability.

"And you'll never lose your arrogance," she stared back at him.

"I have news," he ignored the insult. "Our father is dead."

"You lie."

"His amulet." The general raised a stone talisman that hung from a simple necklace of small whales' teeth bound in black twine.

Pele stood in silence for a moment. Her shimmering eyes reflected the firelight, her body trembled slightly. The *'Goddess of Fire'* she was called amongst her enemies. At that moment, sorrow shed like tears of magma erupting from the broken chambers of her once icy heart. The men could see the emotion coursing through her veins and those who knew her well could discern the familiar silence before she launched into action. The armed warriors tensed their arms and arched their backs, ready to fight.

The proud she-warrior exhaled a deep and shuddering breath as she fell to a knee. With it she expelled the vapour of all her wrath. She slumped weakly, supporting her weight on the palm of her hand. Her braided hair swept the wooden deck. The warriors could not see her face: her stalwart mask now shattered unrecognisably, like her heart, into a thousand splintered shards. She winced slowly in the twisting ache. If for only one stricken moment, she mourned in silence.

Her palm became a fist as she punched the deck and stood quickly, causing the warriors to resume their defensive guard. She inhaled loudly, as if to rejuvenate her life being, and exhaled the very last mist of her sorrow and fragility. With a flick of her hair, she raised her chin towards her brother defiantly. Her face bore the track marks of tears down her sullied cheeks and jaw line.

"Did you have anything to do with his death?" she said.

"You think so little of me, don't you, dear sister?"

"Tell me, you coward!" She stepped forward deftly, inviting the points of the spears.

"No, I did not. He died in his sleep not two moons ago. His last wish was to die in Hawaii, and for you and I to remain close after he was gone."

"Then both his wishes were in vain."

"Not so fast, Pele. Hold one moment," he began his silver tongued tones. "Is this really what you want? Is there not a want in your heart to follow the last wishes of your father? Does this renegade life of meaningless wandering mean so much now that you have spent months tasting its offering?" He motioned towards the dark hull where the companions lay.

"So far it's *your* choices that have been in vain," he continued, "I see it in your face. I see it in your actions when you're with your *comrades*. You look out of place, like a scar across a sands' divide. You do not belong with them. You were destined for greater things, greater things at my side." He had risen from his palpable throne of tapa and moved closer to her.

"My sister, I now offer you one last chance. I am on the brink of victory, on the edge of achieving the greatest position I could ever have dreamed of. Through the wishes of our father, through the clarity of reason, weight of logic and now anticipation of our victory to come – join me once more so we can rule these seas together." His hand was extended out towards her.

For long moments nothing was said. The commanders, Kupe and Siateki, stood like fleshed statues as they watched on and the crackle of the fire hissed and spat. A jeer from warriors on tongiakis close by, echoed across the still night waters as Pele's gaze went from Kamohoali'i to his outstretched hand, then to the licking flames. She then turned towards the uninviting hull where her comrades lay, before glancing over her shoulder.

"See you in hell."

CHAPTER 57

Kao, Ha'apai Islands
Spring, A.D.1121

Before dawn, a light breeze began to gather across the ocean. The eastern horizon was pale with a turquoise tinge heeding the coming sun. The coolest part of the night gave way moments before sunrise and with it conjured new breaths of healthy wind. The breeze teased the flaccid sails and caused some of the wooden frames to knock against the masts. The hollow thumps echoed across the pre-dawn and woke the leaders of the sea crafts. In no time, captains were calling out across the armada of motionless tongiakis, bellowing orders and preparing the warriors for sail. Bodies of men scrambled over the decks like a busy ants' nest.

General Kamohoali'i emerged from his sleeping quarters with a reflection of ambition. Havea and Ganilau appeared and glared at the warriors with terrorizing effect, while without much physical movement, Kamohoali'i's voice thundered across the Pulotulahi armada like a clap of lightning. Warriors jumped to their tasks immediately as if he were personally breathing down their necks. The Fallen Commander leapt to the helm of his vessel and snapped curt orders in the style of a classic military commander. His men, accustomed to his method of command, obeyed him in deft actions. The Weeping Assassin stood at the helm of his vessel and leaned forward as he cursed, spat and screamed at his men. His commanding style was cruel and intimidating, yet produced similar results.

Close by, General Va'iga raised his fist and roared with tremendous volume. His captains, Sooalo and Nam'ulu, on their respective vessels echoed his instructions. The Samoan contingent of over five hundred men in five war tongiakis then synchronized their movement across the water. Their mighty sails easily caught the sea wind and blew into shape. A chorus of cheer erupted. Their drought of favourable breeze was broken and within minutes of the dawn, the Pulotulahi armada of fifteen hundred warriors tamed the wind and headed south on course.

The commotion drew the companions from their hull and a handful of warriors blocked their path with drawn spears.

"Get back in your hole!"

"Oh, come on, give us some fresh air," Vaohoi stepped forward in his zestful manner. "I'm beginning to smell like a dog's ass!" he recoiled as he pretended to smell his armpit.

A couple of the warriors laughed and lowered their spears as a lieutenant walked by and did not appear to be concerned with their emergence. He gave stern orders to the warriors to keep vigilant guard and moved on.

"See? Even he can smell me!" Vaohoi laughed and continued to joke with the enemy.

Adi and Atiogie put their hands on the edge of the hull and looked out over the dawn sea. The wind blew their matted hair and cooled their faces as Talatama stepped up joined them. The giant Samoan put his hand on his shoulder and smiled. It was the first time the prince had surfaced from the dark hull.

"Where are they taking us?" Adi breathed.

"Someplace bad," Atiogie replied.

The prince remained silent, as suddenly a call echoed out across the deck and men momentarily turned their attention to the south. The companions unexpectedly beheld their destination, which lay distant on the horizon.

The vista was a sandy blue cast with outstretched cirrocumulus clouds. In the foreground were cirrus wisps, sporadically stained with violet and perforated by transparency that dashed a golden background. But an aberrant image marred the beauty and struck the companions with trepidation.

Soaring from the sea into the sky to some two kilometres, loomed what appeared to be a gargantuan cumulus cloud. It was dark and full bodied, filled with bulbous muscle and it took the form of a menacing giant standing in the middle of the ocean. But the warriors and companions alike knew well their Pacific kingdom and its nature: this was no natural cloud. It was the billowing smoke from one of the greatest volcanoes across the known seas, Kao.

The mighty stratovolcano was typically cone shaped, rising eleven hundred metres above sea level and possessed a base diameter of six kilometres. It was rocky and showed limited patches of vegetation along its lower flanks, while the upper slopes appeared smooth and bare. From its pointed peak fumed a steady stream of immense smoulder. It ascended into the sky and fuelled the giant smoke cloud emitted from the tumultuous batholith.

"By Hikule'o, it's active again!" one of the lieutenants gasped.

"It's been smoking for a few weeks now," another said.

"When was its last eruption?"

"About thirty years ago, I think."

"Milord, are we -"

"Yes. Keep a steady course and aim to moor on the eastern side of it," Kamohoali'i growled as he turned to the rest of the men.

"See there," he pointed to Kao. "Hikule'o is pleased with our accomplishments! He awaits our arrival and will greet us with godly applause!"

A resonance of a thousand devoted warriors cheered at his words and their efforts doubled for the vessels to increase in speed. The companions exchanged shocked expressions.

"Is he mad?" Vaohoi shook.

"No. He's honouring Hikule'o," Pele said from the dark hull.

"How is he honouring Hikule'o?" The young man peered into the hull to see the she-warrior lying comfortably on her back with her hands behind her head.

"We're being sacrificed to the great Hikule'o. By that I mean we'll be tossed into the mouth of the volcano," she yawned. "It is said to be one of the portals back to the underworld of Pulotu."

"What?" Vaohoi almost fainted.

"Merciful Degei," Adi whispered.

"They can try to throw me in! I'll take a few of them down with me!" Atiogie clenched his massive fists as Talatama turned and disappeared into the dark hull without a word.

On another vessel, the Fallen Commander appeared lost in a distant memory as he spoke to his lieutenant.

"I remember a story my grandfather once told me. He spoke of his great grandfather, who lived in the time of King Aho'eitu. In those days the Tu'i Tonga rule included only half of the island of Tongatapu," Siateki began.

"When was that?" his lieutenant asked.

"Maybe two hundred years ago. He said that when King Aho'eitu was a boy, he and his father witnessed one of the greatest volcano eruptions of our history; an eruption that almost wiped out our people and our very existence. It came not from Kao, but from his older brother, Tofua.

"The island next to Kao?" The lieutenant raised an eyebrow.

"Yes. King Aho'eitu said that prior to the eruption, Tofua was a cone shaped volcano like his younger brother. However he was three times as large as Kao." The Fallen Commander turned to the lieutenant.

"There was an explosion that sent tidal waves in all directions, and darkened the sky for months. Those who survived lived to see the fall of Tofua. Its peak had collapsed during the eruption and snuffed out most of the lava flow. Today, all we see is the cradle of his former self and his belly filled with water like Niuafo'ou."

"Well we may see a similar eruption today or tomorrow," the lieutenant said fearfully.

"We'll see," Siateki responded as he peered over to General Kamohoali'i's vessel.

Within hours, the armada had reached the base of Kao and in the absence of beaches the warriors had tried to search for a safe cove to moor. As far as the eye could see, however, there was no welcome but for jagged boulders at the water's edge. Orders were given to disembark but it was a difficult task. The waves crashed against the high rocks both ceaselessly and violently and as the waves pushed forward, some vessels struck the edges. Curses and insults wailed over the sound of the sea smashing onto the volcanic basalt.

"The winds are favourable." Ganilau raised his rotten face skyward.

"So use it while it lasts," Kamohoali'i said as he prepared to disembark. "It won't take you long to get to 'Eua."

Havea and Ganilau stood together facing the dark general, their fearsome faces perpetuated by their black souls.

"Take those men with you. Seek out and advise Lord Tu'ipulotu of our success and our coming."

"Yes Milord." Ganilau bowed.

"Use stealth this close to the capital, Havea. We're too close to lose this war to carelessness," Kamohoali'i said. "I promise you this though, you will feast upon royal flesh before the next moon."

Havea grinned and licked his black lips while Ganilau laughed. Kamohoali'i never looked more serious in his life.

"Get to land!" he roared as he turned away from his commanders.

When the timing was right with the swell, the Pulotulahi warriors leapt ashore nimbly and were followed by hundreds that filtered from the vessels onto the inhospitable and uneven terrain. Here and there, warriors lost their footing and fell between the rocks or back into the yawning sea. Once the commanders leapt ashore, they ordered the companions to be hauled with haste.

Atiogie lifted Adi into his arms like a child and launched his powerful body onto a large rock platform. Pele and Vaohoi had little trouble negotiating the task but Talatama had difficulty. Still wounded, he was unbalanced and sluggish. He timed his hurdle well but failed to employ the agility needed to land. He grunted as he lost his footing and bounced off the edge of a precipice before a large hand snapped against his wrist with the strength of a shark bite.

"Easy there old friend," the giant Samoan smiled as he pulled the prince to safety.

Talatama keeled over temporarily, combating an unseen pain before finally looking up to his good friend, returning a weak smile.

"Come, let me help you." Atiogie threw Talatama's arm over his shoulder and assisted him to walk.

"You lot!" Siateki yelled to a group of warriors from afar. "Get those prisoners bound with rope! Then get them moving!"

Two large warriors quickly bound their hands together with thin twine, linked them by a long rope around their necks and yanked the tension hard, choking them with brief amusement. They then loosened them slightly, only enough for the companions to breathe. The companions could barely find the voices to curse as they were whipped to commence the ascent.

A handful of helmsmen who remained on-board the vessels steered away from the dangerous edge and disappeared around the cove. The warriors at the fore of the army had begun to weave their way through the maze of rocks. Eventually everyone was following the man in front, snaking past the rocks and through sporadic areas of anaemic shrubbery. It was obvious that the plant life had suffered the effects of volcanic activity.

"What's that awful smell?" Vaohoi screwed his face, the rope having loosened around his neck.

"It's the sulphur in the air," Pele said.

"It smells like one of Atiogie's legendary farts," Vaohoi staggered. "I can hardly breathe."

A nearby group of Pulotulahi warriors sniggered and laughed.

"Do you feel the slight vibration in the rocks? Feel the unnatural heat, the look of these plants?" Pele ran a brittle branch through her hand. "And I saw steam rising from rock pools back at the water's edge."

"I saw it too," Adi said.

"They're all the right signs. Mighty Kao is very close to clearing his throat," Pele said.

The companions paused as they looked up and spied the distant peak. Even the guarding warriors stopped and followed suit. The volcanic cone loomed and growled with threats of peril and demise.

"Then let's choke him and be done with it," Atiogie said as he resumed walking.

CHAPTER 58

The noonday sun scorched the volcanic island and rapidly heated the surface. Men gritted their teeth as they endured the blistering heat on their bare feet and wiped the streaming perspiration from their brows. Bodies were slick with sweat. Mouths were gaping from a combination of choking air and the strenuous climb. At their position, streams of vapour could be seen rising from crevasses on the slope and the tremors had become more frequent.

Only a few hundred metres from the summit, the army of warriors stopped for a brief reprieve. Kamohoali'i sat on a rock ledge, made of basalt and obsidian, while his commanders and warriors swarmed around him. All men were exhausted but showed no signs of complaint. The companions were on their knees catching their breath and wincing against the restraints that bound their hands and necks. The commanders gave the main contingent the permission to sit and recover, as Kamohoali'i took a rag and wiped the greasy sweat from his face.

"Kupe, take a contingent to the peak. Return with your findings," he said as he beckoned for a drink. "We will prepare for the sacrifice when you return."

The Weeping Assassin hesitated before looking around to the other commanders with disapproval, but he was not about to question the order. Siateki snickered at him mockingly.

"Yes, Milord."

Kupe did not have to choose those to accompany him. Scores of his trusted warriors followed his lead without word, and within moments, they disappeared beyond a jagged spine of rocks towards the summit.

"Siateki, find a place to keep the slaves from escaping," Kamohoali'i said after guzzling the contents of a whole coconut.

The Fallen Commander nodded, whistled between his teeth and snapped his fingers towards the warrior guards with custody of the companions. He stared across the immediate terrain and spotted a suitable area. His directions were swift and precise.

The ropes were cut and Talatama landed hard against the rocks in a large pit. The companions tumbled down alongside him with sounds of thumps and groans and a handful of warriors stood above them, leering down in amusement.

"Enjoy your last moments together," one of them said.

"And try not to die just yet," said another as they disappeared from view.

"You bastards!" Vaohoi leapt to his feet and hurled a small stone.

The young warrior jumped onto the closest ledge and scaled the rock wall. He swore to himself in a fit of rage as he climbed.

"Vaohoi! No!" Adi yelled.

When he reached the top of the ten foot wall and clambered to his knees, he was met by two warriors.

"Get back down there!" A foot landed in the centre of his chest that sent him toppling over the edge. Adi screamed. Atiogie stood above the companions and quickly raised his giant arms, caught him from his deadly fall and lowered him to the ground. His expression went pale as he clipped Vaohoi over the head in frustration.

"Well done, Atiogie." Adi showed her appreciation when no one else did.

"What is wrong with you all? How many of you do I need to save today?" he snapped.

"Even when Hikule'o plunges this world into eternal darkness will I not ask for your help," Pele said.

"I've had enough of your arrogance!" the Samoan growled as he pointed.

"Get that filthy hand out of my face," she returned. "Or you'll lose it, you oaf."

"Just try it!"

"That's enough!" Talatama stood red faced.

He shoved his way between them and pushed them aside, his breathing laborious and haggard, his physical pain obvious.

"I would be thankful if both of you were thrown in the lava pit! Rid me of your bickering!" he stood straight and raised his chin.

"Our enemy is there, not in here! We need to work together, as we always have."

"What for? We're doomed! There's no escape," Pele laughed.

"That's right," Atiogie succumbed to the helplessness. "There's no way out of this. We can't fight all of them."

"No. I won't accept that." Talatama's courage began to show after days of despair. "That's not the spirit we need now!"

"And where has your spirit been, Talatama?" Pele sneered.

The prince fell silent as he gazed at the ground, and then engaged all of the companions. His truth could not be suppressed any longer.

"My spirit's been crushed! Mahina's dead! I can't hide it anymore, I loved her, we loved each other! For once in my life I found something pure," he beat his chest as tears welled in his eyes, "And she was ripped from my bare hands!"

"She was a traitor," Pele shot.

"Coming from you," the prince returned, silencing Pele immediately.

"I gave up hope when she died."

"Talatama—" Adi moved forward.

"No, you must all hear this. I was there when Kupe threw her from the cliff. The guilt has crippled me ever since: why wasn't I stronger, quicker, smarter? If I had been, I could have saved her. I've been hopeless every second that's passed, blaming myself for what happened to her, for what she suffered, and not being able to bring her back. But I see now that my hopelessness isn't just harming me. A wise man explained forgiveness to me once. I need to forgive myself for Mahina's death, she can't come back and I can't continue as your leader with the guilt still gauging out my heart and my mind," Talatama paused. "I'm sorry, I wasn't there to look after you when you needed me most."

"No apology is needed." Adi smiled, tears in her eyes.

"You've come back to us now, that's what matters," Atiogie smiled.

"But it doesn't change this situation we're in," Pele returned to herself. "We're still going to die."

"We will not die this way! We'll fight to break free and escape down the slopes to the ships. We'll then—"

"That's ridiculous," Vaohoi said. "It's impossible."

The prince glared at the young boy in surprise. Vaohoi had never contributed to their plans or actions yet had always followed Talatama's decisions. The sudden disagreement killed the prince's momentum.

"He's right, Talatama," Adi finally said. "We cannot achieve that, you cannot achieve that, not in your state. You can barely walk."

The prince inhaled to say something but stopped. He sighed as he sat on a large boulder and hung his head. Vaohoi went and crouched in a corner and hid his face. Pele stood, solemn, in the centre of the pit with her hands on her hips and Atiogie leaned his large frame against the wall with his arms crossed. Adi gazed into oblivion and suddenly her eyes were filled with tears for her beloved Emori. The sudden understanding that she would never see him again filled her with a terrible ache.

Kupe and his warriors came within view of the outer rim of the blistering mouth. The smoke sent chills of their insignificance against such a wonder. It was as though they were tiny insects standing before a large smoking campfire. The tremors had reached a level that made standing difficult. Hot gasses and fumes billowed and flowed through the men with such toxicity, they covered their eyes and mouths with their arms.

"Mighty Hikule'o is with us!" They shouted to be heard over the noise.

Kupe could hardly see with the use of one eye. His other wept profusely as he cringed and cursed at his thoughts. The idea of coming to such a dangerous place was ludicrous and foolhardy. Kamohoali'i was risking his own life and the lives of the army for the sake of a worthless, customary sacrifice. If he had his way, he would simply dispatch the prince and his companions straight.

"Go to the edge of the mouth! See if there's a suitable area for the sacrifice!" Kupe yelled at three of his men. "We will remain here."

The brave warriors nodded and walked forwards into the hot gale. Kupe and his men took partial refuge against a large rock face that shielded them. They watched on as the three daring warriors walked slowly, trying desperately to keep their footing under the tremors and combat the deadly fumes. About ten metres from the mouth, Kupe saw one of the men collapse to the ground forever.

Ignoring the fall of their comrade, the two stronger warriors continued. As Kupe watched on it was difficult to see whether the warriors had made it to the edge of the mouth: the blurry haze of gasses prevented a clear view. They began to see red embers whistle from the edge that carried on the smoke and wind, shooting like falling stars. During a lull in the wind, Kupe caught a glimpse of his men; hey had stopped walking and their entire bodies were a patchwork of black and crimson flesh.

Between breaths it happened. There was an all consuming thunder clap without vibration and Kupe saw his men disintegrate before his eardrums burst. A monumental column of steam, volcanic ash and smoke exploded from the crater. Kupe and his men disappeared in an explosion of tephra that blasted from the mouth in all directions. Within seconds, the column from the eruption had risen over three kilometres into the sky.

Below, the army scattered like frightened children. Kamohoali'i and his commanders bellowed out into the disarray for control, as the earth swayed and shook like the deck of a ship on a stormy night. The sound of the explosion and the grinding earth was terrifying. Men fell into crevices and tumbled down steep cliffs. Large boulders and rock dust rolled down the mountain and through the men. Bodies were hewn and crushed.

Another deafening crack and a devastating pyroclastic cloud rolled down the western flank of Kao. It was a lethal combination of superheated gas and steam that rocketed towards the sea, obliterating anything in its path. Perhaps with the blessing of both deities, Tangaloa and Hikule'o, the deadly plumes narrowly missed the companions and Pulotulahi.

"Prince Talatama! My Prince!" came a stern voice from above the pit.

The companions looked up in disbelief. The Hungan chief peered down at them amid the chaos.

"Kaianuanu? Have you come to reclaim more slaves?" the prince could not contain his delight.

"Forgive my prior ignorance, my Prince," the Hungan warrior said as he threw down a rope.

"What magic is this?" Pele could not believe their luck.

"The magic of hope," Talatama smiled at the she-warrior.

Vaohoi threw his arms in the air and cheered. Atiogie laughed and shook his head as the companions saw someone appear beside Kaianuanu. It was Emori. The Fijian warrior looked down in a stern reflection and caught sight of Adi's anguished face.

"Emori!" she screamed.

The companions scrambled out of the pit into the midst of pandemonium. Hiding between the deep gorges, and beyond view of the Pulotulahi army, were about sixty Vava'u warriors. At their head was a familiar face. Lo'au. The ancient mu'a beamed with joy as he gestured for them to hurry. Vaohoi sprinted forward and leapt into his arms, his eyes brimming with tears.

"Lo'au, you've come," Talatama smiled.

"Kaianuanu said I made a hopeless slave," the old mu'a smiled.

"Destined for greater things perhaps!" the prince chuckled.

"We're not out of trouble yet. But here, these will help." Lo'au motioned to one of the warriors. "Can't have you running around here completely naked."

He directed a warrior unwrap a large tapa blanket on the rocky ground. Within it, were all of the companion's clothing, possessions and weapons. They stood in disbelief.

"How did you -?"

"Never mind, let's just say we commandeered a certain ship before coming ashore."

The companions quickly claimed their combinations of tapa cloth, bracelets, gauntlets and girdles. Atiogie seized up his gargantuan tree-club and caressed it lovingly. Pele snatched together her obsidian axe and her short bow and arrows quickly. Talatama picked up the legendary armour of Sangone and strapped it on before he found the Peace Maker and held it like a child.

"Tangaloa be blessed! Come, my companions, let us escape this madness! " he roared and raised his club in the air.

A great cheer boomed from the companions and the Vava'u warriors.

CHAPTER 59

Amid the mayhem of their escape, Talatama spied Kamohoali'i from a distance. The general was whirling his club in the air and screaming orders, before he glanced in the prince's direction. The recognition of their freedom reflected across his face and it became a mask screwed with rage. His bellows were drowned out by the chaos as he pointed towards the companions.

"This way!" Kaianuanu shouted.

The Hungan chief, the companions and the Vava'u warriors ducked and weaved through the maze of chasms and steaming columns, away from the turmoil. They negotiated the tremor-ridden earth, falling boulders and torrid gasses that blistered at their feet. But it was not long before they heard the enemy on their heels. Bringing up the rear, Talatama twisted around as he ran and spotted a swarm of warriors gaining on them; Kamohoali'i had gained control of his startled men.

"Pele! Atiogie!" the prince shouted.

His companions stopped and knew what they had to do, as he pointed at the crags on either side of the crevasse.

"Adi, Lo'au, keep running! Emori protect them!" Talatama ordered as he took position.

The first group of warriors sprinted between the looming crags, before their heads snapped back in puffs of red mist. The next four stumbled over the fallen bodies and were crushed as the companions leapt out from behind their position. Talatama crushed bone with the Peace Maker, Pele's axe never missed its mark and Kaianuanu finished off the fallen. Atiogie swung his club anew as he stepped directly into the path and faced the oncoming warriors.

"Come, you maggots!" his rage exhaling with the breath.

With the strength of a titan he swept his mighty club to and fro and with each stroke he snuffed a life. Fresh blood spattered across his hulking body and he began to create a pile of corpses across the crevasse. Pele stepped to Atiogie's side and fired her arrows at the oncoming warriors and, for a brief moment, they had defeated the first scouting dozen. But they could hear more advancing.

"Keep moving! Let's go!" Talatama threw his arm forward.

By this time the massive eruption had soared to risen over fifteen kilometres into the sky. It was a dirty grey mass, swollen with angry plumes of black. There were thousands of giant sized tephra and pyroclasts that had been blown into the atmosphere during the eruption, some of which could be seen landing in the sea kilometres away from Kao. The vibrations from the initial explosion had lessened, however, the earth continued to shake.

The companions exited the chasms and crags and arced out into a cleared area. It was barren, covered with millions of tiny pebbles and devoid of plant life. They could see the tongiakis moored in the rough seas just beyond the water's edge. In the distance, the companions could see the larger volcanic island, Tofua. They noticed that there was a small cloud rising from its centre. Talatama prayed as he ran that it too would not erupt.

Lo'au, Adi, Emori and the accompanying Vava'u warriors halted suddenly ahead of the group, as a large contingent of Pulotulahi warriors blocked the path to their escape. The enemy numbers were greater than their own and continued to grow. There was no question for surrender: he would die fighting, the prince swore.

"Companions! To me!" Talatama raised the Peace Maker.

The warriors rushed back to the prince's position and formed a crescent moon facing the enemy. More and more Pulotulahi warriors appeared from the eastern side where their initial porting had been. There were three hundred warriors, then six hundred, then a thousand. The companions could see Kamohoali'i at the apex of the army that approached them slowly. He chuckled as yet more and more of his warriors congregated behind him.

Far to his left was the Fallen Commander, Siateki, with his hundreds. There was the Unarmed Warrior, Omani and his warriors. To his right appeared Kupe and General Va'iga and their hundreds of followers. The Weeping Assassin had narrowly survived the eruption, bearing grievous lacerations. His hair and face was matted with the claret blood that poured from his ears, and down his chest.

The companions looked about in an emotional fusion of hatred and finality. Pele bared her teeth. Atiogie began to breathe like a cornered animal. Vaohoi was at the brink of hysteria. Talatama lifted his chin and regarded them with distain. Even Lo'au gripped his staff in preparation for battle. The enemy began to hoot in a show of intimidation and their howls rose in volume as they began to press forward.

"Talatama – it has been – an honour fighting at your side," Atiogie managed.

"I'll share a cup of kava with you in the underworld, my Prince," Pele suddenly laughed.

"I'm up for that!" Vaohoi squeaked with lunacy.

"No, my dear friends, we will live forever!" Talatama roared from the bottom of his powerful lungs and pointed out to sea.

Many of the enemy close by turned. The companions screamed with elation as they recognised the vessel approaching from the south east, triggering the rest of the Pulotulahi army to turn. No more than a kilometre off shore sailed the mighty Maui Atalaga aboard his war tongiaki. Behind him loomed twenty tongiakis carrying two thousand Rarotongan warriors. Taking the lead on the commanding ship was Prince Whatonga and his proud father, Lord Toi. The united vessels could mean only two things; the truth had been revealed, and bitter gall approached en masse by their dark sails. Talatama's skin crawled with passion. His injuries withered away. He ignored the acrid smell of the volcanic gasses. His senses were heightened and he felt more alive than ever. He was renewed of strength, of purpose. He stabbed his club into the ground and ripped a strip of cloth from his vala and stuffed the long cloth into his mouth. He ran both his hands through his long hair, pulling it into a pony-tail. He then tied his hair back with the cloth and retrieved his weapon.

He turned to his companions and imparted the passion through his eyes. They were instantly inspired.

"For the King! For the Empire! For glory!" the prince bellowed as he charged ahead, the companions at his heels.

In mid charge, the sunlight disappeared and day became as night. The gigantic column had eclipsed the sun. Dark and stormy clouds swelled from Kao's peak as if the sky itself were falling. It was then the torrid ash began to fall. It draped down in a grey curtain around Kao, fading out of sight of the sea, the land, the island itself. In a matter of moments, the companions could scarcely see in front of them. Beyond that was a dark haze, misty and surreal. The army of the Pulotulahi began to vanish in the screen of an ashen miasma.

"Va'iga! Omani! Kupe! Take your men to the landing!" Kamohoali'i roared out before the first rain of ash fell. "Maui Atalaga and those bastards must not make it to shore!"

Talatama materialized out of the curtain of murk and pierced Siateki's regiment like an arrow into flesh. With his surprise attack, he dashed the brains of two warriors before the enemy turned and engaged. Atiogie crashed out of the grey drape like a demon, looming over his foes with the destruction of his club. A spear shot out of the darkness and into the chest of Siateki's lieutenant, as Emori rushed at the Fallen Commander and drove his shoulder through him. The wind from Siateki's lungs was knocked out as he crashed to the ground. The Fijian warrior recovered his spear to finish Siateki but was forced to face oncoming threats.

Siateki clutched his chest as he struggled to breathe again, his other hand searching for his weapon. As he did, Kaianuanu and his

Vava'u warriors plummeted into the main body of his force. The result was the sound of death that pierced the deep groans of the earth. Pele dodged through the moving walls of men, her obsidian axe flashing side to side and striking with clinical precision. Lo'au and Vaohoi remained at the rear of the companions with three Vava'u warriors, waiting to defend Adi should stragglers get through.

Talatama gripped his weapon with both hands, sweeping it to and fro. Through the melee, he felt an occasional ricochet off his Sangone armour. He suddenly felt his energy wane and injuries gnaw at him. He clenched his teeth and blocked with the Peace Maker, countering in a slicing motion. He would not fall victim to his own weakness. He expelled a war cry when he finished the next target his voice echoed by his companions close by.

The warrior prince puffed his chest and walked between the violence of battle. The thick ash fell from the black sky slowly: a stark disparity to the red-rapid action of war. Within moments, every man and woman – friend or foe alike – was completely covered with grey residue. It created the illusion that stone statues of men had come to life and battled in a dreamlike world. It continued to rain down, almost peacefully, but with it came slow suffocation and blindness.

As the battle endured, the combatants began to show signs of choking. Men began to convulse in asphyxiation. The warriors facing Talatama keeled as they were smothered with ash. As the warrior prince continued to slay them, he too began to feel the mucky irritation in his chest. He began to cough slightly, and then choked violently onto his forearm; blood.

"What are you doing, Lo'au?" Vaohoi said.

"If we keep breathing this heavy ash, we'll die," he said as he began to tear lengths of tapa from his possessions.

Adi began to cough as she fell to her knees. The warriors moved to help her.

"Quickly! Wrap this around your nose and mouth!" the mu'a thrust a piece of tapa at the Fijian priestess.

"Vaohoi, quickly take these. Find our comrades. You must hurry!" Lo'au pressed bunches of cloth in the youngster's hands.

Not far away, Talatama and the companions held off a number, four times their own.

"Damn!" the warrior prince cursed as he narrowly defended from an attack.

"Talatama!" Vaohoi yelled as he appeared through the grey haze.

The prince saw the youngster's nose and mouth was covered with a sheet of thin tapa. Vaohoi threw him a length of the same material.

"Put this on!" he said as he disappeared to find the others.

"Good boy," Talatama smiled.

He felt an instant relief as he inhaled the filtered and uncontaminated air. His vision remained irritated however, and he could only focus through constant squinting, but he could breathe! With improved ability and renewed strength, the warrior prince clasped his weapon tightly and resumed the easy killing of suffocating enemies. He rushed through dozens of inflicted warriors and swiftly ended their suffering.

A larger battle materialised through the ashen mist and he observed there were at least one hundred men, all fitted with ragged face visors. The warrior prince's eyes glimmered with battle lust when he spotted Pele and Atiogie in the centre of the struggle. As he quickly approached, he saw Emori and Kaianuanu on the far side of the skirmish. He stopped at the edge of the conflict and a muffled roar exploded under his tapa mask.

"Fight me!" His body was electrified.

Immediately a dozen warriors on the fringe turned and sprinted at him. He shifted askance and struck his first victim before lunging forwards. He blinded another, spun, and almost decapitated the third. Sudden sprays of blood and soot followed every strike. The falling of statue-men continued like the crumbling of their mortar, as Talatama quickly found his rhythm. He fought side to side, back to front, occasionally improvising, sporadically defending instead of attacking. Enemy numbers dwindled.

"Atiogie!" the prince yelled as his giant comrade recognised him through the wet ash and blood. Simultaneously, Pele, Talatama and Emori launched themselves against the dozen warriors battling Atiogie. The relief of the giant warrior was evident and together they made quick work of the foes. As they approached the swarm of battle, Kaianuanu and his Vava'u warriors outnumbered Siateki and his last few men.

By the time they came within reach of the battle, only Siateki and two others remained. They whipped their clubs around wildly, overcome with exhaustion and wounds, defending themselves with every last ounce of desperate effort. A powerful Vava'u warrior stepped forward between their feeble strikes and crushed them. He stepped forward again to finish off the Fallen Commander.

"Stop!" the prince yelled.

The warrior halted and turned to Talatama, before bowing his head. Adi, Vaohoi and Lo'au appeared through the grey mist to join the victorious group. Siateki struggled to see those before him, so covered with soot and ash was he.

"Siateki, it is I, Talatama."

CHAPTER 60

The Fallen Commander had collapsed on his back and reared himself weakly on his elbow. He struggled to shield himself with his club in his right hand, as his chest rose and fell rapidly. Beneath his visor, his gaping mouth could not inhale enough air. He swayed with fatigue and the knowledge of imminent death.

"Talatama, you bastard ..." he exerted his breath hoarsely. "You – you've bested me."

The warrior prince advanced slowly and looked down at Siateki frozen in defence, helpless, beaten. He was suddenly reminded of a time long ago in his youth. The memory was an exact reproduction of that very moment. As a young boy learning to fight during his military training, he duelled with Siateki and had knocked him down. He stared down at the evil man before him and saw his young childhood friend. He remembered Siateki reeling on the ground before smiling up at him.

"Good strike, Talatama. I didn't see that one coming," the boy had said.

The young prince returned the smile and reached down to his friend.

"Here, let me help you, brother," he soothed, as he pulled the young Siateki up and embraced him.

The Fallen Commander failed to rise; he had not the strength for it. His limbs felt as though they were filled with rocks, his blood like mud that coursed slowly through his veins. His tongue hung from his parched mouth and a silence between them was echoed by the distant tremors and the sound of falling ash. Talatama slowly lowered his club, deep in reminiscence.

"If you won't kill him, I will!" Pele stormed forward brandishing her axe.

"No! You will not and neither will I," the warrior prince straightened and regarded Siateki with a dark compassion.

"You and I were once brothers. For that I will spare your life." Talatama glared at him. "You've lived all these years as a rogue, a murderer of innocents, the *'Fallen Commander'*, as a servant of the Pulotulahi. You threw away a promising future years ago, and with it our brotherhood."

"You stole that future from me!" Siateki squirmed helplessly. "You pushed me into the dirt while claiming your victories! You stole my spirit, my ambition, everything! I was nothing more than a worm under your heel!"

"You heaped shame upon yourself. It was not I who drove you from the light. You always allowed your jealousies to consume you, Siateki," Talatama paused. "But after all we've been through, I now pity you."

"I don't need your pity!" the Fallen Commander shrieked and flung dirt at the warrior prince.

He then dropped his own club and collapsed flat on his back. As his body began to rack with emotion he turned on his side and began to sob. Talatama shook his head silently and faced his companions with the sound of roaring battle in the distance.

"Come, Maui-Atalaga needs our help," he said. The companions disappeared through the curtain of ash.

The rain of falling ash extended beyond the shores of Kao, and reached its brother island, Tofua, sweeping out in all directions. The sea had become a littered basin of darkness: the surface was covered with dense silt that crashed on the jagged rocks now coated with grey mud. As the companions arrived at the eastern water's edge, they could see the dozens of vessels moored slightly aground, emptied of warriors. Then suddenly, they heard the blast of Whatonga's conch.

"They made it ashore!" Talatama hastened towards the battle.

They lumbered through the haze blindly, phantoms of shapes appearing here and there, swirls shifting and blowing. Suddenly through the mist ahead, appeared an eerie, reddish glow and they slowed their advance.

"What is that?" Vaohoi said.

It then came into view. Slow, viscous lava crossed their path towards the battle. It hissed and spat as it bubbled towards the sea. Its heat was beyond anything the companions had ever felt. Through the ashen miasma and up the mountain, they spotted more glows approaching. The lava came closer. Walking within metres, they could barely face it.

"Blast! The flow of lava has started. That was incredibly quick," the old mu'a breathed.

"Aaaiieee! My eyes!" Vaohoi shrieked.

"Don't look at it!"

"Hurry! This way!" Talatama quickly led the group past the creeping magma.

Whatonga lifted the tapa that covered his mouth, and raised the conch to his lips before exerting his entire breath through the shell. Its blast pierced the chaos that surrounded them, echoing across the foggy seas. Instantaneously, hundreds of his Rarotongan warriors thrust through the centre of the enemy huddled in an arrowhead formation. As they drove through, the arrow head split and turned outwards, dividing the Pulotulahi warriors. Whatonga and his generals remained at the rear and directed the attack. The Rarotongan lord turned to his generals, with a vision that was blurred with fury and passion.

"To the death!" he roared. "For Mahina!"

The generals resounded his fervour and launched into battle towards Kamohoali'i and the wild Samoan general, Va'iga. Many of the Rarotongan warriors who fought at Niuatoputapu remembered

Va'iga and cleared a berth around him. Intermittently, the evil mercenary would launch himself forward and claim a victim with the deadly combination of his two clubs. He would hold a single handed club in each hand and employ a dexterous recipe of fighting skill; each weapon moving on its own trajectory with double the chances of striking the target.

On the other side of the battle, Kupe swung his legendary rope, sea urchin and coral about his head with one hand, in the other his obsidian dagger. To his left, more engaged with the Rarotongans, was Omani. His feet acted like large clubs, snapping into the heads of his opponents, often leaving them unconscious or dead. Those who came too close to him fell victim to his vicious hand techniques. Clawing hands that ripped at the throat and circular locks that broke joints.

As the battle ensued, few noticed the fast approaching lava flows. Some burning arteries crept slowly, others flowed swiftly. However, the precise number could not be determined because they appeared sporadically, suddenly from the curtains of ash. One thing was certain however: there were too many that had already surrounded the two warring sides. As the Rarotongan forces separated the Pulotulahi army, the division eventually estranged the groups beyond sight of each other. The light tremors continued and there was no sign of the ash fall ceasing.

Talatama and the companions plummeted into the closest warring group. Initially, the Rarotongan warriors turned on them, causing the companions to defend themselves before a Rarotongan lieutenant recognised them and quickly identified them to others mid battle. Talatama hailed the warriors and continued to fight the Pulotulahi enemy when he spotted Kamohoali'i ahead of him. His wrath burned.

"Kamohoali'i!" he raised his club in challenge.

The dark general recognised him immediately and his fury was equalled. He howled and raced through lines of warriors to get to the warrior prince, barrelling over his own soldiers until he clashed against the Peace Maker at force. As Talatama and Kamohoali'i faced off, a clearing formed around them. They circled each other and heaved deeply under their cloth masks. The falling ash between them was slow and deliberate as if mimicking their standoff. Their eyes emanated their fierce spirit behind the tapa masks and through the haze.

"Pity I couldn't throw you in the volcano before it blew!" Kamohoali'i cackled.

"Pity, yes! I wouldn't have got this chance to kill you with my hands!" Talatama returned the sarcastic laugh.

"I'll get just as much enjoyment taking your life at the end of my club!" the general growled as he stepped forwards.

They collided, their clubs clashing hard, ricocheting off each other with a bounce. The general dug his powerful legs into the ashen soil and pounced forwards after a second parry. He overwhelmed the warrior prince, and with his superior weight, knocked him backwards. As he stumbled and tripped, Kamohoali'i tossed his club with all his might. The warrior prince felt a cold blow to the side of his head that stole his hearing. He crashed onto his armour-shelled back, which instantly rolled him to the side. His ears sung a high pitched hum as his hand went to the side of his temple, feeling warm and sticky blood through his fingers.

He squinted. The blurry mass of the general was nearby, bending down to gather his club, while stars glittered all around the falling ash and warring men. Voices, roars and bellows surrounded him as he suddenly realised that he had lost hold of the Peace Maker. He kept shaking his head for clarity as he spread his hands out over the ground. Kamohoali'i approached him, savouring the kill to come.

"And now it ends, Talatama," he said.

"Look out!"

The general whirled around. Blood curdling screams and dreadful howls erupted from a mass of warriors to his left. Then he saw it: a lava flow that flooded through the centre of battle with the speed of a raging river, devouring everything in its path. Men who were trapped gave a petrified expression of terror. The lava took life instantaneously and reduced men to burning liquid in a violent torrid of ruby glow.

Kamohoali'i could say nothing. He throttled his bulky legs, hauling his massive frame as quick as he could. Talatama had barely gained his senses before he realised his single option was to roll out of its path. The blaze of magma ran between the two combatants, ferocious and impartial. The sound of scorched earth hissed and spat as the general swiftly created a safe distance before turning to face it. Talatama escaped the lava flow by metres on his side, curled in the foetal position with his back to the magma. The great shell of Sangone protected his body and repulsed the incinerating heat before the warrior prince gathered his strength and propelled himself further until he could rise to his feet.

Atiogie attacked his Samoan brethren with no quarter. Nam'ulu, lieutenant of the Samoan mercenaries, hacked at the giant with his short club. Every strike rebounded off Atiogie's weapon, occasionally finding his target, but with little results. This did not last long, however, as the constant flurry of attacks infuriated the giant Samoan. With one deafening roar, he swatted his smaller adversary to the ground. His final swing splattered Nam'ulu's brains from his head with a hollow crunch. Suddenly he received a clout to the side of the head, as Sooalo sprinted past. He felt part of his ear hanging by the skin.

The captain of the Samoan mercenaries had duelled with Atiogie in battles past. Their first encounter was years ago in Upolu's north eastern regions, when Atiogie and his father, Lord Feepo, were defending an allied village from General Va'iga, Captain Sooalo and their malevolent warriors. On that day, the righteous warriors prevailed, yet Va'iga and his minions escaped. Later, Feepo told Atiogie that he had known Va'iga since before Atiogie was born, old and stale conflicts from the past. Since that time, the two Samoan forces would engage in sporadic clashes across the Samoan Isles and now into the greater Empire.

The proud son of Lord Feepo held his massive weapon and clenched his strong teeth. He disregarded the abrasion to his head and lost ear, as he faced the captain. Sooalo was only a few years older than Atiogie, and as such, a fierce rivalry had grown between them. The captain held a spear in his hands, his preferred weapon. He lowered the tip towards his enemy and began to circle. Atiogie noticed that Va'iga stood nearby and observed them with keen interest.

"So, boy, of all the places we'd end our bloody conflict, I would never have imagined this!" the general laughed.

"Your deathbed is wherever I can lay you, old man," Atiogie growled.

"Not through me you won't," Sooalo challenged.

"I want you, old man!" Atiogie ignored the captain and pointed to Va'iga. "My father started war with you thirty years ago. I'm going to end it now."

Sooalo exhaled a curt shout and lunged as the giant warrior parried and swung his great club with impressive brawn. But to his astonishment, the captain ducked nimbly, and thrust his weapon again, this time finding his mark. The spear penetrated Atiogie's left chest and sunk in a few inches before exiting. The giant Samoan snarled in pain as he knocked the spear away and stumbled back, allowing the captain to drive his spear again quickly, aiming for Atiogie's heart. But this time he was prepared. He waited and shifted his body at the last moment, catching the end of the spear with his huge hands.

He had dropped his club, and with his superior strength, reefed the spear from Sooalo's hands. Badly wounded and enraged, Atiogie snarled again and flexed his staggering girth, snapping the spear in two. He tossed the broken weapon to the side and advanced on Sooalo barehanded. The captain tried to block Atiogie's fists but his strength was too great. His giant mallets throttled against Sooalo's head and almost knocked him off his feet. Unremitting, the captain struck back and connected two punches to Atiogie's chest and face.

But it was fruitless. Atiogie was a man eighty kilograms heavier than Sooalo and elevated to a point beyond pain. Saliva and blood swayed from his mouth, his face an innocuous mask of wild detachment. Atiogie's elbow crashed upon Sooalo's head with the force of a club, which sent the captain's consciousness wavering. Atiogie's foot then drove through his stomach, sending him sprawling dangerously close to a magma stream. The giant warrior strode to the broken captain and roughly lifted him to his feet. He gripped his hands together, and before any Pulotulahi warriors could engage him, he lumbered his entire weight behind his swinging arms. The incredible impact struck the captain squarely in the chest and lifted him into the air.

Sooalo landed in the lava flow with a dense splash, sending spatters of magma in all directions. In the instant between seconds, there was no reflection of panic on his face as he tried to rise out of the lava. Only in the end, when his body was liquefied beneath him was the terror of his predicament apparent. No smoulder or smoke rose from where he was consumed, his entire being was erased from all existence.

Atiogie stumbled backwards, covering his face in pain from the scorching heat. He eventually lowered his arms and looked for General Va'iga through the rain of ash. The old general had once again, disappeared.

CHAPTER 61

Whatonga stepped over the corpses that lay before him. He strode with purpose; teeth gleaning under a tapa veil, eyes burning bright with the lust of combat. In his right hand he wielded his axe: a shaft of ironwood sporting a chiselled stone in the form of a crescent moon. The haft of the axe was polished and skilfully carved, while the stone married perfectly into the groove bound with twine at its end. He held no weapon in his left. Rather, he used his free hand to counter and trap his opponent's attacks, giving him the opportunity to strike back.

The stone axe was grey, but gleamed with blackish blood. The ash from the eruption discoloured the blood of men, reflecting a disparity of natural hue to sepia. His long black hair, customarily tied back, was free flowing and wild. Regularly stepping from the fray to strategize courses of attack, he had broken position and lunged into the melee. He ignored the coarse shouts from his generals and the compelling voice of his father, Toi, behind in the distance. On this day, Prince Whatonga would change the course of his destiny and the destinies of others forever.

The blurred the shapes of warring men blurred before his eyes. Amid the haze, was the crusted red glow of nearby lava flows. At this time the heat was overwhelming but he had long forgotten his scorched feet and the pain it inflicted. The burning of his skin was naught beside the flame that blazed in his heart for revenge. His vengeance coupled with pains of hatred, scorn and a growing malice took the form of one man. Kupe. Only two days past, Maui Atalaga had led him to Vava'u where he met with Kaianuanu, Lo'au and Emori. Therein he finally learned of Kupe's deceit, his betrayal, and worst of all, his murder of Lady Rongaueroa and Mahina.

Somehow amid the battle, volcanic lava flow and the falling ash, Whatonga managed to find the Weeping Assassin. Kupe stood haggard, though defiant, against his enemies. He was badly wounded, a combination of the initial eruption and subsequent battle. Patches of his old, leathery skin were cut, raw or caked with dry black blood. The deepest lesions on his body glowed like the surroundings of rock and ruby lava. His silvery, shoulder-length hair was matted and his shoulders hunched further forward with injury and fatigue. He stepped over his recent victim and saw Whatonga approach.

"The prodigal son is here to avenge all," he guessed his recent enlightenment.

Whatonga remained silent as he surveyed Kupe, fixing on him with hatred. A hot gust of wind swept down among the warring men and blew the ash in swirls. The two men faced each other, squinting against the hot gust and ashen squall, a defiance of equal proportion hanging in the balance. Kupe threw down dagger and took both hands to his cruel weapon of coral and urchin, before reaching across his face to rip the veil from his mouth. He instantly breathed in the polluted air.

"At last I can finish the job I started with your family," he chuckled as he began to swing his weapon.

"My sister, Mahina," Whatonga said. "You will die for her murder."

"Your sister? So, what about your mother, and your brother, Ruarangi, and your uncle, Hoturapa?"

"What?" Whatonga's fury was replaced with confusion.

The Weeping Assassin revelled in the sudden perplexity that washed across the Rarotongan prince. The evil that coursed through his veins and the memory of his wicked deeds of the past thrilled him. He ignored the signs of his lungs struggling under each breath.

He rejoiced in the evil committed in his life as it came full circle, and cared not for what would happen in moments to come.

"Let me recite the deeds. Thirty years ago, I stole the great tongiaki, Matahourua, from your uncle and with it his willing wife," Kupe chuckled. "And when your uncle and brother attempted to track me down, they became lost at sea and perished. So in essence, I killed them both while making the biggest discovery of new land in the Empire's history!"

"It was you!" Whatonga ripped the veil from his face, remembering the stories of this man's betrayal in his youth.

"Two years ago, plans were construed to include the rest of your family. Your mother was a political ploy, to catch you and your father in my net. Mahina was just a token to direct your attentions of retribution towards Prince Talatama and his companions. Though as you saw, that was a disappointing end."

"And for them all will I slay you!" Whatonga stepped closer.

"But as fate deals, I managed to capture Mahina again," he continued. "Killing her was like savouring a fine meal."

"Spirits of my dead ancestors, give me the strength to take the life of this hell spawn," Whatonga whispered.

"This is not the ending I had planned; it is more than I ever wished for!" Kupe continued to chuckle. "But perhaps it's destiny that I wipe your entire family out from existence, including you."

Whatonga ducked swiftly, evading the deadly swing. The Weeping Assassin smiled, as he maintained the momentum of the weapon and began to circle his prey. His blind eye was sealed shut in a glue of dried tears and filth as he managed to fixate his good eye under the searing winds. The cherry glow from nearby lava blazed across their tattooed skin, as Whatonga shifted his body slowly, maintaining his frontal position, and gripping his axe lightly at his side.

"You're just as weak as your sister. But you'll die on your knees." Kupe swung again, but feinted.

The weapon swung low and caught Whatonga in his left thigh with a crack. The Rarotongan prince felt the urchin spines puncture his skin. It drove deep into his femur, followed by the crude thump of coral, battering his exposed leg. The impact threw him to the ground in agony and sent shattered urchin spines flying. Kupe yanked the weapon back and re-commenced for his final swing as Whatonga's free hand clutched at his leg. The perforated spikes had snapped at the base and remained embedded deep in his flesh.

"Aaaarrrrhh!" Whatonga groaned as he struggled to stand.

The urchin and coral smashed against his arms, while defending his head. Spines ripped into his skin. He stumbled on to his injured leg, but which could not take the weight. He fell again on the ashen ground, sending a puff of grey dust into the air. He cursed angrily to himself. Both strikes should have been easily avoided and he knew he was better than that. But as he tried to rise quickly from the blow, pain shot through his body and he collapsed, muscles shaking with hurt and fatigue. A sudden realisation then came to him. His weakness now would cost him his life. It was the end.

Kupe's chest shot forward with a yelp, as a spear erupted from his solar plexus. He released his weapon in mid spin and the trailing rope shot through the curtain of ash and disappeared. He gave no reflection of surprise but instead, tried to wrench the spear from his back. As he did, he faced his attacker, who had advanced quickly on him. A bone-numbing blow sent his vision spiralling and the sound of crushed limbs echoed through his head. The Weeping Assassin crumpled to the ground for the last time. His attacker looked down on him without pity, as he removed his veil.

"And so I rid my family, and the world, of you, Kupe," Lord Toi said.

At sixty-five, Lord Toi had not engaged in direct battle for two decades. In his prime, he was the most respected warrior chief of the early Empire. Once a great navigator under the command of Warlord Punake, he was a close ally to King Tu'itatui and helped expand the Empire during the years of growth. Though during the later years, his ambition declined, his closeness with the Empire drew apart and he turned recluse. He then allowed his son,

Whatonga, to step forward and claim leadership while he retired from his warrior ways. On this day however, he had not forgotten his instinct for combat.

"T-Toi," Kupe coughed bright blood from his mouth.

"Yes, it is me, old enemy," he nodded. "You can meddle no more. Go now and walk among the damned."

The old warlord turned away to Whatonga, ignoring Kupe's final guttural reply and aided his son to his feet. Once he stood, he limped over to the Weeping Assassin, and without a moment's pause swept the axe across his head, scattering it across the rocks in a messy pulp of hair and teeth. He then fell to his knees against the twitching body and hung his head, as the finality of his vengeance began to evaporate under his skin. Lord Toi watched on silently.

"Whatonga."

"I just need a moment."

As he silently experienced his new born liberation, he spotted a parchment of tapa, wedged in Kupe's fist. Waiting until he caught his breath, he reached down and pried the cloth from the lifeless fingers. As he inspected the parchment, Lord Toi stood behind him and looked about defensively.

"Come, Whatonga, the battle still lingers. It's not safe."

Crude Polynesian symbols and illustrations depicting stars, the sun, sea, unknown animals and symbols were etched crudely in charcoal. The Rarotongan prince instantly identified the cloth as navigational directions and a deep frown etched across his brow. His eyes then widened. In his hand he held the directions to the mythical land Kupe spoke of; the great land he had discovered and returned from all those years ago using his uncle's tongiaki. He carefully tucked the tapa cloth into his girdle and stood slowly.

"Yes, Father, let's go."

Across the barren stage of rock and ash, fewer and fewer men continued battle. The Pulotulahi warriors had been separated from their general, and lacked his leadership in their dwindling numbers. The Rarotongan warriors chased them down mercilessly and spared no one. Shadows of combatants drifted through the snowfall of ash, only to disappear as swiftly. Echoes of men had become faint and distant and eventually a high ranking Pulotulahi warrior called the order for a retreat. All who remained heeded the call.

Talatama faced Kamohoali'i across the smouldering lava flow. The heat caused the air to swell with blurs and searing miasmas. The prince edged away helplessly, unable to cross the breadth of liquid fire. Kamohoali'i broke their fierce stare and turned to combat as the Rarotongan warriors appeared wildly out of the curtain of ash. But they were no match for the veteran warlord. Kamohoali'i took amusement as he slew the men, before turning over his shoulder to Talatama.

"Saved by the blood of the earth, weak prince!" he shouted to be heard over the bleeding earth.

The prince huffed about, frustrated, unable to construct a way to cross the lava. Then, as he glanced back at Kamohoali'i, he saw a single figure appear behind him. This time, however, it was no Rarotongan war party. The young man almost tripped in front of Kamohoali'i when they exchanged glares. The general devoured him with his eyes, relishing the slaughter to come.

"Shit!" Vaohoi said as he began to slowly retreat.

"Don't move. Or you'll not live beyond three steps," Kamohoali'i leered.

Talatama's yelling could not be heard. He jumped and waved in vain to distract the general but with his back to him, Kamohoali'i ignored everything but the consolation of a victim as dear to his heart's hate. Vaohoi summoned all the courage he could muster and raised his small club in defence. The general smirked and attacked, the impact smashing Vaohoi's club in two pieces and sending him wheeling backwards. Kamohoali'i swung again and missed. Vaohoi, pumped with the fear of fighting for his life evaded deftly. But it was the old general's anger and fury that undid Vaohoi's agility. The young man slipped and fell. Kamohoali'i was over him instantly.

The general felt a numbing sensation to the back of his shoulder. It caused him to drop his club and wince. Vaohoi scuttled away to stand at a safe distance as Kamohoali'i's off-hand searched for the pain and found a thin shaft buried deep under his shoulder blade. He turned to face Talatama across the lava flow and recognised the person next to him. Pele slowly lowered her bow and did not reach for another arrow. Kamohoali'i glared at his sister in a mixture of uncertainty and resentment. He stumbled slightly and heard approaching warriors too late. Kaianuanu's club swept over his head and knocked the light from his eyes.

The battle was over. Men who could not board a vessel dived into the grey sea. The patchy vegetation on Kao was on fire. Flames licked from the branches, sending extraneous strands of smoke into the air, lighting up the darkness like torches in the night. In the absence of the sun, the surrounding islands had lowered in temperature. Cold winds blew about the fleeing armada of tongiakis, sending shivers through the companions, who were huddled together on Maui Atalaga's deck. Talatama stood by the folk hero at the helm, as Adi tended to the wounded comrades. Vaohoi had not left Lo'au's side since his encounter, but Pele stood alone at the aft in silence.

Kaianuanu sailed close by with his small entourage of tongiakis. In his main hull was the defeated general, Kamohoali'i. Still unconscious, he was bound tightly and guarded heavily. In other sections of the hull, were additional Pulotulahi prisoners, including the Unarmed Warrior Omani who had been defeated and captured. Talatama had made the decision not to search for the fleeing enemies such as General Va'iga, for he was a mercenary and the defeat would send him sailing back to Samoa with naught but his life. Commander Siateki and other remaining Pulotulahi warriors, who had also fled, posed no threat. The larger force led by Whatonga and Lord Toi followed the companions southward.

As the united forces sailed away from Kao, the ash fall began to lessen. Many gazed back, and witnessed gigantic curtains of steam rising from the coastlines where the lava met the sea. The earth had ceased its tremors and the explosions were silenced. Atop of Kao, further ash clouds had become greyish-white and cream, stretching beyond the stars. The terror, violence and death was over.

CHAPTER 62

Late afternoon set in with the sun hovering over the western horizon. The blend with fine volcanic ash suspended in the atmosphere, created a spectacular sunset of sandy glow. The smell of sulphur still lingered in the sea wind, as the volcanic cloud had been blown beyond the north vista. In the distance, its scattered form became unrecognizable to the high reaching clouds.

The companions and their allies moored their vessels, and camped on a remote beach on the island of Nomuka, a small island in the Ha'apai region about seventy kilometres south of Kao. It had been untouched by the volcanic ash fall, but like all surrounding islands, had suffered minor tsunamis and tremors. The one hundred or so inhabitants of Nomuka rallied within an hour of their arrival and presented the companions with an abundance of food. The allies spread out camps across the beach with circles of fire, according to warrior rank, and in the centre of the beach lay the largest assembly of food, drink and hosts.

Talatama stood with Pele at the tree line. He began to take the Sangone armour off his body during their conversation.

"You know why we didn't, Pele."

"No, I don't. It would have been much wiser to moor on Foa. You know that is my home. We would have received a grander reception and greater aid."

"Pele – you know I trust you with my life. We've been through too much together. But never forget, he is still you brother," Talatama pointed at Kamohoali'i, bound and guarded on the beach.

"And I would have run the risk of a rescue attempt on Foa had we gone there. It's his home too."

"Nonsense! He left Foa decades ago!"

"Is there another reason for this?"

"I want to pay my respects to my father," Pele said after a moment's silence.

"Understood, but it's still too dangerous. Let us return to the capital with Kamohoali'i and I'll accompany you to Alama's tomb."

"I'm going," she said and turned to walk away. "You can't stop me."

"Pele, I need you–" Talatama put his hand on her shoulder, "Stay with us until we arrive at Heketa. Please."

The she-warrior took a deep sigh before the flames subsided and she regarded him with empathy.

"I will stay; do not ask me to stay again."

Talatama watched Pele walk away into the shadows as he heaved off his armour and trudged through the sand towards the chief encampment. Around the fire sat his companions, all washed clean of ash, wounds bound and treated. They had all begun eating and relishing the freshness of the food and after such battle, they felt the very revitalization spread over their weary bodies.

Atiogie ate as though he had not eaten in weeks. Vaohoi ate with Lo'au and was unusually restrained, while Emori and Adi sat nuzzled together in front of the fire, their love for each other renewed again by the recent separation. Maui Atalaga sat by himself gnawing on a large steak, close to Kaianuanu and two of his Hungan lieutenants, all of who enjoyed the crowd of new friends. Talatama noticed that Whatonga and Lord Toi sat in silence and had eaten little, and so took to opportunity to provide company. Whatonga hobbled to greet him. Having the urchin needles painfully removed from his thigh, the Rarotongan prince would be limping for days.

"Prince Talatama, I did not get the chance to tell you ..."

"Yes?"

"I – I thought you should know. Kupe was slain back on Kao," Whatonga said gently. "Mahina has been avenged."

"Thank you. May she rest now in peace," he said and swallowed hard, "Lord Toi, Prince Whatonga. You haven't eaten your fill," he shifted the conversation to avoid more embarrassment.

"Thank you for your kindness, Prince Talatama, but we must leave."

"So soon? Our victory is still young. What demands your time so?"

"We must return to Ngatangi'ia," the two began to leave.

"Wait. My friends, I was about to make a request to you both," the prince recalled. "I call for your accompaniment back to the capital."

"Why?"

"I have many reasons. That which concerns you is in the form of reward."

"We need no prize for our part."

"Then would you prefer personal gratitude and appreciation from my father?"

"Prince Talatama —" Lord Toi began.

"I need your word," Talatama sighed. "Both your word and Prince Whatonga's against the villainy of General Kamohoali'i and his minions. It needs to be heard in the high council."

"Is your word not good enough? Look at him," Whatonga pointed at Kamohoali'i. "His evil ways are as obvious as the nose on his face. Why would your father doubt you?"

"Friends, there is more evil at work here, and it has penetrated the very echelons of the royal house and government. No more than a few months ago, Kamohoali'i was vindicated of his past crimes and pardoned of accusations against him."

"That's madness!"

"There's more, but you must understand, his allies lie deep in the Empire's council. They will certainly thwart my word to vindicate him once more if I don't have your help."

The Rarotongan lords fell silent.

"Please, I insist. Stay with us."

"We can't get involved with the political discord of the Empire, Prince Talatama," Lord Toi began. "I must think of the safety of our small island and its future."

"Lord Toi, you were once one of the greatest commanders in the Empire. Would you turn your back on it now?"

"That was a long time ago, when I had different priorities. The death of my wife and daughter are example enough of my faith in the Empire."

"You should have reported Lady Rongaueroa's kidnapping to the capital," Talatama started. "We could have aided you and used that as proof of Anga'uli's evil."

"Your father is losing control of the Empire, Talatama," Lord Toi said frankly. "Rogue nobles, corrupted warlords, and now you say this evil has found its way into the very house of the king? Your Empire is rotting from the inside out. We island nations have to protect ourselves and look to our own shores."

"I will make it right." Talatama ignored the blatancy and shone with inner strength. "By the blood of the Tu'i Tonga that runs through my veins, I'll end this corruption and restore balance to the Empire."

"Politics is not my arena," Lord Toi looked away, seeing the conviction in the young prince.

"But, Father, I now see what we must do. If our word is not heard, both mother and Mahina's murderer will not face punishment. Their souls will not rest if Kamohoali'i is freed," Whatonga said.

"Kupe has been slain, son." Toi shook his head.

"But his master still lives!" Whatonga pointed at Kamohoali'i again. "We must finish this properly. We must see it to the end."

Lord Toi motioned to his son.

"Excuse us for a moment, Prince Talatama."

"Certainly."

Talatama stood in the firelight and watched them consult one another down by the sea. His mind suddenly went to Mahina and a shuddering feeling rippled through his body, remembering she was now gone and how achingly long ago it seemed. He hung his head momentarily and recalled the magical moments they shared together.

"My Prince," Lo'au called as he approached.

Talatama turned to him just in time to catch a mango.

"There - you must eat," the old mu'a smiled.

"Thank you, old friend," Talatama sniffed.

"Do they discuss their future with us?" Lo'au motioned towards the Rarotongan lords.

"Yes. We need them with us. I think if I have their word, your word, Kaianuanu's, Atiogie's, even Pele or Maui Atalaga's word, then it will sway the mind of the king."

"You've grown wise, oh Prince."

"Hard won", Talatama gazed out to the beautiful sunset.

"Beyond your wisdom, you've learned the greatest power of all – forgiving oneself," Lo'au played with his beard.

Talatama regarded him with a reverence before smiling and meeting his gaze.

"You're a great teacher, old man."

"The greatness of a teacher is reflected only in the success of his pupil," Lo'au patted him on the back as the two chuckled warmly together.

"Prince Talatama," Whatonga and Lord Toi approached.

As they drew near, Lord Toi trudged past in the sand and continued towards the head camp. The dissension was obvious.

"What is your decision?" his expression was solemn.

"My father and I could not agree," Whatonga breathed. "Lord Toi will leave once his warriors are ready. I have decided to stay with you."

"With respect, you have made the right choice, Whatonga. I am thankful to have you with me," Talatama smiled and placed his hand on his shoulder.

"Yes, I'm confident in this decision. Perhaps one day my father will understand."

"Come, let's eat and talk more."

Night fell quickly and the heavens were veiled behind the scattered smoky ash which brought a cooler evening. The moon occasionally peeked out behind clouds marching across the night sky as the allied warriors huddled a fraction closer to the fires and soaked up its warmth. Whatonga had insisted most of the Rarotongan warriors return with his father, before bidding them farewell. Only a handful of them remained to accompany Whatonga to the capital. He promised that he would return to Ngatangi'ia once he and Talatama convinced the king.

Following the hearty feast of grilled pork and delicious fruits, many of the warriors had drifted into slumber and the companions followed suit. Atiogie snored loudly on his back, Emori and Adi slept quietly against each other, and Lo'au and Vaohoi rested easy. Maui Atalaga and Pele lay together away from the fire, staring up at the night sky and exchanged whispers savouring the moment together. Talatama watched from afar, standing down by the water's edge.

He stood with his feet in the water, feeling the soft lapping of the gentle waves. Turning out to sea, he observed the giant shadows of the night clouds lumbering across the distant surfaces. He inhaled deeply, and though he was beyond the point of exhaustion, he felt strangely invigorated. He bent down and cupped a handful of water and brought it to his face and washed it through his long black hair to tie it back. A familiar voice sounded out from the beach, shouting and swearing: General Kamohoali'i. The warrior prince made his way over when he saw the guards surround him.

By the time he stood before the defeated general, some of the guards had struck him across the head. Omani and a few other Pulotulahi warriors were tied down close by.

"That's enough," Talatama motioned for the guards to leave. "What is this racket, traitorous filth?"

"Oh, mighty Prince Talatama," Kamohoali'i grinned. "Do you feel so lofty with your prize, so wealthy?"

"Indeed I do," Talatama said plainly. "Bringing you in will be the end for you, and your evil faction."

"Do you know the game you play, boy?" The general's face turned to malice. "Do you even know the forces that work against you? You cannot win."

"What is this? Some half cooked riddle to lower my guard for an escape?"

"What a fool you are," Kamohoali'i sniggered again. "You see like a newborn."

"Once we're in Tongatapu, I'll drag your hide before the high council and my father. By the words of my allies, and myself your deluded pardon will be stripped and you'll be condemned to death."

"It will take more than the accounts from fools like you to have me killed," Kamohoali'i laughed with Omani.

"More than accounts do I have," Talatama revealed a parchment of tapa from his vala and held it out to Kamohoali'i.

It was the parchment of tapa cloth containing the imperial symbols which the royal spy, Moa'uli'uli, had given the boy Paea prior to his death. On it were the hieroglyphs that Moa'uli'uli recorded, giving clues to what transpired in his last hours: the details of Kamohoali'i's involvement with the Pulotulahi. They were symbols that only the king and his trusted advisors knew how to interpret. It was the evidence Talatama and his men were looking for when they set out for Niuatoputapu long months ago.

Kamohoali'i hid his surprise and laughed with the other Pulotulahi warriors at the parchment. Omani hooted and cackled.

"That is useless, that parchment of tapa, it has nothing on it but a child's scrawling!" the dark general said.

"I doubt that, Kamohoali'i," the prince paused.

"That has nothing that will condemn me, you fool," Kamohoali'i grimaced.

The warrior prince frowned and glanced at the parchment as the Pulotulahi warriors continued laughing. Whatonga and a handful of other men approached and began to surround the prisoners.

"Permission to smash their mouths shut," Whatonga growled, staring at Kamohoali'i.

"No, these fools will not be laughing soon," Talatama turned away from them. "Come, leave them be."

As the warrior prince walked back to the main camp with his men, the Pulotulahi warriors remained giggling to themselves. Once the allies were out of earshot, Kamohoali'i's grin turned to stone while Omani chuckled and shook his head.

"What idiots! Useless piece of tapa—"

"Shut up!" Kamohoali'i snapped, silencing the rest of the men. "Damn it! Cursed gods."

"What's – it doesn't have—"

"No, you buffoon, it doesn't just incriminate me," the general cursed again. "That parchment holds the true identity of Tu'ipulotu, the Dark Lord of the Pulotulahi."

CHAPTER 63

Nuku'alofa, Tongatapu
Summer, A.D.1122

It was a cool late afternoon when Talatama and his allies appeared off the coast of Tongatapu. It was the largest island in the inner Tongan Empire, over two hundred and sixty square kilometres and had been the home of the great Tu'i Tonga for the past two hundred years. It was a predominantly flat island, devoid of any mountains or difficult terrain. This, in addition to the rich volcanic soil, made farming and agriculture simple and unrestricted. It generated mass cultivation, which produced an abundance of food, industry supplies such as timber and tapa, and items for trade.

Within the last sixty years, Tongatapu's population of loyal subjects had soared. During the expansion of the Empire through the reign of King Momo and later, King Tu'itatui, the Empire and its people enjoyed a growing wealth by virtue of tributes and trade. Its borders and influence grew, coupled with a relatively peaceful period within the kingdom. The island had become less a threat to invading islands that promoted population growth and longer living.

His fleet of six tongiakis congregated on the horizon and, soon after, headed towards the northern coasts of the island. As the north-west wind hastened their arrival, the manu'uli sea birds called overhead. Men and women scouring in the shallow reefs for shellfish ceased and gawked, and children on the waterfront raced about with excitement. Talatama stood at the helm with Maui Atalaga, as Atiogie looked from left to right along the great coasts.

"I thought the Heketa was in the east," he said.

"It is, but its moorings are not welcoming. The rocky foreshore is difficult to disembark." Talatama smiled to his big friend.

"Your father didn't plan that well," the Samoan frowned.

"It was my grandfather, Momo, who brought the capital there. It is a beautiful area for the township despite that issue, my friend," Talatama paused. "If I ever become king, I'll move the capital to the shores of the lagoon. It's far better for fleets of tongiakis to moor safely within the sandier banks."

"We stop here, Prince Talatama." Maui Atalaga began to pull back the masts.

"Thank you, directly ahead," the warrior prince pointed. "On that long stretch of beach, just beyond the shore is a small village called Nuku'alofa. I have an old friend who lives there."

The warrior prince and his companions trudged through the shallow water after disembarking. Whatonga and Kaianuanu ensued with their warriors, as an old man armed with a club and a small entourage of servants, walked proudly onto the sandy beach to meet them. The scattering servants bowed to the comrades and immediately offered them food and placed fresh leis around their necks. The old man stopped, and with a piercing gaze, grinned at the warrior prince.

"I thought someone would have killed you by now," he said.

"Who did you swindle for such a peaceful place?" Talatama frowned.

"Oh, you know. Someone wanted me out of the capital not long after King Momo passed away. It wasn't hard."

"Old promises forgotten so soon, old friend. Time catches us all."

"Not yet it hasn't!" The old man blanched. "I found a nice quiet spot here in Nuku'alofa. Time has no meaning for me anymore. I'm not beholden to the court, Empire or your father anymore."

"But perhaps to me you are," the warrior prince smiled. "That is if you're still as hospitable as I remember."

"Do the stone ramparts of the great capital not provide better hospitality? Or perhaps I should take you prisoner and hand you over to your father."

"So it's true: he has issued an order for my arrest."

"Yes, as laughable as that is, no disrespect to your father of course. I don't know what you've done lad, but I guess in my old age I've become more accepting. You know I will always trust you."

"Well in that case, there's no other place I'd rather spend our first night back in the homeland, than in the company of a grumpy old man."

"Ha! The only way this man will be grumpy this evening is if he loses his wager in the duel," he laughed.

"Ah, you're still teaching."

"Well, Takai is my last student."

"Food and lodgings as well as entertainment," he mused.

"Blunt as ever. I suppose I could indulge a member of the royal family, just this once. Just don't tell your father what I'm up to."

Talatama and the old man suddenly laughed and embraced one another strongly.

"It's good to see you, lad."

"And you also, Manusiu, Master Warlord."

Forty years ago, Manusiu was renowned across the Empire as one of the greatest warlords ever to have fought against the Tu'i Tonga. He was the youngest son of King Kaimoeata, one of the last ancestors of the Pulotu Kings. During that time, he had become Lord of Lavengatonga, an ancient capital and township in the east of Tongatapu. Together with his father and allies, Ngongokilitoto, King of Malapo; Naufanua, Queen of Mu'a, and the demonic Fehuluni, he waged a fierce war against King Momo for the rulership of the Tongan Empire. Following three years of civil war, King Momo had proven too great to defeat, and Manusiu agreed to a truce and unite. Recognised for this outstanding leadership and warrior skill, Manusiu was given the title, Master Warlord, and was provided with an armada to expand the great Empire. Following decades of success abroad, Manusiu returned to the capital and became the Empire's teacher of imperial warriors. One of his first students was the small boy, Talatama.

The fale was built atop a large hill close to the waterfront. It was the only hill in the Nuku'alofa area and thus provided a prominent and proud location for the aging warlord. It was surrounded by a myriad of other small thatched fales used by his retainers and slaves. To the southern side of the hill, was a cleared area that was bordered by dense forest. From the cleared area, forest paths lead east to Popua, one of the oldest villages in Tonga. To the south wound another path that led to the distant village of Pea.

Along the area were torches that burned calmly into the cool night. The moon was full. Its face was heavy with ginger on the low horizon, and the morbid shadow of a flying fox colony glided overhead in the twilight. The companions sat comfortably at the head of the main gathering that consisted of Nukualofa's high priest, the village headman and a number of guests. As was the custom, they were presented with a vast selection of cuisines and delicacies unique to Tonga; grilled octopus, steamed lobster and crab, baked fish, mussels and scallops. In addition to the seafood, was crackling pig on the spit and steamed taro, sweet potato, breadfruit and bananas.

Talatama sat next to Manusiu, engaged in constant conversation that centred mainly on war and battles. The warrior prince briefly told the old warlord of the past year and the struggles that had come. He finished with his intent to confront his father with proof against General Kamohoali'i. This had prompted the prince to send a messenger to the king before the banquet, notifying him of their arrival and their planned arrival the next day. In ancient Tongan custom, it was a common courtesy to notify the high council before appearing. .

"Manusiu, I must tell you, I have my suspicions that there is a traitor of the Empire within the capital," Talatama edged towards his old teacher.

"There are always traitors, lad."

"It's more than that. I believe the Dark Lord of the Pulotulahi is a member of the high council."

"Well, you know, I've heard of dark suspicions around the capital at the moment," Manusiu said.

"What have you heard?"

"They're rumours, whispers of corruption in the high ranks, spoken in fear and doubt. I know that's not uncommon but I've felt it myself, something greater at work here."

"What is it?"

"I don't know, young Prince. Something sinister that's beyond my sight," the old man said distastefully. "Be wary, Talatama, I fear you may be walking headlong into this evil scheme."

"I doubt it not."

"Grieved am I that the days of knowing that a fight came at you head on are gone! Now the cowards sneaking in the dark, scheming for murder," Manusiu cursed.

"No one would dare take you on even then!" Talatama laughed.

"No one except the damned Saudeleurians."

"You're not still angry about that? You were too far from reinforcements and the furthest any Tongan army had ever been. Everyone knows that."

Whatonga chose that moment to interrupt, "Manusiu, may I say it's an honour to meet you, my father abounded us with stories of your battles when I was a child."

"You're Toi's boy?"

"Yes." Whatonga smiled.

"You have the same strength in your eyes," the old warlord nodded. "He saved my life more than once!"

The great battle of Nan Madol in the year A.D.1090 was one of the Empire's greatest stories, and its only great defeat. Manusiu was the general in command of the Empire's western armies and his first commander was Lord Toi. They attacked the Saudeleurians on the far island of Pohnpei in the Micronesian Kingdom. Hoping to take the island as a solid foothold in Micronesia, the Saudeleurians withstood the brave Tongan onslaught only by the aid of their great fortress, Nan Madol. For days the Empire was repelled by the giant stone walls of the city, unable to penetrate the outer rim while defending against arrow fire. As a result of the defeat, it marked the limit of the Empire's influence and control in the west. It was Manusiu's last battle prior to returning to Tonga, to become a warlord instructor.

"Enough talk of politics," the old man finally gave the prince and Whatonga a sour look. "Now let us enjoy our entertainment."

Talatama nodded.

"Bring the duellers forward!"

The song and dance ceased at the warlord's order, and the crowds of people formed a circle so that the banquet was at the edge of it. As silence fell on the area, two young men form either side of the crowd appeared, and walked to the centre of the circle. They were naked, and in one hand they each held a short club, in the other was a length of rope. They faced Manusiu and the companions, before bowing with respect. They then presented the ropes towards their honoured guests.

"Bound or unbound?" Manusiu asked Talatama.

"Unbound."

The young warriors bowed again and presented their clubs in a similar fashion.

"To life or death?" Manusiu asked again.

"To life," Talatama did not hesitate. "I've seen enough death in recent times."

The young warriors bowed once more, then faced each other before bowing. They then took their positions and launched at each other. Across the entire Pacific in this period, duels were a typical occurrence between warriors. Regardless of any current warring, tribal conflicts and the expansion of the Empire, duels between individual warriors continued to have a common place in Polynesian society. Often, great warriors would live their lives wandering the oceans, searching for equals to fight against. If a warrior were to hear tales of another, then it was his honour to head out in search of his duel. They were contested mainly for prestige, fame, achieving one's own accomplishments through skill and the honour of being the greatest warrior in the Empire.

Despite the duels resulting in horrendous outcomes, a limited level of civility was acknowledged and respected by all who participated. These were the rules that were agreed upon prior to the duel. Most common were whether the hands were bound with rope or twine, and whether the duel was to the death or not. No warrior would ignore rules of engagement once the duel had begun, for his reputation was always paramount. On some occasions, it was not uncommon for there to be an agreement for no rules at all. However it was deemed, especially in Tonga, that the more rules there were, the greater warrior one would become should he reign victorious.

The two warriors parried each other's attacks, nimbly leaping from side to side, avoiding direct contact. They tested each other, probing out the weaknesses or flaws in the other's ability. Once or twice, a warrior would strike and barely miss his target, which then caused the other to raise his skill. As the skill level rose, so did the concentration and perspiration. For a long while, they seemed equally matched, and with every moment that showed favour to one of the warriors, the next moment the other would level the score.

Dust was kicked up as each warrior slipped or held his ground. Eventually Takai, Manusiu's student, progressively began to lose his strength through inferior fitness. Talatama glanced at Manusiu through the corner of his eye. He could see the old man become tense and shift uneasily, wanting to shout out and encourage his student. But it was forbidden for anyone to jeer or heckle during a duel. It was acknowledged as a sign of esteem to the two warriors in fierce absorption, as a mark of respect for custom and tradition. Even an old warlord like Manusiu did not deny this.

As Takai began to show visible signs of lethargy, the other young warrior began to double his efforts to finish his opponent. The excitement in his eyes shone, the enthusiasm exploded in his chest and the taste of victory filled his mouth. But the expense was a loss of concentration, the precision of his movements and the focus it took to last thus far. Although exhausted, it took Takai one advancement to anticipate as he easily countered and swept his club, striking the underside of the warrior's jaw. There was a snapping sound of teeth and bone before the young warrior's head jolted back. He lost his footing and collapsed onto his back with a crash, before Takai lumbered and stood over him, moaning and clutching his jaw.

Takai then raised his club. The duel was over.

Silence shattered as the crowd erupted in a cheer of jubilation. Women wailed with high pitched cries of joy and men in support of Takai rushed in eagerly, to pat him on the back. The wounded warrior was aided to his feet and helped through the crowd as Manusiu slapped his knee and cackled loudly, pointing out to Talatama how the losing warrior had fallen victim to such a rookie error. The prince nodded in agreement and indulged the old man by suggesting alternative movements that could have been employed. But in truth, Talatama was relieved it was over. If only momentarily, he had lost the stomach for battle. His mind was on more pressing matters and he finally rose to his feet, before politely excusing himself from the continuing celebration.

Talatama appeared out of the shadows towards the Hungan and Rarotongan lieutenants on the coastal side of the hill. With them were one hundred and fifty warriors guarding only five men. Earlier in the night, Talatama made the decision to allocate as many warriors as he could to stand guard over the Pulotulahi prisoners. As they were now on the main island, the risk of their rescue was higher than ever before. The warrior prince nodded and walked past the lieutenants and straight to Kamohoali'i. He did not hold back when he drove his fist into the general's face.

"Who is the Dark Lord within the ranks of the Empire?"

Kamohoali'i recoiled from the strike and spat out blood from his lip.

"Damn you."

Talatama swept another fist across his jaw.

"Speak!" Talatama cocked his fist for another strike.

"You'll never understand, you fool! His identity is withheld even from me," Kamohoali'i lied to avoid more interrogation.

"You filth!" Talatama feigned another blow.

"Even if I knew, I would never tell you, dog. It is kept from me as a last defence. Should I be captured, I cannot betray his identity and therefore preserve his ideals."

"Pig shit! You meet with him, converse with him, sit about and conjure up your evil plans. Do you expect me to believe you don't know his true identity?" the warrior prince used his open hand and slapped Kamohoali'i across his face.

"You tell me then, Unarmed Warrior?" Talatama grabbed Omani by the neck.

"Kamohoali'i speaks the truth, royal filth!" he spat.

Talatama's open hand found its mark across his face too before he recoiled and glared back defiantly. He stepped back from the Pulotulahi warriors and deliberated their answers: a bluff of ignorance. As he did, he was unaware that Kamohoali'i carefully eyed the tapa parchment that was tucked in his vala. The prince stood only arm's reach from him. A moment passed that offered him the opportunity to knock the prince down and covertly snatch the parchment. He could not risk it. He could not jeopardize reinforcing the importance of the parchment should he fail in the attempt. The parchment that contained the secret that he and his Pulotulahi commanders fought to defend, a secret that the dead spy, Moa'uli'uli, had briefly discovered, a secret that could change the course of the Empire's future forever. The general lowered his head and said nothing. He just flexed his thick arms uncomfortably tied behind his back.

CHAPTER 64

Island of "Eua,
Off east coast of Tongatapu

General Va'iga watched his footing as he stepped precariously through the rocky entrance. The moonlight flooded across the beach beyond the cave, but absolute darkness reigned within. Scattered torchlight burned in crevices in far corners of the labyrinth of ancient fissures. It granted barely enough visibility to walk without tripping on the uneven and slippery ground. A horrid stench of bats and their faeces permeated the stale air. The sound of water dripping from giant stalactites and eerie whispers echoed all around.

"We're going to fall out the bottom of the world," stammered one of two quivering Samoan mercenaries, as he followed the general.

"Keep quiet! That's why they call this place the Mouth of Pulotu," Va'iga replied.

The great caves of Tonga were located on the north side of 'Eua, a large island off the eastern coast of Tongatapu. A primordial island from the dawn of time, it was not heavily populated by the Empire because of its mountainous terrain made farming difficult. It was, however, the centre of natural beauty and geographical wonders unlike any other island in the kingdom. This included the giant caves that were a wonder in themselves, and a curse to anyone who dared venture inside. An ancient myth connected to the caves:

somewhere in the multitude of tunnels led a path to Pulotu, the Polynesian underworld.

The torches scarcely gave direction to the Samoan warriors, as they made their way through the caves. General Va'iga noticed in some parts that the cave ceiling was so high it disappeared into the darkness above. Finally, they came to a dark entrance the size of a man, and when Va'iga saw torchlight within, he squeezed through the entryway and gasped at what he saw. The cave chamber seemed as large as a village, its walls obscured by the dark that moved and crept against the firelight. Towards the back of the chamber, was a stone throne with dim torchlight on both sides, enough to draw attention, but subtle enough to keep the man upon the throne in shadow.

Tu'ipulotu, Dark Lord of the Pulotulahi, sat on the throne and leered towards the Samoan warriors. He was adorned in a thick tapa cloak and hood, hiding the features of his face. Gaudy bracelets and jewellery glittered from around his neck and arms in the firelight, products of his long reign of theft and murder. To his sides, were two towering guardians, standing like statues, their disfiguration a permanent exaction of evil.

A few paces from the Dark Lord stood the leper, Ganilau, who observed them with a cold reflection. Alongside the throne and along the walls were fifty or so Pulotulahi warriors. They were unfamiliar to Va'iga, as they were but a portion of the Pulotulahi force that resided in Tongatapu. From the shadows of jagged stalagmites appeared Havea, his tattoos covering his naked form, his head slightly lowered in a transfixed state. His matted hair clung in long heaps, draping slightly over adornment of skulls of human foetuses. The iniquity that radiated from him was confounding. He folded his arms and stared at Va'iga with his black, pitiless eyes.

The Samoan warriors paused, a respectful distance before genuflecting. Va'iga raised his head and addressed the Dark Lord carefully.

"Milord, I come to you from the battle of Kao, with news of Kamohoali'i."

"Speak."

"We suffered defeat at the hands of Talatama and his companions."

Va'iga's words echoed the chamber and out through the tunnels. A long pause followed and the Samoan general swallowed nervously. He could not see the Dark Lord's eyes, though he felt the penetration across his entire being.

"Did you not have Talatama and his companions captured, bound and flogged?" The Dark Lord rose from his throne and stepped towards him.

"Yes, they were – but they were aided by Lord Toi and Prince Whatonga, and Maui Atalaga."

The Dark Lord shot Havea a glance.

"Rarotongan scum. Our losses?"

"Commander Kupe was killed. Commander Siateki is missing. Most of the army was destroyed."

Havea began to gurgle softly, a deep racking building with malevolence.

"And what of your own army, Samoan?"

General Va'iga lowered his head.

"You are nothing but a cheap, beleaguering mercenary and you've proved yourself unworthy to me so far."

"Milord, my men and I follow your rule without question."

"Is that so? You're not interested in jewels, ivory, wealth?" The Dark Lord edged forward.

"N-no milord," Va'iga barely managed.

"Ah, but is your answer of wisdom – or cunning?"

"Milord, I don't underst—"

"My payment is your benefit of the doubt and therefore your lives," the Dark Lord paused. "What use are you to me now? You've already failed me."

Va'iga did not show fear as the Pulotulahi warriors slowly closed in around him and his men.

"Milord, I am humble and contrite," Va'iga bowed low. "I can offer you my unwavering allegiance, in addition to my force of two hundred strong. I yearn for nothing but a Pulotulahi victory!"

Pausing momentarily, the Dark Lord eventually returned to seat himself on his throne. He sat for a long while and said nothing, as the choking silence and dark energy emitting from the Pulotulahi warriors nauseated the old Samoan general. Although he had been in the company of countless immoral counterparts and ruthless leaders throughout his time, he never felt such swell of vice.

In the old days, having warred against rival tribes and sold his skill for carnage, Va'iga was accustomed to bold violence alone. However, it was unlike the deceptive and clandestine ways of the Pulotulahi; murderous, calculating and traitorous, foul and polluted with the stench of a festering malice. The Samoan general could not help but wonder in fascination as to the true motivations of the Dark Lord. It seemed to run deeper than a mere passion for the throne. Did the Dark Lord have a personal vendetta against King Tu'itatui?

"General Va'iga," the Tu'ipulotu suddenly spoke, breaking him from his thoughts.

"Yes, Milord."

"What other news do you bring before I change my mind?"

"Talatama has taken General Kamohoali'i captive along with Commander Omani. They have been brought here to Tongatapu."

"Are they at Heketa?"

"No, Milord. My scouts discovered his camp in the small village of Nuku'alofa. They may take General Kamohoali'i to the king tomorrow."

"Manusiu."

"Milord?"

Tu'ipulotu stood from his mineral throne and placed his big fists on his waist, his laboured breathing became lighter with his mood.

"At last you bear good news," he turned to Ganilau and nodded.

"I will assemble the men. We will attack them at first light and rescue Kamohoali'i." The giant leper growled as he bowed to Tu'ipulotu.

"No, you will not," Tu'ipulotu said.

The Pulotulahi warriors shifted in surprise and Ganilau and Va'iga frowned with confusion. Tu'ipulotu sat again and shook his head.

"You are all my most trusted warriors, dedicated to the cause. Yet you still have not learned what it is to be Pulotulahi," he paused. "Being Pulotulahi is to be cunning: to think before we act on our intentions."

"But, Milord, there's no time —"

"What would you do, Commander?" the Tu'ipulotu glared at Ganilau. "Sail out and rescue Kamohoali'i in a glorious and bloody battle? You would but prove one thing to the king: that Kamohoali'i is Pulotulahi and still loyal to the cause!"

Ganilau lowered his head slowly.

"And in doing so you would expose us. Have you forgotten that Kamohoali'i has been cleared of his past crimes and pardoned by the king? Together with that bumbling fool, Prince Talaiha'apepe, Kamohoali'i's actions are not in question. It is Prince Talatama who is currently wanted for arrest because of the web of lies spun by us. We must keep our faith in that fact."

"Milord, I fear that Prince Talatama may use the word of his new allies to support his case against Kamohoali'i," General Va'iga said.

"And I presume that is the only reason General Kamohoali'i is still alive," the Dark Lord mused. "However, I agree, it's possible that with the weight of his friends' help the king may change his decision. Although I will be there tomorrow at the high council to sway the mind of the king, we must then prepare for the worst."

"Yes, Milord."

"Time is short. It is only a few hours before dawn," the Dark Lord continued. "Send messengers to Tongatapu and summon the rest of our warriors. Tell them to assemble on the island of 'Eua'iki."

"Yes, Milord."

"You will unite with them on the far side of the island. Take precautions not to attract attention with your numbers. I will have spies in the high council who will give you a signal should the decision of Kamohoali'i turn sour," Tu'ipulotu paused. "If that is the case, I want you to send in the entire army to target Prince Talatama and the king."

"Milord? What if Kamohoali'i is killed before we arrive?" Ganilau said. "It will take us time to reach Heketa."

The Dark Lord rose quickly and moved close to Ganilau, so that his words were heard by him alone.

"See no illusion, Ganilau. Should Kamohoali'i fail in this, I consider him an acceptable loss," his voice quivered in anger. "I will not risk the only opportunity I've had in years by exposing our numbers prior to the decision. Should it come to that, your attack must be for all your worth and nothing less."

The leper frowned and eventually nodded slowly.

"Do you understand?" Tu'ipulotu said.

"Yes, Milord. Your will be done."

Ganilau then gave curt orders to a few chosen warriors, before they bowed and disappeared through the exit of the chamber.

"General Va'iga, Commander Ganilau is in charge of the Pulotulahi forces. I want you to provide him with your men and bend to any will of his."

"Without question, Milord!"

"This is your last chance Va'iga. Now go."

The Samoan general bowed low before standing and exiting the chamber with his soldiers. The Dark Lord then beckoned Havea to approach.

"Havea, you know what to do. You must regain possession of the tapa cloth from Prince Talatama. That is your first and foremost task. Do you understand?"

"Yes."

"Then kill as many as you can."

Havea grinned, displaying a crooked mouth of razor teeth.

"Let this be our day of triumph over King Tu'itatui and the Empire," the Dark Lord raised his fist into the air.

As he did, the Pulotulahi warriors erupted in a vociferous roar.

"For Tu'ipulotu! For the Pulotulahi!"

The echo of their cries vibrated against the rocks and burst out into the night like a challenge to the gods themselves.

CHAPTER 65

Dawn. Fledgling rays illuminated the globular clouds that hung in the east. The morning air was humid, heavy like a noonday swelter. The summer day had set in early, and the usual cool, brisk face of daybreak hid away. Scattered stars twinkled, dying low on the northern horizon. Talatama stared at them, deep in thought. He sat on the calm shores of Nuku'alofa and contemplated the day's events in his mind as they would unfold. He recalled Lord Fasi'apule's news back in Samoa - he and his companions were wanted for questioning of the Niuatoputapu massacre. Today he would unveil the true events of Kamohoali'i's lies.

"Prince Talatama."

The warrior prince turned slowly to Adi. Behind her were all his trusted companions: Atiogie, Pele, Lo'au, Vaohoi, Emori and Maui Atalaga. Congregating in support were Prince Whatonga, Kaianuanu and the old warlord Manusiu.

"We're ready to end this with you," the Fijian priestess smiled.

He rose and brushed the sand from his vala to face his friends.

"I suppose I don't have to warn you."

"Not this time, my Prince. We've come so far together. Today we'll finish what we started."

"Then may the gods watch over us." A well of tears glimmered in his eyes. "And bless all you who I call my friends."

They moved forward as one, and embraced the warrior prince firmly. They knew, as he did, they would face whatever the outcome of the day, together.

The royal court was one of the many great structures located in the imperial compound at Heketa. The powerful, wooded columns that supported the massive building stood proud and firm. Surrounding the court were a dozen royal fales that reflected the grandeur of the Pacific island's greatest Empire. They were not adorned with the luxuries of beauty, but perfected by the most breathtaking artistry known.

Every pillar of wood, every sculpture of whale bone and slab of stone was carved, polished and maintained with the utmost diligence. The grass within the entire royal region was trimmed with precision, trees and shrubs that grew in chosen positions were pruned and shaped into natural designs of splendour. The thatching of the structures were layered with care and rotated often to remove any sign of rotting. The summer display of flowers bloomed on every tree and shrub, and splashed colour among the magnificent buildings.

At every entrance, and in all areas, were imperial guards. They stood like the carved statues of the royal fales, embellished with a unique and impressive combination of black robes and high headdresses. Black was the colour of the royals and was a powerful image of strength and imperialism. It was a valuable colour that was difficult to produce from natural substances like browns, yellows and greens. The guards were handpicked warriors of the king, all of who, at one time, would have earned the trust and dependability required to fulfil such a position.

Fortifying the royal compound was an impressive wall of natural flora. The most distinguished craftsmen of agriculture had once been summoned by the king to create such a wonder, rather than use ugly, raw stone and wooden reinforcements. King Momo and later his son, Tu'itatui, embraced a natural taste for design in order to manipulate nature itself. The thick and impenetrable barrier of trees, shrubs and undergrowth had proved its worth for forty years.

Outside the compound was the village of Heketa, home of some ten thousand Tongans. It was a flourishing township that enjoyed the successes of the greater Empire and profited as being the supporting settlement of the royal centre. It was mainly populated with chiefs, lords and high priests, followed by their families, sub servants and slaves. Being a political township with significant domestic power and influence, many citizens of the Empire often made the pilgrimage to seek favour.

The herald called out in a deep, strong voice. It was a calling of respect, and acted as an indication to all those within the royal court, of an impending arrival. On hearing the song, all those within the royal court hushed their conversations and remained seated at their allocated positions. Within the grand hall were the most powerful individuals in the Pacific Ocean at that time in history. Seated along the right side of the court were the military leaders; the commanders of all fifteen Imperial Legions and their accompanying sub commanders. At their head sat the greatest warlord of all time, General Ngongo. Ngongo's precocity in the art of the warrior meant that he had been in battle by the age of seven. At seventy-five, was nothing less than warrior elite and military genius.

To the left side of the court were the fifteen political representatives of all the Tongan villages in the Empire. In addition to these lords, were a handful of chiefs from Samoa, Fiji, Rotuma and Niue and their accompanying diplomats. Towards the end of their side sat High Priest Toutai of Tangaloa, the premier representative of Tangaloa on earth. To his side sat Manusiu, the great warlord and trainer of imperial champions.

In the centre and to the rear of the court were the members of the royal household. First and foremost was Lord Fasi'apule, the wise and powerful brother of King Tu'itatui. To his left sat the regal Prince Talaiha'apepe and the young Prince Lafa with their servants. To his right was the only daughter of the King, the beautiful Princess Fatafehi and her maidens, lacquered in scented oils of sandalwood and floral perfume. The brooding Queen Sialeataongo, the King's sister, and her entourage of old women seemed to tarnish the edge of the assembled family. At the head and principal position within the enormous building, was the ruler of the Empire, King Tu'itatui.

But it was the man who walked through the entrance of the great hall that demanded awe. The Crown Prince strode amid the conclave of men, clad in his mighty war garb. His vala and tapa undergarments beneath his sandalwood girdle were new and fresh. Strapped to his firm torso was the legendary Shell of Sangone, gleaming and charged with magical properties. His high headdress was brushed and cleaned and his bracelets were immaculate. The famous club, the Peace Maker, was tucked into his girdle and had been recently scoured and polished.

However it was not the impressive presentation of his adornments that was noticeable to his kin and countrymen. It was his spirit that shone through the gloom of the aristocratic court like a star in the night sky. Talatama proudly lifted his chin towards the court and stood before all his superiors, before bowing and removing his headdress. It was then that the court saw the difference in his face and all who knew him well, gasped as they observed the extent of new battle scars over his body. His warrior masters nodded in silent acceptance. His sister held her hand over her mouth. His father did not see his young son any longer, he saw a man standing before him.

"Father, my kin, and members of the High Council," the Crown prince began proudly. "I return from a mission that was issued to me and the Fourteenth Legion."

He gave the signal to the guards outside.

"I return successful in investigating the mystery of Niuatoputapu and those responsible for the deaths of thousands, including my entire Fourteenth Legion. I bring you Kamohoali'i, General of the Pulotulahi."

Many gasped. Others shook their heads as two imperial warriors appeared behind the prince and threw Kamohoali'i, bound and wounded, in front of the king. The dark general fell to his knees and growled as he staggered to his feet again.

"That is a serious accusation, Prince Talatama," Toutai, the high priest said.

"An accusation that will require solid proof," Fasi'apule added.

"Prince Talatama, you are aware Kamohoali'i has been pardoned of evil accusations and reinstated as the Guardian of Niuatoputapu," General Ngongo said.

Talatama looked at the men and nodded. He then locked gaze with his father and maintained it.

"A year ago I arrived on the shores of Niuatoputapu to find Kamohoali'i had bribed Noble Anga'uli, using him to establish a foothold in the kingdom. He then staged a battle with the aid of Samoan mercenaries led by General Va'iga. The battle was against the Rarotongan army led by Lord Toi and Prince Whatonga. They had been provoked by the kidnapping and killing of Queen Rongaueroa."

"I discovered his plan to save Niuatoputapu from the Rarotongan onslaught, stage the rescued of Prince Talaiha'apepe and emerge a hero, to be forgiven of all past crimes."

The young prince turned his head, dumbfounded and confused. He stepped forward and frowned at his brother.

"Talatama, he did save me. You weren't there. You didn't see," he said.

"But I was there! I saw his wicked plan unfolding as my men and I fought for our lives!" Talatama's eyes burned into his brother.

"So it's true! You were there during the battle, Prince Talatama. You were involved with the Rarotongan attack," High Priest Toutai began. "It was said to have been orchestrated by you to rescue your Rarotongan lover."

"Ah, yes, I've heard those claims." The prince ignored the anger that boiled inside him. "They're preposterous and unfounded."

"Almost as preposterous and seemingly unfounded as yours against Kamohoali'i?" Fasi'apule returned.

Talatama's eyes narrowed towards his uncle and mentor, uncertain what to make of his comments.

"Indeed not," he said.

472

"Then you deny having a Rarotongan lover?" Toutai pressed.

"I do not."

The hall gasped. Talatama's brothers shifted uncomfortably and Fatafehi stared at her brother in anguish, tears beginning to well in her eyes.

"Her name was Mahina, Princess of Rarotonga. And I loved her with all my heart." Talatama trembled before the court.

"And you had people killed because of her —"

"That's an inconceivable lie!" Talatama snapped and pointed at Toutai. "My love for her was only guilty of naive innocence, and its private nature will not be tainted in this public forum!"

The hall fell silent.

"For countless months following the battle of Niuatoputapu, my companions and I were hunted relentlessly by Kamohoali'i and the Pulotulahi. Many terrible battles did I fight to live and stand before you now. I have the words of my companions who were there and fought valiantly by my side, to vouch for my claims against Kamohoali'i. More than that, the solid proof is in this parchment of tapa," Talatama held out the cloth of symbols.

"And who are these companions whose words we should hear?" Toutai interjected.

"They are not kin, nor are they closely aligned to the Empire," Talatama paused. "Their testimony holder greater weight."

"But this parchment —"

"Perhaps we should hear the voices of your companions then," Fasi'apule said quickly. "If they are here, the high council must hear their words."

"As you wish," the warrior prince said as he tucked the parchment back into his girdle momentarily. "Lo'au?" he called.

The sound of Lo'au's staff thumping on the wooden floor echoed as he walked slowly into the room for the first time in thirty years. The old man was well rested and clad in respectful garments; his long silver hair spiralled down his bearded face and the air of dignity and reverence surrounding him was impossible to ignore. Those old enough to recognise him stared in wonderment. He was a living legend. King Tu'itatui rose from his throne and walked down towards the old man in disbelief.

"No – it cannot be – Grandfather?" the king quietly stammered.

He searched for answers in those around him but his brothers bore similar blank expressions. Toutai frowned.

"You cannot be the Lo'au – not *the* Lo'au of old?" Talatama breathed.

"Long ago." The old man smiled as he knew he would have to explain. "I was once known as Lefolau, a King of the Manu'a Empire, and have carried the name of Lo'au Tuputoka. My daughter, Nua, married King Momo of the Tu'i Tonga, your grandfather. The rest of the story doesn't matter at this time." He then turned to the court. "What matters is that I hereby confirm that Prince Talatama's claims are correct."

"It *is* important! If you are the great Lo'au, then you *are* his kin. Therefore your word cannot hold unsubstantiated weight," Toutai said.

"I will decide that," King Tu'itatui snapped at the high priest.

"Then I call on Atiogie, Chief of 'Aele and Lord of Tuamasaga," Talatama called.

The imperial guards within the great hall straightened when Atiogie entered. The giant man, garbed in his Samoan bracelets, vala and girdle, wore his broad whale bone chest plate with dignity. His hair had been cropped and a vibrant yellow paste had been brushed through it. In his right hand swayed his five foot root of an ironbark tree - his blessed club. When he reached Talatama and Lo'au he paused and bowed to the king.

"I am Atiogie and I am friend to Talatama. What he says is true."

"And what part do you vouch for, Samoan?" Toutai challenged.

The giant warrior lifted his chin and spoke with a rare clarity.

"The story of the Samoan mercenaries is true. I hunted them before the battle at Niuatoputapu. The rest of Talatama's words, as I said, are correct."

"This is nonsense, My King!" Kamohoali'i shouted.

"More must be heard before this can be verified, Your Majesty," Toutai reminded.

"I now call on Prince Whatonga of Rarotonga," Talatama did not let the momentum slow.

The Rarotongan prince walked in quickly and bowed swiftly. He was dressed in a long vala of leaves and wore many iconic bracelets, necklaces and anklets of the Rarotongan islands. His formidable axe was tucked to his side and his hair gleamed and flowed over his tattooed shoulders as he spoke.

"Your Majesty, I am Prince Whatonga of Rarotonga," he said. "Long have our people been allies and Lord Toi, my father, your friend."

"Yes, indeed," King Tu'itatui acknowledged.

"Almost two years ago, my mother Lady Rongaueroa, was kidnapped from our island by the Pulotulahi. She was taken to the island of Niuatoputapu as a prisoner and bait for my men and me. When we arrived to take revenge and steal her back, the Pulotulahi had organised a Samoan army to ambush us. We were temporarily defeated, and my mother was slain."

"Unbeknownst to us, the Pulotulahi conspired against Prince Talatama by feeding us a lie that *he* had killed Lady Rongaueroa while making off with my sister, Mahina."

More gasps and murmurs echoed across the great hall.

"By the time the truth was revealed, Mahina too had been killed," Whatonga paused. "And the man behind all of this, is no other than this piece of garbage standing there," he pointed at Kamohoali'i with anger.

The great hall exploded in an uproar of surprise and revelation.

CHAPTER 66

"How dare you in open court, insult an official of the Empire, which Kamohoali'i still is!" Toutai sneered.

"I dare!" Whatonga growled.

Guards suddenly filed into the great hall and warriors within began to rush protectively in front of the king. The remaining companions, Adi and Emori, Pele and Vaohoi rushed in, frantically pushing and shoving. All of the councils' bodyguards leapt into the rising fray and weapons were drawn. The heat began to boil in the air it seemed.

"Enough!" King Tu'itatui boomed. "Stay your weapons - I will hear the rest of my son's claims!"

"But, Your Majesty," Toutai said.

"Your provocation has been sufficient so far, Toutai," the king glowered.

"Greetings, Your Majesty," Adi and Emori bowed, once the guards had cleared the floor. "I am Priestess Adi, Master of the Snakes and this is my betrothed, Emori, warrior priest. We are both representatives of the Degei. We hail from the Nausori Highlands in Viti Levu."

"I know your grandmaster, Nakaunicina," Tu'itatui said as he settled back into his throne.

"Nakaunicina is my uncle, Your Majesty," Emori said. "And were he to know of us here today, he would send Your Majesty his warm regards."

"We met Prince Talatama on the island of Niuatoputapu also, and can corroborate his claims from that time forward," Adi said in soft tones.

Toutai leered down at the Fijians, holding back a plethora of scrutiny and inquiry.

"Greetings again, Priestess Adi," Lord Fasi'apule nodded. "You are high ranking and revered within your order. As such you are, therefore, forbidden to lie or make false statements. Do you maintain your claim and support Prince Talatama in his?"

"I do," she said without hesitation.

"As do I," Emori added.

"Father," Talatama stepped forward. "I have one more who can confirm my claims, and she is unlike my other companions. She is Pele, sister of Kamohoali'i."

The she-warrior remained silent in front of the king and audience; her face resentful as she looked from the king to her brother. The well of rancour boiled inside her as she recalled the past year of anguish. Her memory of Kamohoali'i's effort to kill her, echoed like a painful wound inside her head. Suddenly she spoke.

"My brother is indeed guilty of all the accusations against him."

Again, the hall exploded in gasps and claims, many cursing her for betraying her kin, unbelievable as it seemed. Others remembered her association with her brother over the years of rebellion and her devotion to him. But it was unheard of for a sister to betray and embarrass a brother in such a way. Pele lowered her head in a mixture of inner turmoil and embarrassment. Her brother glared at her with hatred.

"You will burn in Pulotu for your betrayal, *sister!*"

She could not look at him. The insults and jibes around her began to echo and fade, knowing that her words were the beginning of the end for her brother. She began to feel the great hall close in on her, the shouts and judgments pressing down on her. Harsh curses were thrown at her by chiefs, warriors and other men in the court. She began to shudder at the heckling of the entire council of men.

As she began to tremble, a lone figure entered the great hall and people instantly parted way for him. His presence was irrepressible. The racket of hollow insults drowned out as the man drew near and eyes lowered. Pele discerned the silence and the pressure of the moment ease as outrage gave way to awe. The Polynesian hero walked directly to Pele and placed his hand on her shoulder. She squeezed his hand for support; his very touch instantly consoling her anguish. Maui Atalaga stared at all the startled onlookers, his aura and presence permeating the entire hall.

"Is there anyone here who wishes to speak ill of this woman to me?"

No one spoke. Warriors swallowed uncomfortably, fear welling inside their chests. Chiefs lowered their heads, daring not to speak and Kamohoali'i, Toutai and Fasi'apule looked away with foreboding. Talatama and his companions felt the familiar intensity of the hero pervade all those around him. The old king nodded his head at the folk hero.

"What say you, Kamohoali'i?" the king said, breaking the silence.

"All lies, Your Majesty," he growled, "strung together to implicate me! I have no comrades to vouch for my innocence. They've all been slain by these curs!"

"Bold words from a once infamous criminal," the king quickly returned. "What do you say about their motives if you think they lie?"

"They - I - Prince Talatama is bent on implicating me for the crimes of others! For his shortfall to find the real villain in this tale, he captured me so that he did not come back empty handed!"

"Absurd," the warrior prince blurted.

"I'll not pay the price for your failure," Kamohoali'i continued with his desperate lie. "You've failed!"

"I have heard enough." Tu'itatui stood from his throne. "The decision is made."

The great hall fell silent. He stepped down from his dais and looked across everyone who stood in the hall before clearing his throat. His commanding voice then came loud and deep and behind his beard shone large white teeth.

"For sixty years the great Tongan Empire has grown to unparalleled power across our Pacific Ocean. In this time we have enjoyed the wealth and prosperity that comes with our success. Our raw might as the Empire, however, equally responsible for our accomplishments, has become a double edged weapon. Today is such an example."

"As our force and power is revered across the nations with tribute, we have enjoyed thirty years of peace. As we have grown in might, the danger of our fall comes not from an external enemy, but from enemies from within." Tu'itatui turned to Kamohoali'i.

"The Pulotulahi, although recent in its rise, is such a model for this internal treachery. I only hope that one day light will be shed on its dark motivations, for I do not expect to gain answers from you, Kamohoali'i."

"The words of my son and his companions are impartial and undeniable. I, therefore, renounce your title and find you guilty of sedition," the king paused. "I order your execution without delay. Your death will serve as an example to those remaining loyal to the Pulotulahi."

"But, Father!" Prince Talaiha'apepe reached forward.

As the hall erupted in shouts and cheers, Talatama felt a wave of completion wash over his very being. It was as if the weight of hundreds of innocent deaths were lifted from his conscience. He felt Adi's hand on his shoulder and Atiogie's on the other. The protests from Kamohoali'i were futile and he excised them from his mind as he made his way to his companions with a weary smile of vanquish.

Kamohoali'i was taken away from the great hall as Toutai shook his head at the decision. Talatama glared at him with suspicion. *"He has to be the Dark Lord,"* he thought. The high priest ignored the prince's stare and disappeared behind the dais, as Fasi'apule approached his nephew slowly, a wide grin spanning his face.

"Well done, Talatama," he said.

"Your scrutiny was unexpected, Uncle!" Talatama frowned.

"But necessary, young Talatama. If you are to be king one day, you must justify all your actions and decisions. You must be ready to answer questions and receive criticism when it is given. More so when the lives of others depend on it," Fasi'apule smiled.

"A test," Talatama grinned.

"It was your final test. You have nothing more to learn from me, Prince Talatama." Fasi'apule placed his hand on his shoulder then turned away.

"Talatama," the king stepped down to his eldest son.

"Yes, Father."

"Well done," he looked into his son's eyes. "You have made me proud, my son."

"Thank you, Father. I did what had to be done."

"You did what was necessary for the Empire. You've shown me you have become a man," the king paused. "You've also confirmed another important decision of mine."

"What decision?"

"Enough excitement for one day," he sighed, "We will talk later. Go and see to your brothers and your sister. They have missed you much."

Following an exchange of greetings with his siblings, Talatama and his companions departed the main hall and congregated outside. Atiogie and Vaohoi exchanged playful jabs, Whatonga and the Fijians spoke softly about the decision. Talatama took Lo'au's hands in his and marvelled at the old man with new purpose. Lo'au reflected a humble smile.

"You never told me," Talatama said, "But – but how can you be still alive, by Tangaloa? You must be at least..."

"When I was young, I was once close to death. I was taken to an ancient and secret place, and there I was healed and blessed with longevity, my Prince," Lo'au winked, "I have lived for a long time and lived many lives across countless oceans in the centre of politics, social reform, and hierarchy," the old man breathed. "Long before you were born, I gave that up and decided to dedicate my life to aiding not nations, but individuals."

"But your place is here with us, here with your family."

"I cannot explain it to you, Talatama. We must find our own destiny, seek our own true path. My work here in Tonga was complete a long time ago. It was my time to leave and help others in need."

"I understand."

"Your mother would have been proud of you today," Lo'au smiled and placed his hand gently on the prince's head. "I am proud of you."

"Well, I'm glad this truth came to light before you disappeared again," the prince laughed.

"Excuse me, Milord," came a familiar voice from behind.

Talatama turned wide eyed and speechless.

"I stand before you ready for my orders." Captain Mateitau smiled to his old commander.

"By the gods! How did you – I thought you were killed in Niuatoputapu!" Talatama felt as though he was looking at a ghost of his old captain.

"Kunamoana was slain. I escaped with my life and two others." Mateitau's eyes welled with tears of joy. "Our Fourteenth Legion lives on!"

Talatama reached out, embraced him like a brother and held him long. He released him before grabbing his shoulders.

"Aye, live on it shall!" He beamed. "It is good to see you again, by Tangaloa."

"Prince Talatama!" a chief called from a distance. "You're required here for assistance!"

"Wait here – I'll return shortly."

The prince jogged to the side of one of the main domiciles towards the sea, and as he wheeled around the corner he shuddered to a stop. Three imperial soldiers lay on the ground, slain, five standing above them with bloodied clubs. Next to them was

Kamohoali'i, unbound and grinning from ear to ear. The chief who called Talatama suddenly lunged at him with a spear. The events were too quick for the prince to unleash the Peace Maker tucked into his girdle. He evaded the spear and grabbed the end, engaging in a pulling match with the chief. As he began to call for aid, a throwing club struck him in the side of the head. He released the spear and fell backwards onto the grass, his cracked headdress rolling from his head.

In an instant the chief was above him, raising his arms to drive the spear downwards and all the prince could do was to hold his hands out protectively. The spear struck down and bounced off the Sangone breastplate. He raised the spear again but did not get another strike.

"Talatama!" a familiar voice yelled.

A man struck down the chief with one swift blow, then turned to engage the five soldiers as Talatama rolled to his side with warm blood seeping from his skull. Shifting to his knee, he squinted up at his saviour who had quickly defeated the five warriors and now engaged Kamohoali'i. It was Siateki, the Fallen Commander. Stars sparkled in his vision as he drew the Peace Maker and faced the duel. His old friend fought valiantly against Kamohoali'i, a final representation of yet another betrayal against the Pulotulahi.

"Siateki!"

Suddenly five more men appeared from the bushes, one of them leaping in the air towards the combatants. Omani executed a flying kick that struck Siateki in the back, sending him stumbling forward into Kamohoali'i's club. The Fallen Commander's head jolted as the club swept across, sending blood spattering to the side. The general wasted no time. His club rose and fell over Siateki, turning his head into a soft clump of fragmented bone and skin.

"No!" Talatama screamed.

As Kamohoali'i and his men disappeared through the bush, the companions sprinted around the fale, accompanied by dozens of imperial soldiers. Seeing the prince's bleeding head, they swarmed to him.

"Kamohoali'i's escaped! That way!" he growled at the imperial soldiers before halting in front of Siateki and going to his knees.

He lifted the lifeless body into his arms, as blood from his own head dripped onto Siateki's peaceful face. The images of their friendship through his childhood rushed back, their times of carefree youth, moments of discovery and adventure as young men in the army flooded from his memory. Somehow the evil path he chose later in life was suddenly irrelevant. The act of sacrifice had been his final choice.

"That's -" Atiogie stammered.

"My friend," the prince whispered as he lay the body down.

CHAPTER 67

The warrior prince and his companions reached the main beach of Heketa, about seventy metres to the south east of the compound. Rushing out from the forest path into the open sand, they were suddenly faced with masses of the Pulotulahi, with Ganilau at the head of the force. Kamohoali'i trudged through the shallow water, armed with a new war club and Omani, General Va'iga and the other Pulotulahi lieutenants at his side.

Earlier that morning, Ganilau had assembled a thousand Pulotulahi warriors from around Tongatapu and congregated on the far side of 'Eua'iki. General Va'iga and his Samoan mercenaries had also bolstered the enemy numbers greatly, and on the king's decision that found Kamohoali'i guilty, a Pulotulahi spy had ran to Heketa beach to light a signal fire...an indication that the Dark Lord had failed in swaying the mind of the king. It had taken the main force little time to heed the signal and reach the main island.

The companions slowly unsheathed their weapons while Adi and Lo'au scrambled to find cover amid the trees.

"Vaohoi! Come with us!" the Fijian Priestess said.

"Not this time, Adi. This time I stand with my brothers," the youngster gritted his teeth.

Talatama swiped the Peace Maker and raised it above his head proudly. To his sides ran Atiogie, gripping his gigantic club with both hands, and began to heave like a cornered beast. Whatonga held his gleaming axe eagerly and was ready for battle. Emori ran with Kaianuanu to keep up. Captain Mateitau finally joined the companions with renewed purpose, swearing never to be left behind again. Pele suddenly came rushing through the hundreds of imperial soldiers who had gathered behind the companions. She stood next to Talatama with tracks of tears down her sullied cheeks, peering up at him with resolute determination.

"Let's kill them all," she said.

The prince nodded.

"What is your command, Prince Talatama?" A captain of the Third Imperial Legion pushed his way to the prince.

"Have General Ngongo send for the entire Imperial Army in Nukuleka," he paused. "This time they'll not miss the spoils of war!"

The captain disappeared through the masses of imperial soldiers at Talatama's back and as he did, there ebbed a great silence between the two massive forces. Nothing but the soft lapping of the waves was heard as Talatama engaged Ganilau with a fierce gaze, standing no more than fifty metres apart. The air was electric with anticipation, adrenalin rushing through warriors on both sides.

King Tu'itatui appeared from afar, standing too far inland to come close to danger. He was surrounded protectively by his elite warriors, watching for any sudden attempts at his life. He had appeared at the beach against the wishes of his council, demanding that he partake in the sudden battle. Lord Fasi'apule had physically held him back from launching into the stand-off. His gentle pleas eventually became sibling rows. But their quarrel was short lived by the hands of Princess Fatafehi. She was the king's favourite and possessed the power to sway his mind, especially when beseeching to his compassion.

Talatama raised the Peace Maker above his head again and called out to his soldiers. It was a preparation call for the warrior ritual performed only during times of great battle. His cry was long and loud, and all at once, hundreds of men united their voices with his to a grand crescendo. Then it began: the Tongan war challenge of the ancients.

With their weapons at their feet, the five hundred imperial soldiers led by Talatama slapped their bare chests and swayed their powerful bodies from side to side with ferocity. They raised their hands to the heavens in unison and clawed outwardly to their enemies during the challenge. Their words were synchronized with directed aggression.

'We who are about to die call upon the spirits of the dead in Pulotu,
Watch us as we go bravely into battle for the glory of our people,
Should you be pleased, grant us strength so that we may prevail,
Should you be disappointed, grant us a noble warrior's death!

Come forward, my enemy! Come forward and meet your doom!
We will take your lives with no mercy or remorse!
We will tear your flesh from your bodies with the strength of our god!
Mighty Tangaloa! Be with us!'

As the imperial forces began their war challenge, the Pulotulahi warriors exploded with their own. Led by Ganilau, they echoed returned an equally frightening war challenge, both vicious and terrible. The men tore at their chests and inflicted terrible wounds to themselves with their clubs as the violent dance was heard through their darker verses.

'Bring the heavens, bring the hell, bring it all to the battle on this day,
For you will not live through this hour against we of the Pulotulahi,
We will tear out your eyes so that you will walk the underworld blind,
We will rip out your hearts and feast upon them so that your spirit grows
cold,
We will crush your skull so that the Lord of Darkness takes you forever.

Come and suffer! Come and die!
Peel your flesh, cleave your hearts and pick your bones,
We will feast on your bodies on this day!
Mighty Hikule'o! Be with us!'

The deafening war cries from both sides, in perfect unison, echoed across the land and sea like the voices of the gods themselves. Anyone observing the spectacle was filled with a powerful trepidation, so stirring were the ancient war challenges facing each other.

The last to finish the challenge were the Pulotulahi. No time was spent following their last words. The imperial forces, led by the warrior prince, charged forward in a shrill commotion of war cries. The Pulotulahi sounded their roars and launched into attack, and the human waves crashed together in a discordant confrontation of muscled bodies, violence and death. As the masses then recoiled from the impact, there remained dozens of dead killed within the first seconds.

Then the controlled battle began. The large contingent of imperial soldiers focused through the centre of battle as skirmishes formed and crashed together in groups and occasional duels were fought.

Talatama faced Ganilau. Paired to each other, they were encircled by violence that looked like blurs of spirits flowing through the passage of time. Ganilau began to creep sideways around the warrior prince, interchanging his bloodied club from one hand to another. His own blood had erupted from his leprous welts and it seeped down the stained tapa that bandaged his diseased body. The pain that racked his entire being was focused into the monster's rage: a fury that only the affliction of internal pain could stoke. The giant man's eyes were bloodshot, boiling with carnal wrath and ire.

As tavakes called overhead and the breeze kissed their glistening bodies, the handsome prince stood defiant before the ugly abomination. It was the depiction of good versus evil, light from dark. Ganilau was six inches taller than the prince. At over seven foot and two hundred kilograms, he was a formidable adversary. His black skin was pocked with both the leprous affliction and glistening drops of might. His patchy black hair was haggard and his pink eyes were like those of a wild hog.

Prior to becoming a commander of the Pulotulahi, Ganilau had travelled the Empire as a wandering warrior in search of duels. For a decade he had dominated the island of Viti Levu. No warrior was a match for him. His success was attributed to one thing other than his natural skill and strength: his rage. It was said that during his travels he contracted leprosy from a dying woman, a maiden he had saved from disaster. Though having become cursed with the repulsive disease, he developed a way to combat the pain and suffering. In a way, he was able to channel the excruciating ache into a fury during battle. It drove him beyond the pain threshold of any normal man. In battles, he was impossible to suppress. In a duel, he was relentless.

The warrior prince assailed first. Stepping forward, he sliced the Peace Maker through the air barely missing his target. Ganilau avoided the attack and responded with a flurry of downward strikes. Talatama braced as he blocked with the Peace Maker. *He is powerful,* the warrior prince swore. Ducking and weaving in the soft sand, Talatama attacked again, this time at his legs. He wanted to test the monster's balance and ability to re-position. Suddenly, and in an unexpected move, Ganilau jumped backwards to avoid the attack. But as the prince lunged in advancement, Ganilau leapt back, both his legs kicking Talatama squarely in the chest.

The Sangone armour protected him from the blow but not the force. He was propelled onto his back, and was barely able to avoid Ganilau's follow up attacks. He rolled and jumped to his feet, breathing heavily and feeling his old wound throbbing in his abdomen as he blocked solid attacks again and again. Ganilau paused and rolled his head with a possessed expression - a new rage embodied with the pain of affliction. He rained blows down on the prince with fresh strength, power and intent. It was only seconds before the Peace Maker began to feel heavy, his hands felt a painful tingle caused by the constant crack of wood on wood. He missed a block and the club smashed down on the armour around his shoulder. Talatama pushed away from the monster instantly, recoiling from the strike.

As he stepped backwards, he felt the soft sand beneath his feet become as glue. His legs were stone. But Ganilau did not grant him reprieve. Accustomed to this way of duelling, the leper surged forward knowing the advantage he had as Talatama slipped in the sand, trying to catch his breath. Another block cracked off the Peace Maker. The prince quickly angled himself again, and just in that instant, he saw his father's entourage in the distance.

He knew the king was watching the battle. He sneered and was filled with a renewed spirit and intensity. Ganilau's eyes widened as the warrior prince leapt swiftly and parried his attacks, before spinning and slicing downwards. His strike glided through the monster's defences and cracked upon his chest. But as Ganilau roared in pain, the strike was not a fateful one, and it only stoked his rage. Again Talatama recommenced a duel with the possessed warrior, again draining the strength from the defiant warrior prince.

Despite the inspiration from his father's presence, Talatama knew he could not continue much longer. His mind raced with tactics and strategies as he defended himself and fought against his own exhaustion. In an instant it came to him. He knew what had to be done. One, two, three – his parries echoed through the warring men. The rage: that was the key. Talatama feigned helpless and beaten, which ironically was not far from the truth. He began to raise his hand in defence and allow Ganilau to advance on him easily. He quelled his strength against him and subdued the glimmer of defiance in his own eyes.

In seconds, the results were obvious. Ganilau's rage lessened and the fire in his eyes began to subside. Ganilau saw the prince had become helpless and did not require the rage to continue the fight. He began to snigger and lower his guard. The ruse worked. As he took his eyes from his opponent, Talatama lunged forward with all his might and struck the Peace Maker at Ganilau's legs.

An ear-splitting howl erupted from the leper, like a hound howling at the moon. Ganilau buckled and dropped his club as he fell to the sand. Talatama swiftly reefed the Peace Maker in a downward arc that struck Ganilau directly on the cranium, crumpling the skull inward with a sickening mulch of dark blood. The warrior prince staggered to evade the diseased life flow before the great monster finally collapsed in a heap, staining the yellow sand to claret. The prince, more exhausted than disgusted, quickly ran into the sea and washed the infected blood from his weapon.

"Talatama!" Atiogie bellowed.

"No rest," he cursed. He saw the Samoan waving for his attention further along the beach, pointing to a tongiaki that banked ashore amid the battle. From the bow leapt a demonic figure, soaring through the air and landing in the fray of war. A single blurred movement and all men around the figure collapsed, or were hewn into the lapping waves. The demon stood and arched his back in a roar that could be heard kilometres away. Havea.

Immediately, warriors in his vicinity shook with terror or fled before another moment passed and more imperial warriors were slain effortlessly. Close to him were Kamohoali'i and Omani, capitalizing their fight on the terrorised soldiers. The prince looked about quickly and saw the imperial forces were in trouble; skirmishes up and down the beach were dominated by the Pulotulahi and there were more imperial soldiers lying dead on the sand.

Talatama spied his king's position. The distance was not great and the immediate number of imperial soldiers had waned. Only the king's chosen men surrounded and protected the aged monarch. Now strengthened by Havea, it would not take the Pulotulahi long to reach him. The image of his younger brothers and sister falling under the club was inconceivable. The Imperial Army would not arrive in time.

"My Prince! We're being overrun!" Kaianuanu rushed to his side.

"Quickly, gather all the forces you can and make for the tongiakis. Go now!"

Talatama screamed out to his companions to get their attention as he rushed down to the water's edge. Atiogie and Pele were the first to reach the boats.

"We have to lead the forces away from the beach and the king!" Talatama's bloodied face was full of concern. "Summon as many men as you can and make to the sea!"

CHAPTER 68

Atiogie and Pele swiftly commandeered an imperial vessel as Talatama engaged more Pulotulahi warriors by the water's edge. When he finished off the fourth enemy, he spotted Whatonga and Emori engaged in battle further up the beach with a band of a hundred men. He hesitated and roared out to them, but they were too far away to hear.

"There's no time!" Atiogie shouted.

"My Prince!" Kaianuanu hailed, from one of the half dozen vessels already out into the sea.

"Atiogie's right, Talatama," Pele said.

"Well, hopefully we'll draw most of them away with us!" the warrior prince said as he jumped aboard the vessel.

"Kamohoali'i! You dawdler!" Talatama bellowed. "There lays your champion on the beach, slain by my own hand! Is that the best you can summon from the depths of hell?"

Kamohoali'i and his commanders broke from their blood drunk fray and realised their predicament. He glanced at Ganilau sprawled on the beach, and boiled with fury. Omani paused as he calculated the situation.

"General, we should push forward and kill the king!" he exclaimed.

"Come to me, Kamohoali'i! Is it not your wish to have me slain likewise? Come if you dare!" Talatama screamed himself hoarse.

"You insolent, usurping little bastard," Kamohoali'i fumed as he weighed his two targets.

"The king, Kamohoali'i," Omani pressed.

"There's no reason why we can't take them both," Kamohoali'i returned, red in the face. "Divide the forces! Omani, take General Va'iga and your warriors. Attack the king, and bring me his head!"

"But, Kamohoali'i, we shouldn't divide —"

"You will obey me! We have the advantage!" the general turned to Talatama. "I will tear the spine out of that mongrel Prince myself! Havea! Follow my lead!"

A conch horn trumpeted the divide and direction of the raging battle, while Kamohoali'i, Havea and their men scrambled back onto their vessels. Omani and General Va'iga assembled as many as they could on the bloody beach for a final charge.

"He's taken the bait," Atiogie laughed.

"Good!" Talatama reflected an excited grin. "Helmsman! Take us out to sea!"

The warrior prince signalled Kaianuanu and the rest of the imperial soldiers to follow the lead of his tongiaki before the great sails exploded with wind and launched them across the brine.

"Milord, Kamohoali'i leaves a contingent on the beach. They prepare to attack the king!" Mateitau pointed.

"So long as that demonic Havea is not with them!" the prince winced as he washed the blood from his face.

The convergence of imperial vessels narrowed like an arrowhead as they streamed out to sea but it was not long before the Pulotulahi tongiakis fired out from the beach at incredible knots.

"Blast it, Helmsman! Take an angle to the wind, they're gaining on us!" the warrior prince yelled.

He then whirled to the soldiers on board, armed with bows.

"Take aim, men!" he pointed. "Release!"

A volley of twenty arrows rained down on the closest vessel, striking targets true, but it was not Kamohoali'i's tongiaki. The general had directed his craft between the imperial vessels and land, sailing parallel to them, by using the angle of the wind, he was gaining on them. The prince spied the Pulotulahi leaders and pointed at the vessel anxiously.

"Take aim at that vessel!"

"Milord, it's out of range!" Mateitau shouted over the sea wind.

"Not for me it's not," Pele snarled as she fitted an arrow to her bow and dispatched it straight.

The arrow, like a bolt of lightning, disappeared into the sky. A few seconds later, in the distance, a warrior collapsed from view.

"Yes!" Mateitau and the imperial warriors hooted.

The man standing next to Kamohoali'i jolted back, the arrow pierced straight through his neck. He collapsed backwards and gurgled in agony.

"Damn them!" Kamohoali'i screamed. "Helmsman, set a course for interception!"

Immediately, the vessel took a sharp angle and cut through the blue towards Talatama and his men. The white-wash lathered the bow of the tongiaki and the imperial lead vessel came into sights. Within moments, the tongiakis drew nearer and nearer. Talatama saw their ploy and looked starboard. A few dotted islands separated them from the open ocean.

Onevai and Onevao islands were only a kilometre or two beyond a small reef. He quickly averaged the enemy's number was equal to that of his own, and focused his steely eyes on the islands.

"It ends here," he said to himself, then turned to his warriors. "We make our last stand, men! Prepare to take the beach on Onevai!" He pointed and gave signal to Kaianuanu.

The great tongiakis took a sudden veer north to the island group. The heavy masts swung from port to starboard, almost lifting the second hull from the water. The imperial soldiers continued to rain down arrows upon the bowless enemy, cursing and shouting in frustration. The imperial fleets' change of course had opened the distance between them, giving them more time to get ashore. Once over the reef, the vessels thrust into the soft sands of the larger of the two islands.

The warrior prince and his companions leapt from the tongiaki, sand exploding at their feet as they landed. He sprinted ahead across a wide expanse of beach towards the centre of the islands then stopped and turned to face the sea. Catching his breath, perspiration streamed down his body. He raised the Peace Maker above his head like a beacon, summoning all the imperial warriors to file in behind him.

Atiogie too was slick with sweat, grime and blood. Droplets ran down the Samoan's face as he readjusted his gauntlets for another battle. Pele stabbed her axe into the sand and gathered her braided hair, tying it back with a length of tapa. Her honey skin gleamed in the sunlight and her posture embodied her warrior heritage. Mateitau tore strips of tapa to aid Kaianuanu who had been wounded in the battle at Heketa. The Captain of the Fourteenth Legion observed the bleeding was stemming from a puncture wound at his side. He frowned to Talatama. It was painful enough for him to lean slightly to protect it, but he did not complain.

"Your wound is grave, Kaianuanu. Fall back, get it treated and join the archers."

"No, Milord."

"Kaianuanu?" the prince did a double take.

"We've come a long way together since you came to my island as a slave," the young Hungan chief smiled as he winced with pain. "You've taught me much of honour and victory. I am proud to call you my prince. It will be an honour to die in this glorious battle."

The prince slowly nodded in understanding and tapped the warrior on his shoulder. He turned to Pele and Atiogie with his usual valour.

"May the glory of battle echo the Halls of Pulotu!" the giant Samoan bellowed.

With that, Talatama raised the Peace Maker skyward and roared with skin crawling volume. Filled with an electric rush of adrenalin, a unified camaraderie, and a purpose worth dying for, he was joined by his companions and two hundred imperial warriors.

Every moral fibre of the men was connected in such a way that it lifted their spirits higher and higher.

A hundred metres away, the Pulotulahi contingent landed on the beach and inundated the shallow water with their vessels. As the imperial warriors watched in wait, their actions appeared slowed in time, as Kamohoali'i and Havea hulked across the white sand, fired by the fury of madmen, hooting and howling like animals.

"Charge!" Talatama roared.

The imperial forces accelerated with Talatama at the head. The warrior prince ran with both hands glued to his weapon, eyes fixed on his opponent directly ahead; Kamohoali'i. From a distance he focused on the large man, and as he drew closer, saw the anger on his face. The intent in his wild eyes was unmistakable. He knew Havea was close to the general but never lost his focus.

Suddenly they came together without slowing. At full stride, Talatama swung at Kamohoali'i who did the same. Their clubs clashed together and recoiled as they both hurtled into enemy forces. Mists of blood puffed from the collision and battle cries drowned the sound of death. Brutality ruled over all, as men fought viciously to survive. As the prince weaved his way through his opponents, Atiogie and Pele tried to stay close to him. But as the numbers mulched together, so did all immediate bearing. Skirmishes developed everywhere.

Kaianuanu, Mateitau and a handful of men surrounded Havea and attacked without fear.

"You killed my brother, you bastard," Mateitau shrieked. "Your dread will not work on me!"

They swung their clubs feverishly at the demonic man in the hope of striking him down, but Havea's strength and power was still too much. His cruel club of shark's teeth tore through the warriors like boning a fish. Their cries of death were smutted by his echoing roars. His face was like that of a corpse – marbleized, lifeless, and sickly. He cackled with every pitiless strike that took a life. Mateitau came at him like a storm. His relentless blows were unstoppable, and for a moment, Havea was forced to defend against them. But it took only one missed strike for Havea to gain the upper hand. Mateitau slipped over in his rage and felt the bite of Havea's club across his back. He was sent twirling through the air and landed in a crumpled heap. The Hungan warrior leapt forward with all his might and struck the demon in the chest, but it was not enough. The monster's fist rocketed out and landed on Kaianuanu's chin, shattering it and sending him sprawling. The strikes to his face and wound at his side, proved too great for him to rise. The demon leered down, fangs showing through a frightening visage grin.

"Do your worst," Kaianuanu bravely uttered before Havea ripped the life from him.

Talatama's hair had come loose from the tie and hung freely over his Sangone armour. Blood stained his entire body. He exhaled with every attack and inhaled at every recoil. Each new face that appeared, he engaged impartially, as the Peace Maker sliced through flesh and shattered through bone. He danced to the rhythm of combat, taking moments to search for Kamohoali'i between each predictable engagement. He then realised that none of his companions were close by, let alone Kamohoali'i or Havea. Scores of men repeatedly surrounded him and he was left with little choice but to remain in position.

Only metres away through the crowd of warriors, Pele faced Kamohoali'i. The finality of their mutual hatred, and the journey they took as adversaries, not siblings, had come to an end. A few braids from Pele's hair had come loose and hung down over her stoic face. Blood spattered her skin and her taut limbs gleamed with strength. Kamohoali'i appeared relatively untouched, his great girth saturated with blood and muck.

"This will not end the way I intended it," Pele said.

"It will end with you dead," Kamohoali'i grimaced. "Like our father."

"I was right!" Pele breathed. "You murdered him, didn't you?"

"Of course! My chieftainship had begun to grow since the battle of Niuatoputapu. I couldn't be the Chief of Ha'apai with our father still alive, could I?"

For all the long years they conspired to murder, plunder and steal, Pele never thought the day would ever come to leave her brother's company. Yet here she stood, having left him and joined his enemies, having testified against him before the king. In their past, his every word had commanded her obedience. But now she had become immune to all his callous lies. His words no longer hurt, nor controlled her mind.

"You have shamed yourself beyond redemption, for all eternity," she raised her head to him as a tears rolled down her cheeks.

"Sister, don't tell me that you're still crying over father?"

"My tears are now not for his death, Kamohoali'i," Pele said calmly. "They are for yours."

Kamohoali'i did not see the axe come down. By mere chance he slipped to his left in reflex. The axe missed his head and chopped into his shoulder. The blinding hack almost cleaved the big man's arm from his torso. Ruby red splashed everywhere as he swung and knocked his sister across the head with his forearm. But he did not react to the terrible wound, nor did Pele against his mighty blow. The butt of her axe swung back and connected under the jaw, shattering it with a sound of chewing rocks in one's mouth.

He dropped the club he was never able to raise against her.

He propped himself up using his good arm in time to receive a swinging kick to the chest. It lurched his head forward and from his lips he spat teeth and blood. His great torso slapped against the sand and his arms bounced to his sides helplessly. But Pele was steadfastly ruthless. She raised her deadly axe and thundered it down towards his head.

As it fell, the shaft of the axe was suddenly pushed aside as Talatama moved between them. He swiftly re-directed her attack with the Peace Maker.

"That's enough, Pele," he said quickly.

Ignoring the warrior prince, she again tried to lunge at her brother.

"Pele!" he wrestled with her. "As much as I want him dead too, he must be taken back to the king."

"No!"

"He is beaten! He must -" he intercepted and finally pushed her away. "He must face the punishment of the Empire. That is the only way we can win this sordid war."

The fiery woman screamed in frustration and glared at the defeated general lying prostate on the ground. Rage that she never realised possible began to subside, her breathing slowed and her eyes began to dim. Her sour expression gradually returned, but somehow it was different; there was a mark of concluding acceptance. The proud woman jolted her head back to swing the few braids from her face.

"Take him then, Prince Talatama. Do what you will with him."

"Take this man, bind him quickly. Throw him aboard my tongiaki and wait for me there," the warrior prince called to a group of warriors. "Wrap his wounds so he doesn't die on our way back to the capital."

"I cannot imagine your turmoil." His sincerity to Pele showed through his chestnut eyes.

"My destiny is no longer tied with his, Talatama," she met his gaze and, for the first time, he saw the young woman behind the warrior.

"And you've prevailed," he smiled.

She returned the smile, which was another first.

"For the last honour, would you accompany me to end all this madness?" he said with sober judgment as he gripped the Peace Maker.

"It will be my honour," she snarled.

The two warriors launched into the continuing fray with renewed passion.

CHAPTER 69

The Pulotulahi army were scattered along the beach, heaped with disarray and the Samoan mercenaries mixed among them were in similar disorder. Shortly after Kamohoali'i's departure, the imperial warriors re-grouped inland towards the king for his protection, and about three hundred soldiers formed a line almost as long as the beach itself. Facing the Pulotulahi, the imperial leaders re-positioned to the centre of the force. Standing among them was a couple of captains lead by the old war chief, Manusiu.

To Manusiu's side were Lord Fasi'apule, Prince Whatonga, Emori and Vaohoi. Far behind them, King Tu'itatui had become restless. Surrounded by his bodyguards and his children, he had been ordered by Fasi'apule, not to engage in battle. A long debate had ensued, which concluded in Tu'itatui's frustrated concession. As the war raged on, and war cries echoed across the lands, the aged king was reminded of his earlier days as a warrior and yearned for their return.

From the age of five, known then as Prince Koau, he had been raised as the promising heir to the great King Momo. His destiny was to deliver upon the Pacific Ocean, the greatest oceanic Empire the world had ever seen. He was mentored, tutored and groomed by the greatest minds in the realm, to enforce the dynamic and radical changes that his father had already made to the kingdom. Momo had achieved this through a combination of astute and the might of his own hand, and never before had the Empire grown to such proportions than under his rule.

It had been known from times past that Tu'itatui had been a powerful warrior of immense strength and skill. The decisions earlier in his career were the result of his proactive desire for battle, and all warriors who followed him into war were tangibly inspired. After thirty-five years of his kingship, neither enemy, nor ally, denied the Empire's success was the direct result of his will and the strength of his own back. No rival during the height of his youth could match him in ambition or skill, and now at seventy, the old warrior king still thirsted for battle.

"Father!" Fatafehi cried. "Please don't go!"

"Tangaloa, grant me strength against my enemies," the king boomed with a voice echoing decades.

"You cannot engage in battle, Your Majesty. Respectfully, Lord Fasi'apule's orders remain," Toa, the leader of the bodyguards bowed.

"Who is the king?" he fumed. "Fetch my club!"

"Talaiha'apepe? Tell him! Stop, Father!" Fatafehi pleaded.

"Let him do as he pleases," the young prince replied vacantly.

Talaiha'apepe stood in a trance. He had been publicly embarrassed in the Royal Court when Kamohoali'i's guilt had been decided, for it was he who had endorsed the general's legitimate and noble actions, which took place in Niuatoputapu. It had been he who had made the decision to pardon Kamohoali'i's past crimes and exalt him as a hero. His father looked down upon him with disappointment and regret, regret that he had been swayed by the tarnished view of the young prince. Talaiha'apepe turned on his heel and disappeared.

"Please, Father! I beg you!" Fatafehi threw herself at the king's feet.

"Out of the way, my girl!"

"Your Majesty, please listen to reason!" Toa implored. "You cannot risk the throne to this cut-throat scum! You are too important! Think of your people, of your responsibilities, your family."

The king paused and heaved a long breath. Toa had been his chief bodyguard for more than twenty years and had become like a younger brother. His wisdom and compassion had won him Tu'itatui's trust, not only as a protector but as a friend. Toa's words rang true. Tu'itatui reached out and placed his hand on Fatafehi's weeping head and looked out to the battle with distant eyes.

"Hush, daughter."

Manusiu positioned himself in front of the three hundred warriors, raised his club and summoned from the depths of his chest, a battle howl not heard for over four decades. The men surrounding him were filled with an unspeakable honour; they stood beside one of the most famous warlords in Tonga's history. None of the men had been born in the age when Manusiu tamed the seas and conquered distant lands. Tears rolled down his cheeks as he gave the signal for the men to charge. So moved were the soldiers standing close to Manusiu, they all wept tears of pride and tribute.

The men hurtled into battle, electrified and united with a purpose beyond bloodlust and violent hatred: they charged with honour and tribute to Manusiu. Armed with this powerful inspiration, the men carried the spirits of the dead and all who had died at Manusiu's side during the golden years of the Empire. The great warlord ran into battle fulfilling his last wish, that after all the past peaceful years, he may in the end, find his death in battle.

The two sides collided with the dense impact of human flesh. The imperial soldiers fought with their heads high, beaming with nobility against the barbaric mutineers. Almost immediately, the balance of strength leaned towards the Empire, so passionate were the warriors. The air was electrified; the scene thick with terrible violence and the great yellow expanse of the beach was spattered with red and the dark shadows of men.

Amid the haze of war, Whatonga found General Va'iga. Flooding memories of their encounter back in Niuatoputapu exhilarated the Rarotongan prince as he pointed his axe towards the Samoan general.

"You."

"Yes, it is I," Va'iga glared. "I, who should have killed you back in Niuatoputapu. But you escaped my net."

"Where is your 'net' now, barbarian? How will you best me without your cowardly ambush?"

"I need not those things to slay you, whelp!" he growled.

As Whatonga blocked Va'iga's blow, the clubs slid down the hafts and ripped at his hand. The Rarotongan prince felt pain shoot up his arm as the skin peeled from his fingers. He winced as he pulled back and swiped, missing his target narrowly. Va'iga attacked with greater strength, reefing back each unsuccessful strike to strike again. Whatonga ducked and weaved through the predictable attacks and at last, countered to strike the old general's knee with his axe. Va'iga buckled immediately before receiving a bout to the temple, sending his face plummeting into the sand.

Emori fought with control and calculated strength. Manoeuvring his barbed spear with skill, he was able to hold his ground and keep the enemy at a safe distance. Through the fray, he parried and thrusted, parried and thrusted and occasionally he brought the butt of the spear upwards to strike. His black skin shone with sweat, his eyes burned with concentration and he had now lost count of the men he had conquered. Suddenly, he heard a challenge to him.

"Fijian!" Omani shouted. "We meet again!"

Emori paused and recalled the Battle of the Great Lake. His mouth filled with revulsion.

"Last time you got the better of me," the Fijian walked proud. "This time, I'll take you down."

"I'll use that spear to pick my teeth!" Omani spat.

The Unarmed Warrior ran at the Fijian as sand kicked up from his feet into Emori's face. Once he had broken past the deadly distance of the spear, the Fijian stood exposed to his close quarter strikes. Emori could do nothing but lower his head as a flurry of fists pummelled at his face, and though he pushed back, he collected an elbow to the jaw. Omani danced away from him and allowed him time to recover.

"Pathetic," he teased.

Emori shook his head and glared at his opponent with stars in his eyes. He gripped his spear and lowered it towards the Pulotulahi commander. The challenge was enough to entice Omani again. He shuffled his feet with blinding skill as he closed the distance, occasionally shuddering to a stop, then resuming his feinting movements. His body was like a blur, easily evading Emori's thrusts and again entering past the point of the spear. This time his foot found its mark on Emori's abdomen, keeling the Fijian over, before snapping a blow across his cranium. Emori straightened in pain and watched helplessly as Omani's signature back-kick thundered upon his chest.

Emori's feet flew up with a thick fan of sand, crashing upside-down onto his shoulders and neck, as the world spun. Though he remained conscious, an immense agony ripped across his ribs, inflicting pain when he breathed. He rolled to his side and saw Omani waiting. Thoughts of Adi suddenly drifted across his mind within those brief moments – their future together, their commitment to one another, and their love. At that very moment he knew he was fighting not only for his own life, but for the future with Adi and what may come.

Omani began to move again. He used his powerful legs and leapt into the air above Emori, achieving an incredible height as he shaped up to execute a flying kick. The Fijian's vision blurred as his mind raced with fear. His spear lay just beyond his reach on the red ground. In the blinking of an eye, he exhaled a wounded bellow, stretching out to grasp his spear and raised it so its butt dug into the sand. He leaned back with a panicked expression, his eyes meeting Omani mid flight, comprehending his impending doom as he sailed through the air.

The spear tip sunk into Omani's stomach and erupted from his back with the sound of driving a knife through a raw breadfruit. His feet bounced off the sand on impact and the spear twisted with his body to the side. No words came from Omani's lips, but the agony and sheer surprise was written in his wide eyes. It took only seconds for the life to leave him. Emori rolled onto his back next to his fallen enemy and struggled to breathe with a fractured sternum and four broken ribs.

Manusiu did not possess the strength he once had. But he compensated with his uncanny ability to guess the enemies' movements before they were deployed. It was as if the old warlord could see into the future and foresee their attack. In every instance, he dodged and calculated to the point where an enemy realised too late they were outmanoeuvred. His club always aimed for the head, and using its weighty end, he did not need to employ much muscle.

But his ability to forecast his opponent's attacks did nothing for his endurance. At seventy five, his stamina could not withstand the onslaught of aggressive men a third his age. He felt his strength drain away and the heightened sense of his approaching demise. As he deflected each thrust, he began to stumble. In the end he began to laugh, reliving the days when he felt alive through carnal combat.

The first strike came across his shoulder, shattering the end of his collar bone. Another club bounced off his chest with a crack, yet still he fought on. Wounded, he took two more lives. A spear drove though his back, arching his body in pain as another warrior drove a spear through his chest, immobilising him momentarily. The club dropped from his hand onto the blood-soaked sand and a wide berth of enemy warriors surrounded him. He stumbled forward, appearing to have transcended the physical realm. Blood dribbled from his mouth.

"King Saudeleur..." He gazed into nothingness. "Queen Naufanua."

The enemy warriors watched in confusion.

"King Momo ..." he whispered. "I – I come to you now." He reached out and smiled. "Ahhh, at last we meet again ..."

The old warlord fell to his knees, then to his front. His great spirit drifted from his body and transcended the earthly realm to remain immortal forever.

Talatama staggered from his last duel breathing heavily. His shoulders slouched and he dropped to a knee to look around. The ground was cluttered with the dead. A few battles continued in the distance. The familiar dress of the Imperial Order seemed more prevalent in the living than the Pulotulahi, as he took a deep breath and exhaled, savouring a final victory. Atiogie came to his side, battle wounded and bleeding.

"Talatama, are you hurt badly?"

"I'll live."

"Good to hear, old friend. So may I," he laughed.

The big man helped the prince to his feet, as Pele joined them, having also avoided much injury. "How many lives do you have, my Prince?" she displayed a tired smile.

"One more life for me to take!" Havea loomed over the companions.

"Look out!"

Atiogie shielded Talatama with his giant club in an impact that sent the giant Samoan skidding across the sand. Havea strode towards him for the kill as Pele's axe swept across the terror's arm and with it drew a long line of blood.

He turned to her with an insane indifference to the wound and leered over her with an opened mouth of fangs. The immobilising fear saturated the air like a foul stench, as the fiery warrior leered back. Rare were the moments Havea's power of fear could not be ignored.

"Warrior of fire," his voice echoed, "your destiny lies beyond my control."

"Come devil! I will end your life here!" she beckoned.

"Foolish girl!" he cackled. "You cannot stop me here."

He easily dodged Pele's skilful attacks and moved around her with astonishing speed. Instantly she knew the mistake she had made as he swept his powerful arm up and struck her with all his might. Her body flipped through the air. She crashed to the sand and did not move. Talatama swung with the same strike he used to kill Ganilau. The Peace Maker thundered down upon Havea's chest, cracking into his ribs.

Havea's club swept down and struck the Peace Maker to the side like a twig. Talatama dug his left foot into the sand. He wound up a second swing with all his might, however Havea had mirrored his move. There was a deafening crack and the sound of splintering wood. The impact shattered the end of the Peace Maker; its head spun through the air and thrust into the ground. Talatama felt his spirit break. The club arched and hit him square in the back, bursting in a vociferous, blinding flash as it connected with the Sangone Armour and ricocheted wildly. Yet the strength of the blow was enough to propel the prince across the sand and into a crashed heap. At that very moment, a contingent of thirty imperial warriors swarmed towards Havea and engaged him headlong. For an instant, it seemed that perhaps the sheer numbers could have sewn his demise.

But he rose from the chaos of battle and death like an insufferable demon; his body a cascading portrait of blood, grime and sweat. His muscles were swollen with strength and the fury of the melee, his hair clung together in wet masses of claret. His giant club still bore dozens of shark teeth protruding from its twisted surface, coloured red by its fill of lives taken in the fray. Like a force without reason, an evil judgment that had befallen man on earth, Havea mauled through lives of men like a harvest of crops.

As he tore his club from the broken body of an imperial warrior, he hooted and cackled. With one mighty kick, a soldier flew through the air and landed in the shallow water of Onevai. Blood clouded through the seawater instantly. He regarded the carcass with amusement before he noticed a tongiaki approaching from the east. He recognised the sails, the craft, and the man aboard. For an instant he felt a mortal chill run up his spine. He raised his club and glared in the direction of the tongiaki. A deep roar thundered from the monster like a celestial conch declaring war between heaven and hell.

CHAPTER 70

Atiogie and Pele helped support Talatama as they made their way towards the beach. The battle almost over, the remaining triumphant imperial soldiers joined the three and insisted on caring for their prince. Exalted and exhausted by their victory, they failed to see Havea standing just south of their position on the beach. Talatama shook the soldiers from his sides and grasped the broken Peace Maker that had been reduced to half its size. As he did, all his companions took a fighting stance.

"Talatama!" came a familiar voice from behind.

The group whirled to see Emori and Adi with a dozen imperial warriors running towards them from the northern beach. With them was Prince Whatonga and twenty of his Rarotongan warriors, all readying themselves for more battle.

"You made it." Talatama broke a tired smile.

"Just in time too," Whatonga said tilting his head towards Havea. "Your destiny is filled with war, Prince Talatama."

"So it seems."

"My Prince!" Adi embraced Talatama as she reached him.

The warrior prince saw the terrible state of Emori; the Fijian could hardly stand upright.

"Adi, Emori, stay out of this. You too, Whatonga."

"I fear I cannot aid you in this next battle Talatama," Emori winced.

"Take him to the tree's edge. Seek cover." Talatama tipped his head to Adi. "Whatonga, go with them."

"You may punish me for ignoring a royal command later, but for now we join you till the death," the Rarotongan prince stated.

"So be it."

The Rarotongan's group joined the remnants of the imperial force and slowly progressed towards the evil warrior.

"It's going to take all of us in hope to take Havea down." Atiogie clenched his teeth as he pointed his broken club toward the terror.

"We have to attack him at the same time. Agreed?" Talatama readied himself.

"Talatama," Pele's face was stern. "He took the three of us down in three heart beats. We cannot win this fight."

"Then I'm going to die trying."

He glanced at Pele, Atiogie and Whatonga as they drew closer to Havea and shared the chilling knowledge that this fight may very well be the death of them all. But it was not until a lone tongiaki had made it to the shoreline that the companions noticed it. They stopped in their tracks.

The war tongiaki hardly made a sound as the bow banked on the shore between the companions and Havea. Maui Atalaga leapt from the craft into the knee-high water with ease, his long brown hair waved in the salted sea breeze and his body radiated an atonement of vigour and verve. His face beamed with contentment, joviality almost. In his right hand, the polished darkness of Mohemamahi remained a stark reminder of his purpose and goal.

"It's Maui Atalaga!" Adi shouted from a distance.

"No!" Pele cried out.

Talatama held the warrior by her shoulder and pulled her back.

"Pele, don't. Don't get between this," the prince's voice quivered. "You'll be killed."

"He's right," Atiogie assisted in holding back the she-warrior.

"Oh, Emori..." Adi squeezed the hand of her beloved and hid her face in his chest, "I can't watch."

By this time, the entire Imperial Army had approached from the small village of Nukuleka. General Ngongo and Commander Hi'hiko led the imperial force of almost ten thousand men ashore at Onevai, followed closely by a contingent of the imperial tongiakis carrying Lord Fasi'apule, Prince Talaiha'apepe and High Priest Toutai. They stopped within a few hundred metres of Havea, the leaders recognising him immediately.

Toutai took a few steps forward and halted when he saw Maui Atalaga on the far side of Havea. He licked his lips and wiped sweat from his brow as Lord Fasi'apule and Prince Talaiha'apepe joined him. Squinting under the afternoon sun, thoughts of action raced through their minds as they shifted to remain close to the armed contingents. The companions and the soldiers all looked upon the two mighty warriors with uncontrollable anticipation. The air was electrifying.

Havea was dug into the wet sand like an anchored tree root. His left arm, which wielded his club of terrible destruction, swayed back and forth in preparation of taking a final life.

"So, Maui, you have come at last," Havea's voice forever grinding, forever echoed.

"Havea." Maui Atalaga took measured steps towards his much larger adversary, composed and firm.

"You cannot stop me. I have grown more powerful over the years of being on this earth," Havea cackled.

"I've travelled across the great seas to nations far and wide to find you. You can run no more," Maui Atalaga said as he stopped only metres from the monster.

"Come to me then! Let me taste your flesh," Havea cackled behind rotting, black fangs. "I will take your life, eat your remains and end your line forever."

"To avenge the deaths in my line is my life's greatest honour," Maui Atalaga took Mohemamahi in both hands.

"You've always been smug and too self-assured, just like your father, full of misguided sense of purpose. Maui Fusi Fonua died a coward," Havea kicked sand in his direction.

"It is your mother who fled, a coward, Havea. She taught you well," Maui returned.

Havea crept forward. "No more running, after I kill you, I'll kill your treasured little friends too," he growled and motioned towards the companions.

Maui Atalaga's eyes widened as he saw his dear friends standing anxiously beyond only metres of sand. He felt a dreadful chill run through his heart at the thought of them suffering a fate at the hands of Havea. The fear brought images of Pele at the feet of the malevolent horror.

He barely saw the club sweep up before him like a thunderbolt. He shifted sideways, but not quick enough for the rows of sharks teeth to bounce off the right side of his chest. The sound of ripping skin was followed by a splatter of blood that arced and fell like rain drops into the shallow water. Havea's club came screaming downwards like a falling tree towards his head. This time he saw it coming. The giant club plummeted into the water with an almighty crash, sending an explosion of sand and sea in all directions.

The monster did not compose himself quickly, following his miss, he knew Maui Atalaga had evaded and was regaining his footing behind him. He slowly stood up straight and turned casually towards his enemy.

"You're weak, Maui. Your love of these descendants of worms has made you that way," his voice was curdling. "Now, I will end the Maui line forever."

The clubs came together with a deafening crack that could be heard kilometres away. Maui Atalaga leapt from the water into the air, evading a vicious sideswipe. Another crack of the mighty clubs rang out through the air, thick with hatred and fear. The folk hero rolled across the shallow water and splashed heavily as he gained his footing again.

The warriors stood apart, locked in an intense gaze. Seawater glistened from the muscled and tattooed body of Maui Atalaga, his face an expression of fierce concentration. Havea, having barely moved from his original position, stood inexorable. His breathing had become slightly laboured, unaccustomed to missing opponents with his powerful blows of deadly consequences.

There was no movement between the two combatants. There was no movement between the companions who held their breath, between the ten thousand imperial soldiers who looked on in fascination, or between the princes who glared in anticipation. There was a chilling stillness between the villagers of men, women and children who looked on from the distant shores of Tongatapu. The sea breeze had ceased. The small waves that caressed the shores of Pangaimotu had halted and it seemed the very movement of the clouds above had paused.

The only motions in space and time were the droplets of water over sinew, rolling down their faces and bare bodies; the stream of red that seeped slowly from Maui Atalaga's gaping chest wound; and the trembling rancour that emanated between the eyes of the legendary warriors. Maui Atalaga's brown eyes were a shuddering illustration of absorption and deliberation. Havea's pitiless black eyes were reflected nothing, save his all consuming desire for cruelty and death.

"AAA-YAHHHHH!" Maui Atalaga bellowed a guttural war cry that pierced the silence like the shattering of a thousand celestial stars.

Havea's gaze melted into a cringe of wicked laughter as both warriors moved together against the moments of frozen time. The spatter of water made by Maui Atalaga as he ran towards Havea rose like a cloak of magnificence. It parted, as if to give way to the incredible propulsion. A third crack of wood on wood snapped with a tremendous sound, as Havea parried Maui Atalaga's thrust. Shark's teeth smashed and burst skyward from the impact. Within a fraction of a second, Maui Atalaga maintained his forward movement following the parry and struck Havea in the chest with his shoulder. It caused the giant warrior to break his stance and shift awkwardly to the side. As he did, he allowed the sudden impact of his body to help force a counter attack to Maui Atalaga behind his position.

The giant club hurtled through the air but found no mark. His arm overextended and pulled him off balance: Maui Atalaga was not standing where he thought he was. Mohemamahi did not stop downwards as it drove through Havea's elbow with a sickening crunch. Before the club of sharks teeth even touched the ground, Havea's skull exploded in a pink mist of obliteration. Maui Atalaga's almighty blow sent particles of Havea's head and brains cascading across the beach. All who watched on blinked and expelled a long breath that had been held for almost a minute. Perhaps the greatest duel of all time was finally over.

Adi and Pele jumped up uncontrollably and screamed with joy, tears rolling down their faces. Atiogie raised his broken club towards the sun and chorused a grand bellow of exultation. Emori leaned his weight on his spear and hung his head in relief, and Talatama and Whatonga showed their bold teeth in great laughter of elation. They embraced one another with the rest of the companions. The ten thousand imperial warriors raised their hands in the air and cheered with such climatic force and energy that they could be heard by people at the far end of Nuku'alofa.

Maui Atalaga was on a knee in silent reprieve. He looked down at Havea's body that was being gently rocked by the calm swell. Havea's shattered face had lost the expression of immorality. His black eyes were lifeless, his frightening cringe had faded and all that was left was an ugly, innocuous mask of a terror that had plagued mankind for too long. Blood, the colours of red tinged with black, seeped from the jagged mouth and eyes in what seemed to be the final moments of the great Havea.

"And so it ends," Maui Atalaga said as he stood.

"Farewell, brother." He looked out to sea, "I will be there walking among the stars in Pulotu soon. You have waited long, my fathers. I am coming home now. "

The hero walked slowly out to his tongiaki and pushed the craft to the depths before the companions had the chance to congratulate him. They rushed forward as the tongiaki floated swiftly out to sea.

"Maui Atalaga!" Pele shouted, as she and the others waded into the sea, "No..."

She reached out in anguish towards the man she loved but he did not look back. He gazed out east towards the open sea, adjusted the ropes and sails to catch the air current and smiled in contentment to be alone again on the open brine. Humanity could live again in peace and he could now return to the mystic land beyond the horizon. The nightmare of Havea and the Hikule'o line had ended.

Pele lowered her hands slowly, sank to her knees in the water and sobbed quietly. Talatama gently placed his hand on her head, gazing in the direction of the tongiaki that was now a speck on the fading vista.

"Good bye, Lord Maui."

Maui Atalaga, the last of the ancient heroes of Polynesian folk lore, was never seen again.

CHAPTER 71

The afternoon had grown old. A weary sun lingered in the west, slightly off the horizon, barely colouring the fading sky. Heketa glowed with hundreds of burning torches that shimmered through the village and the royal compound. The outdoor court area was bordered with a stunning selection of trees and flowered shrubs. Lined to the head of the area, were giant totem poles carved with the images of Tangaloa, rising from between five and ten metres high. Adorned in the centre was the famous stone throne of Tu'itatui – 'Esi Makafakinanga.

The Makafakinanga lay within a rectangular mound, surrounded by dressed coral slabs. The slabs had been carefully chiselled to fit together into a neat border that rose only one foot above the ground. The backrest itself was a massive stone tablet, two and a half metres high and weighed almost four tonnes. At the foot of the backrest was a stone seat; two feet by two feet of solid rock and weighing about three hundred kilograms. Covered in flowing decorated tapa cloths, King Tu'itatui sat upon it with his back against the great rock.

Lined along the lengths of the court area were the same military leaders, political representatives, foreign chiefs and accompanying diplomats who had been present earlier in the Royal Hall. A great number of nobles from the outer villages were also present having heard of the recent battle and the attempt on the prince's life. The king's family, Lord Fasi'apule, Prince Talaiha'apepe and the beautiful Princess Fatafehi were beside the king as they beheld the warrior prince standing before them.

Talatama stood, presented to the king and council as he had been before, but in stark difference; he was haggard, covered in grime, dried blood and sand. The pungent smell of sweat and soiled men emanated from him and his companions, his headdress was lost and his long hair held together in clumps of matted mess. Makeshift tourniquets covered his recent wounds and were stained with red. His face was fatigued but contained a deeper strength of purpose. He reefed the wounded Kamohoali'i before the king. Kamohoali'i collapsed in a beaten heap.

"My King, again I present to you the murderer of thousands, the man who has conspired to murder you and precipitate the fall of the Empire. Kamohoali'i, General of the Pulotulahi," he breathed.

A great cheer erupted from the people. The proud faces of his friends and kin beamed with inspiration and his mentor, Fasi'apule, nodded towards him. Fatafehi, tears rolling down her cheeks, was filled with adoration. Lafa jumped up and down, clapping his hands. The companions assembled together behind the warrior prince, filled with a relieved finality and admiration for their leader.

"Kamohoali'i, your fate is sealed," King Tu'itatui said. "May the souls you've murdered finally rest in peace."

"Curse you, Tu'itatui. My legacy will live on. Neither you nor your brat son can change that," Kamohoali'i hissed.

"Toa! Take this filth from my sight!" the king boomed. "And this time, no infractions."

The leader of the king's personal guard stepped forward and whisked orders to a chosen plethora of imperial soldiers. They swarmed around the defeated general and shuffled him to his feet.

"Clear the way!" Toa shouted as he led his men and Kamohoali'i from the reception.

Tu'itatui stood from his stone throne and stepped down to his son, and placing his big hands on his shoulders, showed Talatama the pride in his eyes. He shared the moment with Talatama, one of conclusion, and as the torches flickered light across the old king's bushy beard, he nodded his head in acceptance. Talatama felt like a boy again, when his proud father would congratulate him on a play-fight well done.

"Talatama, you've managed to make this old man a very proud father. I could not have hoped for more fitful an ending."

"Ending, Father?"

"Now is the time that I must enlighten you of that decision I mentioned," he paused and suddenly gestured to all the onlookers, "In front of all these people."

"Your Majesty?" Talatama stepped forward.

King Tu'itatui faced all the nobles, military leaders and chiefs and cleared his throat. His voice was pure and powerful and it carried across the twilight of the entire compound.

"For the last few years I have been deliberating my purpose for our Empire. For so long during my early years, my purpose was so clear to me. I had my destiny laid out before me and I knew what had to be done."

"But for the last ten years I have felt my purpose waver. Wane from its natural path. I began to lose sight of my destiny and the purpose I was to accomplish. Then it came clear: though Tangaloa's purpose for me was a great one, I fulfilled it long ago and thus my purpose had been discharged."

"It became obvious to me that my son had his own destiny ahead of him. Years before Talatama was born, I bore children who died at birth, or as young children. When I was blessed with Talatama, I reserved my joy for fear of losing him as well. As the years passed, I realised I never grew close to him ..." he paused as he regarded his son with emotional eyes.

"While mine was finished, his was just beginning. I began to focus my energy on his growth and push for him to excel in all things. After he passed the stewardship he was offered, I knew he was a man of honour. I then promoted him to Commander of the Fourteenth Legion."

"In the past four years he has proved himself worthy as a Prince of the Empire. Over the last year, after learning integrity, perseverance, hardship and self-sacrifice, he has proven himself worthy as the King of the Empire."

A stunned wave of breaths swept through the court. Talatama stepped forward to his father with an expression of uncertainty.

"After today's events, they leave no doubt in my mind." Tu'itatui turned to his son with pride beaming from his eyes. "And there is no better time or place. At this very moment, I declare that I, King Tu'itatui abdicate from my thirty years as king. I step aside for the rise of my son, the new King of the Empire; his Majesty King Talatama!"

Following a brief pause, an ineffable applause erupted from the council, all those who heard the declaration, and of course, from his companions. Atiogie hooted and cheered at the top of his voice and threw a fist in the air, ignoring diplomats standing aghast close by. Vaohoi leapt in the air and reflected the Samoan's cheer by wrapping his arms around him with a face stretched with lines of joy and excitement. Pele beamed at the warrior prince, her eyes shining with respect and tempered joy. Adi and Emori exchanged jubilant expressions and embraced one another, while Lo'au and Whatonga cheered modestly, but clapped in delight.

"Tonight will mark the coronation of the new king, celebrations will abound!" Tu'itatui shouted, invoking more cheer.

"But, Your Majesty, the proper rituals? The formal coronation must be planned," Toutai ushered to the king.

"No. There is no time to waste. Tonight will be the coronation – in a celebratory night of feasting!"

Talatama smiled at his father and eyed the high priest warily. His suspicions of Toutai were growing greater. Toutai returned a distrustful glare to the prince before turning and disappearing through the wall of council members. He stood quickly and began to follow, but Tu'itatui caught him by the shoulder.

"Where are you going?" he was still brimming with elation. "We must discuss your future!"

"Father, I have my suspicions of Toutai being involved with the Pulotulahi."

"What?" the old king was taken aback, "Nonsense! I've known him for generations."

"But I—"

"I know he can be sharp-tongued and sinister at times, but his loyalty is unquestionable. Now go and get cleaned up for tonight. Understood?"

"Yes, Father."

"Tonight is the most important night of your life son," he smiled.

Talatama sat down by the sea, deep in thought. He could hear the distant commotion of townspeople in preparation for his coronation.

He sat perched on the Heketa rocks, the waves crashing softly below him. He had been washed and scoured, his wounds dressed and his body lacquered with sandalwood oil. But the dull pain of his old wound began to bite again. During the last battle, he had been struck close to it and it still ached. But no matter how clean his body or aggravated old wounds were he felt there was no solace to cleanse the inner turmoil that remained.

Kamohoali'i's defeat was a victory that yielded great rewards, however, the seed that he had planted in Talatama's mind could not be vanquished. It threatened the very future of his kingdom. He heard someone approach from behind but showed no sign: he knew well the cautious steps of his old friend, and newly discovered great-grandfather, Lo'au.

"Thinking again I see," the old mu'a sighed as he sat himself down.

"Mmm."

"You should be preparing for your big night."

Talatama gave him a tired smile, and gazed out again to the northern sea.

"It's not over, Lo'au."

"You've conquered your greatest enemy today. Enjoy your victories, Talatama. Your father taught you that."

"Have I? I feel as though I've felled the poisonous tree but its roots remain."

The old man chuckled, "You're beginning to speak in riddles. At last I've taught you something of philosophy."

"Kamohoali'i and Pele independently spoke of a Dark Lord, Tu'ipulotu." Talatama shifted his body to Lo'au. "Kamohoali'i said the Dark Lord's visions will live on. There's a greater power than Kamohoali'i, and if I don't find who it is, I'll never truly defeat this evil."

The old mu'a sighed and beheld the outstretched sea. He had come to admire the perseverance of the young warrior prince and his strength of will. Over the past year, he had watched him learn the valuable lessons of self-sacrifice, compassion, forgiveness and trust. He had fought by his companions in times of peril, stood by them in times of struggle and put their interests and safety before his. He had suffered personal loss, physical battery and public humiliation through the works of Kamohoali'i, yet still emerged, valiant, the victor.

"Prince Talatama, there is nothing more I can teach you," Lo'au said quietly.

"What do you mean?"

"You have been armed with all the traits, disposition and honour to aid you further. Your only teacher now is experience, your own path, life itself."

It was not the answer Talatama wanted to hear. He sighed and hung his head momentarily and was briefly reminded how fatigued he was. It was only the ardent furore in his mind that drove his body beyond its exhaustion, but he understood Lo'au's meaning. He knew that their paths could not be joined further. He was suddenly filled with a profound humility to have shared such intriguing adventures with him, albeit brief moments in time. He lifted his arm up and placed it on the shoulder of the old mu'a. He smiled widely and pulled him into an embrace.

"I'll not forget your words. Thank you, grandfather."

The celebration of the coronation carried into the night. Too short a time to prepare momentous feasting or prolonged ceremony, the coronation was casual and more akin to a celebration of a battle victory. Tu'itatui was insatiable in laughter, consumption and mood. He threw orders around lavishly, bellowing for more food, entertainment or kava. Talatama, now king, sat adorned in lavish ceremonial tapa. He was crowned with the imposing headdress of red feathers that hung down from his head to shoulder level.

"Bear the weight of the crown with pride and responsibility, my son," Tu'itatui stroked the red feathers, "So much blood has been spilt over it."

Tu'itatui seemed larger than life. He allowed himself to express his delights and indulge without much encouragement. Talatama knew his father had been restless the past few years and it was no secret that he had been grooming him for kingship. But for Tu'itatui not to invest the time to properly prepare a formal coronation was a puzzle.

Talatama neither wanted a pompous coronation nor yearned expressly to inherit the throne. Therefore had little opinion on how the coronation was to be carried out. But he did query himself as to the urgency of it. He surmised that his father was acting on impulse following his triumph, and thought it appropriate to crown him on such a victorious eve. But as he sat beside his father, torchlight flickering across his face, the melody of singing and dancing in the air, the buzz of loud conversation and cheers erupting from the five hundred distinguished guests, his thoughts relapsed to his woes.

Could Toutai the high priest, be Tu'ipulotu, the Dark Lord? He had little concept of how the leader of the Pulotulahi could infiltrate the Royal House for so long and win the trust of his father. If he were the high priest, what could he hope to gain from murdering the king or himself? Surely even if he were to gain power through force, the Empire would not accept a king or leader such as a high priest. The thought of him as the ruler did not fit, for he lacked the charisma for leadership. Talatama sighed. Perhaps it was not Toutai, but someone in the military arm of the Empire. He searched for clues in his mind.

Suddenly it hit him. The tapa parchment! The parchment he had obtained from the children in Niuatoputapu. Perhaps it contained more than Kamohoali'i's involvement, perhaps it gave a clue to Tu'ipulotu's identity!

"...and it is to him that I owe all my inspiration," Tu'itatui engaged all those around him, "Talatama, the king ... "

He turned and saw his son had vanished.

CHAPTER 72

Past the standing guard of more than a dozen warriors, Talatama rushed through the royal fale to his quarters. Laid carefully on the floor were his prized possessions – the broken Peace Maker and the Armour of Sangone. Both had been cleaned of the blood and sand, dried and polished. Next to them were his folded vala and tapa cloak, a new headdress and his girdles. Among the items he had placed together to avoid the servants care, were the whale bone dagger and the ivory ring that had belonged to Mahina. He momentarily forgot his purpose and picked up the ring, caressed it with his fingers and felt the pain of her loss that was still close.

Closing his eyes, he slowly brought the ring to his lips and kissed it, before placing it down to search through the assortment of items he had collected. He passed through it all quickly but there was no tapa parchment with the secret hieroglyphs. His heart sank as he rummaged through the items a second time, then a third. It was not there. Blood boiled to his head as he stood quickly, fuming. When was the last time he had held it? He presented it during his first audience with the king the day before. He remembered revealing it in support of Kamohoali'i's involvement with the Pulotulahi.

But it was Fasi'apule who had quickly changed the subject and re-directed the attention from it. Following that, he recalled placing it back into his garment where it remained during his father's verdict of Kamohoali'i's guilt. But he did not take the parchment to battle in the events that followed. He remembered noticing before battle that it was not on him. Did he give it to someone? Not likely. He could not have dropped it. The new king ran out of the fale and questioned every soldier he could find. He retraced his steps from the royal courthouse to where he was attacked, then down to the beach. It was nowhere to be found.

He stood in the torchlight of the royal compound, deliberating; if it was lost, then the only person who could shed light on it was the General of the Pulotulahi.

"Where are we holding Kamohoali'i?" he shouted to a nearby soldier.

Talatama ran past the main domiciles to the east of the compound. Across the battle pits were four wooden beams made of giant palm, standing twice the height of a man and were placed in a crescent moon shape. A few flamed torches illuminated the area from the darkness of the night. Kamohoali'i was slumped on his knees with his back against the centre beam, his arms and feet bound to the solid timber. The defeated General Va'iga was bound to another beam. Fifty warriors stood sentry in random positions around the captives, scrutinising anyone who approached.

Talatama breathed a sigh of relief and began to make his way over to the general. As he did, his father appeared from the other direction with an entourage of his bodyguards. Tu'itatui saw him immediately and motioned to him.

"There you are! I've been looking all over for you!"

"Sorry, Father, I needed to —"

Talatama saw movement in the corner of his eye and the warriors dropped into guard. When Talaiha'apepe appeared and moved straight to the dark general, the warriors eased. But before anyone could stop him, he raised an obsidian knife and swept it across Kamohoali'i's neck, then plunged it into his chest. Talatama shuddered forward too late.

"Talaiha'apepe!" he shouted in shock as he raced to his brother and snatched the knife from him.

Talatama tossed the weapon and grabbed the dying general by the shoulders, stemming the flow with one hand and shaking with the other to stay conscious.

"No, damn it! Who is Tu'ipulotu! Tell me!"

The fountain of blood pumped out of the deep wound and through Talatama's fingers, saturating his hands. Kamohoali'i's eyes rolled into his skull. He buckled to the ground and within seconds, he was dead. Alarmed murmurs echoed through the warriors as Tu'itatui strode to Talaiha'apepe and scorned him with greater shock than anger.

"Talaiha'apepe! That was not your duty to execute!" he shouted.

The prince glared at his father then at Talatama, his eyes filled with tainted rage and shame. He cursed loudly and pushed his way through the warriors. Silence echoed across the compound. Talatama remained totally overwhelmed.

"Guards!" Tu'itatui pointed. "Take the body and burn it with the rest of the dead."

"Wait, Father, give me a moment. You—" Talatama pointed to a warrior. "Go and fetch Pele. Bring her to me, hurry."

The new king then knelt down next to Kamohoali'i's body and searched through his clothing. The general was dressed in naught but a short vala.

"What are you doing, son?"

"Looking for something."

"He had been disarmed, Talatama." Tu'itatui moved closer.

The warrior prince hung his head after a thorough inspection. He slowly rose and cursed to himself.

"Nothing. There's nothing."

Pele came running with the companions. She hesitated when she saw her brother's corpse, and before kneeling down, she uttered something in a Hawaiian dialect. The companions huddled together and murmured among themselves.

"What happened?" Atiogie stepped next to Talatama.

"I'll tell you later," he approached the she-warrior. "Pele, I grant you the rights for his burial should you so choose."

"I do," she said, her voice a mere whisper.

Talatama nodded and motioned to the warriors before a number of guards swarmed around Kamohoali'i's body. With Pele, they removed it from the area. Tu'itatui shook his head and placed his hand on his son's shoulder. Talatama still frowned in the direction his brother had gone, his face mixed with confusion and astonishment.

"Talaiha'apepe took Kamohoali'i's betrayal as an embarrassment. Perhaps his actions are just as well," Tu'itatui mentioned.

"I'm shocked that he had it in him to kill a man."

"Don't let his actions take away from your efforts today, or the past few months."

"No, Father. It's – it's not that."

"Then what?"

"Sorry, Father, for now, I will take my leave of you. I'll see you back at the feast shortly."

Tu'itatui nodded and swiftly departed with his bodyguards.

"Talaiha'apepe just killed Kamohoali'i," he said as the companions formed around their new king.

"Good," Vaohoi jeered.

"Was there supposed to be a formal execution?" Adi asked.

"No different if he were killed today in the battlefield, I'd say," Emori added.

"No, it's nothing I suppose," Talatama looked over their faces, "Still, he was Pele's brother and we must respect her wishes, regardless of what has happened. She's vulnerable. Her father was killed a month ago, Maui Atalaga is gone and now her brother is dead. Be mindful of that."

The companions nodded solemnly.

"I think I lost the tapa cloth from Niuatoputapu today. I fear it's been stolen. Have any of you seen it?"

"What tapa cloth?" Whatonga frowned.

"No," many said simultaneously.

"But we don't need that anymore anyway," Atiogie said curiously.

Rather than trying to explain, Talatama remained silent. Perhaps he would never discover the true identity of Tu'ipulotu.

"Come, Your Majesty," Lo'au smiled. "There's still much celebrating to do tonight."

"But I have to—"

"Come on Talatama, we must get back to the feast," Atiogie pleaded.

"That's right, Your Majesty," Adi smiled.

The old mu'a took his great-grandson by the arm. "Mahina would want you to celebrate tonight, Talatama," he said. "Celebrate your coronation, our victory and the honoured memory of those lost in battle."

Pele emerged from the darkness to the circle of companions, walking alone and with a resolute stride. The king turned and faced her, in his eyes a glint of sympathy that only a warrior would give to a peer. She returned the silent stare then lowered her head as the companions mirrored a greater compassion.

"Thank you," she said.

Talatama nodded and placed his hand on her shoulder.

"Pele, I was just about to explain to the rest that I must find the tapa parchment that I lost. I need it or—"

"You – that is we...need to return to your coronation," she interrupted, "And enjoy our last night of feasting."

Talatama paused and glanced at his companions. Vaohoi exploded in a burst of laughter and the others joined in contagiously. Atiogie struck Talatama square in the back and Pele frowned to him. The king took a reconciled sigh, abandoning his qualms momentarily. The relief visibly lifted from his shoulders. He raised his head and broke into a warm smile towards his companions. He beckoned Whatonga, Pele and the others to him. The group of them huddled together and embraced.

"Never shall a fellowship like ours end, never shall it fade, never shall it be forgotten," he whispered to them all as they shared the moment together and imparted the respect and affection they had for one another.

"Alright, alright, get off me you oafs." Pele shoved away.

King Talatama and his companions returned to the royal festivities and shared the rewards with each other. Amid the firelight, Atiogie exploded in thunderous laughter and Vaohoi joked and teased. Under the moon and stars, Lo'au and Emori cheered and toasted to the brave moments they had spent together. Over the greatest cuisine the Empire could provide, Adi cherished the memories of their comrades lost along the road. Among the greatest of friends, Pele acknowledged and understood the individual choices they had made throughout the adventure to be righteous and just. In the end, the last moments together as their famous fellowship were treasured by all.

They never shared company again.

PART 4

CHAPTER 73

Ngatangi'ia, Rarotonga
Autumn, A.D.1122

Evening had set in. The teardrop islands of Motutapu, Oneroa and Koromiri sat upon a glassy ocean beyond the mainland. Pushed from the sea, the Ngatangi'ia Mountains reared in spectacular power and beauty. The lush green forests cloaked her back and kissed the sandy shores of the Rarotongan capital. The turquoise water lapped softly on the shore, reflecting the brilliant firelight that spotted as far as the eye could see.

Across the winds were scents of flowers and roasted meat and drums sounded through the cheers and song. Hundreds of Rarotongans milled carefully around the royal seating area, as Lord Toi stood from amongst the dignitaries and approached the people eager to hear their leader's voice.

"Hear me!" he roared. "Hear me!"

A line of warriors either side of the old warrior brought conches to their lips. The deafening and haunting howl of the conches trumpeted across the waters and out to sea, and the shouts and laughter subsided. The music ceased immediately. The entire bay fell silent.

"Hear me," Lord Toi began. "For thirty years I have ruled our heavenly home of Rarotonga. For thirty years I have sought to provide only the best opportunities for my people. Throughout this time I made decisions on behalf of my family for our protection and in order to secure our future. But the road has not always been clear, nor straight," he paused, "Nor easy."

There was no sound but the distant murmur of night insects and the lapping of the calm waves.

"My passion for the sea, like every son of Rarotonga, was the focus and spearhead of these ambitions. Twenty-five years ago, I was appointed as one of four chief commanding navigators of the Empire. I served as General Punake's right hand and conquered from the eastern ocean to the great deserts beyond it. We reaped honour and glory like nothing ever imagined.

"Following this, I returned home and focused my energy into my people and family. I am honoured to have lived as long as I have, and to have lived to see my son, Prince Whatonga become a great man."

A thunderous cheer erupted from the people, before Lord Toi raised both hands to them, silencing their applause.

"But following the death —" he paused, "Following the death of my wife and daughter, and the mourning of their passing, I have been struck anew with a thirst for adventure and discovery! This, of course brings us here together today in preparation for the voyage.

"So without further ado, it is my greatest honour to present the honourable, mighty, His Majesty King Talatama!"

A great roar and clapping of hands rifled through the crowd as Lord Toi stepped aside to Talatama, who stood from his seat. Accompanying him was Princess Fatafehi, her beauty dazzling all as she clung to her brother's arm timidly. To the king's right was Mateitau, his great captain and friend. Following the Battle of Heketa, the king had named him, 'Mateitau Seven Lives', following his consistent luck in avoiding death in battle. To the king's left was the mighty Toa, former bodyguard to King Tu'itatui. As a special guest accompanying the king, was the legendary General Ngongo who stood staunch and proud.

"Thank you, Lord Toi." Talatama gazed across the hundreds of faces in the crowd. "First and foremost, I wish to present the Empire's greatest warrior and general: General Ngongo."

The old man stood and raised his hands to the welcoming people.

"I asked that the General be here with us today for our celebration. For he is the last remaining man to have returned from Aotearoa. Thank you, General Ngongo," the king smiled and motioned for him to return to his seat.

"Now, I wish to share a short prayer my father, King Tu'itatui, used to pray before setting out to the great ocean. He believed it brought him the favour of the gods and much luck.

'Oh mighty Tangaloa hear me and heed my words,
Forever can I hear her calling, the distant lands beyond the horizon,
And the yearning to seek that which cannot be described beneath the
waves,
I cannot suppress the desire to tame your untamed ocean,
Strengthened by the fervour of adventure running through my veins,
And the support of my proud people destined to live eternal across the
seas,
For I fear not the sun nor the sea, nor the stark horizons which hide
golden treasures,
And if we perish before our time is through, let the sea take me back to
her loving womb ... '

"I bless the tongiaki and brave men who are about to embark on this great journey. You go with the hearts and minds of the Tongan people."

When the king stepped back and the people saw he had finished, they rose in a cheer of respect and admiration. He gave a quick nod and smile towards Lord Toi and Prince Whatonga before retiring for the evening.

"Your Majesty!" Whatonga stood. "Where are you going? We've only just begun with the festivities."

"It's time for me to retire, good Prince."

"Here," Whatonga jogged to catch him. "Let me join you."

The two walked along the calm shores of Ngatangi'ia. Mateitau and Toa followed, but allowed a good distance between them. The king and prince strolled past the forty great tongiakis that lay moored, prepared to depart on the voyage at first light. A slight breeze blew across their faces and teased their hair.

"Is something the matter, Your Majesty?" Whatonga peered at Talatama.

"This place ..." the king breathed, "it is filled with the memory of Mahina. I have never been here before but I can feel her sprit here."

"I understand," Whatonga nodded slowly.

The Rarotongan prince had only come to learn of their true love following her death. Although he had heard much of their time together, albeit short lived, Whatonga knew enough to understand that their spiritual connection was powerful and their love deep. The thought of his late sister tugged at his own grief as he pointed over to the water.

"She used to like swimming there as a young girl."

Talatama remained silent as he stared at the water between the mainland and Motutapu. In his mind's eye, he saw the image of a young Mahina playfully swimming with other children. They frolicked in the iridescent water, splashing each other, their laughter echoing across the calm beach. Her face was the same but younger, her beautiful green eyes glimmered in the sunlight, her smile as alluring as it had always been. Her image paused from her play and turned to him. She looked straight at him, through his very eyes. The king shuddered.

"Prince Whatonga, I can no longer remain here. I wish you the best of luck with your journey."

"Your Majesty?"

Talatama grasped Whatonga's forearm and brought him close.

"I – I loved Mahina beyond words – "

"I know."

"- and this place stabs at my heart, Whatonga I cannot stay."

Mateitau and Toa readied themselves when they noticed Talatama turn briskly back towards his quarters. He gave them a short glance.

"We leave immediately. Set a course for Tonga."

Two weeks later, a sunset over the island of Foa in the Ha'apai Islands cast across the sky. Twilight had begun, hazing the late air that seemed to give it dry warmth. The sky was a scattered design of washed velvet with streaks of tangerine. Across the green knoll flowed a tepid breeze, caressing it gently with the promise of a pleasant evening. Atop the knolls that were just beyond the village of Faleloa, were two freshly dug mounds. The earth was a deep auburn, the rich kind that promoted healthy vegetation. Its texture was crumbled and shaped into the rough lengths of men. In the centre of the mounds was posted a three-foot bamboo rod. Its centre was filled with tapa cloth, laced with oil. Its tip burned with a thick yellow flame that cast a strong light over both mounds of soil.

Alone and without ceremony, Pele knelt down in front of the two mounds that were the resting place of her father and brother. She closed her eyes and whispered a prayer to the gods for the great Alama, Chieftain of Ha'apai and the son of Wakea, the great navigator. She asked that the gods join his spirit with Wakea's in the land of eternal rest. Her prayer for Kamohoali'i was one of indifference. She prayed that the evil god Hikule'o grant him favour in the underworld for his unwavering dedication, that which ultimately cost him his life. Her thoughts then went to her own faults and actions when she followed his leadership.

"You'll have to wait longer before you deal with me Hikule'o," she murmured.

Standing in the distance, was a small band of men just beyond the end of the rolling knolls. They were warriors grouped together, their long shadows thrown across the land. Their imperial attire and fine make of tapa flapped gently in the twilight breeze as they watched on. The man in the centre stood stern and foreboding, his arms were across his chest, and though he watched her intently, he occasionally lowered his gaze to the hills. They remained for hours as she lamented, patient, respectful and steadfast. She finally rose and slowly approached them. When she reached their position, she bowed to the King of the Empire.

Talatama and Pele walked down by the north beach of Foa. The white sand dusted across the waterfront and disappeared into aqua sea. Occasional coral shelves jutted from the beach that provided streaks of grey and green across the coast. The soft sound of the lapping waves on the shore was peaceful.

"I never thought it would come to this." The she-warrior gazed out to the open sea.

"Nor I," the king returned.

"When I was young, all I wanted was to make my father and brother proud. Alama was a great teacher. He taught me everything about life."

"He was respected by many."

"I was a little girl when he used to take me down to the beach here and tell me stories about the majestic islands of Hawai'i. My grandfather, Wakea, discovered Hawai'i and countless other islands."

"Tu'itatui spoke highly of Hawai'i. He visited there once with your father before we were born," Talatama said kindly.

"Yes, Alama told me. It was the last time he returned there," she paused. "See here."

Pele pointed to petroglyphs etched in nearby coral shelves. Talatama observed there were dozens of symbols and carvings all about the area, portraying the shapes of animals such as pigs, dogs and turtles, and men.

"He carved these etchings to tell a story. But I tend to think he carved them so that we children, never forgot our wandering spirits," she paused, "That we carve our history into the rock wherever we voyage. Even though he called Ha'apai home, his heart lay out there, beyond the horizon."

Talatama lowered his eyes to the ground and although he knew where the conversation was going, he understood her meaning despite his disappointment.

"It's time for me to embrace that heritage." She turned to him with conviction.

"I was hoping that you would come with Lord Fasi'apule and me. At dawn we're sailing to Viti Levu for Adi and Emori's wedding," he extended nonetheless.

Pele smiled and looked into Talatama's chestnut eyes with femininity rarely expressed.

"Goodbye, Talatama."

She moved and embraced him, as the king returned her affection, holding her strongly. Their relationship an ever change of seasons; respected enemies to trusted companions. Twilight had died and the moon had risen as shadows crept across the darkened coasts of Ha'apai. Talatama's footprints in the sand led away from the beach unaccompanied.

CHAPTER 74

Nausori Highlands, Fiji

Just after noonday, the three imperial tongiakis sailed up the mouth of the great Rewa River. They docked at the small village of Nausori where the tributary diverted inland. The small estuary could only be navigated by river craft provided by the Degei. For long kilometres, the imperial delegation had weaved up through the narrow waterway. The untamed jungle of Viti Levu was a perpetually thick haze of vibrant green on all sides. When the river boats had been set to shore, the delegation continued on foot, following a thin path into the heart of the forest. Brightly coloured parrots squawked overhead and giant blue butterflies littered the air.

For an hour, the delegation had made their way along the high and treacherous mountain path that led higher and higher into the northern Nausori Highlands. Deep jagged chasms yawned around them as they left the humid jungle below. As they rose higher it became noticeably cooler and the buzzing sounds of insects were left far behind. Occasionally, the path offered breathtaking views down the Rewa River to the Pacific Ocean beyond. The trail of black sea-stones wound and twisted, as it rose higher and higher to its peak until the very tops of the Nakombalevu Mountains loomed overhead. The delegation had followed it around a precarious and narrow edge to receive the reward of the climb.

Before them were the two ancient vesi trees that stood proud at the entrance to the mountain glade. The glade, atop the summit of one of the mountain peaks, had been a sacred location for hundreds of years. Its position was enchanting, shouldered by the surrounding mountains that rose majestically, random vesi trees of ancient age and occasional menhirs clothed in green moss. The giant timber totems etched with the Degei symbols marked the glade as consecrated, hallowed by all who visited.

Though on this day, they were decorated with the flowers and flowing sheets of tapa signifying the union of marriage. Beautiful arrangements of ferns, flowers and oceanic jewellery adorned the small fale in the centre of the glade. Its four short beams of ironwood that supported the thatched roof had been entwined with leis of frangipanis. In the four corners of the fale remained the red clay pottery of ancient Lapita design and inside of each, burned the sweet scent of oil and crushed heilala flowers.

The imperial delegation was certainly not the first to arrive as they entered the glade. The area was filled with people. Dozens of Degei priests, draped in their ritual attire, stood stoically about the area. Fijian chiefs and their entourages made up most of the guests, though there were few foreign visitors. The herald announced the arrival of the imperial delegation and all guests ceased their conversations and bowed low.

King Talatama and Lord Fasi'apule walked ahead of their accompanying sixty imperial warriors. They were robed in an impressive combination of regal style and military practicability. Their long black cloaks draped over their armour and their muscular bodies were adorned with precious gauntlets, girdles necklaces and rings. The Sangone Armour gleamed with brilliance under the fine material worn by the king, which procured curious onlookers.

The first to approach the king and his men was the Samoan delegation. Father and son walked together heading the group, the aged and blind, Lord Feepo, and the mighty Atiogie. The groups came together warmly, exchanging cheerful greetings. Atiogie embraced the king like a brother, wrapping his huge arms around Talatama and almost lifting him off the ground. Lord Feepo smiled as he heard his son's show of affection in public. Talatama slapped the giant on the back with a laugh.

"Where's Pele?" Atiogie asked.

Talatama's grin turned solemn and he shook his head.

"Talatama!" Vaohoi appeared from nowhere and jumped at the king.

Talatama laughed as he squeezed the boy in his arms before releasing him to swipe the back of his head.

"Are you keeping out of trouble?"

"No." The youngster frowned as the king returned the suspicious look with a smirk.

"Did Prince Whatonga come?" Vaohoi peeped.

"He couldn't make it back from Ngatangi'ia in time. He's coming through Tonga next moon."

The king went to explain more but his attention was taken by a group of Fijian chiefs who came to greet him. One of the first to be introduced was an old warrior who walked with the assistance of a cane.

"Greetings, King Talatama." He bowed. "I am Chief Naulatikau. I was a friend of your grandfather, King Momo."

"Honourable Chief Naulatikau," Talatama smiled. "You served as a Fijian Warlord during the time of the Empire's Great Expansion."

"Yes that is right." The old chief smiled bearing a mouth of but a few teeth. "I was with the western armies that breeched the Majuroan Kingdoms with General Manusiu."

"Sadly," Talatama's face darkened, "Manusiu died recently. He went to Pulotu with his club in hand."

Grief struck the old warlord's face immediately as his old eyes welled with tears. A Fijian warrior at his side, perhaps his grandson, Talatama thought, placed his hand on Naulatikau's shoulder.

"I'm sorry," the king said softly.

"No, no." Naulatikau wiped the tears from his eyes. "He and I shared many battles and victories together. May he finally rest in peace."

Talatama nodded solemnly before another Fijian chief bowed respectfully to him and then another. Lord Fasi'apule remained at the king's side as they both engaged in formal conversation.

"Honoured guests, on behalf of the Degei Order I welcome you all," an ancient Fijian priest drew everyone's attention.

"For those of you whom I have not had the pleasure of meeting, I am Nakaunicina, Grandmaster of the Degei and I will be presiding over this most glorious ceremony today," he smiled as he stood before a single stone step that led onto the shrine. As he spoke, the guests from around the enchanted glade drew closer to the small shrine in the centre. Within the shrine, the guests could see Adi and Emori standing together facing the people.

"Today is an especially personal day for me, not only because my grandson, Emori, is being married, but also because he's chosen one of our cherished priestesses in the Order; the beautiful Adi.

"For years I have watched their love grow and their dedication to each other become stronger. Eight months ago, they both faced the biggest challenge in their relationship. Adi was charged with starting a temple in faraway Niuatoputapu. This took them apart, and only through the honour of the Order did they submit to our religious calling."

"But as time eternal has taught us, love has no boundaries and so Emori searched for his love across the seas. He found her and discovered she was in peril, and with the aid of others, saved her from a terrible fate." Nakaunicina smiled to the king.

"So despite his choice to forsake his post here in Viti Levu, I have forgiven him in light of his valour. And without further ado, I will hand over to the Master of Ceremonies – High Priest of Tangaloa, Lo'au."

Lo'au stepped forward between Adi and Emori, gowned in the traditional robes of the Tangaloa priest. The material and colour was as remarkable and its design was regal. His whale ivory, shell and obsidian medallion assembled in the image of the sun, the crescent moon and tavakes in flight, hung gently over his robes, and beneath his beard he showed his strong teeth as he spoke. His voice was warm and full of wisdom.

"Honoured guests, you are here today to witness, and partake in, the celebration of matrimony between two special people. The joining of two people in marriage has important spiritual significance. It will bind their dedication to one another and the love they share with each other."

"As I am a High Priest of Tangaloa, as a Master of Ceremony at a Degei wedding, I shall make this unlike both typical religious ceremonies. After all, the celebration of marriage is about love and devotion, not differing faiths."

Lo'au turned to Adi. She was covered in her auburn drapes that flowed elegantly onto the shrine. Her hair was braided with striking white hibiscus flowers and her face was moist with sandalwood oil that emboldened her bronzed skin. Her lips were full and her eyes sparkled with a reflection of sincerity that so typified her personality.

He then turned to Emori. He was adorned in the Degei warrior-priest garments complete with embellishments that displayed his high rank. His hair was worn high and proud from his head with streaks of oil wetting parts of it. His dark, wiry frame threw shadows across his defined musculature, face and jaw line.

The great teacher, Lo'au, turned to the guests and captured their attention with his echoing voice of wisdom.

"All life is struggle. Every living thing in the world, men, animals, and plants struggle to survive by their very existence. We must hunt to eat, we must eat to gain strength, we must have shelter to rest and we must fight others to protect our lives. We live in violent and chaotic times. Life can be the measure of a mere moment, a shifting mood or it can be the difference between guidance and ignorance. Life can be taken in the breath of a word."

"By its very meaning, mortality gives us clarity through these examples. Our moments on this earth are numbered. And whether by the edge of an enemy club or the slow decay of disease, we all perish and never again have our time on this earth. Never again will we feel the morning breeze touch and caress our faces. Never again shall we feel warm sand between our toes, nor savour the sweet smell of fragrant flowers. Never again shall we bear witness to a glorious sunrise, nor hear the tranquil sound of a running river."

"Nor shall we ever experience the feeling of laughter with friends, the closeness between brothers, the honour between warriors, the respect between king and subject nor the reward for living life in truth or valour. But more importantly, never shall we experience the affection between lovers."

"For as cruel and brutal as this world is, life does grant us a few moments of happiness; that comes from our relationships between ourselves as a community, a people and nation. Community is the lifeblood from which our fulfilment derives – and from this develops the most powerful emotion of all – love."

"Love is like the sun that shines on all things, fills us with warmth, touches us all differently and is shared with many in people's lives. But it is the love for a spouse that enriches our lives like no other."

"Some things in life are more difficult to find than others; whale teeth, the vanishing hawks of 'Eua, black pearls of the eastern ocean. Someone who loves you with the utmost affection and devotion, who reflects the burning desire that will not smoulder over time, who will love you and no other, who would sacrifice anything for you, who would die for you."

"What greater gift can someone receive? What more can someone ask in their lifetime than to have someone who is willing to do those things as a reflection of their love? In our world, one needs but to have this love to consider themselves wealthy. To have this suddenly makes the rest of the dark things in life seem irrelevant, and it gives us the ability to rise above the cruelty and pain by keeping guard of the solace within."

"You see, the love I speak of has no boundaries, no rules and no master. It represents an ethereal bond between the two people that cannot be severed. It cannot be taken away, possessed by others or quashed. Even beyond death, the bond can never be broken."

The guests were moved to silence as they gathered. A tear rolled down Talatama's face and his chin seized.

"Do you both, Emori, grandson of Nakaunicina and, Adi, daughter of the Degei, understand and acknowledge that which you both feel for one another? And will you forever respect and value that which is the most pure of all gifts?"

"I do, and will," Emori said proudly.

"I do, and will," Adi's eyes welled with tears of joy.

"And to all those who witness, show Emori and Adi that your support shall guide and protect that which is their gift to one another?"

A haughty cheer rose from the smiling faces of all who watched on.

"Then let us celebrate the formal union of your love!" Lo'au burst into a great smile.

The guests erupted in a cheer of whistling applaud and shouts of approval rung out with clapping. The Fijians broke into a merry song filled with soulful voices and spirited energy. Overflowing with emotion, Emori reached out and swiftly embraced his wife. He lifted her off the wooden floor of the shrine and they broke into laughter of joy. As their lips met, they invited more cheer and jubilation from family and friends.

Fires were lit in the designated fireplaces enclosed with river stones, and steaming food that had been prepared beyond the glade was brought out by scores of local Fijian villagers. Celebratory music filled with voice, drum and pan pipes echoed from the glade across the deep valleys and chasms. The moon rose in the early evening, accompanied by a handful of stars that haloed the peaks of the majestic mountains. The guests of close family, friends and those of the Degei Order were seated comfortably and treated to the highest hospitality.

The night air was warm, even at the altitude of the glade. After tending to the welcoming of the guests, Adi spotted Talatama standing alone beyond the ancient vesi tree and atop a rocky cliff.

The prince leaned over the edge of the crag and gazed up to a full and yellow moon. His heart trembled from Lo'au's words as he reached out and caressed the moon with his fingers. Mahina was the Polynesian word for *'moon'*, and as he reached out to her, he knew he could never touch her again. The ivory ring caught the moonlight, the etched illustration of birds trying desperately to evade giant octopus tentacles rising up from the sea, all so evident.

"My love, I know now what the motif on the ring means..." he shuddered, "Forever were you hunted, but now are you free."

He then pressed his hand against his moist eyes, and hearing Adi approach hastily wiped his face.

"Your Majesty!" Her face beamed as she embraced him.

"You look beautiful," he cuddled her like a sister.

"Talatama, you honour us with your presence. I was worried you wouldn't make it."

"My elevation to the throne doesn't impede me from those I hold dear," he smiled and nudged her.

"I'm glad the others could make it too, of course." She turned and laughed at Atiogie and Vaohoi at to their games by the firelight.

"I was thinking to ask you, did you discover what happened to that Degei captain who deserted you in Niuatoputapu?" the king frowned.

"Duvuduvukulu? Yes, he returned to the Order in Nausori and lied that I had been killed in an accident."

"Humph."

"You can imagine his surprise when the truth was revealed. He was banished from the order, humiliated and shamed."

"A lucky outcome for him. In Tonga he would have been slain."

"Lucky for me, someone saved me back in Niuatoputapu," she smiled to Emori as he joined them and embraced Talatama.

"So what now for you two?" the king smiled.

"We want to start a family," the stole a look to one another, "One of the greatest lessons we've learned during our adventures is, as Lo'au said, we must make the most of every moment. Cherish every day with one another. So we want to have children as a representation of our love."

"You both have my blessing and the blessing of my family." Talatama's teeth shone as he smiled in the moonlight. "What of the Order?"

"We will remain devout and lend our services when we can," Adi said.

"I have land in Nausori where I will build our fale. It is not far from the Bure Kalou of Degei where we can worship."

"I am so very happy for you both -" Talatama put his hands on their shoulders.

"Your Majesty," Lord Fasi'apule interrupted. "May I have a word? It is urgent."

"Certainly," Talatama frowned as he walked away from the married couple.

Lord Fasi'apule led the king over to the entrance of the glade where they could be alone. A dire look reflected in his eyes.

"Talatama, I have received urgent news from the capital."

"What is it?" Talatama flinched. "Is it the Pulotulahi?"

"No. Your father has gone missing."

"What?"

"The runner brought this news in haste," Lord Fasi'apule motioned to a young Fijian boy out of breath, and standing by the totem pole. "Your father has been missing for a few days."

"What else does he say?"

"Princess Fatafehi and the rest of the family are extremely anxious. They're expecting the worst. They call for your return."

"Assemble the men. We leave at once," Talatama said.

As the king strode to his companions to advise them of his departure, Lord Fasi'apule glared down at the Fijian boy and grabbed his chin.

"Say nothing of 'Eua to the king or anyone else, do you understand?" He clenched his teeth in seriousness. "And make sure no one else says anything either. Your life depends on it."

"Yes, Milord," the boy stammered.

CHAPTER 75

Island of 'Eua

At the southern end of 'Eua, was a distinctive landscape of rolling fields. Devoid of trees or jungle, it was instead dotted with numerous rock formations. The coral limestone protruded from the ground in strange arrangements. Standing tall and silent, they overlooked the outstretched southern ocean. At the edge of the field was a sheer drop of fifty metres down to crashing waves. It was an outstanding view. Elevated at some points eighty metres above sea level, sights could be taken virtually in all directions.

In addition to the area being one of beauty and amazement, it had also been a famous location for duels. For one hundred years, the grassy fields had laid witness to countless duels between brave warriors from across the Pacific. It seemed to carry memories of the fallen as one looked across the rolling fields and felt the cool touch of the sea wind.

The noonday sun blanketed the island of 'Eua. As in most areas of the island, it enjoyed a much cooler climate than the mainland of Tonga due to its elevation. The fresh winds swept up from the cliffs and swirled about the grassy fields. A group of a hundred villagers gathered around a saddle in the earth, where two warriors stood. Bound together with a length of rope tied at the wrist, they engaged each other in quick attacks. As in most duels, they tested each other, looking for weaknesses or flaws in one another's ability. Onlooking villagers, as was the custom, remained deathly silent as they watched.

Then in an instant, it was over. Koula, an enormous man with a wild appearance, rocketed his club down onto the chest of his adversary with a crushing thud. The warrior fell to the ground clutching at his sternum, gasping for air and writhing in pain as the villagers exploded in cheer. Having agreed with his adversary the duel was not to the death, Koula untied the rope from his hand and raised his arms in triumph. He was a local hero to the villagers of 'Eua, not for his compassion for his people, but for his dominance in the duel arena.

Koula was a young man of about twenty-two years, standing at almost seven foot tall and weighing close to one hundred and sixty kilograms. His long and haggard hair covered an ugly face; eyes that did not look in the same direction, a huge bulbous nose and patchy facial hair that were outdone by protruding and crooked teeth. His unsightly appearance made him seem older than his age, and certainly did not hinder him in the duel arena. Even so, in only two years, he had attained a successful record as a warrior in duels and had recently celebrated his first year as champion. Many young scallywags and degenerates had formed a gang around him and used his popularity to push their weight around. Across the island of 'Eua, over the past year, they had soon become a feared group.

Koula swaggered to his large group of supporters and revelled in their praise. The young larrikins chanted his name as they threw their arms in the air, apprising anyone who would dare oppose the victory.

"That was a disappointing match. I saw no skill involved whatsoever," came a strong voice from the crowd.

When the comment was not heard, he stepped forward and raised his voice over the clamour of celebration.

"You might as well cheer over stepping on an ant, fools."

Koula's supporters fell silent. Standing ahead of the crowd was an old man, large and well built for his age, and dressed in an old vala and a tattered tapa gown. His grey hair was a mess of untamed frizz and his beard was tousled.

"What did you say, old man?" one of the troublemakers piped.

"Disappointing and pathetic, I said."

"Watch what you say, old timer," Koula said.

"I've not seen you around these parts. You must be new to 'Eua," the troublemaker continued. "In these parts, Koula holds the title of the duel plains."

"Koula possesses nothing but the stench of his own hide."

"Last chance, old man," the Koula leered. "Be gone, before I lose my patience."

"And then what, you'll fight me? Excellent. If you're the champion, I could see nothing more fitting."

"You've a death wish I see! I challenge you to a duel, you old fool!" the degenerate shouted, as he stepped in front of Koula and his gang.

"You? You're an insect, but it will warm me up I suppose."

"You old bastard!"

"No lessons. Rules are, duel to the death," the old man said.

The troublemaker suddenly hesitated. Although his co-degenerates and supporters cheered him on, he suddenly felt the chill of the risk he was taking. Like most cowards, his words were greater than his backbone. The old man threw off his tapa cloak and revealed an awesome club with impressive carvings and designs. People in the crowd gasped at its remarkable make, and an abrupt wave of doubt swept over the villagers and Koula's gang. Even a fool could see that such a club could not belong to a worthless old man. People eyed the stranger warily.

"No rope. Come," the old man beckoned as he stepped into the depression of the grassy fields.

The young degenerate's breath was rapid as his mind raced with a mixture of his own fear and insults to his pride. He wanted to prove his worth to Koula and the gang, that he could back his words. He would show them by killing the old man and sporting his precious club.

He shuffled forward, letting out his best attempt at a ferocious cry.

The old man leapt back then stepped forward quickly. He swept his club at the larrikin's knee and as the youngster moved to block the attack, the old man changed his direction. The club connected to the young man's jaw with a crack, sending him stumbling. The next swing struck the larrikin to the side of the head, producing a crunching sound as blood exploded from his nose, mouth and eyes. Were the strike of greater force, the larrikin's head would have come clean off. His body slumped to the red spattered grass. As the crowd gasped in utter shock, the old man stood back and closed his eyes. He breathed through his nose and exhaled from his mouth, whispering as though gratified by taking a life.

"You old bastard, you'll pay for that," Koula growled as he stepped down into the depression and the gang dragged out the body.

"Good," the old man laughed, still revelling in the fresh kill. "This is what I want."

"You have it," Koula grasped his own club. "Same rules."

"I would not fight otherwise," the old man regarded the young warrior with a strange contemplation.

The champion ignored the cryptic talk and launched with inconceivable speed as the old man stepped back, adapting to the level of aggression. The clubs cracked off each other as he parried. He remained defending against the younger and stronger warrior, weaving, ducking and clashing. The old man's example of his gang member had enraged Koula and had provoked all his skill and fury. Witnessed by dozens of onlookers, his reputation was now at stake; a reputation that had taken him years to build. For all the benefits it provided for him and his gang, he was not about to have a crazy old fool mar it.

Strangely, as the old man perspired under the relentless attacks, his mind and spirit were elsewhere. Times of old battles fought on distant lands and reliving the times of his youth came back to him. The reflection on his face was almost that of pleasure. Inspired by his memories, he broke from defending and swept for Koula's knee. The young warrior shifted and guarded his head. He would not fall from the same trick as his friend. But the old man did not feint. The great club smashed into the warrior's knee with a snap.

Koula screamed in rage.

"Thus my name became widespread," the old man smirked, "If you don't have knees, you cannot stand!"

The old man retreated with a grin across his perspiring face, though his joy was not through the infliction of pain to Koula, but through the delight of the combat itself. The young warrior ignored the pain and limped forwards, attacking again. Imbued with a wild fury like nothing he had previously experienced, Koula pummelled at the old man relentlessly. The old man could not maintain a defence against such carnal aggression, and as he raised his club in defence he caught his fingers between the powerful clash. The bones in his hands shattered like clay pottery. Then with one hand, he weakly held his club high in a last valiant effort to protect himself. There was no fear in the old man's eyes; there was only contentment and fulfilment, a finality that he had been waiting so long for.

With both hands, Koula brought his club down with every ounce of his great strength.

The imperial fleet of five great tongiakis glided around the Kanokupolu point on Tongatapu's western shores. The two lead vessels moved along side to another, as their leaders shouted out over the gap of choppy sea.

"Will you not accompany us to Heketa?" Talatama yelled.

"No, Your Majesty. I've an urgent matter I must attend to in Malapo! I'll meet you in the capital as soon as I can!" Lord Fasi'apule shouted and waved back to Talatama before turning to his Fijian helmsman.

"Pull back, and allow the king to take the lead."

The sea wind was strong, propelling their crafts across the glittering brine with impressive speed. In short moments, the king and his two accompanying tongiakis disappeared around the

Manuka headland. Instead of turning into the lagoon to his home village of Malapo, Lord Fasi'apule pulled sails and drifted his tongiaki just off the island of Oneata. When the king's vessels were long from sight, he turned to his helmsman.

"Set a course for 'Eua."

When Talatama had told his companions of the dire news, it took all his persuasion to have them stay at the wedding ceremony and continue with the celebration. Atiogie and Vaohoi were especially fervent to accompany their king. When they finally conceded to his wishes, they promised to meet him in Heketa a couple of days after.

The king strode into the royal compound with his accompanying warriors.

"Talatama!" A tearful Fatafehi rushed to embrace her brother.

"Alright, it's alright," he reassured her. "What's the latest news?"

"It is Father – he's missing..."

"Leave us," the king tipped his head to his warriors who left them in the royal garden.

"What happened, sister?" Talatama grabbed both her shoulders.

"The day after you left last week – he, he just disappeared," she sobbed.

"Where is Talaiha'apepe?"

"He's here in the compound," she paused, "But Talatama – he's... he's a changed man. I know you haven't spoken to him since he killed Kamohoali'i."

Talatama raised an eyebrow.

"It's as though he just doesn't care anymore."

"Nonsense," he growled and turned to the guards. "Talaiha'apepe? Someone fetch me his hide!"

"Did Father say anything – anything before he disappeared?"

"No. He was happy, Talatama. I haven't seen him that happy since we were children."

The king cursed to himself. He recalled thinking it odd that Tu'itatui rushed the coronation in such an informal manner. He had been acting strangely the last few years and something had changed within him that he had not divulged to anyone. As he churned through the probabilities, Prince Talaiha'apepe appeared through the royal fales. He walked sluggishly and bore an ill look. Talatama gritted his teeth and grabbed his brother by the neck.

"I leave you here in charge of the royal household for a few days – and our father goes missing!" he growled.

Talaiha'apepe did not answer as he glared back at the king.

"What do you have to say for yourself? Where has father gone? What have you done to find him?"

"Let go of me, you bastard. I don't know anything." Talaiha'apepe struck his brothers arms, releasing him from his grip.

"What did you say?" Talatama reached out and grabbed him again.

The young prince tried to deflect the king's attack, as he angrily fought back. But he was no match for his brother's strength. Talatama wrapped his hand around his brother's chubby neck like a vice, before thundering his fist across the jaw, sending him on his backside. Fatafehi threw herself between them.

"Stop! Stop it!" she cried.

Talaiha'apepe crawled backwards, breathing heavily. He glared up at the king with a dark vehemence and spat a mouthful of blood. Talatama stopped himself advancing to strike again; his face was a mixture of fury and frustration.

"Don't ever talk to me like that again," he said, allowing Fatafehi to console him. "I don't know what anger you harbour – whether it's what happened in Niuatoputapu or your public embarrassment. I don't care what it is. But it's compromised my trust in you."

The king turned to walk away but paused, "This is about *our* father. If you can't be helpful, you've my permission to disappear yourself."

Fatafehi crouched down to Talaiha'apepe, comforting him as he remained on the ground, holding his jaw that dripped blood and saliva. They both watched as the king stormed from the garden, calling for his trackers.

Koula and his gang of juveniles sat in their fale not far from Tu'utu'u in 'Eua. They lay like gluttons amid scraps of food and the spoils of personal belongings of dead warriors. They laughed as they threw around a couple of young girls, amusing themselves with undignified and demeaning sexual games. Their den stunk of filth and was crawling with rats fossicking through the garbage.

One of the degenerates noticed a noise coming from outside the fale as they groped with the girls. Suddenly there was a deafening clap of wood and daylight flooded in. The entire front section of the fale collapsed with a crash, as it was torn and dragged away from the rest of the domicile. Two lengths of rope tied to the supporting beams had been pulled simultaneously by a hundred men, as Koula and his gang of fools reeled back like frightened children.

Lord Fasi'apule advanced to the young men with sixty armed Fijian and Tongan warriors behind him, before glaring down at them with a terrifying foreboding. He spotted Koula with his injured knee that had been wrapped with tapa bandages. He reached down and snatched Tu'itatui's club from their treasure and whispered to him with a hint of death on his words.

"Where is his body," Fasi'apule's presence was greater than any ego the young warrior could muster.

"The undertaker. He – he lives at Tu'utu'u, not far from here," he pointed.

Fasi'apule's eyes narrowed and his brow frowned.

"I speak the truth!" Koula pleaded as the dozens of angry warriors congregated around the lord. "He keeps the bodies there until – until either family come to gather the body or he buries them himself!"

Fasi'apule stepped back and turned to his men.

"Half of you, stay here," he directed. "The rest, come with me."

The undertaker's fale was no more than a shack with a small stable to the side for pigs. It was nudged up against a large clump of bushes and coral limestone. The undertaker waddled out of the fale slowly to face an unimpressed Lord Fasi'apule and army of men. He was a filthy man of about forty years, and appeared to be somewhat mentally handicapped.

"You've got a lot of men, Milord," he forced a toothless smile.

"Where is the body, undertaker," Fasi'apule said.

"Oh, I got lots o' bodies," he giggled, his mind that of a five year old child.

"Show me *now*."

He led Fasi'apule into the dilapidated fale and pushed aside a tapa curtain. The foul stench of death punched through the air with staggering weight, as the lord lowered his head and stepped into the dark den. Thrown on the ground, side by side, were five decaying bodies. He spotted Tu'itatui's corpse immediately and it looked as though it had been there a couple of days. He stood in silent mourning. His eyes quickly welled with tears as he stood above the late king's body, discarded so disrespectfully.

"Tu'itatui, you old fool," he said in angst, shaking his head.

He sniffed and swiftly wiped his eyes before turning to the opening, clearing his throat.

"Bring Waqanitoga's body!" he shouted.

"What you – you doing?" the undertaker stuttered.

"Get back!" Fasi'apule's words were so powerful the man yelped as he shuffled away in fear.

Five warriors entered the small shack carrying a large tapa mat. They placed it on the ground and unrolled it, revealing a dead Fijian warrior.

"There," Fasi'apule pointed to Tu'itatui's body.

The warriors switched the bodies and carefully wrapped the late king in the tapa mat, and on count, they lifted the tapa cocoon and marched out of the stable. Lord Fasi'apule stood in the entrance and threatened the undertaker at the end of club. The man was terrified.

"If you tell anyone that we've been here, I'll throw your lifeless body next to the rest of them."

CHAPTER 76

Heketa, Tongatapu
Summer, A.D.1121

Talatama slouched against 'Esi Makafakinanga with a hand on his forehead, shielding the sunlight from his eyes. His head ached as much as the old wound in his abdomen. It had been almost eighteen months since Tu'itatui's disappearance and his coronation. Within that short time, the young king had made crucial decisions that affected the kingship, the people and the Empire. He had subjected himself to an incredible amount of political and social assessments in preparation for massive change. The stress involved with the planning and reconstruction of the Empire was both mentally and physically taxing.

"Your Majesty," Lord Fasi'apule bowed.

"Yes, Uncle," he sighed.

"You must collect your strength," he comforted. "My counsel is yours."

"I was just thinking of father. My challenges today pale in comparison to the challenges he would have faced during the Great Expansion."

"They were different times, young King. And you are a different man with dissimilar traits to your father."

"Mmm."

Seeing his words were not accepted, Fasi'apule continued, "Your father lived in a time of war, Talatama. That time demanded the fire and determination to grow an empire. Your father relished in that. But we now have the pleasure of living in a time of peace. Now your demands are different. They require political verve, tactical planning and the view to propose strategies and designs for a better kingdom. Your father always struggled with those concepts. Never doubt the strength you've shown in the past difficult years."

"I miss him," Talatama nodded in understanding.

"As do I."

Following his return to Tongatapu, and a desperate search for Tu'itatui, the king clung to hope from any lead. He had sent trackers across the entire kingdom in search of the once great king, with no word. No one knew, or had seen, anything. Earlier in the search, rumours had spoken of Tu'itatui travelling to 'Eua, but upon searching the village and digging up shallow graves, Talatama found no trace.

Lord Fasi'apule had been an unwavering support to Talatama and the royal family in more ways than one. As the late king's half-brother, he knew it was his duty to protect Talatama from the truth of what had happened to his father. Working to avoid the political threat to the throne, Fasi'apule had to use his cunning in order to prevent political and social catastrophe.

Foremost it was Fasi'apule's plan to maintain Tu'itatui's anonymity to those in 'Eua and conceal the true circumstances of his death from his family. As Tu'itatui had disguised himself on the island to avoid detection, he had inadvertently strengthened Fasi'apule's effort to keep it that way now. With Tu'itatui's body switched with the that of a Fijian, who had died from illness on their journey to Tonga, and all who knew of the old man's duel, threatened into silence, Talatama's trackers could neither find the true remains of the late king nor speak to anyone about the event.

It was crucial for the secret to be kept from Talatama and the royal family for a number of reasons. Because of the shame of

Tu'itatui's recklessness; he had been the greatest warrior king the Empire had ever seen, and for his demise to be the result of an unruly, young thug, was not only appalling to such an influential leader but an embarrassment to the island nations over whom he ruled.

There was the risk of public scrutiny, of a king who could be killed so easily by a commoner. The effects on the common psyche would have been crippling to Talatama's power and respect he held among his countrymen. It would plant seeds of murder in the minds of future enemies, and shatter the rudimentary foundations of the sacred kings, the Tu'i Tonga and all they represented. It would be seen as a weakness in the eyes of other kings in neighbouring kingdoms and suggest civil unrest, ultimately reducing the esteem of the Empire itself.

Yet despite the pressure to keep his secret plans hidden from virtually everyone, Fasi'apule held no resentment towards his brother for his actions. He had lived by his side for sixty years and knew well the kind of man Tu'itatui was: a warrior and a visionary. He was not endowed with the same philosophical or intellectual gifts Fasi'apule had and indeed he had no need for such traits. His strength of resolve and unrelenting spirit were the metals which forged the will of an Empire and Fasi'apule understood the effect old age had on his brother. Although Tu'itatui was rewarded with peace and prosperity after prodigious years of war and expansion, the enduring peace over long decades began to decay the king's spirit and wear at his soul. He began to suffocate in the world that he had created.

Tu'itatui was said to have been the chosen one of the ancient war god, Tu. His blood was the fire of warfare. He had once told Fasi'apule that he never wanted to die old and sick, that he wanted to die in battle, amid the heat of combat, like his father before him. Fasi'apule had guessed that the Battle of Heketa was the prompt that sealed his fate. When he could not engage in the battle, he was compelled to take a drastic decision. A rushed coronation for

Talatama was done to abdicate quickly, and with the kingship settled, the weight of his actions as ruler was lifted from his conscience. A duel would not have been his ideal choice, Fasi'apule had guessed, but it did nonetheless provide him with the ultimate ending. Should the truth ever be revealed and scrutinised through the eyes of others, Fasi'apule would never forget that after all Tu'itatui had done for his country, he deserved to have his last wish.

Fasi'apule had sailed with Tu'itatui's body back to Malapo following 'Eua. It had been difficult for him to designate a burial site for his brother under the time constraints. He had been summoned back to Heketa to help Talatama with the search. In addition to this, he had to bury Tu'itatui without the knowledge of his fellow villagers. As the Lord of Malapo, and brother to the late king, he was respected beyond questioning, however it was certainly not a burden he wished to bestow on his people. So after cleaning Tu'itatui's body, and with the help of his Fijian warriors, he buried his brother in a provisional grave and, atop it, created a tremendous mound, the size of a small hill.

Four weeks after Tu'itatui's disappearance, Fasi'apule advised the king to convene a formal memorial. He and Talatama had discussed Tu'itatui's motives in disappearing and it took long hours for him to dissuade the king that the Pulotulahi were not to blame. At length, he had convinced Talatama that his father had sailed over the horizon to his doom and the chance of finding him was next to nil. For Talatama, his eventual acceptance that no foul play was to blame lifted a heavy load. But his father's disappearance was a void that could not easily be forgotten.

As such, the king had focused all his attention in planning a memorial site for him, and in the absence of his body to create a royal tomb, Talatama designed a unique monument in dedication of the great king. It was a testament like no other: a representation of strength and enduring power in the form of a trilithon. Despite humble scoffing from his counterparts governing the ambitious concept, Talatama would withstand the seemingly impossible task.

On other matters, King Talatama had made the decision to move the capital to another location. As he planned long ago, his choice was to create a new capital at Mu'a, between the old villages of Malapo and Nukuleka. Lo'au once told Talatama that Mu'a had been the ancient epicentre of the first Tongans who arrived from the great land over the western horizon. Talatama could therefore think of no better place to build the new capital, in addition to its geographical advantages.

"Your Majesty, they're ready for you," Fasi'apule said.

"Excellent, let's go." Talatama was renewed of strength at the prospect of his monument to his father.

The two walked a short distance from the royal court to the memorial site, and when they arrived, there stood a thousand workmen standing to the south of an immense pit. The afternoon sunlight shone across the crater and accentuated its depth. At the bottom, and cleared of earth, was a flat crust of limestone bedrock. Into the bedrock were two large mortises, rectangular cavities chiselled out to a depth of almost two metres.

At the edge of the pit, lay three gigantic limestone slabs draped with a mass of thick ropes. Two of the slabs were exactly the same size: seven metres in length and two metres wide. At one end of these slabs were single carved tenons, and at the other, were vertical square-cut mortises. The third was a smaller slab, six metres long and one and a half metres wide. They were blocks that had been quarried from 'Uvea, some nine hundred kilometres away.

"Master Builder, proceed," King Talatama said loudly.

"Grab the ropes, men!" the old master builder yelled. "First pillar! Four hundred men to the north side, and six hundred to the south! Get moving!"

The muscular army of workers jogged into position with the discipline of soldiers. Many of the labourers were among the largest men on earth: not warriors, but slow moving giants chosen for their incredible strength. A handful were extraordinarily large, some at least eight foot tall and three hundred kilograms of pure might and muscle. When the men were in position, the master builder summoned a voice like no other.

"Heave!"

The ropes pulled taut, as a thousand men stepped back, rope in hand. Then with rhythmic heaves and the strong voices of labourers, the first of the larger slabs, weighing almost thirty-five tonnes began to shift along wooden skids towards the pit. Further and further it dragged until it balanced over the edge of the crater.

"Hold!" The master builder pointed at the four hundred men on the northern side, beads of sweat running down his face.

The four hundred pulled their ropes tied to the opposite end of the slab, and the two groups, taut with groaning ropes pulling at both ends, held the slab in position. Once they had achieved the centre of balance, the master turned to the six hundred.

"Ease!"

He then faced the four hundred men.

"Pull!"

The great slab up-ended. Under the straining sinew of muscle, it was gently lowered into the pit. When the edge of the pillar touched the bedrock, there was a deep, grinding sound of huge pressure. When everyone saw the pillar lay on its own weight in the pit, albeit on an angle, there was a tremendous cheer. King Talatama clapped his hands and smiled broadly to Fasi'apule.

Using his impressive managing ability, the master builder then directed the labour force of thousands to repeat the same feat with the other pillar. Again, the strength and skill of the workers proved remarkable. The second great slab that weighed closer to forty tonnes was eased slowly into the pit on an angle. But the most difficult task was yet come.

The lintel was the third smaller slab of limestone. At almost ten tonnes, its weight was still a chore to drag, especially as the labourers pulled it sideways. Dragging up a mound of earth towards the two partially upright pillars was painstaking, as there would be only once chance to drop the centrepiece into the square mortises. The old master builder ran around to the west end of the pit and monitored the slow pulling of the slab. When one side moved ahead, he would yell out to the other side, to balance the pull.

At last, the lintel was flush with the two pillars and their grooves. The master builder halted the heaving and wiped his perspiring brow. Talatama walked away from Fasi'apule and stood next to him. The master builder licked his lips and faced the six hundred men, raising both hands.

"Both sides, short and sharp... heave!"

The six hundred men on both ends pulled at the same time with a rapid jerk. In one movement, the lintel dropped into the two grooves with a stony crunch. A quick cheer erupted from the labourers. The monument was now one piece: the Trilithon. But it still leaned on a forty-five degree angle. Thirty men then jumped down into the pit to examine the line-up of the joint. When they gave the signal, the pillars were lined up and the master builder gave the orders for the thousand labourers to take up the ropes for the final pull. Talatama stepped in front of the sweat covered men and nodded his head to them with a raised fist.

"Men of Tonga! You are about to be a part of the greatest monument ever built! Pull with all your might!" he roared.

"Heave!" the master builder thundered.

The deep hum of a thousand groans was permeating. The immense labour force dragged the monument upright, at the same time guiding the tenons to the mortises. The grinding of the pillars on the bedrock was like an earthquake. Then suddenly the angle lined up, and dropping in vertically, the two tenons of the two pillars slipped into the deep mortises with an almighty thud. The ground shook, and nearby palm trees swayed. The Trilithon was set into the foundations, which would hold it for a thousand years.

"YYYYAAAAAA!" Talatama punched his fist in the air and veins bulged from his neck.

Ropes were dropped, and the chorus of a thousand men, dozens of watching royal servants and noblemen cheered with such climax that people shed tears. Fasi'apule ran over to Talatama and embraced him like a father. The king then turned to the master builder who was on one knee bowing his head in jubilation. Talatama placed his hand on his shoulder and patted him with restraint.

"Well done."

The old master builder bowed his head with respect.

"In memory of you, father," Talatama looked up to the monument with wet eyes, "And all that you achieved."

Long after King Talatama departed the area, the master builder remained with the monument to correct its standing. Although the tenon pillars had sunk into the two mortises, they were a small fit and there was space between them. The master builder then had to use the force of hundreds to pull the Trilithon straight, so that other men could quickly fill the space with small, limestone chips. Once both mortises had been packed to solidify the foundation, the master builder then ordered the men to fill the pit with earth. The pit was filled and the Trilithon stood immovable, leaving only five metres of the total seven metres of height visible above ground.

Days after, the Trilithon was formally declared a national monument with pomp and celebration. It was protected with a circular border of small limestone slabs, to monumentalise it properly as a dedication to King Tu'itatui and a symbol of the Empire's power, success, ambition and enduring influence. The broken Peace Maker was buried within the monument, laid in two pieces on a bed of heilala flowers. It had been a symbol of power and divinity.

The old Tongans believed that every great weapon possessed its own spirit, a force that imbued it and its owner, with a destiny carved in legend. The Peace Maker, carved from the vesi trees in ancient Pulotu, had paved the way of the Tu'i Tonga for hundreds of years and had taken lives beyond count. Beneath the great arches of the Trilithon, there was no greater a burial site.

CHAPTER 77

Heketa, Tongatapu
Winter, A.D.1123

King Talatama enjoyed his last 'Inasi Festival at Heketa. The next year would see the first 'Inasi in the new capital, Mu'a. The festival was a period where tributes and gifts were brought to the capital by kingdoms within the Empire. Emissaries from all the Melanesian and Polynesian nations sat in the royal courtyard, catered to and spoiled by the servants who were ordered to indulge the noble visitors. Talatama did not subjugate the 'Inasi with the want of gifts, but rather saw it as a time to gather leaders to discuss matters.

It was late afternoon as Lord Atiogie, Matai of the Tuamasaga district of Samoa, approached the king.

"Your Majesty, Lo'au is ready to depart."

"Accompany me, old friend," Talatama nodded and stood down from 'Esi Makafakinanga.

The two warriors, soon after arrived at Heketa beach. There was no bustling fanfare. One of the few on the beach was a familiar face. In two years, Vaohoi had grown a foot, and his boyish features had begun to fade, giving way to manhood. When he saw the king and Atiogie approaching, he smiled broadly, exposing the inner child who would perhaps never leave him.

By his side, were the orphan children of Niuatoputapu; Paea, Heilala and Maka. They had all grown too. Following the coronation, Talatama had sent emissaries to find them, still living in squalor. He brought them to Heketa and claimed them as his adopted children, freeing them from poverty forever. Filled with hope and tears of joy, the children joined the king and remained with him.

Usually standing firm, Fasi'apule showed his age and appeared fragile and tenuous. He walked to the great tongiaki and helped Lo'au throw a large net of green coconuts into the hull. Atiogie jogged ahead of the king to help. Vaohoi met Talatama and embraced him, not having seen him for over a year.

"You've grown again!" King Talatama balked.

"One day I'll be taller than you!"

"That you will," the king ruffled his hair as he walked past to join the others.

The tongiaki sat in the shallow water with its aft banked upon the wet sand. The sun had disappeared behind Tongatapu Island and had painted its masterpiece across the dusty sky. The evening's first stars glimmered amid a lilac horizon and the ocean bade smooth sailing. Lo'au faced the king, breathing heavily, having assisted in loading the last of his supplies aboard the vessel. Talatama noticed his great age all of a sudden.

"You kept this quiet, didn't you?" He smiled as he masked his worry.

"I don't like horded ceremonies," the old mu'a placed his hand on the king's shoulder.

"Where will you go?" Fasi'apule asked.

"I'll sail east, through Rarotonga then on to Ra'iatea. Then perhaps I'll sail until I reach the great forest lands of Mapuche, beyond the eastern stars; a place your father and I once discovered," he smiled to Talatama.

The group chuckled together but returned quickly to the moment. Everyone knew it was an end.

"Master, why – why must you go?" Vaohoi, almost the same height as Lo'au, searched his eyes for answers.

The other three children began to sniff back tears. They owed their lives to the old man and would never forget when he had saved them from starvation in Niuatoputapu over two years ago.

"I must go because my time here is done." Lo'au touched the boy's shoulder. "The Empire is at peace. All whom I love are now safe. I have watched over the generations of Tongan Kings for too long now."

"But, that doesn't mean -" Vaohoi choked with grief.

"There are other people across our beautiful seas who need my help, my làd. I must go to them."

"Who?" Heilala cried.

"Kings, generals," Lo'au spoke tenderly, "Children, orphans, the poor, the persecuted."

The children wept freely, knowing no matter how much they wished with all their hearts, Lo'au would still leave. Deeply sympathetic, he stood above them until, at last, his expression broke and he dropped to his knees with opened arms. The children rushed in and engulfed him. Tears rolled down the old man's face. His heart was breaking. He peered up at the men, his body wrapped with small arms and nesting heads. Talatama, Atiogie and Fasi'apule fought to hold back their sadness.

"Alright, alright, you'll be alright," Lo'au patted their heads and rose to his feet.

He then turned to the men and exchanged brief goodbyes, all unwilling to endure a long and painful farewell. Atiogie was the first to burst into a blithering mess. The giant Samoan almost crushed Lo'au in a howling embrace. Fasi'apule exchanged a formal goodbye, praising him with respect and adoration. Lastly, Lo'au turned to his king, his great-grandson, and friend.

"Rule well, Your Majesty," he said, wiping the tears from his eyes with his forearm.

"You won't come back this time?" Talatama folded his arms, hiding his anguish.

"Not this time."

"Then perhaps – perhaps an old wise man could offer one last piece of advice ..." his eyes began to well.

"I can no longer change the course of destiny, Your Majesty." Lo'au became grave.

"You've said this before," Talatama became frustrated. "What is it you're not telling me? I know you've the gift of foresight."

"You're choices in life so far, Talatama, have been noble and just," Lo'au almost pleaded. "But those decisions have begun to sow the seeds of your undoing."

"I -" the king's eyes shimmered, "I don't understand!"

"It is not for you to understand now, my son." Lo'au took Talatama's hands in his. "You remind me so much of your great grandfather, King 'Afulunga," he reminisced, "Never forget you are the epitome of a noble king: filled with love and compassion for those around you and those of your Empire."

Talatama hung his head in sorrow.

"Forget what I said," Lo'au scolded himself.

"What decision have I made to bring my downfall?"

"Look at me." He searched for the soul behind Talatama's eyes. "To rule others justly, you must first rule your own heart with justice, and you've done that. Continue to do so and you'll become the Empire's greatest and most loved king."

Talatama's eyes brimmed with fresh tears, his shoulders and chest shuddering. Lo'au could not contain his grief as he embraced Talatama hard. The king wept, while his angst and sorrow flowed out of him with heaving breaths. All those around the two great men sunk to their knees and hung their heads. This moment together was their last.

The sky eventually darkened and the sails of Lo'au's tongiaki disappeared into the velvet horizon. The group stood on the shore until there was nothing but the reflection of stars across the night sea and a cool night wind that blew favourably.

* * *

The king and Atiogie sat casually around a smouldering fire in one of the private areas in the royal compound. They sat together as brothers, sharing a light mixture of kava over old tales. They reminisced of their adventures together, of the greatest companionship ever told. They laughed until their ribs ached, and sobbed as they remembered the dark times. Atiogie was due to depart the morning after, to return to Samoa and it was their last evening together.

"Father?" Heilala appeared before the two warriors.

She was dressed in a thick tapa garment with aviary patterns carefully dyed across the surface. It had been a gift from the king when she arrived at Heketa.

"Yes, my Heilala?" Talatama opened his arm so that she could embrace him.

"I'm going to sleep now."

"Alright, good night, my precious," the king smiled.

"Goodnight, Your Majesty," she smiled and kissed him. "Um – Father?"

"What is it, my dear?"

"Remember that parchment? The – the one Paea and I gave you?"

"The tapa parchment in Niuatoputapu?" The king looked surprised.

"Yes, that one. Um, what happened to it?"

"Well, my dear," Talatama frowned towards Atiogie, "Your father lost it one day."

"Oh, but I thought it was important."

"It was! Your father was very upset that he lost it."

"Can you tell me again? Can you tell me why it was important?" Her curiosity was what made her endearing.

"Well, it was very important to Father because it had written on it the name of Father's great enemy."

"But, don't you know your enemy, Father?"

Talatama smiled at her sudden understanding.

"No, Heilala, I didn't know my enemy because it was a secret I couldn't read, and that only that tapa parchment held."

"So now you'll never know? Because you lost it?"

"That's right." Talatama smiled and stroked her hair.

"But, Father ..." The girl's face grew grave, "Aren't you scared your enemy will come one day?"

"Don't worry, my dearest," Talatama kissed her on the forehead, "I think your father might have destroyed that enemy forever—"

"I don't want you to be taken away from me!" She hugged him tightly.

"I think you've seen too many goodbyes in your little lifetime!" he rocked her gently. "Nothing's going to happen to me. Go to sleep now. Go on."

She rose from his lap and walked away hesitantly. Atiogie chuckled to himself as he waved to her.

"You promise, Father?" she asked before she disappeared.

"I promise."

Across the royal courtyard and through the gardens, another private fire lingered. The flames danced and wavered by the night breeze that teased them. The heath was a glowing red. Embers hissed and occasionally floated into the air with the warm smoke. The man sat alone as the fire's only observer, giving the flames his undivided and hypnotic attention. Shades of firelight moved across his face like silhouettes. His eyes were a pool of reflection.

His mind was a hidden world of mystery. Thoughts ran through his mind like a coursing river, doubts like gnawing pain and fears like a burning fever. No one understood the dreams he possessed. No one could fathom the desire he held in his heart. Perhaps no one ever would. The world, filled with the uncertainty of life, the imbalance of justice and unruly leaders could never hope to grasp the concepts he had planned, recruited and killed for.

Prince Talaiha'apepe stood still while staring into the fire. He pulled out something from his clothing and without a second glance, he threw it into the fire and walked away. The tapa parchment, and his secret that was scrolled across it, caught alight immediately. It produced a thin line of smoke that trailed from the fire and weaved into the night sky. Even when his shadow became as one with the darkness, his thoughts permeated the very night.

'One day, they will understand.'

THE END

A Providence Of War

EPILOGUE

The end was a new beginning for all companions. Their time together served as a prequel to destinies they later fulfilled. Their brotherhood was never forgotten to them, nor the deeds or adventures they had shared together. At one brief moment in time, their paths had united for a common purpose upon the most beautiful stage on earth; the Pacific Ocean.

Lord Toi and his son, Prince Whatonga, successfully assembled the fleet required for their grand voyage south. As the journey itself was a great risk, Whatonga expressed his worries to Talatama for the Rarotongan people in his absence. The king had condoned his ambitious expedition and assured him the Empire would oversee Rarotonga's protection and government should they require it.

On a spring morning in A.D.1122, Toi and Whatonga, with the company of a thousand men and women arrived in Aotearoa. Aboard a fleet of forty great tongiakis, they had departed from Ngatangi'ia harbour, using the secret navigational charts Whatonga obtained from Kupe, and began the great voyage towards the south-eastern horizon.

However the journey was not without its struggles. Rough weather during nights separated some of the fleet and others perished in violent storms and cyclones. Finally, six weeks after their departure, the land of the long white cloud came into sight. From the forty great vessels that began the journey, only twelve had survived: Takiumu, Tokomaru, Kurahaupo, Aotea, Tainui, Te Arawa,

Mataatua, Horouta, Tohora, Mamari, Ngatokimatawhaorua and Mahuhu.

The fleet struck the north cape of Aotearoa which Whatonga named Otou, and made camp there for a week. In the following months, Prince Whatonga led the vessels southward until they eventually came to a grand bay and landed at a place he called Whakatane. The Rarotongans, under the leadership of Toi and Whatonga, remained in Aotearoa for the rest of their lives and populated Aotearoa to become the New Zealand Maori.

Accompanied by a few of her loyal warriors, Pele made her own incredible journey to Hawai'i. The first part of her voyage took her to Tahiti, where she lived for a number of years. During her time there, she recruited an army of warriors through the civil wars. Having searched the seas, she was never able to find her wandering lover, Maui Atalaga, with whom she secretly hoped to be reunited.

Heartbroken, Pele vowed never to fall in love again, and from that point onwards, she sought to manipulate men to her will. She continued on a downward spiral, becoming more violent and cruel. Her exceptional skill as a warrior never wavered, and she quickly gained the respect of kings and leaders alike. She captured the hearts of men through her inspirational talents and charismatic magnetism, and in time, became a woman of legendary status.

As such, she sparked the second major migration of Polynesians to Hawaii. In the year A.D.1126, Pele successfully led a fleet of adventurers north on a three month voyage, reaching Kauai, northern most island of Hawaii. On her arrival, her fleet of adventurers were attacked by the natives from nearby islands. Following a short massacre by the hands of Pele and her warriors, she was shocked to find that her lineage had been decimated by civil unrest. No remains of her family had survived.

This incited the first Hawaiian wars between the new migrants, led by Pele and the local Hawaiians, whom they named the 'Menehune'. The bloody wars lasted for four years, in which time more migrations from Tahiti arrived to fuel Pele's war effort. But in the course of consistent bloodshed, she had begun to lose control of her mind. She became terribly severe, merciless and cruel, resulting in the death of hundreds of innocents. She had single-handedly defeated the Menehune on all the major islands, and subjugated them into slavery. The last King of the Menehune surrendered and sailed off to the west with the remainder of free peoples.

During the Hawaiian wars, Lo'au had travelled from Tonga to Eastern Polynesia where ministered to the victims of civil unrest in the Tahitian islands. In a few short years, he created and fostered a form of government that promoted peace and prosperity. As a result, the Tahitians, who had modified his name to Pa'au, made him an unwilling chief of the Bora Bora Island. During this short period, Pa'au adopted Pili, a young chieftain's son who had become an orphan of the civil unrest in Tahiti.

Pa'au had become aware of the popular migrations to Hawaii and regarded them with dislike. It was not until the young, adventurous Pili encouraged Pa'au to join the last migration north that he finally went. The two set sail in company of two hundred adventurers and landed in Hawaii long months after. What they discovered was shocking brutality under the leadership of the mighty Pele and her generals who had, at the time, conquered all of the Hawaii islands.

Pele had gone mad in her lust for bloodshed, and were it not for Pa'au, the Menehune would have suffered a terrible fate of genocide. When Pele and Pa'au met again, Pele was instantly mollified by his presence. To the surprise of her generals, and unaware of their past in Tonga, she obeyed Pa'au's commands, most of which saw the end of the wars. Pa'au's influences turned the Hawaiian's cruel existence into a stratified culture and secure social system. Sadly, not long after, Pa'au, the saviour of hundreds, and who had had seen the rise and fall of empires, died at the age of 106 years. He was buried as a king in Hawai'i.

Pili became a great king in later years and founded the dynasty from which Kamehameha descended twenty-eight generations later.

Pele deserted her leadership status shortly after. Madness had engulfed her mind, and legend had it, that she vanished into the volcano of Halema'uma'u on the island of Hawaii. In the years following, she would terrorize anyone who came close and eventually faded into mythology, as Pele; the goddess of fire.

Following the return to his homeland with the captive General Va'iga, Lord Atiogie accompanied by Vaohoi, was hailed a hero across the Samoan islands. Shortly after, his father, Lord Feepo, abdicated to allow Atiogie to become the primary chief of the 'Aele region where he remained. Atiogie married his sweetheart, Tauaiupolu, in a beautiful ceremony that included guests such as King Talatama, Adi, Emori and Vaohoi. They grew old together and raised a large family, bearing powerful sons: Vagana, Savea, Tuna, Fata, Leaupepe and Patu. Vaohoi decided to remain in Samoa and in time, became a great chief himself.

The friendship between Talatama and Atiogie lasted for the rest of their lives. Atiogie ruled the region in prosperous years of peace and harmony. His sons, however, were to be instrumental in the changing period of the Empire and its king in the decades to come; an unfortunate irony in light of Talatama and Atiogie's closeness.

Months after Lo'au's departure, King Talatama succeeded in moving the capital from Heketa to Mu'a. In painstaking planning and management, the entire royal household and all its structures were transported twenty kilometres by sea, to the ancient settlement of Mu'a. The new capital was located on the calm shores of the great lagoon, which made the Empire's fleet accessible, as well as vessels of trade from other islands. Fatafehi supported Talatama in this move. She had become restless since the time of Tu'itatui's disappearance and claimed that the noisy shores of Heketa added to her growing insomnia.

As the shadow of the Pulotulahi had disappeared after Kamohoali'i's defeat, Talatama disregarded any plausible threat of their influence, especially as he never discovered the identity of

Tu'ipulotu. Unbeknownst to him, Talaiha'apepe plotted to exact revenge. During a friendly contest of duelling, the king was duped into engaging an agent of the Pulotulahi, secretly advised by Talaiha'apepe. The evil prince gave the agent precise information to strike at Talatama's old wound, in order to kill him.

The duel was stopped by Lord Fasi'apule but the agent, feigning an accident, had already struck Talatama in the abdomen. The blow caused internal bleeding, which Talatama ignored for the first few days. Following the third day, however, the king fell violently ill and called for his old friend, Atiogie. Shocked by the news of Talatama's illness, Atiogie rushed from Samoa, but arrived too late. The great King Talatama had died hours prior. He was twenty-four years old. An epic funeral was held and the much loved young king of honour and integrity was mourned by all across the Empire.

The Samoan lord, overcome with grief, fumed at the royals and exclaimed that the king had been slain. He sparked strife within the royal household by throwing blame to those closest to Talatama, and as such, was sent away until the death could be properly investigated. Lord Fasi'apule commenced an inquiry, even though on the face of it, he appeared to have died from illness. Fasi'apule's thorough investigation eventually implicated Talaiha'apepe as the murder suspect, which meant he could not release his findings to the family, let alone the public.

In the interim, however, and in the interests of the people, Fasi'apule had to organize the coronation of another king. Bitterly reminded of the difficulty he faced when Tu'itatui was killed, Fasi'apule struggled again to avoid political and social upheaval. But as Talaiha'apepe was the prime suspect, he could not elevate him to become the new king. As a result, he created the illusion that a new king, by the name of Tamatou, had been crowned. He ordered the master artisans to carve the image of a man seated on a throne made of to'a wood. When the image was complete, they placed the new king far from public view and draped it with black tapa to create the illusion. Meanwhile, Fasi'apule was caught in a stalemate; he could not directly prove it had been Talaiha'apepe's plan to kill the late king.

Short years after his death, Fasi'apule released the prince from his suspicion and allowed him to take the throne. Lord Atiogie was infuriated with this decision, marking the moment as the time he forever removed himself from the Empire's dealings. Talaiha'apepe in the meantime, did not want to be seen taking the throne as Talatama's brother, as the Tu'i Tonga father to son tradition was so strong. As such, he carried the deception Fasi'apule created and declared that King Tamatou had suddenly died, and that he was the only son. Therefore, he proclaimed his kingship as a son rather than a brother.

Appalled with his actions, Lord Fasi'apule resigned from formal office and retired to his land in Malapo, where he lived out the rest of his years. King Talaiha'apepe immediately cast the children of Niuatoputapu back to the island when he gained the Crown. Lord Atiogie later heard this, retrieved the children and returned with them to Samoa. The implementation of the ruthless traditions of the Pulotulahi with an iron fist thus began the dark and turbulent years of King Talaiha'apepe and his son, Talakaifaiki. This historically, over the next two hundred years, marked the end of the Empire's enduring influence.

HISTORICAL NOTE

The ancient Tongans in this period were known to have been extremely powerful and enterprising. Twentieth century excavations resulting in accidental resurfacing of ancient human bones in Tonga were common. Findings were astounding. Skeletons of enormous size with the dimensions of giant men described in the book are not exaggerated. This coupled with their known ferocity, even up to the late eighteenth century, would have created terrifying foes in great numbers. I have no doubt that in addition to their advanced voyaging skills, it was not difficult for the ancient Tongans to conquer most of that which they discovered. This lent to the rise of their dominance.

Many of the main characters in the book are historical. Prince Talatama, King Tu'itatui, Prince Talaiha'apepe, Lord Fasi'apule, Princess Fatafehi were all recorded as having lived in this period. The mighty Samoan warrior, Atiogie, and his father, Lord Feepo, are recorded in Samoan histories with certainty and it was Atiogie's sons who led the rebellion against King Talakaifaiki sixty years later, spawning one of Samoa's most powerful families of today, the Malietoa.

Prince Whatonga and Lord Toi, as well as Kupe, were pioneers in their voyages to New Zealand and are extensively recorded in New Zealand historical texts. Maori legend regarding Kupe, who was historically the first to reach New Zealand, tells of his shrewd actions in stealing the tongiaki, betraying the owner, *Harapua*, and stealing his wife to conduct the voyage. There was no doubt that, in addition to other tales, he was an obvious choice as a villain for the book.

Maui Atalaga of the Maui line was a hero from the family that came from the original peoples of Pulotu. Much like the legends of Hercules in Greek mythology, the Maui brothers were often spoken of as mortals with god-like abilities and strength. They are often recounted as folklore heroes, capable of great deeds and, of course, over time were elevated to godlike status. Like his nemesis, the dreaded Havea who was historically purported to be Maui's cousin, he preceded the first overlords, such as the first Tu'i Tonga, Aho'eitu.

The witch Mo'unga was, of course, fictional. However her supernatural abilities are based on well-known legends. In the 1990's, an Australian media group presented a story in Tonga showing a strange ceremony where certain village people were able to, not only summon sharks by way of calling, but place flowered lei's around their necks and caress them. When I viewed this program, I was inspired to include a more exaggerated version in this book.

Though the Fijians, Adi and Emori, were purely fictional, they represented an extremely influential religion of that period; the Degei. History shows Degei was the largest religion in the Fijian islands and had temples all over the country. Pele was taken from the mythological Hawaiian Pele 'Goddess of Fire'. Maintaining uniformity with my belief that many of these ancient Polynesian deities were once historical people, Pele and her brother, Kamohoali'i, provided an interesting addition to the book. The other connection with the Hawaiian Islands was the discovery of petroglyphs on the north tip of Foa, Ha'apai in 2008. The petroglyphs have striking similarities to petroglyphs found in Hawaii, however pre-date them by centuries. This, of course, supported the fictional addition of having Pele return to Hawaii following Foa.

Lo'au is perhaps better known in Polynesian legend than most. Modern Tongan historians believe Lo'au was a Samoan, or at least a foreigner, a theory I support. I take it one step further and suggest that Lo'au could have been the king, of the powerful Tu'i Manu'a. This Samoan kingship is said to have existed in the Manu'a islands of Samoa hundreds of years prior to the Tu'i Tonga. Historians assert the Tu'i Manu'a had already declined by the time of Aho'eitu, and perhaps having come from a well experienced ruling line, Lo'au was able to influence the early King Momo, Tu'itatui's father, in making changes to the Tongan hierarchical system, as outlined in the first chapter. Lo'au's daughter, Nua, then married Momo, thus making him Talatama's great-grandfather. Interestingly, there are parallels of Lo'au in other islands. Pa'au, as mentioned in the Epilogue, was a chief in the Bora Bora Islands and led a migration to Hawaii.

As I mentioned previously, though the plot is fictional, it was my intention to weave historical and mythological events throughout the book. Arguably, the most famous is the quest of Fasi'apule to find the Shell of Sangone in Samoa. This story is well remembered and has been used in classical Tongan poems and music. The riddles between Fasi'apule and the old dwarf, Lafaipana, are perhaps the highlight of the account, and we know that the Shell of Sangone existed. So it is said, a piece of it had been carved into a helu *(hair comb)* that can be seen today at the Tonga Museum in Nuku'alofa, Tonga. Continuity of the shell was lost when the last Tui' Tonga Laufilitonga gave it away in Fiji in the mid-nineteenth century. It was not until years later, that King George Tupou I retrieved the remains of the shell and returned them to Tonga.

The circumstances surrounding the death of King Tu'itatui has a couple of versions in Tongan history. Being recklessly killed in a common duel at 'Eua by a warrior unaware of his identity, is perhaps the most well known. It is said that Fasi'apule returned from Fiji and replaced the king's body with that of a Fijian's before the locals discovered the identity. This was done perhaps out of embarrassment, as detailed in the book, and he was subsequently buried in Fasi'apule's home village of Malapo.

The secret of Prince Talaiha'apepe as Lord Tu'ipulotu was a fictional direction for the plot. I was inspired by the historical puzzle of Talatama's sudden death (said to have died young) that was preceded by 'King Tamatou'; a carved wooden 'doll'. Legends say that Talaiha'apepe had wanted this wooden doll to represent Talatama's son *(because he died childless)* and that following an unknown period, he announced Tamatou had died and that he would take the throne as his son. There are metaphorical theories surrounding this unusual story however it does raise a plethora of questions as to why it happened. Fictionally it was not a difficult choice to illustrate the ultimate jealousy of the young prince as an anchor to this historical conundrum.

All of the locations in the book currently exist with the exception of Maka Vela in Niuafo'ou. There are two islands on Vai Lahi today, though to speculate a volcanic eruption since is not farfetched. If this was the case, it is plausible that different islands within the lake existed a thousand years ago. As for the sea level, modern science tells us that it was the same as today, making it easy to detail areas that are present nowadays. The volcanos of Tafahi, Kao and Tofua are still active. The Falls of Papapai-tai is a tourist attraction in Samoa, as are the amazing caves in 'Eua. The underwater cave in Vava'u is a popular dive spot and the buried remains of Castle Ha'afuluhao on Mt Talau near Neiafu can still be seen. The ancient pyramid, 'Temple of Pulemelei' in Savai'i Samoa, is currently the subject of ongoing archaeological digs.

Lastly the immortal Ha'amonga a Maui' or Tongan Trilithon is perhaps the most definitive representation of this period, and arguably, the greatest monument the ancient Tongans ever built, with the exception of the great langis. The dimensions and details of its construction in Chapter 76 are the most agreed upon, in addition to the number of men it would have taken to assemble it (as the ancient Tongans had no wheels, horses, cattle or beasts to haul the stones). Its original purpose has attracted many theories still debated today: a royal gateway to a construct of seasonal identification. I chose to support the ideal that it was constructed as a monument – a bold statement, symbol and representation of Tonga's incredible power at the time. Fictionally, this assimilated with the demise of Tu'itatui and was thus incorporated with Talatama's lament.

My personal fascination with the Tu'i Tonga stems from a personal connection to ancient ancestry. Taumoefolau, my great-great-grandfather, from whom my surname has its origin, was the grandson of the 37th Tu'i Tonga, Ma'ulupekotofa who inherited the title around A.D.1770's. Thus, from a lineage of father to son, I am able to connect a line back to the very characters that appear in this story.

But in a greater vein, my passion for this ancient period is fuelled by two aspects; the nature of its obscurity, an epoch so coloured with grandeur yet so remote in the living memory of my people who never had the benefit of written records, and the goal of glorifying our legends and tales through the medium of *historical fiction* in hope that these stories and their heroes are not forgotten, but remembered.

J.T

A Providence Of War